LOVER REBORN

BY J. R. WARD

THE BLACK DAGGER BROTHERHOOD SERIES

Dark Lover

Lover Eternal

Lover Awakened

Lover Revealed

Lover Unbound

Lover Enshrined

The Black Dagger Brotherhood:
An Insider's Guide

Lover Avenged

Lover Mine

Lover Unleashed

Lover Reborn

NOVELS OF THE FALLEN ANGELS

Covet

Crave

Envy

J.R.WARD

LOVER
REBORN

A NOVEL OF THE BLACK DAGGER BROTHERHOOD

 NEW AMERICAN LIBRARY

New American Library
Published by New American Library, a division of
Penguin Group (USA) Inc., 375 Hudson Street,
New York, New York 10014, USA
Penguin Group (Canada), 90 Eglinton Avenue East, Suite 700, Toronto,
Ontario M4P 2Y3, Canada (a division of Pearson Penguin Canada Inc.)
Penguin Books Ltd., 80 Strand, London WC2R 0RL, England
Penguin Ireland, 25 St. Stephen's Green, Dublin 2,
Ireland (a division of Penguin Books Ltd.)
Penguin Group (Australia), 250 Camberwell Road, Camberwell, Victoria 3124,
Australia (a division of Pearson Australia Group Pty. Ltd.)
Penguin Books India Pvt. Ltd., 11 Community Centre, Panchsheel Park,
New Delhi - 110 017, India
Penguin Group (NZ), 67 Apollo Drive, Rosedale, Auckland 0632,
New Zealand (a division of Pearson New Zealand Ltd.)
Penguin Books (South Africa) (Pty.) Ltd., 24 Sturdee Avenue,
Rosebank, Johannesburg 2196, South Africa

Penguin Books Ltd., Registered Offices:
80 Strand, London WC2R 0RL, England

First published by New American Library,
a division of Penguin Group (USA) Inc.

First Printing, April 2012
10   9   8   7   6   5   4   3   2   1

 REGISTERED TRADEMARK—MARCA REGISTRADA

LIBRARY OF CONGRESS CATALOGING-IN-PUBLICATION DATA:

Ward, J. R., 1969–
Lover reborn: a novel of the Black Dagger Brotherhood/J. R. Ward.
p. cm.
ISBN 978-0-451-23584-8
1. Vampires—Fiction. I. Title.
PS3623.A73227L694 2012
813'.6—dc23   2011046870

Set in Garamond
Designed by Patrice Sheridan

Printed in the United States of America

PUBLISHER'S NOTE
This is a work of fiction. Names, characters, places, and incidents either are the product of the author's
imagination or are used fictitiously, and any resemblance to actual persons, living or dead, business estab-
lishments, events, or locales is entirely coincidental.
The publisher does not have any control over and does not assume any responsibility for author or
third-party Web sites or their content.

DEDICATED TO: YOU—

it has been so long,

too long,

since you have had a home.

ACKNOWLEDGMENTS

With immense gratitude to the readers of the Black Dagger Brotherhood and a shout-out to the Cellies!

Thank you so very much for all the support and guidance: Steven Axelrod, Kara Welsh, Claire Zion, and Leslie Gelbman. Thank you also to everyone at New American Library—these books are truly a team effort.

Thank you to all our Mods for everything you do out of the goodness of your hearts!

With love to Team Waud—you know who you are. This simply could not happen without you.

None of this would be possible without: my loving husband, who is my adviser and caretaker and visionary; my wonderful mother, who has given me so much love I couldn't possibly ever repay her; my family (both those of blood and those by adoption); and my dearest friends.

Oh, and the better half of WriterDog, of course.

GLOSSARY OF TERMS
AND PROPER NOUNS

abstrux nohtrum (n.) Private guard with license to kill who is granted his or her position by the king.

ahvenge (v.) Act of mortal retribution, carried out typically by a male loved one.

Black Dagger Brotherhood (pr. n.) Highly trained vampire warriors who protect their species against the Lessening Society. As a result of selective breeding within the race, Brothers possess immense physical and mental strength, as well as rapid healing capabilities. They are not siblings for the most part, and are inducted into the Brotherhood upon nomination by the Brothers. Aggressive, self-reliant, and secretive by nature, they exist apart from civilians, having little contact with members of the other classes except when they need to feed. They are the subjects of legend and objects of reverence within the vampire world. They may be killed only by the most serious of wounds, e.g., a gunshot or stab to the heart, etc.

blood slave (n.) Male or female vampire who has been subjugated to serve the blood needs of another. The practice of keeping blood slaves has recently been outlawed.

the Chosen (pr. n.) Female vampires who have been bred to serve the Scribe Virgin. They are considered members of the aristocracy, though they are spiritually rather than temporally focused. They have little or no interaction with males, but can be mated to Brothers at the Scribe Virgin's direction to propagate their class. Some have the ability to prognosticate. In the past, they were used to meet the blood needs of unmated members of the Brotherhood, and that practice has been reinstated by the Brothers.

chrih (n.) Symbol of honorable death in the Old Language.

cohntehst (n.) Conflict between two males competing for the right to be a female's mate.

Dhunhd (pr. n.) Hell.

doggen (n.) Member of the servant class within the vampire world. *Doggen* have old, conservative traditions about service to their superiors, following a formal code of dress and behavior. They are able to go out during the day, but they age relatively quickly. Life expectancy is approximately five hundred years.

ehros (n.) A Chosen trained in the matter of sexual arts.

exhile dhoble (n.) The evil or cursed twin, the one born second.

the Fade (pr. n.) Nontemporal realm where the dead reunite with their loved ones and pass eternity.

First Family (pr. n.) The king and queen of the vampires, and any children they may have.

ghardian (n.) Custodian of an individual. There are varying degrees of *ghardians*, with the most powerful being that of a *sehcluded* female.

glymera (n.) The social core of the aristocracy, roughly equivalent to Regency England's *ton*.

hellren (n.) Male vampire who has been mated to a female. Males may take more than one female as mate.

leahdyre (n.) A person of power and influence.

leelan (adj.) A term of endearment loosely translated as "dearest one."

Lessening Society (pr. n.) Order of slayers convened by the Omega for the purpose of eradicating the vampire species.

lesser (n.) De-souled human who targets vampires for extermination as a member of the Lessening Society. *Lessers* must be stabbed through the chest in order to be killed; otherwise they are ageless. They do not eat or drink and are impotent. Over time, their hair, skin, and irises lose pigmentation until they are blond, blushless, and pale eyed. They smell like baby powder. Inducted into the Society by the Omega, they retain a ceramic jar thereafter into which their heart was placed after it was removed.

lewlhen (n.) Gift.

lheage (n.) A term of respect used by a sexual submissive to refer to her dominant.

Lhenihan (pr. n.) A mythic beast renown for its sexual prowess. In modern slang, refers to a male of preternatural size and sexual stamina.

lys (n.) Torture tool used to remove the eyes.

mahmen (n.) Mother. Used both as an identifier and a term of affection.

mhis (n.) The masking of a given physical environment; the creation of a field of illusion.

nalla (n., f.) or ***nallum*** (n., m.) Beloved.

needing period (n.) Female vampire's time of fertility, generally lasting for two days and accompanied by intense sexual cravings. Occurs approximately five years after a female's transition and then once a decade thereafter. All males respond to some degree if they are around a female in her need. It can be a dangerous time, with conflicts and fights breaking out between competing males, particularly if the female is not mated.

newling (n.) A virgin.

the Omega (pr. n.) Malevolent, mystical figure who has targeted the vampires for extinction out of resentment directed toward the Scribe Virgin. Exists in a nontemporal realm and has extensive powers, though not the power of creation.

phearsom (adj.) Term referring to the potency of a male's sexual organs. Literal translation something close to "worthy of entering a female."

princeps (n.) Highest level of the vampire aristocracy, second only to members of the First Family or the Scribe Virgin's Chosen. Must be born to the title; it may not be conferred.

pyrocant (n.) Refers to a critical weakness in an individual. The weakness can be internal, such as an addiction, or external, such as a lover.

rahlman (n.) Savior.

rythe (n.) Ritual manner of assuaging honor granted by one who has offended another. If accepted, the offended chooses a weapon and strikes the offender, who presents him- or herself without defenses.

the Scribe Virgin (pr. n.) Mystical force who is counselor to the king as well as the keeper of vampire archives and the dispenser of privileges. Exists in a nontemporal realm and has extensive powers. Capable of a single act of creation, which she expended to bring the vampires into existence.

sehclusion (n.) Status conferred by the king upon a female of the aristocracy as a result of a petition by the female's family. Places the female under the sole direction of her *ghardian*, typically the eldest male in her household. Her *ghardian* then has the legal right to determine all manner of her life, restricting at will any and all interactions she has with the world.

shellan (n.) Female vampire who has been mated to a male. Females generally do not take more than one mate due to the highly territorial nature of bonded males.

symphath (n.) Subspecies within the vampire race characterized by the ability and desire to manipulate emotions in others (for the purposes of an energy exchange), among other traits. Historically, they have been discriminated against and, during certain eras, hunted by vampires. They are near extinction.

the Tomb (pr. n.) Sacred vault of the Black Dagger Brotherhood. Used as a ceremonial site as well as a storage facility for the jars of *lessers*. Ceremonies performed there include inductions, funerals, and disciplinary actions against Brothers. No one may enter except for members of the Brotherhood, the Scribe Virgin, or candidates for induction.

trahyner (n.) Word used between males of mutual respect and affection. Translated loosely as "beloved friend."

transition (n.) Critical moment in a vampire's life when he or she transforms into an adult. Thereafter, he or she must drink the blood of the opposite sex to survive and is unable to withstand sunlight. Occurs generally in the mid-twenties. Some vampires do not survive their transitions, males in particular. Prior to their transitions, vampires are physically weak, sexually unaware and unresponsive, and unable to dematerialize.

vampire (n.) Member of a species separate from that of Homo sapiens. Vampires must drink the blood of the opposite sex to survive. Human blood will keep them alive, though the strength does not last long. Following their transitions, which occur in their mid-twenties, they are unable to go out into sunlight and must feed from the vein regularly. Vampires cannot "convert" humans through a bite or transfer of blood, though they are in rare cases able to breed with the other species. Vampires can dematerialize at will, though they must be able to calm themselves and concentrate to do so and may not carry anything heavy with them. They are able to strip the memories of humans, provided such memories are short-term. Some vampires are able to read minds. Life expectancy is upward of a thousand years, or in some cases even longer.

wahlker (n.) An individual who has died and returned to the living from the Fade. They are accorded great respect and are revered for their travails.

whard (n.) Equivalent of a godfather or godmother to an individual.

*"The quick and the dead are all the same.
Everyone's just looking for home."*

—Lassiter

LOVER REBORN

Spring

ONE

"The bastard's taking the bridge! He's mine!"

Tohrment waited for an answering whistle, and when it came, he tore off after the *lesser*, his shitkickers slamming into puddles, his legs going piston, his hands fisting hard. He passed Dumpsters and parked POSs, scattered rats and homeless people, jumped over a barricade, vaulted over a motorcycle.

Three a.m. in downtown Caldwell, New York, gave you just enough obstacles to keep shit amusing. Unfortunately, the little gnat of a slayer up ahead was taking him in a direction he didn't want to go in.

As they hit the entrance ramp to the westbound bridge, Tohr wanted to kill the fool—natch. Unlike the blocks of privacy you could find in the maze of alleys around the clubs, you were guaranteed traffic over the Hudson, even this late. Okay, sure, the Herbert G. Falcheck suspension special wasn't going to be choked with cars, but there were going to be a few—and God knew every human behind the wheel had a goddamn iPhone these days.

There was one rule in the war between the vampires and the Lessening Society: Stay the fuck away from humans. That race of nosy, upright

orangutans was a complication waiting to happen, and the last thing anyone needed was widespread confirmation that Dracula wasn't a product of fiction, and the walking dead weren't just a TV show that didn't suck.

Nobody wanted to frontline on the network news, the papers, the magazines.

Internet was fine. No credibility there.

This down-low tenet was the single thing that the enemy and the Black Dagger Brotherhood agreed upon, the one deference that was given by both sides. So, yeah, the slayers could, say . . . target your pregnant *shellan*, shoot her in the face, and leave her for dead, taking away not just her life, but your own. But God forbid they rile up the humans.

'Cuz that would just be wrong.

Unfortunately, this directionally challenged, hydraulic-legged motherfucker up here hadn't gotten the memo.

Nothing a black dagger in the chest couldn't fix.

As a growl rose up his throat and his fangs elongated in his mouth, Tohr dug deep and tapped a reserve of high-octane hatred, his gas tank refilling, his flagging energy instantly renewed.

It had been a long road back from the nightmare of his king and his brothers coming to tell him that his life was over. As a bonded male, his female was the beating heart in his chest, and in the absence of his Wellsie, he was a ghost of who he had once been, form without substance. The only thing that animated him was the chase, the capture, and the kill. And the knowledge that he could wake up the next night and find more to take down.

Other than *ahvenging* his dead, he might as well be in the blessed Fade with his family. Frankly, the latter would be preferable—and who knew, maybe he'd get lucky tonight. Maybe in the heat of a fight he'd suffer a catastrophic mortal injury and be relieved of his burdens.

A male could only hope.

The blare of a car horn followed by a chorus of screeching rubber was the first sign that Captain Complication had found what he was looking for.

Tohr got to the top of the ramp's rise just in time to catch a quick visual of the slayer bouncing off the hood of a Toyota nothing-special. The impact stopped the sedan dead; didn't slow down the slayer in the slightest. Like all *lessers*, the bastard was stronger and more resilient than he'd been as a mere human, the black, oily blood of the Omega giving him a bigger engine, tighter suspension and better handling—as well as racing tires in this case.

Its GPS sucked, for real, though.

The slayer sprang up out of his roll across the pavement like a professional stuntman and, naturally, kept going. He was injured, though, that noxious baby-powder smell of his more pronounced.

Tohr came up to the car just as a pair of humans popped their doors, scrambled out, and started flapping their arms like something was on fire.

"CPD," Tohr yelled as he ripped past them. "In pursuit!"

This calmed them down, and lined up damage control. It was virtually guaranteed that they'd now become a peanut gallery with all kinds of Kodak inclinations, and that was perfect—when this was all over, he'd know where to find them so he could scrub their memories, and take their cell phones.

Meanwhile, the *lesser* appeared to be gunning for the pedestrian walkway—not his best move. If Tohr had been in the dumb-ass's position, he'd have taken over that Toyota and tried to drive off—

"Oh . . . come *on* . . ." Tohr gritted out.

Apparently, the bastard's goal wasn't the walkway, but the lip of the bridge itself: The slayer jumped up and over the fencing that contained the pedi-way, and landed on the thin ledge on the far side. Next stop: the Hudson River.

The slayer looked behind himself, and in the peachy glow of the sodium lights, his arrogant expression was that of a sixteen-year-old boy after he'd sucked down a six-pack of beer in front of his friends.

All ego. No brains.

He was going to jump. The fucker was going to jump.

Fidiot. Even though the Omega's joy juice gave the slayers all that power, it didn't mean the laws of physics went out the window for them. Einstein's little ditty about energy equaling mass times acceleration was still going to apply—so when the dipshit hit the water, he was going to get blown apart, sustaining substantial structural damage. Which wouldn't kill him but would incapacitate the hell out of him.

Fuckers couldn't die unless they got stabbed. And they could spend eternity in a purgatory of decomposition.

Boo-frickin'-hoo.

And before his Wellsie's murder, Tohr probably would have let it go. On the sliding scale of the war, it was more important to wrap those humans up in an amnesiac bullshit blanket and head over to help John Matthew and Qhuinn, who were still handling business back in that alley. Now? There was no pulling out: One way or the other, he and this slayer were going to do a meet-and-greet.

Tohr leaped over the guardrail, hit the walkway, and bounced up onto the fence. Locking a clawhold into the links, he swung his lower body over the top, and landed his shitkickers on the parapet.

The *lesser*'s beery bravado fizzled a little as he started backing away.

"What, you think I'm afraid of heights?" Tohr said in a low voice. "Or that five feet of chainlink is going to keep me from you?"

The wind howled against them, plastering their clothes to their bodies and whistling through the steel girders. Far, far, far down below, the inky waters of the river were nothing but a vague, dark stretch, like a parking lot.

Gonna feel like asphalt, too.

"I got a gun," the *lesser* yelled.

"So take it out."

"My friends are coming for me!"

"You don't have any friends."

The *lesser* was a new recruit, his hair and eyes and skin having yet to pale out. Lanky and twitchy, he was likely a drug user who suffered from brain-fry—which was no doubt why he'd fallen for the pitch to join the Society.

"I'll jump! I'll fucking jump!"

Tohr palmed the handle of one of his two daggers and withdrew the black blade from his chest holster. "So quit yakking and start flying."

The slayer looked over the edge. "I'll do it! I swear I'll do it!"

A gust gave them a blast from a different direction, sweeping Tohr's long leather coat out over the free fall. "Don't matter to me. I'll kill you up here or down there."

The *lesser* peered over the edge again, hesitated, and then let 'er rip, leaping to the side and hitting all that nothing-but-air, his arms pinwheeling as if he were trying to keep his balance so he landed feetfirst.

Which at this height would probably just drive his thighbones up into his abdominal cavity. Better than swallowing his own head, however.

Tohr resheathed his dagger and prepared for his own descent, taking a deep breath. And then it was . . .

As he went over the edge and took that first gasp of antigravity, the irony of the bridge jump wasn't lost. He'd spent so much time wishing for his death to come, praying for the Scribe Virgin to take his body and send him up to be with his loved ones. Suicide had never been an option; you took your own life, you couldn't get into the Fade—and that was the only reason he hadn't cut his wrists, sucked on the business end of a shotgun, or . . . jumped off a bridge.

In his descent, he let himself enjoy the idea that this was it, that the impact coming in a second and a half was going to be the end of his suffering. All he had to do was reposition his trajectory so he was in a dive, then not protect his head and let the inevitable happen: blackout, likely paralysis, death by drowning.

Except that kind of goner-for-good couldn't be his end result. Whoever made the call on these things would have to know that, unlike the *lesser*, he had an out.

Calming his mind, he dematerialized himself from the free fall—one moment gravity had a death grip on him; the next he was nothing but an invisible cloud of molecules that he could will in any direction he wanted.

Next door, the slayer hit the water not with the *splash!* of someone going off the side of a pool, or the *ker-chunk* of somebody working a diving board. The fucker was like a missile hitting a target, and the explosion registered in the form of a sonic cracking as gallons of displaced Hudson River shot up into the brisk air.

Tohr, on the other hand, chose to re-form himself on top of the massive concrete support to the right of the impact site. Three . . . two . . . one . . .

Bingo.

A head popped up downstream of the still-bubbling entrance point. No arms moving in an attempt to regain access to oxygen. No legs kicking. No gasping.

But it wasn't dead: You could run them over with your car, beat them until your own fist broke, rip their arms and/or legs off, do whatever the hell you wanted . . . and they would still be alive.

Fuckers were the ticks of the underworld. And there was no way he wasn't getting wet.

Tohr shrugged off his trench coat, folded it carefully, and left it nestled in the juncture where the upper part of the support met its broad, aquatic base. Getting in the drink with that on his back was a drowning recipe; plus he had to protect his forties and his cell phone.

With a couple of bounding leaps, so he could get enough momentum to put him over open water, he threw himself into dive formation, his arms pointed above his head, his palms together, his body straight as an arrow. Unlike the *lesser*, his penetration was elegant and smooth, even though he came at the surface of the Hudson from a good twelve- to fifteen-foot drop.

Cold. Really frickin' cold.

After all, it was late April in upstate New York—which was still a good month away from anything remotely balmy.

Exhaling through his mouth as he stroked up from the depths, he fell into a powerful freestyle. When he got to the slayer, he locked a grip onto the jacket and began pulling the undead weight to shore.

Where he would finish this. So he could go look for the next one.

As Tohr went off the side of the bridge, John Matthew's own life flashed before his eyes—sure as if he were the one whose shitkickers had left solid ground in favor of nothing-but-net.

He was on the shore, under the exit ramp, when it happened, in the process of finishing off the slayer he'd been chasing: From out of the corner of his eye, he saw something go into a fall from the great height above the river.

It hadn't made sense at first. Any *lesser* with half a brain would know that wasn't a good escape route. Except then everything had become too clear. A figure was standing on the lip of the bridge, leather coat billowing around like a shroud.

Tohrment.

Noooooooo, John had shouted while making no sound at all.

"Mother*fucker*, he's going to jump," Qhuinn spat from behind him.

John lunged forward, for all the good that would do, and then screamed mutely as the closest thing he had to a father jumped.

Later, John would reflect that moments like this had to be what people said of death itself—as you one-plus-oned the series of events that were unfolding, and the math added up to certain destruction, your mind flipped into slide-show mode, showing you clips of life as you had always known it:

John sitting at Tohr and Wellsie's table that first night after he'd been adopted into the vampire world . . . The expression on Tohr's face as the blood results had announced that John was Darius's son . . . That nightmarish moment when the Brotherhood had arrived to tell them both that Wellsie was gone . . .

Then came images from the second act: Lassiter bringing a shriveled shell of Tohr back from wherever he had been . . . Tohr and John finally losing it together over the murder . . . Tohr gradually working his strength up . . . John's own *shellan* appearing in the red gown that Wellsie had mated Tohr in . . .

Man, destiny sucked ass. It just had to barge in and piss all over everyone's rose garden.

And now it was taking a shit in the other flower beds.

Except then Tohr abruptly disappeared into thin air. One moment he was all fly-be-free; the next, he was gone.

Thank God, John thought.

"Thank you, baby Jesus," Qhuinn breathed.

A moment later, on the far side of a pylon, a dark arrow sliced into the river.

Without a glance or a word between them, he and Qhuinn tore off in that direction, getting to the rocky shore just as Tohr surfaced, grabbed the slayer, and started to swim in. As John got into position to help drag the *lesser* onto dry land, his eyes locked on Tohr's grim, pale face.

The male looked dead, even though he was technically alive.

I got him, John signed as he leaned in, nabbed the closest arm, and heaved the soaking-wet slayer out of the river. The thing landed in a heap and did an excellent impression of a fish, eyes bulging, mouth gaping, little clicking sounds coming from its wide-open gullet.

But whatever, Tohr was the issue, and John looked the Brother over as he emerged from the water: Leather pants were sticking like glue to thighs that were thin, muscle shirt was second-skinned to a flat chest, cropped black hair with that white stripe was standing straight up even though it was wet.

Dark blue eyes were locked on the *lesser*.

Or studiously ignoring John's stare.

Probably both.

Tohr reached down and grabbed the *lesser* by the throat. Baring fangs that were viciously long, he growled, "Told you."

Then he outted his black dagger and started stabbing.

John and Qhuinn had to step back. It was either that or get a paint job.

"He could just hit the damn chest," Qhuinn muttered, "and get this over with."

Except killing the slayer wasn't the point. Desecration was.

That sharp black blade penetrated every square inch of flesh—except for the sternum, which was the lights-out switch. With each slashing blow, Tohr exhaled hard; with every jerk free, the Brother inhaled deep, the rhythm of respiration driving the gruesome scene.

"Now I know how they make shredded lettuce."

John rubbed his face, and hoped that was the end of the commentary.

Tohr didn't slow down. He just stopped. And in the aftermath, he listed to the side, propping himself up by throwing a hand out to the oil-soaked dirt. The slayer was . . . well, shredded, yeah, but he wasn't finished.

There'd be no helping out, though. In spite of Tohr's obvious exhaustion, John and Qhuinn knew better than to mess with the end game. They'd seen this before. The final strike had to be Tohr's.

After a couple of moments of recovery, the Brother lurched back into position, double-handing the dagger and lifting the blade over his head.

A hoarse cry tore out of his throat as he buried the point in the chest of what was left of his prey. As bright light flashed, the tragic expression on Tohr's face was illuminated, a comic book rendering of his twisted, horrific features, caught for a moment . . . and an eternity.

He always stared down into the illumination, even though the impermanent sun was too bright to look into.

After it was done, the Brother slumped sure as if his spinal column had turned to putty, his energy disappearing. Clearly, he needed to feed, but that subject, like so many others, was a no-go.

"What time is it," he got out between breaths.

Qhuinn snagged a peek at his Suunto. "Two a.m."

Tohr looked up from the stained ground he'd been staring at, focusing his red-rimmed eyes on the part of downtown they'd just come from.

"How about we go back to the compound." Qhuinn took out his cell phone. "Butch isn't far away—"

"No." Tohr shoved himself back and sat on his ass. "Don't call anyone. I'm fine—just need to catch my breath."

Bull. Shit. The guy was not any closer to fine than John was at the moment. Although, granted, only one of them was dripping wet in a fifty-degree gust.

John shoved his hands into the Brother's field of vision. *We're going home now—*

Wafting over on the breeze, like an alarm breaking through a silent house, the scent of baby powder tickled into each of their noses.

The stench did what all that breathing on the ground couldn't: It got Tohr onto his feet. Gone was the logy disorientation—hell, if you'd pointed out to him that he was still wet as a fish, he probably would have been surprised.

"There're more," he snarled.

As he took off, John cursed at the maniac.

"Come on," Qhuinn said. "Let's get our run on. This is going to be a long night."

TWO

"Take some time off . . . relax . . . enjoy yourself. . . ."

As Xhex muttered to a peanut gallery of antique furniture, she walked out of the bedroom and into the bath suite. And back again. And . . . back once more into marble-landia.

In the bath she and John now shared, she stopped by the pond-deep Jacuzzi. Next to the brass faucets, there was a silver tray with all kinds of lotions and potions and girlie what-the-fuck. And that wasn't the half of it. By the sinks? Another tray, this one full of perfume by Chanel: Cristalle, Coco, No. 5, Coco Mademoiselle. Then there was the fine wicker basket of hairbrushes, some with short naps, others with pointy bristles or spiky metal crap. In the cupboards? A lineup of OPI nail polish bottles in enough variations on cocksucking pink to give even Barbie a nosebleed. As well as fifteen different brands of mousse. Gel. Hair spray.

Really?

And don't get her started on the Bobbi Brown makeup.

Who the hell did they think had moved in here? One of those Kardashian nut jobs?

And on that note . . . Christ, she couldn't believe she now knew Kim, Kourtney, Khloe, Kris; the brother, Rob; stepfather, Bruce; little sisters Kendall and Kylie; as well as the various husband(s), boyfriend(s), and that kid Mason—

Meeting her own eyes in the mirror, she thought, Well, wasn't this interesting. She'd managed to blow her brains out with E! Entertainment Television.

Certainly less messy than a sawed-off, and the results were the same.

"That shit needs to come with a warning label on it."

As she stared at her reflection, she recognized the buzzed-off black hair, and the pale skin, and the tight, hard body. The clipped nails. The absolute lack of makeup. She even had her own clothes on, the black muscle shirt and leather pants a uniform she'd put on every night for years.

Well, except for a couple of evenings ago. Then she'd worn something else entirely.

Maybe that gown was the reason for all the fembot stuff that had shown up after the mating ceremony: Fritz and the *doggen* may have assumed she'd turned over a new leaf. Either that or it was all just part of the standard, newly mated *shellan* welcome wagon.

Turning away, she put her hands up to the base of her throat, to the big, square diamond John had bought her. Set in sturdy platinum, it was the only piece of jewelry she could ever imagine wearing: tough, solid, able to withstand a good fight and stay on her body.

In this new world of Paul Mitchell, and Bed Head, and Coco's stinky stuff, at least John still got her. As for the rest of them? Can you say "education"? Not the first time she'd played teacher to a bunch of males who thought that just because you had breasts, you belonged in a gilded cage. Anyone tried to turn her into a *glymera* chickadee? She'd just saw through the gold bars, set a bomb on the base of the stand, and hang the steaming remains from a chandelier in the foyer.

Heading into the bedroom, she opened the closet and pulled out the red gown that she'd worn during that ceremony. Only dress she'd ever put on—and she had to admit she'd enjoyed the way John had taken it off with his teeth. And yeah, sure, the nights lounging around had been great— first break she'd had in forever. All they'd done was have sex, feed from each other, eat great food, and repeat with bouts of sleep.

But now John had gone back out into the field—whereas she wasn't due to start fighting until tomorrow evening.

This was just twenty-four hours, a delay, not a dead end.

So what the hell was her problem?

Maybe all the chicky-chicky was just triggering her inner bitch for no good reason. She wasn't cooped up, nobody was making her change herself, and that Kardashian car accident of a marathon on the boob tube was her own damn fault. As for the beauty stuff? The *doggen* were just trying to be nice, in the only way they knew how.

Not a lot of females like her. And not just because she was half *symphath*—

Frowning, she cranked her head around.

Letting the satin fall from her hands, she went for the emotional grid that was outside in the hall.

With her *symphath* senses, the three-dimensional structure of sadness and loss and shame was as real as any building you could drive by, look around, or walk through. Unfortunately, in this case, there was no fixing the damage to the supports, or the hole in the roof, or the fact that the electric system wasn't operational anymore: As much as she experienced a person's emotions as if they were a private home, there were no subcontracting workers to come in and repair what was wrong, no plumbers or electricians or painters for this shit. The homeowner had to perform their own improvements on what was broken, battered, and busted; no one else could do it for them.

As she stepped out into the hall of statues, Xhex had a tremor go through her own little house. Then again, the robed, limping figure up ahead was her mother.

God, that still felt weird to say, even if only in her head—and it didn't really apply on so many levels, did it?

She cleared her throat. "Good evening . . . ah . . ."

It didn't sound right to throw out *mahmen* or mom or mommy. No'One, the name the female went by, wasn't comfortable, either. Then again, what could you call somebody who had been abducted by a *symphath*, violently forced to conceive, and then trapped by biology to bear the result of the torture?

First and last name: I and Sorry. Middle name: Am.

As No'One shifted around, the hood that was in place covered her face. "Good evening. How fare thee?"

The English was stiff across her mother's lips, suggesting the female would have done better speaking in the Old Language. And the bow that she gave, which was utterly unnecessary, was lopsided, likely because of whatever injury that caused the uneven gait.

That scent she threw off was not anything by Chanel. Unless they'd recently added a Tragedy line.

"I'm well." Try restless and bored. "Where are you going?"

"To tidy up the sitting room."

Xhex sucked back a wince of don't-go-there. Fritz didn't let anyone but fellow *doggen* lift a finger in the mansion—and No'One, in spite of the fact that she had come here to attend to Payne, was staying in a guest room, eating at the table with the Brothers, and accepted here as the mother of a mated *shellan*. She was not a maid by any standard.

"Yeah, ah . . . how'd you like to . . ." Do what? Xhex wondered. What could the two of them possibly do together? Xhex was a fighter. Her mother was . . . a ghost with substance. Not a lot of common ground there.

"It is all right," No'One said gently. "These are awkward—"

Thunder roared through the foyer below, sure as if clouds had formed, lightning flashed, and rain had started to piss down. As No'One recoiled, Xhex glared over her shoulder. What the hell was—

Rhage, a.k.a. Hollywood, a.k.a. the biggest and most beautiful of the Brothers, all but leaped up onto the second-floor balcony. As he landed, his blond head shot around in her direction, his teal eyes on fire.

"John Matthew called. It's all hands on deck downtown. Get armed and meet us at the front door in ten minutes."

"Hot damn," Xhex hissed as she smacked her palms.

When she turned back to her mother, the female was trembling, and trying not to show it.

"It's okay," Xhex said. "I'm good at fighting. I'm not going to get hurt."

Nice words. Except that wasn't what the female was worried about, was it: Her grid was showing fear . . . of Xhex.

Duh. Given that she was a half-breed *symphath*, of course No'One would think "dangerous" before "daughter."

"I'll leave you alone," Xhex said. "Don't worry."

As she jogged back toward her bedroom, she couldn't ignore the fact that her chest was killing her. But then, she couldn't ignore reality, either: Her mother hadn't wanted her.

And still didn't.

And who could blame her.

*   *   *

From beneath the brim of her hooded robe, No'One watched the tall, strong, merciless female she had birthed rush off to fight against the enemy.

Xhexania didn't seem fazed at all by the idea that she would be facing deadly *lessers*: Indeed, that sneer she had shown upon the Brother's command suggested she would relish it.

No'One's knees went weak as she thought about what she had brought forth into the world, this female with power in her limbs and vengeance in her heart. No female of the *glymera* would respond such as that; then again, they would never be asked.

But the *symphath* was in her daughter.

Dearest Virgin Scribe . . .

And yet, as Xhexania had spun around, there had been an expression quickly hidden on her face.

No'One hurried forth, limping down the hallway to her daughter's room. At the heavy door, she knocked softly.

It was a moment before Xhexania opened up. "Hey."

"I am sorry."

There was no reaction. That showed. "What for?"

"I know what it is to be unwanted by parents. I do not wish you to—"

"It's okay." Xhexania shrugged. "Not like I don't know where you're coming from."

"I—"

"Listen, I have to get ready. Come in if you like, but be warned: I'm not dressing for tea."

No'One hesitated at the threshold. Inside, the room was well lived-in: The bed was mussed; there were leather pants draped on chairs; two sets of boots were on the floor; a pair of wineglasses were set on a table over in the corner by the chaise lounge. All around, the bonding scent of a full-blooded male, dark and sensuous, lingered in the air.

Lingered on Xhexania herself.

There was a series of clicks and No'One looked around the jamb. Over at the closet, Xhexania was putting some kind of nasty-looking gun through its paces. She was utterly competent, slipping it into a holster under her arm and taking out another. And then it was the bullets and a knife—

"You're not going to feel any better about me if you keep standing there."

"I did not come for myself."

That broke the flow of those hands. "Why, then."

"I saw the look on your face. I do not want that for you."

Xhexania reached in and pulled out a black leather jacket. As she yanked the thing on, she cursed. "Look, let's not pretend either one of us wanted me born, okay? I absolve you, you absolve me, we were the victims, blah, blah, blah. We need to stipulate that and move along our separate ways."

"Are you sure that is what you want."

The female froze, then narrowed her eyes. "I know what you did. The night of my birth."

No'One took a step back. "How . . ."

Xhexania pointed to her own chest. "*Symphath*, remember." The fighter came forward, her gait like a prowl. "That means I get into people— so I can feel the fear you have right now. And the regrets. And the pain. Just standing in front of me, you're right back where you were when it all happened—and yeah, I know you buried a dagger in your stomach rather than face a future with me. So like I said, how about you and I just avoid each other, and save both of us the hassle?"

No'One lifted her chin. "Indeed, you are a half-breed."

Dark brows popped. "Excuse me?"

"You sense but a portion of what I feel for you. Or perhaps you do not wish to acknowledge, for your own reasons, that I might wish to care for you."

In spite of the fact that the female was strung with weapons, she abruptly seemed vulnerable.

"In your gruff self-protection, do not cut off avenues for us," No'One whispered. "We do not need to force closeness if it is not there. But let us not stop it from blooming if there is a chance. Perhaps . . . perhaps you shall just tell me this night if there is some small way I can help you. We shall start there . . . and see what transpires."

Xhexania broke off and walked around, her tight, hard body more like a male's, her dress more like a male's, her energy masculine. She stopped when she was in front of the closet and, after a moment, pulled out the skirting of the red gown Tohrment had given her for the night of her mating.

"Have you cleaned the satin?" No'One asked. "And I am not suggesting you have sullied it. Fine fabric must be cared for, however, in order to be preserved."

"I'd have no idea where to start on that one."

"Allow me, then?"

"It'll be fine."

"Please. Allow me."

Xhexania looked over. In a low voice, she said, "Why in God's name would you want to do that?"

The truth was as simple as four words, as complex as an entire language. "You are my daughter."

THREE

Back in downtown Caldwell, Tohr shed the cold and the aches and the exhaustion that gumshoed him and went in pursuit once again: The scent of fresh *lesser* blood was like cocaine in his system, buzzing him up and giving him the strength to carry on.

Behind him, he heard the other two closing in, and knew damn well they weren't seeking enemy—but good fucking luck trying to get him back to the mansion. Dawn was the only thing that could do that.

Besides, the more wiped out he was, the better shot he had at actually sleeping for an hour or two.

As he rounded the corner of an alley, his shitkickers skidded to a halt. In front of him, seven *lessers* were circling a pair of fighters, but the centerpieces were not Z and Phury, or V and Butch, or Blaylock and Rhage.

That was a scythe in the left one's hands. A big-ass, sharply honed scythe.

"Son of a bitch," Tohr muttered.

The male with the curving blade had his feet planted on the pavement like he was a god, his weapon poised, his ugly face smiling in anticipation as if he were about to sit down to a good meal. Next to him, a vampire

Tohr hadn't see for aeons was nothing like the guy he'd once met in the Old Country.

Looked as though Throe, son of Throe, had fallen in with a bad crowd.

John and Qhuinn pulled up on either side of him, and the latter glanced over. "Tell me that isn't our new neighbor."

"Xcor."

"Was he born with that puss or did someone make it for him?"

"Who knows."

"Well, if that was supposed to be a nose job, he needs a new plastic surgeon."

Tohr looked over at John. "Call them off."

Excuse me? the kid signed.

"I know you texted the brothers back at the house. Tell them it was a mistake. Right now." When John started to argue, he cut off the conversation. "You want there to be an all-out war here? You call the Brotherhood in, he calls his bastards in, and suddenly we're balls to the wall without any strategy. We'll handle this by ourselves—I'm fucking serious, John. I've dealt with these boys before. You haven't."

As John's hard stare met his own, Tohr had the sense, as always, that they had been in these situations together far, far longer than just the past few months.

"You gotta trust me, son."

John's response was to mouth a curse, get his phone out and start hitting the buttons.

And at that moment, Xcor tweaked that there were visitors. In spite of the number of *lessers* ahead of him, he started laughing. "It's the bloody Black Daggers—and just in time to save us. You want us on our knees?"

The slayers spun around—big mistake. Xcor didn't waste a moment, striking with a circling sweep, hitting two of them in the lower back. That was his free shot. As the pair fell to the ground, the others split into two camps, half heading for Xcor and Throe, half gunning for Tohr and his boys.

Tohr let out a roar and met the onslaught with his bare hands, leaping forward and locking onto the first slayer that got in range. He went for the head, grabbing on hard, before putting up his knee and cracking the fucker's face open. Then he wheeled the thing around and threw the loose body skullfirst into the side of a Dumpster.

As the ringing faded, Tohr faced off at the next in line. He'd have preferred to have gone more with the fist action, but he wasn't going to dick around: At the far end of the alley, seven more newbies were dropping like snakes from a tree, dripping down the front of a chain-link fence.

He ripped out both daggers, set his boots in the pavement, and assessed an offensive strategy for the fresh arrivals. Man . . . say what you would about Xcor's ethics, social skills, and *GQ* eligibility; the motherfucker could fight. He was swinging that scythe around like it weighed less than a pound, and he had a knack for judging distance—*lesser* parts were flying all over the place, hands, a head, an arm. The bastard was incredibly effective, and Throe wasn't incompetent, either.

Against all odds, and the choice of any of them, Tohr and his crew fell into a rhythm with the bastards: Xcor drove the first round into the waiting blades at the head of the alley, while his lieutenant held the second wave in place so no one got blocked in. After Tohr, John, and Qhuinn picked the tide off, one by one the other slayers were sent to the slaughter— freshly wounded.

Whereas there had been showboating in the beginning, now this was work. Xcor wasn't doing any flashy moves with his wide blade; Throe wasn't jumping around; John and Qhuinn were in the zone.

And Tohr was knee-deep in revenge.

These were nothing but new recruits—so it wasn't like the slayers were offering much in the way of skills. The sheer numbers, however, were such that the tide could turn—

A third squadron popped over the fence.

As they landed one after the other on the payment, Tohr regretted his order to John. That had been vengeance talking. Fuck the shit with avoiding a BDB vs. Band of Bastards showdown; he'd wanted to save the kills for himself. The result? He'd put John's and Qhuinn's lives in danger. Xcor and Throe—they could die tonight, tomorrow, a year from now, whatever. And as for himself—well, you could jump off a bridge in a thousand different ways.

But his boys . . . ? They were worth saving. John was someone's *hellren* now. And Qhuinn had a lot of living ahead of him.

It wasn't fair for his death wish to put them in early graves.

Xcor, son of an unknown sire, had his lover in his hands. His scythe was the only female he had ever cared for, and tonight, as he faced off against what started as seven of the enemy, and then grew to fourteen, and then swelled to twenty-one, she repaid his loyalty with a performance unparalleled.

As they moved together, she was an extension of not just his arms, but his body, his eyes, his brain. He was not a soldier with a weapon; united, they were a beast with mighty jaws. And as they worked, he knew this was what he had missed. This was why he had come across the ocean unto the New World: to find a new life in a new land where there was still plenty of the old, worthy enemy.

Upon his arrival, however, his ambitions had identified an even loftier goal. And it meant the other vampires in this alley were in his way.

At the opposite end of the alley, Tohrment, son of Hharm, was something worth seeing. As much as Xcor hated to admit it, the Brother was an incredible fighter, those whirling black daggers catching the ambient light, those arms and legs shifting positions fast as a heartbeat, that balance and execution—sheer perfection.

If he had been one of Xcor's males, the Brother might well have had to be killed so that Xcor could retain his prime position: It was a basic tenent of leadership that one eliminated those who presented a potential challenge to one's position . . . although it wasn't as if his band were incompetents—after all, one had to eliminate the weak as well.

The Bloodletter had taught him that and so much more.

At least some things had proven not to be lies.

There would never be a place for the likes of Tohrment in his band of bastards, however: that Brother and his ilk would not slum themselves for a shared meal, much less any professional association.

Though one cohesed briefly, this night. As the fight progressed, he and Throe fell into a cooperation with the Brothers, funneling *lessers* in small groups into blade range, whereupon they were dispatched to the Omega by the other three.

Two Brothers, or Brotherhood candidates, were with Tohr, and both were larger than him—in fact, Tohrment, son of Hharm, was not as broad as he had once been. Mayhap from recovery of a recent injury? Whatever the cause, Tohr had chosen his backups wisely. The one on the right was a tremendous male, the size of whom proved that the Scribe Virgin's breeding program had had a point. The other was more the girth and vertical of Xcor and his males—which was to say he was not small. Both worked seamlessly and without hesitation, showing no fear.

When it was finally done, Xcor was breathing hard, his forearms and biceps numb from exertion. All who had fangs were standing. All who had black blood in the vein were gone, sent back to their evil maker.

The five of them stayed in their positions, weapons still in hand as they panted, eyes peeled for any signs of aggression from the other side.

Xcor glanced at Throe and nodded ever so slightly. If others from the Brotherhood had been called in, this was not the kind of showdown they would come out of alive. If these three engaged? He and his soldier had a chance, but there would be injuries.

He did not come to Caldwell to die. He came here to be king.

"I look forward to seeing you again, Tohrment, son of Hharm," he announced.

"Leaving so soon?" the Brother countered.

"Did you think I would bow before you?"

"No, that would require class."

Xcor smiled coldly, flashing his fangs as they elongated. His temper was held in check by his self-control—and the fact that he was already begining to work on the *glymera*. "Unlike the Brotherhood, we lowly soldiers actually work during the night. So instead of kissing the ring of antiquated custom, we're going to seek and eliminate more of the enemy."

"I know why you're here, Xcor."

"Do you. Mind reader?"

"You're going to get yourself killed."

"Indeed. Or mayhap it shall be the other way around."

Tohrment shook his head slowly. "Consider this a friendly warning. Go back where you came from before what you set in motion rolls you right into an early grave."

"I like where I am. The air is bracing on this side of the ocean. How's your *shellan*, by the way."

The cold draft that surged forward was what he wanted: He'd heard through the convoluted grapevine that the female Wellesandra had been killed in the war some time ago, and he wasn't above using any weapon he had to throw off the enemy.

And the shot was a good one. Immediately, the bookends on either side of the Brother stepped in and grabbed on. But there would be no fighting or arguing. Not this eve.

Xcor and Throe dematerialized, scattering themselves into the chilly spring night. He was not worried that they would be followed. That pair was going to make sure Tohr was okay, which meant they were going to dissuade him from a half-cocked, angry whim that might possibly lead to an ambush.

They had no way of knowing he couldn't access the rest of his troops.

He and Throe regained their forms on top of the tallest skyscraper in the city. He and his soldiers had always had a rallying point such that the band could be reunited from time to time during the night, and this towering rooftop was not only easily visible from all quadrants of the battlefield; it seemed apt.

Xcor liked the view from on high.

"We need cell phones," Throe said over the din of the wind.

"Do we."

"They have them."

"The enemy, you mean?"

"Aye. Both of them." When Xcor said nothing further, his right-hand male muttered, "They have ways of communicating—"

"That we do not require. If you allow yourself to rely on externals, they become weapons over you. We have done just fine without such technology for centuries."

"And this is a new era in a new place. Things are different here."

Xcor glanced over his shoulder, trading the view of the city for the sight of his second in command. Throe, son of Throe, was a fine example of breeding, all perfect features, and comely body that, thanks to Xcor's lessons, was now not merely decorative, but useful: For truth, he had grown hard over the years, finally earning the right to declare his sex as that of male.

Xcor smiled coldly. "If the Brothers' tactics and methods are so successful, why did the race get raided?"

"Things happen."

"And sometimes they are the result of mistakes—fatal ones." Xcor resumed his perusal of the city. "You might consider how easily such errors can be made."

"All I'm saying—"

"This is the problem with the *glymera*—always looking for the easy way out. I thought I beat that tendency out of you years ago. Do you require a refresher?"

As Throe shut the fuck up, Xcor smiled more broadly.

Focusing on the expanse of Caldwell, he knew that dark though the night was, his future was bright indeed.

And paved with the bodies of the Brotherhood.

FOUR

"**W**here the hell are they finding all these recruits?" Qhuinn asked as he walked around the fight scene, his boots slapping through the black blood.

John barely heard the guy, even though his ears were working just fine. With the departure of those bastards, he was sticking by Tohr's side. The Brother seemed to have recovered from that uncalled-for kick in the nuts Xcor had just nailed him with, but it was still waaaaay break time.

Tohr wiped his black blades off on his thighs. Took a deep breath. Seemed to pull out of an inner suck hole. "Ah . . . the only thing that makes sense is Manhattan. You need a big population. With a lot of bad seeds on the periphery."

"Who the hell is this *Fore-lesser?*"

"A little shit, last I heard."

"Right up the Omega's alley."

"Smart, though."

Just as John was going to broach the whole Cinderella-turning-into-a-pumpkin thing, his head shot around.

"More," Tohr said on a growl.

Yeah, but that wasn't the problem.

John's *shellan* was out in the alleys.

Instantly, everything went from his mind; his toilet bowl flushed. What the hell was she doing out? She wasn't on rotation. She should be home—

As the stench of fresh, breathing *lesser* entered his nose, a deep inner conviction clawed into his chest: *She shouldn't be out here at all.*

"I need to get my coat," Tohr said. "Stay here and I'll go with you."

Fat. Chance.

The instant Tohr dematerialized back to the bridge, John took off, his shitkickers pounding the asphalt as Qhuinn shouted something that ended with, "You cocksucker!"

Whatever, unlike Tohr's wild, crazy, maniac diversions, this was *important.*

John cut through the alley, shot down a side street, jumped across two lines of parked cars, bolted into a detour. . . .

And there she was, his mate, his lover, his life, squaring off against a quartet of *lessers* in front of an abandoned rooming house—flanked by a big, loudmouthed blond traitor.

Rhage should *never* have recruited her. John had said reinforcements— he sure as shit hadn't meant his Xhex. And second of all, he'd told them to stay home, at Tohr's request. What the fuck were they—

"Hey!" Rhage called out cheerfully. Like he was inviting them to a party. "Just thought we'd take the air tonight in beeeeautiful downtown Caldwell."

Right. This was one moment when being mute sucked. *You fucking ass—*

Xhex turned her head around to look at him—and that was when it happened. One of the *lessers* was tucking a knife, and the sonofabitch had both a good arm and great aim: The blade flew through the air, hilt over point.

Until it came to a sudden stop . . . in Xhex's chest.

For the second time in one evening, John screamed without making a sound.

As his body surged forward, Xhex whipped around to the slayer, an expression of rage tightening her features. Without losing a beat, she grabbed onto the handle and tore the weapon out of her own flesh—but how long would her strength last? That was a direct hit—

Jesus Christ! She was going to try to take care of the bastard. Even injured, she was going to go after him tooth and nail . . . and get herself killed in the process.

The one thought that shot through John's mind was that he didn't want to be like Tohr. He didn't want to walk that stretch of hell on earth.

He didn't want to lose his Xhex tonight, tomorrow night, any night. Ever.

Opening his mouth, he roared all of the air out of his lungs. He wasn't conscious of dematerializing, but he was on that *lesser* so fast that going ghost and re-forming was the only explanation. Locking onto the thing's throat with his palm, he pushed the piece of shit backward off its feet and let his own weight follow. When they hit the ground, he head-butted its face, smashing the nose, and likely breaking a cheekbone or an eye socket.

No stopping there.

As black blood splashed up all over him, he bared his fangs and tore into the enemy with his teeth while he held the thing down. The destructive instinct was so finely tuned and focused, he would have kept going until he was chewing on pavement—but then his rational side sent up a hi-how're-ya.

He needed to assess Xhex's injuries.

Taking out a dagger, he raised his arm high and locked eyes with the slayer. Or what was left of the *lesser*'s pair of peepers.

John buried that blade so deep and hard that after the flash and bang faded, he needed a two-handed grip and a full-body pull to free the weapon out of the asphalt. Scrambling around, he prayed to see Xhex—

She was more than up on her feet. She was engaging another one of the quartet—even though there was a growing red stain on the front of her chest, and her right arm was hanging loose.

John nearly lost his mind.

Leaping up, he threw his body between his mate and the enemy, and as he shoved her out of the way, he took a hit meant for her—a solid swing with a baseball bat that rang his church bell and made him momentarily lose his balance.

Exactly the kind of thing that would have knocked her flat and put "paid" to her coffin.

With a quick shift, he reestablished equilibrium, and then caught the second try at turning him into a homer with both hands.

Quick punch forward and he slammed the *lesser* in the face with its own Louisville slugger, giving the undead a split second of show tunes in its head. Then it was domination time.

"What the hell!" Xhex hollered at him as he forced the slayer onto the ground.

No good way to communicate, considering his hands were locked on the *lesser*'s throat. Then again, it wasn't going to help them for her to know what was on his mind.

With a quick stab, John dispatched the slayer back to the Omega and got up. His left eye, the one that had gotten corked with the bat, was starting to swell, and he could feel his heartbeat in his face. Meanwhile, Xhex was still bleeding.

"Don't you *ever* do that to me again," she hissed.

He wanted to jab his finger in her face, but if he did, he couldn't talk. *Then don't fight when you're injury-injer-injured!*

Christ, he couldn't even communicate, his fingers clogging up over words.

"I was just fine!"

You're fucking bleeding—

"It's a flesh wound—"

Then why can't you lift up your arm!

The pair of them were closing in on each other, and not in a good way, their jaws jacked forward, their bodies hunched in aggression. And when she didn't counter him on his last potshot, he knew he'd guessed right— knew, too, that she was hurting.

"I take care of myself, John Matthew," she spat. "I don't need you looking over my shoulder because I'm a female."

I would have done the same for one of the Brothers. Well, mostly he would have. *So don't push that feminist bullshit on me—*

"Feminist *bullshit*?!"

You're the one making it about your sex, not me.

Her eyes narrowed. "Oh, really. Funnily enough, I'm not persuaded. And if you think my standing up for myself is a goddamn political statement, you mated the wrong *goddamn* female."

This is not about your being female!

"The fuck it isn't!"

On that note, she inhaled deep, as if to remind him that his bonding scent was so strong, it knocked out even the stench of all the *lesser* blood splattered around.

John bared his fangs and signed, *It's about your stupidity creating a liability on the battlefield.*

Xhex's mouth cranked open—but then, instead of countering, she just stared up at him.

Abruptly, she crossed her good arm over her chest and focused out over his left shoulder, slowly shaking her head back and forth.

Like she was regretting not just what had happened a moment ago, but maybe meeting him in the first place.

John cursed and went to pace around, only to find that everyone else in the alleyway—and that would be Tohr, Qhuinn, Rhage, Blaylock, Zsadist, and Phury—was watching the show. And what do you know, each of the males wore an expression that suggested he was really, truly, completely, and utterly glad that John's last statement hadn't come out of *his* piehole.

Do you mind, John signed with a glare.

On cue, the bunch of them started milling about, looking up at the dark sky, down at the pavement, across at the brick walls of the alley. Manly muttering floated over on the stinky breeze, as if they were a convention of movie critics discussing what had just been screened.

He didn't care what their opinions were.

And in this moment of anger, he didn't care what Xhex's was, either.

Back at the Brotherhood mansion, No'One had her daughter's mating dress in her arms—and a *doggen* planted in front of her, thwarting her quest for directions to the second-story laundry room. The former was welcome; the latter was not.

"No," she said again. "I shall take care of this."

"Mistress, please, it is a simple thing to—"

"Then letting me tend to the gown will be no problem for you."

The *doggen*'s face fell so far, it was a wonder he didn't have to look up to meet her eyes. "Perhaps . . . I shall just check with Superior Perlmutter—"

"And perhaps I shall tell him how helpful you were in showing me the cleaning supplies—and how much I appreciated your fine service unto me."

Even though her hood was up and shielding her face, the *doggen* seemed to gauge her intention clearly enough: She wasn't budging. Not to this member of the staff or any other. His only option was to throw her over his shoulder and carry her off—and that would never happen.

"I am—"

"Just about to lead the way, aren't you."

"Ah . . . yes, mistress."

She bowed her head. "Thank you."

"May I take the—"

"Lead? Yes, please. Thank you."

He was not holding the dress for her. Or cleaning it. Or hanging it up. Or redelivering it.

This was between her and her daughter.

With dejection worthy of a castaway, the servant spun about and started walking, taking her down the long corridor that was marked by beautiful marble statuary of males in various positions. Then it was through a pair of swinging doors at the end, to the left, and through another set of doors.

At this point, everything changed. The runner on the hardwood flooring was no longer an Oriental, but a plain, well-vacuumed cream. There was no art on these pristine creamy walls, and the windows were covered not with great swaths of color with fringe and tassels, but heavy bolts of cotton in the same pale color.

They had entered the servant portion of the mansion.

The juxtaposition had been the same at her father's manse: One standard for the family. One standard for the staff.

Or at least she had heard it was as such. She had never gone to the back side of the house when she had lived therein.

"This should be"—the *doggen* opened a pair of doors—"everything you seek."

The room was the size of the suite she had had at her father's estate, big and spacious. Except there were no windows. No grand bed with a matching set of handmade furniture. No needlepoint rugs in peaches and yellows and reds. No closets full of fashions from Paris or drawers of jewels or baskets of hair ribbons.

This was where she belonged now. Especially as the *doggen* described the sundry white contraptions as washing machines and dryers, and then detailed the operation of the ironing boards and irons.

Yes, the servants' quarters rather than the guest accommodations were her home, and had been ever since she had . . . found herself in a different place.

In fact, if she could convince someone, anyone, to let her have a room down in this part of the mansion, it would be preferable. Alas, however, as the mother of the mated *shellan* of one of the household's prime fighters, she was accorded privilege that she did not deserve.

The *doggen* began to open cupboards and closets, showing her all manner of equipment and concoctions that were described variously as steamers and stain removers and pressers. . . .

After the tour was completed, she went over and rose up awkwardly on her good foot to link the top of the gown's hanger upon a knob.

"Are there any stains of which you are aware?" the *doggen* asked as she flounced out the skirting.

No'One proceeded to go over every square inch of the full bottom, the bodice, the capped sleeves. "There is only this that I can see." She bent down carefully so as not to put a lot of weight on her weak leg. "Here where the hem meets the floor."

The *doggen* did likewise and inspected the faint darkening on the fabric, his pale hands so sure, his frown one of concentration instead of confusion. "Yes, the manual dry cleaner, I think."

He took her to the far side of the room and described a process that was easily going to fill hours. Perfect. And before she allowed him to depart, she insisted that he stay at her side for the first couple of treatments. As this made him feel more useful, it worked for the both of them.

"I believe I am ready to continue on my own," she said eventually.

"Very well, mistress." He bowed and smiled. "I shall go down and endeavor to ready Last Meal. If you should need anything, please call me."

From what she had learned since her arrival, that required a telephone—

"Here," he said, over by the counters. "Press 'star' and 'one' and ask for me, Greenly."

"You have been most helpful."

She looked away quickly, not wanting to see him bow to her. And she didn't try for a deep breath until the door shut behind him.

Now alone, she put her hands on her hips and let her head hang for a moment, the pressure in her chest making it difficult to fill her lungs.

When she had come here, she expected to struggle—and she was, just not with the things she had anticipated.

She hadn't considered how difficult it would be to exist in an aristocratic house. The home of the First Family, in fact. At least when she had been up with the Chosen, there had been other rhythms and rules, with no one below her. Here? The lofty position people forced upon her cut off her oxygen a lot of the time.

Dearest Virgin Scribe, mayhap she should have asked the servant to stay. At least the innate need for composure had given her a draw in her ribs. With no one to hide from, however, she fought for breath.

The robe was going to have to come off.

Limping over to the doors, she went to lock them, but found there was no bolting mechanism. Not what she was expecting.

Opening them a crack, she put her head out and double-checked the long hallway.

All the servants would be downstairs preparing food for the people of the house. Even more significant, there was no way anyone but *doggen* would be in this part of the mansion.

She was safe from other eyes.

Ducking back in, she loosened the tie around her waist, removed her hood from the crown of her head and then stripped herself of the weight she bore anytime she was in public. Ah, glorious relief. Reaching her arms up high, she stretched her shoulders and her back, then pulled her neck from side to side. Her last reclamation was to lift the heavy braid of her hair and put it over her shoulder, relieving some of the pull at her nape.

Save for that first night that she had come unto this house and confronted her daughter—as well as the Brother who had tried to save her life so long ago—no one had seen her features. And no one would henceforth. Ever since that brief revelation, she had been e'er covered, and she was going to stay that way.

Proof of identity had been a necessary evil.

As always, she wore beneath her robing a simple linen sheath she had made herself. She had a number of them, and when they grew too thin, she recycled them as towels to dry herself with. She wasn't sure where she would find the fabric for replacements here, but that was no problem. In order to refresh herself so that she did not need to feed, she went regularly to the Other Side, and she could get what she needed then.

So different the two places were. And yet in either, her hours were the same: infinite, solitary—

No, not entirely solitary. She had come to this side to find her daughter, and now that she had, she was going to . . .

Well, tonight, she was going to clean this gown.

Stroking the fine fabric, she couldn't stop the memories from bursting forth, a geyser, unwelcomed.

She had had gowns like this. Dozens of them. They had filled the closet of her nighttime quarters, those beautifully kitted-out rooms that had had the French doors.

Which had proved to be less than secure.

As her eyes misted over, she fought the pull of the past. She'd been through that black hole too many times to count—

"You should burn that robe."

No'One wheeled around so fast, she nearly tore the dress off the worktable.

In the doorway was a massive male with blond-and-black hair. Verily, he was so big he filled the double-size jambs, but that was not the astonishing thing.

He appeared to gleam.

Then again, he was covered with gold, hoops and studs marking his ears, his eyebrows, his lips, his throat.

No'One dived for what normally covered her, and he stood calmly as she girded herself with the robe.

"Better?" he said softly.

"Who are you."

Her heart beat so fast that the three words came out in a rush. She wasn't good with males in enclosed spaces, and this was very enclosed, and he was very male.

"I'm a friend of yours."

"Then why have I yet to make your acquaintance."

"Some people would say you're lucky to have been spared," he muttered. "And you've seen me at meals."

She supposed she had. She typically kept her head down and her eyes on her plate, but yes, in the periphery, he had been there.

"You're very beautiful," he said.

There were two things that kept her from completely panicking: First, there was no speculation in that deep voice of his, no masculine heat, nothing that made her feel preyed upon; and second, he had shifted his position so he was lounging back against the jamb—leaving her room to bolt out if she had to.

As if he knew what made her nervous.

"I've been giving you some time to settle in and get your bearings," he murmured.

"Why would you have cause to do that."

"Because you're here for a very important reason, and I'm going to help you."

The male's bright white, pupil-less eyes held hers, even though her face was in shadow . . . as though he were not merely looking at her, but into her.

She took a step back. "You do not know me."

At least that was a truth so solid she could plant her feet on it: Even if whoever this was was familiar with her parents, her family, her lineage, he did not know her. She was not who she had once been: the abduction, the birth, her death had wiped that slate clean.

Or had broken it to pieces, more accurately.

"I know that you can help me," he said. "How about that."

"Are you looking for a maid?"

Hard to imagine, given the number of staff in this household—but that was beside the point. She didn't want to serve a male in any kind of intimate way.

"No." Now he smiled, and she had to admit he looked a little . . . kind. "You know, your default doesn't have to be servile."

She kicked her chin up a notch. "All work is honorable."

That was a fact that she had missed before everything had changed. Dearest Virgin Scribe, she'd been a spoiled, overpampered, entitled brat. And the shedding of those ugly, jeweled robes of self-inflation had been the only good thing that had come out of it all.

"Not maintaining to the contrary." He tilted his head, as if he were imagining her in a different place, with different clothes. Or maybe he just had a stiff neck; who knew. "I understand you're Xhex's mom."

"I am the female who birthed her, yes."

"I heard that Darius and Tohr put her up for adoption after she was born."

"They did. They sheltered me through my convalescence." She skipped the part about her taking the latter's dagger and putting it to use upon her own flesh: she had already spoken o'er much to this male.

"You know, Tohrment, son of Hharm, spends a lot of time looking in your direction at meals."

No'One recoiled. "I am certain you are wrong."

"My eyes work just fine. As do his, apparently."

Now she laughed, the hard, short burst breaking out of her throat. "I can assure you, it is not because he fancies me."

The male shrugged "Well, friends can disagree."

"With all due respect, we are not friends. I do not know you—"

Abruptly, the room was infused with a golden glow, the light so buttery and delicious, she felt her skin prickle with warmth.

No'One took a further step back as she realized it was not an optical illusion courtesy of all the jewelry he wore. The male was the source of the illumination, his body, his face, his aura like a banked fire.

As he smiled at her, his expression was that of a holy man. "My name's Lassiter, and I'll tell you all you need to know about me. I'm an angel first and a sinner second, and I'm not here for long. I'll never hurt you, but I'm prepared to make you pretty goddamn uncomfortable if I have to, to get my job done. I like sunsets and long walks on the beach, but my perfect female no longer exists. Oh, and my favorite hobby is annoying the shit out of people. Guess I'm just bred to want to get a rise out of folks—probably the whole resurrection thing."

No'One's hand crept up and held her robe together in a tight grip. "Why ever are you here?"

"If I told you now, you'd just fight it tooth and nail, but let's just say I believe in full circles—I simply didn't see the one we're in until you came along." He gave her a little bow. "Take care of yourself—and that beautiful dress."

With that, he was gone, drifting away, taking the warmth and the light with him.

Slumping back against the counter, it took her a while to realize her hand hurt. Looking down, she observed it from a distance, seeing the white knuckles and the rigid flesh against the robe's lapels as if it were someone else's appendage.

It was always thus when she regarded any part of her body.

But at least she could command her flesh: Her brain ordered the hand attached to the arm that plugged into the torso to release and relax.

As it obeyed, she glanced back over to where the male had stood. The doors were closed. Except . . . he hadn't shut them, had he?

Had he even been here?

She rushed over and looked out into the hall. In all directions . . . there was no one.

FIVE

After nearly two hundred years of having been mated, Tohr was pretty familiar with the way arguments between pigheaded fighters and hot-tempered females went. And how ridiculous was it to have a case of the nostalgias over the way John and Xhex were hairy-eyeballing each other.

God, he and his Wellsie had gone a few good rounds during their day. Just one more thing to mourn.

Dragging his exhausted brain back on track, he stepped in between the pair, figuring the situation needed a reality injection. If it had been any other two, he wouldn't have wasted his breath. Romance was not his business—whether it was going well or badly—but this was John. This was . . . the son he'd once hoped to have.

"Time to go back to the compound," he said. "You both need treatment."

"Stay out of this—"

Stay out of this—

Tohr reached over and clamped a hold on the nape of John Matthew's neck, squeezing those tendons until the male was forced to look at him. "Don't be an asshole about this."

Oh, sure, it was okay for you to be an asshole—

"You got it, kid. That's the privilege of age. Now shut up and get in the fucking car."

John frowned as if he'd just noticed Butch had rolled up in the Escalade.

"And you," Tohr said in a softer tone. "Do everyone a favor and get that shoulder dealt with. Afterward, you can call him a fuck-twit, an ass-hat, and any other thing that strikes you—but right now, that injury of yours is reknitting in three or four different bad ways. You need to see our surgeons fast, and as you are a reasonable female, I know you see the merits of what I'm saying—"

Tohr took his forefinger and shoved it in John's face. "Shut. Up. And no, she's going to get herself back to the compound. Aren't you, Xhex. She's not getting in that SUV with you."

John's hands started going, but they stopped when Xhex said, "Okay. I'll head north now."

"Good. Come on, son." Tohr shoved John in the direction of the SUV, prepared to pick him up by the short hairs if he had to. "Time to have a little ride."

Man, John was so pissed off, you could have fried an egg on his forehead.

Tough. Shit. Tohr whipped open the passenger-side door and packed the fighter into the front seat like he would have an overnight duffel, or a set of golf clubs, or maybe a bag of groceries.

"Can you do the seat belt yourself like a big boy—or should I work it for you?"

John's lip curled up, his fangs making a reveal.

Tohr just shook his head and propped an arm on the SUV's black body paint. Man, he was fucking tired. "Listen to me—as a male who's been in your boots with this kind of thing a million times, you two have to have some space right now. Separate corners, a little calm-down—then you can talk shit through and . . ." His voice got gruff. "Well, makeup sex is fantastic, if memory serves."

John Matthew's mouth formed a couple variations on *fuck*. Then he slammed his head back against the rest. Twice.

Mental note: Have Fritz check for structural damage to the seat.

"Trust me, son. The pair of you are going to do this from time to time, and you might as well start to deal with it rationally now. Took me a good fifty years of making shit worse till I figured out a better way to handle arguments. Learn from my mistakes."

John's head cranked over, and he started to mouth, *I love her so much. I'd die if anything happened to h—*

When he stopped short, Tohr took a deep breath through the pain in his chest. "I know. Trust me . . . I know."

Shutting the door with a clap, he went around to Butch's side. When the window was put down, he said quietly, "Drive slow and take the long route. Let's try to have her in and out of surgery before he gets there. Last thing we need is him riding Manny's ass in the OR."

The cop nodded. "Hey, you want a ride back? You don't look so hot."

"I'm fine."

"Are you sure you know what those two words mean?"

"Yup. Later."

When he turned away, he saw that Xhex was gone, and knew there was a good probability she had done what she'd said she was going to. Even though she was as pissed off as John, it was doubtful she'd be stupid about her health, or their future.

Females, after all, were not just the fairer sex, but the fairly reasonable one. Which was the only reason the race had survived this long.

As the Escalade eased off at a snail's pace, Tohr anticipated all the fun Butch was going to have on the way home. Hard not to feel sorry for the poor bastard.

Annnnnnd then he faced off at his peanut galley. Looked like the cop from Boston wasn't the only one about to get an earful, and sure enough, each one of the males lobbed a sentence back at him:

"Time to go back to the training center."

"You need treatment."

"You are a reasonable male, and I know you see the merits of what I'm saying."

"Don't be an asshole."

Rhage summed up the regurgitation with two words: "Kettle. Black."

Fucking hell. "Did you guys plan that out?"

"Yeah, and if you don't fight us"—Hollywood bit down on his grape Tootsie Pop—"we'll do it again—only with the dance moves this time."

"Spare me."

"Fine. *Unless* you agree to home it, we *will* rock the dance moves." To prove the point, the moron linked his palms behind his head and started doing something obscene with his hips. Which was backed up by a series of, "Uh-huh, uh-huh, ohhhh, yeeeeeeeaaaah, who's your daddy . . ."

The others looked at Rhage like he'd grown a horn in the middle of his forehead. Nothing unusual there. And Tohr knew that, in spite of this ridiculous diversion, if he didn't cave, the lot of them would crawl so far up his ass, he'd be coughing up shitkickers.

Also nothing unusual.

Rhage wheeled around, shoved out his butt, and started slapping his moneymaker like it was bread dough.

The only advantage? Whatever shit he was spouting was muffled.

"For the love of the Virgin Scribe," Z muttered, "put us out of this misery, and go the fuck home."

Someone else chimed in, "You know, I never thought there were advantages to being blind. . . ."

"Or deaf."

"Or mute," somebody added.

Tohr looked around the periphery, hoping that something that smelled like three-day-old sandwich meat would jump out of the shadows.

No luck.

And next thing you knew, Rhage would break into the robot. Or the Cabbage Patch. Or go Twist and Shout on their asses.

His brothers would never forgive him.

An hour and a half . . .

It took one hour and thirty cocksucking minutes to get back home.

As far as John could figure, the only way the trip could have taken longer was if Butch had detoured through Connecticut. Or maybe Maryland.

When they finally pulled in front of the great stone mansion, he didn't wait for the Escalade to get parked—or even slow down. He unlocked the door and leaped out while the SUV was still crusing. Landing in a flat-out run, he took the stone steps up to the front entrance in a single leap, and after ripping into the vestibule, shoved his face so tightly into the security camera, he almost broke the lens with his nose.

The massive bronze portal opened fairly quickly, but damned if he could have said who did the honors. And the incredible rainbow-colored foyer with its marble and malachite columns and its lofty painted ceiling made no impression at all. Neither did the mosaic tiles on the floor that he crossed at a dead run, or the calls of his name from who-the-fuck-knew.

Hitting the door that was tucked underneath the grand staircase, he plowed into the underground tunnel that connected to the training center,

punching in pass codes so viciously it was a wonder he didn't break the keypads. Entering through the back of the office's supply closet, he vaulted around the desk, shot out through the glass door, and—

"She's being operated on now," V announced from fifty yards away.

The Brother was standing outside the main examination room's doorway, a hand-rolled between his teeth, a lighter in his gloved hand.

"It'll be another twenty minutes or so."

As a *shhhh-ch* rose up, a little flame made an appearance, and V brought the heat to the tip of his cigarette. When he exhaled, the scent of Turkish tobacco wafted leisurely down the hall.

Rubbing his aching head, John felt like he'd been put in a metaphorical time-out.

"She's going to be fine," V said on a stream of smoke.

No reason to rush now, and not just because she was on the table. It was pretty damn obvious that V had been put out in the hall as a living, breathing doorstop: John wasn't getting in that room until the Brother let him.

Probably smart. Given his mood, he'd have been perfectly capable of breaking the door down cartoon-style, leaving nothing but the outline of his body in the panel—and naturally, that was what you wanted in the middle of scalpel-palooza.

Robbed of a target, John dragged his sorry ass down to the Brother. *They put you out here, didn't they.*

"Nah. Just a cigarette break."

Yeah, right.

Settling against the wall next to the male, John was tempted to give the back of his head a workout against the concrete, but he didn't want to risk making any noise.

It was too soon, he thought. Too soon for him to be locked out of yet another procedure of hers. Too soon for them to be fighting. Too soon for the tension and the anger.

Can I try one of those? he signed.

V cocked a brow, but didn't try to talk sense into him. The Brother just pulled out a pouch and some cigarette papers. "You want to do the honors yourself?"

John shook his head. For one thing, although he'd watched V's rolling procedure countless times, he'd never tried anything like it before. For another, he didn't think his hands were steady enough.

V took care of things in the work of a moment, and as he gave the coffin nail over, he flicked his lighter.

They both leaned in. Just before John connected the cigarette to the flame, V said, "Word of advice. These have a kick, so don't suck too hard—"

Holy hypoxia, Batman.

John's lungs didn't just reject the onslaught; they had a seizure over it. And as he coughed his bronchial tubes up, V took the offending item from him. Helpful—meant he could brace both palms on his thighs as he bent over and retched.

When the stars faded from his watering eyes, he looked over at V . . . and felt his balls shrivel up and hibernate in his lower gut. The Brother had taken John's hand-rolled and added it to his own, drawing on both of them at the same time.

Great. Like he didn't already feel like a pussy.

V held the pair out between his fore- and middle fingers. "Unless you want to give it another go?" When John shook his head, he got a nod of approval. "Good call. A second drag and your next stop's the wastepaper basket—and not to toss your Kleenex, true."

John let his ass slide down the wall until the linoleum floor came up and caught his tailbone. *Where's Tohr? He come home yet?*

"Yup. I sent him to go eat. Told him he wasn't allowed back here until he had a sworn affidavit that he'd sucked down a full meal with dessert." V took another drag and talked out the fragrant smoke. "I nearly had to drag him up there myself. He's there for you, for real."

He nearly got himself killed tonight.

"Same could be said for all of us. It's the nature of the job."

You know with him it's different.

A grunt was all he got in return.

As time passed, and V smoked like a big shot, John found himself wanting to ask the unaskable.

Teetering on the brink of propriety, desperation eventually threw him over the edge. Whistling softly so Vishous would look over, he used his hands carefully.

How does she die, V. As the Brother stiffened, John signed, *I've heard you sometimes see these things. And if I knew it was old age, I could handle this stuff about her in the field so much better.*

V shook his head, his dark brows going down over his diamond eyes, the tattoo at his temple shifting its shape. "You shouldn't make any changes

to your life based on my visions. They're just a snapshot of a moment in time—which could be next week, next year, three centuries from now. It's occurrence without context, not a when and where."

With his throat closing up, John shot back, *So she does die violently.*

"I didn't say that."

What happens to her? Please.

V's eyes shifted away so that he was staring across the concrete hallway. And in the silence, John was both terrified of, and starved for, whatever the Brother was seeing.

"Sorry, John. I made the mistake of telling someone this information once. It relieved him in the short term, it truly did, but . . . in the end, it was a curse. So, yeah, I know firsthand that opening this can of worms doesn't get anyone anywhere." He glanced over. "Funny, most people don't want to know, true? And I think that's good and the way it's supposed to be. That's why I can't see my own death. Or Butch's. Or Payne's. Too close. Life's meant to be lived blind—that's how you don't take shit for granted. The crap I see isn't natural—it ain't right, kid."

John felt a great hum start up in his head. He knew the guy was talking sense, but he was tingling with the need to know. One look at V's jaw, however, told him he was barking up the wrong tree if he pushed the issue.

Nothing was going to come back at him.

Except maybe a fist.

Still, it was horrible to stand on the lip of such knowledge, knowing that it was out there in the world, a book that should not, must not be read—that he nonetheless was dying to have in his palms.

It was just . . . his whole life was in there with Doc Jane and Manny. Everything he was, and would ever be, was on that slab of a table, out like a light, getting repaired because the enemy had hurt her.

As he closed his eyes, he saw the madness in Tohr's face as the Brother attacked that *lesser*.

Yes, he thought, he now knew down to his marrow precisely how the male felt.

Hell on earth made you do some pretty fucked-up shit.

SIX

pstairs in the formal dining room, the food that Tohr ate with the others was all texture, no taste. Likewise, the conversation percolating up around the table was just sound without relevance. And the people to his left and to his right were two-dimensional sketches, nothing more.

As he sat with his brothers and the *shellans* and guests of the mansion, everything was a distant, hazy blur.

Well, almost all of it.

There was only one thing in the vast room that made any impression on him.

Across the porcelain and the silver, on the far side of the bouquets of flowers and the curling candelabra, a robed figure sat motionless and self-contained in a chair precisely opposite his own. With that hood up in place, the only thing that showed of the female underneath was a pair of delicate hands that, from time to time, cut a piece of meat or forked up some rice.

She ate like a bird. Was silent as a shadow.

And why she was here, he hadn't a clue.

He had buried her back in the Old Country. Underneath an apple

tree, because he had hoped the fragrant blooms would ease her in her death.

God knew she had had nothing easy at the end of her life.

And yet now she was alive again, having arrived with Payne from the Other Side, proof positive that when it came to the Scribe Virgin and the granting of mercies, anything was possible.

"More lamb, sire?" a *doggen* asked at his elbow.

Tohr's stomach was packed tighter than a suitcase, but he was still feeling loose in the joints and sloppy in the head. Considering that eating more was better than the ordeal of feeding, he nodded.

"Thanks, man."

As his plate was refilled with meat, and he volunteered for more rice pilaf, he looked around at the others just to give himself something to do.

Wrath was at the head of the table, the king presiding over everything and everybody. Beth was supposed to be in the other armchair at the far end, but instead, and as usual, she was in her *hellren*'s lap. As was also typical, Wrath was more interested in paying honor to his female than feeding himself: Even though he was fully blind now, he fed his *shellan* from his plate, lifting his fork and holding it so that she leaned in and accepted what he provided.

The pride he so clearly had in her, the satisfaction he took from caring for her, the goddamn warmth between them transformed his harsh, aristocratic face into something almost tender. And from time to time he bared his long fangs, as if he were looking forward to getting her alone and sinking into her . . . in a variety of ways.

Not the kind of thing Tohr needed to see.

Swinging his head around, he caught Rehv and Ehlena sitting side by side, doing the lovey-dovey. And Phury and Cormia. And Z and Bella.

Rhage and Mary . . .

Frowning, he thought of how Hollywood's female had been saved by the Scribe Virgin. She'd been on the lip edge of dead, only to be pulled back and given a long life.

Down in the clinic, Doc Jane was the same. Dead, but returned, with nothing but good years ahead of her and her *hellren*.

Tohr's eyes locked on the robed figure across from him.

Anger boiled in his distended stomach, adding to the pressure: That fallen-from-grace aristocrat, now going by the name No'One, was fucking back as well, granted the gift of life anew by the goddamn mother of the race.

His Wellsie?

Dead and gone. Nothing but memory and ashes.

Forevermore.

As his temper started really buzzing, he wondered who you had to bribe or blow to get that kind of dispensation. His Wellsie had been a female of worth, just like these other three—why hadn't she been spared. Why the fuck wasn't he like those other males, looking forward to the rest of his years.

Why hadn't he and his *shellan* been granted mercy when they needed it most. . . .

He was staring at her.

No . . . he was glaring at her.

Across the table, Tohrment, son of Hharm, was focused on No'One with hard, angry eyes, as if he resented not just her presence in this house, but the very breath in her lungs and the beat of her heart.

The expression did not favor his features. Indeed, he had aged so much since last she had seen him, even though vampires, especially those of strong lineage, appeared to be in their mid- to late twenties until just before they died. And that was not the only change in him. He was suffering from a persistent weight loss—no matter how much he ate at the table, he did not carry enough flesh on his bones, his face marked with hollowed cheekbones and a too-sharp jaw, his sunken eyes smudged with shadows above and below them.

His physical infirmity, whatever it was, hadn't stopped him from fighting, however. He hadn't changed before the meal, and his damp clothes were stained with red blood and black oil, visceral reminders of how all the males spent their nights.

He had washed his hands, however.

Where was his mate? she wondered. She had seen no evidence of a *shellan*—perhaps he had remained unattached all these years? Surely if he had a female, she would be here to support him.

Ducking her head further under her hood, she placed her fork and knife to the side of her plate. She had no more appetite for food.

Nor was she hungry for echoes from the past. The latter, however, was nothing she could politely refuse. . . .

Tohrment had been as young as she when they had spent all those months together in that fortified cabin in the Old Country, taking refuge against the cold of the winter, the wet of the spring, the heat of the summer, and the drafts of the autumn. They had had four seasons of watching her belly swell with life, a complete calendar cycle in which he and his mentor, Darius, had fed, sheltered, and cared for her.

It was not how her first pregnancy should have gone. It was not how a female of her background should have lived. It was not anything that the fate she had intended for herself would have e'er provided.

Arrogant of her to have assumed anything, however. And there had been, and still was, no going back. From the moment she had been captured and ripped away from her family, she had been forever altered sure as if acid had been splashed upon her face, or her body had been burned beyond recognition, or she had lost limbs or eyesight or hearing.

But that was not the worst of it. Bad enough that she had been tainted at all, but that it had been by a *symphath*? And that the stress had triggered her first needing?

She had spent those four long seasons under that thatched roof aware that there was a monster growing inside of her. Indeed, she would have lost her social station if it had been a vampire who had abducted her and cheated her family of the most valuable thing about her: her virginity. Previous to her abduction, as the daughter of the Council's *leahdyre*, she had been a highly valuable commodity, the kind of thing that was sequestered and brought out for admiring at special occasions like a fine jewel.

In fact, her father had been making arrangements for her mating to someone who would have provided her with a lifestyle even higher than that to which she had been born. . . .

With terrible clarity, she recalled that she had been tending to her hair when the soft clicking sound from the French door had registered.

She had put the brush down on her makeup table.

And then the latch had been released by someone other than herself. . . .

In quiet moments since then, she sometimes imagined that she had gone down to her subterranean quarters with her family that night. She hadn't been feeling well—the precursor, likely, to her needing period—and had stayed upstairs because there was more to distract her from her restlessness up above.

Yes . . . she pretended sometimes that she had followed them down into the basement and, once there, had finally told her father about the strange figure that often appeared outside of her bedroom on the terrace.

She would have saved herself.

Saved the warrior across from her this anger of his . . .

She had used Tohrment's dagger. Right after the birth, she had snapped and taken the weapon from him. Unable to bear the reality of what she had brought into the world, incapable of drawing one more breath in the destiny she had been condemned to, she had turned the blade upon her own stomach.

The last thing she had heard before the light had claimed her was him screaming—

The screech of his chair getting shoved back made her jump, and everyone at the table went silent, all eating halting, all movement ceasing, all conversation cutting off as he prowled out of the room.

No'One lifted her napkin and blotted her mouth under her hood. Nobody looked over at her, as if they had all failed to notice his fixation on her. But from down at the far end, the angel with the blond-and-black hair was staring right at her.

Shifting her eyes from him, she saw Tohrment come out of the billiards room across the foyer. He had a bottle of some dark liquid in each hand, and his grim face was nothing short of a death mask.

Closing her lids, she reached deep, trying to find the strength she was going to need to approach the male who had just left so abruptly. She had come here to this side, to this house, to make amends with the daughter she had abandoned.

There was another who needed an apology, however.

And though words of contrition were the ultimate goal, she would begin with the dress, returning it to him as soon as she finished cleaning and pressing it with her own hands. Comparatively, it was such a small thing. But one had to start somewhere, and the gown was clearly a generational one from his bloodline, given to her daughter to wear, as she had no other family.

Even after all these years, he continued to take care of Xhexania.

He was a male of worth.

No'One was quieter about her departure, but the room fell silent once more as she rose from her seat. Keeping her head down, she left not through the archway, as he had, but through the butler's door that led into the kitchen.

Limping past the ovens and counter spaces and busy, disapproving *doggen*, she took to the rear stairwell, the one that had simple whitewashed plaster walls and pine stairs—

"It was his *shellan's*."

The soft leather sole of her slipper shoe squeaked as she wheeled around. Down below, the angel stood at the bottom step.

"The dress," he said. "That was the gown that Wellesandra wore on the night they were mated nearly two hundred years ago."

"Oh, then I shall return it to his mate—"

"She's dead."

A cold shiver went down her spine. "Dead . . ."

"A *lesser* shot her in the face." As No'One gasped, his white eyes didn't blink. "She was pregnant."

No'One threw her hand out for the rail as her body swayed.

"Sorry," the angel said. "I don't sugarcoat shit, and you need to know what you're walking into if you're going to give that back to him. Xhex should have told you—I'm surprised she didn't."

Indeed. Although it wasn't as if they had spent much time together— and they had plenty of topics of their own to tiptoe around.

"I did not know," she said eventually. "The seeing bowls on the Other Side . . . they never . . ." Except she hadn't been thinking of Tohrment when she had gone to them; she'd been worried about and focused on Xhexania.

"Tragedy, like love, makes people blind," he said, as if he could read her regrets.

"I'm not going to take it to him." She shook her head. "I've done enough damage. Presenting him with his . . . mate's gown . . ."

"Is a nice gesture. I think you should return it to him. Maybe it'll help."

"Do what," she said numbly.

"Remind him that she's gone."

No'One frowned. "As if he has forgotten?"

"You'd be surprised, my fair one. The chain of memory needs to be broken—so I say bring the dress to him, and let him take it from you."

No'One tried to imagine that exchange. "How cruel—no, if you're so interested in torturing him, you can do it yourself."

The angel cocked a brow. "It's not torture. It's reality. Time's passing and he needs to move on, fast. Take the gown to him."

"Why are you so interested in his affairs?"

"His destiny is my own."

"How is that possible?"

"Trust me, I didn't set it up like this."

The angel stared at her as if daring her to find falsity in anything he had stated.

"Forgive me," she said roughly. "But I have done enough harm to that fine male. I shan't be a part of anything that hurts him."

The angel rubbed his eyes as if he had a headache. "Goddamn it. He doesn't need coddling. He needs a good hard boot in the ass—and if he doesn't get one soon, he's going to *pray* to be in the shithole he's in now."

"I do not understand any of this—"

"Hell is a place of many levels. And where he's headed is going to make this stretch of agony seem like nothing but spikes under fingernails."

No'One recoiled and then had to clear her throat. "A way with words you have not, angel."

"Really. You don't say."

"I can't . . . I can't do what you wish me to."

"Yes, you can. You have to."

SEVEN

When Tohr had hit the billiards room bar, he hadn't bothered to check which bottles he took. Up on the second-floor landing, however, he learned that the one in his right hand was Qhuinn's Herradurra, and the one in his left was . . . *Drambuie*?

Okay, right, he might be desperate, but he still had taste buds, and that shit was nasty.

Striding down to the sitting room at the end of the hall, he swapped the latter for some good old-fashioned rum—maybe he'd pretend the tequila was Coke and put the two together.

In his room, he shut the door, cracked the seal on the Bacardi, and opened his gullet, sucking the hooch down. Pause for swallow and breath. Repeat. Annnnd repeat . . . and one more good one. The line of fire from his lips to his gut was kind of nice, like he'd deep-throated a lightning strike, and he kept the rhythm going, taking air when he had to as if he were doing the freestyle in a pool.

Half the bottle was gone in about ten minutes, and he was still standing just inside his room. Which was pretty stupid, he supposed.

Unlike getting drunk, which was pretty necessary.

He put all the booze down and fucked around with his shitkickers until he got them off. Leathers, socks, muscle shirt followed the trend. When he was naked, he walked into the bathroom, turned on the shower, and got in with both bottles in his hands.

The rum lasted through the shampoo and soap-up routine. When he started the rinse cycle, he opened the Herradurra and had at it.

It wasn't until he got out that he began to feel the effects, the sharp edges of his mood recontouring and sprouting the peach fuzz of oblivion. Even as the tide came in to claim him, though, he kept up with the drinking as he went dripping wet into his room.

He wanted to go down to the clinic and see about Xhex and John, but he knew that she was going to make it, and they were going to have to sort stuff out on their own. Besides, his mood was toxic, and God knew, they'd had enough of that going around between the pair of them back in the alley.

No need to share the wealth.

He let the duvet dry his body. Well, that and the heat seeping gently through the vents in the ceiling. The Herradurra lasted a little longer than the rum—probably because his stomach had gone SRO between all the booze and the big dinner. When the tequila was done for, he put the bottle on the bedside stand and arranged his limbs comfortably—which wasn't tough. At this point, he could have been packed into a FedEx box and felt okay about it.

Closing his eyes, the room started to go on an easy little spin, as if his bed was right over a drain and everything was slowly funneling out.

You know . . . considering how well this was rolling along, he was going to have to remember the safe out. The pain in his chest was nothing but a dim echo; his blood hunger was quelled; his emotions were placid as a marble countertop. Even when he slept, he didn't get this kind of respite—

The knock on his door was so soft, he thought it was just the beat of his heart. But then it repeated. And repeated again.

"Goddamn, fucking hell . . ." He jacked his head off the pillow and hollered, "*What.*"

When there was no answer, he shot up to his feet—"Whoa. Yeah, okay . . . *hello.*"

Catching himself on the bed stand, he knocked the empty Herradurra on the floor. Wow. His center of gravity was now split between the pinkie toe of his left foot and the outer piece of his right ear. Which meant his body wanted to go in two directions at once.

Getting to the door was like ice-skating. On a Tilt-A-Whirl. With a helicopter as headgear.

And the knob was a moving target, although how that door was shifting from side to side in its frame without breaking was a mystery.

Yanking the thing wide, he barked, "What!"

There was nobody there. But what he saw sobered him up.

Across the hall, hanging from one of the brass sconces, was his Wellsie's red waterfall of a mating dress.

He looked to the left and saw no one. Then he looked to the right and saw . . . No'One.

Down at the far end of the hall, the robed female was going as fast as her limp would allow her, her frail body shifting awkwardly under those folds of rough cloth.

He probably could have caught her. But, shit, he'd obviously scared the crap out of the female, and if he'd been unfit for conversation at the dinner table, he was now unfitter-er.

See? He was even making up words now.

Plus he was buck-ass naked.

Weaving his way out into the corridor, he stood in front of the gown. The thing had obviously been cleaned with care and prepared for storage, its sleeves stuffed with tissue paper, its hanger one of those jobs that had a padded insert for the bodice.

As he looked at the dress, the effects of the alcohol made it seem as if the skirting was caught in a breeze, the bloodred fabric waving to and fro, the weight catching the light and reflecting it back at him at various angles.

Except he was the one moving, wasn't he.

Reaching up, he lifted the hanger from where it had been slung over the sconce, and carried the gown inside his room, shutting his door behind them both. Over at the bed, he laid the dress out on the side that Wellsie had always preferred—the one farthest from the door—and carefully arranged the sleeves and the skirting, making minute adjustments until it was in perfect position.

Then he willed the lights off.

Lying down, he curled on his side, putting his head on the pillow opposite the one that would have supported his Wellsie's head.

With a shaking hand, he touched the satin of the filled-out bodice, feeling the whalebones set within the fabric, the structure of the dress built to enhance a female's gentle, curving body.

It was not as good as her rib cage. Just as the satin was not as good as her body. And the sleeves weren't as good as her arms.

"I miss you. . . ." He stroked the indentation of the gown where her waist would have been—should have been. "I miss you so much."

To think she had once filled this dress out. Had lived inside of it for a brief time, nothing but a camera shot of one evening in both their lives.

Why couldn't his memories bring her back? They felt strong enough, powerful enough, a summoning spell that should have had her magically reinflating the gown.

Except she was alive only in his mind. Ever with him, always out of reach.

That's what death was, he realized. The great fictionalizer.

And just as he would have reread a passage in a book, he remembered their mating day, the way he had stood so nervously to one side of his brothers, fidgeting with his satin robe and his jeweled belt. His blooded sire, Hharm, had yet to come around, the reconciliation that had arrived at the end of his life still a century in the making. But Darius had been there, the male looking over at him every second or two, no doubt because he'd been worried Tohr was going to pass the fuck out.

Which had made two of them.

And then Wellsie had shown. . . .

Tohr slipped his palm down to the satin skirting. Closing his eyes, he imagined her warm, vital flesh filling out the gown once again, her breath expanding and contracting the confines of the bodice, her long, long legs holding the skirting up off the floor, her red hair curling down to the black lace of the sleeves.

In his vision, she was real and she was in his arms, looking up at him from under her lashes as they had danced the minuet with the others. They'd both been virgins that night. He'd been a fumbling idiot. She'd known exactly what to do. And that was pretty much the way things had continued throughout their mating.

Although he'd gotten pretty goddamn good at the sex, pretty fucking fast.

They had been yin and yang, and yet exactly the same: He'd been a sergeant with the Brotherhood, she'd been the general at home, and together, they'd had it all. . . .

Maybe that was why it had happened, he thought. He'd had too much luck and so had she, and the Scribe Virgin had had to level that score.

And now here he was, empty just like the dress, because what had filled both him and this gown was gone.

The tears that came out of his eyes were silent, the kind that seeped out and soaked the pillow, traveling over the bridge of his nose and falling free to drop one after another like rain from the lip of a roof.

His thumb went back and forth over the satin, as if he were rubbing her hip as he had when they'd been together, and he moved his leg over so that it was on top of the skirting.

It wasn't the same, though. There was no body underneath, and the fabric smelled like lemons, not her skin. And he was, after all, alone in this room that was not theirs.

"God, I miss you," he said in a voice that cracked. "Every night. Every day . . ."

From across the dark bedroom, Lassiter stood in the corner next to the highboy, feeling like crap while Tohr whispered to the dress.

Scrubbing his face, he wondered why . . . *why* in the hell, of all the ways he could have gotten free of the In Between, did it have to be this one.

The shit was starting to get to him.

Him. The angel who didn't give a shit about other people, the one who should have been a claims adjuster or a personal injury lawyer or anything on the earth where screwing others was an asset in his course of work.

He should never have been an angel. That required a skill set he didn't have, and couldn't fake.

Back when the Maker had approached him with an opportunity to redeem himself, he'd been too focused on the idea of getting free to think about the particulars of the assignment. All he'd heard was something along the lines of, "Go to earth, get this vampire back on track, set that *shellan* free," yada, yada, yada. . . . After which he'd be released to go about his business instead of stuck in the land of neither-here-nor-there. Seemed like a good deal. And in the beginning, it was. Show up in the woods with a Big Mac, feed the sorry bastard, drag him back here . . . and then wait until Tohr was strong enough physically to start the process of moving on.

Good plan. Except then came the stall-out.

"Moving on" was more than just fighting the enemy, apparently.

He'd been losing hope, about to throw up his hands . . . when suddenly that female No'One appeared in the house—and for the first time, Tohr actually focused on something.

Which was when light dawned on Marblehead: "Moving on" was going to require another level of participation in the world.

Sure. Fine. Dandy. Get the guy laid, great. Then everyone won—most especially Lassiter himself. And, shit, the instant he'd seen No'One without that hood up, he'd known he was on the right track. She was astonishingly beautiful, the kind of female who made even a male who wasn't interested in anything like that stand a little straighter and jack his slacks up. She had paper white skin, and blond hair that would have come down to her hips if it hadn't been braided. With lips that were pink, and eyes that were a lovely gray, and cheeks that were the color of the inside of a strawberry, she was too bright to be real.

And clearly she was perfect for other reasons: She wanted to make amends, and Lassiter had been assuming that with any luck, nature would take its course and everything would fall into place . . . and she would fall into the Brother's bed.

Sure. Fine. Dandy.

Except, whatever. This . . . display . . . across the way? Not sure, not fine, not dandy.

That kind of suffering was a canyon, a purgatory of its own for someone who had not died. And damned if the angel had any clue how to drag the Brother out of it.

Frankly, he was having enough trouble just playing witness.

And on that note, he hadn't planned on respecting the guy. After all, he was on a mission, not here to get buddy-buddy with his key to freedom.

Trouble was, as the acrid scent of the male's agony rose up and filled the room, it was impossible not to feel for him.

Man, he just couldn't fucking take this.

Spiriting himself out into the corridor, he walked alone down the hall of statues to the head of the great staircase. Planting his ass on the top step, he listened to the sounds of the house. Down below, the *doggen* were cleaning up after Last Meal, their cheerful running commentary like chamber music in the background, all bippity-boppity, busy-busy. Behind him, in the study, the king and queen were . . . "working," so to speak, Wrath's bonding scent thick in the air, Beth's hitched breathing very quiet. The rest of the house was relatively quiet, the other Brothers and *shellans* and guests retiring for sleep . . . or other things along the lines of what the royal couple were up to.

Lifting his eyes, he focused on the painted ceiling that was high above the mosaic floor of the foyer. Over the heads of the depicted warriors on

their fearsome, grimacing steeds, the blue sky and white clouds were kind of ridiculous—after all, vampires couldn't fight during the day. But, whatever, that was the beauty of representing reality instead of being in it: When you had the paintbrush in your hand, you were the god you wished ruled your life, capable of picking and choosing among fate's catalog of wares and destiny's deck of cards to your prolonged and sustained advantage.

Peering into the clouds, he waited for the figure he was looking for to appear, and soon it did.

Wellesandra was seated in a vast, desolate field, the endless gray plain studded with large boulders, the merciless wind blowing at her from all directions. She was not doing as well as she had been when he'd first seen her. Beneath the gray blanket that she clutched to herself and the young, she had grown paler, her red hair fading to a dull stain, her skin going pasty, her eyes no longer any discernible shade of sherry brown. And the babe in her arms, the tiny, swaddled bundle, didn't move as much anymore.

This was the tragedy of the In Between. Unlike the Fade, it wasn't meant to be forever. It was a way station to a final destination, and everyone's was a little different. The only thing that was the same? If you stayed too long, you couldn't get out. No eternal grace for you.

You just transitioned into a *Dhund*-like nothingness, with no chance of ever getting free of the void.

And these two were reaching the end of their rope.

"I'm doing the best I can," he said to them. "Just hold on . . . fucking hell, just *hold on*."

EIGHT

The first thing Xhex did when she checked back into consciousness was look for John in the recovery room.

He wasn't in the chair across the way. Wasn't on the floor, propped up in the corner. Wasn't on the bed beside her.

She was alone.

Where the hell was he?

Oh, yeah, sure. He crawled all over her in the field, but then he left her here? Had he even come back for her operation?

With a groan, she considered rolling onto her side, but with all the IV lines in her arm and wires on her chest, she decided not to fight her plugins. Well, and then there was the happy fact that someone had drilled a large bore hole in her shoulder. A number of times.

Lying there with a snarl on her face, everything about the room annoyed her. The blow of the heat from the ceiling, the whirring sound of the machines behind her head, the sheets that felt like sandpaper, the rock-hard pillow and the too-soft mattress . . .

Where the fuck was John?

For the love of God, she may have made a mistake mating him. The

loving him thing was what it was—no changing that, and she wouldn't want to. But she should have known better than to make things official. Even though the traditional sex roles of vampires were changing, thanks in large part to Wrath loosening up the Old Ways, there was still a load of patriarchal shit surrounding *shellans.* You could be a friend, a girlfriend, a lover, a co-worker, a car mechanic, for fuck's sake, and expect your life to be your own.

But she feared that once your name was in the back of a male—and worse, a full-blooded warrior male—things changed. Expectations shifted.

Your mate started getting up in your face and thinking you couldn't take care of yourself.

Where *was* John?

Fed up, she shoved herself off the pillows, took out her IV and clipped the end so that the saline and whatever else didn't drip all over the floor. Next she silenced the heart monitor behind her, and then ripped the pads off her chest with her free hand.

She kept her right arm immobilized against her rib cage—she just needed to walk, not wave a flag.

At least she didn't have a catheter.

Putting her feet on the linoleum, she stood up carefully and gave herself props for being such a good little patient. In the bathroom, she washed her face, brushed her teeth, used the loo.

When she came back out, she expected to see John in one of the two doorways.

Nope.

Going around the end of the bed, she took things slowly, because her body was logy from the drugs, the operation, and the fact that she needed to feed—although shit knew, scoring John's vein was the last thing she was interested in. The longer he stayed away, the more she didn't want to see his hairy ass.

Goddamn it.

Over at the closet, she opened the paneled doors, ditched her johnny, and changed into some scrubs—which, of course, were not her size, but male-sized. And wasn't that a metaphor. As she struggled to dress with one hand, she cursed John, the Brotherhood, the role of *shellans,* females in general . . . and especially the shirt and pants, as she struggled to one-handedly roll up the bottoms that pooled around her feet.

As she marched for the door, she studiously ignored the fact that she was looking for her mate, and instead focused on the songs going through her head, little a cappella versions of such happy Top 40 hits as "What

Gave Him the Right to Call Her Out on the Field," "How in the Hell Could He Have Left Her Down Here Alone," and the ever-popular standby "All Males are Morons."

Doo-dah, doo-dah.

Tearing open the door, she—

Across the corridor, John was sitting on the hard floor, knees peaked like tent poles, arms crossed around his chest. His eyes met hers the instant she made an appearance—not because he looked her way, but because he had been focused on the space she would fill long before she had actually come out.

The ranting in her brain silenced: He looked like he had been through hell and had carried the flames of the devil's living room back in his bare hands.

Unwrapping his arms, he signed, *I thought you might like your privacy.*

Well, shit. There he went, ruining her bad temper.

Shuffling over, she eased herself down beside him. He didn't help her, and she knew he was doing that on purpose—as a way to honor her independence.

"Guess this was our first fight," she said.

He nodded. *I hated it. The whole thing. And I'm sorry—I just . . . I can't explain what came over me, but when I saw you injured, I snapped.*

Her exhale was long and slow. "You were okay with me fighting. Right before we were mated, you said you were cool with it."

I know. And I still am.

"You sure about that."

After a moment, he nodded again. *I love you.*

"Me, too. I mean, you. You know."

But he hadn't really answered her, had he. And she didn't have the energy to follow up any further. The pair of them just sat on that floor in silence until eventually she reached out and took his hand.

"I need to feed," she said roughly. "Will you . . ."

His eyes shot to hers and his head bobbed. *Always*, he mouthed.

She got to her feet without his aid and extended her free hand to him. When he took her palm, she summoned her strength and pulled him up. Then she led him into the recovery room, and locked the doors with her mind as he sat down on the bed.

He was rubbing his palms on his leathers as if he were nervous, and before she could go over to him, he jumped up. *I need to shower. I can't get close to you like this—I'm covered in blood.*

God, she hadn't even noticed he was still in his fighting clothes. "Okay."

They traded places, she heading for the edge of the mattress, he going for the bathroom to turn on the hot water. He left the door open . . . so as he stripped off his muscle shirt, she watched his shoulders bunch and twist.

Her name, Xhexania, was not just tattooed, but carved in beautiful symbols across his back.

As he bent down to draw off his leathers, his ass made a stupendous appearance, his heavy thighs flexing as he shucked one leg and then the other. When he got in the shower, he went out of eyeshot, but he returned soon thereafter.

He was not aroused, she realized.

First time for that. Especially as she was about to feed.

John wrapped a towel around his hips and tucked the end in at his waist. As he turned to her, his grave eyes made her sad. *Would you like me to put on a robe?*

What the hell had happened to them? she thought. And for fuck's sake, they had been through too much just to get to what should be the good stuff only to screw it up.

"No." She shook her head and wiped her eyes. "Please . . . no . . ."

As he came forward, he kept that towel right where it was.

When he got in front of her, he sank down onto his knees and put up his wrist. *Take from me. Please let me take care of you.*

Xhex leaned in and clasped his hand. Passing her thumb back and forth over his vein, she felt the connection rise between them once again, that link that had been sliced through in the alley reknitting, an injury healing.

Reaching out, she clasped the back of his neck and brought his mouth to hers. Kissing him slowly, thoroughly, she spread her legs, making room for him as he eased forward, his hips finding the place that was his and his alone.

When the towel hit the floor, her hand went to his sex—and found that it had hardened.

Just as she wanted it to.

Stroking him, she curled her upper lip, exposing her fangs. Then, tilting her head to the side, she ran one razor-sharp tip up his neck.

His huge body shuddered—so she repeated the motion, this time with her tongue. "Come up on the bed with me."

John wasted no time, filling the space she vacated as she pushed herself back to make room for him.

Lot of eye contact. As if they were both reacquainting themselves with each other.

Taking his hand, she put it on her hip as she rolled into him, and as their bodies made contact, his grip tightened, his bonding scent flaring.

She'd intended to keep things slow and low-key. But their flesh had a different plan. Need grabbed the reins and took over, and she struck his throat with a powerful lunge, taking what she had to have to survive and be at her strongest—and also marking him in her own way. In response, his body jacked against her own, his erection wanting inside of her.

While she took great drags on his vein, she struggled to get her scrubs off—but he took care of that for her, gripping the waist and yanking the pants so hard the fabric split on a clean, screaming rip. And then his hand was right where she wanted it to be, moving against her core, slipping and sliding, teasing and then entering her. Working herself against his long, penetrating fingers, she found a rhythm that was guaranteed to get them both off, her moans competing in her throat with the blood she was downing at an alarming rate.

After her first orgasm, she shifted around—with his help—and straddled his hips. She needed to stay relatively still to keep locked on his throat, but he took care of the motion side of things, pumping up against her, closing in and retreating, creating that friction they both wanted.

When she came a second time, she had to retract her mouth from his flesh and call out his name. And as he pulsed deep within her, she stopped moving and absorbed the sensation of the kicking and jerking, so familiar, and yet so fresh.

Jesus . . . what an expression he had . . . his eyes squeezed shut, his teeth bared, the muscles in his neck straining, all while a streak of delicious red left the puncture marks she had yet to lick closed.

When his lids finally opened, she stared hard at the blissed-out haze in those blue eyes of his. His love for her wasn't just emotional; there was an undeniable physical component to it. That was the way bonded males worked.

Maybe he couldn't have stopped himself in that alley, she thought. Maybe that was the beast inside the civilized shell, the animal part of vampires that separated the species from those watered-down humans.

Dipping low, she licked at his neck, lapping the wounds shut, savoring the taste that clung to the inside of her mouth and the expressway of her throat. Already she could feel the power coursing out from her gut, and this was just the beginning. As her body absorbed what he had given her, she was just going to feel stronger and stronger.

"I love you," she said.

With that, she drew him up off the pillows so she was sitting in his lap, his arousal pushing even deeper inside her core. Palming the back of his neck with her free hand, she brought him to her vein and held him in place.

He didn't need any more urging than that—and the pain that came with his strike was a sweet sting that carried her right back over the edge of release, her sex milking him into another orgasm, working against his shaft, squeezing him, pulling at him.

John's arms locked around her, and the sight of them out of the corner of her eye made her frown. They were huge, bulging limbs that, in spite of how strong she was, could lift more, strike harder, punch faster. They were bigger than her thighs, thicker than her waist.

Their bodies were not, in fact, created equal, were they. He was always going to be more powerful than her.

A reality, sure. But how much someone could bench-press was not the determining factor when it came to competence in the field; nor was it the only way to judge a fighter. She was just as accurate a shooter, just as good with a dagger, and equally furious and tenacious when faced with prey.

She simply had to make him see that.

Biology was one thing. But even males had a brain.

When the sex was finally over, John lay beside his mate, utterly sated and sleepy. It would probably be a good idea to scrounge up some food, but he didn't have the energy or inclination.

He didn't want to leave her. At this moment. Ten minutes from now. Tomorrow, next week, next month . . .

As she curled into him, he snagged a blanket from the side table and draped it over the two of them, even though the combination of their body heat was keeping them pretty damn toasty.

He was well aware of when she fell asleep—her breathing changed and her leg twitched from time to time.

He wondered if she was kicking him in the ass in her dreams.

He had shit to work on; that was for sure.

And no one to go to talk about it—it wasn't like he could ask Tohr for anything more than the advice he'd gotten on the fly tonight. And everybody else's relationships were perfect. All he ever saw at the dining table were happy, smiling couples—hardly the sounding board he was looking for.

He could just picture the response: *You're having problems? Really? Huh, that's weird . . . maybe you could call in to the radio or some shit?*

The only thing that would change would be whether that was delivered by someone with a goatee, a pair of wraparounds, a mink duster, a Tootsie Roll in his piehole. . . .

He had this moment of peace, though. And he and Xhex could build on it.

They were going to have to.

You were okay with me fighting. Right before we were mated, you said you were cool with it.

And he really had been. But that was before he'd seen her cut right in front of him.

The thing was . . . and as much as it pained him to admit this . . . the last thing he wanted to be was the Brother he admired the most. Now that he had Xhex properly, the idea of losing her and stepping into Tohr's boots was the single most terrifying thing he'd ever faced.

He had no idea how the Brother was getting out of bed every night. And frankly, if he hadn't already forgiven the guy for taking off and disappearing right afterward, he would have now.

He thought of that moment when Wrath and the Brotherhood had come to them in a group. He and Tohr had been in the office here at the training center, with the Brother calling home time and time again, hoping, praying for something other than voice mail. . . .

In the corridor outside the office, there were fissures in the massive concrete walls—in spite of the fact that the damn things were eighteen-inch-thick concrete: Tohr's release of energy from his anger and pain had been so great he had literally exploded himself to God only knew where, shaking the subterranean foundation until it cracked.

John still didn't know where he'd gone. But Lassiter had brought him back in bad shape.

He remained in bad shape.

Selfish though it was, John didn't want that for himself. Tohr was half the male he had once been—and not just because he'd lost weight—and though no one would have shown pity to the guy's face, each and every one of the fighters felt it behind closed doors.

Hard to know how much longer the Brother was going to last out

there with the enemy. He was refusing to feed, so he was weakening, yet every night he went into the field, his need for revenge getting sharper and more consuming.

He was going to get himself killed. End of.

It was like triangulating the impact of a car into an oak tree: a simple matter of geometry. You just drew out the angles and trajectories and *boom!* There was Tohr, dead on the pavement.

Although, shit, he'd probably take his last breath with a smile, knowing he was finally going to be with his *shellan*.

Maybe that was why John was as stressed about the Xhex thing as he was. He was close to other people in the house, to his half sister, Beth, to Qhuinn and Blay, to the other Brothers. But Tohr and Xhex were his go-to people—and the idea of losing them both?

Fuuuuuck.

Thinking about Xhex in the field, he knew that if she was out there in those alleys, fighting the enemy, she was going to get hurt again. They all did from time to time. Most of the injuries were near misses, but you never knew when that line was going to be crossed, when a simple hand-to-hand engagement would get away from you and you'd find yourself surrounded.

It wasn't that he doubted her or her capabilities—in spite of that pot-shot that had come out of his mouth tonight. It was the odds he didn't like. Soon enough, if you rolled the dice over and over again, you were going to come up snake eyes. And in the larger scheme of things, her life was more important than one more fighter out in the field.

He should have thought about this a little more before going all, *Yeah, sure, I'm tight with you fighting. . . .*

"What are you thinking about?" she asked in the darkness.

As if what was banging through his brain had woken her up.

Rearranging himself, he put his head next to hers and shook it back and forth. But he was lying. And she probably knew it.

NINE

The following evening, Qhuinn stood in the far corner of Wrath's study, wedged into the juncture of two pale blue walls. The room was huge, a good forty feet long and forty feet across, and it had a ceiling lofty enough to give you a nosebleed. But space was getting tight.

Then again, there were a dozen or so big people packed in around the prissy French furniture.

Qhuinn knew from the French shit. His dead-and-gone mother had liked the style, and back before he'd been disavowed from his family, he'd been yammered at ad nauseam about not sitting on her Louis-the-somethingth crap.

At least that was one area where he hadn't been discriminated against in his own house—she'd wanted only her and his sister to park it in those delicate seats. He and his brother had not been permitted. Ever. And his father had been tolerated with a grimace, likely only because he'd paid for the stuff a couple hundred years before.

Whatever.

At least Wrath's command central made sense. The king's chair was as

big as a car and probably weighed as much as one, its rugged yet elegant carvings marking it as the throne of the race. And the huge desk in front of him wasn't exactly fit for a girl, either.

Tonight, and as usual, Wrath looked like the killer he was: silent, intense, deadly. Your basic anti–Avon lady. Beside him, Beth, his queen and *shellan*, was composed and serious. And on the other side, George, his Seeing Eye dog, was looking . . . well, kinda postcard-y. But then golden retrievers were like that: picturesque, pretty, and pettable.

More Donny Osmond than dark overlord.

Then again, Wrath more than made up for that one.

Abruptly, Qhuinn dropped his mismatched eyes to the Aubusson rug. He did not need to see who was standing on the far side of the queen.

Ah, hell.

His peripheral vision was working far too well tonight.

His slut of a cousin, his cocksucking, suit-wearing, Montblanc-up-the-ass cousin Saxton the Magnificent, was standing next to the queen, looking like a combination of Cary Grant and some model in a goddamn cologne ad.

Not that Qhuinn was bitter.

Because the guy was sharing Blay's bed.

Nah.

Nope. Not at all.

The cocksucker—

With a wince, he thought maybe he should switch that insult to something a little farther away from what the two of them . . .

God, he couldn't even go there. Not if he wanted to breathe.

Blay was also in the room, but the guy was staying away from his lover. He always did. Whether it was in these meetings, or outside of them, they were never closer than three feet apart.

Which was the only saving grace to living in the same house as the pair of them. Nobody ever saw them lip-locked or even holding hands.

Although . . . it wasn't as if Qhuinn didn't lie awake during the day anyway, torturing himself with all kinds of Kama Sutra shit—

The door of the study opened and Tohrment came dragging in. Man, he looked as if he'd been rolled out of a moving car on the highway, his eyes like piss holes in the snow, his body moving stiffly as he went over to stand next to John and Xhex.

At the arrival, Wrath's voice cut through the convo, shutting everyone up. "Now that we're all here, I'm going to can the bullshit and turn this over to Rehvenge. I got nothing good to say about any of this, so he'll be more efficient at briefing you."

As the Brothers got to muttering, the massive, Mohawked motherfucker plugged his cane into the floor and got to his feet. As usual, the half-breed was dressed in a black pin-striped suit—God, Qhuinn was starting to despise anything that had lapels—and a mink duster to keep him warm. With his *symphath* tendencies kept in control, thanks to regular hits of dopamine, his eyes were violet, and mostly un-evil.

Mostly. He really wasn't someone you wanted as an enemy, and not just because, like Wrath, he was the leader of his people: His day job was being king of the *symphath* colony up north. Nights he spent here with his *shellan*, Ehlena, living *la vida* vampire. And never the twain shall meet.

It went without saying that he was a highly valuable asset to the Brotherhood.

"A number of days ago, a letter was sent out to every head of the remaining bloodlines." He reached into the mink and took out a folded sheet of what looked to be old-fashioned parchment. "Snail mail. Handwritten. In the Old Language. Mine took a while to reach me because it went to the Great Camp up north first. No, I have no idea how they got the address, and yes, I have confirmed that everybody got one."

Balancing his cane against the delicate sofa he'd been sitting on, he opened the parchment with his fingertips, like he didn't enjoy the feel of the thing. Then in a low, deep voice, he read each sentence in the ancient language it had been composed in.

My old, dear friend,

I am writing to advise you of my arrival in the city of Caldwell with my soldiers. Although we have long tallied in the Old Country, the dire events of the previous few years in this jurisdiction have made it impossible for us to remain, in all good conscience, where we have previously established our domicile.

As you perhaps have heard from relations overseas, our strong efforts have eradicated the Lessening Society in the motherlands, making it safe for our fair race to flourish in peace and security there. Clearly, it is time I bring this stout arm of protection to bear on this side of the ocean—the race here in these parts has sustained untenable losses, ones that mayhap could have been avoided if we had been here sooner.

*I ask for nothing in return for our service to the race,
although I would appreciate the opportunity to meet with you
and the Council—if only to express my sincerest condolences at all
you have borne since the raids. It is a shame that things have come
to this—the commentary is sad upon certain segments of our
society.*

With kindest regard,
Xcor

When Rehv was done, he folded the paper up and disappeared it. No
one said a thing.

"That was my reaction, too," he muttered dryly.

This opened the floodgates, everybody talking at once, the curses
flowing rich and heavy.

Wrath made a fist and banged on his desk until the lamp jumped, and
George went into hiding under his master's throne. When order was finally
restored, it was like a stallion brought under control with a bit; a tenuous
respite, more like a pause in the bucking and rearing than a true settle-
down.

"I understand the bastard was out last night," Wrath said.

Tohrment spoke up. "We engaged with Xcor, yes."

"So this is not a fake."

"No, but it was written by someone else. He's illiterate—"

"I'll teach the fucker to read," V muttered. "By cramming the Library
of Congress up his ass."

As grunts of approval threatened to turn into more outbursts, Wrath
pounded on his desk again. "What do we know about his crew?"

Tohr shrugged. "Assuming he's kept the same ones on, they're a total
of five. Three cousins. That porn star Zypher—"

Rhage harrumphed at that. Clearly, even though he was now very
happily mated, he felt like the race had one, and only one, sex legend—and
it was him.

"And Throe was with him in that alley," Tohr smoothed over. "Look,
I'm not going to lie—it's clear that Xcor's making a play against . . ."

When he didn't finish the statement, Wrath nodded. "Me."

"Which would mean us—"

"Us—"

"Us—"

More voices than you could count uttered that one word, the single syllable coming from every corner of the room, every seat cushion, every flat plane of wall someone was up against. And that was the thing. Unlike Wrath's father, this king had been a fighter and a Brother first—so the bonds that had been formed were not out of some artifact of prescribed duty, but the fact that Wrath had stood beside them all in the field and saved their asses personally at one time or another.

The king smiled a little. "I appreciate the support."

"He needs to die." When everybody looked at Rehvenge, the guy shrugged. "Plain and simple. Let's not bullshit around with protocol and meetings. Let's just take him out."

"Don't you think that's a little bloodthirsty, sin-eater?" Wrath drawled.

"From one king to another, know that I'm giving you the middle finger right now." And he was, with a smile. "*Symphaths* are known for efficiency."

"Yeah, and I can feel where you're coming from. Unfortunately, the law provides that you have to make an attempt on my life before I can bury you."

"That's where this is headed."

"Agreed, but our hands are tied. My ordering the assassination of what is otherwise an innocent male is not going to help us in the eyes of the *glymera*."

"Why do you need to be associated with the death?"

"And if that bastard's innocent," Rhage spoke up, "I'm the fucking Easter bunny."

"Oh, good," someone quipped. "I'm calling you Hop-along Hollywood from now on."

"Beasty Bo Peep," somebody else threw out.

"We could put you in a Cadbury ad and finally make some money—"

"People," Rhage barked, "the point is that he is *not* innocent and I'm *not* the Easter bunny—"

"Where's your basket?"

"Can I play with your eggs?"

"Hop it out, big guy—"

"Will you guys fuck off? Seriously!"

As various cottontail comments were lobbed like Jell-O at a food fight, Wrath had to pound the desk another time or two. It was obvious where the humor was coming from: The stress was so high, if they didn't blow off a little steam, shit was going to get grim fast. It didn't mean the Brother-

hood wasn't focused; if anything, they all felt like Qhuinn did—socked in the gut.

Wrath was the fabric of life, the basis for everything, the living, breathing structure of the race. After the brutal raids by the Lessening Society, what was left of the aristocracy had fled Caldwell to their safe homes out of town. The last thing the vampires needed was further fragmentation, especially in the form of a violent overthrow of the rightful ruler.

And Rehv was correct: That was where this was going. Hell, even Qhuinn could see the path: Step one, create doubt in the minds of the *glymera* about the Brotherhood's ability to protect the race. Step two, fill the "void" in the field with those soldiers of Xcor's. Step three, create allies on the Council and stir up anger and lack of confidence against the king. Step four, dethrone Wrath and weather the storm. Step five, emerge as the new leader.

When order in the study was finally reestablished, Wrath looked downright nasty. "Next one of you mouthy assholes makes me pound my desk again, I'm throwing you the fuck out." On that note, he reached down, picked up the cowering ninety-pound retriever, and settled George in his lap. "You're freaking out my dog and it's pissing me off."

As the animal put his big boxy head in the crook of the king's arm, Wrath stroked all that silky, blond fur. It was absolutely incongruous, the tremendous, cruel-looking vampire calming that handsome, gentle dog, but the two had a symbiotic relationship, trust and love thick as blood on both sides.

"Now, if you're ready to be reasonable," the king said, "I'll tell you what we're going to do. Rehv is going to stall the guy for as long as he can."

"I still think we should put a knife in his left eye," Rehv muttered, "but in the alternative, we've got to hold him in place. He wants to see and be seen, and as *leahdyre* of the Council, I can stonewall him up to a point. His voice in the ears of the *glymera* is not what we need."

"In the meantime," Wrath announced, "I'm going to go out and meet personally with the heads of the families, on their turf."

At this, there was an explosion in the room, irrespective of his warning: People jumped out of their seats, throwing up their dagger hands.

Bad idea, Qhuinn thought, agreeing with the others.

Wrath let them go for a minute, like he'd expected this. Then he resumed control of the meeting. "I can't expect support if I don't earn it— and I haven't personally seen some of these people in decades, if not

centuries. My father met with folks every month, if not every week, to resolve disputes."

"You're the king!" someone bit out. "You don't need to do shit—"

"You see that letter? It's the new world order—if I don't respond proactively, I'm undermining myself. Look, my brothers, if you were out in the field, about to face the enemy, would you fool yourself about the landscape? Would you lie to yourself about the layout of the streets, the buildings, the cars, or whether it was hot or cold, raining or dry? *No.* So why should I bullshit myself that tradition is something I can take cover behind in a shoot-out? Back in my father's time . . . that shit was a bulletproof vest. Now? It's a sheet of paper, people. You gotta know that."

There was a long period of silence, and then everyone looked at Tohr. Like they were used to turning to him when shit got sticky.

"He's right," the Brother said gruffly. Then he focused on Wrath. "But you gotta know you're not doing this alone. You need to have two or three of us with you. And the meet-and-greets have to be staggered over a period of months—cram them in too tight and you look desperate, but more to the point, I don't want anyone getting organized to do a hit on you. Sites must be prescreened by us, and . . ." At this, he paused to glance around. "You need to be aware that we're going to be trigger-happy. We will shoot to kill when your life's on the line—whether it's a female or a male or a *doggen* or the head of a family. We will not ask permission, or merely wound. If you can live with those terms, we will let you do this."

Nobody else could have laid down the rules like that and walked without a limp afterward: The king gave out orders to the Brotherhood, not the other way around. But this was the new world, as Wrath had said.

The male in question ground his molars for a while. Then grunted. "Agreed."

As a collective exhale hit the airwaves, Qhuinn found himself looking over at Blay. Aw, hell, talk about a suck zone—this was why he avoided the guy like the plague. Just one glance and he was locked on, all kinds of reactions rolling through him, until the room spun a little—

For no good reason, Blay's eyes flipped up and met his.

It was like getting goosed in the ass with a live wire, his body spasming to the point where he had to hide the reaction by coughing while he glanced away.

About as smooth as a crater. Yup. Fantastic.

". . . and in the meantime," Wrath was saying, "I want to find out where these soldiers are staying."

"I can take care of that," Xhex spoke up. "Especially if I hit them in the daytime."

All heads turned in her direction. Beside her, John stiffened from head to foot, and Qhuinn cursed under his breath.

Talk about your showdowns . . . except hadn't the pair of them just had one?

Man, sometimes he was really glad he didn't do relationships.

Not again, John thought to himself. For fuck's sake, they'd just gotten back on speaking terms, and now *this*?

If he'd thought fighting side by side with Xhex was trouble, the idea of her trying to infiltrate the Band of Bastards on their home turf put him on the edge of a seizure.

As he let his head fall back against the wall, he realized that everyone and their dog was staring at him. Literally—even George's brown eyes were trained in his direction.

"Are you kidding me," Xhex said. "Are you frickin' kidding me."

Even after she spoke, nobody looked at her. It was all about John: Clearly, as he was her *hellren*, they were seeking his approval—or not—about what she'd put out there.

And John couldn't seem to move, stuck in the cold quagmire between what she wanted and where he didn't want them to end up.

Wrath cleared his throat. "Well, that's a kind offer—"

"Kind offer?" she spat. "Like I'm inviting you to dinner?"

Say something, he told himself. Put your flapping hands up and tell her . . . What? That he was on board with her going to find six males with no consciences? After what Lash had done to her? What if she was captured and . . .

Oh, Jesus, he was cracking up over here. Yes, she was tough and strong and capable. But she was as mortal as anybody else. And without Xhex, he wouldn't want to be on the planet at all.

Rehvenge snagged his cane and pushed himself up. "Let's you and I talk—"

"Excuse me?" Xhex bit out. " 'Talk'? Like I'm the one who needs a mental readjustment? No offense, but bite me, Rehv. The bunch of you need me to do what I can to help."

As all the other males in the room started looking at their shitkickers and loafers, the *symphath* king shook his head. "Things are different now."

"How."

"Come on, Xhex—"

"Are you people insane? Just because my name's in his back, I'm suddenly a prisoner or some shit?"

"Xhex—"

"Oh, no, nope, you can fuck off with that be-reasonable tone." She glared at the males, and then focused on Beth and Payne. "I don't know how you two stand it—I really don't."

John was trying to think of what he could say to derail the collision, but what a waste of time. Two trains had already made head-on contact and there was twisted metal and steaming engine parts everywhere.

Especially as Xhex marched for the door like she was prepared to claw it apart just to prove a point.

When he went to follow her, she pegged him with a hard eye. "If you're coming after me for any other reason than to let me go after Xcor, you need to stop right where you are. Because you belong with this anachronistic group of misogynists. Not at my side."

Lifting his hands, he signed, *It is not wrong to want to keep you safe.*

"This is not about safety—it's about control."

Bullshit! You were hurt less than twenty-four hours ago—

"Fine. I have an idea. I want to keep *you* safe—so how about *you* stop fighting." She glared over her shoulder at Wrath. "You gonna back me up, my lord? How about the rest of you fools? Let's put the skirt and the panty hose on John, shall we? Come on, back my ass up. No? You don't think that would be 'fair'?"

John's temper flared, and he just . . . He didn't mean to do what he did. It just happened.

He stomped his boot, creating a thunderous noise, and pointed . . . directly at Tohr.

Awkward. Horrid. Silence.

Kind of like he and Xhex had not only dragged their dirty laundry out in front of everyone, but he'd managed to drape their sweat socks and stained shirts all over Tohr's head.

In response? The Brother just crossed his arms over his chest and nodded, once.

Xhex shook her head. "I gotta get out of here. I gotta clear my head. John, if you know what's good for you, you will *not* follow me."

And just like that, she was gone.

In the aftermath, John rubbed his face, pushing his palms in so hard he felt like he was rearranging his features.

"How 'bout everybody head off for the night," Wrath said softly. "I want to talk to John. Tohr, you hang."

No need to ask twice. The Brotherhood and the others left like someone was out in the courtyard stealing their cars.

Beth stayed behind. So did George.

As the doors shut, John looked at Tohr. *I'm so sorry—*

"Nah, son." The male stepped forward. "I don't want where I'm at for you, either."

The Brother put his arms around John, and John went with it, collapsing into the once massive body . . . that nonetheless managed to hold him up.

Tohr's voice was steady in his ear: "It's okay. I got you. It's all right. . . ."

John put his head to the side and stared at the door his *shellan* had walked out of. He wanted to go after her with every fiber of his being—but those fibers were also what were ripping them apart. In his mind, he understood everything she was saying, but his heart and his body were ruled by something separate from all that, something bigger and more primordial. And it was overriding everything.

It was wrong. Disrespectful. Old-fashioned in a way that he never thought he could be. He didn't think females should be sequestered, and he believed in his mate, and he wanted her . . .

To be safe.

Period.

"Give her some time," Tohr murmured, "and we'll go after her, okay? You and I will go together."

"Good plan," Wrath said, "because neither of you is going out in the field tonight." The king held up his palms to cut off the arguing. "Really?"

That shut them both up.

"So are you okay?" the king asked Tohr.

The Brother's smile wasn't warm in the slightest. "I'm already in hell—shit's not going to get any hotter just because he's using me as an example of where he doesn't want to be."

"You sure about that."

"Don't worry about me."

"Easier said than done." Wrath motioned his hand, like he didn't want to go any further on all that. "We done?"

As Tohr nodded and turned for the door, John gave the First Family a bow and then went after the male.

He didn't have to rush. Tohr was waiting for him out in the corridor. "Listen to me—it's cool. I'm serious-"

I'm just . . . so sorry, John signed. *About everything. And . . . shit, I miss Wellsie—I really miss her.*

Tohr blinked for a moment. Then in a quiet voice, he said, "I know, son. I know you lost her, too."

Do you think she would have liked Xhex?

"Yeah." A shadow of a smile hit that harsh face. "She only met her once, and it was a while ago, but they were cool, and if there had been time . . . they'd have gotten along great. And man, on a night like tonight, we could have used the female backup."

Too right, John signed, as he tried to imagine approaching Xhex.

At least he could guess where she would go: back to her own place on the Hudson River. That was her refuge, her private space. And when he showed up on her doorstep, he could only pray she didn't throw him out on his ass.

But they had to resolve this somehow.

I think I'd better go alone, John signed. *This is probably going to get ugly.*

Make that uglier, he thought.

"Fair enough. Just know that I'm here if you need me."

Wasn't that always the way, John thought as they parted. Almost as if it had been centuries of their knowing each other, instead of merely a matter of years. Then again he guessed that was what happened when you crossed paths with someone you were really compatible with.

Felt like you'd been with them forever.

TEN

"I shall do it."

As No'One spoke up, the group of *doggen* she had sneaked in behind turned like a flock of birds, all at once. In their modest staff room, there were males and females both among the assembled, each dressed properly for his or her role whether it was cook or cleaner, baker or butler. She had found them when she had gone for an idle stroll, and who was she not to take advantage of an opportunity.

The one who was in charge, Fritz Perlmutter, looked like he was about to faint. Then again, he had been her father's *doggen* all those years ago, and had had particular struggles with her defining herself in a servile role. "My fine lady—"

"No'One. My name is No'One now. Please address me as that and that alone. And as I said, I shall take care of the washing down in the training center."

Wherever that was.

Indeed, last night with that dress had been a benediction of sorts, the task busying her hands and giving her a focus that passed the hours with alacrity. It had once been the same on the Other Side, her manual

labor the only thing that calmed her and imparted structure to her existence.

How she had missed having a purpose.

For truth, she had come here to serve Payne, but the female wanted none of that. She had come here to try to connect with her daughter, but the female was newly mated, with vital distractions. And she had come here in search of some kind of peace, only to be driven mad with inactivity since her arrival.

And that was prior to her near run-in with Tohrment early this morning.

At least he had taken the dress, though. It was gone from where she had hung it when he had answered her knock with such gruff—

Abruptly, she noted that the butler was looking at her expectantly, as if he had just said something that required a response.

"Please take me down there," she said, "and show me the duties."

Given the way his old, wrinkled face fell even further, she gathered that was not the reply he had been hoping for.

"Mistress—"

"No'One. And you, or one of your staff, can show me now."

The assembled masses all looked worried, as if mayhap rumors of the sky falling had suddenly become reality.

"Thank you," she said to the butler. "For your facilitation."

Clearly recognizing that he was not going to win, the head *doggen* bowed low. "But of course I shall, mist— Ah, No— Er . . ."

When he couldn't get out her proper name, as if the appropriate title of "mistress" was required to blaze the trail up his windpipe, she took pity on him.

"You are most helpful," she murmured. "Now, lead on."

After dismissing the others, he took her out of the staff room, through the kitchen, and into the foyer by virtue of yet another door that was new to her. As they proceeded, she recalled her previous, younger self, the haughty daughter of a bloodline of means who had refused to cut up her own meat, or brush her own hair, or dress herself. What a waste. At least now that she was no one and had nothing, she was clear on how to pass the hours meaningfully: work. Work was the key.

"We go through herein," the butler pronounced as he held wide a hidden door beneath the grand staircase. "Allow me to provide you the codes."

"Thank you," she replied, memorizing them.

As she followed the *doggen* into the long, thin tube of an underground

tunnel, she thought, yes, if she was going to stay on this side, she needed to busy herself with chores, even if it offended the *doggen*, the Brotherhood, the *shellans*. . . . Better that than the prison of her own thoughts.

They exited the tunnel by stepping through the back of a closet and passing into a squat room that had a desk and metal cabinets and a glass door.

The *doggen* cleared his throat. "This is the training center and medical facility. We have classrooms, a gym, locker room, weight room, physical therapy area, and a pool, as well as many other amenities. There are staff who take care of the deep cleaning of each section"—this was said sternly, as if he did not care that she was the guest of the king; she was not mucking about with his schedule—"but the *doggen* who took care of the laundry has gone upon bed rest, as she is *mitte doggen* and it is no longer safe for her to be on her feet. Please, we are this way."

As he held open the glass portal, they went out into the corridor and headed to a double-doored room that was kitted up identically to the laundry she had used the night before in the main house. Over the next twenty minutes, she received a refresher on how to operate the machines, and then the butler reviewed with her a map of the facilities so she knew where to collect the bins and where to return what she had tended to.

And then, after a stiff silence, and stiffer adieu, she was blissfully alone.

Standing in the middle of the utility room, surrounded by washing machines and dryers and tables to fold upon, she closed her eyes and took a deep breath.

Oh, the lovely solitude, and the fortunate weight of duty settling upon her shoulders. For the next six hours, she had nothing to think of but white towels and sheets: finding them, putting them in machines, folding them, returning them to their proper places.

There was no room for the past or her regrets here. Just the work.

Gripping a rolling bin, she wheeled the blue fabric receptacle out into the corridor and began making her rounds, beginning with the clinic and returning to the laundry when there was no more space left in her transport. After she got the first load into a deep-bellied washer, she went out again, passing into the locker room and finding a mountain of white. It took her two trips to get all those towels, and she made a pile of them in the center of the washer room, beside the drain in the gray concrete floor.

Her final stop took her to the very far left, all the way down the corridor to the pool. As she went along, the wheels on her cart made a little whistling noise, and her feet shuffled unevenly, her grip on the bin's lip giving her some added stability and helping her to go faster.

When she heard music coming from the swimming area, she slowed. Then stopped.

The strains of notes and voices made no sense as all members of the Brotherhood and their *shellans* were gone for the night. Unless someone had left the music on after they had finished their time in the water?

Pushing her way into a squat anteroom tiled with mosaics of athletic males, she got hit with a wall of warmth and humidity so heavy, it was as if she had stepped up against a velvet drape. And all around, there was a strange, chemical smell in the air, one that made her wonder what they treated the water with—on the Other Side, everything had stayed permanently fresh and clean, but she knew that was not the case on earth.

Leaving the bin to wait in the lobby, she walked forward toward a vast, cavelike space. Reaching out, she touched the warm tiles on the wall, running her fingers over the blue skies and rolling green fields, but skipping any of the loinclothed males, with their archery bows, and their fencing staffs, and their running poses.

She loved the water. The floating buoyancy, the easing of the aches in her bad leg, the sense of brief freedom—

"Oh . . . my . . ." she gasped as she turned the corner.

The pool was four times the size of the largest bath on the Other Side, and its water was a shimmering pale blue—likely because of the tiles that skinned its deep belly. Black lines ran lengthwise, denoting lanes, and there were numbers going down the stone lip, clearly marking depth. Up above, the ceiling was domed and covered in more mosaics, and there were benches against the walls, providing places to sit. Echoing around, the music was louder, but not overly so, and the mournful tune possessed a pleasing resonance.

Given that she was alone, she couldn't resist going over and testing the temperature with her bare foot.

Tempting. So very tempting.

But instead of giving in, she refocused on her duties, going back to her bin, rolling it over to a large wicker basket, and then transferring her body weight in damp terry cloth.

When she turned to go, she paused and stared at the water again.

There was no way the first round of sheeting had finished its washing cycle. It had at least forty-five minutes left according to what the machine had reported.

She checked the clock that was mounted on the wall.

Perhaps just a few minutes in the pool, she decided. She could use the relief from the aching in her lower body, and there was nothing she could do relative to her job for the next little bit.

Grabbing one of the fresh, folded towels, she double-checked the anteroom. Went farther down and looked out into the corridor.

Nobody was about. And now was the time to do this—the staff would be concentrating on cleaning the second floor of the mansion, as they had to get that work done between First and Last Meals. And there was no one getting treated at the clinic, at least for the moment.

She had to make this fast.

Limping back to the shallow end, she unfastened her robe and drew off the hood, stripping down to her undersheath. After a brief hesitation, she removed the sheer liner as well—she would have to remember to bring a second with her if she wanted to do this again. Better to remain modest.

As she folded her things, she deliberately stared at her twisted calf, tracing the roping scars that formed an ugly relief map of mountains and valleys in her flesh. Once, the lower leg had worked perfectly and been as lovely as many an artist could have drawn. Now it was a symbol of who and what she was, a reminder of a fall from grace that had made her a lesser person . . . and, over time, a better one.

Fortunately, there was a chrome handrail by the steps, and she gripped it for balance as she slowly entered the warm water. Upon the descent, she recalled her braid and wound the heavy length around and around the top of her head, tucking in the loose end so that the beehive held in place.

And then . . . she glided.

Closing her eyes in bliss, she gave herself over to weightlessness, the water a temperate breeze wafting across her flesh, her body held kindly in the pool's peaceable palms. As she stroked out into the center, she threw away her resolve not to get her hair wet, and rolled over onto her back, sweeping her hands in circles to keep herself afloat.

For a brief time, she allowed herself to feel something, opening the door to her senses.

And it was . . . good.

Left behind at the mansion for the night, Tohr was off-roster, stuck inside and hungover: a bad-mood trifecta if he'd ever seen one.

The good news was that with most people gone or going about their business, he didn't have to inflict the toxicity on anybody else.

On that note, he headed for the training center, dressed in nothing but his swimming trunks. Having heard that most hangovers were caused by dehydration, he'd decided not only to go to the pool and submerge himself . . . but to bring some liquid refreshment with him. And how was that for healthy.

What had he grabbed? Oh, good, vodka—he liked that straight up, and hey, it looked like water.

Pausing in the tunnel, he took a swig of V's Goose, and swallowed—

Fuck. The sound of John's shitkicker hitting the floor, like some god-forsaken bell tolling, was something he was never going to forget. Just like the kid's finger pointing at him.

Time for another swallow . . . and hey, how about one more.

As he resumed his trek toward what was probably going to be a drowning party, he recognized that he was a walking cliché: He'd seen his brothers in this shape from time to time, weaving around with a sour, fuzzy head, a bad attitude, and a bottle of knockout juice grafted to their palms. Back before Wellsie had been taken from him, he'd never really understood the whys.

Now? Duh.

You did what you had to do to get yourself through the hours. And the nights when you couldn't go out and fight were the worst—unless, of course, you were facing off against all the day's bright, glowing no-go. That was even more wretched.

As he came out of the office and zeroed in on the pool, he was glad he didn't have to fake the expression on his face, or watch his language, or chill his temper.

Pushing open the door to the anteroom, his blood pressure lowered as that warm, welcoming wave of humidity came over him. The music helped, too: From out of the sound system, U2 was filling the air, old-school *The Joshua Tree* echoing around.

His first clue that something was off was the pile of rags at the shallow end. And maybe if he hadn't been hitting the liquor, he might have put two and two together before he—

Floating in the center of the pool, a female was faceup on the top of the water, her naked breasts glistening, her nipples tight in the warm air, her head back.

"Fuck."

Hard to know what made the bigger noise: his f-bomb or the Goose bottle hitting the tile floor . . . or the splash out in the middle as No'One jacked up and spluttered, covering herself while she tried to keep her head above water.

Tohr spun around and put his hands over his eyes—

On the pivot, broken glass sliced into the ball of his bare foot, the pain pitching him off balance—not that he needed any help with that, thanks to his having sucked face with the vodka. Throwing out a hand, he went to catch himself on the tile floor—and ended up slicing open his right palm as well.

"Fucking hell," he shouted, shoving himself free of the shards.

As he rolled onto his back, No'One scampered out of the water and dragged her robe around her naked flesh, that long braid swinging free as she jerked the hood into place.

With another curse, Tohr brought his palm up to check the injury. Great. Right in the center of his dagger hand, two inches long, and the bitch was a couple of millimeters deep.

God only knew what he'd done to his foot.

"I didn't know you were here," he said without looking up or over at her. "I'm sorry."

From out of the corner of his eye, he got a visual of No'One approaching, her bare feet making appearances under the hem of her robe.

"Don't come any closer," he barked. "There's glass all over the place."

"I shall be right back."

"Fine," he muttered, as he brought up his foot for a look-see.

Fantastic—longer. Deeper. Bleeding more. And there was still bottle in it.

With a growl, he took hold of the little glass triangle and pulled the thing out. His blood on the shard was red as a blush, and he turned the piece from side to side, watching the light play through it.

"Thinking of taking up surgery?"

Tohr glanced over at Manny Manello, MD, human surgeon, mated *hellren* of V's twin. The guy had come with a first-aid kit, as well as his signature I-run-the-world attitude.

What was it with surgeons? They were almost as bad as warriors. Or kings.

The human crouched down beside him. "You're leaking."

"No shit."

Just as he was wondering where No'One was, the female came in with a broom, a rolling trash bin, and a dustpan. Without looking at him or the human, she began sweeping carefully.

At least she'd put shoes on.

Jesus Christ . . . she had been really fucking naked.

As Manello poked and prodded at the injured hand, and then started numbing and stitching, Tohr watched the female out of the corner of his eye—no direct viewing. Especially not after—

Jesus . . . like, *really* fucking naked—

Okay, time to stop thinking about that.

Focusing on her limp, he noticed that it was pretty damn pronounced, and wondered if she'd hurt herself in that great rush to get out of the pool and get clothed.

He'd seen her frantic before. But only once . . .

It had been the night they'd gotten her away from that *symphath*.

He'd killed the bastard. Shot her captor right through the head, dropping him like a stone. Then he and Darius had packed her into a carriage and headed back for her family's house. The plan had been to return her to them. Take her to her blood. Give her to those who by all rights should have helped her heal.

Except when they'd gotten close to that stately mansion, she'd bolted out of the carriage even though the horses had been going at a clip. And he'd never forget the sight of her in that white nightgown, streaking across a field, running like she was being chased even though the capture part was over.

She'd known she was pregnant. That was why she'd taken off.

She'd had the limp then, too.

That had been her only attempt to escape. Well, until the one after the birth, the one that had worked.

God . . . he'd been nervous around her during the months they'd stayed together at Darius's. He'd had zero experience with females of any worth: Yeah, sure, he'd grown up around them while he'd been with his mother, but that had been as a child, as a pretrans. The instant he'd gone through his transition, he'd been ripped out of his home and thrown into the sink-or-swim pit of the Bloodletter's training camp—where he had been too busy trying to stay alive to worry about the whores.

He hadn't even met Wellsie in person at that point. His promise to her had been an obligation his mother had assumed for him when he'd been twenty-five, before she'd even been born—

With a jerk, he hissed, and Manello looked up from his needle and thread. "Sorry. You want more lidocaine?"

"I'm fine."

No'One's hood shifted position sharply as she glanced over. After a moment, she resumed her broom work.

Maybe it was the alcohol kicking in, but he suddenly didn't give a shit about pretenses. He let himself openly stare at the female as the good doctor finished up on the palm.

"You know, I'm going to have to get you a crutch," Manello muttered.

"If you tell me what you need," No'One said softly, "I shall bring it here for you."

"Perfect. Go to the equipment room at the far end of the gym. In the PT suite, you'll find the . . ."

As the guy gave her instructions, No'One nodded, that hood of hers moving up and down. For some reason, Tohr tried to picture her face, but it was hazy. He hadn't seen her properly in centuries—that brief flash just now didn't count, because it had been from a distance. And when she'd done the reveal to Xhex and him before the mating ceremony, he'd been too rocked to pay full attention.

But she was blond; he knew that. And she'd always liked the shadows—or at least, she had in Darius's cabin. She hadn't wanted to be looked at then, either.

"Okay, doing good," Manello said as he inspected his repair job. "Let's wrap this and move on to the next."

No'One returned just as the surgeon was taping the tail end of the gauze in place.

"You can watch if you like."

Tohr frowned until he realized that Manello was addressing No'One. The female was hanging back, and sure as if that hood of hers was a face with expressions, he could tell she was worried.

"Just a warning, though." Manello moved downward. "This is worse than the hand—but the palm is more important, because that's what he fights with."

As No'One hesitated, Tohr shrugged. "You can see anything you like, assuming your stomach's up for it."

She went around and stood behind the doctor, crossing her arms into the sleeves of her robe so that she looked like some kind of religious statue. Except she was very much alive: When he winced as the needle went in with the anesthetic, she seemed to burrow into herself.

Like his being in pain affected her.

Tohr shifted his eyes away for the duration.

"All right, you're done," Manello said sometime later. "And before you ask, I'll give you a 'yeah, probably.' Given how fast you guys heal, you should be good to go tomorrow night. For fuck's sake, you're like cars—

take a beating, go into the body shop, next thing you know, back out on the road. Humans take so damn long to get over things."

Uh-huh, right. Tohr wasn't quite ready to put himself in Dodge Ram territory. The exhaustion he was lugging around with him meant he needed to feed—and that these relatively minor injuries could take a while to repair themselves.

Aside from that one session from Selena, he hadn't taken a vein since—

Nope. Not going there. No need to open that door.

"No walking on this foot," the surgeon ordered on as he snapped off his gloves. "At least until dawn. And no swimming."

"No problem." Especially on the latter. After what he'd just seen floating in the middle of the goddamn thing, he might never go in the pool again. Any pool, for that matter.

The only thing that saved his having walked in on her from being a complete mess was the fact that there had been nothing sexual on his side. Yeah, he'd been shocked, but that didn't mean he wanted to . . . you know, bang her or some shit.

"One question," the doctor said as he rose up and held out his hand.

Tohr accepted the palm and was a little surprised to find himself pulled solidly to his feet.

"What."

"How did it happen?"

Tohr glanced over at No'One—who looked away so quickly, she turned her whole body in the opposite direction.

"Bottle slipped out of my hand," Tohr muttered.

"Ah, well—accidents happen." The yeah-sure tone suggested the guy didn't believe the fudge for a second. "Call me if you need me. I'm down in the clinic for the rest of the night."

"Thanks, man."

"Yup."

And then . . . he and No'One were alone together.

ELEVEN

As No'One watched the healer go, she found herself wanting to take a step back from Tohrment. It seemed as if, in the absence of any other parties, he had suddenly gotten closer. And much, much larger.

In the silence that transpired, she had the sense that they should be speaking, but her mind was clouded. *Mortified* did not begin to cover it, and she had some instinct that if she could just explain herself, mayhap she could make that feeling go away.

In the meantime, too much of his physical form registered for comfort. He was so tall—inches and inches, a whole foot taller than she was. And his body was not reedy as hers was: Although he was thinner than she remembered from before, and a great deal lighter than his Brothers, he was still broader and more muscled than any male member of the *glymera* ever had been. . . .

Where was her tongue? she thought.

And yet even as she wondered that, all she could do was measure the brutal width of his shoulders, and the massive contours of his heavy chest, and those long, viciously muscled arms. It was not because she considered him comely, however. She was abruptly frightened of all that physical power—

Tohrment was the one who took a step back, his face registering disgust. "Don't look at me like that."

Shaking herself, she recalled that this was the male who had gotten her free. Not someone who had ever hurt her. Or would. "I am sorry—"

"Listen up, and I want to make this clear. I'm not interested in anything from you. I don't know what kind of game you're playing—"

"Game?"

His powerful arm shot out as he pointed to the pool. "Lying in wait for me to come down here—"

No'One recoiled. "What? I was not waiting for you or anyone else—"

"Bullshit—"

"I checked first to make sure I was alone—"

"You were naked, floating there like some kind of whore—"

"*Whore?*"

Their raised voices ricocheted around like bullets, crossing paths as they interrupted each other.

Tohrment jutted himself forward on his hips. "Why did you come here?"

"I work as a laundress—"

"Not the training center—this goddamn compound."

"I wanted to see my daughter—"

"Then why haven't you spent any time with her?"

"She is newly mated! I have tried to make myself available—"

"Yeah, I know. Just not to her."

The disrespect in that deep voice made her want to shrink away, but his unfairness gave her a backbone. "I had no way of knowing that you were going to enter herein. I thought all were gone for the night—"

Tohrment closed the distance between them. "I'm going to say this only once. There's nothing here for you. The mated males in this house are bound to their *shellans*, Qhuinn's not interested, and neither am I. If you've come looking for a *hellren* or a lover, you're out of luck—"

"I want no male!" Her shouting shut him up, but that wasn't nearly enough. "I shall say *this* only once—I would kill myself afore I ever accept another male into my body. I know why you hate me, and I respect your reasons, but I do *not* want you or any other of your persuasion. *Ever.*"

"Then how about you start by keeping your goddamn clothes on."

She would have slapped him if she could have reached that high. Her palm even started to tingle.

But she did not jump up to wipe the terrible expression off his face with force. Lifting her chin, she said with as much dignity as she could, "In the event you have forgotten what the last male did to me, I can assure you I have not. Whether you choose to believe me or prefer a delusion, that is not my doing—or my concern."

As she limped past him, she wished for once that her leg was what it had been before: Pride was far better served by an even gait.

Just as she got to the anteroom, she looked back at him. He had not turned about, so she addressed his shoulders . . . and the name of his *shellan*, which was carved in his very skin. "I shall never go near that water again. Clothed or unclothed."

As she wobbled to the door, she was shaking from head to foot, and it wasn't until she felt the cold slap of the air out in the corridor that she realized she had left the rolling trash bin, the sweeper, and her sheath behind.

She was not going back for them, that was for certain.

In the laundry room, she closed herself in and leaned against the wall by the doors.

Abruptly, she felt like she was suffocating, and ripped the hood from her head. Indeed, her body was hot, and not because of the heavy layer she wore. An internal burn had taken root and used her gut for kindling, the heated smoke from that fire filling her lungs, crowding out the oxygen.

It was impossible to reconcile the male she had known in the Old Country with the one she saw now. The former had been awkward, but never, ever disrespectful, a kind, gentle soul who somehow excelled at his brutal endeavors in the war—whilst retaining his compassion.

This current iteration was but a bitter shell.

And to think she'd assumed preparing that dress would be of any benefit?

She'd have better luck moving the mansion with her mind.

In the wake of No'One's pissed-off departure, Tohr decided that short of the fact John Matthew hadn't managed to cut himself on the hand and foot thus far tonight, it looked like Tohr and the kid had a lot in common: Courtesy of their tempers, both were now dressed in the Captain Asshole costume—which included, for no extra charge, the cape of disgrace, the booties of shame, and keys to the Fuck Up mobile.

Christ, what had come out of his mouth?

In the event you have forgotten what the last male did to me, I can assure you I have not.

With a groan, he pinched the bridge of his nose. Why in the world would he think, for even a second, that female would have any sexual interest in a male?

"Because you assumed she was attracted to you and it freaked you out."

Tohr closed his eyes. "Not now, Lassiter."

Naturally, the fallen angel paid no attention to the verbal POLICE LINE—DO NOT CROSS tape. The blond-and-black idiot walked over and sat down on one of the benches, putting his elbows on the knees of his leathers, his odd white eyes steady and grave.

"It's time you and I had a little talk."

"About my social skills?" Tohr shook his head. "No offense, but I'd rather take advice from Rhage—and that's saying something."

"Have you ever heard of the In Between."

Tohr awkwardly pivoted around on his good foot. "I'm not interested in a class on fractions. Thanks."

"It's a very real place."

"So is Cleveland. Detroit. Beautiful downtown Burbank." He'd been a *Laugh-In* fan in the sixties. So sue him. "But I don't need to know about them, either."

"It's where Wellsie is."

Tohr's heart stopped in his chest. "What the hell are you talking about?"

"She is not in the Fade."

Okay. Right. He probably should follow that one up with, "What the *fuck* are you talking about?" Instead, all he could do was stare at the guy.

"She's not where you think she is," the angel murmured.

Through a dry mouth, he managed, "You're saying she's in hell? Because that's the only other option."

"No, it isn't."

Tohr took a deep breath. "My *shellan* was a female of worth, and she's in the Fade—there's no reason to think she'd be in *Dhund*. As for myself, I'm through with jumping down people's throats tonight. So I'm going to walk out that door over there"—he pointed in the direction of the anteroom just to be helpful—"and you're going to let me go. Because I'm not in the mood for this."

Turning away, he started hobbling, using that single crutch No'One had brought in.

"You're pretty goddamn sure of something you don't know shit about."

Tohr stopped. Closed his eyes again. Sent up a prayer for an emotion, any emotion, other than the urge to kill.

No luck.

He glanced over his shoulder. "You're an angel, right. So you're supposed to be compassionate. I just accused a female who was raped until impregnated of being a whore. Do you honestly think I can handle being circle jerked about my *shellan* right now?"

"There are three places in the afterlife. The Fade, where loved ones are reunited. *Dhund*, where the unjust go. And the In Between—"

"Did you hear what I just said?"

"—which is where souls get stuck. It's not like the other two—"

"Do you care?"

"—because the In Between is different for everybody. Right now, your *shellan* and your young are stuck because of you. That's why I've come— I'm here to help you, help them get where they belong."

Man, this was a fine time to have a fucked-up foot, Tohr thought, because he suddenly had no sense of balance whatsoever. Either that or the training center was spinning on the axis of the house.

"I don't understand," he whispered.

"You've got to move on, my man. Stop holding on to her so she can go—"

"There is no purgatory, if that's what you're suggesting—"

"Where the fuck do you think I came from?"

Tohr cocked a brow. "You really want me to answer that."

"Not funny. And I'm serious."

"No, you're lying—"

"You ever wonder how I found you in those woods? Why I've stuck around? Have you asked yourself for a moment why I'm wasting time on you? Your *shellan* and your son are trapped and I was sent here to get them free."

"Son?" Tohr breathed.

"Yeah, she was carrying a little boy."

Tohr's legs went out from underneath him at that point—fortunately, the angel jumped forward and caught him before he broke something.

"Come here." Lassiter maneuvered him over toward the bench. "Park it and put your head between your knees—your color's gone to hell."

For once, Tohr didn't put up a fight; he let his ass go down and allowed himself to get pretzeled by the angel. As he opened his mouth and tried to breathe, he noticed for no good reason that the tiles on the floor weren't a solid aqua blue, but had multicolored specks in them of white and gray and navy.

As a big hand started making circles on his back, he was strangely comforted.

"A son . . ." Tohr lifted his head a little and swept his palm down his face. "I wanted a son."

"So did she."

He looked over sharply. "She never told me that."

"She kept quiet because she didn't want you to get all fat-chested about having two males in the house."

Tohr laughed. Or maybe it was a sob. "She would so do that."

"Yeah."

"So you've seen her."

"Yeah. She's not doing well, Tohr."

Abruptly, he felt like . . . "I'm going to be sick." Which was better than crying. "Purgatory?"

"The In Between. And there's a reason that no one knows about it. If you get out, you're in the Fade—or *Dhund,* and your experience of where you were is forgotten, a bad memory that fades. And if your window closes, you're stuck there forever, so it's not like you're filing any reports on the landscape."

"I don't understand—she lived a good life. She was a female of worth who was taken early. Why wouldn't she go into the Fade?"

"Did you hear what I said? Because of you."

"Me?" He threw his hands up. "What the fuck did I do wrong? I'm living and breathing—I didn't off myself and I'm not going to—"

"You haven't let her go. Don't deny it. Come on, look what you just did to No'One. You walked in on her naked, through no fault of her own, and you tore her head off because you thought she was hitting you with a case of the hot-and-bothereds."

"And it's somehow wrong that I don't want to be ogled?" Tohr frowned. "Besides, how the hell do you know what just happened."

"You don't honestly think you're ever alone anymore, do you? And the problem isn't No'One. It's you—you don't want to be attracted to her."

"I *wasn't* attracted to her. I'm *not.*"

"But it's okay if you are. That's the point—"

Tohr reached over, grabbed the front of the angel's shirt, and yanked their heads together. "I got two things to say to you. I don't believe a thing you're telling me, and if you know what's good for you, you'll shut the fuck up about my mate."

As Tohr shoved free and got to his feet, Lassiter cursed. "You don't have forever with this, buddy."

"Stay the hell out of my room."

"Are you willing to bet her eternity on your anger? Are you really that arrogant?"

Tohr glared over his shoulder . . . except the son of a bitch was gone: There was nothing but air on the bench where the angel had been. And it was hard to argue with that.

"Whatever. Fucking whack-job."

TWELVE

When Xhex walked into the Iron Mask, she felt like she was stepping back in time. For years, she had worked in clubs like this, weeding through desperate people like this, keeping her eyes peeled for trouble . . . like this little knot of tension that had formed up ahead.

Directly in front of her, two guys were squaring off, a pair of Goth bulls all but pawing at the ground with their New Rocks. Just to the side, a chick with black-and-white hair, glittery cleavage, and a dumb-ass getup involving buckled straps of black leather was looking pretty damn satisfied with herself.

Xhex wanted to slap her upside the head and send her packing just for that attitude alone.

The real problem, however, was not this bonehead with the breasticles, but the two pieces of meat who were about to go Dana White on each other. The concern was not so much what they did to each other's noses or jawlines; it was the other two hundred people who were basically behaving. Male bodies flying backward in twelve different directions could knock a lot of bystanders on their asses, and who needed that?

She was about to step in when she reminded herself that this wasn't her job anymore. She was no longer responsible for these asshats and their libidos and their jealousies, their drug dealing and doing, their sexual exploits—

Annnnnnd here was Trez "Latimer," taking care of it anyway.

The humans in the crowd saw the Moor as simply one of them, just bigger and more aggressive. She knew the truth, however. That Shadow was far more dangerous than any of the Homo sapiens could have guessed. If he'd wanted to, he could have ripped their throats out in the blink of an eye . . . then thrown the carcasses on a spit over a fire, basted them for a couple of hours, and had them for dinner with an ear of corn and a bag of chips.

Shadows had a unique way of disposing of their enemies.

Tums, anyone?

As Trez's bulk made an impression, the dynamic onstage changed instantly: Dipshit chippie took one look at him and appeared to forget the names of the two guys she'd whipped up into a tizzy. Meanwhile, the pair of boozing bozos cooled off a little, stepping back and reevaluating their situation.

Good plan—they were one second away from having it forcibly re-evaluated for them.

Trez's eyes met Xhex's for a heartbeat, and then he focused on his three patrons. As the female tried to sidle up to him, flashing her eyes and her breast tissue, she made all the impression of a strip steak to a vegetarian: Trez was vaguely disgusted.

Over the din of the music, Xhex only caught a few words here and there, but she could have guessed the script well enough: *Don't be an ass. Take it outside. First and only warning before you're* persona non grata.

At the end of it, Trez practically had to peel the harpy off him with a crowbar—somehow, she'd grafted herself onto his arm.

Shaking her off with a, "You can't be serious," he stepped up. "Hey."

That slow, sexy smile of his was the problem, of course. And the deep voice didn't help. Or that body.

"Hey." She had to smile back. "Female problems again?"

"Always." He glanced around. "Where's ya man?"

"Not here."

"Ahhhhh." Pause. "How you?"

"I don't know, Trez. I don't know why I'm here. I just . . ."

Reaching out, he put a heavy arm around her shoulders and drew her up against him. God, he smelled the same, a combination of Gucci Pour Homme and something that was altogether *him*.

"Come on, girlie," he murmured. "Back to my office."

"Don't call me 'girlie.'"

"Okay. How 'bout 'buttercup.'"

She snaked an arm around his waist and leaned her head on his pec as they started walking together. "You like your balls where they are?"

"Yeah. I don't like the way you're lookin', though. I prefer you feisty and pissed off."

"Me, too, Trez. Me too . . ."

"So we're good on the 'buttercup'? Or do I have to get even tougher with you? I'll pull out 'pookie' if I have to."

In the way back of the club, next to the locker room where the "dancers" changed in and out of their street clothes, Trez's office had a door on it like a meat locker. Inside, there was a black leather couch, a big metal desk, and a lead-lined blanket chest that was bolted to the floor. That was it. Well, aside from the purchase orders, receipts, phone messages, laptops. . . .

It felt like a million years since she'd been around all this.

"Guess iAm hasn't been here yet," she said, nodding to the mess on the desk. Trez's twin would never have stood for it.

"He's over at Sal's cooking until midnight."

"Same schedule, then."

"If it ain't broke . . ."

As they settled in, he in his thronelike chair, she on the couch, her chest hurt.

"Talk to me," he said, his dark face serious.

Propping her head on her hand and crossing her leg ankle to knee, she fiddled with the laces on her shitkicker. "What if I told you I wanted my old job back?"

In her peripheral vision, she watched him recoil a little. "I thought you were fighting with the Brothers."

"So did I."

"Wrath not exactly comfortable with a female in the field?"

"John isn't." As Trez cursed, she exhaled hard. "And as I'm his *shellan*, what he says goes."

"He actually looked you in the eye and—"

"Oh, he did more than that." When a threatening growl percolated

through the air, she waved her hand. "No, nothing violent. The argument—arguments weren't a party, though."

Trez sat back. Drummed his fingers on the clutter in front of him. Stared at her. "Of course you can come back—you know me. I'm not bound by any vampiric notion of propriety—and ours is a matriarchal society, so I've never understood the misogyny of the Old Ways. Am worried about you and John, however."

"We'll work it out." How? She hadn't a clue. But she wasn't giving her fear that they wouldn't be able to any more credibility by putting it into words. "I just can't sit in that house doing nothing, and I don't want to even lay eyes on the bunch of them. Shit, Trez, I should have known this mating thing was a bad idea. I'm not cut out for it."

"Sounds like you're not the one creating the problem. Although I do get where he's coming from. If anything happened to iAm, I'd go fucking mental—so it's not a good idea for he and I to fight side by side."

"You do anyway."

"Yeah, but we're stupid. And it's not like we go out looking for hand-to-hand every night—we got office jobs that keep us busy, and it's only if something finds us that we take care of it." He opened a desk drawer and threw her a set of keys. "There's one last empty office down the hall. If that detective from CPD homicide comes around again about Chrissy and that dead boyfriend of hers, we'll deal with it if we have to. Meanwhile, I'll put you back on the payroll. Timing's good—I could use some help organizing the bouncers. But—and I mean this—there's no long-term obligation. You can leave whenever you want."

"Thanks, Trez."

The two of them stared across his desk.

"It's going to be okay," the Shadow said.

"You sure about that."

"Positive."

About a block and a half away from the Iron Mask, Xcor stood in the lee of a tattoo parlor, the red, yellow, and blue glow from its neon sign getting in his eyes and on his nerves.

Throe and Zypher had gone into the establishment about ten minutes ago.

But not for ink.

By all that was holy, Xcor would have preferred for his soldiers to be anywhere else on a mission for anything else. Unfortunately, one couldn't negotiate with the need for blood—and they had yet to find a reliable source for it. Human females would do in the pinch they were in, but the strength didn't last nearly as long, and that meant the hunt for victims was nearly as frequent as that for food.

Indeed, they had been here only a week, and he could feel the lagging effect on his flesh already—back in the Old Country, they had had proper vampire females that they had paid to be of service. Here, they currently didn't have that luxury, and he feared it would be a while before they did.

Although if he became king, the problem would be solved.

As he waited, he shifted his weight back and forth on his boots, his leather coat making a subtle creaking noise. On his back, concealed in her holster but ready for use, his scythe was as impatient as he was.

Sometimes he could swear the thing talked to him: For instance, from time to time, a human would pass by the opening of the alley he was in; maybe it was a loner striding quickly, or a woman lollygagging as she tried to light a cigarette in the wind, or a small group of revelers. Whatever the variant, his eyes tracked them as prey, noting the way their bodies moved and where they might be hiding any weapons and how many bounding leaps it would take to put himself in their paths.

And all the while his scythe whispered to him, urging him to take action.

Back in the Bloodletter's time, humans had been fewer and less robust, good for both target practice and as a source of sustenance—which was how that race of tailless rats had ended up with so many vampire myths. Now, however, the rodents had taken over the palace of the earth, becoming a threat.

Such a shame he couldn't go to work on Caldwell properly. Take it over not just from the great Blind King and the Brotherhood, but the Homo sapiens, too.

His scythe was ready; that was for certain. She all but tingled on his back, begging to be used in that voice that was sexier than anything his ears had actually heard from a female.

Throe emerged from the shop and came into the alley. Immediately, Xcor's fangs elongated, his cock getting hard not because he was interested in sex, but because that was just what his body did.

"Zypher's finishing up with them right now," his lieutenant said.

"Good."

As a metal door opened down the way, both of them ducked their hands into their leather dusters and gripped guns. But it was just Zypher . . .

with a triumvirate of ladies, all of whom were about as attractive as garbage next to a dinner plate.

Beggars, choosers and all that, however. Besides, each had the fore-most requirement: a neck.

On the approach, Zypher was grinning, but being careful not to flash his fangs. In his accent, he drawled, "This is Carla, Beth, and Linda—"

"Lindsay," the one on the far end called out.

"Lindsay," he corrected, reaching over and pulling her in closer. "Girls, you met my friend—and this is my boss."

The soldier didn't bother with names—why waste the breath? Yet re-gardless of the improper introduction, they seemed excited: Carla, Beth, and Lin-whatever-the-fuck smiled at Throe, all green-light in the eye . . . until they looked at Xcor

Even though he was mostly in the shadows, a security light had been motion-activated above the door they'd come out of, and clearly they didn't like what they saw. Two of them dropped their eyes to the ground. The other just got busy fiddling with Zypher's leather jacket.

The intrinsic rejection was not an unheard-of reaction. In fact, no fe-male had ever looked upon him with approval or attraction.

Fortunately, he couldn't care less.

Before the silence could get awkward, Zypher said, "Anyhow, these lovely ladies are about to go to work—"

"At the Iron Mask," Lin-whatever spoke up.

"—but they've agreed to meet us out here at three o'clock."

"When we get off," one of them tacked on.

As the trio fell into a set of annoying, naughty giggles, Xcor was no more interested in them than they were in him. Indeed, his ambitions were far loftier than the likes of Zypher's. Sex, like taking blood, was an incon-venient biological function, and he was far too smart to ever fall for that romance bullshit.

If one was determined to go that route, castration was easier, less pain-ful, and just as permanent.

"So, do we have a date?" Zypher said to the woman.

The one who'd all but crawled into his clothes whispered something that brought his head down. As his brows tightened, it wasn't hard to figure out what the gist was, and the woman didn't look too unhappy about his answer.

She purred.

Then again, that was what unspayed alley cats did, Xcor supposed.

"It's a date," the vampire said, glancing at Throe. "I have promised that we shall take care of these three very nicely."

"I've got what we need."

"Fine. Good." He swatted the ass of one, then another. The third, the woman trying to get into his coat, he tilted back and kissed hard.

More giggling. More coy looks that were not entirely about the fact that these were prostitutes on the way to getting paid.

Just as they were leaving, each one of the women looked back at Xcor, their expressions suggesting he was like a disease they were soon to be exposed to. He wondered who was going to get the short end of the stick when they all reconvened—because sure as the day was long and the nights always too short, he was going to have one of them.

It simply cost extra in these kinds of situations.

"Fine specimens of virtue," Xcor said dryly when he was alone with his soldiers.

Zypher shrugged. "They are what they are. And they'll be good enough."

"I am endeavoring to find us proper females," Throe said. "It is not easy, however."

"Mayhap you need to work harder." Xcor looked up to the sky. "Now let us get to work. Time is wasting."

THIRTEEN

*W*hore? *Whore?*

As No'One cast herself unto the Other Side and reentered the Sanctuary she had spent centuries in, she could get neither that word nor her anger out of her head.

Down below, in the training center, clean laundry had never been folded so viciously, and when she had finished her duties, staying in the mansion for the daylight hours had not been possible.

This was her only other destination.

And it was about time to come here to refresh herself anyway.

Standing in the field of colorful flowers, she took deep breaths . . . and prayed that she would be left alone. The Chosen were a kindly lot of sacred females and they deserved better than what she had to offer even a casual passerby—fortunately, they were mostly over on the Far Side now with the Primale.

Hitching up her robing, she started to walk, marching through the perpetually blooming tulips with their fat hats in vibrant, jewel-like hues. She kept going until her bad leg started to protest. And then still she continued to promenade.

The Scribe Virgin's precious territory was bound on all four sides by a thick forest, and peppered with classically styled buildings and temples. No'One knew every roof, every wall, every path, every pool—and now in her fury, she made a broad circle about it all.

Anger animated her, driving her forward toward . . . nothing and nobody. And yet nonetheless she surged on.

How could he who had seen her suffer ever call her that? She had been a virgin violently robbed of the gift she had intended to give whomever she would have mated.

Whore!

Indeed, Tohrment was not the male she had once known—and as the thought occurred, she reflected that in this they were the same. She, too, had shed an earlier incarnation of herself, but unlike him, her current persona was an improvement.

After a while, her leg ached so much she had to slow down . . . and then stop. The pain was a great clarifier, making the environment she was actually in supersede the one she had left down below but kept with her.

She was standing afore the Temple of the Sequestered Scribes.

It was unoccupied. As had all the other buildings been.

As she looked around, the true depth of the quiet sank in. The landscape was utterly unoccupied. It was as if, in a rake of irony, the vibrant color that had finally come hereto had not just replaced the pervasive white, but chased away all the life.

Recalling the past, when there had been so much to tend to, she realized that in truth, she had gone to the Other Side not just to seek her daughter, but to find another place where she could busy herself to exhaustion so that she did not think overly much.

Here she had nothing to do.

Dearest Virgin Scribe, she was going to go mad.

Abruptly, an image of Tohrment, son of Hharm's naked shoulders filled her mind until she was blinded by it.

𝔚𝔈𝔏𝔏𝔈𝔖𝔄𝔑𝔇𝔕𝔄

The name was carved on the breadth of his musculature in the Old Language, the marking of a true union of bodies and souls.

After having something like that ripped away by fate, he was no doubt as ruined as she herself was. And she had been angry at first, too. When she had arrived here after her death and was shown her duties by the

Directrix, her numbness had melted away, revealing a fire of rage. There had been nothing to lash out at except for herself, however—and she had done that for decades.

At least until she had come to realize the "why" of her fate, the purpose behind her tragedy, the cause of her salvation.

She had been given a second chance so that she could be born anew into a role of service and humility, and learn the error of her previous ways.

Pushing the temple's door wide, she limped into the lofty room, where the rows of desks and rolls of parchment and flares of feather quills were. At each station, in the center of the workspace, was a round crystal bowl filled three-quarters of the way with water so pure that it was nearly invisible.

Indeed, Tohrment was suffering as she had, perhaps just starting the journey she felt as though she had completed over too many years to count. And though her anger was an easy emotion to feel in the face of his unjust accusation, understanding and compassion were the harder, more valuable stances to take . . .

She had learned this from the example the Chosen set.

Although understanding required knowledge, she thought, staring at one of the bowls.

As she stepped forward, she was uneasy with the quest she was about to initiate, and she chose a station far, far in the back, away from both the doors and the cathedral-size leaded windows.

Sitting down, she found no dust on the surface of the desk, nor minute debris within or upon the water, nor dried-up ink in the bottle—in spite of the fact that it had been a long while since the room had been filled with females seeking out the events of the race down below and recording the history that appeared unto their kindly eyes.

No'One picked up the bowl, holding it with her palms, not her fingers. With barely perceptible movement, she began to circle the water, picturing Tohrment's back as clearly as she was able.

Soon enough, a story began to unfold, told in moving pictures that were trussed in living color, and animated by love.

She had never before thought to search him and his life out in the bowls. The few times she had come here, it had been to check on her family's fortunes and the course of her daughter's life. Now, though, she knew it had been too painful for her to look into the pair of warriors who had given her shelter and protected her.

In her final, most cowardly act, she had betrayed them both.

On the surface of the water, she saw Tohrment with a red-haired female of grand stature—they were waltzing, she in that red gown, he robe-less and showing off the fresh scarification that spelled out her name in the Old Language. He was so happy, incandescently so, his love and bonding making him shine like the North Star.

There were other scenes that followed, drifting down through the years, from when it had been all new between them to the comfort that came with familiarity, from small abodes to larger ones, from good times where they laughed together to hard times when they argued.

It was the very best that life had to offer anyone: a person to love and be loved by, with whom you carved meaning in the oak trunk of time's perennial passing.

And then another scene.

The female was in a kitchen, a lovely, gleaming kitchen, standing before a stove. There was a pan on the heat, some meat cooking therein, and she had a spatula in her hand. She wasn't looking downward, however. She was star-ing into the space afore her, her eyes unfocused as smoke began to curl up.

Tohrment appeared across the way, rushing into the doorway. He called out her name and grabbed a small towel, going over to a fixture on the ceiling and whisking the cloth back and forth with vigor as he winced as though his ears hurt.

Over at the stove, Wellesandra jumped to attention and shoved the burning pan from the red-hot coil. She began speaking, and though there was no sound associated with the pictures, it was clear she was making apologies.

After all was settled and calmed and no longer afire, Tohrment leaned back against the counter, crossed his arms over his chest, and spoke for a bit. Then he went silent.

It was a long while before Wellesandra answered. In the previous pic-tures of their life, she had always appeared to be strong and direct . . . now her expression was hesitant.

When she finished her reply, her lips pursed together and her eyes locked on her mate.

Tohrment's arms gradually unfolded until they hung limp by his sides, and his mouth grew lax as well, his jaw unlatching to fall open. His eyes blinked repeatedly, open and shut, open and shut, open and shut. . . .

When he finally moved, it was with the grace of someone who had broken every bone in his body: He lurched across the distance that sepa-rated them and fell to his knees before his *shellan*. Reaching up with shak-ing hands, he touched her lower belly as tears watered his eyes.

He didn't say a word. Just gathered his mate to him, his big, strong arms enveloping her waist, his wet cheek coming to rest on her womb.

Above him, Wellesandra started to smile . . . beam, really.

Down below her happiness, however, Tohr's face was cast in lines of terror. As if he knew, even then, that the pregnancy she rejoiced in was doom for all three of them—

"I thought I'd find you on this side."

No'One whipped around, the water in the bowl splashing out onto her robe, the image ruined.

Tohrment stood in the doorway sure as if her invasion of his privacy had called him forth to protect what was rightly his. His temper had dissipated, but even in the absence of anger, his gaunt face was nothing close to what she had just seen of him.

"I've come to apologize," he said.

She carefully put the bowl back, watching as the choppy surface of the water calmed down and the level slowly rose to what it had been, replenished from an unknown, unseeable reservoir.

"I figured I'd wait until I sobered up a little—"

"I've been watching you," she said. "In the bowl. With your *shellan*."

That shut him up.

Getting to her feet, No'One smoothed her robe even though it fell as it always did, in straight, shapeless folds of cloth. "I understand why you are in a foul way and quick to temper. It is in the nature of a wounded animal to strike out at even a friendly hand."

When she looked up, he was frowning so deeply, his brows were a single line. Not exactly an opening for conversation. But it was time to clear the air between them, and as with the debridement of a festering wound, one could expect it to hurt.

The infection must be wrestled from the flesh, however.

"How long ago did she die?"

"Killed," he said after a moment. "She was killed."

"How long."

"Fifteen months, twenty-six days, seven hours. I'd have to check a watch for the minutes."

No'One walked over to the windows and looked out over the bright green grass. "How did you find out she had been taken from you?"

"My king. My brothers. They came to me . . . and they told me she had been shot."

"What happened after that?"

"I screamed. I took myself somewhere, anywhere else. I cried for weeks in the wilderness alone."

"You didn't perform a Fade ceremony?"

"I didn't come back for nearly a year." He cursed and scrubbed his face. "I can't believe you're asking me this shit, and I can't believe I'm answering."

She shrugged. "It is because you were cruel to me at the pool. You feel guilty, and I feel like you owe me something. The latter makes me bold and the former loosens your lips."

He opened his mouth. Shut it. Opened it again. "You're very smart."

"Not really. It is obvious."

"What did you see in the bowls?"

"Are you sure you wish me to say?"

"All of it plays in my head on an endless loop. Not gonna be a news flash, whatever it is."

"She told you she was pregnant in your kitchen. You fell to the floor before her—she was happy, you were not."

As he blanched, she wished she'd shared one of the other scenes.

And then he surprised her. "It's weird . . . but I knew it was bad news. Too much good fortune. She wanted one so badly. Every ten years we fought about it when she had her needing. Finally, it got to the point where she was going to leave me if I didn't agree to let her try. It was like choosing between taking a bullet or a blade—either way, I knew . . . somehow I was going to lose her."

Using the crutch, he hobbled over to a chair, pulled it out, and sat down. As he awkwardly maneuvered his injured foot around, she realized they had yet another thing in common.

She approached him slowly and unevenly and sat at the desk beside him. "I am so sorry." When he seemed a bit surprised, she shrugged once again. "How can I not offer condolences in the face of your loss? In truth, after seeing you both together, I don't think I shall ever forget how much you loved her."

After a moment, he murmured hoarsely, "That makes two of us."

As they fell silent, Tohr stared at the small, hooded figure sitting so still next to him. They were separated by about four feet, each parked at one of the scribing desks. But they seemed closer than that.

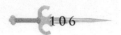

"Take your hood off for me." As No'One hesitated, he tacked on, "You saw the best of my life. I want to see your eyes."

Her pale hands lifted, and they shook ever so slightly as she removed what covered her face.

She didn't look at him. Likely couldn't.

With dispassionate focus, he measured the spectacular angles of her features. "Why do you wear that all the time."

She took a deep breath, the robe rising and falling such that he was forced to remember she was probably still naked under it.

"Tell me," he demanded.

As she squared her shoulders, he thought that anyone who believed this female was weak had another think coming.

"This face"—she motioned around her perfectly angled jaw and her rosy, high cheeks—"is not who I am. If people see it, they treat me with a deference that is inappropriate. Even the Chosen did so. I cover it up because if I don't, then I am propagating a lie, and even if it grinds upon only me, that is enough."

"You have quite a way of putting things."

"Is the explanation not sufficient."

"It is." When she went to raise the thing up again, he reached out and put his hand on her arm. "If I promise to forget what you look like, will you keep it down? I can't judge your mood as well when you're hiding— and in case you haven't noticed, we're not exactly talking about the weather here."

She kept her hand on one half of the hood, as if she couldn't let go. And then she locked her eyes on him—so directly he recoiled.

It was the first time she'd really looked at him, he realized. Ever.

Speaking with likewise candor, she said, "Just so that you and I are utterly clear with each other, I have no interest in any male. I am sexually repulsed by your kind, and that includes yourself."

He cleared his throat. Pulled at his muscle shirt. Shifted in the chair.

Then he took a slow, relieved breath.

No'One continued, "If I have offended you—"

"No, not at all. I know it's not personal."

"It truly is not."

"To be honest, it makes things . . . easier. Because I feel the same way."

At this, she actually smiled a little. "Two peas in a pod are we, indeed."

They were quiet for a time. Until he said abruptly, "I'm still in love with my *shellan*."

"Why wouldn't you be. She was lovely."

He felt himself smile for the first time in . . . so long. "It wasn't just her looks. It was everything about her."

"I could tell by the way you stared at her. You were enthralled."

He picked up one of the quills and checked out the fine, sharp cut of its tip. "God . . . I was nervous that night we were mated. I wanted her so badly—and I couldn't believe she was going to be mine."

"Was it arranged?"

"Yeah, by my *mahmen*. My father didn't care about that kind of thing—or for me, for that matter. But my mother took care of things the best she could—and she was smart. She knew if I got a good female, I'd be set for life. Or at least . . . that was the plan."

"Is your *mahmen* alive?"

"No, and I'm glad she isn't. She wouldn't have . . . liked any of this."

"And your father?"

"He's dead, too. He disowned me until he got close to the grave. About six months before he died, he called me to him—and I wouldn't have gone but for Wellsie. She made me, and she was right. He formally reclaimed me on his deathbed. I'm not sure why it was so important to him, but there you go."

"What about Darius? I have not seen him around—"

"He was killed by the enemy. Just before Wellsie was." As she gasped and put her hand to her mouth, he nodded. "It's been hell, really."

"You are all alone," she said in a small voice.

"I have my brothers."

"Do you let them in."

With a short laugh, he shook his head. "You are hell's bells with the rhetoricals, you know that?"

"I am sorry, I—"

"No, don't apologize." He put the quill back in its holder. "I like talking to you."

As he heard the surprise in his own voice, he laughed harshly. "Man, I'm just making all kinds of charm points with you tonight, aren't I." Slapping his thighs to end their conversation, he got to his feet with the help of the crutch. "Listen, I also came here to do a little research. Do you know where the library is? Damned if I can find it."

"Yes, of course." As she stood, she swept that hood up over her head again. "I shall take you there."

While she went past him, he frowned. "You're limping worse than usual. Did you get hurt?"

"No. When I move around too much, it aches."

"We could take care of that down below—Manello is—"

"Thank you, but no."

Tohr threw out a hand and stopped her before she went out the door. "The hood. Leave it down, please." When she didn't respond, he said, "There's no one here but us. You're safe."

FOURTEEN

As John Matthew stood on the shores of the Hudson River about fifteen minutes north of downtown Caldwell, he felt like he was a thousand miles away from everyone.

At his back, he had the prevailing breeze as well as a small hunting cabin that, if you didn't know what it was, you'd write off as something not worth the effort to knock over. The place was a fortress, however, with steel-reinforced walls, an impenetrable roof, bulletproof windows . . . and enough firepower in its garage to make half the population of the city see God up close and personal.

He had assumed Xhex would come here. Been so convinced, he hadn't bothered to track her.

But she wasn't—

A flare of headlights off to the right brought his head around. A car was coming down the lane, slowly approaching the cabin.

John frowned as he got an earful of the engine: low, deep, a mean growl.

That was no Hyundai or Honda. Couldn't be a Harley, too smooth.

Whatever the hell it was meandered by and kept going, all the way to

the tip of the point where that big-ass house had been put up. A few moments later, lights began to go on inside the mansion, illumination pouring out of its curved porches and stacked, three-story straightaways.

Damn thing looked like a spaceship about to take off.

Not his biz. And it was time to go, anyway.

With a mute curse, he scattered his molecules and zeroed in on the armpit of Caldie, that stretch of bars, strip clubs, and tattoo places down around Trade Street.

The Iron Mask had been Rehvenge's second club, a dance/sex/drug facility created to cater to a Goth demographic unserviced by his first establishment, ZeroSum—which had had more of a Eurotrash kind of vibe.

There was a line to get in—always was—but the two bouncers, Big Rob and Silent Tom, recognized him and let him in ahead of everyone else.

Velvet drapes, deep-seated couches, black lights . . . women in black leather with white makeup and hair extensions down to their asses . . . men clustered in groups, strategizing on how to get laid . . . moody music with lyrics that made you think fondly of eating a bullet.

But maybe that was just his mood.

And she was here. He could sense his blood in Xhex, and he headed through the crowd, zeroing in on the signal.

As he got to the unmarked door that led into the staff-only part of the club, Trez stepped out of the shadows. Natch.

"What's doing," the Shadow said, offering his palm.

The two clapped a grip, knocked shoulders, and slapped each other's backs.

"You here to talk to her?" When John nodded, the guy opened the door. "I gave her the office beside the locker room next to me. Go on back—she's just checking her staff reports—"

The Shadow stopped abruptly, but he'd said enough.

Jesus Christ . . .

"Ah, yeah, she's back there," the guy muttered, like he was sooo staying out of this one.

John ducked in and strode down the corridor. When he got to a closed door, he didn't see a sign with her name on it, but wondered how long that would last.

And he knocked, even though she had to know he was here.

When she called out, he pushed in—

Xhex was in the far corner, bent over and pulling at something on the floor. As she looked up with a glare, she froze; which told him that, in fact, she hadn't noticed he'd arrived.

Great. She was so into her new old job, she'd forgotten about him already.

"Ah . . . hey." Glancing back down, she resumed what she was doing, yanking at—

An extension cord whipped out from underneath the file cabinet, the sharp-toothed end going flying.

Before it ripped around and caught her a good one, he leaped forward, snatched a hold on the thing, and took the hit himself, the sting of pain lighting off on his rib cage.

"Thanks," she said as he handed it over and stepped away. "It was jammed back there."

So . . . you're going to work here now?

"Yeah. I am. I don't think that other option is realistic. And"—her eyes got hard—"if you try to tell me I can't—"

God, Xhex, this is not what we are. He motioned back and forth over the desk that separated them. *This is not us.*

"Actually, I guess it is, because we're here, aren't we."

I don't want to stop you from fighting—

"But you have. Let's not pretend otherwise." Xhex sat down in the office chair and leaned back, a squeak rising up. "Now that you and I are mated, the Brothers, even your king, take their cues from you—no, wait, I'm not finished." She closed her eyes as if exhausted. "Just let me talk this out. I know they respect me, but they respect a mated male's prerogative over his *shellan* more. It's not specific to the Brotherhood—it's the very fabric of vampire society, and no doubt it's because a bonded male is a dangerous animal. You can't change that, and I can't live like that, so yeah, this is where we are."

I can talk to them, make them—

"They're not the root problem."

John felt a sudden urge to punch a wall. *I can change.*

Abruptly her shoulders dropped, and her eyes, those gunmetal gray eyes, grew stark. "I don't think you can, John. And neither can I. I'm not going to sit home and wait for you to come back at dawn every night."

I'm not asking you to do that.

"Good, because I'm not going back to the mansion." As John felt the

blood drain out of his head, she cleared her throat. "You know, that whole bonding thing . . . I know you can't help it. I was pissed off when I left, but I've been thinking it over ever since then, and— Shit, I know if you could feel different, be different, you would. The reality is, though, we could spend another miserable couple of months figuring that out, and learn to hate each other in the process—and I don't want that. You don't want that."

So you're done with me, he signed. *Is that it?*

"No! I don't know— I mean, fuck." She threw her hands up. "What else am I going to do? I'm so frustrated with you, with me, with everything—I'm not sure I'm even talking any sense."

John frowned, finding himself in the same tough spot she was in. Where was the middle road?

There is more to us than this, he signed.

"I want to believe that," she said sadly. "I really do."

On impulse, he walked around the desk and stood over her. Gripping the armrest, he turned the chair toward him and put out both his palms, offering them to her.

There was no demand. No aggression. She would choose or not choose.

After a moment, Xhex placed her hands in his, and when he pulled her up, she didn't fight him.

Slipping his arms around her, he brought her close—and then moving with power, he bent her off balance, holding her in his powerful arms, keeping her from the floor.

With eyes boring into hers, he brought their lips together once, briefly. When she didn't slap him, kick him in the nuts, or bite him, he dropped his head and took her mouth properly, plying her to open for him.

When she did, he melded her body to his and kissed the ever-living shit out of her. One of his hands ended up on her ass, squeezing; the other got clamped on the back of her neck. As a groan came up her throat, he knew he'd proved his point.

Although he had no immediate solution to the bonded-male situation, he knew this connection between them was a for-sure, in a world that had suddenly seemed filled with maybe-not.

He stopped the kiss. He put her back down where she had been sitting. He went to the door.

Text me when you want to see me again, he signed. *I'm giving you your space, but know this: I* will *wait forever for you.*

*   *   *

Good thing for the chair, Xhex thought as the door closed behind John.

Yeah, wow. Whatever her head was cramped up with, her body was as fluid and easy as warm air.

She still wanted him. And he'd made his point. They did fit together—at least like that.

Holy hell, did they fit together.

Shit, what to do now?

Well, one idea . . . would be to text him to come back, lock them in together, and break in her new office improperly.

She even reached for her phone.

In the end, however, she texted something altogether different.

We'll figure this out. Promise.

Putting the phone down, she knew it was up to her and John to find their own future—work it out of the unforgiving, rocky shoals of passing time in a way that fit what they both needed.

She'd assumed that would be fighting side by side with him and the Brotherhood, and so had he.

Maybe that was still the way. Maybe it wasn't.

As she looked around her office, she wasn't sure how long she would be here—

The knock that interrupted her was a single strong one.

"Yeah," she called out.

Big Rob and Silent Tom walked in, looking as they always did—like they were about to drop some hotshot on his head for behaving badly. And as much as she was still focused on John, it was good to have some business-as-usual up in her face. She had spent a lot of nights making sure a club ran smoothly.

This she could do.

"Talk to me," she said.

Naturally, Big Rob did the obliging. "There's a new player in town."

"In what line of business?"

The guy tapped the side of his nose.

Drugs. Wonderful—but hardly a surprise. Rehv had been the kingpin for a decade, and now that he'd departed the scene? Opportunity, like nature, hated a vacuum—and money was a great motivator.

Frickin' great. The underworld of Caldwell was already a three-legged table from hell; more instability they did not need.

"Who is it?"

"No one knows. He's come out of, like, nowhere, and just bought half a million in powder from Benloise, in cash."

She frowned. It wasn't like she doubted her bouncer's sources, but that was a lot of product. "Doesn't mean it's going to be sold in Caldwell."

"We just picked up this from a disorderly in the men's bathroom."

Big Tom tossed a cellophane packet on the desk. The thing was your standard-issue quarter-ounce serve-up, except for one little detail. It was stamped with a red ink seal.

Fuck . . .

"I got no idea what that writing thingy is."

Of course he didn't. It was a character in the Old Language, one that didn't have an equivalent in English. Typically it was stamped on official documents, and it represented death.

The question was . . . who was trying to take Rehv's place—who happened to be of the race?

"The guy you got this from, did you let him go?" she asked.

"He's waiting for you in my office."

Xhex got up and came around the desk. Nailing Big Tom in the arm with a quick punch, she said, "I always did like you."

FIFTEEN

Up in the Sanctuary, No'One led Tohrment to the library, and expected to leave him to his investigations, whatever they might be. When they arrived at their destination, however, he opened the door for her, and beckoned her forward.

Of course, she stepped over the threshold.

The temple of books was long and thin and tall, built rather on the dimensions of a folio standing on its end. All around, leather-bound volumes, filled with the careful strokes of generations of the Chosen, were set in white marble cases in chronological order, the stories therein nonfictional accounts of lives lived far down below, and witnessed upon water's transparent screen.

Tohrment stood for a moment, his crutch keeping him stable as he cocked his bandaged foot up.

"What are you looking for?" she asked as she glanced at the nearest shelves. The sight of the volumes made her wonder about the future of keeping the past. With the Chosen exploring the real world, they were not recording as much, if at all. This long tradition could well be lost.

"The afterlife," Tohrment replied. "Any idea if there's a section on that?"

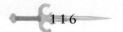

"I believe the chronicles are arranged by year, not subject."

"You ever hear of the In Between?"

"Of what?"

He laughed with a hard edge as he hobbled forward and began inspecting the stacks. "Exactly. We got the Fade. We got *Dhund*. Two opposite ends that I assumed were the only choices when you die. I'm looking for any evidence that there's another option. Damn it . . . yup—these are chronological, not by subject. Is it different elsewhere?"

"Not that I'm aware."

"Any index system?"

"Only by decade, I believe? I am not an expert, however."

"Shit, it could take years to go through all this."

"Perhaps you should speak with one of the Chosen? I know that Selena was a scribe—"

"No one needs to know about this. It's about my Wellsie."

The irony of that phrasing seemed lost upon him. "Wait . . . there is another room."

Leading him down the center aisle, she then took him left, into what was essentially a vault. "This is the most sacred place—where the lives of the Brotherhood are kept."

The heavy doors resisted the invasion, at least when she tried to open them. Before Tohrment's strength, however, they yielded to reveal a tight, tall room.

"So she kept us locked away," he said dryly as he inspected the names on the spines. "Look at these. . . ."

He drew out one of the volumes and cracked the spine. "Ah, Throe— father of the current Throe. Wonder what the old man would think of who his son's in bed with."

As he replaced the volume, she made no bones about staring at him, his brows tight in concentration, his strong yet refined fingers handling the books with care, his body leaning into the shelving.

His dark hair was thick and glossy, and cut very short. And that white stripe in front seemed shockingly out of place—until she thought of his tired, haunted eyes.

Oh, those eyes of his. Blue as the sapphires in the Treasury—and just as precious, she supposed.

He was very handsome, she realized.

Funny, the fact that he was in love with someone else made it possible for her to even assess him on that level: With him feeling as he did for his *shellan*, he was . . . safe. To the point where she no longer felt awkward that he had seen her unclothed. He would never regard her with anything sexual. That would be a violation of his love for Wellesandra.

"Is there anything else in here?" he said, bending low while balancing on the crutch. "I just see . . . biographies of Brothers . . ."

"Here, allow me to help."

Together they went through it all, and found no reference volumes pertaining to heaven or hell. Just Brother after Brother after Brother . . .

"Nothing," he muttered. "What the fuck is a library good for if you can't find anything in it?"

"Perhaps . . ." Gripping the lip of a shelf, she awkwardly bent downward, tracking the names. Finally, she found what she was looking for. "We could search your own."

Crossing his arms over his chest, he appeared to gird himself. "She'd be in there, wouldn't she."

"She was a part of your life, and you are the subject."

"Pull it."

There were several devoted to him, and No'One slid the most current one out. Cracking the spine, she flipped past the lineage declaration in the front, and scanned through the various pages that were focused on his prowess in the field. When she got to what had been written last, she frowned.

"What does it say."

In the Old Language, she read aloud the date and then the notation: "'*Upon this eve, he did lose his mated* shellan, *Wellesandra, who was with young, from the earth. Subsequently, he extricated himself from the communal society of the Black Dagger Brotherhood.*'"

"That's it?"

"Yes."

She turned the book around so he could read for himself, but he slashed his hand through the air. "Jesus Christ, I get ruined, and that's all they wrote."

"Perhaps they were being respectful of your grief." She put the book away. "Surely that is best kept private."

He didn't say anything further, just stood there, pitched against the crutch that kept him up on his feet, his angry eyes locked on the floor.

"Talk to me," she said softly.

"Fucking hell." As he rubbed his eyes, the exhaustion radiated out of him. "The only peace I have in this whole nightmare is that my Wellsie's in the Fade with my son. That's the one thing I can live with. When I get

crazy, I tell myself she is safe, and better I go through the grief than her—better that I'm the one doing the missing down here on earth. 'Cuz, hey, the Fade is supposed to be all peace and love, right? Except then that angel comes along and starts talking about some kind of In Between—and now, suddenly, my single solace is . . . poof! And to top it off? I have never heard of the place and I can't verify it—"

"I have an idea. Come with me." When he just stared at her, she wasn't about to take no for an answer. "Come."

Tugging on his arm, she drew him out of the vault and back into the main part of the library. Then she went deep into the stacks, ticking down the dates of the volumes, locating the most recent ones.

"What was the day when she . . ." When Tohrment gave her the month and day again, she pulled out the appropriate volume.

Leafing through, she felt his looming presence above her—and was not threatened. "Here—here she is."

"Oh . . . God. What."

"It just says . . . yes, the same as it was noted in your volume. She was lost from the earth . . . wait a moment."

Going backward, then forward, she traced the histories of the other females and males who had died on that date: So-and-so passed unto to the Fade . . . unto the Fade . . . unto the Fade. . . .

When No'One looked up at him again, she felt a moment of true fear. "In fact, it does not say she is there. The Fade, that is."

"What do you mean—"

"It just says that she is lost. It does not say that she is in the Fade."

Deep in the cold, gritty heart of Caldwell, Xcor tracked a single *lesser*.

Traveling over a park's dead, scratchy grass, he moved silently behind the undead, scythe in hand, body poised for striking. This was a stray, one who had broken from the pack that he and his band of bastards had attacked earlier.

The thing was obviously injured, its black blood leaving a trail that was, as it turned out, eminently obvious.

He and his soldiers had killed all its colleagues back in the alleys; then they had taken some souvenirs upon Xcor's command, and he had split off to find this lonesome deserter. Throe and Zypher, meanwhile, had gone back to the tattoo shop to organize the females for feeding, and the cousins had returned to base camp to tend their battle wounds.

Mayhap, if the women were dispatched with suitable alacrity, they could find another squadron of the enemy before dawn—although *squadron* was the wrong word. Too professional. These current recruits were nothing like the ones in the Old Country back in the heyday of the war there; fresh from their inductions, these hadn't even paled out, and they didn't seem to be well organized or capable of working together during an engagement. Further, their weapons were largely of the street variety: box cutters, switchblades, bats—if they had guns, the pistols were mismatched and often ill shot.

It was a cobbled-together army the strength of which appeared to be mainly in numbers. And the Brotherhood could not beat them? Such a disgrace.

Refocusing on his prey, Xcor began to close the distance.

Time to finish this work. Get fed. Go back out.

The commons they had entered was down by the river, and rather too well lit for Xcor's tastes. Too out-upon-the-open as well: Dotted with picnic tables and round fifty-five-gallon drums for trash disposal, it didn't offer much in the way of shelter from prying eyes, but at least the night was cold enough to drive the humans with any credibility indoors. There would always be transients around, of course. Fortunately, they tended to stay in their own worlds, and if they didn't, no one would pay them any mind.

Up ahead, the *lesser* was on a concrete pathway that, instead of leading him to safety, was just going to deliver him to his demise—and he was ready for his final act. He was beginning to list from side to side, one arm throwing out uselessly for balance that would remain elusive, the other locked on its midsection. At this rate, it was going to drop to the ground soon, and where was the fun in that—

A sob broke through the muted sounds of the night.

And then another.

It was crying. The goddamn thing was crying like a female.

Xcor's wave of anger rose so fast, he nearly choked. Abruptly, he resheathed his scythe and took out his steel dagger.

Once a matter of business, now this was personal.

At his will, the sidewalk's lights on their long-necked poles started to go out one by one both in front of and behind the slayer, the darkness closing in until finally, through even his weakness and pain, he noticed that his time had come.

"Oh, fuck . . . no . . ." The thing spun around in the illumination of the last lamp. "Christ, no . . ."

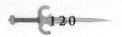

His face was stark white, as if he had stage makeup on, but it was not because he had been a slayer long enough to turn pale. Young, only eighteen or twenty, he had tattoos around his neck and down his arms, and if memory served, he'd been fairly competent with a knife—although it had been obvious during hand-to-hand that that was more instinct than training.

Clearly he'd been an aggressor in his previous incarnation; his initial show of force had proven that he was used to opponents who backed down after a first strike. The time for his strength and ego had passed, however, and these pathetic tears proved what he was at his core.

As the final light, the one that was over him, went out, he screamed.

Xcor attacked with brutal force, launching his great weight into the air and latching onto the thing as he shoved it backward to the grass.

Clapping a palm on its face, he buried the knife in the shoulder and pulled away, ripping through tendon and muscle, shearing across bone. Hot breath exploded up as the *lesser* screamed again—proving anew that even the undead had pain receptors.

Xcor leaned down and put his mouth to the male's ear. "Cry for me. Cry away . . . cry hard until you can't breathe."

The bastard took the direction and ran with it, weeping openly with great hoarse grabs of air and quaking exhalations. Reigning above the show, Xcor absorbed the weakness through his pores, pulling it in, holding it tight in his own lungs.

The hatred he felt went beyond the war, beyond this night and this moment. Soul deep, and marrow blistering, his disgust made him want to draw and quarter the former human.

But there was a more fitting end to this.

Flipping the thing over onto its stomach, he shoved both of his knees in between its tight thighs, and spread its legs as if it were a female about to get fucked. Rearing up over its prone body, he pushed its face into the grass.

And then he went to work.

No more raising the knife high and stabbing downward. Now was the time for precision and careful follow-through with his dagger.

As the *lesser* struggled pitifully, Xcor cut through the collar of its sleeveless shirt, then put his blade between his teeth and ripped the cloth in two, exposing the thing's shoulders and back. A tattoo of some kind of urban scene was done with respectable competence, the ink shown off to great effect by the skin's smooth surface—at least where black, oily blood didn't cloud the picture.

Weeping and harsh gasping caused the image to distort and resume its shape, distort and resume, as if it were a moving picture poorly screened.

"Such a pity to ruin this piece," Xcor drawled. "It must have taken a long time to get done. Must have hurt as well."

Xcor put the blade's razor point to the nape of the thing's neck. Piercing the skin, he went ever deeper, until he was stopped by bone.

More crying.

He put his mouth to the fucker's ear again. "I'm just revealing what everyone can see."

With a sure and steady stroke, he drew the knife downward, tracing the orderly stacks of vertebra whilst his prey squealed like a pig. And then he shifted his knees to the back of the slayer's legs, planted a palm on the thick of its shoulder . . . and reached in to lock a grip on the top of the spine.

What transpired as he threw all his strength upon his goal was nothing that a human could live through. The *lesser*, however, remained animated, even though afterward, respiration was no longer possible for him, and he would not be able to stand ever again: his core infrastructure, that which had defined his posture and his mobility, his height and girth, was now hanging from Xcor's hand.

The slayer was still crying, tears seeping from its eyes.

Xcor sat back, and breathed heavily from the exertion. It would be a fine thing to leave this weakling here in its current state, its destiny to be a spineless waste forever, and he took a moment to enjoy the suffering and imprint this vision of punishment in his mind.

Remembering back through the years, he recalled being in a similar position. Reduced to raw emotion, down on the ground, naked and degraded.

You are as worthless as your face. Get out.

The Bloodletter had been coldly dismissive, his subordinates efficient and pitiless: Xcor's arms and legs had been gripped and he had been carried to the mouth of the war camp's cave—whereupon he had been tossed out as if they were removing horse excrement.

Alone and in the cold white snow of winter, Xcor had lain where he had landed much as this slayer was, incapacitated, at the mercy of others. He had been faceup, however.

Indeed, that hadn't been the first time he'd been cast out. Starting with the female who had birthed him; then going through to the last orphanage he had stayed in, he'd had a long history of being denied. The war

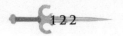

camp had been his final chance to find any community, and he had refused to be expelled from its confines.

He'd had to earn his way back in by bearing pain. And even the Bloodletter had been impressed at what he'd proven he could withstand.

Tears were for the young and females and castrated males. Too bad the lesson was wasted on this piece of—

"You've been busy."

Xcor looked up. Throe had come out of nowhere, no doubt materializing to the scene.

"Are the women ready," Xcor demanded gruffly.

"It's time."

Xcor endeavored to gather his strength. He had to take care of this mess—there was no leaving a twitching corpse behind for humans to find and extrapolate over until their heads exploded.

"There is a lavatory o'er there." Throe pointed across the lawn. "Finish this and let us wash you."

"As if I am a babe?" Xcor glared at his lieutenant. "I think not. You go back to the whores. I shall be there shortly."

"You can't bring your trophies."

"And where would you suggest I leave them." His tone suggested "up your ass" was an option, at least from his point of view. "Go."

Throe disapproved, and disagreed, but nonetheless—and per protocol—he nodded and spirited away.

Left on his own, Xcor spared the desecrated carcass one last look. "Oh, get over yourself."

The urge to further punish the weakness gave him the energy to stab the thing through the chest. The instant the steel tip penetrated, there was a pop, a flare . . . and then nothing but a stain on the grass where the *lesser* had lain.

Dragging himself to his feet, he took the spine of his prey and put it in his shoulder satchel with his other trophies.

It did not fit, one end protruding out the cinched top.

Throe had a point about the grisly bag of keepsakes. Damn it.

Dematerializing to the top of the bathroom shed, he left his trophies under the contours of the ventilation system and willed himself inside, where the sinks and the toilets were. He was quite sure the place smelled of fake air freshener, but nothing was able to penetrate the cloying, spoiled-meat stink of his prey.

Motion-activated lights came on as he moved around, creating a fluorescent haze. The basins were stainless steel and rudimentary, but the water ran cold and clean, and, leaning down, he cupped his hands and splashed his face once. Twice. Again.

So dumb to waste time on this tidy-up, he thought. Those prostitutes would remember nothing. And it wasn't as if washing would improve the comeliness of his features.

On the other hand, best not to scare them into flight: Dragging them back was such a bore.

As he lifted his head, he saw himself in the crude metal sheets that were supposed to be mirrors. Even though the reflection was dull, he noted his ugliness and thought of Throe just now. In spite of the fact that the soldier had been out fighting all night, his handsome visage had appeared fresh as a daisy, his well-bred looks overshadowing the reality that he had slayer blood on his clothes and had been scraped and bruised.

Xcor, however, could have taken rest for two weeks straight, eaten a large meal, and fed from a fucking Chosen, and he would still appear as repulsive.

He rinsed his face one more time. Then looked around for something to use as a wipe-off. All there appeared to be were machines bolted into the wall for drying one's hands with hot air.

His leather duster was filthy. The loose black shirt underneath was the same.

He left the facility with cold water dripping from his chin, reappearing up top on the roof. His bag was not secure enough here, and he was going to have to leave his scythe and his coat somewhere very safe.

As exhaustion dogged him, he thought . . . such a bloody fucking nuisance, all this.

SIXTEEN

Up high above the chaos of Caldwell, in the silent marble library of the Chosen, Tohr had a scream in his head that was so loud, it was a wonder that No'One didn't cover her ears from the din.

He threw his hand out. "Give me that."

Taking the volume from her, he forced his eyes to focus on the characters of the Old Language that had been so carefully constructed.

Wellesandra, mated of the Black Dagger Brother Tohrment, son of Hharm, blooded daughter of Relix, passed from the earth on this night, taking with her her unbirthed young, a son of some forty weeks.

Reading the short passage, he felt as if the whole event had happened a mere moment ago, his body submerging in that old, familiar river of grief.

He had to go over the symbols a couple of times before he could concentrate not only on what was there, but what wasn't.

No mention of the Fade.

Sifting through other paragraphs, he sought the notations of other passings. There were a number. . . .

Passed from the earth unto the Fade. Passed from the earth unto the Fade. Passed from the—he flipped the page—*earth unto the Fade.*

"Oh, God . . ."

As a screeching noise echoed around, he did not lift his eyes. But abruptly, No'One started pulling on his arm.

"Sit, please sit." She yanked hard. "Please."

He let himself go, and the stool that she had dragged over caught his weight.

"Is there any chance," he said in a guttural voice, "that they simply forgot to put it in?"

There was no need for No'One, or anybody else, to answer that question. The sequestered Chosen had had a sacred job, something they did not fuck up. And that kind of "oopsie" would be a big one.

Lassiter's voice knocked on his inside door: *That's why I've come—I'm here to help you, help her.*

"I have to go back to the mansion," he mumbled.

Next move was to get to his feet, but that didn't go well. Between a sudden weakness in his body and that fucking foot, he slammed into one of the stacks, the contour of his shoulder pushing a wave into the books whose spines were so carefully arranged. Annnnnnnd then it was a case of the floor tipping in the opposite direction, pitching him into free air.

Something small and soft got in the way of his falling. . . .

It was a body. A diminutive female body with hips and breasts that suddenly, shockingly imprinted on him even through the freak-out.

Instantly, the vision of No'One in that pool, her naked form glistening and wet, exploded like a land mine in his brain, the detonation so great that it blasted its way through everything that had been driving him.

It happened so fast: the contact, the memory . . . and the arousal.

Underneath the fly of his leathers, his cock punched out to its full length. Without apology.

"Let me help you back into the chair," he heard her say from a vast distance.

"Don't touch me." He pushed her off. Stumbled away. "Don't get anywhere near me. I'm . . . losing it. . . ."

Floundering his way down the stacks, he couldn't breathe, couldn't . . . stand himself. . . .

As soon as he was free from the library, he raced away from the Sanctuary, returning his faithless body to his bedroom at the mansion.

He was still erect when he got there.

Duh.

Staring down at his button fly, he tried to find another explanation. Maybe he'd thrown a clot? A cock clot . . . or maybe . . . shit . . .

There was no way he could be attracted to another female.

He was a bonded male, goddamn it.

"Lassiter," he looked around. "Lassiter!"

Where the fuck was that angel?

"Lassiter!" he bellowed.

When there was no reply, no burst-through-the-door, he was stuck alone . . . with his hard-on.

Rage curled his right hand into a fist.

With a vicious swing, he punched himself where it counted, nailing himself in the *cojones*—

"Fuck!"

It was like getting hit with a wrecking ball, and his skyscraper went down, the pain buckling him so fast he ate carpet.

As he retched and tried to push himself up on his knees, all the while wondering if he hadn't done some serious internal damage, a dry voice filtered in through the ow-ow-ows.

"Shit, that musta hurt." The angel's face entered his line of watery vision. "On the plus side, you could probably sing Alvin's part on a Christmas CD."

"What . . ." Hard to talk. But then it was hard to breathe. And every time he coughed, he wondered if his balls were coming up his throat. "Tell me . . . the In Between . . ."

"You want to wait until you're not hypoxic?"

Tohr snapped out a hand and gripped the angel's biceps. "Tell me, motherfucker."

It was a universal truth among males that anytime you saw a guy get it in the nuts, you experienced a shot of phantom pain in your own croquet set.

As Lassiter crouched beside the Brother's pretzel of a body, he was feeling a little nauseous himself, and he took a moment to cup what hung between his legs—just to reassure the boys downstairs that however much of an iconoclast he was, some things were sacred.

"Tell me!"

Impressive that the guy could still summon the energy to yell. And, yeah, there was no maybe-later-after-you-recover option with a son of a bitch who could punch himself like that.

No reason to pad shit, either. Natch.

"The In Between is not really the jurisdiction of the Scribe Virgin or the Omega. It's the Maker's territory—and before you ask, that would be the creator of all things. Your Scribe Virgin, the Omega, all of it. There's a couple ways of ending up there, but mostly it's because you won't let go or because someone won't let go of you."

When Tohr was silent, Lassiter recognized the signs of brain-fry and took pity on the poor son of a bitch.

Placing a hand on the Brother's shoulder, he said gently, "Breathe with me. Come on, we'll do it together. Let's just breathe shit out for a minute. . . ."

They stayed there for the longest time, Tohr bowed around the front of his hips, Lassiter feeling like a plank.

In his long life, he had seen suffering in all its forms. Disease. Dismemberment. Disenchantment on epic scales.

Staring at his outstretched hand, he realized he had become detached from it all. Hardened by overexposure and personal experience. Separated from any compassion.

Man, he was the wrong angel for the job.

Helluva situation the pair of them were in.

Tohr's eyes lifted, and they were so dilated, if Lassiter hadn't known they were blue, he would have said they were black.

"What can I do . . . ?" the Brother moaned.

Oh, man, he couldn't stand it.

Abruptly, he got up and went to the window. Outside, the landscape was discreetly lit, the gardens far from resplendent in their nascent state. Indeed, spring was a cold, cruel incubator, summer's wallowing warmth months off.

A lifetime away.

"Help me help her," Tohr said hoarsely. "That's what you told me."

In the silence that followed, he had nothing. No voice. No thoughts, even. And this was in spite of the fact that unless he pulled something out of his ass, he was headed back to a hell custom-made for him, with no hope of escape. And Wellsie and that young were stuck in theirs. And Tohr was stuck in his.

He'd been so arrogant.

It had never dawned on him this wasn't going to work. When he'd been approached, he'd been flippant, confident, and ready for the aftermath—which had been all about freedom for himself.

A struggle had never occurred to him. The concept of failure had not been anywhere near his radar screen.

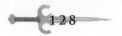

And he'd never expected to give two shits about what happened to Wellsie and Tohr.

"You said you were here to help me, help her." When there was no reply, Tohr's voice lowered. "Lassiter, I'm on my knees here."

"That's because your balls are in your diaphragm."

"You told me—"

"You don't believe me, remember."

"I saw. In the books on the Far Side. She is not in the Fade."

Lassiter stared out at the gardens and marveled at how close to life they were—in spite of how shriveled and decrepit they appeared, they were about to burst forth and sing for spring.

"She is not in the Fade!"

Something grabbed him, spinning him around and slamming him ass-first into the wall so hard, if he'd had his wings on, they would have been snapped off.

"She is not there!"

Tohr's face was twisted into a facsimile of its features, and as a hand clamped on his throat, Lassiter had a moment of clarity. The Brother could kill him, right here, right now.

Maybe that was how he ended up in the In Between again. Couple of head shots, then maybe a snapped neck, and poof! You failed. Hello, infinite nothingness.

Funny, he'd never even considered going back. Probably should have.

"You'd better open your fucking mouth, angel," Tohr growled.

Lassiter traced that face again, measured the power in that body, took the temperature of the rage. "You love her too much."

"She is my *shellan*—"

"Was. Goddamn you, *was*."

There was a heartbeat of silence. Then a crack, and a light show, and a lot of pain. As well as a little wobble of the knees—not that he'd have admitted that.

The bastard had coldcocked him.

Lassiter shoved the guy off him, spit blood out on the carpet, and thought about hitting back. Fuck the fighting, though. If the Maker was going to reclaim him, then the Be All and End All was going to have to come get him; Tohr was not going to be airmailing him in.

Time to get the hell out of this room.

As he headed for the door, the muttered cursing from behind him was easily ignored. Especially given that he was wondering whether one of his eyes was hanging by its optic nerve.

"Lassiter. Fuck, Lassiter—I'm sorry."

The angel wheeled around. "You want to know what the problem is?" He pointed right into the guy's puss. "*You* are the problem. I'm sorry you lost your female. Sorry you're still suicidal. Sorry that you have nothing to get out of bed for—or get into bed for. I'm sorry that you've got a boil on your ass and a toothache and goddamn fucking swimmer's ear. *You* are alive. *She* is not. And your hanging on to the past is putting you both in an In Between."

Catching his flow, he marched up to the cocksucker. "You want the fine print? Well, here it goddamn is. She is fading out—not heading for the Fade. And you are the reason it's happening. This"—he motioned around the male's stringy body and his bandaged foot and hand—"is why she's there. And the longer you hold on to her, and your old life, and every-thing you lost, the less of a chance she has of getting free. You are in charge here, not her, not me—so how about you punch yourself again next time, asshole."

Tohr dragged a shaking hand down his face, like he was trying to sand off his features. And then he clasped the front of his muscle shirt—right over his heart. "I can't just stop . . . because her body did."

"But you're acting like it happened yesterday, and I've got no sense this is going to change." Lassiter went over to the bed where the mating gown was laid out. Fisting the satin, he dragged the thing off by the thick skirt and shook it. "This is not her. Your anger is not her. Your dreams, your fucking pain . . . none of it is her. She is *gone*."

"I know that," Tohr shot back. "Do you think I don't know that?"

Lassiter shoved the gown forward, the satin falling like a rain of blood. "Then say it!"

Silence.

"Say it, Tohr. Let me hear it."

"She is . . ."

"*Say it.*"

"She is . . ."

When nothing came back at him, he shook his head and tossed the gown on the bed. Muttering under his breath, he went for the door again. "This is going nowhere. Unfortunately, the same is true for her."

SEVENTEEN

As dawn grew near, Xhex wrapped up her first night back in her old boots. The pace of the hours had been good, the Ping-Pong nature of dealing with a fuckload of people in an enclosed space with alcohol in the mix making the time pass fast enough. It was also good to be Alex Hess, head of security, once again—her own female, even if the name she used among the humans was fake.

And it was frickin' fantastic not having the Brotherhood breathing down her back.

What was not so hot was the fact that everything felt flat, like life had been bulldozed in preparation for the paving trucks to come.

She'd never heard of females doing the bonding thing. But as usual, that didn't mean she wasn't an outlier. And bottom line, without John by her side, everything seemed to be just a big, resounding *meh*.

A quick check of her watch told her there was one hour left of true darkness. Man, she wished she'd come in on her bike so she could can the headlight and roll through the shadows at ridiculous speeds. The Ducati was locked up tight in her garage, however.

She wondered if there was a rule against *shellans* riding.

Probably not . . . As long as she was sidesaddle, dressed in armor plating, and had a helmet made of reinforced, skid-resistant Kevlar, they'd probably let her go a few circles around the fountain in front of the house.

Vroom-vroom. Fucking wheeeeeeee.

Leaving her office, she locked the thing up with her mind so she didn't have to worry about keys—

"Hey, Trez," she said as her boss emerged from the ladies' locker room. "I was just coming to look for you."

The Shadow was tucking his crisp white shirt into his black slacks, and looking a little more relaxed than usual. A second later, one of the working girls came out from behind the door with a glow on her like she'd been hand-polished.

Which was probably not far from the truth.

At least her clueless expression told Xhex that Trez was keeping things on the DL. But still . . . you shouldn't feed where you worked. Complications could arise.

"I'll see you tomorrow night," the woman said with a loopy smile. "I'm late. Meeting friends."

After the girl went out the back, Xhex looked at Trez. "You should use other sources."

"It's convenient and I'm careful."

"Not safe. Besides, you could scramble her mind."

"I never use the same one twice." Trez put an arm around her. "But enough about me. You off?"

"Yeah."

Together, they ambled down to the door the woman had used. God . . . it was old times all over again, as if nothing had happened since the last time they'd closed up together. And yet Lash had happened. John had happened. The mating had—

"I'm not going to insult you by offering to escort you home," Trez murmured.

"So you like your legs right where they are, huh."

"Yup. They fill out my pants just fine." He did open the door for her, the cold air rushing in like it was trying to get away from itself. "What do you want me to tell him if he hits me up."

"That I'm fine."

"Good thing lying isn't a problem for me." When she went to argue, the Shadow just rolled his eyes. "Don't waste your breath or my

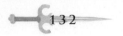

time. Go home and get some sleep. Maybe things will be better tomorrow."

By manner of reply, she gave him a quick hug, and stepped into the darkness.

Instead of dematerializing north, she wandered along Trade Street. Everyone was in closing mode: the clubs were spitting out their last few patrons—who looked about as attractive as masticated gum; the tat shop was clicking off its neon sign; the Tex-Mex restaurant had already battened down its hatches.

Shit grew seedier as she kept going, everything getting gloomier and grungier until she arrived at the blocks-long stretch of abandoned buildings. With the downturn in the economy, businesses were drying up like roadkill, and lessees were fewer and farther between—

Xhex stopped. Sniffed the air. Looked to the left.

The unmistakable scent of male vampire wafted over from a deserted walk-up.

BBFO, or Before Brotherhood Freak-out, she would have pursued it— gone in, checked to see if any of them needed help, found out what the Brothers were doing.

Now she just kept going, walking onward with her head held high. They didn't want her help—no, that probably wasn't accurate. They'd seemed fine with her until John had had issues. It was more like they no longer felt comfortable with her—

Up ahead about two blocks, a massive figure stepped out into her path.

She halted. Took a deep breath. Felt a prickling in her eyes.

On the breeze drifting down to her, John's unmistakable bonding scent was a dark spice that wiped out the stink of the city and the wretched sting of her unhappiness.

She started walking toward him. Fast. Faster . . .

Now she was running.

He met her halfway, falling into a jog as soon as he saw her pick up the pace, and they slammed into each other.

Hard to know whose mouth found whose, or whose arms were cinched tighter, or who was the desperate one.

But then, in this they were equals.

Breaking the kiss, she groaned, "My cabin."

The second after he nodded, she was out of there and so was he . . . and they re-formed outside her place.

No waiting to go inside.

He fucked her standing up, against her door, in the cold.

It was all so fast and frantic, her ripping her leathers down until she got one leg free, him breaking the buttons on his fly. Then she was spread wide and locked on his hips and he was buried to the base in her core.

He pounded into her so hard that her head banged on the door like she was trying to break into her own house. And then he bit her on the side of the neck—but not to feed, to hold her in place. He felt so much bigger inside of her, stretching her to the point where he strained her capacity. She needed that. At this moment, on this night, she needed him raw and un-chained and a little painful.

Hell, yeah, she did—and that was exactly what she got.

When he came, his hips locked against hers, his erection kicking up a storm deep within her, spurring her own orgasm.

And then they were in the cabin. On the floor. Her legs cranked apart, his mouth on her sex.

With his hands clamped on her thighs, and his still-erect cock sticking out of his open fly, he went down on her with a furious tongue, lashing at her, penetrating her, taking what he'd just had.

The pleasure was unbearable, a kind of agony that had her throwing back her head and contorting on the floor, her palms squeaking on the linoleum as she struggled unsuccessfully to keep herself from riding backward—

The orgasm plowed through her so violently that as she shouted his name, bright lights flickered across her vision. And he didn't relent in the slightest. As the onslaught continued, she was pretty sure that at some point he bit her on the inner leg, at that juncture where the thick vein went down to feed the lower half of her. But there was too much sucking, too much releasing, too much . . . everything to know or care.

When John finally stopped and lifted his head, they were in the far corner, nearly into the living room. Oh, what a picture. Her mate's face was flushed, his mouth glossy and puffy, his fangs so long he couldn't close his jaw—and she was likewise wrung out, her breathing ragged, her sex throbbing with its own heartbeat.

He was still erect.

Too bad she barely had the energy to blink—because he deserved one heck of a payback. . . .

Except he seemed to know exactly what she was thinking. Rising up between her open legs, he gripped himself and began to stroke.

With a moan, she arched and rolled her hips. "Come all over me," she said through gritted teeth.

John worked himself, his palm locked around his thick shaft, a clicking sound rising up as he pumped. His massive thighs split wide as he shoved his knees farther apart for balance, the muscles in his forearm standing out in harsh relief as he went harder and faster. And then he was barking something in a soundless way, his body going rigid as hot jets splashed all over her sex.

Just the thought of herself wet and messy was almost enough to make her come again. But the sight of him making it happen? Sent her right over the edge once more . . .

"She's going to need an extra two hundred if she does him."

Xcor stood off to the side during negotiations with the whores, making certain that he was in the shadows—especially now that Throe had reached the tricky part of his being accommodated. No reason for the reminder of what he looked like to drive the price even higher.

Only two of the three girls had shown up at this abandoned house down on Trade Street, but apparently number three was on her way—although courtesy of her being late, she had been handed the short straw: him.

Her friends were taking care of her, though—unless, of course, they intended to take a cut of the increase. After all, good whores, like good soldiers, tended to look out for themselves.

Abruptly, Zypher stepped into the woman who was doing the talking, clearly prepared to use his physical assets to conserve financial ones. As the vampire trailed a fingertip along the girl's collarbone, she appeared to fall into a trance.

It was not mind games on Zypher's part. Females of both races couldn't help themselves around him.

The vampire dipped toward her ear and spoke softly. Then he licked up her throat. Behind him, Throe was as he always was, silent, watchful, patient. Waiting his turn.

Ever the gentlemale.

"Okay," the woman said breathlessly. "Just fifty more—"

At that moment, the door opened wide.

Xcor and his soldiers put hands into their coats, finding their weapons, prepared to kill. But it was just the prostitute who was late.

"Hey, girl, heeeeeeeeeey," she said to her friends.

Standing in the doorway with a floppy jacket pulled over her whore clothes, and the bad sense of balance of a drunk, she was obviously on something, her face suffused with the blissed-out expression of the newly drugged.

Good. She'd be easier to deal with.

Zypher clapped his hands. "Shall we get down to business."

A giggle came from the one next to him. "I love your accent."

"Then you can have me."

"Wait, me, too!" A giggle from someone else. "I love it, too!"

"You're going to take care of my fellow soldier—my friend. Who is going to pay you all now."

Throe stepped forward with the cash, and as he doled it out into waiting palms, the whores seemed more focused on the two males as opposed to the money.

A professional role reversal that Xcor was willing to bet didn't happen very often.

And then the pairing off occurred, with Throe and Zypher drawing their prey into separate corners, whilst he was left with the whore who was fuzzy.

"So are we going to do this?" she said with a practiced smile. Indeed, the fact that her eyes were softened by drugs made the expression almost real.

"Come to me."

He held his hand out of the darkness.

"Oh, I like it." She sidled over, exaggerating the shift of her hips. "You sound like . . . I don't know what."

When she put her palm against his, he pulled her to him—except then she jerked back.

"Oh—er . . . um . . . okay."

Turning her face to the side, she rubbed her nose, and then pinched it as if she couldn't stand the smell of him. Logical. It took more than a rinse with water to get *lesser* blood off someone. Naturally, Throe and Zypher had taken a moment to flash home and get cleaned up. He, however, had stayed to fight.

Dandies. Both of them. On the other hand, their women were not already looking for an escape.

"It's okay, though," she said with resignation. "But *no* kissing."

"I was unaware I had suggested such a thing."

"Just so we're clear."

As moans began to rise up, Xcor stared down at the human. Her hair was loose around her shoulders, looking stringy and pulled-through. Her makeup was heavy and smudged at the lip line and in the corner of one eye. Her perfume was sweat and—

Xcor frowned, as he caught an unwelcomed scent.

"Now, listen," she said, "don't give me that look. It's my policy and you can—"

He let her ramble on as he reached out and lifted one side of the blond tangle, exposing her throat. . . . Nothing but smooth skin. And on the other side . . .

Ah, yes. There they were. Two puncture marks right on her jugular.

She had already been used tonight by one of his kind. And that explained the fogginess and the musk his nose was picking up on.

Xcor laid the hair back where it had been. Then he stepped away.

"I can't believe you're being so pissy," she mouthed off. "Just because I won't kiss you—I'm not giving the money back, you know. A deal's a deal."

Someone was having an orgasm, the sounds of pleasure so rich and lush that the symphony transformed, for however briefly, the abandoned walk-up into a proper boudoir.

"But of course you may keep the cash," he murmured.

"You know what, fuck you, you can have it back." She threw the wad at him. "You smell like a sewer and you're ugly as sin."

Whilst the bills bounced off his chest, he inclined his head briefly. "As you wish."

"Fuck you."

The alacrity with which she changed from bliss to bitch suggested this kind of mood swing was not uncommon to her. One more reason to keep things professional between oneself and the female sex—

As he bent down to pick up the money, she drew back her foot and tried to kick him in the head.

Not smart. With all his warrior training and years of combat experience, his body defended itself without his conscious mind giving any commands: The whore was caught by the ankle, yanked off balance, and slammed into the floor. And before he was aware of even moving, he had her spun onto her belly and had taken that fragile neck of hers in the thick crook of his arm.

Whereupon he was prepared to break it.

No more aggression from her. Now she whimpered and begged.

He immediately relented, jumping free of her, then helping her shuffle back against the wall. She was hyperventilating, her chest pumping up and down so hard she was liable to rupture her false breasts against the cups of her brassiere.

As he loomed over her, he thought of how the Bloodletter would have handled the situation. That male wouldn't have let her get past the no-kissing proposition—he would have taken what he wanted on his terms, and to hell with how much it might have hurt her. Or whether it killed her.

"Look at me," Xcor commanded.

When those wide, shell-shocked eyes lifted to his, he erased her memory of being here, putting her in a trance. Instantly her respiration calmed, her body resuming its loose, relaxed composure, her frantic, jerky hands stilling.

Gathering up the money, he put it in her lap. She deserved it for whatever bruises she was going to have in the morning.

Then with a groan, Xcor sank down and arranged himself against the wall next to her, stretching his legs out and crossing them at the ankles. He had to go pick up his satchel of goodies and his scythe at the skyscraper, but at the moment, he was too exhausted to move.

No feeding for him tonight, however. Even with the hypnosis.

If he took the vein of the woman next to him, he was liable to kill her: He was viciously hungry, and he didn't know how heavily she had been tapped. For all he knew, her loopiness was low blood pressure.

Across the way, he watched his soldiers fucking, and he had to admit the rhythms of the bodies were erotic. Under different circumstances, he imagined Zypher would have merged the two pairings into one large tangle of arms and legs, breasts and hands, cocks and slick slits. Not here, though. The room was filthy, not secure and cold.

Easing his head back against the wall, Xcor closed his eyes and kept listening.

If he fell asleep, and his soldiers questioned whether he had fed, he would just use the other vampire's aftermath to explain away their concern.

And there would be time to sink his teeth into another source later.

In truth, he hated feeding. Unlike the Bloodletter, he got no thrill from forcing himself upon women and females—and God knew, none of them had ever come willingly unto him.

He supposed he owed his life to prostitutes.

As someone else started to orgasm again, this time one of his soldiers—

Throe, if he had to guess—he imagined himself with a different face, a handsome face, a comely face that summoned females rather than sent them screaming.

Mayhap he should be removing his own spine.

But that was the beauty of inner thoughts. No one had to know your weaknesses.

And once you'd finished dwelling on them, you could toss them into the mental trash bin they belonged in.

EIGHTEEN

Quinn had never been good at waiting. And that was when shit was going okay. Considering he'd just lied twice about where John Matthew was?

Not a happy camper.

As he loitered at the hidden door by the grand staircase—so he could duck into the tunnel if anyone came by—he had the best view of the foyer you could get. Which meant when the vestibule's door opened, he got an eyeball full of his absolutely *favorite* couple: Blay and Saxton.

He should have known his luck wouldn't have had it otherwise.

Blay held the way open, like the gentlemale he was, and as Saxton stepped through, the bastard tossed a lingering, half-lidded stare over his shoulder.

Man, that kind of "look" was worse than the pair of them sucking face in public.

No doubt they'd been out for a nice meal and then gone back to Saxton's place for a little play of the sort that was hard to have here in the mansion. Total privacy was not something you could find on a bet around the compound—

As Blay removed his Burberry coat, his silk button-down pulled wide, and showed off a bite mark on his neck. And on his collarbone.

God only knew where else he had them. . . .

Abruptly, Saxton said something that made Blay blush, and the slightly shy, reserved laugh that followed made Qhuinn want to throw the fuck up.

Great, so the slut was a comedian, and Blay liked his jokes.

Fantastic.

Yup.

On that note, Saxton went up the stairs. Blay, on the other hand, came around the—

Shit. Qhuinn wheeled away and lunged for the door, hands scrambling to get the latch free.

"Hi."

Qhuinn's hands stilled. His body stilled. His heart . . . stilled.

That voice. That soft, deep voice he'd heard nearly all his life.

Straightening his spine, he fucked off the escape idea, turned around, and faced his former best friend like the male he was. "Hi. Have a good night?"

Shit, he wanted to take that one back. As if the guy hadn't?

"Yes, and you?"

"Yeah. Good. John and I went out. He's back now, and we're going to go hit the weight room. He's getting changed."

Tough to know whether the lying or the burn in his chest was making him so chatty.

"No Last Meal for you?"

"Nah."

Cue crickets in the background. The *Jeopardy!* theme. A nuclear bomb—not that Qhuinn would have noticed even a mushroom cloud at this point.

God, Blay's eyes were so damned blue. And . . . holy crap, the two of them were actually alone. When was the last time that had happened?

Oh, yeah. Right after Blay had hooked up with his cousin for the first time.

"So you've taken out your piercings," Blay said.

"Not all of them."

"Why? I mean . . . they were always, like, *you*, you know?"

"Guess I don't want to be defined that way anymore."

As Blay's brows popped, Qhuinn's kind of wanted to do the same. He'd expected something else to come out of his piehole. Something like, "Meh." Or, "Whatever." Or, "I still got 'em where it counts, don't you worry."

After which he could honk his package, and snort like he had balls the size of his head.

No wonder Saxton seemed attractive.

"So, yeah . . ." he said. Then cleared his throat. "So how are things with . . . you guys?"

Cue second trip to the heavens for those red eyebrows. "I'm good—we're . . . ah, good."

"Good. Ah . . ."

After a moment, Blay glanced over his shoulder, toward the door into the butler's pantry. Clearly, it was the beginning of a back-away.

Hey, as you leave, Qhuinn wanted to say, *will you do me a favor? I think my left ventricle is on the floor, so don't step on it as you pull out? Thanks. Great.*

"Are you feeling okay?" Blay murmured.

"Yeah. I'm going to go work out with John." He'd already said that. Fuck. This was a train wreck. "So there you go. Where you headed?"

"I'm going to go . . . get some food for Sax and myself."

"No Last Meal for you guys, either. Guess we have that in common." Someone bust out the pom-poms and cheer for the team. Yay. "So, yeah, enjoy yourself. Selves, I mean—"

Across the foyer, the vestibule door swung wide and John Matthew came in. "Son of a bitch," Qhuinn muttered. "The bastard is finally back."

"I thought you said he was—"

"I was covering. For us both."

"You weren't together? Wait, you get caught without being with him—"

"It was *not* my choice. Trust me."

As Qhuinn beelined for Mr. Independent, Blay was right with him, and John took one look at the pair of them and his *ahh*-satisfied expression got ghost sure as if someone had booted him in the ass with a nine iron.

"We need to talk," Qhuinn hissed.

John glanced around like he was looking for a bunker to jump into. Yeah, well, tough balls for him; the foyer was essentially empty of furniture, and the dumb bitch couldn't jump far enough to reach the dining room.

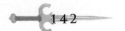

Qhuinn, I was going to call—

Qhuinn grabbed the guy by the back of the neck and shoved him face-first into the land of pool and popcorn. Just past the threshold, John pushed free and went gunning for the bar. Picking up a bottle of Jack, he ripped the thing open.

"Do you think this is a fucking joke?" Qhuinn jabbed at the tattooed tear that was under his eye. "I'm supposed to be with you every second of the night and day, asshole. I've been lying for you for the last forty minutes—"

"It's true. He has."

As Blay spoke up from behind, it was a surprise. And kind of nice.

I went to see Xhex, okay. Right now, she's my priority.

Qhuinn threw up his hands. "Great. So when V is stabbing my pink slip into my chest, you can still feel good about yourself. Thanks."

"John, you can't light-head stuff like this." Blay went around and grabbed a glass, like he was afraid their buddy was going to suck the bottle down whole. "Give me that."

He took the booze, poured a healthy dose, and . . .

Drank it himself.

"What," he muttered as he got stared at. "Here, take it back if you want."

John took a swig and then stared into space. After a moment, he shoved the Jack in Qhuinn's direction.

Rolling his eyes, Qhuinn muttered, "At least this is the kind of apology I'll accept."

As he took the bottle, it dawned on him that it had been ages since the three of them had been together. Back before their transitions, they'd spent every night after training in Blay's old room at the guy's parents' house, pissing away the hours playing video games and drinking beer and talking about the future.

And now that they were finally where they'd wanted to be? Everyone was going in a different direction.

Then again, John was right. The guy was properly mated now, so of course his focus was somewhere else. And Blay was having a rockin' good time with Saxton the Slut.

Qhuinn was the only one pining for the GODs.

"Fucking hell," he muttered to John. "Let's just forget it—"

"No," Blay cut in. "This is *not* okay. You cut the shit, John—you let him come with you. I don't care if you're going to be with Xhex or not. You owe this to him."

Qhuinn stopped breathing, focusing everything he had on the male who had been his best friend and his never-been lover . . . and the ever-after that was never going to happen.

Even after all the things that had gone on between them, and all the fuckups on his end, which were legendary, Blay still had his back.

"I love you," Qhuinn blurted into the silence.

John lifted up his hands and signed, *I love you, too. And I'm really fucking sorry. This thing with Xhex and I has . . .*

Blah, blah, blah. Or, *Blah, blah, blah,* as the case was with the ASL.

Qhuinn wasn't hearing a thing. As John went on and on, explaining his sitch, Qhuinn was tempted to interrupt and cop to not just what he'd said, but who he'd said it to. Except all he could think of was Blay coming in with Sax, and that f-in' blush.

It took everything he had in him to look at John and squeeze out, "We can work it out, all right? Just let me follow you—I won't look, I promise."

John was signing something. Qhuinn was nodding. Then Blay started pulling away, taking a step back and then another and then a third.

More conversation. Blay talking.

And then the male turned and strode out. To get food. To go up to Saxton.

A low whistle made him shake himself and focus on John.

"Yeah. Sure."

John frowned. *You want to have a parking ticket stapled to your fore-head?*

"What?"

Sorry, I had a feeling you weren't tracking. Guess I was right.

Qhuinn shrugged. "Look at it this way, I don't feel like coldcocking you anymore."

Oh, good. Bonus. But Blay is right. I won't do this again.

"Thanks, man."

Drink?

"Yeah. Good idea. Great one." He headed around the bar. "Matter of fact, I'll get my own bottle."

NINETEEN

"She's dead."

At the sound of the male voice, Lassiter looked over his shoulder. Across his bedroom, Tohr was standing in the doorway, holding himself up by the jambs.

Lassiter put down the fleece he'd been packing. The suitcase routine wasn't because he could take any of his shit with him, but rather, because it seemed only fair to get his stuff in order for the summoning that was coming: After he got sucked back into the In Between, the staff was going to have to ditch the clothes he'd worn and the few things he'd collected.

The Brother entered and shut them in together.

"She's dead." He limped over and sat on the chaise lounge. "There, I said it."

Lassiter lowered his ass down on the bed and stared at the guy. "And you think that's enough."

"What the fuck do you want from me?"

He had to laugh. "Please. If I were running this show, you'd have had her back down here months ago and I'd be long fucking gone."

Tohr laughed a little in surprise.

"Aw, come on, my man," Lassiter muttered. "I don't want to screw you. You're too flat chested, for one thing—I'm a boob man. And for another, you're a good guy. You deserve better than this."

Now Tohr looked downright shocked.

"Oh, for fuck's sake." Lassiter got up and went back to the open drawers of the dresser. Pulling out a pair of leathers, he messed them up, and then folded them again.

Futzing around with his hands was supposed to help his brain focus. Didn't work all that well, though. Maybe he should just slam his head into the wall.

"Going somewhere?" the Brother asked after a while.

"Yeah."

"Giving up on me?"

"I told you. I don't make the rules here. I'm going to get pulled out, and it's going to be sooner rather than later."

"Pulled out to where?"

"Where I was." He shuddered, even though it was a pussy move. But an eternity of isolation was hell for a guy like him. "It's not a trip I'm looking forward to making."

"Would you be going where . . . Wellsie is?"

"I told you, everyone's In Between is different."

Tohr put his head in his hands. "I can't just turn myself off. She was my life. How the hell do I—"

"You can start by not trying to castrate yourself with a fist when you get a hard-on for another female."

When the Brother didn't say anything, Lassiter had a feeling the guy had teared up. And yeah, wow, didn't that make things awkward. God. Damn.

Lassiter shook his head. "I'm the wrong angel for this job, for real."

"I never cheated on her." Tohr inhaled sharply through his nose, the sniff entirely manly, as sniffles went. "Other males . . . even bonded ones, I mean, they look at females from time to time. Maybe they screw around a little on the side. Not me. She wasn't perfect, but she was more than enough to keep me satisfied. Hell, when Wrath needed someone to keep an eye on Beth back before they were mated? He sent me. He knew I wouldn't come on to her, not just out of respect for him, but because I wasn't going to be interested in the slightest. I have literally never had an instant when I thought of anyone else."

"You did tonight."

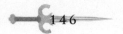

"Don't remind me."

Well, at least he copped to it. "Which is why I'm about to take my one-way trip to Never-coming-back Land. And your *shellan* is staying where she is."

Tohr rubbed the center of his chest like it hurt. "Are you sure I didn't die and go to this In Between already? Because this sure as shit feels like what you've described. Suffering but not *Dhund*."

"I don't know. Maybe some people aren't aware they're in it—but my directive was clear as a bell, and it was all about you letting go so she could move on."

Tohr dropped his hands like he was so done with the world. "I never thought there was going to be something worse than her dying. I couldn't fathom any course of events that would hurt more." He cursed. "I should have known that fate is sadistic as well as endlessly inventive. Imagine— my fucking some female gets the one I love into the Fade. Fabulous equation. Just frickin' fantastic."

That wasn't the half of it, Lassiter thought. But why bring it up now.

"I have to know something," the Brother said. "As an angel, do you believe that certain people are cursed from the start? That some lives are just doomed right out of the box?"

"I think . . ." Shit, he didn't go this deep. This was *not* him. "I—ah, I think that life runs on a set of odds that are spread out over the heads of every living, breathing bastard on the planet. Chance is unfair by definition, and random."

"So what about this Creator of yours? Doesn't He play a role?"

"Ours," he muttered. "And I don't know. I don't put much stock in anything."

"An angel who's an atheist?"

Lassiter laughed a little. "Maybe that's why I keep getting into trouble."

"Nah. That part's because you can be a real asshole."

They both chuckled. Then sat in silence.

"So what's it going to take?" Tohr asked. "Honestly, what the hell is destiny going to want from me now?"

"The same as any endeavor. Blood, sweat, and tears."

"That's it," Tohr said dryly. "And here I was thinking it could just be an arm or a leg."

When Lassiter didn't reply, the Brother shook his head. "Listen, you gotta stay. You *have* to help me."

"It's not working."

"I'll try harder. Please."

After an eternity, Lassiter felt his head nod. "Okay. Fine. I will."

Tohr exhaled long and slow, like he was relieved. Showed what he knew; they were all still in trouble.

"You know," the Brother said, "I didn't like you when I first met you. I've thought you were a jackass."

"The feeling was mutual. Although not the jackass part—and it wasn't personal. I don't like anyone, and as I said, I don't really believe in anything."

"Even though you're staying to help me?"

"I don't know . . . I guess I just want what your *shellan* does." He shrugged. "End of the day, the quick and the dead are the same. Everyone's just looking for home. Plus . . . I don't know, you're not so bad."

Tohr went back to his own room sometime later. When he got to his door, he found his crutch propped against the panels.

No'One had returned it to him. After he'd left it behind on the Other Side.

Picking the thing up, he went into his room . . . and half expected to find her naked on his bed, ready for some sex. Which was completely ridiculous—on too many levels to count.

Parking himself on the chaise lounge, he stared at the gown that Lassiter had handled so roughly. The fine satin was bunched up in waves, the disorder creating a wonderful, shimmering display over on the bed.

"My beloved is dead," he said out loud.

As the sound of the words faded, something was suddenly, stupidly clear: Wellesandra, blooded daughter of Relix, was never filling out that bodice again. She was never going to put the skirting over her head and wriggle into the corset, or free the ends of her hair from the lace-ups in the back. She wasn't going to look for matching shoes, or get pissed off because she sneezed right after she put her mascara on, or worry about whether she was going to spill on the skirting.

She was . . . dead.

How ironic. He'd been mourning her this whole time, and yet somehow missing the point that was most obvious. She was not coming back. Ever.

Getting up, he went across and gently gathered up the dress. The skirting refused to obey, slipping out of his hands and jumping back down to the floor—doing what it wanted and taking control of the situation.

Just as his Wellsie had always done.

When he had a moderate handle on everything, he carried the gown over to the closet, opened the double doors, and hung the glorious weight on the brass rod.

Crap. He was going to see it every time he went in here.

Pulling it free, he shifted it over to the other side, so it was in the darkness behind the two suits that he never wore and the ties that had been bought for him not by his mate, but by Fritz.

And then he closed the closet up tight.

Back at the bed, he lay down and shut his eyes.

Moving on didn't have to involve sex, he told himself. It just didn't. Accepting the death, letting her go to save her, that he could do without the benefit of . . . any kind of naked-female thing. After all, what was he going to do? Head out into the alleys, find a whore, and fuck her? That was a bodily function like breathing. Hard to see how that was going to help.

Lying still, he tried to picture doves being released from cages, and waters bursting from dams, and wind blowing through trees, and . . .

Fucking hell. It was like the insides of his eyelids were playing the goddamn Discovery Channel.

But then just as he was drifting off, the images changed, shifting to water, lazy blue-green water that had no current. Calm. Warm water. With humid air all around. . . .

He wasn't sure exactly when he fell asleep, but the image turned into a dream that started with a pale arm, a lovely pale arm floating on the water, the lazy blue-green water that had no current. Calm. Warm—

It was his Wellsie in the pool. His beautiful Wellsie, her breasts peaked as she floated, her tight stomach and flaring hips and bare sex licked with wetness.

In the dream, he saw himself breaching the pool, walking down short steps, the water getting into his clothes—

Abruptly, he stopped and looked at his chest.

His daggers were strapped on. His guns under his arms. His ammo belt locked on his hips.

What the hell was he doing? This shit got wet and it was useless—

That wasn't Wellsie.

Holy shit, that was *not* his *shellan*. . . .

With a shout, Tohr jacked upright, ripping free of the dream. Slapping his hands on his thighs, he expected to find wet leather. But no, none of it had been real.

His arousal was back, however. And a thought he refused to give credence to surfaced and stank in the back of his mind.

As he stared down at his sex and cursed, the strong length of it made him think of the countless times he'd used it for pleasure and fun . . . and procreation.

Now he just wanted it to go limp and stay that way.

Settling back against the pillows, sorrow settled on him like a physical weight as he recognized the truth that the angel had spoken. He had not, in fact, let his Wellsie go on any level.

He . . . was the problem.

Summer

TWENTY

From the vantage point behind binoculars, the mansion on the far side of the Hudson River looked enormous, a massive stack-on-stack of floors that sat boldly upon a rocky bluff. On every of its levels, lights glowed through glass panels, as if the thing had no solid walls.

"Quite a palace," Zypher remarked in the thick, balmy breeze.

"Aye," came a reply over on the left.

Xcor dropped the binocs from his eyes. "Too much exposure to daylight. 'Tis a roasting waiting to happen."

"Mayhap he kitted out the basement," Zypher said. "With more of those marble tubs . . ."

Given the tone of his voice, the soldier was imagining females of different sorts in water with suds, and Xcor shot him a glare before resuming the watch.

Such a waste this was. Assail—son of one of the greatest Brothers there had ever been—could have been a fighter, a warrior, mayhap even a Brother, but his fallen Chosen mother had forced another path upon him.

Although one could argue if the bastard had had any cock at all, he would have forged his own destiny in pursuits other than those of marble

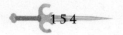

tubing. As it stood, however, he was simply another useless drain upon the species, a dandy with naught worthwhile to do with his nights.

Although that could all change this evening.

Under these clouded skies, against the backdrop of flashes of lightning, this male was significant, at least for a short time. Granted, the circumstances of his relevancy might cost him his life, but if the history books served their purposes, he could well be remembered for playing a small role in the great turning point of the race.

Not that he knew any of this, of course.

Then again, one didn't expect chum to be aware it was attracting sharks.

Scanning the rolling grounds once again, Xcor decided the lack of trees and shrubs was the result of the clearing process prior to construction. No doubt an aristocrat would want manicured gardens; the fact that it made the house more difficult to get up close to was not the kind of thing Assail would consider.

The good news was that although it was likely there was steel in the structure of the house—as part of support beams, floor pinnings, roof joists—at least one could get in and out through all that glass.

"Ah, yes, here is the proud homeowner now," Xcor growled at the figure of a male striding out into the grand living room.

Not even drapes to hide his presence. It was as if he were a hamster in a cage.

The male deserved to die for being this stupid, and indeed, on Xcor's back, his scythe began to hum a little dirge.

Xcor increased the binoculars' magnification. Assail was taking something out of his breast pocket—a cigar. And naturally, the lighter was a gold one. He probably thought fire, like packaged meat, came only from stores.

It was going to be a pleasure to kill him.

Along with the others who would soon show up here.

Indeed, the *glymera*'s Council had effectively stonewalled Xcor and his Band of Bastards. No invitation to a meeting. No greeting by its *leahdyre*, Rehvenge. Not even an official response to the letter that had been sent in the spring.

At first, this had frustrated him to the point of violence. But then a little birdie had begun to chirp in his ear, and another path had been revealed.

The best weapon in a war was often not a dagger, a gun, or even a cannon. It was something that was invisible and deadly—yet not poisonous gas. It was something that was utterly weightless and yet had gravity beyond measure.

Information, solid, verified information, from a source inside your enemy's camp, was atomic-bomb powerful.

His missive to the Council had in fact been received, and what was more, it was being taken seriously. The great Blind King, whilst saying nothing, had immediately commenced meeting with the heads of all the remaining bloodlines—in person, at their places of residence.

Bold move in a time of war—and it proved Xcor's challenge had a basis in reality: A king did not risk his life like that unless he was out of touch with his subjects and being forced to reconnect.

In retrospect, it was even better than a meeting with the Council. There were a limited number of its members left, and all of them had known abodes. Wrath had already had audiences with the majority, and, thanks to that little birdie, Xcor was well aware of who was left.

Shifting his focus around, he assessed the roof. The porches. The chimney on the near side.

According to Xcor's source, Assail had arrived back in the spring, assumed ownership of this sieve of a homestead, and . . . that was all the aristocrats knew. Well, other than the odd notables that the male had brought no one with him—no family, no staff, no *shellan*—and that he kept to himself. Both were unusual for a member of the *glymera*, but then mayhap he was waiting to see how things fared in this new environment afore bringing his blood to him and entertaining others of his ilk. . . .

There had been a younger brother, hadn't there? Also coddled by that fallen Chosen mother of theirs. Perhaps a half sister of some ill repute?

Behind him, Xcor heard his soldiers stretch, their leather creaking, their weapons shifting. Up above, storm clouds continued to release intermittent flashes of light, with the base drum of thunder remaining as yet in the distance.

He should have assumed from the very beginning that it would come down to this: If he wanted Wrath off the throne, he was going to have to do it himself. Relying on the *glymera* for anything more than unfounded delusions of grandeur had been a mistake.

At least he had his in on the Council. In the aftermath, when things got messy, he was going to need the support. Fortunately, there were more people who agreed with him than did not: Wrath was nothing but a fig-

urehead, and whereas in times of peace that was tolerable, in this era of war and strife it was insupportable.

The Old Ways could keep that male where he didn't belong for just so long. In the meantime, Xcor would wait for the proper moment, and strike decisively.

It was time for Wrath's reign to be relegated to a soon forgotten footnote.

"I hate waiting," Zypher muttered.

"'Tis the only virtue that matters," Xcor shot back.

In the foyer of the Brotherhood's mansion, everyone was gathering to go out for the night, the males milling around at the foot of the grand staircase, their weapons gleaming on their chests and at their hips, their brows drawn over cold eyes, their bodies mincing about like those of stallions whose hooves could not be stilled.

From the shadows outside the butler's pantry, No'One waited for Tohrment to come down and join them. He was usually among the first, but of late he had tarried longer and longer—

There he was, at the head of the second-floor landing, clad in black leather.

As he descended, he took the banister casually.

She was not fooled.

He had grown e'er weaker over the last few months, his body wasting away, until it was clear that only his will for vengeance animated him.

He was starved for blood. And yet he obviously refused to yield to that demand of the flesh.

So thus she nervously waited and watched at the beginning of every night and the end: Every sundown she hoped he would come down finally refreshed. Every near-to-dawn, she found herself praying he arrived back alive.

Dearest Virgin Scribe, he—

"You look like shit," one of his Brothers said.

Tohrment ignored the comment as he went over to stand next to the massive young male who had mated Xhexania. The pair were a team, from what she could tell, and she was grateful for it. The younger had to be a full-breed, in spite of his nomenclature, and she had heard many references to his prowess in the field. Further, that particular fighter was never alone: Behind him, as faithfully as a reflection, was a downright nasty-looking soldier, one with mismatched irises and a calculation to his stare that suggested he was as smart as he was strong.

She had to believe that both would intercede if Tohrment were in danger.

"Enjoying the view? I'm not."

She hissed and spun around, her robe's hem flaring out. Lassiter had come through the pantry without her knowing and was filling the open doorway, his blond-and-black hair and his gold piercings catching the light of the fixture above him.

His knowing eyes were always something to escape from, but at least at the moment, that white stare was not on her.

Crossing her arms over her chest and tucking her hands into the robe's sleeves, she resumed her own regard of Tohrment. "In truth, I do not know how he is still fighting."

"It's time to stop pussyfooting around with him."

She wasn't entirely sure what that meant, but took a guess. "There are Chosen here who make themselves available for feeding. Surely he could use one of them?"

"You'd fucking think."

Standing in concert, their focus wavered for but a moment as Wrath, the Blind King, appeared at the head of the stairs and walked down to the assembled. He was dressed for war, too, and his beloved dog was not with him—he was led now by his queen, the two in such synchronization that they moved with the same posture, gait, poise.

Tohrment had had that once, she thought.

"I wish there was some way of helping him," she murmured. "I would do anything to see him with aid as opposed to alone in his suffering."

"Do you mean that," came a dark response.

"Of course."

Lassiter put his face in her vision. "Do you *really* mean that."

She went to take a step back, but found herself blocked by the jamb. "Yes . . ."

The angel put his palm out for her to clasp. "Swear to it."

No'One frowned. "I do not understand—"

"You maintain you would do anything—I want you to swear to that." Now those white eyes burned. "We've stalled out since the spring, and we didn't have endless time back then. You say you want to save him, and I want you to commit to that—no matter what it takes."

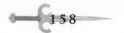

Abruptly, as if the memory had been purposely put in her mind—perhaps by the angel, more likely by her conscience—she remembered those moments after her birthing of Xhexania, when her physical pain and her mental anguish had been one and the same, the balance finally equalized as the agony in her heart for all she had lost was made manifest in her very core. . . .

Unable to bear her burdens, she had taken Tohrment's dagger from his chest holster and used it in a way that had made him scream.

His hoarse cry had been the last thing she'd heard.

Staring up at the angel, she wasn't stupid, and she was no longer naive. "You are suggesting I feed him."

"Yeah. I am. It's time to take this to the next level."

No'One had to steel herself before she looked back at Tohrment. But as she took in his frail body, she came to a resolve: He had buried her . . . so surely she could force herself to accept him at her vein in order to give him life.

Assuming he would agree to take what was offered.

Assuming she could make herself.

Indeed, even in the hypothetical, her body trembled at the thought, but her mind rejected the response of her flesh. This was not a male interested in anything from her. In fact, he would be the only male she could safely feed.

"A Chosen's blood would be purer," she heard herself say.

"And get us nowhere."

No'One shook her head, refusing to read anything into that statement. Then she took the angel's hand. "I shall serve his blood needs, if he comes to me."

Lassiter bowed ever so slightly. "I'll take care of that part. And I'm going to hold you to this."

"You shall not have to. My vow is my vow."

TWENTY-ONE

Standing in the foyer with his brothers, Tohr had a bad feeling about the way the night was going to go. Then again, he'd woken up from that dream of his Wellsie and the young, the one he had had from time to time, but only truly understood since Lassiter had provided the context. He knew now that the two were in the In Between, huddled under a gray blanket in the midst of a dark gray landscape that was cold and unyielding.

They were gradually moving off into the distance.

The first time he'd had the vision, he'd been able to pick out each individual hair on his *shellan*'s head . . . and the quarter-moon whites at the tips of her fingernails . . . and the way the blanket's rough fibers caught the strange, ambient light . . .

As well as the contours of the tiny bundle she cradled against her heart.

Now, though, she was yards off, the gray ground between them something that he tried to cross, but was unable to cover. And just as dire, she had lost all color, her face and hair now tinted with the gray of the prison she was trapped in.

Naturally, he'd been insane when he woke up.

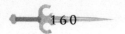

For fuck's sake, he'd done everything he could to move on in the last few months: Put the dress away. Gone down for First and Last Meals. Tried cocksucking yoga, transcendental bullcrap, and even gotten on the Internet to research grief stages and other psychobabble bullshit.

He'd attempted to not think of Wellsie consciously, and if his subconscious burped up a memory, he quashed it. When his heart ached, he pictured those f-in' white doves released from cages, and dams bursting, and shooting stars, and a bunch of other dumb-ass metaphoricals that belonged on motivational posters.

And still he'd had that dream in shades of gray.

And still Lassiter was here.

It wasn't working—

"Tohr? You with us," Wrath barked out.

"Yeah."

"You sure about that." After a moment, Wrath's wraparounds swung back to the rest of the group. "So we do this. V, John Matthew, Qhuinn, and Tohr on me. Everyone else in the field, ready to come in as backup."

There was a shout of agreement from the Brothers, and then they were all filing through the vestibule.

Tohr was the last through the door, and just as he got to the jambs, something made him stop and look over his shoulder.

No'One had stepped out from somewhere, and stood on the edge of the depiction of the apple tree in the floor, her hood and robe making her seem like a shadow that had suddenly gone 3-D.

Time slowed and then ground to a halt as he met her eyes, some strange pull keeping him where he stood.

In the intervening months since the spring, he had seen her at meals, had forced himself to speak with her, had pulled out chairs and helped to serve her as he did the other females in the house.

But he hadn't been alone with her, and he'd never touched her.

He felt like he was touching her now, for some reason.

"No'One?" he said.

Her arms unfolded from out of her sleeves and her hands lifted to the hood that covered her face. With grace, she revealed herself to him.

Her eyes were luminous and a little scared, her features as perfect as they had been back in the spring at the Sanctuary. And down lower, her throat was a perfect, pale column of flesh . . . which she touched lightly with fingertips that trembled.

From out of nowhere, hunger struck him hard, the need reverberating through his body, lengthening his fangs, parting his lips—

"Tohr? What the fuck?"

V's sharp voice broke the spell, and with a curse, he looked over his shoulder. "I'm coming—"

"Good. 'Cuz the king's waiting for you, true."

Tohr glanced back across the foyer, but No'One was gone. As if she had never been.

Rubbing his eyes, he wondered if he'd imagined the whole thing. Had he exhausted himself to the point of hallucination—

If he was seeing things, it wasn't exhaustion, some part of him pointed out.

"Don't say another word," he muttered as he brushed past his brother. "Not one goddamn thing."

As V started talking under his breath, it was obviously a litany of all of Tohr's faults, real and imagined, but whatever. At least that shit was keeping the fucker's mouth busy as they strode out toward Wrath, John Matthew, and Qhuinn.

"Ready," Tohr announced.

None of them needed to about-fucking-time him verbally. Their expressions were loud enough.

Seconds later, the five of them rematerialized on the rolling lawn of a house so big you could keep an army in it. Tragically, only the owner was in residence, because that was all that was left of the bloodline.

They had been to so many houses like this over the last few months. Too many. And the stories were all the same. Families decimated. Hope gone. Those left behind limping, not living.

The Brotherhood did not take for granted that these visits were welcome, even though, naturally, no one turned down the king. And they did not take chances: With their guns in their hands, the formation they assumed as they approached the door was with Tohr in front of Wrath, V to the rear, John at the king's dagger hand, and Qhuinn on the other side.

Two more meetings like this to go and they could take a breather—

What went down next proved that tits up could happen in an instant.

Abruptly, the world started spinning, the sprawling antique house twisting and turning sure as if it had eggbeaters for a foundation.

"Tohr!" someone barked out.

A hand grabbed him. Somebody else cursed.

"Has he been shot?"

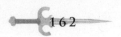

"Motherfucker—"

With a curse, Tohr shoved everyone off of him and regained his balance. "For chrissakes, I'm fine—"

V crawled so far up into his grill, the bastard was practically inside his nose. "Go home."

"Have you lost your mind—"

"You're a liability here. I'm calling in for backup."

Tohr was ready to argue, but Wrath just shook his head. "You need to feed, my brother. It's time."

"Layla's prepared for it," Qhuinn tacked on. "I've been keeping her going on this side."

Tohr looked at the four of them and he knew he'd lost. Christ, V already had his phone to his ear.

He also knew on some level they were right. But, God, he didn't want to face that ordeal again.

"Go home," Wrath commanded.

V put his cell away. "Rhage's ETA is—bingo."

As Hollywood appeared, Tohr cursed a couple of times. But there was no fighting them . . . or his reality.

With all the enthusiasm of someone facing a limb amputation, he returned to the mansion . . . to go find the Chosen Layla.

Fuck.

Through his binoculars, Xcor watched the venerable Assail stride into a massive kitchen and pause at a window that faced the direction of the bastards.

The male was still sinfully handsome with dark, viciously black hair and tan skin. Features were so aristocratic, he actually looked intelligent— although that was the thing with the *glymera*. Often people with fine countenances and fit bodies were mistakenly assumed by others to have the brains to match.

As the vampire fell into some kind of activity, Xcor frowned and wondered if he wasn't seeing things. Alas . . . no. It appeared that the male was indeed checking the mechanism of a gun as if he were used to doing so. And after he tucked the weapon under that precisely tailored black suit jacket, he picked up another and went through the same motions.

Strange.

Unless the king had warned him there could be trouble on the visit?

But no, that would be daft. If you were the seat of power for the race, you would not want to appear under siege.

Especially if in fact you were.

"He's departing," Xcor announced as Assail appeared to head for the garage. "He is not meeting Wrath. At least not tonight—or certainly not here. Let us cross the river. Now."

In a flash, they dematerialized, reassuming their forms in the stand of pines at the edge of the property.

He'd been wrong about the landscaping, Xcor realized. There were circular patches all over the lawn where the grass was filling in, and here, around the back of the house, there was a neatly stacked pile of not simply logs, but whole trees.

As well as an ax buried in a stump, and a bow saw . . . and corded wood newly cut for burning.

So the male had some *doggen*, at least. And apparently a respect for how important it was to not provide coverage for attackers. Unless the removals had been for the sake of the view?

Not much but forest on this side of the house.

Indeed, Assail did not appear to be the average aristocrat, Xcor thought grimly. The question was why.

The door to the garage bay closest to the house began to rise soundlessly, its ascent unleashing an ever-broadening pool of light. Inside, a powerful engine revved, and then some variety of low-slung, shiny black thing eased out in reverse.

As the vehicle stopped dead and the door began to descend, it was clear Assail was waiting patiently for the house to be secured before he left.

And then when he took off, it was not fast; and it was not with his headlights on.

"We follow him," Xcor commanded, collapsing the binoculars and securing them at his belt.

By dematerializing at intervals, they were able to track the male down the river toward Caldwell. The pursuit presented no challenge at all: In spite of being behind the wheel of what appeared to be a sports car of some speed, Assail seemed to feel no urgency . . . which, under other circumstances, Xcor would have chalked up to the male being a typical aristocrat with nothing better to do than look good in a leather seat.

But mayhap not so in this case. . . .

The car stopped at all the red lights, avoided the highway, and pen-

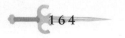

etrated the downtown area's alleys and streets with the same lack of alacrity.

Assail went left, then right . . . left again. Another left. Still more turns, until he was in the oldest part of the city thicket, where the brick office buildings were dilapidated, and missions and food kitchens serving the homeless were more common than for-profit businesses.

A more circuitous route there could not have been taken.

Xcor and his band of bastards kept on him by flashing from rooftop to rooftop, a practice that became tricky as the conditions degraded.

Except then the car stopped in a tight alley between a tenement house that had been condemned and the crumbled shell of a walk-up. As Assail got out, he puffed on his cigar, the sweet smoke drifting up on the currents of air to Xcor's nose.

For a moment, Xcor wondered if they had been lulled into a trap—and as he went for his gun, his soldiers did likewise. But then a large black sedan made a fat turn and rolled into the lane. As it halted afore him, Assail's preferred positioning became clear. Unlike the new arrivals, the vampire had parked at the head of a four-way, so that he could go in any direction.

Wise if one wanted to get away.

Humans emerged from the other car. Four of them.

"You here alone?" the one in front asked.

"Aye. As you asked."

The humans shared looks that suggested the male's compliance was crazy. "Do you have the money?"

"Aye."

"Where is it?"

"In my possession." The male's English was similar to Xcor's—thickly accented—but there the comparison ended. That was a high-class drawl down there, not a rough brogue. "Have you my goods."

"Yeah, we got it. Let's see the cash."

"After I inspect what you have brought me."

The man doing the talking took out a gun and pointed it at the vampire's chest. "That's not the way we're going to do this."

Assail released a puff of blue smoke and rolled the cigar between the tips of his fingers.

"Did you hear what I said, asshole?" the human barked as the three behind him disappeared hands into their suit jackets.

"Aye."

"This is going to be done the way *we* want, asshole."

"That would be 'Assail,' kind sir."

"Fuck you. Gimme the cash."

"Hm. Indeed. So you have demanded."

Abruptly the vampire's eyes locked on that human's, and after a moment, the autoloader in that meaty palm began to vibrate ever so slightly. Frowning, the guy focused on his hand, as if he were sending it a command.

"That is not how *I* do business, however," Assail murmured.

That gun muzzle gradually began to move, shifting away from the vampire and moving in a broad circle farther and farther afield. With growing panic, the man gripped his own wrist, as if he were fighting another, but naught of his effort derailed the changing trajectory.

Whilst the weapon was gradually turned on its own operator, the other men began to shout and shuffle about. The vampire said nothing, did nothing, remaining utterly calm and in control as he froze those three in place, locking their bodies but not their faces. Oh, those expressions of panic. Rather delightful.

When the gun was up to the man's temple, Assail smiled, flashing white teeth that gleamed in the darkness.

"Permit me to show you how I do business," he said in a low voice.

And then the human pulled the trigger and shot himself in the head.

As the body dropped to the pavement and the sound of the shot echoed around, the remaining men's eyes drew wide in horror even as their bodies remained immobilized.

"You," Assail said to the one closest to the sedan. "Bring me what I bought."

"I-I-I . . ." The man swallowed hard. "We don't got nothing."

With hauteur worthy of a king, Assail countered, "I'm sorry, what did you say."

"We dint bring nothing."

"And why not."

"Because we was going to . . ." The man had to take another stab at swallowing. "We was going to . . ."

"You were going to take my money and leave me for dead?" When there was no reply, Assail nodded. "I can see the value in that. And no doubt you'll understand what I must do now."

While the vampire puffed on his cigar, the man who had been speaking began to reposition his own gun, the muzzle ending up upon his temple.

One by one, three more shots rang out.

And then the vampire sauntered over and extinguished his cigar in the dead mouth of the first to go down.

Xcor laughed softly as Assail returned to his vehicle.

"Do we follow him?" Zypher asked.

Wasn't that the question. There were *lessers* to fight here in the downtown area, and there was no reason to care if Assail was making money off the addictions of humans. Still, there was a lot of night left to be utilized, and there might as yet be a meeting between the male and the king forthcoming.

"Aye," Xcor replied. "But only myself and Throe. If there is a rendezvous with Wrath we will find you."

"This is why we all need cell phones," Throe said. "Faster, better coordination."

Xcor ground his teeth. Since their arrival in the New World, he had allowed Throe to engage one such cellular, and no others: A fighter's sense of smell and hearing, his instinct honed by training and practice, his knowledge of his enemy and himself, these did not come with a monthly bill, the need for recharging, or the threat of being laid aside and lost or stolen.

Ignoring the commentary, Xcor ordered, "The rest of you go forth and find the enemy."

"Which one," Zypher said with a hearty laugh. "There are a growing number from which to choose."

Indeed. For Assail was not behaving like an aristocrat. He was acting like a male who might be trying to build some kind of empire of his own.

It was entirely possible this member of the *glymera* was Xcor's kind of vampire. Which meant he might well have to be eliminated at some point—and not simply as collateral damage.

There was room for only one king in Caldwell.

TWENTY-TWO

𝕬s Tohr resumed form at the Brotherhood mansion, he was pissed off at the world. Rankly ugly. Rattlesnake mad.

Pushing his way into the vestibule, he prayed that Fritz just released the lock remotely and didn't go the personal route. No one needed to see him like this—

His prayers were answered as the inner door gave way, and he marched into the foyer to an audience of nobody: All around the first floor the house was silent, the *doggen* taking the opportunity to attend to the upstairs bedrooms before beginning preparations for Last Meal.

Shit. He probably needed to text Phury about where Layla was—

On a sudden, gripping instinct, his head cranked around on the top of his spine, his eyes focusing on the dining room.

Some inner cue told him to get walking, the impulse carrying him through the arches, past the long, glossy table . . . and out the flap door into the kitchen.

No'One was at the counter cracking eggs into a ceramic bowl.

Alone.

She stopped in midstrike, her hood coming up and turning to face him.

For some reason, his heart started beating hard. "Did I imagine you?" he said.

"I'm sorry?"

"Did I imagine you in the foyer before I left."

No'One slowly lowered her hand, the egg saved from shattering. Temporarily. "No. You did not."

"Take your hood off again."

It was not a question, but a demand—the kind of thing Wellsie would never have stood for. No'One, on the other hand, solemnly obeyed him.

And there she was, revealed to his eyes, her cap of blond hair terminating in the start of that rope-thick braid, her pale cheeks and eyes luminous, her face. . . .

"I told Lassiter . . ." She cleared her throat. "Lassiter asked me if I would feed you."

"And you said."

"Yes."

All of a sudden, he pictured her in that pool, floating on her back, utterly naked, with the water's pervasive tongue licking at her warm flesh.

Everywhere.

Tohr threw out a palm and braced himself on a cupboard. Hard to know what was rocking him most: the sudden need to be at her throat, or his utter despair at the thought of it.

"I am still in love with my *shellan*," he heard himself say.

And that remained the problem: All the resolving in the world, all the turning-the-new-leaf-and-letting-go shit, hadn't changed his emotions in the slightest.

"I know," No'One replied. "And I am glad."

"I should use a Chosen." He took a step closer to her.

"I know. And I agree. Their blood is purer."

He took another step forward. "You are from a good bloodline."

"Was," she said starkly.

As the fragile expanse of her shoulders began to tremble ever so slightly—like she had sensed his hunger—the predator in him awoke. Abruptly, he found himself wanting to jump over the island she was standing at, just so he could . . .

Do what?

Well, that was obvious.

Even though his heart and his mind were nothing but an empty ice-skating rink, frozen over and flat as fuck, the rest of him was alive, his body throbbing with a purpose that threatened to mow down good intentions, proper decorum . . . and his grieving process.

As he took yet more steps to her, he had a horrifying thought that this was what Lassiter had meant by letting go: In this moment, he had left Wellsie behind. He was aware of nothing except the diminutive female in front of him who was fighting to stay in place as she was stalked by a Brother.

He stopped only when he was no more than a foot away from her. Looking down past her bent head, his eyes locked on the fragile pulse at her jugular vein.

She was breathing as hard as he was.

And as he inhaled, he caught a scent.

It was not fear.

Dearest Virgin Scribe, he was enormous.

As No'One stood in the lee of the great warrior who had come upon her, she felt the heat coming off his massive body sure as if she were in front of a raging fire. And yet . . . she was not burned. And she was not afraid. She was warmed in someplace so deep, so buried within her, that she did not immediately recognize it as part of her internal makeup.

All she knew for sure was that he was going to take her vein within moments and she was going to let him—not because the angel had requested it of her, and not because she had vowed to, and not to make up for something in the past.

She . . . wanted him to.

As a hiss boiled out of him, she knew Tohrment had opened his mouth to expose his fangs.

It was time. And she did not pull up her sleeve. She loosened the top of her robe, peeled it wide to her shoulders, and tilted her head to the side.

Giving him her throat.

Oh, how her heart beat.

"Not here," he growled. "Come with me."

Taking her hand, he drew her into the butler's pantry and closed them in. The squat, cramped room was lined with shelves of colorful canned fruits and vegetables, the still, warm air smelling of freshly milled grains and the dry, cakey sweetness of flour.

As the overhead light came on and the door locked itself, she knew they had been willed so by him.

And then he just stared at her as his fangs elongated even further, the twin white tips peeking out from under his parted upper lip, his eyes glowing.

"What do I do?" she said hoarsely.

He frowned. "What do you mean?"

"What do I . . . do for you?" The *symphath* had taken what he'd wanted and to hell with her. And her father had naturally never permitted any male to feed from her. Was there a certain way to—

Abruptly, Tohrment appeared to pull out of the vortex, something jarring him back to a different consciousness. And yet even so, his body remained fully engaged, his weight shifting from one boot to the other, his hands curling into fists and releasing, curling . . . and releasing.

"Have you never . . ."

"My father was saving me. And when I was abducted . . . I have never done this properly before."

Tohrment put a hand up to his head as if he had an ache within it. "Listen, this is—"

"Tell me what to do."

As he trained his eyes on her once again, she thought his name was indeed apt. Lo, how he was tormented.

"I need this," he said, as if speaking to himself.

"Yes, you do. You are so gaunt that I ache for you."

Except he was going to stop this, she thought as his stare grew dull. And she knew why.

"She is welcome in this space," No'One said. "Bring your *shellan* unto your mind. Let her take my place."

Anything to help him. For Tohrment's great kindnesses toward her earlier self, and fate's cruel machinations against him, she would do anything for him to be made right.

"I may hurt you," he said harshly.

"No worse than I have already survived."

"Why . . ."

"Stop talking. Stop trying to think. Do what you must to take care of yourself."

There was a long, tense silence. And then the light went off, the little room going dim, with the only illumination that which bled through the milky glass panels of the door.

She gasped.

He breathed harder.

And then an arm linked around the back of her waist and jerked her forward. As she hit his chest wall, it was as if she had been thrown against rock, and she blindly put her hands out to grab onto something—

The flesh of his arms was smooth and hot, the skin thin over hard muscles.

Tugging. Tugging on her braid. Then wrenching . . . and her hair was unbound, her scalp spared the stretch and pull of the binding, the release drawing her head back.

A large hand speared in through her tresses, tangling them, pulling downward. And as her neck stretched further, her spine was forced to follow until she was held up entirely by the strength of him.

Disoriented and off balance, she momentarily lost her purpose, just as he had before darkness had been wrought.

Searching for his face, she found it. But there was no grounding to be had. She could not see the features, could not find him in the male body she was up against.

Instantly, his visage became nothing but anonymous planes and angles. And his body was not that of Tohrment, the Brother who had attempted to save her, but some stranger.

There was no turning back, however, no undoing the spin of the wheel she had unleashed.

His grip, his arms, his body tightened up even more until she was crushed against him. And as she stiffened, he brought his head downward, a chuffing growl emanating from that deep rib cage of his, a dark, rich scent nearly permeating her sense of fear.

There was another hiss, followed by a razor-thin scratch that started at her collarbone and rose e'er higher.

Panic o'ertook her.

His presence, his hold on her, the fact that she couldn't see properly, everything about the experience shifted her back into the past, and she started to struggle.

Which was when he struck.

Violently.

No'One cried out and attempted to push away, but his fangs were already in deep, the pain sweet like a bee sting. And then the sucking, the powerful sucking that was accompanied by a wild trembling in his body.

Something hard protruded from his hips. Pressed into her belly.

Using all her strength, she tried again to get free, but her efforts were a countervailing breeze in the face of a hurricane gale.

And then . . . his pelvis began to move against her, gyrating, that

arousal of his pushing at her robe, searching for a way inside as he took deeply from her, groans of satisfaction rising up in the air between them.

He did not even feel her fright, so consumed was he.

And her conscious mind could not regrasp the fact that she had wanted this from him.

Staring up toward the ceiling, she recalled other times she had fought to no avail, and prayed, as she had before, for this to pass soon.

Dearest Virgin Scribe, what had she done . . .

The body against Tohr's yielded everything there was to give, blood, breath, and flesh. And goddamn them both, but he took, took hard and ravenously, drinking deep, and wanting more than just the vein.

He wanted the core of this female.

He wanted in her as he drank from her.

And this was true even as he was acutely aware that this was not his Wellsie. Her hair didn't feel the same—No'One's fell in smooth lengths, not thick curls. Her blood didn't taste the same—the rich flavor against his tongue and the tang at the back of his throat were altogether different. And her body was thinner and more delicate, not robust and powerful.

But he still wanted her.

His godforsaken cock was roaring without excuse—ready to take and take and . . . own, as well. At least sexually.

Shit, this fireball of want and need was nothing like the pale anemic feeding he'd had with the Chosen Selena. This was what it should be, this abandonment, this shedding of the civilized skin to reveal the animal at the marrow.

And goddamn him, he went with it.

Repositioning No'One, he let his hold around her waist go downward until he was gripping her lower back, and then her hip . . . and then her ass.

Abruptly, he pushed her into the glass cupboards, the panes on the doors rattling. He didn't mean to be rough, but it was impossible to fight the need. And worse, in the recesses of his mind, he didn't want to.

Lifting his head, he let out a roar that stung even his own ears, and then he bit her again, his control snapping at the feast of his starved senses.

The second bite was higher and closer to her jaw, and his sucking became even more intense, her nourishment speeding to the fibers of his muscles, strengthening him, restoring him, making him physically whole once more.

The sucking . . . fuck him, the *sucking* . . .

When he finally lifted his head, he was drunk on her, his mind spinning for different reasons than from blood hunger. Next would be the sex, and he actually looked around for a bed.

Except . . . they were in the butler's pantry? What the hell?

Christ, he couldn't even remember how all this had happened.

He was sure, however, that he didn't want her bleeding out, so he dropped his head to her throat. Elongating his tongue, he stroked up the column he had nailed twice, feeling velvet and tasting her and smelling her—

The scent that entered his nostrils was not a commercial perfume.

And it was not a female's lush arousal, as he had sensed in the beginning.

She was terrified.

"No'One?" he said, as he felt her trembling for the first time.

With a hoarse cry, she began to sob, and in his shock, he went momentarily numb. Then, as sensation returned, he felt all too clearly her nails clawing into the backs of his upper arms, her delicate body trying to get free.

He let her go immediately—

No'One slammed into the corner cupboard and then went for the door, jerking at the knob, rattling it so forcibly the opaque glass was liable to break.

"Hold on, I'll let you—"

The instant he sprang the lock she took off, flying through the kitchen and out the other side as if she were running for her dear life.

"Shit!" He tore after her. "No'One!"

He didn't care who heard him as he called her name again, his voice echoing up through the dining room's high ceiling as he blew past the long table and then shot into the foyer.

As she ripped across the depiction of the apple tree in the floor, he recalled the memory of her that night they had tried to bring her home to her father's, her nightgown streaming behind her, turning her into a ghost as she ran across the moonlit meadow.

Now her robe streamed behind as she headed for the stairs.

Tohr's panic was running so high he dematerialized in pursuit, reassuming form halfway up and yet still not in front of her. Continuing to chase her on foot, he followed her past Wrath's study, and down the hall to the right.

The second she got to the bedroom she stayed in, she threw herself inside and slammed the door.

He got to the wooden panels just in time to hear the lock turn.

As her blood raced through his system, giving him the power he had been missing, and the appetite for food he hadn't had, and the clearest head that had plugged into his spine for ages, he remembered everything he hadn't during the time he'd been at her throat.

She had given herself willingly, generously, and he had taken too much, too fast, in a dark room where he could have been anyone but the one she had agreed to feed.

He'd scared her. Or worse.

Pivoting, he put his back to her door and let his knees loosen until his ass caught the floor. "Fuck me . . . fucking hell . . ."

God*damn* him.

Oh, wait, that had already happened.

TWENTY-THREE

Just before closing time at the Iron Mask, Xhex was in her office and shaking her head at Big Rob. On her desk between them were three more packets of that cocaine with the death symbol on it. "Are you kidding me with this shit?"

"Pulled it off a guy ten minutes ago."

"Did you keep him?"

"Within the bounds of what's legal. Told him I was processing paperwork. Didn't exactly mention to him that he was free to go—fortunately, he's so drunk he's not worried about his civil rights."

"Let me go talk to him."

"He's where you like them."

She headed out and hung a left. The interrogation room was at the far end of the hall, and it didn't have a lock on the door—last thing they needed was trouble with the CPD. Make that more trouble: Given what went down under this roof every night, the police were known to nose around from time to time.

Opening the door, she cursed under her breath. The guy sitting at the table was slumped over onto himself, his chin down on his chest, his arms

hanging loose, his knees out to the sides. He was dressed like an old-fashioned dandy in steam-punk style, sporting a black slim-fit suit and a white shirt with a high lace collar—and naturally, something was off about the threads. The fabric, for one thing. The fact that none of it was handmade, for another. The buttons . . . But that was what happened when humans who liked to pretend dipped their toes in historical waters. They got shit wrong every time.

Shutting the door quietly, she walked over to him in silence, curled up a fist . . . and *slammed* it on the table to wake him up.

Oh, look, he had a little cane to complete his outfit. And a cape.

As the guy flipped backward and teetered on two chair legs, she caught the ebony walking stick on the fly and let gravity decide what to do with the human—

How. Cute. In his open mouth, two porcelain fang-like projections had been glued onto his canines. Guess that made him feel even more Frank Langella.

She sat down just as he landed flat on his back, and she studied the silver skull at the top of the cane while he dragged himself off the floor, righted his dumb-ass costume as well as the chair, and parked it once again. As he smoothed his jet-black hair, the roots showed mouse brown.

"Yes, we're letting you go," she said before he asked. "And as long as you tell me what I want to know, I won't get our friends down at the CPD involved."

"Okay. Yeah. Thanks."

At least he didn't pretend to have an English accent. "Where'd you get the coke?" She put a hand up as he opened his yap. "Before you tell me it was your friend's and you're just keeping it for him, or that you borrowed the coat and it was in the pockets, the police aren't going to believe that bullshit any more than I do—but I guarantee they'll get to hear the lie."

There was a long silence during which she stared at him. He'd even put in red contacts to make his irises appear to be glowing.

She wondered if he'd ever tried to dematerialize through a wall.

She was ready to help him give it a go.

"I made the buy on the corner of Trade and Eighth. About three hours ago. I don't know the guy's name, but he's usually there every night between eleven and twelve."

"Does he only sell the shit marked with that symbol?"

"Nah." The guy seemed to relax, his Jersey accent growing stronger. "He'll move just about anything. Back in the spring, I sometimes couldn't get the coke. But, I don't know, last month or so he's had it every time. It's what I like."

Was the Dracula routine his rebellion against GTL? she wondered.

"What name does it go by?" she said.

"Dagger. It fits who I am." As he motioned down his getup, his red-stoned pinkie ring caught the light. "I'm a vampire."

"Reallllly. I thought they didn't exist."

"Oh, we're very real." He gave her the once-over, his eyes going Lothario. "I could introduce you to some people. Bring you into the coven."

"Isn't that for witches?"

"I have three wives, you know."

"Sounds crowded at your house."

"I'm looking for a fourth."

"Nice offer, but I'm married." As she said the words, her chest ached. "Happily, I might add."

She wasn't sure for whose benefit that was tacked on. God, John—

The knock on the door was soft. "Yeah," she said over her shoulder.

"You got a visitor."

The instant the reply hit her ears, her body flared to life, and abruptly she was ready to usher this trick-or-treat motherfucker out the door head-first.

John was early tonight, which was fine with her.

"We're done," she announced, getting to her feet.

The human rose up, his nostrils flaring. "God, your perfume is . . . amazing."

"Don't bring that shit into my house again, or next time we're not going to do any talking. Clear?"

Opening up the door, she got hit with her mate's bonding scent: Those dark spices were barreling down the hall . . .

And there he was, at the other end, standing tall outside her office.

Her John.

As his head came around toward her, he dipped his chin and smiled, his eyes looking a little evil. Which meant he was more than ready for her.

"You're beautiful," the faker breathed as he stepped forward.

She was about to brush him off when John caught sight of the horny little fucker.

This did not go over well.

Her bonded male came prowling down the hall, his shitkickers loud enough to drown out the bass beat from the club proper.

Her buddy with the caps and the cape was still focused on her, but that didn't last. As he got a load of the nearly three-hundred-pound, jacked-up force of nature riding up on him, he actually shrank into himself and took cover behind Xhex.

Manly. Yup. Real stud material.

John stopped at the door and blocked all escape, those beautiful blues of his downright vicious as he glared over her shoulder at the human.

God, she wanted to fuck him, she thought.

With a casual wave, she provided introductions. "This is my husband, John. John, this was just leaving. Do you want to escort it out, honey?"

Before the faker could respond, John bared his fangs and let out a hiss. It was the only sound he could make besides a whistle, but it was better than words—

"Oh, man," Xhex muttered as she stepped aside sharply.

The wannabe had just pissed himself.

John was more than happy to take out the garbage. Dumb-ass human, looking at his female like that? The bastard was lucky John was so sexed up. Otherwise he'd have taken the time to break a leg or an arm just to make a point.

Clamping a hold on the nape of the guy's neck, he frog-marched the leering son of a bitch over to the rear exit, kicked open the door, and dragged him into the back parking lot.

Some version of, "Oh, God, please don't hurt me," was coming out of that mouth, and with good goddamn reason. Only the thinnest veil of common sense was keeping John from murder.

As there was no way to command the guy to look at him, John spun the POS around, grabbed him by the shoulders, and lifted him up until his cute patent leather black shoes hung in the breeze.

Meeting eyes that had some kind of ridiculous fake red color over them, John willed the poser into a trance, and wiped clean the memories of those fangs that had been flashed. Then . . . well, it was tempting to implant a little ditty about how vampires really did exist and were coming after him.

Good dose of induced paranoia would put a quick end to this charade the fucker was living.

Then again, it wasn't worth the effort. Especially not when he could be inside his female right now.

With a final shake, he let the guy go, sending him off at a dead run. Fucker was scrawny; exercise would do him good.

As John turned back to the club, he saw Xhex's Ducati parked flush against the building under a security light, and damn . . . He imagined her straddling all that power, lying low on the engine, gunning the bike around a dead man's curve. . . .

He stalked over to the door and found it open, with her standing in it.

"I thought you were going to tear his throat out," she drawled.

She was totally aroused.

As John came up to her, he didn't stop until her breasts were against his chest, and she didn't budge in the slightest—which naturally juiced him even more. God, she was hot to begin with, but this self-imposed separation they were rocking was making him even more desperate to be with her.

"You want to come in my office," she said on a growl. "Or do it out here?"

When he just nodded like the dumb handle he was, she laughed. "How about inside so we don't scare the children."

Yeah, for most humans, sex didn't involve drawing blood.

As she led the way, he watched her hips sway and wondered if in fact it was anatomically possible for a person's tongue to drag on the floor.

The instant they were locked in together, he was all over her, kissing her hard as his hands made fast work of shoving up her shirt. As her fingers speared into his hair, he bent down and sent up a prayer of thanks that she never bothered with a bra.

With her nipple in his sucking mouth and one hand between her legs from the back, he laid her out on top of the paperwork on her desk. Next move was to peel off her leathers, and then he was sprung and penetrating her.

Fast, furious fucking, the kind that rearranged furniture and probably called attention to itself, was always the opening gambit. Second time was slower. Third time was that sensuous crap that got shot with a blurry lens in movies.

It was your typical way of handling a banquet: gorge to take the edge off; concentrate on favorites; finish off with a delicate aperitif—

They came at the same time, he bending over her, she wrapping her long legs up around his hips, both of them holding on as tight as they could.

In the midst of the jerking releases, he happened to lift his head and look up. Across the way, there was a file cabinet, and an extra chair . . . and for some reason, he noticed for the first time that the wall was made of concrete blocks and painted black.

Same stuff that he'd stared at for the last couple months. And none of it had registered.

Now, though, the fact that it was not her home or his hit him hard.

She hadn't invited him back to her place on the river since they'd had that first all-out session after their separation.

She hadn't come to the mansion, either.

Closing his eyes, he tried to reconnect with what his body was still up to, but all he got were vague sensations of pulsing below his belt. Popping his lids, he wanted to look at her face, but she had arched back and all he could see was the point of her chin. And some time cards. For her bouncers.

Who could be right outside the door, listening to them.

Shit . . . this was seedy.

He was having an illicit affair . . . with his own mate.

In the beginning, it had been so exciting, like they were dating in a way they hadn't done when they'd first gotten together. And he'd assumed it would always be that fun.

Except there had been shadows all along, hadn't there.

Squeezing his eyes shut, he realized he would so rather do this in a bed. Their mated bed. And it wasn't because he was old-fashioned; he missed her sleeping beside him.

"What is it, John?"

He cracked his lids. He should have known she'd have a bead on where he was at—*symphath* abilities aside, she knew him as no one else did. And now, as he met her gunmetal gray eyes, a stab of sadness nailed him in the chest.

He really didn't want to talk about it, though. They had too little time together.

He kissed her deep and long, figuring that was the best kind of distraction for both of them—and it worked. As her tongue met his, he began moving inside of her again, the long strokes taking him out to the brink, then easing him in all the way. The rhythm was slow but inexorable, and he, too, got swept away to a place where his head quieted down.

The release was a gently cresting wave this time, and he rode it out with a kind of desperation.

When it had passed, as all orgasms did, he became acutely aware of the distant, muffled pounding of music, and the clipping of heels out in the hall, and the far-off ringing of a cell phone.

"What's wrong?" she said.

As he disengaged their bodies, he noticed that they were both mostly dressed. When was the last time they'd been fully naked?

Jesus . . . it had been during that period of bliss after their mating. Which seemed like a distant memory. Maybe about another couple.

"Did everything go okay with Wrath tonight?" she asked as she pulled up her pants. "Is that what it is?"

His brain struggled to focus, but fortunately, his hands were working just fine, and not only to get his button fly done up. *Yeah, the meeting went okay. Hard to judge, though. The* glymera *are all about appearances.*

"Mmm." She never had much to say about things involving the Brotherhood. Then again, given where they stood about her fighting, he was surprised she brought his work up at all.

How's it going for you tonight? he signed.

She picked up something that she'd been lying on, a little baggie. "We have a new drug dealer in town."

He caught what she tossed over, frowning at the symbol stamped on the cellophane. *What the hell? This is . . . the Old Language.*

"Yup, and we have no clue who's behind it. But I promise you this, I'm going to find out."

Let me know if I can help.

"I got this."

I know.

The stretch of silence that rang out served to remind him of where they were—and were not.

"You're right," she said abruptly. "I haven't had you to my house on purpose. It's hard enough to have you leave me from here."

I could stay with you. I could move in, and—

"Wrath would never allow it—rightfully so, I might add. You're a very valuable commodity to him, and my cabin is hardly as secure as the mansion. Besides, what the hell would we do with Qhuinn? He deserves a life, too—and at least where you stay he has some autonomy."

Alternate days, then.

She shrugged. "Until that becomes not enough? John, this is what we have—and it's better than a lot of people get. You don't think Tohr would kill to be able to—"

It's not enough for me. I'm greedy, and you're my shellan, *not just a booty call.*

"And I can't go back to the mansion. I'm sorry. If I do, I'll end up hating them—and you. I'd like to pretend I can self-actualize this shit away, and be all, 'I'll just do me,' but I can't."

I'll talk to Wrath—

"Wrath's not the issue. They take their cues from you. All of them."

When he didn't reply, she came up to him, put her palms on his face, and stared into his eyes. "This is the way it has to be. Now go so I can close up. And come back to me first thing tomorrow night. I'm already counting down the minutes."

She kissed him firmly.

And then turned away and left the office.

TWENTY-FOUR

No'One woke up to a great, horrifying scream, the kind of thing that accompanied bloody murder.

It took her a moment to realize she was making the sound, her mouth stretched wide, her body strung tight, her lungs burning as she exhaled.

Fortunately, she had left the lights on, and she frantically looked around at the bedroom's toile-covered walls and drapery and bedspread. Then she focused on her robe . . . yes, she had her robe on, not a thin nightgown.

It had been a dream. A dream . . .

She was *not* in a root cellar in the earth.

She was *not* at the mercy of the *symphath*—

"I'm sorry."

Gasping, she jerked back against the padded headboard. Tohrment was standing just inside the room, the door closed behind him.

"Are you okay?" he said.

She yanked her hood up into place, hiding beneath it. "I . . ." Memo-

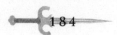

ries of what had happened between them made it hard to think clearly. "I am . . . well enough."

"I can't believe that," he said in a hoarse way. "God . . . I'm so sorry. There's no excuse for what I did. And I won't come near you ever again. I swear . . ."

The anguish in his voice bit into her as surely as if it were her own. "It's all right—"

"The hell it is. I even gave you a nightmare—"

"What awoke me was not you. It was . . . from before." Taking a deep breath, she said, "It's strange, I have not dreamed of the . . . what happened to me . . . ever. I have thought of it often, but when I sleep, I have only darkness."

"And just now?" he gritted out.

"I was back underground. In the root cellar. The smell down there— dearest Virgin Scribe, the *smell.*" Wrapping her arms around herself, she felt the draft sure as if she were once again behind that rough oak door. "Salt licks . . . I'd forgotten the salt licks."

"I'm sorry?"

"There were salt licks down there for the animals—that is why my scars stuck with me. I'd always wondered if maybe he'd used some kind of *symphath* power or something to alter my skin. But no, there were salt licks, and salting meats." She shook her head. "I'd forgotten about them until now. Forgotten so many precise details—"

As a growled curse came out of him, she glanced up. Tohrment's expression suggested he wished he could kill that *symphath* all over again— but he covered it up, as if he didn't want to upset her.

"I don't think I ever told you I was sorry," he said softly. "Back then, in the cottage with Darius. He and I were both so sorry that you had—"

"Please, let us speak no longer upon the subject. Thank you."

In the awkward silence that followed, his stomach rumbled.

"You should eat," she murmured.

"Not hungry."

"Your tum—"

"Can go to hell."

Staring up at his still figure, she was astounded by the difference in him: even after such a short time, the color was back in his face, his posture was straighter, his eyes much more alert.

The blood was such a powerful thing, she thought.

"I will feed you again." As he regarded her as though she had lost her mind, she kicked up her chin and met his stare. "Absolutely, I will do it again."

To see this improvement in him in such a short time, she would endure those moments of terror anew. She was e'er trapped by her past, but oh, the change in him: her blood had freed him from his fatigue—and that was going to keep him alive out in the field.

"How can you say that?" His voice was gruff to the point of cracking.

"It is simply the way I feel."

"Obligation shouldn't take you that far down into your personal hell."

"That is for me to choose, not you."

His brows drew in hard. "You were a lamb to the slaughter in that pantry."

"If that were true, I would not be breathing right now, would I."

"Did you like the dream you just had? Have fun with it?" As she recoiled, he stalked across to the shuttered windows and stared with fixation as if he could see through them to the garden. "You're more than a maid or a blood whore, you know."

With proper hauteur, she informed him, "To serve others well is a noble endeavor."

Looking over his shoulder, his eyes found hers in spite of the hood. "But you're not doing it to be noble. You're under that robe hiding your beauty and your station to punish yourself. I don't think it has anything to do with some kind of an altruistic streak."

"You do not know me or my motivations—"

"I was aroused." At that she blinked. "You had to have known that."

Well, yes, she had. But—

"And if I am at your vein again, that's going to happen. Again."

"You were not thinking of me, though," she pointed out.

"Would that make a difference."

"Yes."

"You sure about that," he said dryly.

"You didn't do anything about it, did you. And that one feeding is not going to be enough—you must know that. It has been too long for you. You have already come so far, but you are going to need more soon."

As he cursed, she lifted her chin once more, unwilling to back down.

After a long while, he shook his head. "You are so . . . odd."

"I shall take that as a compliment."

*   *   *

From across the bedroom, Tohr stared down at No'One and had to respect the shit out of her—even though it was clear she was nuts: She was utterly unbowed, in spite of the fact that she had bite marks on her neck, had woken up screaming, and was facing off with a Brother.

Christ, when he'd heard that scream, he'd all but broken down the damn door. Visions of her with another knife of some kind, doing hell's own amount of damage, had thrown him into action. But all there had been was her on the middle of that bed, oblivious to anything but whatever was playing in her head.

Salt licks. Fucking hell.

"Your leg," he said gently. "How did it happen."

"He put a steel cuff around my ankle and chained me to a beam. When he . . . came to me . . . the cuff bit into me."

Tohr closed his eyes against the images. "Oh, God . . ."

He wasn't sure what to say after that. He just stood there, powerless, saddened . . . wishing that so many things had been different in both of their lives.

"I think I know why we're here," she said abruptly.

"Because you screamed."

"No, I mean . . ." She cleared her throat. "I've always wondered why the Scribe Virgin brought me to the Sanctuary. But Lassiter, the angel, is right. I am here to help you, as you helped me long ago."

"I didn't save you, remember. Not at the end."

"You did, though." He was shaking his head when she cut him off. "I used to watch you sleep—back in the Old Country. You were always to the right of the fire, and you slept on your side facing me. I spent hours memorizing the way the low glow from the peat played over your closed eyes and your cheeks and your jaw."

Suddenly, the room seemed to retract in on them both, growing tighter, smaller . . . warmer. "Why?"

"Because you weren't like the *symphath* at all. You were dark and he was pale. You were big and he was thin. You were kind to me . . . and he was not. You were the only thing that kept me from going completely mad."

"I never knew."

"I did not want you to know."

After a moment, he said grimly, "You always planned on killing yourself."

"Yes."

"Why not do it before the birth?" Man, he couldn't believe how candid they were getting.

"I did not want to curse the babe. I had heard the rumors about what happened if you took matters into your own hands, and I was prepared to accept the consequences for myself. But the unborn? It was coming into the world in such sadness to begin with, but at least it could make of its destiny what it could."

And yet she had not been cursed . . . maybe because of her circumstances—God knew, she had suffered enough on her way to the exit.

On that note, he shook his head again. "About the feeding. I appreciate your offer, I really do. But somehow, I can't imagine a repeat of that scene downstairs is going to do either of us any good."

"Admit that you feel stronger."

"You said you haven't dreamed of that shit since it happened."

"One dream is not—"

"It's enough for me."

That chin of hers went up again, and damned if that habit wasn't . . . well, not appealing, no. No, it was not appealing.

Really.

"If I can live through the events," she said, "I can get through the memories."

In that moment, staring across the room at her show of will, he felt a tie to her, sure as if a rope had linked the pair of them chest-to-chest.

"Come to me again," she announced. "When you are in need."

"We'll see about that," he dismissed. "Now, are you . . . okay? Here in this room, I mean? You can lock the door—"

"I shall be all right, if you come to me again."

"No'One—"

"It is the only way I have to make things right with you."

"You don't have to make anything right. Honest."

Turning away, he went to the door, and before he stepped out, he glanced over his shoulder. She was staring at her entwined hands, that hooded head of hers bowed.

Leaving her with what little peace she had, he took his grumbling stomach to his room and disarmed. He was righteously starved, his appetite for food carving a bottomless pit out of his lower torso—and though he would have preferred to ignore the demand, he didn't have a choice. Ordering up a tray from Fritz, he thought of No'One, and told the *doggen* to make sure she got some eats as well.

Then it was shower time. After he turned on the water, he undressed and left the clothes on the marble floor where they landed. He was in the process of stepping over the mess when he saw himself in the long mirror over the sinks.

Even to his uncaring eye, it was obvious his body had rebounded, the muscles tightening under his skin, his shoulders back where they should be instead of down around his diaphragm.

Too bad he didn't feel better about the recovery.

Getting into the glass-enclosed space, he stood under the jets, braced his arms out, and let the water run off his flesh.

When he closed his eyes, he found himself back in the pantry, at No'One's throat, working her vein. He should have taken her wrist, not her throat—matter of fact, why hadn't he—

Abruptly, the memory went full-bore on him, the tastes and scents and feel of that female against him shutting his mind down and cranking up his senses.

God, she had been . . . a sunrise.

Opening his eyes, he stared down at the erection that had made itself known at the first image. His cock was in proportion to the rest of him—which meant it was long, thick, and heavy. And capable of going for hours.

As it strained in a demand for attention, he feared the arousal was like the hunger in his gut: going nowhere until he did something about it.

Yeah, whatever on that. He was not some posttrans with a perma-boner and a hairy palm. He could choose whether or not he jerked off, for fuck's sake—and that would be a big NO.

Snagging the bar of soap, he sudsed up his legs, and wished he was V—no, not with the black candles and shit. But at least if he had that vampire's mind, he could think of, like, the molecular makeup of plastic, or the chemical composition of fluoride toothpaste, or . . . how gasoline powered cars.

Or he supposed he could think of dudes—which, given that he wasn't attracted to them, might well lead to a merciful deflation.

The problem was, he was just Tohrment, son of Hharm . . . so he was stuck trying to remember how to make Toll House cookies: He didn't know shit from Shinola about science, he didn't give a crap about sports, and he hadn't read a newspaper or watched the TV news in years.

Plus those were the only goddamn anything he knew how to make . . . what did you put in them? Butter? Crisco? Spackle?

As nothing came to him, he began to worry that his Food Network channel was not only incompetent, but wasn't going to do shit for his dumb handle.

He gave it another shot. And could only remember how to open the goddamn bag of chips.

Stalled, stiff at the hips, and despaired, he closed his eyes . . . and thought of his Wellsie, naked and in their bed. Of how she tasted and felt, of all the ways they'd been together, of all the days spent interlocked and panting.

Gripping himself, he pinned the pictures of his mate to the forefront of his mind, plastering them over anything that had to do with No'One. He didn't want that other female in this space; he might have to take care of business, which he didn't want to do, but he could damn well set boundaries.

He sure as hell couldn't pick his fate, but his fantasies were totally up for grabs.

Stroking his shaft, he tried to remember everything about his red-haired beauty: the way her hair had looked across his chest, the gleam of her bare sex, how her breasts had peaked when she was on her back.

It was just part of a history book, though, and the illustrations had faded—as if his mind had lifted the ink from the pages.

His concentration lost, he popped open his lids and got a hi-how're-ya of his hand wrapped around that stupid-ass arousal, trying to pump off something, anything.

It was like milking a Coke machine—getting him nowhere. Well, except for a vague sting where the skin got pinched at the head.

"God*damn* it."

Dropping the whole bad idea, he got busy with the soap, running the bar over his chest and under his armpits.

"Sire?" Fritz called out from the other room. "Would you require aught else?"

He was *not* asking the *doggen* for porn. That was *blech* on so many levels. "Ah, no, thanks, my man."

"Very good. Have a blessed sleep."

Yeah. Right. "You, too."

After the outside door was shut again, Tohr shampooed his head like he supposed all males did: Squeeze out a crapload, rub it into your hair like you were trying to get a stain out of a carpet, and then stand under the spray forever because you'd used too much of whatever Fritz had bought you.

Later, he would decide it would have been best to keep his eyes open.

As soon as he shut his lids to keep the suds out, the warm rush down his torso turned into hands, and the urge to orgasm came back even stronger than before, his cock throbbing, his balls getting tight—

Instantly, he was downstairs in the pantry again, his mouth locked on No'One's smooth throat, his suction and swallowing filling his belly, his arms squeezing her hard against his body. . . .

Your shellan *is welcome here.*

He shook his head at the sound of her voice in his inner ear. But then he realized that was the answer.

Regripping himself, he told his brain that the images were of his Wellsie. That the feeling, the sensation, the scent, the taste . . . it was his Wellsie, not another female.

It was not a memory.

It was his mate back to him—

The release was so sudden, he actually recoiled, his eyes going wide, his body jerking not from the orgasm but the surprise that, yes, in fact, he was actually having one in RL, not in some dreamscape.

As he stroked himself and rode the crest, he watched himself come, his sex doing what it was supposed to, kicking out jets that hit the wet marble wall and the glass pane of the door.

The sight was less erotic than biological.

It was just a function, he realized. Like breathing and eating. Yeah, it felt good, but so did a deep breath: in this vacuum of emotion, in this lonely shower, it was really just a series of ejaculations that coughed through his prostate.

Feelings gave sex meaning, whether it was in a fantasy or with your mate . . . or if you were with someone you didn't like all that much, for that matter.

Or didn't want to want, an inner voice pointed out.

When his body was done, he feared it was just a round-one situation, because he was still every bit as erect as he had been when this had started. But at least he didn't feel like he had cheated on his mate. In fact, he didn't feel anything at all, and that was good.

Rinsing off, he got out, dried himself with a towel . . . and took the stretch of terry cloth with him into the bedroom.

He was pretty certain that after he ate, things were going to get messy when he lay down, and not from any kind of indigestion.

But it was . . . okay. As okay as he could ever get, he supposed.

The sex he'd had with his mate had been monumental, shattering, fireworks-making—transformative.

This shit was about as sexy as a head cold.

As long as he didn't think of . . .

He stopped himself and cleared his throat, even though he wasn't speaking out loud.

As long as he didn't think of anyone else of the female persuasion, he was good.

TWENTY-FIVE

The following evening, Xcor stood in the recessed doorway of a brick building in the heart of downtown. Set back by nearly three feet, the space formed a coffin of sorts, providing him shadows to conceal himself with, as well as cover from stray bullets.

On his own, he was utterly and completely pissed off as he surveyed the area and kept an eye on the sleek black car he had followed.

Lifting his forearm, he checked his watch. Again. Where were his soldiers?

Splitting off from the group to follow Assail had brought him here, but before he had departed, he'd told the others to find him after they had finished their first round of fighting—a locating task that shouldn't have been difficult. All they had to do was rooftop-to-rooftop surveillance in the part of the city where drug dealing was at its most prevalent.

Not hard a'tall.

And yet here he was, alone.

Assail was still inside the building opposite, likely consorting with more of the ilk that he had killed the night before. The place of business he'd entered was ostensibly an art gallery, but Xcor was old-fashioned, not naive. All manner of goods and services could be contracted out of any sort of "legitimate" establishment.

It was nearly an hour later when the other vampire finally re-emerged, and the light over the back exit caught his densely black hair and his predatorlike features. That low-slung car he ambulated in was parked off to the side, and as he walked around it, a pinkie ring of some sort flashed.

Moving as he did, dressed in black as he was, he looked . . . exactly like a vampire, actually. Dark, sensuous, dangerous.

Pausing at the car's door, he put his hand inside his jacket to get his keys—

And turned around to face Xcor with a gun. "Do you honestly think I don't know you're watching me?"

That pronunciation was so old-world and so very thick, the accent turning the words into practically a foreign language—or what would have been one if Xcor wasn't so intimately familiar with the original dialect.

Where were his *fucking* soldiers?

As Xcor stepped out, he had an autoloader of his own, and it was not without satisfaction that he watched the other male recoil slightly as recognition dawned.

"Did you expect a Brother, mayhap?" Xcor drawled.

Assail did not lower his muzzle. "My business is my own. You have no right to shadow me."

"My business is whatever I determine it to be."

"Your ways will not work here."

"And what 'ways' are those?"

"There are laws here."

"So I have heard. And I am fairly confident you are breaking several in your endeavors."

"I refer not to human ones." As if those were entirely irrelevant—and at least on that they could agree. "The Old Law provides—"

"We're in the New World, Assail. New rules."

"According to whom?"

"Me."

The male narrowed his eyes. "O'erstepping already?"

"Your conclusion is your own."

"Then I shall let it stand. And I shall take my leave of you now—unless you have plans to shoot me. In which case, I shall take you with me." He lifted up his other hand. In it was a small black handset. "Just so we're clear, the bomb that is wired to the undercarriage of my car will go off if my thumb contracts—which is precisely the kind of autonomic jerk that will occur if you put a bullet in my chest or my back. Oh, and mayhap I should mention that the explosion has a radius that more than includes where you are, and the detonation is so efficient, you will not be able to dematerialize out of the zone fast enough."

Xcor laughed with genuine respect. "You know what they say about suicides, don't you. No Fade for them."

"It's not suicide if you shoot me first. Self-defense."

"And you're willing to test that out?"

"If you are."

The male appeared utterly unconcerned with the choice, at peace with living or dying, uncaring of the violence and pain—and yet not unplugged, either.

He would have made an exceptional soldier, Xcor thought. If he hadn't been castrated by his mommy.

"So your solution," Xcor murmured, "is mutual self-destruction."

"What is it going to be?"

If Xcor had had his backup in place, there would have been a better way to handle this. But no, the bastards were nowhere around. And it was a fundamental tenet of conflict that if you were facing a well-matched enemy, who was well-provisioned and well-couraged, then you did not engage—you retreated, remarshaled, and lived to fight under circumstances more favorable to your own victory.

Besides, Assail had to be kept alive long enough so that the king could come to see him.

None of this sat well, however. And Xcor's mood, already dark to begin with, went utterly black.

He didn't say anything further. He simply dematerialized to another alley about half a mile away, letting his departure speak for itself.

As he re-formed by a shut-up newsstand, he was furious with his soldiers, his ire from the confrontation with Assail transferred and magnified as he thought of his males.

Initiating a search of his own, he went from abandoned building to club to tattoo parlor to tenement until he found them at the skyscraper: As he took form, they were all there, loitering as if they had naught better to do.

Violence replaced the very veins in his body, threading throughout him—to the point where he began to feel the hum of insanity within the confines of his skull.

It was the blood hunger, of course. But the root cause did nothing to temper the emotions.

"Where the fuck were you?" he demanded, the wind ripping around his head.

"You told us to wait here—"

"I told you to come find me!"

Throe threw up his hands. "Goddamn it! We all need phones, not just—"

Xcor launched himself at the male, grabbing him by the coat and throwing him up against a steel door. "Watch. Your. Tone."

"I am right in this—"

"We are *not* having this discussion again."

Xcor shoved himself away and walked off from the male, his duster getting thrown to the side from the hot, gale force blowing o'er the city.

Throe, however, would not leave it alone. "We could have been where you wanted us to be. The Brotherhood has cell—"

He wheeled around. "Fuck the Brotherhood!"

"You'd have better luck doing that if we had methods of communication!"

"The Brotherhood are weak for their technological crutches!"

Throe shook his head, all aristocrat-who-knew-better. "No, they're in the future. And we can't compete with them if we're in the past."

Xcor curled his hands into fists. His father—rather, the Bloodletter—would have pushed the son of a bitch right off the side of the building for this insolence and insubordination. And Xcor did take a step forward toward the male.

Except no, he thought with cold logic. There was a more useful way to handle this.

"We go into the field. Now."

As he leveled his stare at Throe, there was one and only one acceptable response—and the others knew this, judging from the way they got their weapons out and readied themselves to engage the enemy.

And ah, yes, Throe, ever the dandy who appreciated social order, even in a military situations, naturally followed suit.

But then again, there were other reasons for him to follow orders over and above an affinity for consensus: It was that debt that he believed he

would be working off forever. It was his commitment to the other bastards, which had grown over time and was mutual—to a point.

And, of course, it was his dearest, departed sister, who was, in a way, still with him.

Well, she was more with Xcor in practicality.

Upon his nod, he and his soldiers traveled in sprays of loose molecules down into the system of alleys. As they went, Xcor recalled that night long ago when a fine gentlemale approached him in a dirty part of London for a deadly purpose.

The disposition of the request had been rather more involved than Throe had contemplated.

To get Xcor to kill the one who had defiled his sister had required much more than just the shillings in his pocket. It had required his whole life. And servicing the debt had turned him into something so much more than a member of the *glymera* who had happened to have a Brotherhood name: Throe had lived up to his blooded legacy, far surpassing any expectations.

Far surpassing *every* expectation: In truth, Xcor had struck the deal to use the male as an example of weakness to the others. Throe was supposed to have been a humiliated foil for the true soldiers, a downtrodden, whining pussy who was broken over time and then made to serve them.

Not where they had ended up.

Down at ground level, the alley they re-formed in was rank and sweaty from the summer's heat, and as his soldiers fanned out behind him, they filled the confines from brick wall to brick wall.

They always hunted in a pack; unlike the Brotherhood, they stuck together.

So all of them saw what happened next.

Unsheathing one of his steel daggers, Xcor gripped the handle hard. Spun around to Throe.

And sliced the male in the gut.

Someone shouted. Several cursed. Throe curled around the wound—

Xcor caught the male's shoulder, retracted the weapon, and stabbed again.

The scent of fresh vampire blood was unmistakable.

There needed to be two sources, not just one, however.

Resheathing his dagger, he pushed Throe backward so that the male fell flat on the ground. Then he took one of Throe's blades from its holster and ran the sharp edge down the inside of his own forearm.

Wiping his wound all over Throe's upper body, he then forced the bloodied dagger into the soldier's hand. Then he crouched down, locking vicious eyes with the male.

"When the Brotherhood finds you, they will take you in and treat you—and you are going to find out where they live. You are going to tell them that I betrayed you and you want to fight with them. You will ingratiate yourself with them and find a way to infiltrate their domicile." He jabbed a finger in the male's face. "And because you're so fucking committed to the exchange of information, you're going to tell everything to me. You have twenty-four hours and then you and I shall reconvene—or the remains of your sweet sister are going to come to a disgraceful end."

Throe's eyes popped wide in his pale face.

"Yes, I have her." Xcor leaned down even farther, until they were nose-to-nose. "I have had her with us all along. So I say unto you, do *not* forget where your allegiances lie."

"You . . . bastard . . ."

"You got that right. You have until tomorrow. Top of the World, four a.m. Be there."

The male's eyes burned as they met his own, and the hatred in them was answer enough: Xcor had the ashes of the male's dead, and they both knew that if he was capable of sending his second in command into the belly of the beast, tossing those powdered remains into a garbage bin or a dirty toilet or the fry basket in a McDonald's was nothing special.

The threat of all that was, however, more than enough to cuff Throe.

And just as he had back in another era, so, too, would he now sacrifice himself for whom he had lost.

Xcor shot up and spun around.

His soldiers were standing shoulder-to-shoulder, a wall of menace that faced him squarely. But he was not worried about insurrection. They had each been raised, if one could call it that, by the Bloodletter—taught by that sadistic male the art of fighting, and of retribution. If they were surprised, it should have only been because Xcor had not done this sooner.

"Go back to camp for the rest of the night. I have a meeting to attend to—if I return to find any of you gone, I will hunt you down and not leave you injured. I will finish the job."

They left without looking at Throe—or him, for that matter.

Wise choice.

His anger was sharper than the blades he had just used.

*   *   *

As Throe was left alone in the alley, he positioned his hand flat against his abdominals, exerting pressure to reduce the blood loss.

Although his body was crippled with pain, his vision and hearing were preternaturally acute as they trained on his environment: The buildings arching above him were tall and without lights. The windows were narrow and had thick, rippled glass. The air smelled of cooking meat, as if he were not far from a restaurant that grilled a great deal. And off in the distance, he heard the horns of cars and the rush of the brakes on a bus and a woman laughing shrilly.

It was still early in the night.

Anyone could find him. Friend. Foe. *Lesser*. Brother.

At least Xcor had left him with his dagger in his hand.

With a curse, he rolled over onto his side and tried to push himself upright—

Didn't that solve the problem of everything registering so brightly and loudly. Upon a fresh onslaught of agony, the world receded, the bomb exploding in his gut of such magnitude that he wondered if he hadn't ruptured something.

Easing back to where he'd been, he thought Xcor might well be incorrect. Mayhap this alley was a coffin for him, rather than a serving plate for the Brotherhood.

Indeed, whilst he lay in his suffering, he realized he should have known better. He had grown to be at ease around that male, in the same way one who handled tigers might become lax: He'd taken for granted certain patterns of behavior, finding in them a misguided safety and predictability.

In reality, the danger had not dissipated, but grown.

And as it had been from the very first moment with Xcor, he remained trapped by the circumstances that had brought them together.

His sister. His beautiful, pure sister.

I have had her with us all along.

Throe moaned, but not from his wounds. How had Xcor gotten the ashes?

He had assumed his family had performed a proper ceremony and taken care of her as was appropriate. And how could he have known otherwise? He had not been permitted to see his mother or his brother once the deal had been struck, and his father had passed ten years before.

The unfairness was legion: In death, one would hope for her to have the peace she deserved. After all, the Fade had been created for souls as light and lovely as hers had been. But without having had the ceremony—

Dearest Virgin Scribe, she could have been denied entrance.

This was a new curse upon him. And her.

Staring up at the sky, of which he could see nearly naught, he thought of the Brotherhood. If they did find him before he died, and if they did take him in as Xcor assumed, he would do as he was required to. Unlike the others in the Band of Bastards, he had his own fealty, and it was not to the king or Xcor or his fellow soldiers—although in truth, it had begun to swing in the direction of those males.

No, his allegiance was to another . . . and Xcor knew that. Which was why that despot had made the effort long ago to gather some further assurance against Throe extricating—

At first he assumed the stench upon the warm breeze was from a garbage bin, the result of the wind switching direction and catching the odor of some abandoned food waste. But no, there was a telltale sweetness in the horrid bouquet.

Lifting his head, he looked down his body and across yards and yards of pavement. At the end of the alley, three *lessers* stepped into view.

Their laughter was his death knell, and yet he found himself smiling, even as flashes of dull light suggested that knives had been taken out.

The idea that fate had thwarted Xcor's plan seemed a perfectly acceptable note to go out on. Except his sister . . . how could he help her if he were dead?

As the slayers approached, he knew that what they were going to do to him would make the pain in his stomach seem like nothing more than a stubbed toe.

But he had to fight, and he would do so.

Until the last beat of his heart and the final exodus of his breath, he would fight with all that he was for the one thing he had left to live for.

TWENTY-SIX

Goddamn it, but Tohr noticed a difference in himself. Much as he hated to admit it, as he, John, and Qhuinn headed into their quarter of the downtown area, he was stronger, nimbler . . . clearheaded as a motherfucker. And his senses were back: No more wonky balance problems. His vision was spot-on. And his hearing was so good he could catch the scratching paws of rats as they scrambled for cover in the alleys.

You never realized how thick your fog was until it lifted.

Feeding was undeniably powerful, especially given his kind of work, and yup, he clearly needed a new profession. Accountant. Lint picker. Dog psychic. Anything where you sat on your ass all night long.

Then again, he couldn't *ahvenge* his Wellsie doing any of those. And after everything that had happened last night, from what had gone down in the pantry, to what he'd done to himself after he'd finally gone to bed, he felt like he had things to make up to her for.

Christ, the fact that No'One had given him such strength made him think that Wellsie's memory had been violated in some manner. Stained. Eroded.

When he'd fed from the Chosen Selena, it hadn't bothered him as much—maybe because he'd still been in shell-shock mode . . . more likely because he hadn't been aroused in the slightest, before, during or afterward.

Fucking hell, he was so ready for a fight tonight.

And fewer than three blocks later, he found what he was in search of: the scent of *lessers*.

As he and the boys fell into a silent jog, he didn't get out any of his weapons. With the mood he was rocking, hand-to-hand was what he was after, and if he was lucky—

The scream that cut through the dull sounds of distant traffic was not made by a female. Low and ragged, it could only have come out of a masculine throat.

Screw the quiet-approach routine.

Breaking into a sprint, he shot around the corner of an alley and ran smack into a wall of scents that he had no trouble processing: vampire blood—two kinds, both male. Slayer blood—one kind, rank and nasty.

Sure enough, up ahead, there was a male vampire down on the asphalt, two slayers up on their feet, and one *lesser* lurching around, having obviously just been nailed in the face. Which explained the holler.

That was all the intel he needed to go on.

Bolting forward, he sent himself flying and locked onto one of the *lessers*, catching the bastard around the neck with his arm and Pop-Tarting him into the air with a yank. As gravity took care of biz and slammed the enemy down onto the pavement faceup, the temptation was to kick the crap out of him—but with somebody injured in the middle of the alley, this was an emergency situation. He outed one of his daggers, nailed the fucker in the chest, and reestablished his fighting stance before the flash faded.

Over on the left, John was taking care of the *lesser* with the leak in his cheek, stabbing him back to his unholy maker. And Qhuinn had picked up on number three's option, swinging him around and throwing him headfirst at a wall.

With no more of the enemy to engage, at least for the moment, Tohr jogged over to the downed male.

"Throe," he breathed as he got a load of the guy.

The soldier was on his back, clutching his gut with the hand that wasn't on his dagger. Lot of blood. Lot of pain, given that tortured expression.

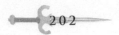

"John! Qhuinn!" Tohr called out. "Keep your eyes peeled for company of the Bastard variety."

As he got a whistle and a "Roger that" in reply, he got down on his haunches, and felt for a pulse. The flickering he found was not a good sign.

Easing back, he met a pair of sky blue eyes. "You gonna tell me who did this to you? Or let me play Q and A all by my lonesome."

Throe opened his mouth, coughed some blood, and closed his eyes.

"Okaaay, I'm going to guess your boss. How'm I doing?" Tohr lifted up the guy's hand and got a gander at the gut wound. Make that wound*s*. "You know, you never belonged with that motherfucker."

No response, but the guy wasn't out cold—his respiration was too quick, the panting indicating the kind of pain that came only with consciousness. Whatever, though. Xcor was the only explanation. The Band of Bastards always fought in a single squadron, and they never would have left a soldier behind—unless Xcor had ordered them to.

Besides, two kinds of vampire blood? Had to have been a dagger-to-dagger conflict.

"What happened? The pair of you get into it over what to have for Last Meal? Dress code? Or was it something more serious. Homer versus Fred Flintstone?"

He made quick work disarming the soldier, removing two good, serviceable guns, plenty of ammo, multiple knives, a length of choking wire, and—

"Watch it," he barked as Throe's arm came up. Catching it easily, he forced it back down with hardly any effort. "Quick moves are going to make me finish the job Xcor started."

"Shin blade . . ." came the croaked response.

Tohr popped up the pants, and, hello, more metal.

"At least he kept you well supplied," Tohr muttered as he got out his cell phone and dialed the compound.

"I have a situation," he said when V picked up.

After some quick back-and-forth with his brother, he and Vishous decided to bring the SOB to the training center. After all, the enemy of your enemy could be your friend . . . under the right circumstances. Besides, the *mhis* that surrounded the compound could scramble anything from GPS to Santa Claus. No way the Band of Bastards would find the guy, if this happened to be a setup.

Ten minutes later, Butch arrived with the Escalade.

Throe didn't have much of an opinion about being lifted up, carried over, and laid down in the backseat: The fucker was finally out cold. The good news was that it meant he wasn't an immediate threat—but it would be a bene to get him back alive.

Bargaining chip? Intel source? Footstool . . .

The repurposing options were endless.

"Just the kind of passenger I like," Butch said as he got behind the wheel again. "No chance he's going to try to backseat drive."

Tohr nodded. "I'm coming with you—"

The first gunshot that went off came from John's forty, and Tohr immediately went back into fight mode, throwing the Escalade's door shut, at the same time he went for his own weapon.

Second shot was from the enemy, whoever it was.

Lunging for cover behind the bulletproof SUV, Tohr nonetheless pounded on the quarter panel to get the cop to take the fuck off. Throe was too valuable to lose over something as ho-hum as a squadron of *lessers*. Worse, it could be the Bastards.

As the brother hit the gas, Tohr was left with his ass in the breeze, but he took care of that quick, ducking into a roll, becoming a tight, moving target that would be harder to hit.

Bullets followed him, except the guy with the trigger finger didn't know how to lead prey—the pinging off the pavement closed in on him, but not quick enough. And as he came up to a Dumpster, he tore behind the thing, prepared to return fire, as soon as he knew where his boys were.

Silence in the alley—

No, that wasn't quite right.

Dripping, like something was leaking out of the iron belly of the massive trash bin, made him frown and take a quick look down.

It wasn't the Dumpster.

Shit. He'd been hit.

Like a computer running a scan, he went into his body and identified the sources of the damage. Torso, left side, at the ribs. Upper arm, underside, four inches below his pit. And . . . that was about it.

He hadn't even felt the hits, and he wasn't drained by them, not by the pain or the blood loss. Goddamn feeding—it was like pouring jet fuel in your tank. And of course, it helped that the bullets hadn't caught anything important—they were surface grazes only.

Putting his head out around the Dumpster, he couldn't see anyone in the alley, but he could sense slayers all around, taking cover. At least he

didn't smell any fresh blood other than his own. So John and Qhuinn were okay, thank God.

The lull that followed got on his nerves.

Especially as it persisted.

Man, someone had to kick this fight into high gear again—Butch was heading back with a ticking time bomb in his cargo hold, and Tohr wanted to be there when the brother got to the compound.

More of the *Jeopardy!* theme.

From out of nowhere, that god-awful scene from the butler's pantry hit him again, his hunger and No'One's struggles and his body's reaction ripping through him—

A great clawing anger bit him in the ass, ruining his concentration, pulling him out of the fight—and putting him exactly where he didn't want to be.

As his brain scrambled and his chest burned, he wanted to scream.

Instead, he chose another way to force his mind somewhere else.

Putting both guns up in front of him, he jumped out from behind the Dumpster.

Talk about a lightning rod. Triggers were pulled. Lead went flying. And he was the target.

As his shoulder kicked back, he knew he was struck again, but he didn't pay any attention. Zeroing in on the source, he discharged both semis at the dark corner, squeezing off round after round as he walked forward.

Someone was yelling but he couldn't hear it—didn't hear it.

He was on autopilot.

He was . . . invincible.

When the call came in to the medical staff, No'One was in the training center's main exam room, delivering a stack of freshly folded scrubs that were straight from the dryer and still a little warm.

Over at the desk, Doc Jane leaned into her phone. "He's what? Can you repeat that? Who? And you're bringing him *here?*"

At that moment, the door to the outside corridor burst wide and No'One took an involuntary step back. The Brothers Vishous and Rhage filled the room as they barged in—and the fighters were grim, their eyes darkened, their brows down, their bodies tight.

There were daggers in their right hands.

"Wait, yes, they're here. What's your ETA? Okay, yup, we'll be ready for him." Jane hung up and looked over at the males. "Guess you guys are in charge of security."

"Damn straight." Vishous nodded at the operating table. "So I can't assist you."

"Because you're going to have a knife to the throat of my patient."

"You got it. Where's Ehlena?"

Conversation bloomed as Doc Jane began gathering equipment and staff, and in the chaos that followed, No'One prayed nobody noticed her. Who was being brought in—

As if Vishous read her mind, he looked in her direction. "All nonessential personnel have to leave the training compound—"

The desk phone went off again with a shrill sound, and the healer Jane put it up to her ear once more. "Hello? Qhuinn? What is— What? He did *what*?" The female's eyes shot to her mate, her cheeks going pale. "Tell me how bad? And he needs transport? Do you have— Thank God. Yeah, I'll take care of it."

She hung up and spoke in a hollow voice. "Tohr is hit. Multiple times. Manny!" she called out. "We've got another incoming!"

Tohrment?

Vishous cursed. "If Throe put even one slug into him—"

"He walked into gunfire," Jane cut in.

Everyone froze.

As No'One threw a hand out to the wall to steady herself, Rhage said softly, "Excuse me?"

"I don't know much more than that. Qhuinn just said that he stepped out from under cover, put up two forties, and just . . . walked forward into a spray of gunfire."

The other doctor, Manuel, came flying in from next door. "Who we got now?"

There was a lot more conversation at that point, deep voices mixing with the female's higher tone. Ehlena, the nurse, arrived. Two more Brothers.

No'One sank farther back into the corner by the supply cabinet, staying out of the way as she stared at the floor and prayed. When a pair of huge black boots intruded upon her line of vision, she just shook her head, knowing what would be said to her.

"You need to go."

Vishous's voice was steady and sure. Almost kind, which was a new one.

Lifting her chin, she met icy, diamond eyes. "Verily, you will have to kill me and drag my body out of here if you wish me to leave."

The Brother frowned. "Look, we're bringing in a dangerous—"

A sudden, subtle growling appeared to surprise the male. Silly, she thought, considering he was making the—

No. He was not.

She was. That warning was rising up out of her own chest, breaching her own lips.

Cutting the sound off, she pronounced, "I shall stay. Which room are you treating him in?"

V blinked, as if he were dumbfounded and unfamiliar with the sensation. After a moment, he looked over his shoulder at his mate. "Ah, Jane— where are you working on Tohr?"

"Right here. Throe's going into our second OR—fewer doors, so there's less of an escape risk."

The Brother turned away and walked off, but it was just to get a stool and bring it over to her. "This is in case you get tired of standing."

Then he left her be.

Dearest Virgin Scribe, who walked into enemy fire unprotected? she wondered.

The answer, when it came to her, made her gut seize up: someone who wanted to be killed in the line of duty. That was who.

Mayhap it would be better if Layla fed him. Less complicated—no. Not less so. The Chosen was incredibly beautiful, without a deformity of any sort. Yes, he had stated that he wanted no one in a sexual manner, but a male's resolve could be sorely tested by a female who looked like that. And any such response would kill him.

No'One was better for him.

Yes, that was right. She would handle his needs.

As she continued to justify things to herself, the fact that the idea of him at the fair Chosen's throat made her curiously violent was nothing she wanted to examine too closely.

TWENTY-SEVEN

Throe came awake in a void. He had no sight, no hearing, and no feeling in his body, as if the surrounding darkness had claimed him in his entirety.

Ah, so this was *Dhund*, he thought. The opposite of the illuminated Fade. The shadowy place where those who had sinned upon the earth were locked for eternity.

This was the Omega's hell, and indeed, it was hot.

His belly was on fire—

"No, you're wrong. That *lesser* was shot from above, too. Someone else was at the scene."

Throe's senses came quickly upon him, ushering away the void sure as sunrise over the landscape—but he was careful not to change his breathing or move: That male was not one of his fellow soldiers.

And neither was the second who spoke: "What are you talking about?"

"When I went over to stab him back to the Omega, he was riddled with bullets, some of which could only have been discharged from a van-

tage point above him. I'm telling you, the top of his skull, his shoulders, that shit was a mess."

"Any of our boys up there?"

"Not that I'm aware of."

A third voice said, "Nope. We were all at ground level."

"Someone else took the fucker out. Tohr put some lead into him, sure, but that wasn't all—"

"Shut it. Our guest's come around."

With the ruse over, Throe opened his eyes. Ah, yes. This was not *Dhund*—but damn close to it: The whole of the Black Dagger Brotherhood lined the walls of the room he was in, the males staring at him with aggression in their marrow. And that was not all. There were some others with them, soldiers, clearly . . . as well as that female, the one who had killed the Bloodletter.

As well as the great Blind King.

Throe focused on Wrath. The male had on dark spectacles, but even so, the consuming stare behind those lenses felt very obvious. Indeed, the most important vampire on the planet was as he had always been, a massive fighter, with the cunning of a master strategist, the expression of an executioner, and a body strong enough to follow through on both of those accounts.

Aptly named, he was.

And Xcor had chosen a very, very dangerous adversary.

The king stepped up to the bedside. "My surgeons saved your life."

"I do not doubt it," Throe rasped out. Dearest Virgin Scribe, his throat was sore.

"So the way I look at it, under normal circumstances, a male of worth would owe me. But given who you're in bed with, the normal rules don't apply."

Throe swallowed a couple of times. "My first allegiance, my only . . . one . . . is to my family—"

"Some fucking family," the Brother Vishous muttered.

"My blooded relations, that is. My . . . beloved sister—"

"I thought she was dead."

Throe glared at the fighter. "She is."

The king stepped in between the pair of them. "Yada, yada, yada— here's the deal. You'll be released when you're well enough, free to go out and tell the world that me and my boys are as compassionate and fair as Mother fucking Teresa, in spite of who your boss is—"

"*Was.*"

"Whatever. Bottom line, you're welcome to stay in one piece—"

"Unless you pop shit," Vishous interjected.

The king glared at the Brother. "—as long as you act like a gentleman. We'll even get you someone to feed from. The sooner you're out of here, the better."

"And if I wanted to battle alongside you?"

Vishous spit on the floor. "We don't take traitors—"

Wrath's eyes whipped around. "V. Shut your motherfucking face. Or you're out in the hall."

Vishous, son of the Bloodletter, was not the kind of male anyone addressed like that. Except, apparently, for Wrath. In this case, the Brother with the tattoos on his face and the perverted reputation and the hand of death did exactly what he was told. He shut the fuck up.

Which said volumes about Wrath. Did it not.

The king turned back. "But I wouldn't mind knowing who cut you."

"Xcor."

Wrath's nostrils flared. "And he left you for dead?"

"Aye." On some level, he still couldn't believe it. Which marked him as stupid. "Aye . . . he did."

"Is that the reason your own blood is your allegiance now?"

"No. That has e'er been true."

Wrath nodded and crossed his arms over his chest. "You tell the truth."

"Always."

"Well, good thing you quit them now, son. The Band of Bastards is kicking at a hornets' nest the likes of which they will not walk away from."

"Verily . . . there is nothing I can say that you do not already know."

Wrath laughed softly. "A diplomat."

Vishous cut in with, "Try dead animal—"

Wrath's hand shot up into the air, the black diamond of the king's ring flashing. "Somebody get that mouth out of this room. Or I'll do it."

"I'm fucking leaving."

After the Brother marched out, the king rubbed his forehead. "Okay. Enough with the talking. You look like shit—where's Layla?"

Throe began to shake his head. "I have no need for blood—"

"Bullshit. And you are not dying on our watch just so Xcor can accuse us of killing you. I'm not giving him that kind of weapon." As the king started for the door, Throe realized for the first time that there was a dog at the male's side—wearing a halter that Wrath grasped. Was he truly blind? "Needless to say, this is going to be witnessed— Oh, hey, Chosen."

Throe's entire brain shut down as a vision entered the room. An absolute . . . vision. Tall, and fair of hair and eye, dressed in a white robe, it was indeed a Chosen.

Such a beauty was she, he thought. A sunrise that lived and breathed . . . a miracle.

And she was not alone, as was appropriate for a gem such as herself. By her side, Phury, son of Ahgony, was a wall of protection, his face screwed down so tight, it appeared as if mayhap she was his? He even had a black dagger in his hand—although it was discreetly held by his thigh, undoubtedly so the female did not see it and grow alarmed.

"I'll leave you to this," Wrath said. "But if I were you, I'd watch yourself. My boys here, they're a little twitchy."

After the great Blind King left with the blond dog, Throe was alone with the Brothers, the soldiers . . . and that female.

As she came forward into the room, her smile was a wellspring of peace and femininity in the midst of the vile trappings of war and death, and if he hadn't been lying down, he'd have sunk to his knees in awe.

It had been so long since he had been 'round any female of worth. Verily, he had grown too used to the whores and the prostitutes, whom he treated like ladies out of habit, but not concern.

His eyes teared up.

She reminded him of who his sister should have been.

Phury stepped up in front of her, blocking the view as he leaned down and put his mouth right to Throe's ear. As he squeezed Throe's biceps until it screamed in pain, the Brother growled softly, "You get hard and I'll castrate you as soon as she leaves."

Well . . . if that wasn't crystal clear. And a quick glance around the room suggested that Phury wasn't the only one who would come after him. The other Brothers would fight for pieces of his dead carcass if he became aroused.

Straightening to his full height, Phury smiled at the female as if there was nothing of any concern going on. "This soldier is very grateful for the gift of your vein, Chosen. Aren't you."

The "asshole" went unsaid. And the grip that once again tightened on Throe's upper arm was just as hidden and emphatic.

"I am e'er grateful, your grace," he breathed.

At that, the Chosen smiled at Throe, stealing his breath. "If I may be in even a small way helpful to a male of worth such as yourself, I am blessed. There is no greater service to the race than fighting the enemy."

"I can think of at least one more," somebody said under their breath.

As Phury motioned her to come to the bedside, Throe could only stare up into her face, his heart struggling to decide whether to pound or stop altogether. And whilst he imagined what she could possibly taste like, he tried not to lick his lips—for surely that would fall under the prohibited-activities list. He also sternly reminded his sex to stay flaccid or lose its two stupid best mates.

"I am not worthy," he said softly to her.

"Damn fucking straight," someone growled.

The Chosen frowned over her shoulder. "Oh, but surely he is. Anyone who wields a dagger with honor against the *lessers* is worthy." She looked down at him again. "Sire, may I serve you now?"

Oh . . . damn.

Her words went straight to his cock: Right up the shaft, which thickened instantly, to the tip, which promptly stung with need.

Throe closed his eyes and prayed for strength. And bad aim for the Brothers. Neither of which would likely be granted—

Her wrist was close to his lips—he could smell it.

Eyes flaring open, he saw her fragile vein within striking distance—and, merciful Virgin Scribe save him, all he could think about was reaching out to her, caressing her smooth cheek—

A black blade forced his arm back down. "No touching," Phury said darkly.

Well . . . at least if that was all the Brother was worried about, obviously he had not caught on to the issue below the waist. And short of agreeing to have himself neutered, Throe would do anything to have this happen—so no touching was good.

No touching was fine with him. . . .

As Tohr lay in his bed, he came awake with the thought it was a little early to be sleeping. Shouldn't he be out fighting? Why was he—

"Get Layla in here stat," a male voice barked. "We can't operate until his blood pressure is up—"

Say what? Tohr wondered. Whose blood pressure was bad . . . ?

"She'll be there ASAP," came a far-off response.

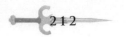

Were they talking about him? Nah, they couldn't be—

As he popped opened his eyes, the industrial chandelier hanging right over his face cleared things up fast. This wasn't his bedroom; this was the clinic in the training center. And they *were* talking about him.

Everything came back in a flash. Him stepping out from behind that Dumpster. His body getting drilled as he walked forward, opening fire. Him shooting until he stood over the slumped, stinking form of that slayer.

After that, he'd wobbled back and forth, like a stick only partially drilled into the ground.

Then it had been lights out.

With a groan, he went to push himself up, but his palm slipped on the padding of the gurney. Guess he was leaking—

Manello's handsome puss popped into his line of vision, replacing the bright-and-shiny of the light fixture. Wow—check out that expression. The bastard looked like someone had just gotten him tickets to Disneyland. Surprise!

"You shouldn't be conscious."

"That bad, huh."

"Maybe a little worse. No offense, but what the fuck were you thinking?" The good surgeon pivoted and jogged to the door, shoving his head out into the corridor. "We need Layla in here! Now!"

At that, there was some conversation, but he couldn't track any of it, and not because he was injured. In spite of all the owie-owie, his body had a huge opinion about who he was going to feed from—and as far as it was concerned, as lovely as the Chosen was, it was *not* going to be her.

And it was a shock to realize why.

He wanted No'One. Even though it wasn't fair—

"I shall do it. I shall take care of him."

At the sound of No'One's voice, Tohr gritted his teeth, and felt a surge go through him. Turning his head, he looked past the rolling tables of operating instruments . . . and there she was in the far corner, her hood in place, her body still, her hands churning under the robe's sleeves.

The instant he saw her, his fangs elongated, and his body filled out its own skin, the residual numbness receding and revealing all kinds of sensation: pain at the side of his neck, his ribs, and under his arm; tingling at the tips of his canines sure as if he had already struck; hunger in his gut— for her.

Starvation in his cock—for her.

Shit.

He quickly camo'd the arousal by yanking the surgical drape around and holding it to the front of his hips.

"Okay, you shouldn't be able to sit up," Manny muttered.

Was he? Oh, hey, check it . . . And as for the doctor's second dose of surprise? Nice guy, but he was being a dumb-ass human when it came to the feeding thing. With this kind of hunger for that particular female? Tohr was frickin' Superman, capable of bench-pressing a Hummer while he juggled Smart Cars with his free hand.

He was worried about No'One, though. Last time had been such an epic fail.

Except from across the room, she just nodded at him, as if she knew exactly what he was worried about, and was ready to follow through anyway.

For some reason, her courage made his eyes sting.

"Leave us," he told the surgeon without looking at the man. "And don't let anyone in until I call for you."

Cursing. Muttering. All of which he ignored. And as he heard the door finally shut, he took firm control of his instincts, the knowledge that he was alone with her tempering all that drive to feed: He was not going to hurt or scare her again. Period.

No'One's reedy voice cut through the silence. "You're bleeding so badly."

Oh, man, they must not have cleaned him up yet. "It looks worse than it is."

"Then you should be dead."

He laughed a little. Then laughed a little more—and blamed the ha-has on blood loss. 'Cuz none of this shit was funny.

As he rubbed his face, he hit a raw patch and had to lie back—which made him wonder whether he might be in trouble—and not the sexed-up variety. How many bullets were in him? How close had he come to dying?

No offense, but what the fuck were you thinking?

Shaking all that off, he extended his hand and beckoned her. As she closed in on him, her limp was pronounced, and, when she reached the table, she leaned her hip against the edge like maybe her leg was bothering her.

"Let me get you a chair," he said, making a move to get up.

Her delicate hand eased him back. "I'll do it."

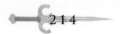

As he watched her limp across the way, it was obvious she was in pain. "How long have you been standing?"

"Awhile."

"You should have left."

She rolled the stool over and groaned as she took the weight off her feet. "Not until I knew you were home safe. They said . . . that you walked into the line of fire."

God, he wished he could see her eyes. "It's not the first time I've done something stupid."

Like that somehow made things better? Idiot.

"I do not want you to die," she whispered.

God. Damn. The heartfelt emotion in those words left him nonplussed.

As the silence ruled once again, he stared into the shadow created by the hood, thinking of that moment when he'd stepped out from behind that Dumpster. Then he went back farther into his memory. . . .

"You know what? I've been mad at you for years." As she appeared to recoil, he tempered his tone. "I just couldn't believe what you did to yourself. We'd come so far, the three of us, you, me, and Darius. We were a kind of family, and I think I've always felt like you betrayed us in a way. But now . . . after I've lost all I have . . . I understand the why. I truly do."

Her head dipped down. "Oh, Tohrment."

He reached out and covered her hand with his own. Except then he noticed his was bloody and stained, a horrific travesty against the purity of her skin.

When he went to pull away, she held on and kept them together.

He cleared his throat. "Yeah, I guess I understand why you did it. At that moment, you couldn't see anyone but yourself. It wasn't to hurt the other people around you—it was ending your own suffering because you simply couldn't fucking stand it another minute."

There was a long moment of quiet, and then she said quietly, "When you walked out into those bullets tonight, were you trying to . . ."

"That was just about the fighting."

"Was it?"

"Yeah. Only doing my job."

"Given the reactions of your Brothers, they appear to think that is not in the description of duties."

Shifting his eyes upward, he caught the reflection of them in the stainless-steel contours of the operating chandelier, him laid out and leaking, her curled in and hooded. Their forms and figures were distorted, bent, twisted out of shape because of the uneven reflecting surface, but the image was accurate in more ways than one: Their destinies had been such as to make them both grotesque.

Strangely, their two hands clasped were the clearest of all, that image being caught on a straightaway.

"I hated what I did to you last night," he blurted.

"I know. But that is no reason to kill yourself."

True. He had more than enough cause for that from elsewhere.

Abruptly, No'One took her hood off, and he instantly zeroed in on her throat.

Shit, he wanted that vein, the one that ran up so close to the surface.

Chat time was over. The hunger was back, and it wasn't just about biology. He wanted to be at her flesh again, drinking not simply to cure his wounds, but because he liked the taste of her, and the feel of her fine skin at his mouth, and the way his fangs punctured in deep and let him take part of her into him.

Okay, maybe he'd fibbed a little about that bullet shower. He absolutely had hated hurting her—but that wasn't the only reason why he'd walked into all that lead. The truth was, she was calling something out of him, some kind of emotion, and those feelings were starting to turn gears inside of him that were rusted and cranky from lack of use.

It terrified him. *She* terrified him.

And yet, looking at her strained face right now, he was glad he'd come back from that alley alive. "I'm happy I'm still here."

The breath she exhaled was relief made manifest. "Your presence eases many, and you are important in this world. You matter a great deal."

He laughed awkwardly. "You overestimate me."

"You underestimate yourself."

"Ditto," he whispered.

"I'm sorry?"

"You know exactly what I mean." He punctuated that with a squeeze of her hand, and when she didn't reply, he said, "I'm glad you're here."

"I'm glad *you* are here. It's a miracle."

Yeah, she was probably right. He had no idea how he'd gotten out of that one alive. He hadn't been wearing a vest.

Maybe his luck was changing.

Little late in the game, unfortunately.

Staring up at her, he took in her lovely features, from her dove gray

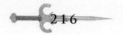

eyes to her pink lips . . . to the elegant column of her throat and the pulse that beat beneath her precious skin.

Abruptly, her gaze went to his mouth. "Yes," she said. "I will feed you now."

Heat and raw power resurged in his body, jerking his hips up and over-solving that blood pressure problem of the surgeon's. But all the off-the-chain was still a no-go. The part of him that wanted things from her, things that she wasn't going to be comfortable giving anybody . . . things that were all about what he had done in the shower and in his bed alone during the day . . . was not getting airtime here.

Besides, his mind and his heart weren't interested in any of that shit, and this was another reason she was perfect for him. Layla might well take his body up on the arousal; No'One never would. And there were worse betrayals to his *shellan* than wanting the unattainable. At least with No'One, and thanks to his self-control, those impulses would forever be just a fantasy, a harmless, unrealized, masturbation fantasy that had no more substance in his real life than porn on the Internet—

God help you, a small voice pointed out, if she ever wants you back.

Too right. But as she appeared to hesitate, he was certain that was never going to happen.

In a guttural voice, he told her, "I'm in no hurry. And know this, the lights will stay on this time . . . and I will take from your wrist only as much as you care to give me."

TWENTY-EIGHT

As No'One sat beside Tohrment, she heard herself say once again, "Yes . . ."

Dearest Virgin Scribe, something had changed between them. In the thick, charged air that separated their bodies, some kind of heat was sparking, the current of electricity warming her skin from the inside out.

This was totally different than when she had been in the dark of the pantry with him, struggling against the past's perennial stranglehold.

Tohrment cursed softly. "Shit, I should have them clean me up first."

As if he were naught but a countertop that had been spilled upon, or a bolt of cloth that required laundering.

She frowned. "I care not what you look like. You breathe and your heart beats—that is all that matters to me."

"You have very low standards for males."

"I have no standard for males. For you, however, if there is health and safety, I am at peace."

"God damn," he said softly. "I really don't get it . . . but I believe you."

" 'Tis the truth."

Staring at their entwined hands, she thought about what he had said . . . about the past, about the cobbled-together family the three of them had formed in the Old Country.

About how she had shattered that for them all, including her daughter.

Indeed, she had always viewed the resurrection she had been given as an opportunity for penance for taking her own life, but yes, she realized once again, now there was another purpose to serve.

She had hurt this male, but she had also been granted the opportunity to help him.

It was the Scribe Virgin's fundamental tenet at work: all things coming full circle so that balance could be retained.

Assuming she *could* help him, that was.

With a sense of purpose, she looked down his body—or what she could see of it under the surgical sheeting. His chest was padded with muscle, a star-shaped scar marking one pectoral, and his abdomen was ribbed with strength. All along, there were a number of bruises that she didn't want to guess the causes of, and small round holes that scared her.

But what was happening below his waist captured her eyes. He was holding the blue sheeting in place over his hips as if hiding something, his forearm and hand tightening up as she stared.

"Don't worry about that," he said in a guttural voice.

He was aroused, she thought.

"No'One, come on—meet my eyes. Don't look down there."

The temperature in the room shot up even higher, to the point where she considered taking off her robing. And abruptly, as if he could read her mind, his pelvis rolled in an arch that was . . . sensuous.

"Oh, fuck—No'One, you gotta not go there."

A strange anticipation threaded through her veins, making her head buzz and her stomach feel vaguely sick. And yet she had no cognition of not feeding him; if anything, she wanted his mouth on her even more.

With that thought, she brought her wrist up and over his lips.

His hiss was quick, the bite was fast, the pain sweet as the prick of a hundred tiny needles. And then . . . he was sucking, his warm, wet mouth fitting a seal against her flesh and pulling at her rhythmically—

He moaned. Deep in his throat, he moaned in pleasure, and as he did, her heart jumped in her chest and then beat even faster. More of that heat, insidious and suffusing, bloomed on the underside of her skin, her mind growing woolly and her body getting languid.

As if Tohrment sensed the changed in her, he moaned again, his head craning, his chest rising, his eyes rolling back into his head. And then he began making mewing noises, the supplication fitting not at all with his tremendous size, the plaintive sounds rising repeatedly up from his throat, alternating with his swallows.

With the lights on, and her arm her own to retract, her panic flared only briefly, before being dismissed wholly. There was just too much of Tohrment in this for her to mistake him for anyone else, and the well-lit room they were in had nothing in common with that root cellar: All was bright and clean, and this male at her vein . . . was very much vampire and nothing even remotely *symphath*.

The more at ease she grew, the more aware she became.

His hips were moving all the while now.

Under the sheeting she would soon be washing, beneath the cup of what was now both of his palms, his pelvis was gyrating. And every time it did, his abdominals tightened and his torso arched . . . and those noises grew a little louder.

He was deeply aroused.

Even terribly injured, his body was ready for mating—desperate for it, if the way he moved was any indication. . . .

At first, she didn't understand the tingling that came over her, numbing her up and hypersensitizing her at the same time. Mayhap it was the fact that she had given him two feedings in less than a day . . . But no. As Tohrment's hands tightened anew at the front of his hips, as he gripped himself even harder through the sheeting, it was clear his sex had cried out for attention and he had been forced to give it some—

The sparkling returned even more keenly as she realized he was rubbing himself.

No'One's own lips parted as breathing became difficult, and under her robing, the warmth cranked up even higher and focused in her lower gut.

Dearest Virgin Scribe, she was . . . aroused. For the first time in her life.

As if he could read her mind, his eyes shot to hers. Confusion was in them. And an eerie darkness that seemed to be near to fear. But there was also more of that heat, so much more . . .

Whilst she met his glowing stare, one of his hands unlatched from down below and traveled up his chest. When he touched her forearm, it was not to keep her in place or restrain her, but to stroke her flesh softly, slowly.

Breathing became impossible.

And she did not care.

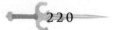

His fingers running lightly over her skin were intoxicating, drawing her closer to this flame that she could not see. Closing her eyes, she allowed herself to fly far away from any worries or preoccupations, until she knew nothing but the sensations in her body.

Indeed, as she fed him, she was fed herself, a part of her innermost soul nourished for the first time. . . .

Eventually she heard licking and realized he was done.

She wanted to tell him to continue.

To beg him, was more like it.

Raising heavy lids, she could not focus her eyes, and that seemed only appropriate. The world was fuzzy and so was she . . . boneless and fuzzy, with honey in her veins and cotton batting in her brain.

Tohrment was anything but, however.

He seemed sharp as a blade, his muscles straining now not just in his hips but his whole body, from his biceps to his abdominals—even his feet beneath the sheeting stood up straight.

His other hand, the one that had been stroking her, returned to below his waist. "I think you'd better go."

His voice was so deep, she frowned as she tried to decipher the words. "Have I done something wrong?"

"No, but I'm about to." He grit his white teeth as his hips moved up and back under the sheet. "I have to . . . *Fuck.*"

And that was when his meaning became clear.

"No'One, please . . . I've got to . . . I can't keep it back much longer. . . ."

His massive body was so beautiful in this particular agony: Even though he was bloodied and wounded and bruised, there was something undeniably sexual about the way he ground his teeth and arched upon the table.

For a moment, her nightmare with the *symphath* threatened to come back, terror trying to gain traction at the edge of her consciousness. But then Tohrment moaned and bit down on his lower lip, those long white canines tearing into the soft pink flesh.

"I do not want to go," she said roughly.

His face squeezed up tight, another curse breaching his lips. "You stay and you're going to have a hell of a show."

"So . . . show me."

That got his attention, his eyes snapping back to hers, his body freezing. As he blinked, he did not otherwise move.

In a harsh tone, he blurted, "I'm going to make myself come. Do you know what that means? Orgasm?"

Thank the Virgin Scribe for the chair, No'One thought. Because between that graveled voice, and his heady scent, and the erotic way he was holding on to himself, even her good leg had no strength to support what little weight she had.

"No'One, do you understand?"

The part of her that had woken up was what answered: "Yes. I do. And I want to watch."

He shook his head as if he intended to argue. Except then he said no more.

"Ease yourself, warrior," she told him.

"Oh, Jesus . . ."

"Now."

As she commanded him, a thrall appeared to come over him: Below his waist, under the sheeting, one of his knees came up toward his body, his thighs splitting wide as his grip secured that vital place that defined him as uniquely male.

What happened next defied description. He worked himself against the balled sheeting, rolling his hips, pushing down, his body gathering momentum—

Oh, the sounds: from the rasp of his breath to his moans to the squeak from under the table.

This was the male animal in the throes of passion.

And there was no going back.

For either of them.

Faster. Greater pressure with his hands, until his chest stood out, the anatomy appearing carved, rather than made of flesh. And then he cursed in an explosion of breath and jerked up against the grasp he had on his sex. His spasms had her clutching her own chest and breathing in a pant, as if what was happening to him was replicated within her own form. Indeed, what miracle was this? Tohrment appeared to be in pain, and yet showed no evidence of wanting what racked him to end—if anything, he drew it out, shifting his hips ever more.

Until it was done.

In the aftermath, the only sound in the room was their breathing, at first quite loud, then growing quieter and quieter, until they were still.

As her heightened senses receded, her mind came forth, and the same seemed to be true for him. Releasing his hands from below his

waist, he revealed a wetness on the sheeting that had not been there before.

"Are you okay?" he said roughly.

She opened her mouth. Her voice lost, all she could do was nod.

"You sure about that?"

It was so hard to put into words what she was feeling. She was not
threatened, to be sure. But she was also not . . . right.

She was spinning and antsy. Inside her head. Outside of it. "I am
so . . . confused."

"What about?"

The bullet wounds in his flesh had her shaking her head. This was not
the time to talk. "Let me get the healers. You need to be attended to."

"You're more important than that. Are you all right?"

Given the stubborn line of his jaw, it was clear he wasn't budging. And
no doubt if she left to get the surgeon, he would follow her and leave a trail
of blood he did not have to spare.

She shrugged. "I just never expected to . . ."

As she went no further, the realities of their situation returned to her.
That arousal, that satisfaction that he'd found . . . it had been about his
shellan, hadn't it. She had told him that Wellesandra was welcome between
them, and he'd made it amply clear that he wanted no one but that female:
Whilst he had appeared to be focusing on her, in all likelihood he had
merely projected the image of someone else.

It had had nothing to do with her.

Which really shouldn't have bothered her. It was, after all, exactly
what she had told him she wanted.

So why did she feel so curiously deflated?

"I am fine." She met him in the eye. "I swear to it. Now, may I please
get the healers? I will take no true full breath until they care for you."

His eyes narrowed. But then he nodded. "Okay."

She smiled stiffly and turned away.

Just as she got to the door, he said, "No'One."

"Yes?"

"I want to return the favor to you."

Well, didn't that stop the female in her tracks.

Kind of made Tohr's heart freeze, as well.

As No'One stood at the door with her back to him, he couldn't believe what had come out of his mouth—but it was the goddamned truth, and he was determined to follow through on it.

"I know you go to the Sanctuary to take care of your blood needs," he said, "but that can't be enough. Not tonight. I've taken so much from you in the last twenty-four hours."

When she didn't reply, he caught her scent and had to tamp down an answering growl in his throat. He wasn't sure she knew it in her mind, but her body was clear: It wanted what he could provide to her.

Badly.

Except . . . God, what was he getting into? He was going to feed someone other than his Wellsie?

God help you if she ever wanted you back. . . .

No, no, noooooo, this wasn't about sex. It was about him taking care of her after she had allowed him at her vein. It was just blood—which was unsettling enough, fuck him very much.

You sure about that, the small voice shot back.

Just as he was about to fuck-off himself again, Lassiter's *fakakta* lecture came back to him: You *are alive.* She *is not. And your hanging on to the past is putting you both in an In Between.*

Tohr cleared his throat. "I mean it. I want to be there for you now. It's simple biology—"

Oh, really? that voice demanded.

Fuck off—

"Excuse me?" she said, shooting a stare over her shoulder, her brows to the ceiling.

Great, so he wasn't just talking to himself.

"Look," he said, "come to me after they're done patching me up. I'll be in my room right afterward."

"You may be more injured than you know."

"Nah, I've been here before. Lots of times."

She lifted the hood into place. "You need your strength to recover."

"You've given me more than enough for the two of us. Come with me—I mean—" Shit. Fuck. "Come *to* me."

There was a long pause. "I'll get the healer."

As No'One left, he let his head fall back—and as it slammed into the gurney's hard pillow, the thud reverberated through his skull. The sting felt good. So he did it again.

Manello strode into the exam room. "You two finished in here?"

The guy's tone was snark-free, something Tohr would have appreciated more if it didn't just dawn on him that he'd come all over the sheet.

"Okay, let's do this, big man." The surgeon snapped on a pair of latex specials. "I took X-rays while you were out cold, and I'm happy to report you only have two slugs in you. Chest and shoulder. So I'm going to go in, perform a lead-ectomy, and then stitch up the other sets of entrance and exit wounds. Piece of cake."

"I need to clean up first."

"That's my job, and trust me, I got enough distilled water to hose all that dried blood off and still wash a car afterward."

"Yeah . . . um . . . I'm not talking about that kind of mess."

Cue the screeching tires. As Manello's expression went from relaxed to resolutely professional, it was obvious that the message had been received.

"Sounds good. How about I get you another sheet?"

"Yeah. Thanks." Fucking hell. He was blushing. Either that or he'd been shot in the face, too, and was only just now noticing.

As a clean sheet awkwardly changed hands, neither one looked at the other—and then Manello got studiously busy over at a stainless-steel rolling table, checking the needles and thread and scissors and sterile packs that had been laid out.

Amazing how sex could turn two fully grown adult males into teenagers.

Tohr tidied himself up and told his hard-on to can it. Unfortunately, his cock seemed to be speaking another language, because the thing stayed hard as a crowbar. Maybe it was deaf?

He was kind of done throwing fists at it.

Dumping the dirty cloth on the floor, he covered himself with the fresh one. "I'm, ah, ready."

The good news was that at least he hadn't been hit in the thigh, so Manello was going to stay above the waist.

"Good," the doc said as he came back over. "Now, I think we can handle this all locally, and the fewer drugs the better. So I'd like to take a shot at not putting you out cold, okay?"

"I don't care, Doc. You just do you."

"I like your attitude. And we're going to start with this one on your upper chest. This may sting as I numb you up—"

"*Fuuuuck.*"

"Sorry about that."

"Nothing you can do." Well, other than taking a spike and nailing him to the table.

As Manello settled into his work, Tohr closed his eyes and thought of No'One. "I don't have to stay down here after this, do I?"

"If you were a human? Absolutely. But this shit's already healing up. Goddamn, you guys are amazing."

"So I can go right back to the mansion."

"Well, yeah . . . eventually." There was a resounding *bonk!*—as if the guy had dropped one of the lead slugs on the tray. "I think Mary wanted to check in with you first."

"Why?"

"She just wants to, you know, check in."

Tohr focused a glare on the guy. "Why."

"Do you realize how lucky you are that you didn't end up—"

"I don't need to 'talk' to her, if that's what you're getting at."

"Look, I'm not going to get in the middle of this."

"I'm fine—"

"You got yourself shot up tonight."

"Hazard of the job—"

"Bullshit. You are not 'fine,' and you do need to 'talk' to someone. Asshole." On the *fine* and the *talk*, the human gestured with his hands, doing air quotes in spite of the fact that his fingers were busy holding instruments.

Tohr shut his eyes in frustration. "Look, I'll follow up with Mary when I can . . . but right after this, I'm busy."

In reply, the surgeon covered all kinds of mental health territory, most of which was punctuated by f-bombs.

Not Tohr's problem, though.

TWENTY-NINE

Over to the east, in the thick of Caldwell's farm country, Zypher sat in silence upon his top bunk. He was far from alone in the Band of Bastards' basement accommodations. The three cousins were with him, each as capable of conversation as he was, but likewise not inclined to indulge.

There was no real movement among them. No sounds except for the whispers of his whittling knife as he cleaved it into soft wood again and again.

No one was sleeping.

Whilst dawn settled over the land and claimed its illuminative dominion, their thoughts were similarly subsumed, the weight of the actions of their leader settling heavily upon them.

It was not at all unfathomable that Xcor had so brutally stabbed Throe for his insubordination. It was not unbelievable that he had then ordered the rest of them away such that their fellow soldier was left for dead for the enemy.

And yet he somehow could not understand it. And clearly, neither could the others.

Throe had always been the glue that bound, a male of worth with more honor than the rest of them had put together . . . as well as a way with logic that had landed him in the role of facilitator with Xcor: Throe was typically on the front lines with their cold, calculating leader, the only voice that could get through to the male—well, usually. He'd also been the translator between all of them and the rest of the world, the one with Internet access who had found this house and was trying to get them females of the race to feed from, the one who coordinated money and servants.

He was right about the technology, too.

Except Xcor had snapped, and now . . . if slayers hadn't gotten Throe in that alley, the Brothers might well have killed him just on principle.

Then again, there was going to be a price on all of their heads soon. It was only a matter of time. . . .

Examining his carving, he thought it was a piece of crap, no more obviously a bird than it had been as a thick maple stick. Indeed, he had no artistry in his hands, his eyes, or his heart. This was just a way to pass the time whilst he was busy not sleeping.

Indeed, he wished there was a female around. Fucking was his best talent, and he'd been oft known to pass hours between the legs of a maid with great effect.

He could certainly use the distraction.

Tossing the hunk of wood to the foot of his bunk, he examined his blade. So pure and sharp, capable of so much more than poorly rendering a wretched swallow.

He hadn't liked Throe at all at first. The male had come to the Band of Bastards on a rainy evening, and he'd looked as out of place as he was: a dear boy among death dealers, standing outside a hovel that no doubt he wouldn't have stabled a horse in.

From his top hat to his perfectly buffed-up shoes, they had all despised every inch of him.

And then Xcor had had them draw straws to find out who would beat him down first. Zypher had won, and had smiled as he'd cracked his knuckles and gotten ready to hand the male's masculinity to his royal self on a silver plate.

Throe had flailed at the first couple of punches that had come at him, providing no proper defense and absorbing the blows in his head and gut. But sooner than was at all expected, something had clicked within him—his stance had changed for no good reason, his fists coming up, his body filling out those fancy clothes in an altogether different way.

The turnabout had been . . . nothing short of extraordinary.

Zypher had kept fighting the male, throwing out combinations of punches that were abruptly parried . . . and, after a bit, returned, until he himself had had to step up his efforts.

That dandy had been learning, right then and there, even as his fine clothes had gotten shredded and torn, even as he had become soaked by the rain and his own blood.

During that very first fight, and at each succeeding one, he had demonstrated an uncanny ability to assimilate. Between the initial fist that had been thrown at him, to the moment when he had finally landed on his ass with exhaustion, he had evolved more as a fighter than soldiers who had spent years in the Bloodletter's war camp.

They had all stood around Throe as he sat there in the mud, his chest heaving, his pretty face bruised, his top hat long lost.

Standing over the male, Zypher had spit the blood out of his mouth . . . and then he'd leaned down and offered his palm. The dandy had still had much to prove—but he'd been no lackey during that fight.

In fact, no lackey had he e'er proved to be.

'Twas strange to feel any allegiance to someone of the aristocracy. But Throe had earned the respect time and time again. And he had long been one of them now—although that may well have ended on several levels tonight.

Zypher turned his knife back and forth, the candlelight on its blade a beautiful thing, as lovely as when it fell upon the skin of a female's inner thigh.

Xcor had used one of these for what it was intended—to cut, to maul, to kill—but his target? Considering all that Throe did for them, their leader, in his rage, had done more harm than good. Indeed, Xcor's blood hunger was making him mercurial. And with a mind like his and plans such as he had, that was not a good combination—

The back of Zypher's neck tickled, one of the spiders that lived with them eight-legging across his nape. Reaching around with a curse, he scrubbed at his flesh, destroying the thing.

He should probably try for some sleep. In truth, he had been waiting up for Xcor's return, but dawn had long since arrived and the male had not come back. Mayhap he was dead, the Brotherhood having caught him out alone. Or perhaps one of those clandestine meetings he had with that member of the *glymera* had gone sour.

Zypher was surprised to find he didn't care. He rather hoped, as a matter of fact, that Xcor never arrived home again.

It was a big change in his thinking. Back when the Band of Bastards had first come together in the Old Country, they had been a mercenary lot, each out only for themselves. The Bloodletter had been the only one capable of uniting them: that killing machine, who had had no humanity to temper any of his urges, had been the rawest male to ever walk in a soldier's boots, and they had individually followed him as a symbol of freedom and strength in the war.

After all, there was no way the Black Dagger Brotherhood would ever take any of them.

Over time, however, bonds had grown. Regardless of how Xcor thought of things, the soldiers who fought under him had developed loyalties . . . and they extended even to the former aristocrat, Throe.

"'Re ye gonna talk with him?" Syphon asked softly from down below.

He and Syphon had shared bunks for aeons, with Zypher always on top. It was the same with the females and women as well, and they were a good pair. Syphon could keep up: in the bed, on the floor, against a wall . . . in the field as well.

"Aye. If he comes home."

"Wouldnae kill m' if he dint." The brogue was thick in that deep voice, putting a different twist on the syllables. And it was the same for the male's cousins. "He shouldnae done that."

"Aye."

"You dinnae haft t' stand up to him y'self."

"No, I'll take care of it."

The grunt that came in reply suggested that there was backup available at a moment's notice and he might well need it. Xcor was as ugly a fighter as he was a lover—

"Damn spiders," Zypher muttered as he slapped at the back of his neck again.

"We should 'ave done aught," somebody said in the dimness.

It was Balthazar.

And a rumble of *aye*s rippled through the candlelight.

"We shan't sit idly by again," Zypher announced. "And shan't do so the now."

Assuming the fucker came back. Which, if he didn't, would not be because he had second thoughts or regrets about what he'd done. Not Xcor. He was as decisive as his blades.

One thing was clear, however: If Throe was dead, Xcor was going to have a mutiny on his hands. Hell, that might be true regardless of whether that soldier lived. No one was going to put their heads on the chopping block in pursuit of the throne for someone who didn't honor the bonds of—

Zypher smacked the nape of his neck so hard, someone remarked, "If you'd prefer some floggers, we have 'em."

Wetness on his palm made him bring the thing forward—

Blood. Red blood. A lot of it.

Damn it, he must have been bitten by the fucker. Putting his other hand up, he investigated the area, probing with his fingertips—

A droplet hit the back of his wrist.

Looking up to the floor joists above him, his cheek caught the next one that fell through a small crack in the hardwood.

He was off his bunk with knives in both hands before there was another.

The others went on instant alert, not even proffering a question—just seeing him ready to fight called them up out of their beds and to attention.

"You're bleedin'," Syphon whispered.

"It's not me. Someone's upstairs."

Zypher inhaled in an attempt to catch a scent, but all he could smell was the musty, clinging stench of the damp underground.

"Could the Brotherhood have delivered Xcor back to us?" somebody breathed.

In a matter of seconds, guns were checked and armor plates were strapped on chests.

"I go first," Zypher announced.

There was no argument—then again, he was already at the base of the sturdy stairs, and beginning to ascend. The others followed him, and even though the lot of them easily weighed a total of seventy-two stone, they went up without making a sound, no creaks or groans of old wood tipping their hand. Or their feet, as it were.

At least until they got to the top. The final three planks were set badly on purpose so as to give away any infiltration. He skipped them by dematerializing directly to the steel-reinforced door that was locked into a steel frame set into four walls that had steel mesh nailed to the plaster.

No way anyone could get in or out the easy way.

With care, he gently threw the steel bolt and cranked the knob. Then he eased the way open a quarter of an inch.

The scent of fresh blood rushed into his nose and his sinuses, so thick he tasted sweet metal in the back of his throat. And he recognized the source.

It was Xcor. And there was nothing and no one else with him: no stench of *lesser*, no dark spice of a male vampire, no pathetic cologne of a human.

Zypher motioned for the others to stay back. He was going to need them to save his ass if his nose had misinformed him.

Opening the door on a quick, soundless shove, he stepped out into the artificial darkness created by the boards and drapes that covered all the windows—

Across the chipped tile of the kitchen and the dusty hardwood of the hall, in the far corner of the living room, in a circle of honey-colored candlelight . . . Xcor sat in a pool of blood.

The soldier was still dressed in his fighting clothes, his scythe and his guns set beside him on the floor, his legs outstretched, his bare and bloodied forearms resting on his thighs.

There was a steel dagger in his hand.

He was cutting himself. Over and over with the blade of his killing knife, he was cutting his ropy, strong arms such that they dripped from too many striped wounds to count. But that was not the shocker. There were tears on the male's face. Running down his cheeks, falling off his jaw and chin, mixing with what seeped from his flesh.

Words, hoarse and low, drifted over. ". . . goddamn pussy . . . crying, worthless, pussy . . . stop it . . . *stop it* . . . you did what you had to do to him . . . goddamn pussy . . ."

It appeared as though someone else had developed a bond with Throe.

Indeed, their leader was abject in his misery and his regret.

Zypher slowly backed up through the door and shut it again.

"What?" Syphon demanded in the darkness.

"We need to leave him be."

"Xcor's alive then?"

"Aye. And he's suffering at his own hand, for the right reason—spilling his blood for whom he offended so mortally."

There was a grumble of approval, and then everyone turned around and descended.

It was a start. But there was a long way yet to go to regain their loyalty. And they needed to learn what had happened to Throe.

Sitting upon the hard floor, in a pool of his own blood, Xcor was stretched thin between his training at the hands of the Bloodletter and his . . . heart, he supposed.

Odd at this age to discover that he actually had one of those, and difficult to count its discovery as a blessing.

It seemed more a badge of failure. The Bloodletter had taught him well the requirements of a good soldier, and emotions other than rage, vengeance, and greed were not part of that lexicon: Loyalty was something you demanded of your subordinates, and if they did not provide it to you and you alone, you did away with them as malfunctioning weapons. Respect was given solely in response to your enemy's strength, and simply because you did not want to be bested by an underestimation of the opposition. Love was associated only with the acquisition and successful defense of your power—

Digging the red-stained knife blade into his skin again, he hissed as the pain tingled through his arms and legs, making his head buzz and his heartbeat flicker.

As fresh blood welled, he prayed that it would carry out of his body the confusing tangle of regret that had claimed him shortly after he had left Throe upon that pavement.

How could this all have gone so awry . . .

The chaos, indeed, had started when he had not departed from that alley.

After he had sent his males away from Throe, he had intended to do the same . . . but had ended up lurking upon the rooftop of one of the buildings, staying hidden whilst he watched over his soldier. Ostensibly, he told himself that it had been because he wanted to ensure that the Brothers found his second in command, not the Lessening Society—because the information he needed was on the former enemy rather than the latter one.

Except as he had watched Throe writhing in pain on the asphalt, limbs cocking at odd angles as he sought relief in repositioning, the reality of a proud warrior rendered defenseless had seeped into him.

For what reason had he caused such agony?

As the winds had rushed against Xcor, clearing his head and cooling his anger, he'd realized his actions sat uncomfortably within him. Unbearably.

As the slayers had arrived, he had outted his gun, prepared to defend the very male he had disposed of. But Throe had made a formidable first strike . . . and then the Brothers had come and acted as predicted, dispatching the *lessers* with ease, picking up Throe and putting him in the back of a black vehicle.

In that moment, Xcor had resolved not to follow the SUV. And the reason he so chose was an anathema as measured against his prior actions.

Throe would get treated with great competence back at the Brotherhood's lair.

Say what one would about how the fuckers preferred luxury, he knew they had access to superior medical care. They were the king's private guard; Wrath would not provide them with anything less. If he followed them, with the idea of infiltrating their compound? They might well discover him and fight him along the way, instead of get Throe to the help he needed.

Indeed, Xcor stayed away for the wrong reason, the bad reason, an unacceptable reason—in spite of all his training, he found himself choosing Throe's life over ambition: His anger had taken him in one direction, but his regret had led him in another. And the latter one was what won out.

The Bloodletter no doubt had turned in his grave.

Decision made, he had languished in the rubble of night and his intentions when gunfire had lit up the alley even before the vehicle Throe was in had had a chance to depart.

As he'd gathered his wits, there had been a brief lull . . . and then Tohrment, son of Hharm, had walked out into the center of the lane, eschewing cover, becoming a target to the newly arrived *lessers* even as he discharged his firearms at them.

It was impossible not to respect that.

Xcor had been directly above the slayer who had commenced to fire back upon the Brother—and yet even as the enemy's bullets had been driven into the male, Tohrment continued to lead with both barrels, undeterred, unwavering.

One shot to the head and he would be done forever.

Motivated by something he had refused to name, Xcor had dropped to his belly, snaked over to the lip of the building, and extended his own gun, emptying his clip upon the *lesser* who was behind cover, putting to rest any possibility of the Brother's death. It had seemed like an appropriate reward for that manner of courage.

Then he had dematerialized out of the area and walked the streets of Caldwell for hours, the Bloodletter's teachings banging on his inner door, demanding to be let in so that they could extinguish the sense that what he had done to Throe had been wrong.

The regret had just intensified, however, festering under his skin, redefining his relationship with his soldier . . . as well as the male he had once called *Father*.

The conception that he might not be cut from the same cloth as the Bloodletter had rankled. Especially given that he had set himself and his bastards on a collision course with the Blind King—and execution of that plan was going to require the kind of strength that came only from the compassionless.

In fact, it was too late to back out of that course now, even if he wanted to—which he did not. He still intended to take down Wrath—for the simple reason that the throne was for the taking, no matter what the Old Laws or blind tradition dictated.

But when it came to his soldiers, and his second in command . . .

Refocusing upon his forearms, habit and a blind search for himself had him once again applying his blade unto his flesh, dragging the point up against its cutting side so that the damage was ragged, unclean, and properly painful.

It was getting increasingly difficult to find fresh skin.

Hissing through his clenched teeth, he prayed for the pain to reach his core. He needed it to burrow through his emotions in the way the Bloodletter's remembered voice had never failed to, strengthening him, giving him a clear mind and a cold heart.

It was not working, however. The pain just redoubled in his heart, amplifying the betrayal he had wrought upon a good male with a good soul who had served so very well.

Slick with his own blood, swimming in his own torture, he reapplied the blade again and again, waiting for the old, familiar clarity to come. . . .

And when it did not, he found himself arriving at the realization that, if he ever got the chance, he would set Throe free, finally and forevermore.

THIRTY

As Tohr lay in his bed alone, he was aware of nothing except the heartbeat in his cock. Well, that and the smell of fresh-cut flowers from Fritz doing his midday vase routine out in the hall.

"Is this what you want from me, angel?" he asked aloud. "Come on, I know you're here. Is this what you want?"

To emphasize the question, he put his hand under the covers and let it drift down his chest and his belly until it got to the front of his hips. As he gripped himself, he couldn't suppress the racking arch that rocked his spine or the groan that rose in his throat.

"Where the fuck are you?" he growled, unsure in the dim glow who he was talking to. Lassiter. No'One. The merciful Fates—if there were any.

On some level, he couldn't believe he was waiting for another female—and the fact that the tipping balance between urgency and guilt was quickly shifting to the former was a—

"If you say my name while you do that, I'm going to throw up a little in my mouth."

Lassiter's voice was rough and disembodied as it came from the far corner of the room where the chaise was.

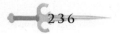

"Is this what you meant." God, was that really him? Tohr wondered. Hungry, impatient. Cranky because he was juiced up.

"It's a better direction than you walking out into a bullet shower—" There was a shuffling sound. "Hey, no offense, but do you mind if you put both your palms where I can see 'em?"

"Can you make her come to me."

"Free will is what it is. And palms, motherfucker? If you don't mind."

Tohr outted both his arms and felt compelled to declare, "I want to feed her, not fuck her. I wouldn't put No'One through that."

"I suggest you let her make up her own mind about the sex." The guy coughed a little bit—but then, yet again, fucking was an awkward subject between guys if they were talking about females of worth. "She may have her own ideas."

Tohr thought back to the way she had looked at him in the clinic when he'd worked himself out. She had not been afraid. She had appeared captivated. . . .

He wasn't sure how to handle that—

His body arched on its own, as if to say, *The fuck you don't, buddy.*

As another cough sounded out, Tohr laughed a little. "You have allergies to those flowers?"

"Yeah. That's it. I'm going to leave you now, 'kay?" There was a pause. "I'm proud of you."

Tohr frowned. "What for?"

When there was no answer, it was clear the angel had already taken off—

A soft knocking at the door shot Tohr upright, and he barely felt the pain of his wounds: He knew exactly who this was. "Come in."

Come to me.

The door opened a crack, and No'One slipped inside, shutting them in with each other.

As he heard the click of the locking mechanism, his body shut his mind down completely: It was going to feed her . . . and, God help them both, fuck her if she let him.

For one brief moment of lucidity, he thought he should tell her to go, so they could be spared the aftermath when sex cooled down and heads cleared up . . . and two people learned that those Molotov cocktails that had seemed like such a fun, exciting idea to make and throw, had, in actuality, decimated their landscapes.

Except he just extended his hand to her.

After a moment, she reached up and removed her hood. As he re-memorized her face and form, he saw that she was nothing like his Wellsie. She was smaller and more delicately built. Fair of coloring instead of vibrant. Proper instead of blunt.

He liked her, though. And it was easier, in a strange way, that she was so different. Less of a chance of ever replacing his beloved in his heart with this female: Even though his body was aroused, that was the least important marker of connection. Males with the kind of bloodline he had, when in good health and well fed, as he now was, could get hard over a sack of potatoes.

And No'One, in spite of her opinion of herself, was a hell of a lot more attractive than root vegetables. . . .

Christ, the romance was just *awesome* all up in here. Wasn't it.

She approached slowly, her limp barely noticeable, and when she got to the edge of the mattress, she looked down at his bare chest, his arms, his stomach . . . and went even lower with her eyes.

"I'm aroused again," he said in a guttural voice. And fuck him, but you'd think he brought that up to warn her off. The truth? He was hoping to get that look back, the one that had been on her face when he'd made himself come—

And, what do you know . . . there it was: heat and curiosity. No fear.

"Should I take your wrist from here?" she asked.

"Come on the bed," he all but growled.

She stretched up one knee onto the high mattress, and then awkwardly tried to bring the other one with it. Her bad leg threw her off balance, however, and she pitched forward—

Tohr caught her easily, grabbing her shoulders and keeping her from falling on her face. "I've got you."

And wasn't there a double meaning in that one.

Deliberately, he pulled her over him so that she was poised above his pecs. Man, she didn't weigh a thing. Then again, she never ate much.

He was not the only one who needed to feed properly.

Except then he just stopped, to give her time to adjust. He was a lot of male, and he was aroused as shit, and he had scared her more than enough already. As far as he was concerned, she could take all the time in the world to make sure she knew who was with her—

Abruptly, her scent changed, shifting into the heady spectrum of female awakening. In response, his hips rolled underneath the covers, and she craned a glance over her shoulder, watching his body react.

If he'd been a gentlemale, he would have hidden the response and made sure that this was just about repaying her the service she had given to him. But he was feeling so much more *male* than *gentle*.

On that note, he lowered her onto his chest, angling her so that her mouth hit his jugular.

Skin.

Warm male skin against her lips.

Warm, clean, vampire skin that was golden brown, not pasty white. That smelled of spice, and strength, and . . . something so erotic, her body had returned to that volcanic place.

As she breathed in, the scent of him—that male scent—produced an unprecedented reaction. Everything went instantly instinct, her fangs dropping from her upper jaw, her lips parting, her tongue coming out as if it intended to taste.

"Take it, No'One. . . . You know you want to. Take me. . . ."

Swallowing hard, she pushed herself up from him and met his burning eyes. There were too many emotions to decipher in them, and the same was true with his voice and his expression. This was not easy for him; then again, this was his marital room, where he had no doubt been with his mate a thousand times.

And yet he wanted her. It was obvious in the tension of his body, in that arousal that even beneath the covers she could see.

She knew the troubled crossroads he stood upon, torn between contradictions: She was the same. She wanted this, but if she fed from him now, things were going to progress, and she was not sure she was prepared for where it would take them both.

Except she was not going to turn away. And neither was he.

"Do you not wish me at your wrist," she said in a voice that was nothing like her own.

"No."

"Then where do you want me." It wasn't a question. And, dearest Virgin Scribe, she didn't know who was talking to him like that—low, seductive, demanding.

"At my throat." His words were even lower, and he moaned as her eyes went back to where he had seemed to deliberately put her.

This mighty warrior wanted to be used by her. As he lay back against the pillows, his huge body appeared to be in that strange thrall she had seen before, held captive by invisible binds that were nonetheless impossible for him to break out of.

His eyes stayed on hers as he tilted his head to the side, exposing his vein . . . on the side opposite of where she was. So that she would have to stretch across his chest once more. Yes, she thought, she wanted that, too . . . except before she made any kind of move, she gave her inner core a chance to panic. The last thing she wanted was to become overwrought and undone in the midst of this.

Nothing bubbled up from the depths. For once, the present was so alive and captivating that the past was not even an echo or a shadow—she was, in this moment, wiped clean.

And very clear about what she wanted.

No'One reached out her arm and stretched herself thin as she surmounted the impossible expanse of his torso. His size was nearly a joke, the juxtaposition of their bodies absurd—and yet she was not afraid. The hard pads of his pectorals and the broad beam of his shoulders were nothing to be threatened by.

They merely served to sharpen her hunger for his vein.

His body arched upward as she laid herself upon him, and oh, the heat. Boiling up through his skin and magnifying her body's need, sure as a simmer was made into a rioting fervor.

It had been so long since she had struck any male. And back in her earliest past, it had been done only under the strict supervision of not just her father, but the other males of her bloodline: Indeed, throughout all of it, there had been a ceremonial feel, biology tempered by society and social expectation.

She had never been aroused. And if the fine, gentlemale she'd used had been, he had wisely shown no such reaction.

This was everything that the former experiences had not been.

This was raw, and wild . . . and very sexual.

"Take from me," he commanded, his jaw locking, his chin lifting, his throat becoming even more exposed.

As she brought her head down, she shook from head to foot, and she struck with no grace whatsoever—

This time, the moan came from her.

His taste was like nothing she could recall, a screaming roar in her mouth, over her tongue, down her throat. His blood was so much purer

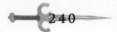

and stronger than that which she had had, and oh, the power of him. It was as if the potency of his warrior's body poured into hers, transforming her into something so much more than she had ever been before.

"Take more," he urged in a rough voice. "Take everything. . . ."

She did as he commanded, readjusting the angle of her head so that her seal was even more perfect. And as she drank with renewed gusto, she found herself becoming acutely aware of the weight of her breasts as they rested on his chest. And of the ache in her gut that no matter how much she took in seemed only to get sharper. And of the languid nature of her legs . . . as if all they wanted to do was fall open.

For him.

The reversal of her tense rigidity was so complete, it felt irreversible, and what did that matter? So consumed was she that she cared for naught but more of what she was getting.

THIRTY-ONE

Zohr orgasmed shortly after No'One's first strike. There was just no stopping the contraction of his balls or the pulsing shocks that traveled up his shaft or the explosion that blew out the head of his cock as he jerked underneath the sheets.

"Fuuuuuck . . . *No'One* . . ."

As if she knew what had just happened, and what he was asking permission for, she nodded against his throat. Then went so far as to take his wrist and push his hand under the sheet.

No asking twice on that one.

Spreading his legs, he stroked his rigid length in a rhythm that matched the pulls on his vein. And as he released again, his arousal kicking like mad, he dipped down, gathered his sac, and squeezed hard. Pleasure and pain became a fun-house mirror, the distorting reflection of one against the other amplifying everything from the feel of the fangs in his neck to his below-the-waist eruptions.

The sense of letting go, of putting aside the pain he struggled with night and day, was such a fucking relief. He was the lake temporarily

melted and free from its ice cover, and he reveled in his openness to her, the way he let himself lie there beneath her slight body, captured and held by her dainty weight and her powerful bite.

It had been so long since he had felt anything good deep in the permafrost of his soul. And because he knew that all of his burdens would be waiting for him when this halcyon sunrise faded, he drew himself even more into the experience, deliberately clothing himself in all the sensations.

When No'One finally retracted her fangs, the drawing lick of her tongue as it sealed the puncture wounds made him come all over again: the wet, warm drag over his skin translated down his body to his erection, which kicked and bucked, sending out more of what already covered his lower belly and soaked the sheets.

He stared up into her eyes as he orgasmed, biting down on his lower lip, kicking his head back—so that she knew exactly what he was doing.

And that was when he knew . . . she wanted some for herself.

Her luscious scent told him so.

"Will you let me make you feel good?" he said hoarsely.

"I . . . I do not know what to do."

"Is that a yes?"

"Yes . . ." she breathed.

Rolling onto his side, he gently pushed her against the mattress. "All you have to do is lie there—I'll take care of everything."

The ease with which she complied was a humbling surprise—and an immediate cue, as far as his libido was concerned, to get her naked, mount her, and come all over her.

Not going to happen. For so many reasons.

"I'll go slowly," he groaned, wondering which of them he was speaking to. And then he thought . . . fuck, yeah, he was going slowly. He wasn't sure he could remember what to do to a female—

From out of nowhere, a shadow crossed through his mind, jumped out of his brain, and barged in between them, darkening the moment.

With a sad ache, he realized he couldn't remember precisely when he and Wellsie had been together for that final time; if he'd known their future, he would have paid much greater attention to so much.

No doubt, it had been one of those comfortable, forgettable, but ultimately profound sessions in their mated bed, with both of them half-awake and happy to ride the currents—

"Tohrment?"

The sound of No'One's voice scrambled him, threatening to completely derail what was happening in the present. Except then he thought of Lassiter . . . and he thought of his *shellan* in that gray underworld, trapped in that desolate field of dust.

If he stopped now, he was never going to come back to this moment, this potential, this situation again with No'One . . . with anyone else. He was going to get permanently stuck on the road out of his grief—and Wellsie would never be free.

Damn it, as with so many things in life, you had to push through the obstacles, and this was the big one. It also wasn't going to last forever. He'd had well over a year of mourning and grief, and there were decades and centuries of it in front of him. For the next ten minutes, fifteen minutes, hour—however long this lasted—he needed to stay only in the here-and-now.

Only with No'One.

"Tohrment, we can st—"

"May I loosen your robe?" His voice sounded dead to his own ears. "Please . . . let me see you."

When she nodded, he swallowed hard and brought a shaking hand to the tie of her robe. The thing loosened with little or no help from him, and then the folds were free of her sheath-covered body.

His sex kicked hard at the sight of her barely concealed from his eyes, his hands . . . his mouth.

And that reaction told him that unfortunately . . . or fortunately . . . he could do this. He was *going* to do this.

Sliding his hand around her waist, he paused. Wellsie had had such a lush body, all feminine curves and female strength that he had loved so much. No'One wasn't like that.

"You have to eat more," he said harshly.

As her brows came together and she appeared to retract from him, he wanted to punch himself in the head. No female needed to hear about shortcomings at a time like this.

"You're very beautiful," he said, eyes probing the thin fabric that covered her breasts and her hips. "I just worry about you. That's all."

As she relaxed again, he took his time, stroking her through the simple linen coverlet she wore, slowly moving over onto her belly. That image of her suspended upon the crystal palm of the pool's blue water, floating with

her arms out, her head back and her breasts tight at the tips made him groan.

And gave him a specific direction.

Trailing his fingertips upward, he brushed the bottom of her breast—

The hiss she let out and the sudden arch told him that the contact was more than welcome. But there was no hurrying. He'd done that down in the pantry; not going to happen again.

With languid ease, he went higher until his forefinger surmounted her nipple. More hissing. More arching.

More exploring.

His body was roaring, his cock straining against the covers, against his self-control, against the tempo. But he was keeping things under wraps down below—and shit was going to stay that way. This was about her, not him, and the quickest way to flip that table would be to get his naked body anywhere near her.

It had to be her blood in him. Yeah, that was it. That was the cause of his crazy urge to mate. . . .

When No'One was thrashing her legs on top of the duvet, and she had gripped his forearm with her nails, that was when he cupped her whole breast, switching his thumb for his forefinger as he stroked her.

"Do you like," he drawled as she gasped.

The reply she eventually gave him was nothing but a bunch of sounds; then again, all that erotic straining gave him his real answer.

She *really* liked the way she felt.

Encircling the small of her back with his arm, he gently lifted her up to his mouth. He had a moment's hesitation before he latched on, just because he could not believe he was actually doing this to someone: It had never occurred to him that he would have any kind of sex life outside of memories, but here it was, up close and personal, so to speak, that electric connection sparking, his body naked and aroused, his mouth about to taste someone different.

"Tohrment . . ." she moaned. "I do not know what I am . . ."

"It's okay. I got you . . . I got you."

Dropping his head, he parted his lips and brushed at her nipple through the sheath, going back and forth, back and forth. In response, her hands dug into his hair, feeling good against his scalp, tightening, scratching.

Shit, she smelled fantastic, her scent lighter and more citrusy than Wellsie's . . . yet still like rocket fuel in his veins.

A lick brought him the rasp of the cloth and the hint of paradise—so he lapped at her again. And again. And again.

Sucking her into his mouth, he pulled on her nipple, tugging upward as he fell into a rhythm. And while she held on even harder to him, he moved his hands all around her body, learning her hips and her outer thighs, her belly, that tiny rib cage.

The bed made a subtle creaking noise, the mattress giving under him as he moved closer to her . . . and brought their lower bodies together.

It was time to take this up a notch.

This was why females got that look in their eyes when they thought about their mates.

No'One finally understood why, when a *hellren* walked into a room, his *shellan* straightened a little and wore a secret smile. This was the cause of the shared glances between the two halves of the species. This was the urgency to get the mating ceremony done with, and the guests fed and danced, and the house shut up for the day.

This was why happily mated couples sometimes did not come down for First Meal. Or Last Meal. Or any meals in between.

This feast of the senses was the ultimate sustenance for the species.

And something she had never believed she would know.

The reason she was able to enjoy it? In spite of the frantic demand in both of their bodies, Tohr was so careful with her. Even though he was obviously aroused, and so was she, he did not rush: His self-control was a set of steel bars over their collective mating instincts, his tasting and tempo as unhurried and unthreatening as the graceful fall of a feather through still air.

It was rather driving her nuts, actually.

But she knew it was for the good. Frustrated as she was, she knew this was the right way, for there was no possibility of confusing who she was with or whether she wanted this—

The sensation of his wet mouth sealed upon her breast made her cry out and score his scalp. And that was before he began to suckle at her.

Around her nipple, he said, "Will you open your legs for me?"

Her thighs obeyed before her lips could form an acquiescence, and the laugh she got in response was a deep rumble of satisfaction in his chest. He also wasted no time. Relocking his mouth onto her breast, his palm slipped down to the top of her thigh and drifted over to the inside.

"Lift your hips for me," he said before licking at her nipple some more.

She obeyed immediately, so lost in anticipation that she couldn't comprehend why he'd asked. Except then there was a soft brush all around her legs.

The sheath. He was moving the sheath up—

His touch returned, brushing over the top of her thigh, going downward . . . before moving once again to the inside. . . .

Oh, the lack of barrier. As if it had not already been good enough.

In response, her pelvis arched and strained and got nowhere when it came to urging him to the heat he would ultimately claim. Verily, under his diverted ministrations, the blooming at her core shifted into something edgy, the welling sensation changing into a sharp-edged need, the pain of which was much like that of the strikes he'd taken at her vein.

The first touch of her sex was nothing but a passover that had her crying out for more. The second was a slower shift. The third was a—

She shot her hand down and covered his, pushing him against her heat.

His moan was unexpected, suggesting that the feel of her might have made him orgasm himself—yes, she could tell by the way his body spasmed that he had found another release, his hips jerking beneath the blankets in a way that made her think of penetration.

Repeated, vigorous penetration.

"Tohrment . . ." Her voice was ragged, her brain clogged, her body the only thing that was clear on anything.

It was a while before he could answer her with something other than heaving breath. "Are you okay?"

"Help me. I need . . ."

He brushed his lips against her breast and inched his hand away. "I'll take care of it. Promise. Just a little longer."

She didn't know how much "longer" she could stand before her body blew apart.

Except then he taught her that there were even greater heights of frustration.

Eventually, the rubbing started just as it all had, slowly, lightly, a tease rather than a bona fide touch. But thanks be to the great Scribe Virgin, it didn't stay that way. As he subtly increased the pressure at the top of her sex, she was reminded of the way he had pleasured himself in the clinic, his hands pushing down at his hips, his body creating friction until something snapped and the pleasure crested—

The orgasm was more powerful than anything she had ever felt: Not even the pain she had known at the hands of the *symphath* came close to the pleasure that bucked through her lower body, reverberated up her torso, and echoed out to the tips of her fingers and her toes.

She knew earth. She knew the Sanctuary.

But this . . . was heaven.

THIRTY-TWO

As No'One orgasmed, Tohr's cock released again, the feel of her slick sex and her hips jerking and her voice crying out putting him waaaaay over the threshold: She was wet; she was open; she was ready for him.

She was luscious.

And as she rubbed herself against his hand, he wanted his mouth on her and his tongue up inside her so he could swallow what he had given her.

In fact, if she hadn't been locked against him so tightly, he would have moved into position right away, heading down her body and finding her with his lips. But there was no going anywhere at the moment. Not until both their rides were over and their muscles had unlocked from their bones.

Except . . . she didn't let go of him.

Even after her release had passed, her arms retained their shockingly strong hold on his neck.

When she started to shake, he felt every tremor.

At first he wondered if it was the passion returning, but it was quickly obvious that wasn't the case.

No'One was crying softly.

As he tried to pull back, she just gripped him more tightly, tucking her head against his chest and burrowing in. Clearly, she wasn't afraid of him, or hurt by him. But, God, still . . .

"Shh . . ." he whispered as he put his big palm on her back and began circling in gentle strokes. "It's okay. . . ."

Actually, that one was a lie. He wasn't sure if anything was okay. Especially as she started to sob in earnest.

Given there was nothing he could do but stay with her, he dropped his head close to hers and yanked the duvet off his legs to cover her up and keep her warm.

She cried forever.

He would have held her even longer than that.

It was odd . . . providing her with a grounding place grounded himself, giving him a purpose and focus that was just as strong as the sexual ones had been only moments before. And in retrospect, he should have known this was coming. What had just happened was probably the first and only sexual experience she'd ever consented to. Female of worth from a high-blooded family? No way she would have been permitted to even hold hands with a male.

That *symphath*'s violence had been all she'd ever known.

Goddamn him, he wanted to kill that bastard again.

"I don't . . . know why . . . I cry," she said eventually, the words dodging past her harsh exhales.

"I've got you," he murmured. "For as long as it takes, I got you."

But the emotions were passing, her breathing easing, the sniffling not quite as prevalent.

It was all over after one last shuddering inhale. Then she was still and so was he.

"Talk to me." He continued stroking her back. "Tell me where you're at."

She opened her mouth as if she meant to answer, but then just shook her head.

"Well, I think you're very brave."

"Brave?" She laughed. "How well you do not know me."

"Very brave. This couldn't have been easy for you—and I'm honored that you let me . . . do what I did to you."

Her face assumed a picture of confusion. "Why ever for?"

"It takes great trust, No'One—especially for someone with what happened to you in their background."

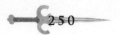

With a frown, she seemed to retreat into herself.

"Hey," he said, putting his forefinger under her chin. "Look at me." When she did, he traced her face lightly. "I wish I had something philosophical or poignant or . . . anything . . . to help you put shit in perspective. I don't, and I'm sorry for that. I know this, though. It takes true courage to break through the past, and you did that tonight."

"I suppose we both have courage then."

His eyes shifted away. "Yeah."

There was a period of quiet, as if the past had sucked all of the energy out of both of them.

Abruptly, she asked, "Why is the aftermath so awkward? I feel so . . . apart from you."

He nodded, thinking, Yeah, sex could be weird like that, even if there weren't complications of the kind they were rocking: Even if you didn't go all the way, the shattering closeness that was shared seemed to make the return to normal feel like distance in spite of the fact that you were lying side by side.

"I should go back to my room now," she said.

He pictured her down the hall, and thought that it seemed too far away. "Don't. Stay here."

In the dim light, he could see she was frowning again. "Are you certain?"

He reached up and tucked away a blond escapee from her braid. "Yeah. I am."

They stared at each other for the longest time, and somehow—maybe it was the vulnerable look in her eyes, maybe the line of her mouth; maybe he was reading her mind—he knew exactly what she was wondering.

"I knew it was you," he said softly. "The entire time . . . I knew it was you."

"And that was . . . okay, to use your expression?"

He thought back to his mate. "You're nothing like Wellsie was."

When he heard her clear her throat, he realized he'd spoken out loud. "No, what I mean is—"

"You don't have to explain." Her sad smile was so full of compassion. "You truly don't."

"No'One—"

She held up her hand. "There's no need to explain—by the way, the flowers in here are gorgeous. I've never smelled such a bouquet."

"They're out in the hall, actually. Fritz changes them every two days. Listen, can I do something for you?"

"Have you not done enough," she countered.

"I'd like to bring you some food."

Her graceful brows peaked. "I wouldn't wish for you to trouble yourself—"

"But you are hungry, right?"

"Well . . . yes . . ."

"So I'll be back in a minute."

He shifted off the mattress quick, and unconsciously braced himself for the world to tilt wildly. But there was no light-headedness, no need to reclaim his balance, no loopy shit. His body was raring to go as he walked around the foot of the bed—

No'One's eyes fell upon him, and the expression on her face stopped him dead in his tracks.

That speculation was back in her eyes. Hunger, too.

He hadn't considered whether there was ever going to be a repeat when it had been happening. But given the way she stared at him . . . the answer would appear to be a big "yes," at least from her point of view.

"Do you like what you see," he asked in a too-deep voice.

"Yes . . ."

Well, didn't that get him hard: Below his waist, his cock shot right back to attention—and damned if her eyes didn't lock on and watch the show.

"I have other things I want to do to you," he growled. "That could be just the beginning. If you want."

Her lips parted, her eyelids sinking low. "Do you want that?"

"Yeah, I do."

"Then I would say . . . yes, please."

He nodded once at her, as if they had struck some kind of deal. Then he had to force himself away from the bed.

Going over to the closet, he pulled on a pair of jeans and went for the door.

"Anything in particular?" he asked before he left.

No'One slowly shook her head, her lids still low, her mouth still parted, her cheeks still flushed. Man . . . she had no idea how enticing she looked in that big, rumpled bed, her robe draping off the side of the mattress, her neat-as-a-pin hairdo feathered with blond wisps, her scent as strong and seductive as ever.

Maybe food could wait. Especially as he noticed that her bare legs were showing in the midst of the tangled duvet.

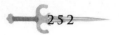

Yeah, he had plans for them. Over-the-shoulder kinds of plans—

Abruptly, she yanked the covers over her crippled one, hiding it from him.

Tohr marched right back over to her, and resolutely pulled the duvet back where it had been. Tracing the badly healed wounds with his fingertips, he met her squarely in the eye.

"You're beautiful. Every inch of you. Don't think for a moment there's anything wrong with you. We clear?"

"But—"

"Nope. I'm not hearing that." Bending down, he pressed his lips to her shin, her calf, her ankle, tracing the scars, caressing them. "Beautiful. All of you."

"How can you say that," she whispered, blinking back tears.

"Because it's the truth." Straightening, he gave her a final squeeze. "No hiding from me, okay. And after I feed you, I think I'm going to have to show you just how serious I am."

That made her smile . . . and then laugh a little.

"That's my girl," he murmured. Except . . . shit, she wasn't his. What the hell had come out of his mouth?

Forcing himself back to the door, he stepped out into the corridor, shut her in and—

"What the fuck?" Lifting his lower leg, he inspected the bottom of his bare foot. There was silver paint on it.

Glancing at the runner, he found a trail of . . . silver paint heading down the hallway toward the second-story balcony.

With a curse, he wondered which of the *doggen* was working on what part of the house. Good thing stains made the poor bastards cheerful; otherwise Fritz was going to be pissed.

Following the line of drops to the head of the great staircase, he descended to the foyer along with them.

The mess went right out into the vestibule.

"Sire, good day. Do you require anything?"

Tohr turned to Fritz, who was coming through the dining room with some floor polish. "Hey, yeah. I need to get some food. But what's up with the paint? You guys doing something obscene to the fountain out there?"

The butler shuffled over and frowned. "There is no one painting anywhere in the compound."

"Well, someone's pulling a Michelangelo." Tohr sank down on his haunches and dragged a finger through one of the little pools . . .

Wait a minute—not paint.

And the shit smelled like flowers.

Fresh flowers?

In fact, it was the scent that had been in his room.

As his eyes shot to the door to the vestibule, he thought of the shower of bullets he had walked into. And worried that a miracle hadn't been the reason he wasn't dead, after all.

"Get Doc Jane, stat," he barked to the *doggen*.

Ah, yeahhhh, Lassiter thought as he rolled over on hot stone and started to sun his bare ass. That's what's up. . . .

All things considered, it had been a good day to get shot at.

Well, night, rather.

Make that season.

Thank the Maker it was summer: Lying on the front steps of the mansion, the brilliant July megawatts beat down on him, the rays healing his bullet-ridden body. Without it? He might well have died again—which was not the way he wanted to meet up with his boss. Indeed, the sunlight was to him what blood was to the vampires; a necessity that he really enjoyed. And as he bathed in the stuff, the pain faded, his strength returned . . . and he thought of Tohr.

What a dumb-ass, pulling a move like that in the alley. What in the name of all that was holy had the fucker been thinking?

Whatever. There had been no way he was going to let that bastard walk into all that gunfire without protection. The pair of them had come too far to crap out just as progress was being made.

And now, thanks to his having turned himself into a pincushion, Tohr and No'One were having sex.

So all had not been lost. He was, however, seriously thinking of punching that Brother in the balls as payback. For one, that shit had stung like a motherfucker. For another, if this had been December? He might not have made it—

The sound of the heavy front door swinging open brought his head up and around. Doc Jane, that fantastic healer of theirs, burst out like she'd planned on having to run some distance.

She skidded to a halt so she didn't trip over him. "There you are!"

Oh, look, she'd brought her fun box with her, the little red cross denoting emergency supplies.

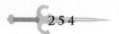

"Helluva time to get a tan," she murmured.

He rested his head back down, his cheek lying flat on all that warm rock. "Just takin' my medicine like a good little patient."

"Mind if I examine you?"

"Will your mate kill me if you see me naked?"

"You are naked."

"You're not looking at my business side." When she just loomed over him without further comment, he muttered, "Fine. Whatever—but don't stand in my sun. I need it more than I need you."

She put the box down next to his ear and got on her knees. "Yeah, V told me a little about how you work."

"I'll bet. You know, he and I have had our go-arounds." The SOB had even saved him once—which had been a miracle given how much they hated each other. "We've got history."

"He mentioned that." Her words were spoken with distraction, as if she were checking his holes out. "You might have some lead left in you—do you mind my rolling you over?"

"The lead doesn't matter. My body will consume it—provided I get enough sunshine on my shoulders."

"You're bleeding badly still."

"It's going to be okay."

And he was beginning to think that wasn't a lie. After it had all happened, he'd kept himself invisi and had hidden in the passenger seat of the Mercedes that had taken Tohr back to the clinic. Minute he'd arrived at medical central, he'd stolen some bandages and gone mummy on his own ass so he didn't bleed all over the place. There'd been no reason to hurry outdoors—there had been no sunlight available at that point—or at least not enough to make a difference. Besides, he'd thought he'd just walk it off.

Nope. It was shortly after he'd gone up to that bedroom with Tohr that he'd recognized he was in trouble. Breathing got harder. Pain got hotter. Vision started to fritz out. Fortunately, the sun had fully risen by then.

And he would have had to leave about the time No'One showed up anyway—

"Lassiter. I want to see the front of you."

"That's what all the girls say."

"Do you expect me to roll you over? 'Cuz I will."

"Your mate's not going to like this."

"As if that's going to bother you?"

"True. It actually makes it worth the effort."

With a groan, he shoved his palms into the shimmering silver pool of blood beneath him, and flopped over like the side of beef he was.

"Wow," she breathed.

"I know, right? Hung like a horse."

"If you're really nice—and you live through this—I'll promise not to tell V."

"About my size."

She laughed a little. "No, that you assumed I'd look at you in any fashion other than professionally. Can I bandage any of these?" She touched him lightly on the pec. "Even if I leave the bullets in, maybe it would slow the bleeding?"

"Not a good call. Sunshine and surface area are what it's about. And I'm going to be fine. As long as we don't cloud up."

"Should we be getting you a tanning bed?"

Now he laughed—which made him cough. "No, no—has to be the real thing."

"I don't like the sound of that rattle."

"What time is it?"

"One twenty-six."

"Come out in another thirty minutes and see where we're at."

There was a period of quiet. "Okay. I will. Tohr will want an—" Her phone went off, and she answered it with, "I was just talking about you. Yup, I'm with him, and he's . . . bad, but he says he's taking care of himself. Of course I'll stay with him—no, I'm good on supplies, and I'll call in another twenty minutes. Fine, ten." There was a long pause and then she took a deep breath. "It's—ah—it's a lot of gunshots. In his chest." Another pause. "Hello? Hello, Tohr— Oh, good, I thought I'd lost you. Yeah—no, listen, you gotta trust me. If I thought he was in danger, I'd drag him kicking and screaming into the foyer. But to be honest, I'm watching him heal as we speak—I can see his internal bruising dissipating with my own eyes. Okay. Yup. Bye."

Lassiter didn't make any comment on all that; he just stayed where he was, eyes closed, body solar-paneling its way back to health.

"So you're the reason Tohr got out of that alley alive," the good doctor murmured after a while.

"I don't know what you're talking about."

THIRTY-THREE

"Sorry, my man, but you only get one feeding. That's what I've been told."

As Throe lay in the bed he'd been strapped to, he was not surprised at the human doctor's response to his inquiry. Strength in a prisoner did not work in the Brotherhood's favor. The problem was, he wasn't recovering very well, and more blood would help.

Of course . . . if he were to feed, would it not be just a lovely coincidence that he'd get to see that Chosen once more before he left.

She was close by. He could sense her. . . .

"In fact, I believe plans are being made for your imminent departure. Night's falling soon enough."

Mayhap if he simply refused to move?

No, that would likely not slow the Brotherhood down. They would just handle him like any other variety of refuse.

The human surgeon left thereafter—how ever were they using a human, by the way?—and then he was alone again.

When the door reopened, he didn't bother cracking his lids. It wasn't the Chosen—

The click of metal on metal close to his ear got his attention. Popping his eyes wide, he stared into the barrel of a .357 Magnum.

Vishous's gloved finger was attached to the trigger. "Wakie, wakie."

"If you turn me out now," he said weakly, "I'm not going to make it."

In this, he told the truth. Having lived off the weak sustenance of human females for as long as he had, he was not in a position to heal himself of wounds this serious so quickly.

Vishous shrugged. "Then we'll deliver you to Xcor in a pine box."

"Best of luck with that, mate. I shall not tell you where to find him." Although not because of Xcor. He didn't want his fellow soldiers—or more properly, his *former* comrades—to be attacked unaware. "You can torture me if you wish. But nothing shall escape my lips."

"I decide to torture you and a whole lot will come up, trust me."

"So proceed—"

The surgeon got between them. "Okaaaay, let's relax before I need to go get my needle and thread again. You"—he nodded to Throe—"shut the fuck up—this is not a boy who needs encouragement when it comes to bloodletting. And as for the release of him?" He focused on the Brother. "My patient has a point. Look at his vitals—he's hanging by a thread. I thought the whole point of this was to make sure he lives? Bottom line, he's going to need another shot at the vein thing. Either that or a week or two of recovery time."

The Brother's icy eyes shifted to the machines that beeped and flashed behind the bed.

As the fighter cursed under his breath, Throe smiled to himself.

The Brother left without a word.

"Thank you," Throe said to the healer.

The man frowned. "It's just my clinical opinion—believe me, I can't wait to get you the fuck off my turf."

"Fair enough."

Once again left alone, he waited with anticipation. And the fact that no one came in for a while told him that the Brothers were arguing about his fate.

Likely a lively discussion.

When the door was finally thrown wide, his nostrils flared, and his head whipped to the side . . . there she was.

As lovely as a dream. As heavenly as the moon. As real as it got.

Flanked by the Brothers Phury and Vishous, the Chosen smiled at him sweetly—as if she were entirely unaware that those males were pre-

pared to tear him apart if he so much as sneezed in her direction. "Sire, I am told you require more?"

I require all of you, he thought as he nodded to her.

Approaching the bed, she went to sit down next to him, but Phury bared his fangs over her head and Vishous subtly trained that gun on his crotch.

"Here," Phury said, redirecting her to a chair with finesse. "You'll be much more comfortable in this."

Not at all true, as now she had to reach up to him. Yet the Brother's voice was so charming and easy, it made the statement seem to have veracity.

Whilst she brought up her arm, Throe wanted to tell her she was beautiful, and that he'd missed her, and that he'd worship her if she gave him a chance. But he liked his tongue in his mouth—not sliced off and ground into the floor.

"Why ever do you look at me like that?" she said.

"You are so beautiful—"

Over her shoulder, Phury bared his fangs again, his face transforming into nothing short of total violence.

Throe did not care. He was getting another taste of ambrosia, and these two males wouldn't do anything truly horrible in front of the fair Chosen.

Who was currently blushing up a storm—and didn't that make her all the more resplendent.

As the Chosen stretched forward and put her wrist to his mouth, his arms jerked against the chains that bound him—and there was a moment of confusion for her as she heard the rattle. There was nothing to see above the blankets, however; everything was covered up beneath what kept him warm.

"'Tis just the bedsprings," he murmured.

She smiled again and repositioned her wrist o'er his mouth.

Embracing her with his eyes, he struck as carefully as he could, not wanting to hurt her even in the smallest way—and as he drank, he stared at her face, committing it to memory so that he could hold it close in his heart.

Because this was likely the last time he would ever see her.

Indeed, so torn he was between thanking the Scribe Virgin for having this female come into his life even for a moment, and yet viewing these two chance meetings as a kind of curse.

She was going to stay with him, he feared. Haunting him as sure as any ghost . . .

Too soon it was over, and he was retracting his canines from her fragrant flesh. He licked once, twice, stroking at her with his tongue—

"Okay, that's enough." Phury gathered her up from the chair, smiling at her with true warmth. "You go find Qhuinn now—you're going to need some strength."

This was true, Throe thought with a stab of guilt. Indeed, she looked pale and seemed slightly woozy. Then again, she had fed him twice in as many hours.

He wished his name was Qhuinn.

Phury escorted her to the door and sent her off with kind words in the Old Language. And then he turned back . . . and made sure that the lock was in place.

The fist came flying at him from the side, and given his brief impression of black leather, it was clearly the Brother Vishous's.

And the resulting crack was so loud it was as if a log had been snapped in half.

Then again, he'd always had a sturdy jaw.

As cathedral bells rang in Throe's head and he spit out blood, Vishous said grimly, "That is for looking at her like you were fucking her in your mind."

Across the room, the Brother Phury likewise curled up a fist and started smacking it into the open palm of his free hand. As he approached, he said in a nasty tone, "And this is to make sure you don't follow up on that bright idea."

Throe smiled at them both. The more they beat him . . . the more likely he would have to feed again.

They were right, too: He did want to be with her—although "making love" was a far better term.

And those moments with her were so worth whatever they gave him. . . .

Up at the mansion, Tohr sat on the bottom step of the grand stairwell, his elbows on his bent knees, his chin on a fist, his cell phone faceup next to him.

His ass was numb.

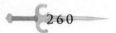

In fact, after having sat where he had for the last—how long? five hours?—he was probably going to have to get Doc Jane to surgically remove the carpet fibers from his caboose—

The security check-in station let out a beep, and he burst up, striding over to the panel, double-checking the screen, releasing the door lock.

Lassiter came in alone, likely because Doc Jane had returned to the Pit. And the angel was naked as a jaybird . . . and just frickin' fine. No bullet holes, no scars, no contusions.

"You keep looking at me like that and you'd better buy me dinner afterward."

Tohr glared at the angel. "What the hell were you thinking?"

Lassiter shook his finger. "You, of all people, do not need to ask me that. Not about last night."

On that note—and utterly unconcerned about the nakey—Lassiter sauntered into the billiards room and headed for the bar. The good news was that at least when he was behind the thing pouring liquor, his longshoreman and those two buoys were not in full view.

"Scotch? Gin? Bourbon?" the angel asked. "I'm having an Orgasm."

Tohr rubbed his face. "Can you never say that word around me when you're buck-ass nekkid?"

That set off a round of, "Orgaaaaasmmm, orgaaaaasmmm, orgaaaasmmm," to the tune of Beethoven's Fifth. Fortunately, the fruity bullshit the fucker put into his glass cut the chorus off as he swallowed it on a oner.

"Ahhhhh . . ." The angel smiled. "Think I'll have another. Care for one? Or did you have enough this afternoon."

A quick mental picture of No'One's breast in his hand made his cock hop all over that plan. "Lassiter, I know what you did."

"Outside? Yeah, the sun and I get along. Best doctor there is—and no copay. Woo-hoo."

More with the drinking. Which suggested that bravado might just be a little forced.

Tohr parked it on one of the stools. "Why the hell did you put yourself in front of me?"

The angel went about making himself number three. "I'll tell you the same thing I did Doc Jane—I got no clue what you're talking about."

"Those were bullet wounds all over you."

"Were they?"

"Yeah."

"Can you prove it?" Lassiter did a little turn with his arms up. "Can you prove I was even hurt?"

"Why deny it?"

"This isn't a denial if I have no fucking clue what you're going on about."

With another charmer of a smile, he bottomed up again. And then immediately started making number four.

Tohr shook his head. "If you're going to get plastered, why can't you do it like a real man."

"I like the taste of fruit."

"You are what you drink."

The angel glanced up at the clock. "Shit. I missed *Maury*. But I DVR'd *Ellen*."

Lassiter went over and stretched out on the leather couch—and Tohr counted himself lucky that the bastard at least had the decency to wrap a throw blanket around his naughty bits. As the television came on, and Ellen DeGeneres danced down a row of housewives, it was obvious that conversation was not on the angel's to-do list.

"I just don't get why you did it," Tohr muttered.

It was so unlike the guy, always out for himself.

At that moment, No'One appeared in the arches of the room. She was in her robe with the hood in place, but Tohr saw her naked and undone, and his body juiced to life.

As he slid off the stool and went to the female, he could have sworn Lassiter murmured, "That's why."

Approaching the female, he said, "Hey, did you get the food?"

"Yes," she whispered. "But I was worried when you didn't come back. What happened?"

He glanced back at Lassiter. The angel appeared to have passed out, his breathing even, the remote resting on his chest in a lax hand, the drink beading up with condensation on the floor beside him.

But Tohr didn't trust the out-cold appearance.

"Nothing," he said roughly. "It's . . . nothing. Let's go upstairs and have a rest."

As he turned her away with a subtle touch on her shoulders, she said, "You sure?"

"Yeah." And they really were going to rest. He was suddenly exhausted.

He spared one last glance over the shoulder as he headed into the foyer. Lassiter was exactly where he'd been . . . except there was the smallest hint of a smile on his face.

Like everything had been worth it, as long as Tohr and No'One were together.

THIRTY-FOUR

As the night wore on, Throe walked the streets of Caldwell by himself, unarmed, dressed in hospital scrubs . . . and stronger than he'd been since he'd arrived in the New World.

His beating at the hands of those two Brothers had healed up almost immediately, and the Brotherhood had released him shortly after that second feeding.

He still had a number of hours before he was due to meet Xcor, and he passed the time with his own thoughts, walking in running shoes that had been a gift from the enemy.

During his stay with the Brotherhood, he had learned nothing about where their facilities were located. He had been unconscious when brought into their compound—and locked in a van with no windows when he'd left. After a drive of some time, no doubt due to a circuitous route, he'd been deposited by the river, and left to his own devices.

Naturally, the van had had no license plate, and no distinguishing features. And he'd had the sense that he was being watched—as if they were waiting to see if he tried to follow it as it departed from him.

He did not. He stayed where he was until it had driven off . . . and then he had started upon his walkabout.

Xcor's brilliant maneuver had succeeded in gaining naught. Well, aside from likely saving Throe's life. What little he had discovered about the Brotherhood was nothing that couldn't have been guessed at: Their resources were extensive, judging by the amount and sophistication of the medical equipment he'd been treated with; the number of people he'd seen or heard walking in the hall was just as impressive; and security was taken very seriously. Indeed, theirs appeared to be an entire community, hidden from human and *lesser* eyes alike.

Everything had to be underground, he thought. Well guarded. Camouflaged to appear as if it were nothing in particular; for even during the raids, when so many of the race's homes had been found and wiped out, there had been no rumor that the king's household had been hit.

So Xcor's plan had yielded little on Throe's part but animosity.

And for a moment, he questioned whether he would show up to meet his former leader or not.

In the end, he knew such rebellion would remain unrealized. Xcor had something Throe wanted—the only thing, really. And as long as those ashes were retained by the male, there was naught to be done but grit one's teeth, duck one's head, and push onward. It was, after all, what he had been doing for centuries.

Except he would not make the same mistake twice. Only an idiot would not recall this visceral reminder of where things really stood between them.

The answer was to get the remains of his sister back. And as soon as he did? He would miss his fellow soldiers in the same manner he ached for his family, but he would take himself out of the Band of Bastards—forcibly if need be. Then perhaps he would put down some roots somewhere else in America—there would be no returning to the Old Country. He might be too tempted to try to revisit his bloodline, and that would not be fair to them.

Toward the end of the night, at around four a.m. judging by the moon's position, he dematerialized to the rooftop of the skyscraper. He had no weapons on which to draw for protection—but he had no intention of fighting. As far as he had been taught, his sister could not enter unto the Fade without the proper ceremony so he had to live long enough to bury her.

As soon as he did, however . . .

Up high above the streets and other buildings of the city, in the curiously silent stratosphere where there were no horns or shouts or rumbles of delivery trucks coming in early, the wind was strong and bracingly chilly in spite of the humidity in the air and the warm temperature. Overhead, thunder rumbled and lightning skipped along the underside of storm clouds, promising a wet beginning to the day.

When he'd started his journey with Xcor, he had been a gentlemale better tutored in the fine art of leading a female upon the dance floor—as opposed to engaging in hand-to-hand combat. But he was no longer who he had been.

Accordingly, he stood out in the open without cowardice or apology, feet braced and arms at his sides. There was no weakness in the line of his chin, the contour of his chest, or the straight angle of his shoulders, and no fear in his heart at what might step out to greet him. All of that was because of Xcor: Throe had technically been born male, but it wasn't until he had run afoul of that fighter that he had truly learned how to live up to his gender.

He would always owe that to the soldiers he had been with for so long—

From behind the mechanicals, a figure stepped out, the wind catching a long coat and blowing it free from a heavy, deadly body.

Instinct and training overrode intent as Throe fell into a fighting stance, prepared to face his—

As the male took a step forward, the light from the fixture above the rooftop door caught his face.

It was not Xcor.

Throe did not ease his stance. "Zypher?"

"Aye." Abruptly, the soldier lurched forward, and then broke into a run to close the distance between them.

Before Throe knew it, he was encompassed in a rough embrace, held in arms as strong as his own, against a body as big as his own.

"You live," the soldier breathed. "You are alive. . . ."

Awkwardly at first, and then with a strange desperation, Throe latched onto the other fighter. "Aye. Aye, I am."

With an abrupt shove, he was pushed back and examined from head to foot. "What e'er did they do unto you?"

"Nothing."

Those eyes narrowed. "Be in truth with me, brother. And afore you answer, one of your eyes is still black-and-blue."

"They provided me with a healer, and a . . . Chosen."

"A Chosen?!"

"Aye."

"Mayhap I should try to get stabbed."

Throe had to laugh. "She was . . . like nothing on this earth. Fair of hair and skin and countenance, ethereal, though she lived and breathed."

"I thought they had been fabricated."

"I do not know—mayhap I have romanticized it. But she was exactly as rumors describe them—lovelier than any female your eyes have beheld."

"Do not torture me thus!" Zypher grinned briefly, and then regained his seriousness. "Are you well."

Not a question—a demand.

"They treated me as a guest for the most part." Indeed, except for the shackles and the beat-down—although given that they were protecting a precious gem's virtue, he had to say he approved of what they had wrought upon him. "But aye, I am recovered fully, thanks to their healers." He looked around. "Where is Xcor."

Zypher shook his head. "He's not coming."

"So you are to kill me then." Odd that the male would task another with what surely he would relish.

"Fuck, no." Zypher unshouldered one side of a rucksack. "I am to give you this."

From out of the pack, Zypher produced a large, square brass box with ornate markings and inscriptions.

Throe could only stare at the thing.

He had not seen it for centuries. In fact, he had not known it had been taken from his family until Xcor had threatened him with it.

Zypher cleared his throat. "He told me to tell you he releases you. Your debt to him is settled and he is returning your dead unto you."

Throe's hands shook badly—until they accepted the weight of his sister's ashes. Then they were steadied.

As he stood there in the wind and drizzle, poleaxed and unmoving, Zypher paced about in a tight circle, his hands on his hips and his eyes on the gravel that covered the skyscraper's roofing panels.

"He hasnae been the same since he left you," the soldier said. "This morning, I found him cutting himself to the bone from the mourning."

Throe's eyes shot over to the male he knew so well. "Indeed?"

"Aye. He did so all day long. And this night, he has not even gone out to fight. He is back at the safe house, sitting by himself. He ordered everyone but me away, and then gave me this."

Throe brought the box even closer to his body, holding it tightly. "Are you sure I am the cause for such upset," he said dryly.

"Very much so. In truth, he is not like the Bloodletter in his heart. He wants to be—and he is capable of much against others that I personally am not. But to you, to us . . . we are his clan." Zypher's stare was filled with candor. "You should come back to us. To him. He shall not act thus again—those ashes are your proof. And we need you—not just because of all you do, but who you have become to us. It has been but twenty-four hours and we are broken without you."

Throe glanced up at the sky, at the storm, at the violent, churning heavens above. Having once been damned by circumstance, he couldn't believe he would even consider being damned by consent.

"We will all be incomplete without you. Even him."

Throe had to smile a little. "Did you e'er think you would say such."

"No." The laugh that floated over upon the gusts was deep. "Not about an aristocrat. But you are more than that."

"Thanks to you."

"And Xcor."

"I'm not sure if I'm ready to give him any credit."

"Come back with me. See him. Rejoin your family. Much as it might pain you this night, you are as lost without us as we are without you."

In response, Throe could only stare out over the city, its lights like that of the stars that were eclipsed up above.

"I cannot trust him," he heard himself say.

"He has given you your freedom this night. Surely that means something."

"We are all facing death sentences if we continue. I saw the Brotherhood—if they were formidable before in the Old Country, that is nothing compared to their resources now."

"So they live well."

"They live smart. I couldn't find them even if I wished. And they have extensive facilities—they are a force to be reckoned with." He glanced over. "Xcor will be disappointed with what I have learned—which is nothing."

"He said no."

Throe frowned. "I don't understand."

"He stated he wishes to know none of it. You shall never get an apology from him directly, but he has given you the key to the binds that entangle you, and he will accept no information from you."

A brief anger shafted through him. Then what had it all been for?

Except . . . mayhap Xcor hadn't considered that he'd feel the way he did. And Zypher was right; the idea of not being with those males was . . . like a death. After all these years, they were all he had.

"If I come back, I could be a security risk. What if I've made a secret pact with the Brotherhood. What if they are here." He motioned around. "Or perhaps waiting elsewhere to follow me?"

Zypher shrugged with complete disregard. "We've been trying to meet up with them for months. Such a confluence would be welcome."

Throe blinked. And then started to laugh. "You people are crazy."

"Shouldn't that be 'we'?" Abruptly, Zypher shook his head. "You would never betray us. Even if you hated Xcor with your whole being, you would never compromise the rest of us."

That was true, he thought. As for hating Xcor . . .

He stared down at the box in his arms.

There had been many times over the years when he had wondered at the turns and twists of his fate.

And it appeared tonight he was going to wonder anew at his destiny.

He had been unsure about the course against Wrath, but now that he had seen that Chosen female, he rather liked the idea of o'ertaking the throne and finding her and claiming her for himself.

Bloodthirsty? Yes, indeed—his earlier self would have never thought in such ways. But his newer self had gotten used to taking what he wanted, the cloak of civility having grown threadbare after years without his tending its delicate fibers.

If he could get to Wrath, he could find her again. . . .

Abruptly, he felt his mouth move and heard his own voice in the wind: "He is going to have to allow me to buy cell phones."

Xcor stayed home all night long.

The problem was the damage to his forearms. He hated the fact that they had yet to heal, but he was smart enough to know that he could barely use them. Indeed, just gripping the spoon to feed himself soup was proving difficult.

A dagger against an enemy would be an impossibility. And then there was the infection risk.

It was the damn blood thing. Again. Mayhap if he had taken the time to feed from that whore back in the . . . fates, had it been in the spring?

Frowning, he performed an uneasy addition, one that yielded far too great a sum. No wonder he remained in difficult straits . . . and good thing he wasn't completely blood crazed.

Or was he? Thinking back upon what he had wrought with Throe, it was difficult not to judge his actions by that condemning catchall.

With a curse, he hung his head, exhaustion and a strange kind of en-nui settling upon his shoulders—

The back door at the kitchen opened, and given that it was too early for his soldiers to return, he knew that it was Zypher with the update on Throe's departure.

"Was he all right?" Xcor asked without looking up. "Did he get off safely?"

"He is and he did."

Xcor's eyes shot up. Throe himself was in the archway, standing tall and proud, his eyes alert, his body strong.

"And he returneth safely," the male finished in a grim tone.

Xcor immediately refocused on his soup and blinked hard. From a vast distance, he watched as the spoon in his hand shook out its contents.

"Did Zypher not tell you," he muttered gruffly.

"That I was free? Aye. He did."

"If you wish to fight, I shall set aside my meal."

"I don't know that you're up to anything but feeding yourself the now."

Damn sleeveless shirts, Xcor thought as he turned his arms inward so that less of the damage showed. "I could muster if need be. Where are your boots?"

"I don't know. They took everything I had."

"Were you treated well."

"Well enough." Throe came forward, the boards beneath his feet creaking. "Zypher said you wanted to know none of what I've seen."

Xcor just shook his head.

"He also said that I would never get an apology out of you." There was a long pause. "I want one. Now."

Xcor put aside his soup and found himself searching the wounds he had given himself, recalling all that pain, all that blood—which had dried brown on the floorboards beneath him.

"And then what," he said in a rough voice.

"You'll have to find out."

Fair enough, Xcor thought.

Without grace—not that he had any, anyway—he rose to his feet. At his full height, he was unsteady for too many reasons to count, and the off-balance feeling got even worse as he met the eyes of his . . . friend.

Looking Throe in the face, he stepped up and put out his palm. "I am sorry."

Three simple words spoken loud and clear. And they didn't go nearly far enough.

"I was wrong to treat you as I did. I am . . . not as much of the Blood-letter as I thought—as I have e'er wanted to be."

"This is not a bad thing," Throe said quietly.

"When it comes to the likes of you, I would agree."

"And the others?"

"The others as well." Xcor shook his head. "That would be as far as it goes, however."

"So your ambitions have not changed."

"No. My methods, though . . . they will ne'er be the same."

In the silence that followed, he had no clue what he was going to get in return: a curse, a punch, a wretched row. The instability struck him as more than fair.

"Ask me to return to you as a free male," Throe demanded.

"Please. Come back, and you have my word—though it be worth less than a pence—that you shall be accorded the respect you have long deserved."

After a moment, his palm was engulfed. "All right then."

Xcor released a shuddering breath, one born out of relief. "All right, indeed."

Releasing the fighter's hand, he bent down, picked up his mostly untouched bowl of food . . . and offered what little he had to Throe.

"You will allow me to transform communications," the male said.

"Aye."

And that was that.

Throe accepted the soup and went over to where Xcor had been sitting. Sinking down to the floor, he put the brass box on the far side of himself and began to eat.

Xcor joined him on the stain of the blood he had shed during the day, and in silence, they completed their reunion. But it was not over, at least not on Xcor's part.

His regret stayed with him, the heaviness of the burden of his actions altering him forever, like an injury that had scarred over and healed wrong.

Or rather, in this case . . . healed right.

Autumn

THIRTY-FIVE

No'One awoke in an earthquake.

Beneath her, the mattress was all a-jumbling, the great force of the disturbance pitching pillows this way and that, sending covers flying, the cold air barging in against her skin—

Her consciousness quickly redefined the cause of the chaos. It was not the earth moving, but Tohrment. He was flailing beside her as if fighting against ties that bound him to the bed, his massive body jerking uncontrollably.

He'd had that dream again. The one he refused to speak of, and which, therefore, had to concern his beloved.

The glow from the bathroom caught his naked body as he landed on his feet, the clenched muscles of his back throwing hard-lined shadows, his hands curled in fists, his thighs engaged as if he were about to spring forward.

As he caught his breath and got his bearings, the name that was carved into his skin in a graceful arch expanded and contracted, almost as if the female was alive again:

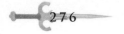

WELLESANDRA

Without a word, Tohrment stalked into the bathroom, closing the door, cutting off the illumination . . . and her.

Lying in the dark, she listened to the water start to run. A quick glance to the bedside clock indicated it was about time to get up, and yet she stayed where she was.

How many days had she spent in this bed of his? A month's worth. No, two . . . mayhap three? Time had ceased to have meaning to her, the nights wafting by like fragrance on a summer's breeze.

She supposed he was her first lover.

Except . . . he refused to take her fully.

Moreover, even after all this time together, he did not allow her to touch him. Nor did he sleep under the covers with her. Or kiss her on the mouth. And he did not join her in the tub or the pool, or watch her dress with lingering eyes . . . and he did not hold her when they slept.

Still, he was generous with his sensual talents, taking her time and time again to that place of transient bliss, always so careful with her body and her releases. And she knew it pleased him, as well: His body's reaction was too powerful to hide.

It seemed greedy to want more. But she did.

In spite of all the mad heat they called up from each other, in spite of the way he freely fed from her and she did the same from him, she felt . . . stalled. Trapped in a place that was short of an ultimate destination. Even though she had found structure in her nights working down at the compound, and relief and anticipation every dawn when he came back in health and strength, she was . . . quagmired. Restless.

Unhappy.

Which was why she had finally requested a visitor to come to the compound this evening.

At least she could make some progress somewhere. Or so she hoped.

Slipping out from the pocket of warmth she herself created, she shivered even though the heating units were on. The inconsistent temperature was one thing that she had yet to get used to on this side—and the only thing about the Sanctuary that she missed. Here, there were times when she was o'erheated, and others when she had a chill, the latter more prevalent now that September had arrived and ushered in with it the early frosts of fall.

As she pulled on her robe, its folds were cold, and she trembled within the fabric's cloying embrace. She made sure she was always dressed whenever she was out of bed. Tohrment had never said as much, but she had the sense that he preferred her as such: As much as he appeared to enjoy the feel of her, his eyes avoided her nakedness and ducked away, too, when they were in public—even though surely his Brothers knew that she stayed with him.

She had a feeling, even though he had said he knew it was her whom he pleasured, that he tried to find his *shellan* in her body, in their experiences together.

Any reminder to the contrary would be difficult for him.

Slipping her feet into her leather moccasins, she hesitated before leaving. She hated that he was in extremis, but he would never talk to her about it. In fact, lately, he did not speak much when she was around him, even though their bodies were fluent in whatever language it was they communicated in. Indeed, nothing good could come out of her lingering, especially given the mood he had to be in.

Forcing herself to the door, she put her hood up and her head out, looking both ways before stepping into the corridor and shutting him in by himself.

As usual, she left without making a sound.

"Lassiter," Tohr hissed into the bathroom mirror. When there was no reply, he splashed his face with cold water again. *"Lassiter."*

As he closed his eyes, he saw his Wellsie in that gray landscape. She was even farther away from him, off now in the distance . . . harder than ever to reach as she sat so still among those boulders of gray stone.

They were losing ground.

"Lassiter—where the *fuck* are you?"

The angel finally made an appearance over on the edge of the Jacuzzi, a box of Freddie Freihofer's chocolate-chip cookies in one hand, a long-tall of milk in the other.

"Want one?" he said, jogging the calorie payload. "They're right out of the fridge. So much better cold."

Tohr glared at the guy. "You told me I was the problem." When all he got was chewing, he had the urge to feed the whole box to the bastard. At once. "She's still there. She's nearly *gone*."

Lassiter put the spoil-your-dinner aside, like maybe he'd just lost his appetite. And when he simply shook his head, Tohr had a moment of panic.

"If you've bullshitted me, angel, I'm going to kill you."

The other male rolled his eyes. "I'm already dead, idiot. And might I remind you that your *shellan's* not the only one I'm trying to get free—my destiny is hers, remember. You fail, I fail—so I'm not incented to fuck with you."

"Then why the hell is she still in that horrible place?"

Lassiter threw up his hands. "Look, man, it's going to take more than a couple of orgasms. You've got to know that."

"Jesus *Christ*, I can't do much more than I am—"

"Really." Lassiter's eyes narrowed. "You sure about that."

As their stares clashed, Tohr had to look away—as well as reassess any privacy he assumed he and No'One had.

Fuck that; they'd had a hundred orgasms together, so . . .

"You know as well as I do how much you haven't done," the angel said softly. "Blood, sweat and tears, that's what it's going to take."

Lowering his head, Tohr rubbed his temples, feeling like he was going to scream. Fucking bullshit—

"You're going out tonight, yeah?" the angel murmured. "So when you get back, come find me."

"You're with me anyway, aren't you."

"Don't know what you're talking about. Let's meet after Last Meal."

"What are you going to do with me?"

"You say you want help—well, I'm going to give it to you."

The angel got to his feet and sauntered toward the bathroom's door. Then doubled back and got his frickin' cookies. "Until dawn, my friend."

Left by himself, Tohr briefly considered the merits of punching the mirror—but then figured he might endanger his chances of going out and finding some *lessers* to kill. And right now? That prospect was the only thing keeping him in his own skin.

Blood. Sweat. Tears.

Cursing, he took a shower, shaved, and went out into the bedroom. No'One was already gone, likely so that she could make it down to First Meal separately from him. She did this every night, even though the show of discretion couldn't possibly fool anybody.

You know as well as I do how much you haven't done.

Damn it to hell, Lassiter probably did have a point—and not just about the whole sex thing.

As he thought about it, he realized he never explained himself to

No'One. Like, there was no way she didn't know that he'd had a nightmare again—him popping off the bed like it was a toaster and moody-ing around was a neon sign in the room. But he never talked about it with her. Never gave her an opening to ask about it.

He didn't really talk to her about anything, actually. Not his work out in the field. Not his Brothers. Not the ongoing struggles the king was having with the *glymera*.

And there were so many other distances that he maintained . . .

At his closet, he ripped out a pair of leathers, stepped into them, and—

The waistband jammed at his thighs. And when he pulled them again, they stayed put. Yanking them even harder, they . . . split at the fly into two halves.

What. The. Fuck.

Goddamn pieces of shit.

He grabbed another pair. And ran into the same problem—his thighs were too big for them.

Going through his closet, he checked all his sets of fighting clothes. Now that he thought about it, things had been getting tighter lately. Jackets constricting his shoulders. Shirts ripped under the armpits at the end of the night. Thighgate.

Glancing over his shoulder, he caught his reflection in the mirror over one of the dressers.

Damn, he was . . . back to the size he had once been. Strange that he hadn't noticed until tonight, but his body, now on a regular feeding schedule, had blown out to its previous dimensions, his shoulders corded with muscle, his arms bulging, his stomach rippled, his thighs swollen with power.

No'One was responsible for this. It was her blood in him making him this strong.

Turning away, he went over to the phone by the bed, ordered up another pair of leathers in a bigger size, stat, and then parked it on the chaise.

His eyes locked on the closet.

The mating dress was still in it, pushed to the rear, hanging where he had put it when he'd resolved to try to move on.

Lassiter was right: He hadn't taken things as far as he could. But, God, having sex with someone else? As in actual sex? There had only ever been his Wellsie.

Shiiiiit . . . this nightmare he was in just kept getting more "mare."

But, God, that vision as he'd woken up, of his *shellan* ever farther

away . . . even more faded . . . her exhausted eyes tortured and gray as the landscape.

The knock on the door was too strong to be Fritz.

"Come in."

John Matthew peered around the jamb. The kid was dressed for fighting, his weapons on, his mood dark.

"Going out early?" Tohr said.

No, I've switched shifts with Z—just wanted you to know that.

"What's wrong?"

Nothing.

What a lie. The truth came out in the sharp edges to the kid's words, his hands forming the positions of ASL with hard corners on the letters. And he wouldn't look anywhere but the floor.

Tohr thought of the messy bed across the way, and the fact that No'One had left one of her spare sheaths on the chair over by the bureau.

"John," he said. "Listen . . ."

The kid didn't look at him. Just stood there in the open doorway, head down, brows down, body twitching to leave.

"Come in a minute. And shut the door."

John took his time and crossed his arms when he was done closing them in.

Crap. Where to start.

"I think you know what's going on here. With No'One."

None of my business, came the signed response.

"Bullshit." At least that got him some eye contact—too bad, since he promptly stalled out on the reveal. How could he explain what was going on? "It's a complicated situation. But no one's taking Wellsie's place." Shit, that name. "I mean—"

Do you love her?

"No'One? No, I don't."

So what the hell are you doing here—no, don't answer that. John paced around, hands on hips, weapons catching the light in subtle flashes. *I can guess.*

In a sad way, Tohr thought, the anger was honorable. A son protecting the memory of his mother.

God, that hurt.

"I've got to move on," Tohr whispered hoarsely. "I have no choice."

The fuck you don't. But like I said, it's none of my business. I gotta go. Later—

"If you think for one moment that I'm having a party in here, you're too wrong."

I've heard the sounds. I know exactly *how much fun you're having.*

As he took off, the door shut with a crack.

Fantastic. This night got any better and someone was going to lose a leg. Or a head.

THIRTY-SIX

Generally speaking, the scent of human blood wasn't nearly as interesting as that of a *lesser* or a vampire. But it was equally recognizable, and something that you had to pay a little attention to.

As Xhex threw a leg over her Ducati, she sniffed the air again.

Definitely human, coming from west of the Iron Mask.

Checking her watch, she saw she had a little extra time before her meet-and-greet, and whereas in the normal course of business she wouldn't give any kind of mess involving humans even a drive-by, in light of current events in the black-market trade, she dismounted, took her key, and dematerialized in that direction.

Over the last three months, there had been a rash of killings downtown. Well . . . duh on that. But the ones she had been interested in were not the sloppy gang-related drive-bys, or the heat-of-passion trigger fingers, or the drunken hit-and-runs. Her group fell into the fourth big catchall—drug related.

Except not in your run-of-the-mill kind of way.

The deaths were all suicides.

Middlemen were capping themselves left and right—and really, what were the chances that so many of those motherfuckers would develop a conscience at the same time? Unless, of course, someone was putting a moral additive in the Caldwell water system. In which case Trez would be out of business on a couple of different levels—and he wasn't.

The human police were flummoxed. The news media had gone national. The politicians were all excited and getting up on their stumps.

She'd even tried to do some Nancy Drewing herself, but her timing had always been of the day/late, dollar/short variety.

Then again, she already knew the answer to a lot of those human questions: That Old Language symbol for death on those packets was the key. And gee whiz . . . the more guys who ate their own bullets, the more those stamps had appeared. They were even starting to show up on heroin and Ecstasy packaging now, not just cocaine.

The vampire in question, whoever he or she was, was gradually staking their claim. And after a busy summer season of influencing human filth to take themselves out of the gene pool, they'd managed to kill off an entire demographic in the drug trade: All that were left were street-corner retailers . . . and Benloise, the big-fish supplier.

As she took form behind a parked van, it was clear that she'd gotten to the scene right after it had all gone down: There were two guys making like mud puddles on the asphalt, lying faceup with unseeing eyes. Both had guns in their hands and holes in the fronts of their brains, and the car that the RIPs had come in was still going at an idle, its doors open, steam rising from its tailpipe.

None of that was what she cared about, however. What she was really interested in was the male vampire getting into a sleek Jaguar, his black hair flashing blue in the overhead light of an archway.

Guess her day/dollar ratio was on an upswing.

With a quick shift, she re-formed in front of his car, and thanks to the fact that he had no headlights on, she caught a good look at his face in the glow from the dashboard.

Well, well, well, she thought, as his head shot up to her.

The slow laugh that came out of the male belonged with the summer nights: deep, warm—and dangerous as coming lightning. "The fair Xhexania."

"Assail. Welcome to the New World."

"I had heard you were here."

"Likewise." She nodded at the bodies. "I understand that you've been performing a public service."

The vampire assumed an evil expression, one she had to respect. "You give me credit where it may not be due."

"Uh-huh. Right."

"You can't tell me you care about these rats without tails?"

"I care that your product has been in my club."

"Club?" Elegant brows peaked over those cold eyes. "You work with humans?"

"Keep them in line is more like it."

"And you don't approve of chemicals."

"The more they're under the influence, the more annoying they are."

There was a long pause. "You look good, Xhex. But you always did."

She thought of John and the way he'd handled that vampire wannabe a couple of months ago. It would be a different scenario with Assail—John would have much more fun with a worthier opponent, and Assail was capable of anything. . . .

With a shot of pain, she abruptly wondered whether her mate would even bother fighting for her now.

Things were different between them, and not in a good way. All those summertime resolutions to stay close and connected had faded under the grind of their nightly jobs, those short bursts of seeing each other seeming to create more distance than they cured.

Until now, in the cold weather of fall, their visits were harder, less frequent. Less sexual, too.

"What's the matter, Xhex," Assail said softly. "I can smell pain."

"You overestimate your nose—and your reach, if you think you can take over Caldwell so fast. You're trying to fill some big-ass shoes."

"Your boss, Rehvenge's, you mean."

"Precisely."

"Does that mean you'll come work for me when I finish cleaning house?"

"Not on your life."

"How about on yours?" He tempered that one with a smile. "I've always liked you, Xhex. If you ever want a real job, come find me—I don't have a problem with half-breeds."

Annnnd didn't that little ditty make her want to kick him in the teeth. "Sorry, I like where I'm at."

"Not according to your scent, you don't." As he turned the car engine on, the subtle growl foretold all kinds of horses under the hood. "I'll see you around."

With a casual wave, he shut himself in, revved the engine, and tore off without putting on his lights.

As she stared at the dead he'd left behind, she thought, well, at least she had a name now, but that was the extent of the good news. Assail was the kind of male you didn't turn your back on for an instant. A chameleon without a conscience, he could be a thousand different faces to a thousand different people—with no one ever knowing the real him.

For example, she didn't believe he found her attractive for one moment. It was just a comment to put her off balance. And it had worked; just not for the reason he'd intended.

God, John . . .

This shit between them was killing them both, but they were stalled out. Unable to make things work; unable to let things go.

It was a mess.

Flashing back to her bike, she mounted, put her sunglasses on to protect her eyes, and took off. As she headed out of downtown, she blew past a fleet of CPD squad cars with their lights flashing and sirens blaring, going as fast as their tires would take them toward where she had just been.

Have fun, boys, she thought.

Wonder if they had a protocol for multiple suicides by now.

She herself headed north toward the mountains. It would have been more efficient to just dematerialize, but she needed to air her head out, and there was nothing like doing eighty on a rural road to get your skull clean as a whistle. With the cold air shoving her aviators back onto her nose, and her biker's jacket forming a second skin across her breasts, she gunned the engine even harder, stretching out flat over the bike, becoming one with the machine.

As she closed in on the Brotherhood's mansion, she wasn't sure why she'd agreed to this. Maybe it was just surprise at the request. Maybe she wanted to run into John. Maybe she was . . . looking for something, anything, that was a change from this fog of sadness she was living in.

Then again, maybe the fact that she was meeting with her mother meant shit was only going to get worse.

About fifteen minutes later, she turned off the road and ran smack into the *mhis* that was always in place. Slowing down, so she didn't hit a deer or a tree, she gradually ascended the mountain's rise, stopping at the series of gates that were similar to the ones that led to the training center entrance.

There was barely a delay at each of the security cameras; she was expected.

After she passed through the last barricade, and started on the wide turn that led to the courtyard, her heart relocated to her gut. Dayum, the huge stone house still looked the same. But come on, like it would have changed at all? There could be a nuclear bomb shower along the northeast coast and the place would still be solid.

This fortress, cockroaches, and Twinkies. All that would be left.

She parked the Ducati just beyond the stone steps that went up to the front door, but she didn't dismount. Looking at the arching jambs, the massive carved panels, the glowering gargoyles that had cameras in their mouths—there was no welcome mat in sight.

Enter at your own risk was the point.

A quick check of her watch told her what she already knew: John would already be out for the night, fighting in the part of town she had just left—

Xhex cranked her head to the left.

Her mother's grid was out back, in the gardens behind the house.

This was good. She didn't want to go inside. Didn't want to walk across the foyer. Didn't want to remember what she had been wearing, thinking, dreaming of when she'd been mated.

Dumb-ass fantasy of what life was going to be like.

Dematerializing to the far side of the barrier hedge, she had no trouble orienting herself. She and John had wandered out here in the spring, ducking beneath the budding branches of the fruit trees, breathing in the forgotten smell of fresh earth, holding each other against the chill that they knew was not long for the air.

So much possibility back then. And given where they were now, it seemed kind of fitting that all of summer's warmth was gone, that vital blooming period missed altogether: Now the leaves were on the ground, the branches were bare once again, and everything was about hunkering down.

Well, wasn't she a Hallmark card tonight.

Zeroing in on her mother's grid, she went along the side of the house, passing by the French doors of the billiards room and the library.

No'One was down at the pool's edge, a still figure spotlit by the blue glow of water that was yet to be drained.

Wow . . . Xhex thought. Something big had changed with the female, and whatever the shift was, it had altered much of her emotional super-structure. Her grid was jumbled up, but not in a bad way; more like a house that was undergoing extensive renovations. It was a good start, a positive transformation that was probably a long time in coming.

"Attaboy, Tohr," Xhex murmured under her breath.

As if she had heard, No'One looked over her shoulder—and that was when Xhex realized that the hood that was always up was down, her moth-er's cap of smooth blond hair suggesting that the stuff was braided, with the long end tucked under the robing.

Xhex waited for fear to light up that grid. And waited. And waited . . .

Holy shit, something *really* had changed.

"Thank you for coming," No'One said as Xhex approached.

That voice was different. A little deeper. Surer.

She had been transformed in a lot of ways.

"Thanks for inviting me," Xhex replied.

"You look well."

"As do you."

Stopping in front of her mother, she measured the way the flickering light from the pool played across the female's perfectly lovely face. And in the quiet that followed, Xhex frowned, information flooding through her sensory receptors, the picture filling out.

"You are stuck," she said, thinking that was kind of ironic.

Her mother's brows flared. "As a matter of fact . . . I am."

"Funny." Xhex looked at the sky. "Me, too."

Staring up at the strong, proud female in front of her, No'One felt the strangest connection to her daughter: as the restless reflections from the pool played over tough, grim features, those gunmetal gray eyes held an edgy frustration similar to her own.

"So you and Tohr, huh," Xhex said casually.

No'One put her hands up to her hot blush. "I do not know how to respond to that."

"Maybe I shouldn't have brought it up. It's just—yeah, it's all over your mind."

"Not really."

"Liar." There was no accusation, though. No censure. Just a statement of fact.

No'One turned back to the water and reminded herself that as a half *symphath*, her daughter would know the truth even if she didn't say a word.

"I have no right to him," she murmured, looking at the pool's churning surface. "No right to any of him. But that is not why I asked you to come—"

"Says who?"

"I'm sorry?"

"Who says he's not yours."

No'One shook her head. "You know all the whys."

"No. I don't. If you want him and he wants you—"

"He does not. Not . . . in all ways." No'One brushed at her hair even though it was already back off her face. Dearest Virgin Scribe, her heart was beating so hard. "I can't . . . I shouldn't speak of this."

It felt safer not to utter a syllable to a soul—she knew Tohr wouldn't like to be speculated about.

There was a long silence.

"John and I aren't doing well."

No'One glanced over, brows up at her daughter's candidness. "I . . . I had wondered. You have been long gone from here, and he has not looked happy. I had hoped for . . . a different outcome. On many levels."

Including between the two of them.

And indeed, it was true what Xhex had said. They were each stalled—not exactly the accord one would wish for. However, she would take any commonality that presented itself.

"I think you and Tohr make sense," Xhex said abruptly, as she began to wander down the edge of the pool. "I like it."

No'One arched her brows again. And reassessed the no-talk rule. "Truly?"

"He's a good male. Steady, reliable—damn tragic about what happened to his family. John's been worried about him for so long—you know, she was the only mother John had. Wellsie, that is."

"Did you ever meet her?"

"Not formally. She wasn't the type to hang out where I worked, and God knew I was never welcome where the Brotherhood was. But I was aware of her reputation. Tough cookie—really blunt, a female of worth in that regard. I don't think the *glymera* were big fans of hers, and the fact that she didn't care about them was just another thing to recommend her, in my opinion."

"Theirs was a true love story."

"Yeah, from what I hear. Frankly, I'm surprised that he's been able to move on, but I'm glad he has—it's done you a world of good."

No'One took a deep breath and smelled dry leaves. "He has no choice."

"I'm sorry?"

"It is not my story to tell, but suffice it to say, if he could choose another path, any other, he would."

"I don't understand what you're getting at." When No'One didn't fill in with explanations, Xhex shrugged. "I can respect the boundaries."

"Thank you. And I'm glad you came."

"I was surprised you wanted me here—"

"I have failed you too many times to count." As Xhex visibly recoiled, No'One nodded. "When I first arrived herein, I was overwhelmed by so much, lost though I spoke the language, isolated though I was not alone. I want you to know, however, that you are the real reason I came—and tonight, it is time that I apologized to you."

"For what?"

"For abandoning you at your very beginning."

"Jesus . . ." The female rubbed her short hair, her powerful body wincing in place, as if she were having to force herself not to bolt. "Ah, listen, there's nothing to apologize for. You didn't ask to be—"

"You were a young, newly born unto the world, without a *mahmen* to care for you. I left you to fend for yourself when you could do little more than cry for warmth and succor. I am . . . so sorry, my daughter." She put her hand up to her heart. "It has taken me too long to find my voice and my words, but know that I have practiced this for hours in my head. I want what I say to you to be correct, because everything has been wrong between you and me from day one—and it is all my doing. I was so selfish, and I lacked courage, and I—"

"Stop." Xhex's voice was strained. "Please . . . just stop—"

"—was wrong to ever turn my back on you. I was wrong to wait this long. I was wrong about everything. But this." She stamped her foot. "This night I reveal to you all my faults, so that I may also pledge you my love, however imperfect and unwanted it is. I do not deserve to be your mother, or to call you daughter, but mayhap we may form a kind of . . . friendship. I can understand if this is unwanted as well, and I know that I have no

right to demand anything from you. Just know that I am here, and my heart and mind are open to learning about who you are . . . and what you are."

Xhex blinked once, and then stayed silent. As if what had been spoken to her had come over a bad radio frequency and she was forced to extrapolate meaning.

After a moment, the female said roughly, "I'm a *symphath*. You know that, right? The term 'half-breed' doesn't mean shit when the 'half' is sin-eater."

No'One kicked up her chin. "You are a female of worth. That is what you are. I care naught for the composition of your blood."

"You were terrified of me."

"I was terrified of everything."

"And you have to see that . . . male in my face. Every time you look at me, you have to remember what was done to you."

At that, No'One swallowed hard. She supposed that part was true, but it was also the least important thing going forward: it was more than time to make this about her daughter. "You are a female of worth. That is what I see. Nothing more . . . *and nothing less.*"

Xhex blinked again. A couple of times. Then faster.

And then she lunged forward, and No'One found herself enveloped in a strong, sure embrace.

She did not hesitate for a moment to return the gesture of affection.

As she held on to her daughter, she thought, yes, indeed, forgiveness was best expressed through contact. Words could not give nuance to the sensation of holding what she had eschewed in a moment of great agony, of having her blood against her, of supporting the female, even just briefly, whom she had so selfishly wronged.

"My daughter," she said in a voice that cracked. "My beautiful, strong . . . worthy daughter."

With a shaking hand, she cupped the back of Xhex's head and turned the female's face to the side, so that she held her upon her shoulder as she would have a babe. Then with soft, gentle strokes, she smoothed the short hair.

It was impossible to say that she was grateful for anything that *symphath* had done to her. But this moment took the sting away, this vital moment when she felt as if the circle that had started to be drawn in her womb had finally been completed, two halves that had long tarried apart, coming to cleave once more.

When Xhex eventually pulled back, No'One gasped. "You bleed!"

Reaching up to her daughter's cheek, she cleared away the red drops with her hands. "I shall get Doc Jane—"

"Don't worry about it. It's just . . . yeah, nothing to worry about. It's the way I . . . cry."

No'One put her hand on her daughter's face and shook her head in wonder. "You are nothing like me." As the female looked away sharply, she said, "No, that is good. You are so strong. So powerful. I love that about you—I love all about you."

"You can't mean that."

"Your *symphath* side . . . it is a blessing of sorts." As Xhex began disagreeing, No'One cut her off. "It gives you a layer of protection against . . . things. It gives you a weapon against . . . things."

"Maybe."

"Definitely."

"You know something? I was never mad at you. I mean, I understand why you did what you did. You brought an abomination into the world—"

"Do not *ever* use that word around me," No'One barked. "Not when it comes to yourself. Are we clear."

Xhex laughed in a throaty way, putting her palms up in defense. "Okay. Okay."

"You are a miracle."

"More like a curse." When No'One opened her mouth to argue, Xhex cut her off. "Look, I appreciate this whole . . . thing. I really do—I mean, it's really good of you. But I don't believe in butterflies and unicorns, and neither should you. Do you know what I've been for the last . . . God, as many years as I can remember?"

No'One frowned. "You have been working in the human world, no? I believe I overheard that at some point?"

Xhex lifted her pale hands, flexing the fingers into claws and releasing them. "I've been an assassin. I've been paid to hunt people down and kill them. There's blood all over me, No'One—and you need to know that before you go planning any kind of rosy-rosy reunion for us. Again, I'm glad that you asked me to come here, and you are more than totally forgiven for everything—but I'm not sure you have a realistic picture of me."

No'One tucked her arms into the sleeves of her robe. "Are you . . . engaged in that practice now?"

"Not for the Brotherhood or my old boss. But with the job I have at the moment? If I had to revisit that skill set, I would without hesitation. I protect what's mine, and if anyone gets in the way, I will do what I have to. That's how I am."

No'One studied those features, that stark expression, that tense, muscled body that was more like a male's . . . and saw what was behind the strength: There was a vulnerability to Xhex, as if she were waiting to be turned away, shut out, shoved aside.

"I think that's just fine."

Xhex actually jumped. "What?"

No'One kicked up her chin once more. "I am surrounded by males who live by those rules. Why should it be any different for you because you are female? I'm rather of proud of you, actually. Better to be the aggressor than the aggressed upon—I should much rather have you of that mind than any other."

Xhex took a shuddering breath. "God . . . damn . . . you have no idea how badly I need to hear that right now."

"I shall be pleased to repeat it, if you would like?"

"I never thought . . . well, whatever. I'm glad you're here. I'm glad you called. I'm glad you . . ."

As the sentence was not finished, No'One smiled, a bright, shining light striking up within her chest. "Myself as well. Mayhap, if you have . . . how do they say, time off? We could tarry some hours away together?"

Xhex started to grin a little. "Can I ask you something?"

"Anything."

"You ever been on a motorcycle?"

"What's that?"

"Come around to the front of the house. Let me show you."

THIRTY-SEVEN

Zohr came back at the end of the evening with two dirty daggers, no ammunition, and a bone bruise on his right calf that made him limp like a zombie.

Fucking tire irons. Then again, payback to that particular *lesser* had been kind of fun. Nothing like sanding the face off your enemy to lighten the mood.

Asphalt was his friend.

It had been a hard night fighting for all of them, a late one, too—both of which were good. The hours had sped by, and even though he stank like spoiled meat from all the black blood, and his new pair of leathers were going to have to be stitched up on one side, he felt better than he had when he'd headed out.

Fighting and fucking, as Rhage had always said. Those were the two best mood stabilizers there were.

Too bad the fact that he was more chilled out didn't mean anything was different. The same shit was waiting for him as he came home.

Stepping through the vestibule, he began the disarming ritual, undoing his chest holster, his shoulder holster, his gun belt. The scent of freshly

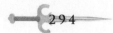

cooked lamb with rosemary filled the foyer, and a quick glance into the dining room showed that the *doggen* had set everything up properly, the silver gleaming, the crystal sparkling, people already beginning to gather for Last Meal.

No'One wasn't among them as was usually the case.

Jogging up the stairs, he couldn't deny the arousal that got harder and harder the higher he went. But the erection didn't exactly make him happy.

You know as well as I do how much you haven't done.

When he got to his door, he gripped the knob and closed his eyes. Then, forcing the panels wide, he said, "No'One?"

Her shift would have been over for about an hour—Fritz had insisted that she have some time to ready herself for dining, something she had fought initially, but seemed to have been taking advantage of lately, as the Jacuzzi was always damp at its drain when he came back after fighting.

He hoped he wouldn't catch her in the tub. He wanted a shower, and didn't know how to handle the two of them in the bathroom naked together.

You know as well as I do—

"Shut. Up." He dropped his weapons and started to shuck his muscle shirt and his shitkickers. "No'One? You here?"

Frowning, he leaned into the bathroom, and found a whole lot of nobody.

No fragrance in the air. No draining water in the tub. No towels out of place.

Weird.

With a scattered head, he went back out into the corridor, hit the grand staircase and put the hidden door underneath it to good use. As he went through the underground tunnel, he wondered if she was in the pool.

He hoped she wasn't. His cock prayed she was.

For godsakes, he didn't know what the fuck to think anymore.

Except . . . she wasn't floating, naked or otherwise, on its surface. And she wasn't where the washers and dryers were. Not in the weight room or the locker room or the gym restacking towels. Not in the clinic area putting fresh scrubs in the shelving, either.

She wasn't . . . there.

His trip back to the mansion took half the time of the jog out, and when he got to the kitchen, all he found was a shitload of *doggen* doing the dinner scurry.

Stretching his senses out for the first time, he discovered . . . she wasn't anywhere in the mansion.

A striking panic went through him, making his head hum—

No, wait, that was the sound of a . . . motorcycle?

The deep, rumbling growl made no sense. Unless Xhex had come home for some reason—which was good news for John—

No'One was out in front of the house. Right now.

Tracking his blood in her veins, he ran out across the foyer, shot through the vestibule, and . . . stopped dead on the top step of the entrance.

Xhex was on her Ducati, her black leather form fitting perfectly with the bike. And right behind her? No'One was sharing the seat, her hood off, her hair a frizzy mess, her smile as bright as the sun.

The expression changed as she saw him, tightening up.

"Hey," he said, feeling his heart rate start to return to normal.

Behind him, he sensed someone else come out of the vestibule. John.

Xhex glanced at her mate and nodded, but did not cut the engine. Looking over her shoulder, she said, "You okay there, Mom?"

"Yes, indeed." No'One dismounted awkwardly, her robe resettling down at her feet as if it were relieved to have the joyride over with. "I shall see you tomorrow night?"

"Yup. I'll pick you up at three."

"Perfect."

The two females shared a smile that was so easy, he nearly teared the fuck up: Some kind of something had been reached between them . . . and if he couldn't have his Wellsie and son back . . . yeah, he would want No'One to find her true family.

Looked like a step in the right direction had been taken.

As No'One walked up the steps, John traded places with her, going down to the bike. Tohr wanted to ask her where they'd gone, what she'd done, what had been said. But he reminded himself that sleeping arrangements notwithstanding, he didn't have a right to any of that.

Which told him exactly how far they hadn't come, didn't it.

"You have fun?" he said as he backed up and held the door open for her.

"Yes, I did." She gathered the hem of her robe and limped into the vestibule. "Xhex took me for a motorcycle ride—or is it motorbike?"

"Either one works." Death trap. Donor cycle. Whatevs. "Next time, you wear a helmet, though."

"Helmet? As in an equestrian one?"

"Not exactly. We're talking about something a little sturdier than vel-vet with a chin strap. I'll get you one."

"Oh, thank you." She smoothed the wisps that were all over her cap of blond hair. "It was so . . . exhilarating. Like flying. I was scared at first, but she went slowly. Later, though, I learned to love it. We went very fast."

Well, didn't that make him want to shit in a bag for the rest of his life.

And for once, he found himself wishing she was afraid. That Ducati was nothing but an engine with a goddamn seat bolted to it. One bounce off the back, and that delicate skin of hers would be nothing but red paint for the road.

"Yeah . . . that's great." In his head, he started to give her a safety lec-ture that revolved around the fundamentals of kinetic energy and medical terms like *hematoma* and *amputation*. "You ready to eat?"

"I'm famished. All that fresh air."

In the distance, he heard the roar of that bike taking off, and then John came in looking like death.

The kid went directly to the billiards room, and ten to one, he wasn't after a handful of honey-roasted—but there would be no talking with him. He'd made that pretty damn clear at the beginning of the night.

"Come on," Tohr said. "Let's go sit down."

The usual din of conversation around the table quieted as they came through the arches, but he was too focused on the female walking ahead of him to care. The idea that she'd been out in the world on her own, roar-ing along in the night with Xhex, made her seem . . . different.

The No'One he knew would never have done something like that.

And, shit . . . for some reason, his body juiced at the thought of her in clothes other than that robe of hers, straddling that bike, her hair free from that braid and trailing into the night.

What would she look like in jeans? The good kind . . . the kind that hugged a female's ass, and made a male want to do some riding of the non-cycle variety.

Abruptly, he pictured her naked and up against the wall, her legs spread, her hair unbraided, her hands cupping her breasts. Like a good boy, he was on his knees, his mouth on her sex, his tongue licking at that place he had learned so much about with his fingers.

He was sucking on her. Feeling her against his face as she arched up and got tight—

The growl that came out of him was loud enough to echo in the silent room. Loud enough to bring No'One's surprised face around over her shoulder. Loud enough to make him seem like a total ass.

To cover his tracks, he made elaborate work out of pulling her chair from the table. Like the shit was brain surgery.

As No'One sat down, her own arousal drifted up into his nose, and he nearly had to strangle himself to keep another growl from vibrating up out of his chest.

Parking it in his own seat, his erection got pinched big-time behind his fly, and that was just fine. Maybe the blood supply would get cut off and the bitch would deflate—except . . . well, going on the cock-ring theory, the opposite would likely be true.

Fantastic.

He picked up his napkin, snapped it free of its elaborate fold, and—

Everyone was looking at him and No'One. The Brotherhood. Their *shellans*. Even the *doggen* who had yet to start serving.

"What," he muttered, as he laid the damask across his lap.

Annnnd that was when he realized that he wasn't wearing a shirt. And No'One hadn't put up her hood.

Hard to know who was getting more attention. Probably her, as most folks hadn't seen her without her face covered—

Before he knew it, his upper lip curled off his elongated fangs, and he met each one of the males in the eye, hissing at them low and nasty. In spite of the fact that they were all happily mated. And his brothers. And he had no right to be territorial.

Lot of brows went up. A couple of folks asked for another shot of whatever they were drinking. Someone started whistling casually.

As No'One quickly put her hood back into place, awkward conversations about the weather and sports sprouted.

Tohr just rubbed his temples. Hard to know what was giving him his headache.

There was so much to choose from.

In the end, the meal passed by without further incident. Then again, short of a food fight or a fire in the kitchen, it was hard to imagine what could have been a worthy second act to his playing rattlesnake at the Brotherhood.

When things broke up, he and No'One beat feet out of the dining room—but not for the same reason, evidently.

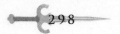

"I have to go to work now," she said as they came up to the staircase. "I was gone all evening."

"You can catch up at nightfall."

"That wouldn't be right."

As he found himself on the verge of telling her she should go to bed instead, he realized that in the last few months, No'One had spent time only with him: Yeah, sure, she had worked, but she did that alone, and at meals she stayed quiet.

Come to think of it, when they were upstairs, they were either hitting it or asleep. So she didn't really interact with him, either.

"Where did you and Xhex go?"

"All over. Down to the river. Into town."

He closed his eyes briefly at the "into town" bit. And then had to wonder why he had never taken her anywhere. Whenever he was off rotation, he was down in the gym or reading in bed, waiting for her to be done. It had never dawned on him to do anything with her out in the world.

That's because you've been hiding her as best you can, his conscience pointed out.

Whatever. She was always working—

"Hey, wait a minute, why don't you get any evenings off?" he demanded with a frown as he did the math. Shit, what the hell was that butler doing, working this female to the bone—

"Oh, I do, but I never take them. I don't like to simply sit around."

Tohr rubbed an eyebrow with his thumb.

"If you'll excuse me," she murmured, "I'll go down to the training center and get started now."

"When will you be finished."

"Probably about four in the afternoon."

"Okay." As she turned away, he put a hand on her forearm. "Ah, listen, if you go into the locker room during daylight hours, always knock and announce yourself, 'kay?"

The last thing anyone needed was her getting a gander at one of his naked brothers.

"Oh, of course. I always do."

As she disappeared around the corner, he watched her go, her limping form carrying an innate dignity that he abruptly felt he hadn't been honoring.

"We have a date, remember?"

Glancing to the right, he shook his head at Lassiter. "Not in the mood."

"Tough shit. Come on—I've got it all set up."

"Look, no offense, but I'm not good company now—"

"When are you ever?"

"I really don't—"

"Blah, blah, blah. Shut the fuck up and get your ass in gear."

As the angel grabbed hold and pulled, Tohr gave up the fight and allowed himself to be dragged up the staircase and down the hall of statues—and out the other side. They went past his room, past the boys' rooms, past Z and Bella and Nalla's suite. Out into the staff quarters. Over to the entrance to the movie theater.

Tohr stopped dead. "If this is another *Beaches* marathon, I'm going to Bette your ass until you can't sit down."

"Aw, look at you! Trying to be finny."

"Seriously, if you have any compassion in you at all, you'll let me go to bed—"

"I have peanut M&M's up there."

"Not my style."

"Raisinets."

"Feh."

"Sam Adams."

Tohr narrowed his eyes. "Cold?"

"Downright icy."

Tohr crossed his arms over his chest and told himself he was not pouting like a five-year-old. "I want Milk Duds."

"Got 'em. And popcorn."

With a curse, Tohr yanked open the door and ascended into the dimly lit red cave. The angel made everything seamless once they got up there: Deep-dish ass palaces engaged. Sam Adams with backups on the floor in a bucket with ice. An embarrassing caloric display with, yup, a yellow box of Milk Duds. And the damn popcorn.

They sat down side by side, and kicked up the footrests.

"Tell me this isn't a fifties-era sex-ed film," Tohr muttered.

"Nah. Popcorn?" the angel said as he hit *play* and offered a bowl. "Extra butter—the good plastic kind, too. Not that bullshit real cow crap."

"I'm okay right now."

Up on the screen, some movie studio's intro played along with a bunch of credits. And then there were two old people sitting on a couch. Talking.

Tohr took a pull of his beer. "What the hell is this?"

"*When Harry Met Sally.*"

Tohr lowered the longneck from his mouth. "What?"

"Shut it. After this, we're going to watch an episode of *Moonlighting*. Then *An Affair to Remember*—the old-school one, not that stupidity with Warren Beatty. Then *The Princess Bride*—"

Tohr hit the switch by his hip and straightened the chair up. "Okay. Right. Have fun with this—"

Lassiter hit *pause* and clamped a hard hand on his shoulder. "Sit the fuck back. Watch and learn."

"What? How much I hate rom-coms? How 'bout we just stipulate that and let me go."

"You're going to need this."

"For my second career as a pussy?"

"Because you have to remember how to be romantic."

Tohr shook his head. "No. Nope. Not going to happen . . ."

As he hopped on the over-my-dead-body train, Lassiter just kept shaking his head. "You gotta remember it's possible, buddy."

"The hell I do—"

"You're stalled, Tohr. And whereas you might have time to fart around, Wellsie doesn't have that luxury."

Tohr shut up. Sat back. Started to pick off the label on his beer. "I can't do that, man. I can't pretend to feel . . . that way."

"Kind of like you can't have sex with No'One? Just how long do you plan on going on like you are?"

"Until you disappear. Until Wellsie's free and you're gone."

"And how's that working for you. You like that dream you woke up with today?"

"Movies aren't going to help," he said after a moment.

"What else are you going to do? Jack off in your room until No'One comes back from work—then jack off next to her? Oh, wait, let me guess—pace around aimlessly. Because it's not like you've ever done that before." Lassiter shoved the bowl he'd offered into Tohr's face. "What the fuck is it going to cost you to hang here with me. Shut up and eat your half of the popcorn, asshole."

Tohr accepted what was in his grill only because it was either that or he ended up with Orville all over his lap.

One hour and thirty-six minutes later, he had to clear his throat as

Meg Ryan told Billy Crystal that she hated him in the middle of a New Year's Eve party.

"Sauce on the side," Lassiter said as he got up. "The answer to everything."

A minute later, young Bruce Willis came onscreen, and Tohr sent up a prayer of thanks. "This is much better. We need more beer, though."

"Got it."

A case of lager later and they had blown through two epis of *Moonlighting*, including a Christmas one where the cast and crew sang along with the actors in the last scene.

Which did *not* make him clear his throat again.

Really. It didn't.

Then they tried to get through *An Affair to Remember*. At least until Lassiter took pity on them both and started to rock the fast-forward button.

"Chicks say this is the greatest," the angel muttered, as he hit the button again and whoever it was started speed-emoting. "Maybe this one was a mistake."

"Amen on that."

Okay, the princess movie did not suck—that shit was funny in places. And, yeah, it was . . . cool when the pair got together at the end. Plus he liked Columbo as the granddad. But he couldn't really say any of it was turning him into a Casanova.

Lassiter glanced over. "We're not done yet."

"Just keep beering me."

"Ask and ye shall receive."

The angel handed him a freshie and disappeared into the control room to switch DVDs. As he came back down to where they were sitting, the screen lit up with—

Tohr jacked forward in his seat. "What the hell!"

As Lassiter's big body cut through the projection onto the screen, a gigantic pair of flapping breasts covered his face and chest. "*Adventures in the MILFy Way*. A true classic."

"It's porn!"

"Duh—"

"Okay, I am *not* sitting through this with you."

The angel, still standing up, shrugged. "Just wanted to make sure you know what you're missing."

Moans rumbled through the surround sound as those boobs . . . those frickin' *boobs* looked like they were slapping Lassiter in the piehole—

Tohr covered his eyes at the horror. "No! Not doing this!"

Lassiter cut off the movie, the sounds disappearing. And a quick intrafinger check indicated that it was a stop, not a pause, mercifully.

"I'm just trying to get through to you." Lassiter sat down, cracked open a beer, and looked tired. "Man, this angel crap . . . it's so fucking hard to influence anything. I've never had a problem with free will before, but for shit's sake, I wish I could just *I Dream of Jeannie* you to where you need to be." As Tohr winced, the angel muttered, "It's okay, though. We'll get you there somehow—"

"Actually, I'm cringing at the vision of you in a pink harem costume."

"Hey, I have a great ass, I'll have you know."

They drank beer for a while until a Sony logo started to appear at random points on the screen. "You ever been in love?" Tohr asked.

"Once. Never again."

"What happened." When the angel didn't answer, Tohr shot a look over. "Oh, so it's fine for you to be all up in my dark-and-dirty, but you can't return the favor?"

Lassiter shrugged. Opened yet another beer. "You know what I think?"

"Not unless you tell me."

"I think we should try another epi of *Moonlighting.*"

Tohr exhaled long and slow and had to agree. It didn't suck watching movies with the guy, talking over the dialogue while drinking Sam Adams and eating crap food. In fact, he could not remember the last time he'd ever just . . . hung out.

Of course, it must have been with Wellsie. If he'd had downtime, he'd always spent it with her.

God, how many days had they frittered away, mindlessly checking out in front of the television, watching reruns and crappy cable movies and droning newscasts. They'd held hands, or she'd lain on his chest, or he'd played with her hair.

Such wasted time, he thought. But when they'd been in that suck zone of minutes and hours, it had been . . . a simple, easy kind of bliss.

One more thing to mourn.

"How about something later in Willis's career?" he said roughly.

"*Die Hard?*"

"You set it up and I'll put another fire in the hole at the popcorn machine."

"Deal."

As they both rose and headed for the back, him to the candy and soda counter, Lassiter to the control booth, Tohr stopped the guy.

"Thanks, man."

The angel gave him a knock in the shoulder, and then went about getting some yippee-ki-yay-motherfucker on deck. "Just doing my job."

Tohr watched the angel's blond-and-black head duck through the narrow doorway.

Fuck free will was right. And as for him and No'One?

It was tough to think about what was coming next. Hell, when he'd first hooked up with her, it had taken the hide right off of him to ride through all the emotions just so he could accept her vein, give her his, and be with her to the extent he had.

If he took this any farther?

The next level was going to make that shit look like a walk in the park.

THIRTY-EIGHT

t was twelve noon when Xcor's cellular device went off, and the
soft chiming roused him from his light sleep. With awkward jabs,
he hunted and pecked around for the green send button, and after
he hit it, he put the thing to his ear.

In practice, he hated the damn things. In practical terms, they were
an incredible benefit, one that made him question why he had ever been
so resistant.

"Aye," he demanded. When a haughty voice answered him, he smiled
into the dim candlelight of the basement. "Greetings, gentlemale. How
fare thee this day, Elan?"

"What . . . what . . ." The aristocrat had to marshal more breath.
"Whatever have you sent me?"

His source on the Council had a rather high voice to begin with; the
care package that had obviously just been opened lifted the male's tone
into the stratosphere.

"Proof of our work." As he spoke, heads began to lift off of bunks, his
Band of Bastards waking, listening. "I did not want you to think that we

had overestimated our effectiveness—or, the Scribe Virgin preserve us, been untruthful with respect to our activities."

"I . . . I . . . Whatever shall I do with . . . this?"

Xcor rolled his eyes. "Mayhap some of your servants could parcel it up and share it among your fellow Council members. And then I imagine your carpet will need to be cleaned."

Inside the three-foot-by-three-foot cardboard box he'd had delivered, Xcor had put some of the souvenirs of their kills, all manner of bits and pieces of *lessers*: arms, hands, that spinal column, a head, part of a leg. He had been saving them up, preparing for the right moment to both shock the Council . . . and prove that the job was getting done.

The gamble was that the grotesque nature of his "gift" would backfire and they would be viewed as savages. The potential payoff was that he and his soldiers would be seen as effective.

Elan cleared his throat. "Indeed, you have been . . . rather busy."

"I realize that it is grisly, but war is a grisly business that you should merely be the beneficiary of, not a participant in. We need to save you—" Until you are no longer useful. "—from such unpleasantness. I should like to point out, however, that that is but a small sampling of the very many we have killed."

"In truth?"

The bit of awe there was gratifying. "Aye. You may be assured that we fight every night for the race, and we are highly successful."

"Yes, clearly, you are . . . and I would stipulate that I require no more 'proof,' as it were. I will say, however, that I was going to call you late this afternoon anyway. The final appointment with the king has been scheduled."

"Oh?"

"I called the members of the Council because I have scheduled for this evening a gathering—keeping it informal, of course, so that there is no procedural requirement to include Rehvenge. Assail has indicated he cannot attend. Clearly, he must have an audience with the king—or he would come unto my home."

"Clearly," Xcor drawled. Or rather, clearly not. Given Assail's nightly pursuits, which had only intensified since the summer, he was likely busy enough. "And I thank you for the information."

"When the others arrive, I shall exhibit this . . . display," the aristocrat said.

"Do that. And tell them that I am ready to meet with them at any time. You just call upon me—I am your servant in this as in all things. In fact," he paused for effect, "it shall be an honor to associate with them under your introduction—and together, you and I may ensure that they understand adequately the vulnerable state they are in under the rule of the Blind King, and the safety that you and I can provide for them."

"Oh, yes, indeed . . . yes." The gentlemale perked up at all that verbiage—which was precisely why it had been used. "And I am very appreciative of your candor."

Amazing when calculation was mistaken for that.

"And I for your support, Elan." As Xcor hung up the phone, he glanced over his soldiers and then focused on Throe. "After sunset, we coalesce upon Assail's property once again. Mayhap it will come to aught this time."

As the others growled their readiness, he mutely raised his cell phone . . . and inclined his head to his second in command.

"Sire, we have arrived. The door is shutting behind our vehicle."

As Fritz's voice came through the van's intercom, the butler's report wasn't a news flash, even though Tohr couldn't see anything of where they were from his vantage point in the back.

"Thanks, man."

Drumming his fingers on the floor's Duraliner, he was still buzzed from all those beers he'd had with Lassiter, and his stomach was a sour pit thanks to that marathon of plastic butter and Milk Duds.

Then again, maybe the nausea was more about where they were.

"Sire, you are free to extricate yourself."

Tohr crab-walked to the double doors, and wondered why the hell he was doing this to himself. After he and Lassiter had finished their homage to John McClane, the angel had taken off to go crash, and Tohr had . . . come up with this great idea, for no apparent reason.

Opening the way out . . . he stepped into his darkened garage and closed things up behind him.

Fritz put his window down. "Sire, mayhap I shall just wait here."

"No, you go. I'm going to hang until sunset."

"Are you certain the drapes are pulled indoors."

"Yup. That's protocol, and I trust my *doggen*."

"Mayhap I shall simply go through and double-check?"

"That's really not—"

"Please, sire. Do not send me home to face your king and your Brothers without my knowing you are safe."

Hard to argue with that. "I'll wait here."

The *doggen* hustled his old bones out from behind the wheel and headed across the way with admirable speed—probably because he was worried Tohr would change his mind.

As the butler slipped into the house, Tohr wandered around, inspecting his old lawn equipment, his rakes, his salt for the driveway. The Stingray convertible had been relocated to the mansion's garage . . . back on the night he'd brought Wellsie's gown over for Xhex.

He hadn't wanted to return here to drop off the dress after it had been cleaned and pressed.

Wasn't sure he wanted to be here now.

"All is secure, sire."

Tohr pivoted away from the empty space where the Corvette had been parked. "Thanks, man."

There was no waiting for the butler to leave before he went in—too much sunlight on the other side of the garage doors. So with a final wave, he pulled himself together . . . and walked into the back hall.

As the door clamped shut behind him, the first thing he saw in the mudroom was their winter coats. The damn parkas were still hung up on pegs, his, Wellsie's, and John's.

John's was tiny, because he'd been just a pretrans back then.

It was like the damn things were waiting for them all to come home again.

"Good luck with that," he muttered.

Bracing himself, he kept going, entering the kitchen that had been Wellsie's dream.

Fritz had thoughtfully left lights on, and the shock of seeing everything for the first time since the deaths made Tohr wonder if it wouldn't have been better to come in in the dark: The countertops they had chosen together, and that massive Sub-Zero she had loved so much, and that table they had bought online at 1stdibs.com, and the set of shelves he had put up for her cookbooks . . . all of it was on display, gleaming and clean as the day it had been installed/delivered/assembled.

Shit, nothing had changed. Everything was *exactly* as it had been the night she had been killed, his *doggen* keeping after the dust and that was it.

Walking over to the built-in desk, he forced himself to pick up a Post-it note with her handwriting on it.

Tues: Havers—checkup, 11:30.

He dropped the pad and turned away, seriously questioning his sanity. Why had he come here? What possible good could come out of this?

Wandering around, he went through the living room, the library, and the dining room, making a loop of the first floor's public rooms . . . until he felt like he couldn't breathe, until the alchie buzz was beyond gone and his vision and his sense of smell and his hearing were unbearably acute. Why was he—

Tohr blinked as he found himself in front of a door.

He'd come full circle, back to the kitchen.

And he was standing at the way into the basement.

Ah, shit. Not this . . . he wasn't ready for this.

The truth was, Lassiter and his dumb-ass movies had done more damage than good. All those couples up on the screen . . . even though they were contrived instruments of fiction, some of them had filtered into his brain, and triggered all kinds of things.

None of which had been about Wellsie.

Instead, he'd thought only about those days with No'One, the two of them straining with all those blankets between their bodies, she looking up at him as if she wanted so much more than he was giving her, he holding back out of respect for his dead . . . and maybe because he was a fucking coward at his core.

Probably equal bits of both.

Given what was banging around in his head, he'd had to come here. He needed memories of his beloved, images of his Wellsie that maybe he'd forgotten, a powerful blast from the past to compete with what felt like a betrayal in the present.

From a vast distance, he watched his hand reach out and grab the doorknob. Twisting to the right, he pulled the heavy, painted steel panel wide. As the motion-activated lights came on in the stairwell, he was hit with a whole lot of cream: the steps that went downward were carpeted in a mellow buff, and the walls were painted likewise, everything calming and serene.

This had been their sanctuary.

The first step was the equivalent of jumping off the lip of the Grand Canyon. And number two wasn't any better.

He still felt that way when he got to the bottom and there was no more descent to be had.

The basement of the house followed the first-floor plan, although only two-thirds of the space was finished with a master suite, a gym, a laundry, and a minikitchen fleshed out, and the rest functioning as storage.

Tohr had no idea how long he stood there.

Eventually, though, he walked forward, toward the closed door up ahead. . . .

The fact that he opened the thing into a black hole seemed absolutely right—

Fuuuuck, it still smelled like her. Her perfume. Her scent.

Stepping inside, he closed himself in and braced himself as he hit the wall switch, bringing up the overheads gradually.

The bed was made.

Likely by her hands: Even though they had staff, she had been the kind of female who liked to do things herself. Cooking. Cleaning. Folding laundry.

Making their bed at the end of every day.

There wasn't a lick of dust on any of the surfaces, not the dressers, his and hers . . . not the nightstands, his with the alarm clock, hers with the phone . . . not the desk with the computer that they had shared.

Goddamn, he couldn't breathe.

To take a little break from his crucible, he went into the bathroom with the idea of catching up on the oxygen requirements of his body.

He should have known better. She was all over the tiled space, too; just as she was all over the house.

Opening one of the cabinets, he picked up a pump bottle of her hand lotion and read the label, back and front—something he had never done when she'd been alive. He did the same with one of her backup shampoo bottles, as well as a jar of bath salts that . . . yup, smelled just as he remembered, lemon verbena.

Back to the bedroom.

Over to the walk-in closet . . .

He wasn't sure exactly when the shift occurred. Maybe it was as he went through her sweaters that were stacked in the cubbies. Maybe it was as he stared at her shoes in their neat, marching order on the tilted shelves. Maybe it was as he trolled through her blouses on their hangers, or no, her slacks . . . or maybe the skirts or the dresses . . .

But eventually, in the silence, in his aching loneliness, in his perennial grief . . . it dawned on him that this was all just stuff.

Her clothing, her makeup, her toiletries . . . the bed she had made, the kitchen she had cooked in, the house she had made their own.

It was only stuff.

And just as she was never going to fill out her mating gown again, she was never coming back here to claim any of this. It had all been hers and she had worn it, and used it, and needed every bit of it—but it wasn't her.

Say it—say that she's dead.

I can't.

You're the problem.

Nothing he had done in his mourning process had brought her back. Not the agony of reminiscing, not the mindless drinking, not the worthless weak tears or the resistance to another female . . . not the avoidance of this place, or the hours sitting alone with an empty hole in his chest.

She was gone.

And that meant that all of this was just stuff in an empty house.

God . . . this was not at all what he had expected to feel. He had come here to pave over No'One. Instead? All he'd found was a collection of inanimate objects with no more power to transform where he was at than they could walk and talk on their own.

Although, considering where Wellsie was, the idea that he had been looking for a way to stop the connection with No'One was craziness. He should be rejoicing at the idea he was thinking of another female.

Instead, it still felt like a curse.

THIRTY-NINE

Back at the Brotherhood mansion, No'One sat upon the bed she shared with Tohrment, her robe lying on the duvet next to her, her shift covering her flesh.

Silent. So silent this room was without him.

Wherever was he?

When she had returned herein following her work down in the training center, she had expected to find him waiting upon her, warm and mayhap asleep upon the duvet. Instead, the covers were all arranged, the pillows ordered at the headboard, the extra comforter, the one he used to warm himself, still folded neatly at the foot of the mattress.

He had not been in the weight room, the pool, or the gym. Nor had he been in the kitchen when she had stopped briefly to gather a refreshment for herself. Or the billiards room or library.

And he had not appeared for First Meal, either.

The knob turned and she jumped—only to release a deep, easing exhale. Her blood in the warrior's body announced his arrival even before his scent came upon her nose or his body filled the jambs.

He still didn't have a shirt on. Or boots upon his feet.

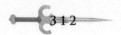

And his stare was dark and desolate as the corridors of *Dhund*.

"Where have you been," she whispered.

He ducked both her eyes and the question by going into the bathroom. "I'm late. Wrath's called a meeting."

As the shower came on, she gathered her robe and drew it over her shoulders, knowing that he was uncomfortable with her in any manner of undress out of bed. But that wasn't the cause of his mood; he'd been as such afore he'd even looked her way.

His beloved, she thought. It had to have something to do with his beloved.

And she should probably leave him be.

But she did not.

When he came out, he had a towel wrapped around his hips, and he went directly to the closet without sparing her a glance. Propping a palm on the doorjamb, he opened up and leaned in, the name upon his shoulders spotlit under the ceiling fixture above him.

Except he didn't take any clothing out. He hung his head and fell still.

"I went home today," he said abruptly.

"Today? As in . . . during the daylight hours?"

"Fritz took me."

Her heart beat hard at the thought of him exposed to sunshine—Wait, hadn't they lived together here?

"We had our own place," he said. "We didn't stay here with everyone else."

So this was not his mated room. Or his mated bed.

When he didn't say anything further, she prompted, "What did you . . . find there?"

"Nothing. Absolutely fucking nothing."

"It had been emptied of your things?"

"No, I left it all exactly as it was the night she died. Down to the dishes that are clean in the dishwasher, the mail on the counter, the mascara she left out right before she took off for the last time."

Oh, the agony for him, she thought.

"I went there looking for her, and all I got was an exhibition of the past."

"But you are never far from her—your Wellesandra is ever with you. She breathes in your heart."

Tohrment pivoted around, his eyes hooded, intense. "Not like she used to."

Abruptly, she straightened under his gaze. Fiddled with the edge of her robe. Crossed her legs. Uncrossed them. "Why are you looking at me like that."

"I want to fuck you. That's why I went back home."

As No'One's face registered high-octane shock, Tohr didn't bother to temper the truth with pretty words or apologies or any kind of fanfare. He was just too done with everything: fighting his body, arguing with destiny, wrestling with an inevitability that he had been refusing to yield to for too long.

Standing in front of her, he was naked in a way that had nothing to do with a lack of clothes. Naked and tired . . . and hungry for her—

"Then you may have me," she said in a soft voice.

As her words sank in, he felt himself pale. "Do you understand what I said?"

"You were blunt enough."

"You're supposed to tell me to go to hell."

There was a short pause. "Well, we do not have to proceed."

No rancor. No begging. No disappointment—it was all about him and where he was at.

How could she be so . . . kind? he wondered.

"I don't want to hurt you," he said, feeling like he wanted to return the favor.

"You won't. I know you are still in love with your mate, and I do not blame you. What you had with her is a once-in-a-lifetime love."

"What about you?"

"I have no need or desire to take her place. And I accept you just as you are, in any fashion you choose to come to me. Or not, if that is the way it must be."

Tohr cursed as a part of his pain unexpectedly eased. "That isn't fair to you."

"Yes, it is. I am happy to simply have time with you. That is enough—and more than I could ever have expected out of my fate. These past few months have been a complicated joy that I wouldn't have traded anything for. If it must end, then at least I've had what I did. And if it goes further then I am luckier than I deserve. And . . . if it puts you in some small way at peace then I have served my only purpose."

As she fell silent, that quiet dignity of hers slayed him, it truly did.

And it was with a sense of utter unreality that he walked over to her, bent down and took her face into his palms.

Rubbing her cheek with his thumb, he stared into her eyes. "You are . . ." His voice broke. "You are such a female of worth."

No'One put her hands up to his thick wrists, her touch soft and light. "Listen to my words and believe them. Do not worry about me. Take care of your heart and your soul first—that is what matters most."

Kneeling in front of her, he worked his way in between her legs, filling the space he created with his body. As always with her, he felt both awkward and at ease being so close.

With his eyes, he traced her face, that beautiful, kind face. And then he zeroed in on her lips.

Moving slowly, he leaned in, not really sure what the hell he was doing. He had never kissed her. Not once. For all he knew about her body, he knew nothing of her mouth, and as her eyes flared, it was obvious she had never expected the intimacy.

Tilting his head to the side, he shut his lids . . . and closed the distance until he met a whole lot of velvet.

Softly, chastely, he pressed in and pulled back.

Not enough.

Dipping down again, he lingered at her mouth, brushing, plying. Then he abruptly broke off the contact and shoved himself to his feet. If he didn't stop now, he wouldn't at all, and he was already running late for Wrath and his brothers. Besides, this wasn't about a quick sex session.

It was more important than that.

"I have to get dressed," he told her. "I have to go."

"And I shall be here when you return. If you want me to be."

"I do."

Turning away, he wasted no time in throwing his clothes on or gathering his weapons, and as soon as he nabbed his leather jacket, he had every intention of going right out the door. Instead, he stopped and looked at her. She had her fingertips up to her lips, her eyes wide and full of wonder . . . as if she had never felt anything even close to what she just had.

He went back to the bed. "Was that your first kiss?"

She blushed in the most lovely pink, her eyes dropping shyly to the carpet. "Yes."

For a moment, all he could do was shake his head at everything she had been through.

Then he leaned down. "You gonna let me give you another?"

"Yes, please . . ." she breathed.

He kissed her longer this time, lingering on her lower lip, even clipping it gently with one of his fangs. At the contact, heat exploded between them, especially as he pulled her up against his body, holding her harder than he should given how many weapons were hanging off his torso.

Before he took her standing up, he forced himself to put her back on the bed. "Thank you," he whispered.

"What ever for?"

All he could do was shrug because so much of his gratitude was too complicated to give voice to. "I guess for not trying to change me."

"Never," she said. "Now be safe."

"I will."

Out in the hall, he closed the door quietly and took a deep breath. . . .

"You all right, my brother?"

He shook himself and glanced over at Z. The male was likewise dressed for fighting, but he was coming down the hall from the opposite direction of his suite.

"Ah, yeah, sure. Yourself?"

"I was sent to get you."

Right. Got it. And he was glad it was Z. Undoubtedly the guy was well aware of his fucked-up mood, but unlike some of the others—*cough*Rhage*cough*—he would never pry.

Together, they walked down the hall and entered the king's study, arriving just as V said, "I don't like this. The one vampire who's fucked us off for months suddenly calls from out of the blue and says he's ready to see you?"

Assail, Tohr thought, while he settled against the bookshelves.

As his brothers muttered different variations on the not-so-hot theme, he put his game head on and agreed completely. Too much of a coincidence—

From behind the great desk, Wrath's expression went stone-cold, and just the look on that face quieted the room: He was going, with or without the rest of them.

"Fucking hell," Rhage bitched. "You can't be serious."

Cursing under his breath, Tohr figured he might as well cut past the argument stage: given the thrust of Wrath's jaw, the brothers were going to lose in any contest of will. "You are wearing a Kevlar vest," he told the king.

Wrath bared his fangs. "When have I not."

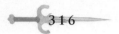

"Just needed to be clear on that. What time do you want to leave?"

"Now."

Vishous lit up a hand-rolled and blew out smoke. "Fucking hell is right."

Wrath stood up, grasped George's halter, and came around from the throne. "I want just a regular squadron of four. We go there with too many guns and it's going to look like we're nervous. Tohr, V, John, and Qhuinn are going to be on first string."

Made sense. Rhage with his beast was too much of a wild card. Z and Phury were technically off rotation tonight. Butch needed to be on standby with the Escalade. And Rehv wasn't in the room, which meant his day job of being king of the *symphaths* had taken him up north again.

Oh, and Payne? Given what she looked like, she was liable to fritz Assail's circuits out, rendering him too stupid to speak. Like her twin, she tended to make a big impression on the opposite sex.

Everyone would just be a text away, however, and Wrath was right: They brought the whole fan-damn-ily and that was going to send the wrong message.

As everybody filed out and hit the grand staircase, there were all kinds of under-the-breath grousing, and at the bottom, weapons were rechecked and holsters tightened an extra notch.

Tohr glanced across at John. Qhuinn was on the kid's ass tighter than a pair of pants, and that was a good thing as it was obvious that all was still not well in John's world: he smelled like his bonding scent, but looked like death.

The king bent down and talked to George for a moment. Then he grabbed his queen and kissed her like he meant it. "I'll be home before you know it, *leelan*."

While Wrath walked through the crowd and disappeared into the courtyard without aid, Tohr went over to Beth, took her hand, and gave it a squeeze. "You don't worry about a thing. I'm gonna bring him back as soon as it's over—in one piece."

"Thank you—God, thank you." She put her arms around him and hugged him hard. "I know he's safe with you."

As she sank to her haunches to comfort the anxious retriever, Tohr headed for the door, slowing down as he joined the traffic jam of brothers at the vestibule. Waiting to file through, he glanced up at the second-floor balcony. No'One was at the head of the stairs, standing by herself, that hood of hers down.

The braid needed to go, he thought to himself. Hair as beautiful as hers was meant to catch the light and shine.

He lifted his hand in a wave, and after she echoed the good-bye, he ducked out and emerged into the cold night.

Standing close, but not too close to John, he waited for Wrath to give the nod, and then he dematerialized with the king and the boys to a peninsula on the Hudson just north of Xhex's cabin.

As Tohr re-formed in the midst of a thin beard of forest, the air was bracingly cold and smelled of fallen leaves and the wet rocks of the shoreline.

Up ahead, Assail's contemporary mansion was a true showpiece, even from this rear view by the garages. The palatial structure had two main floors, with a porch that went all the way around, everything angled and windowed to provide as much of a view of the water as possible.

Dumb-ass place for a vampire to live. All that glass in the daylight?

Then again, what could you expect from a member of the *glymera*.

The house had been prescreened, as each of the other locations for the meetings had been, so they were familiar with the layout on the exterior— and V had broken in and surveyed the inside as well. Report: Nothing much in there, and clearly that hadn't changed. In the lights that glowed from the ceilings, there was a whole lot of nothing much in the furniture department.

It was as if Assail lived in a display case featuring himself.

And yet apparently the guy had done a few smart things. According to V, all those glass panels were threaded with fine steel wires, in the manner of a car window defroster system, so there was no dematerializing in or out. He'd also cleared the lawn that circled the place so that if anything or anybody approached, they'd be sitting ducks.

On that note, Tohr let his instincts and senses roam . . . and had a grand total of nada hit his radar screen. Nothing moved that wasn't supposed to: just tree limbs and leaves in the breeze, a deer about three hundred yards away, his brother and the boys behind him.

At least until a car came down the narrow, paved driveway.

Jaguar, Tohr guessed by the engine sound.

Yup, he was right. Black XKR. With blacked-out side windows.

The long-nosed convertible went by, stopped at the garage door nearest to the mansion, and then eased inside as the panels rose. Assail, or whoever it was behind the wheel, did not can the engine or get out of the car right away. He waited for the door to drop back into place behind him, and as it did, Tohr noticed there were no windowpanes in the thing. The shit was also a shade ever so slightly off from the trim on the rest of the house. Same with the other five bays.

He'd added those doors since he'd moved in, Tohr thought.

Maybe the SOB wasn't a total moron.

"Okay, I'll head over to the front door." V's diamond eyes flashed. "I'll give you a signal . . . or you'll hear that lightweight scream like a girl. Either way, you know what to do."

Annnnnd off he went, dematerializing around the corner of the house. It would be better to have eyes on him, but Wrath was the most important part of this, and the tree line in the back was the only cover there was to be had.

As they waited, Tohr got his gun out, and so did John Matthew and Qhuinn. The king was dripping with forties, but his matched sets stayed put. Way too defensive to have him with a gat in his hand.

But your personal guard? Part of the cocksucking job description.

Keeping sharp, he wished, yet again, that they could leave the king at home for the pregame process, but Wrath had flat-out no'd that idea months ago. Too galling, no doubt, given that, unlike his father, he'd been a fighter before he'd taken the throne—it was just, fucking hell, moments like this made you want to peel your own face off.

Tohr's cell phone went off three tense minutes later: *Kitchen door by the garage.*

"He wants us at the back entrance," Tohr said, putting the thing away. "Wrath, that's fifty yards straight ahead."

"Roger that."

The four of them dematerialized and reappeared on the rear stoop in a flanking formation that provided as much protection to Wrath as possible: Tohr was right in front of the king, John to his right, Qhuinn to his left. V immediately assumed the rear.

And right on cue, Assail opened the door.

FORTY

Zohr's first impression of their host was that Assail hadn't changed at all. He was still big enough to be a Brother, with hair so dark he made V seem like a blond. And his clothes were, as always, formal and perfectly tailored. He was also as cagey as ever, his stare shrewd and hooded . . . seeing too much, capable of too much.

Another fine addition to the continent.

Not.

The aristocrat smiled in a way that didn't reach his eyes. "I'm guessing that's Wrath in the middle of all those bodies?"

"Show some fucking respect," V snapped.

"Compliments are the condiment of conversation." Assail turned away, leaving them to come through the jambs by themselves. "They just get in the way—"

Wrath dematerialized right in the guy's path, moving so fast they met chest-to-chest.

Baring fangs long as daggers, the king growled low. "Watch your mouth, son. Or I'll make it impossible for you to throw any more bullshit around."

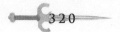

Assail stepped back, his eyes narrowing like he was reading Wrath's vital statistics. "You're not like your father."

"Neither are you. Unfortunately."

As V shut the door, Assail went for his inside pocket—and immediately had four gun muzzles pointed at his head. As he froze, his eyes went from weapon to weapon.

"I was getting out a cigar."

"I'd do it slowly if I were you," Wrath murmured. "My boys wouldn't mind dropping you where you stand."

"Good thing we're not in my living room. I love that rug." He glanced over at V. "You sure you want to do this here in the mudroom?"

"Yeah, bitch, I am," Vishous ground out.

"Window phobia?"

"You were about to light up," Wrath said. "Or get lit up. How about we solve that one first and then talk about your sieve of a house."

"I like the view."

"Which could be me standing over your grave," V announced as he nodded at the guy's disappeared hand.

Cocking a brow, Assail pulled out a long Cuban, and made a point to show it to everybody. Then he went into a side pocket, took out a gold snipper, and held it up to his well-armed peanut gallery.

"Anyone care to join me? No?" He clipped the end off and lit up, seemingly unconcerned that his head was still in the crosshairs.

After a couple of puffs, he said, "So I want to know something."

"Don't give me an opening like that," V muttered.

"Is that why you finally called me?" Wrath asked.

"Yes, it is." The vampire rolled his cigar back and forth between his thumb and forefinger. "Do you have any intention of altering the laws concerning commerce with humans?"

Leaning to the side, Tohr did a flash scan of what he could see of the rest of the house—which wasn't much: modern kitchen, a hint of the dining room, a living room out the far side. Finding no one moving through the empty rooms, he refocused.

"No," Wrath said. "Provided the business stays under the radar, you can do what you want. What kind of commerce are you in."

"Retail."

"Of what?"

"Does it matter."

"If you're not answering, I'm going to assume drugs or women." Wrath frowned when there was no reply. "So which one is it."

"Women are too much trouble."

"That drug shit is tough to keep under the radar."

"Not the way I take care of things."

V piped up. "So you're the reason middlemen have been capping themselves in alleys."

"No comment."

Wrath frowned again. "Why bring this up now?"

"Let's just say I've run into one too many interested parties."

"Be more specific."

"Well, one of them's about six feet tall. Brush-cut dark hair. Name rhymes with sex, and her body's built for it."

Oh, no, you didn't, Tohr thought—

The hiss that came out of John brought everyone's head around. And what do you know, the guy's eyes were trained on Assail as if, at least in his mind, he was already ripping the male's throat out.

"I beg your pardon," Assail drawled. "I didn't know you were acquainted with her in some manner."

Tohr growled on behalf of his son—even though they were estranged. "He's a fuck of a lot more than just acquainted. So you can blow that speculation out your ass—and while you're at it, stay away from her."

"She was the one who came to me."

Greeeeeeeeeeeeeeat. That went over like a lead balloon—

Before shit got out of hand, Wrath held up his palm. "I don't give a fuck what you do with humans—provided you clean up any messes. But if you get tagged, you're on your own."

"What about our species interfering with my commerce."

Wrath smiled a little, his cruel face showing absolutely no humor. "Having trouble defending your territory already? Guess what. You can't have what you can't keep."

Assail inclined his head. "Fair enough—"

The shattering of glass sounded out behind them all, cutting through everything, crushing time down to a crawl: gunfire.

With a mighty lunge, Tohr went airborne, his massive body flying over the Spanish tile, his target: Wrath.

As a *rat-tat-tat-tat-tat* spray of bullets hit the back of the house, he tackled the king to the floor, covering his brother with as much of his body

as possible. Everyone else, including Assail, likewise hit the ground and shuffled for cover against various walls.

"My lord, are you hit?" Tohr hissed in Wrath's ear as he hit *send* on the text alarm.

"Maybe the neck," came a groaned response.

"Lie still."

"You're all over me. Exactly where do you think I'm going."

Tohr twisted his head around to eyeball where everybody was. V was all about Assail, his hand locked on the guy's throat, his weapon tight on their host's temple. And Qhuinn and John were back-flatted on either side of where they'd come in, covering the outside as well as the entryway into the kitchen.

The cold breeze coming through the broken windowpane in the door did not provide any particular scent, and that proved who it was: Slayers would have stunk up the place given that both the prevailing wind and the shot came from the north.

It was Xcor and his Band of Bastards.

But come on, like they didn't know that already. That single shot had to have come from a rifle, and had to have been aimed at Wrath through those fucking panes in the door—and it had been a long while since the Lessening Society had shown any finesse in their attacks.

"You were supposed to keep this meeting private, vampire," V said in a deadly tone.

"No one knows you're here."

"Then I'll assume you ordered an assassination all by your lonesome."

He was going to shoot the motherfucker, Tohr thought without caring. Right here, right now.

Assail kept it cool, squaring off at the Brother so that the gun muzzle was now pointed at the center of his forehead. "Fuck you—that's why I wanted to do this out in the living room. That's bulletproof glass out there, asshole. And P.S., I'm hit, you fool."

The male lifted his arm and showed off his dripping right hand, the one that had been holding the cigar.

"So maybe your friends have bad aim."

"That was *not* bad aim. I'm a target, too—"

More bullets sprayed the back of the house, finding their way in through the cutout in the door. Fucking hell, thermal pane was good against the New York winters, but it didn't do shit to stop Remington's best.

"How you doing?" Tohr whispered in Wrath's ear as he checked his phone for a response from his other brothers.

"Fine. You?" Except the king coughed . . . and, man, there was a rattle in his lungs.

He was bleeding somewhere along his respiratory tract—

Moving fast as a gasp, Assail slipped out of V's hold, and streaked across the back of the mudroom, heading for a door that had to let out into the garage. "Don't shoot! I've got a car you can take him in! And I'm killing all the lights in the house."

As everything went dark, Vishous dematerialized on top of the guy, taking him down and grinding his face into the tile. "I'm going to kill you now—"

"No," Wrath ordered. "Not until we know what's going on."

In the shadows, V grit his teeth and glared at the king. But at least he didn't hit the trigger. Instead, he put his mouth to their host's ear and growled, "You better think twice before you go for any exits again."

"Then do it yourself." This came out as, "*Vhen do ith y'selth.*"

Vishous glanced over at Tohr, the pair of them locking eyes. When Tohr gave a subtle nod, the other brother cursed . . . then reached up and popped open the garage door. The automatic lights were still on from Assail's having come home earlier, and Tohr caught sight of four cars: The Jaguar. A Spyker. A black Mercedes. And a black van with no side windows.

"Take the GMC," Assail grunted. "Keys are in the ignition. It's bulletproof all the way around."

As everything went silent outside, John and Qhuinn began pumping rounds off through the broken glass, falling into a steady, alternating rhythm, just to make sure that someone didn't try and dematerialize inside.

Shit, their ammo wasn't going to last long.

Tohr cursed the lack of options, as well as the fact that he'd gotten no reply from the Brotherhood—

"We got this," Qhuinn said, not turning away from the door. "But we need the other Brothers here before you try to leave."

"I've already alerted them," Tohr muttered. "They're on the way."

At least, he hoped they were.

Assail's voice rose above the gunshots. "Take the goddamn van. I'm not fucking with you."

Tohr pegged the guy with hard eyes. "If you are, I will skin you alive."

"I'm *not.*"

Given that there were no further assurances to be had, Tohr rolled off

Wrath and helped the king into a crouching position. Shit . . . blood at the side of his neck. Lot of it. "Keep your head down, my lord, and follow my lead."

"You don't say."

Moving as quickly as he dared, Tohr started them across the floor, steering the king over to the wall so that Wrath could put a hand out and orient himself.

"Washing machine," Tohr said, pulling him out to avoid the boxy machine. "Dryer. Door six feet. Four. Two. Step down."

As they went by Assail, the male was watching them. "Jesus, he really is blind."

Wrath pulled up short and unsheathed his dagger, pointing it directly into the guy's face. "But my hearing works just fine."

Assail probably would have recoiled, but he was stuck between the hard wall, a bullet and a sharp point—not a lot of room to maneuver. "Yes. Indeed."

"This meeting isn't over," Wrath said.

"I don't have anything else."

"I do. You watch yourself, son—this little go-around proves to have your fingerprints anywhere near it, and your next house is a pine box."

"It wasn't me. I swear to it—I'm a businessman, pure and simple. I just want to be left alone."

"Greta fucking Garbo," V bit out as Tohr urged Wrath back into motion.

In the garage proper, Tohr crabbed it across the bald concrete with the king, going around the other vehicles. When they got to the van, he checked the thing out, then popped the back double doors and shoved the most powerful vampire on the planet in there like he was a piece of luggage.

As he reshut the panels, he spared one moment to take a deep breath. Then he ripped around to the driver's side and got in. The interior light stayed on for a bit after he took his seat, and yes, the keys were right where Assail had said. And yeah, there had been some serious modifications to the vehicle: two gas tanks, reinforced steel crash cage, thick glass the girth of which suggested it was indeed bulletproof.

There was a sliding partition that separated the back from the front, and he opened it far enough so he could monitor the king.

With his hearing on overdrive, the dripping of blood in the van seemed as loud as the gunshots that had caused it. "You're hit bad, my lord."

All that came back at him was that cough.

Fuck.

John was ready to kill.

As he stood to the left of that goddamn back door, the thick muscles of his thighs were twitching, and his heart was going bronco in his chest. His gun, however, was steady as a stone.

The Band of Bastards had initiated the attack from where the Brotherhood had started out: on the far side of the cleared lawn, in the forest behind the house.

Hell of a shot, he thought. That first rifle bullet had punctured the door's windowpane and gone right for Wrath's head, even though there had been a number of people standing around.

Too close. Waaaaay too close.

These guys were true professionals—which meant they had to be gearing up for a second engagement . . . and not from this angle that was guarded so well.

As Qhuinn kept pulling his trigger in a slow, even motion, John leaned back and looked through the archway into the kitchen.

Whistling low, he caught Qhuinn's eye and nodded in that direction.

"Roger that—"

"John, you don't go out there alone," V said. "I'll watch the back door as well as our host."

"What if they come through the opening?" Qhuinn asked.

"I'll pick 'em off one by one."

Hard to argue with the guy. Especially as the Brother trained his second gun right where Qhuinn and John had been shooting through.

That was the end of any further convo.

John and Qhuinn fell into flanking position and took off together. Using the moonlight as a guide, they streaked through the professionally equipped kitchen, and tried every door they came to. Locked. Locked. Locked.

The dining, living, and family rooms turned out to be one massive expanse, kind of like a football field that had been outfitted at a home show. The good news was that there were ornate columns at regular intervals that supported the ceiling over the expanse, and he and Qhuinn used them for cover as they darted out, checked sliding glass doors, and ducked back again.

Everything was locked: As they worked the circle of the giant room, shit was tight as a tick on all sides. But God, all that glass . . .

Stopping short, he leveled his gun muzzle at a stretch of it, whistled twice to signal to V . . . and popped off a test shot.

No shattering. Not even a cracking. The ten-by-six-foot pane simply caught the bullet and held it, like the thing was nothing more than ABC gum.

Assail hadn't lied. At least not about that.

From the back of the house, their host's voice was distant but clear. "Close and lock the door at the base of the stairs to the second floor. Fast."

Roger. That.

John let Qhuinn sweep the bathrooms and the office as he beat feet over to a black-and-white marble staircase. Sure enough, tucked into the wall was a stainless-steel, fireproof panel that, when you pulled it out, smelled like fresh paint, as if it had been recently installed.

There were two locks on it, one so you could isolated yourself upstairs, one for doing the same downstairs.

As he got the thing into place and secured, he had to have some respect for how Assail handled security measures.

"This place is a fortress," Qhuinn said as he came out of another bathroom.

Cellar? John mouthed so he didn't have to reholster his gun.

Like he read minds, Assail called out, "The basement door is locked. It's in the kitchen by the second fridge."

They darted back in the direction they'd started out in, locating another one of those steel jobbies that happened to already be slid into place and bolted.

John checked his phone, and saw the group text that Rhage had sent out: *Hvy fghtn dwntwn—b thr ASAP.*

Fuck, he breathed as he flashed the screen to Qhuinn.

"I'm going out there," the guy announced as he jogged for one of the sliders. "Lock the door after me—"

John lunged for the fighter, snagging a hold. *The hell you are,* he mouthed.

Qhuinn shook off the iron grip. "This is a cluster-fuck waiting to happen, and Wrath *has* to be taken to the clinic." As John cursed in silence, Qhuinn shook his head. "Be reasonable, buddy. You're the backup for V with Assail, and the pair of you have to keep the interior secured. Likewise, that van has to get moving because the king's bleeding. You need to let me go out there and do what I can to secure the area—we can't spare anybody else."

John cursed again, his mind churning for other options.

In the end, he clapped his best friend on the side of the neck and brought their foreheads together for a brief moment. Then he let go and backed the fuck off—even though it nearly killed him.

Bottom line, his first duty was to save the king, not his best friend. Wrath was the mission critical here, not Qhuinn.

Besides, Qhuinn was a deadly son of a bitch, fast on his feet, good with a gun, great with a knife.

You had to trust those skills. And the bastard was right: They were sorely needed in this situation.

With a final nod, Qhuinn slipped out of a glass door, and John closed and locked it behind him . . . leaving the male on his own.

At least the Band of Bastards would likely assume everyone was in the house and staying there—they had to know that backup would be coming, and in most situations, people waited for their reinforcements to arrive before they marshaled a counterattack.

"John! Qhuinn!" V called out. "What the hell is going on out there!"

John jogged back to the mudroom. Unfortunately, there was no effective way to communicate without losing his weapon—

"Shit, Qhuinn went out there alone, didn't he."

Assail laughed softly. "And I thought I was the only one with a death wish."

FORTY-ONE

irectly after Syphon pulled the trigger on his long-range rifle, Xcor's first thought was that the male may well have killed the king.

Standing in the shelter of the forest, he was amazed at his soldier's accuracy: The bullet had sailed across the lawn, blown out the glass pane of the door . . . and dropped the king like a bag of sand.

Either that or the king had chosen to take cover.

There was no way of knowing whether the disappearance was a defensive reaction or the collapse of a male gravely injured.

Mayhap both were true.

"Open fire," he commanded into the newfangled transistor at his shoulder. "And assume second positions."

With practiced precision, his soldiers went into action, the ringing sound of gunfire providing cover as everyone but him and Throe shifted in various directions.

The Brotherhood would be arriving at any moment, so there was little time to batten down the hatches and prepare for conflict. Good thing his soldiers were well trained—

All at once, the house went dark—smart. It made them more difficult to isolate as targets, although given the way all the glass except for that back door's had withstood bullets, it appeared as though Assail was far more tactical than your average *glymera* waffle-about.

Car bombs notwithstanding.

In the lull that followed, Xcor had to assume that if the king were alive and completely unhit, Wrath would dematerialize through the opening in the back door, get out of the area, and the others would attack. If the king was injured, they would hunker down and wait for the other members of the Brotherhood to arrive and provide cover for a drive-out. And if the Blind King were dead? They would stay with the body to protect it until the others got here—

A gun went off in the interior. One shot, the flash of which appeared to the left.

They were testing the glass, he thought. So Assail was either dead or they didn't trust him.

"Someone is coming out," Throe said by his side.

"Shoot to kill," Xcor ordered into his shoulder.

There was no reason to take a chance at a capture: Anybody fighting alongside the Brotherhood would be trained to withstand torture, and therefore not a good candidate for information gathering. More to the point, this situation was a powder keg about to explode, and reducing the number of the enemy was the most important goal; taking prisoners was not.

Gunfire rang out as his bastards tried to pick off whoever had departed, but naturally the fighter dematerialized so it was unlikely they were hit—

The Brotherhood arrived all at once, the massive fighters taking positions all over the exterior of house, as if it had been scoped out previously.

Gunfire was traded, with Xcor aiming for the pair on the roof whilst his others focused on the dark shapes moving around the porches as well as any who might be coming up from behind in the woods.

He needed to get in the path of any vehicle that attempted to get away from the house.

"I shall cover the garage," he spoke into his transistor. "Hold positions."

Glancing over his shoulder at Throe, he ordered, "You back up the cousins at the north."

As his soldier nodded and took off, Xcor ducked and did the same,

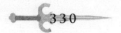

shifting his position by running, as he was too keyed up to dematerialize: If they tried to take Wrath out by vehicle because he was injured, Xcor *had* to be the one who got the satisfaction of preventing the king's escape . . . and finishing the job as necessary. The garage, therefore, was his best vantage point: The Brothers would have to commandeer one of Assail's vehicles as they appeared to have arrived without any—and Assail would offer the aid. He had no allegiance to any particular group—not the Band of Bastards, not the Council, probably not even the king. But he wouldn't want to bear the price of someone else's vendetta against Wrath.

Xcor set up behind a massive boulder that sat at the edge of the asphalt square behind the house. Taking out a small, convex strip of metal that was polished to a high shine, he positioned the mirror on the rock so he had a view of whatever was behind him. And then he waited.

Ah, yes. Right again . . .

As gunfire continued to ring out, the garage door farthest to the right opened, the protection it offered disappearing panel by panel.

The van that backed out had no windows in its rear portion, and he was willing to bet that, like the house, its flanks were impenetrable by anything less than an antiaircraft missile.

It was entirely possible, of course, that this was a ruse.

But he was not going to miss the opportunity in the event that it wasn't.

Flicking his eyes up, he checked behind him, then refocused on the van. If he jumped out into its path, he might get a shot into the engine block through the front grille—

The attack that came from behind was so swift, all he felt was an arm locking around his throat and his body getting hauled backward. Shifting instantly into hand-to-hand self-defense mode, he stopped the male from snapping his neck by elbowing the shit out of the fighter's gut, and then taking advantage of the momentary stun to spin around.

He had a brief impression of mismatched eyes . . . and then it was all about the fighting.

The male attacked with such ferocity, the punches were like getting rained upon by cars. Fortunately, he had outstanding balance and reflexes, and crouching low, he took the male by the thighs and tackled him hard. Riding that massive lower body down to the ground, he jumped upward and worked the fighter's face until there was blood not just on his knuckles, but flying in the air.

His superior position did not last. In spite of the fact that the soldier couldn't possibly see clearly, he somehow caught one of Xcor's wrists and held on to it. With brute strength, he yanked back, brought Xcor within range, and head-butted so hard, for a moment the world went incandescent sure as if the trees around them had fireworks for branches and leaves.

An abrupt shift in gravity told him that he was being rolled, but fuck that. He stopped the momentum by throwing out a leg and digging his boot into the ground. As he strained against a great weight on his chest, he saw the black van screeching off like a bat out of hell down the driveway.

Anger at a missed chance at the king gave him extra power, and he rose up onto his feet with the male draped across his shoulders, a shawl of soldier.

Unsheathing his hunting knife, he stabbed around the back of his own torso, and he knew he hit something, given the resistance and the cursing. But then that grip around his neck returned, challenging his airway, making him work even harder for oxygen.

The large rock he'd taken cover behind was about a meter away, and he headed for it, his boots clomping across the lawn. Spinning about, he slammed the male once . . . twice. . . .

On the third time, just before he was about to black out, the grip loosened. With sloppy disorientation, he freed himself just as a bullet whistled by his head, so close he felt a stripe of heat on his scalp.

Behind him, the soldier fell down upon the grass, but that wasn't going to last—and a quick glance around at the gunfight being waged told him that if he and his bastards stayed much longer, there would be catastrophic casualties—yes, they would take out some of the Brotherhood with them, but only at a tremendous cost to their own numbers.

His gut instinct told him Wrath had already left. And damn it, even if half the Brotherhood was in or around that van—and if the king was being transported away, some of them were undoubtedly shadowing the vehicle—there were still plenty of Brothers left here at the river's edge to do vital damage to him and his males.

The Bloodletter would have stayed and fought.

He, however, was smarter than that: If Wrath was mortally injured, or if that was his body, Xcor was going to need his band of bastards for the second phase of his takeover.

"Retreat," he barked into his shoulder piece.

He hauled back his combat boot and kicked that downed, mismatched-eyed motherfucker on the ground—to make sure the male stayed where he was.

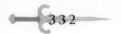

Then he closed his eyes and forced himself to calm . . . calm . . . calm. . . .

Life and death turned on whether he could get himself into the right frame of mind—

Just as another bullet whizzed by his skull, he felt himself take wings . . . and fly.

"How we doing back there?"

Tohr yelled out the question as he forced the van into yet another curve in the road. The POS cornered like it was on a coffee table with bad legs, rocking to and fro until even he felt a little nauseous.

Wrath, meanwhile, was playing marble-in-a-jar in the back, the king rolling around and flailing his arms to catch himself.

"Any chance—" Wrath lurched in the other direction and coughed some more. "You can slow . . . this bus down?"

Tohr looked in the rearview mirror. He'd kept the partition open so he could keep an eye on the king, and in the glow from the dashboard, Wrath was white as a sheet. Except for where the blood stained the skin of his throat. That was red as a cherry.

"No slowing down—sorry."

If luck was on their side, the Brotherhood was keeping the Band of Bastards fully occupied at the house, but who the fuck knew. And he and Wrath were on the wrong side of the Hudson River with a good twenty minutes of driving in front of them.

And no backup.

And Wrath . . . shit, he really didn't look good.

"How you doing?" Tohr called out again.

There was a longer pause at that point. Too long.

Gritting his teeth, he triangulated the distance to Havers's clinic. Fuck, it was nearly equidistant—so gunning for that facility in the hopes of finding somebody, anybody with medical training wasn't going to save much time.

From out of nowhere, Lassiter appeared in the passenger seat—right out of thin air.

"You can put your gun down," the angel said dryly.

Shit, he'd pulled his heat on the guy.

"I'll take the wheel," Lassiter ordered. "You deal with him."

Tohr was out of that seat belt and doing the driver shuffle in a heart-beat, and as the angel took over, it was clear the guy was fully armed. Nice touch. "Thanks, man."

"No problem. And here, let me shed some light on the subject."

The angel began to glow, but only toward the back. And . . . god-damn . . . when Tohr stepped through the partition, what he saw in the golden illumination was death on four hooves coming for the king: Wrath's breathing was shallow and coming in puffs, his neck cords strain-ing with the effort it was taking him to get oxygen down into his lungs.

That gunshot in the neck was compromising the airway above the Adam's apple. Hopefully it was just swelling; worst case, he was bleeding from an artery and drowning in his own blood.

"How far from the bridge," he barked out to Lassiter.

"I can see it."

Wrath was running out of time. "Don't slow down. For anything."

"Got it."

Tohr knelt beside the king and ripped off his own leather jacket. "I'm going to see if I can help you, my brother—"

The king grabbed his arm. "Don't . . . get . . . panties . . . in a wad."

"I'm not wearing any, my lord." And he was not being paranoid about the danger they were facing. If the king didn't get some help with the breathing thing, he was going to die before anyone addressed whatever else was wrong.

Snapping into action, he tore open the king's coat, stripped off the front of the Kevlar vest—and was only mildly reassured to find nothing doing on that big chest. The problem was the neck wound, and yup, closer inspec-tion suggested the bullet was lodged in there somewhere. Christ only knew precisely what was wrong. But he was pretty sure that if he could open up an air access point below the injury, they might have a fighting chance.

"Wrath, I gotta get you breathing. And please, for the love of your *shellan*, don't fight me about the trouble you're in. I need you to work with me, not against me."

The king fumbled with his hand at his face, eventually finding his wraparounds and shoving them out of the way. As those incredibly beauti-ful, bright green eyes locked on Tohr's own, it was as if they worked.

"Tohr? Tohr—" Clicking, desperate clicking as the king tried to draw breath. "Where . . . you?"

Tohr captured that flapping palm and squeezed it hard. "I'm right

here. You're going to let me help you breathe, okay? Nod for me, my brother."

When the king did, Tohr shouted up to Lassiter, "Keep it real steady up there until I say so."

"Hitting the bridge right now."

At least they had a straightaway.

"Real steady, angel, we clear?"

"Roger that."

Unsheathing one of his daggers, he put it on the carpeted floor by Wrath's head. Then he shed his water pack and ripped it apart: Taking the flexible plastic tubing that snaked from the mouthpiece to the bladder, he drew the thing out flat and cut it at both ends; then he blew the water out of the inside.

He leaned down to Wrath. "I'm going to have to cut it into you."

Shit, the breathing was even worse, nothing but hitches.

Tohr didn't wait for consent or even acknowledgment. He palmed his knife and, with his left hand, probed the soft, fleshy field between the terminals of the king's collarbones.

"Brace yourself," he said hoarsely.

It was a damn shame he couldn't sterilize the blade, but even if he'd had a bonfire to draw it through, he didn't have time for the thing to cool down: Those jerking breaths were getting quieter, instead of louder.

With a silent prayer, Tohr did exactly as V had trained him: He pressed the sharp point of his dagger through the skin to the tough tunnel of the esophagus. Another quick prayer . . . and then he cut deep, but not too deep. Immediately thereafter, he shoved the flexible hollow tubing into the king.

The relief was fast, the air rushing out with a little whistle. And right thereafter, Wrath sucked in a proper breath, and another . . . and another.

Planting a palm on the floor, Tohr focused on keeping that tube right where it was, sticking out of the front of the king's throat. When blood started to seep from around the site, he ditched the prop-up routine and pinched the skin around the plastic lifeline, keeping the seal as tight as possible.

Those blind eyes with their pinprick irises found his, and there was gratitude in them, like he'd saved the guy's life or something.

But they'd have to see about that. Every subtle bump that registered through the van's suspension made Tohr mental, and they were still too far from home.

"Stay with me," Tohr murmured. "Stay right here with me."

As Wrath nodded and closed his eyes, Tohr glanced over at the Kevlar vest. The damn things were designed to protect vital organs, but they were not a home-safe guarantee.

On that note, how the hell had they managed to get the van out of there at all? Surely Xcor's soldiers would have been manning the garage—those bloodthirsty bastards would have known that that was the only escape route for an injured king.

Somebody must have covered it—no doubt one of the Brothers arriving in the nick of time.

"Can you drive any faster?" Tohr demanded.

"I got the pedal to the metal." The angel looked back. "And I don't care what I have to mow over."

FORTY-TWO

No'One was down in the training center, pushing along a bin full of clean linens to the recovery beds, when it happened again.

The phone rang in the main exam room, and then she heard through the open door Doc Jane talking fast and pointedly . . . and using the name "Tohr"—

What began as a hesitation turned into a dead stop, her hands tightening on the bin's metal rim, her heart beating hard as the world tilted wildly, spinning her round and round—

Down at the far end of the hallway, the office's glass door burst wide and Beth, the queen, skidded into the hallway.

"Jane! Jane!"

The healer stuck her head out of the examination room. "I'm on the phone with Tohr right now. They're bringing him in right away."

Beth tore down the corridor, her dark hair streaming out behind her. "I'm ready to feed him."

It took a moment for the implications to sink in.

Not Tohr, it wasn't Tohr, not Tohr . . . Dearest Virgin Scribe, thank you—

But Wrath—not the *king*!

Time became as a rubber band, stretching endlessly, the passing minutes slowing down to a crawl as people from the household began to arrive—except then suddenly, a terminal extension was reached and *snap!* everything became a blur.

Doc Jane and the healer Manuel flew out from the examining room, a rolling gurney between them, a black duffel bag with a red cross jangling off the male's shoulder. Ehlena was right with them, with more equipment in her hands. And so was the queen.

No'One whispered down the hall in their wake, running on the balls of her leather slippers, catching the heavy steel door that led out into the parking lot and squeezing through before it closed. At the curb, a van with blackened windows screeched to a halt, steam curling up from its tailpipe.

Voices—harried and deep—fought for airspace as the vehicle's rear doors were popped wide and Manuel the healer jumped inside.

Then Tohr got out.

No'One gasped. He was covered with blood, his hands, his chest, his leathers, everything stained red. Except he seemed otherwise all right. It had to be Wrath's.

Dearest Virgin Scribe, the king—

"Beth! Get in here," Manuel hollared. *"Now."*

After Tohr helped the queen inside, he stood by the open doors with his hands on his hips, his chest rising and falling fast, his bleak stare trained on the treatment of the king. No'One, meanwhile, loitered on the periphery, waiting and praying, her eyes going back and forth from Tohr's horrible, fixed expression to the dark recesses of the van. All she saw of the king were his boots, tough, thick soled, and black, the tread on them deep enough to make grooves in set concrete—at least when a male as great as he was wearing them.

Would that he would walk tall once again.

Wrapping her arms around herself, she wished she was a Chosen, a sacred female who had a line to the Scribe Virgin, some way of approaching the mother of the race for special dispensation. But she was no one like that.

All she could do was wait with the ring of others who had formed by the van. . . .

There was no way of knowing how long they worked upon the king in that vehicle. Hours. Days. But eventually Ehlena repositioned the gurney as close as possible and Tohr hopped back in the rear.

Wrath was carried forth by his loyal Brother and laid out flat upon the white-sheeted mattress—which would not stay so pure for long, she feared, as she measured the king's neck: Red was already seeping through layers of gauze at the side.

Time was of the essence—but before they could roll him inside, the great male grabbed onto Tohr's ruined shirt and then started motioning to his throat. Abruptly he made a fist, and then opened his palm upward as if he were holding something.

Tohr nodded, and looked at the doctors. "You need to try to take the bullet out. We have to have that thing—it's the only way we're going to be able to prove who did this."

"What if it compromises his life?" Manuel asked.

Wrath started shaking his head and pointing again, but the queen overruled him. "Then you will leave it right where it is." As her mate glared at her, she shrugged. "Sorry, my *hellren*. I'm sure your Brothers will agree—you need to survive first and foremost."

"That's right," Tohr growled. "The lead is less important—besides, we already know who's to blame."

Wrath started working his mouth—except there was no speaking, because . . . there was a tube sticking out of his throat?

"Good, glad that's settled," Tohr muttered. "Have at him, will you?"

The healers nodded and off they all went with the king, the queen staying right with her male, speaking to him in soft, urgent tones as she jogged alongside. Indeed, as they passed through the doors into the training center, Wrath's eyes, pale green and glowing, were locked, but unfocused, on her face.

She was keeping him alive, No'One thought. That connection between the two of them sustaining him just as much as anything that the physicians were doing. . . .

Tohr, meanwhile, also stayed with his leader, passing by without even looking at her.

She didn't blame him. How could he see anything else?

Reentering the corridor, she wondered if she shouldn't try to get back to work. But no, there was no possibility of that.

She just followed the group down until the whole lot of them, including Tohr, disappeared into the operating room. Not daring to intrude, she tarried outside.

It was not long before she was joined by the rest of the Brotherhood.

Tragically so.

Over the next hour, the horrors of war were all too evident, the risks to life and limb made manifest by the injuries that presented themselves as the Brothers came in from the field at a trickle.

It had been a rabid gunfight. At least, that was what they said to their mates, all of whom gathered to comfort them, anxious faces, horrified eyes, panicked hearts drawing the couples tightly together. The good news was that each and every one of them came home, the males, and the lone female, Payne, all returned safe and got treated.

Only to worry about Wrath.

The last to arrive was among the worst injured but for the king—to the point that at first, she didn't recognize who it was. The thatch of dark hair and the fact that John Matthew was carrying him informed her it was likely Qhuinn—but one certainly wouldn't know that going by his face.

He had been beaten severely.

As the male was delivered to the second operating room, she thought of the mangled mess of her leg and prayed that the healing ahead for him, for them all, was nothing like hers had been.

Dawn eventually arrived, but she knew this only because of what the clock on the wall read. Intermittent glimpses of the various dramas were provided when OR doors were opened and closed, and eventually, those treated were released into healing rooms, or permitted to ambulate themselves back to the main house—not that any of them left. They all settled as she did against the concrete walls of the corridor, sitting vigil not just for the king, but for their fellow fighters.

Doggen brought food and drink to those who could eat, and she helped pass trays laden with fruit juices and coffee and tea. She brought pillows to ease strained necks, and blankets to cut the draft on the hard floor, and tissues—not that anyone was crying.

The stoic nature of those males and their mates was a kind of power in and of itself. Yet she knew, in spite of their forbearance, that they were terrified.

Still other members of the household arrived: Layla, the Chosen. Saxton, the lawyer who worked with the king. Rehvenge, who always made her nervous even though he had never been anything but perfectly polite to her. The king's beloved retriever who wasn't allowed into the operating room, but was comforted by all and sundry. The black cat, Boo, who snaked around the stretched-out boots, and padded over laps, and was petted in passing.

Late morning.

Afternoon.

Late afternoon.

At five-oh-seven, Doc Jane and her partner, Manuel, finally appeared, removing their masks from their exhausted faces.

"Wrath is doing as well as can be expected," the female reported. "But given that he was treated in the field, we've got twenty-four hours of watching for infection ahead of us."

"You can deal with that, though," the Brother Rhage spoke up. "Right?"

"We can treat the shit out of it," Manuel said with a nod. "He's going to pull through—that tough bastard won't have it any other way."

There was an abrupt war cry from the Brotherhood, their respect and adoration and relief so very obvious. And as No'One breathed her own sigh of relief, she realized it was not for the king. It was because she did not want Tohr to sustain any more losses.

This was . . . good. Thanks be to the Scribe Virgin.

FORTY-THREE

At first, Layla could not comprehend what she was looking at. A face, yes, and one that she supposed she knew by shape. But its composite features were distorted to such an extent that she would not have been able to identify the male had she not known him so well.

"Qhuinn . . . ?" she whispered as she approached the hospital bed.

He had been stitched up, little lines of black thread snaking down his brow and across his cheek, his skin shiny from swelling, his hair as yet matted with dried blood, his breathing shallow.

Looking to the machines over the bed, she heard no alarms ringing, saw nothing flashing. That was good, yes?

She would feel better if he replied to her. "Qhuinn?"

On the bed, his hand turned over and released its tight crunch to reveal his broad, flat palm.

She put her own upon it and felt him squeeze. "So you are in there," she said roughly.

Another squeeze.

"I need to feed you," she moaned, feeling his pain as her own. "Please . . . open your mouth for me. Let me ease you. . . ."

As he complied, there was a cracking sound, as if the joints of his jaw weren't working properly.

Scoring her own vein, she carried her wrist to his bruised, parted lips. "Take from me. . . ."

At first, it was clear he had difficulty swallowing, so she licked one of the puncture marks shut to slow the flow. As he gained momentum, she bit herself once again.

She fed him for as long as he would let her, praying that her strength would become his own, and be transformed into a healing force.

How had this happened? Who had done this to him?

Given the number of gauze-wrapped limbs out in the hallway, it was obvious the *lessers* had sent a brutal force out into the streets of Caldwell upon the eve. And Qhuinn had certainly taken on the toughest, meanest member of the enemy forces. He was like that. Unflinching, always willing to put himself on the line . . . to the point where she worried about that vengeful streak of his.

It was such a fine distinction between courage and deadly recklessness.

When he was finished, she closed her wounds and pulled up a chair, sitting beside him with her palm against his once more.

It was a relief to watch the miraculous transformation of the injuries on his face. At this rate, they would soon be nothing but surface wounds, barely noticeable upon the morrow's arrival.

Whatever damage he had internally would likewise be discharged.

He was going to survive.

Sitting with him in silence, she thought about the pair of them, and the friendship that had sprouted from that misplaced adoration of hers. If anything happened to him, she would mourn him as a brother of her own blood, and there was naught that she would not do for him—further, she had the keen sense that the same was true on his side as well.

Indeed, he had done so much for her. He had taught her to drive and to fight with her fists, to shoot a gun and operate all manner of computer equipment. He had shown her movies and exposed her to music, bought her clothes that were other than the traditional white robe of the Chosen, took time to answer her questions about this side and make her laugh when she needed to.

She had learned so much from him. Owed him so much.

So it seemed . . . ungrateful . . . to feel dissatisfied with her lot. But of late she had experienced a strange irony: The more she was exposed to, the emptier her life felt. And yet as much as he urged her in opposite directions, she still looked upon her service to the Brotherhood as the most important thing she could do with her time—

As Qhuinn tried to reposition himself, he cursed from discomfort, and she reached out to calm him, stroking back his stringy hair. Only one eye of his worked, and it shifted over to her, the light behind the blue color exhausted and grateful.

A smile stretched her lips and she brushed his busted-up cheek with the very tips of her fingers. Strange, this platonic closeness they shared—it was an island, a sanctuary, and she valued it so much more than whatever heat she had once felt for him.

The vital link also made her aware of how much he suffered, watching his beloved Blay with Saxton.

His pain was ever present, coating him as his very flesh did and binding him in the same way, defining his contours and straightaways.

It made her resent Blay at times, even though it was not her place to judge: If there was one thing she had learned, it was that the hearts of others were known only to themselves—and Blay was, at his core, a male of worth—

The door opened behind her, and over her shoulder the male in her thoughts appeared as if summoned by her ruminations.

Blaylock was not uninjured himself, but he was far better off than the male on the bed—at least on the outside. Internally was a matter altogether different: still fully armed, he appeared far, far older than his years. Especially as he took in his fellow soldier.

He stopped short just inside the room. "I wanted to know how you . . . he . . . is doing."

Layla refocused on Qhuinn. His working eye was locked on the redheaded male, and the regard he paid the other no longer pained her—well, not in the sense that she wanted it for herself.

She wished for Qhuinn this soldier. She truly did.

"Come in," she said. "Please—we're done here."

Blay was slow in approaching, and his hands went to random buckles—on his holster, on his belt, on the leather strapping around his upper thigh.

His composure was retained, however. At least until he spoke. Then his voice quavered. "You dumb son of a bitch."

Layla's brows sunk into a glare, even though Qhuinn hardly needed someone like her to defend him. "I *beg* your pardon."

"According to John, he went out of that house into the Band of Bastards. Alone."

"Band of Bastards?"

"The ones who tried to assassinate Wrath tonight. This dumb son of a bitch took it upon himself to go out right into the middle of them, all alone, like he was some kind of superhero—it was a miracle he didn't get himself killed."

She immediately transferred her glare to the bed. Clearly, the Lessening Society had a new division, and the idea that he had exposed himself in such a way made her want to yell at him. "You . . . dumb son of a bitch."

Qhuinn coughed a little. Then a little more.

With a stab of fear, she jumped up. "I shall get the doctors—"

Except Qhuinn was laughing. Not choking to death.

He laughed stiffly at first and then with growing expression, until the bed shook from the hilarity that only he saw.

"I find no levity in this," she snapped.

"Nor I," Blay cut in. "What the hell is wrong with you?"

Qhuinn just continued to laugh, enjoying himself over the Scribe Virgin only knew what.

Layla glanced over at Blay. "I find myself rather wanting to hit him."

"It'd be redundant at this point. Wait until he's better, then have at him. Matter of fact, I'll hold him down for you."

"Right . . . thing . . . to do . . ." Qhuinn groaned out.

"I agree." Layla put her hands on her hips. "Blay is absolutely right—I shall punch you later. And you taught me exactly where one needs to strike a male."

"Nice," Blay muttered.

After they all fell silent, the intense way the males stared at each other made her heart light up. Mayhap they could find an accord now?

"I shall go forth and check the others," she said quickly. "To see if anyone else requires feeding—"

Qhuinn reached out and snagged her hand. "You?"

"No, I'm fine. You were more than generous enough last week. I feel very strong." She bent down and kissed his forehead. "You just rest. I'll check on you later."

On her way past Blay, she said softly, "You two talk. I'll tell everyone to leave you be."

As the Chosen departed, Blay could only stare in disbelief at the back of her perfectly coiffed head.

When he'd walked into the room, the connection between Qhuinn and that female had socked him in the gut: all that eye contact, that hand-holding, the way she curved her elegant body toward him . . . the way that she and she alone sustained him.

And yet . . . it appeared as if she wanted him to be by himself with Qhuinn.

It made no sense. If anyone was incented to keep the pair of them apart, it was her.

Refocusing on the male, he thought, God, those injuries were hard to look at, even though they were in the process of healing.

"Who did you go up against?" he asked roughly. "And don't bother arguing—I spoke to John as soon as I got home. I know what you did."

Qhuinn lifted a swollen hand and made an X.

"*Xcor* . . . ?" As the guy nodded, he grimaced like the movement made his head hurt. "Don't—yeah, don't force yourself."

Qhuinn waved the concern off in his classic, nothing-doing kind of way. On a rasp, he said, "S'okay."

"What made you go out there against him?"

"Wrath . . . was hit . . . knew Xcor's ego—he'd have to be . . ." Big breath, one that rattled on its way out. ". . . the guy to prevent the king from leaving. Bastard had to . . . had to be incapacitated . . . or Wrath would never . . ."

"Have gotten out of there alive." Blay rubbed the back of his neck. "Holy shit—you saved the king's life."

"Nah . . . lot of people . . . did that."

Yeah, he wasn't so sure about that. Back at Assail's, it had been total chaos—the kind of out-of-control that easily cut both ways: had the Band of Bastards not retreated shortly after the Brotherhood arrived, there would have been heavy losses on both sides.

Staring down at Qhuinn, he had to wonder what kind of shape Xcor was in. If he looked like this? The bastard was at least the same, probably worse.

Blay shook himself, aware that he had been standing at the edge of the bed in silence. "Ah . . ."

Back long ago, a lifetime ago, there had never been silences between them. Except . . . they had been boys then. Not fully transitioned males.

Different standard, he supposed.

"I guess I should leave you," he said. Without leaving.

This could so easily have gone a different way, he thought. Xcor's ability to kill was well-known—not by Blay personally, but he'd heard the

stories from the Old Country. Besides, for chrissakes, anyone with enough balls not only to talk about going against Wrath, but to actually put a bullet in the king?

Deadly or stupid. And the latter didn't count in this case.

Qhuinn could easily have been hit by a lot more than multiple fists.

"Can I get you anything?" Blay said. Except, duh, the guy couldn't eat, and he'd already been fed.

Layla had taken care of that.

Man, if he was brutally honest with himself—and it seemed as if *brutally* was the word of the day—there were times when he resented the Chosen, even though that was a colossal waste of emotion. He had no right to feel cranked, especially given what he and Saxton got up to on a very regular basis. Especially given that nothing was going to change on Qhuinn's side.

You almost died tonight, he wanted to say. *You dumb son of a bitch, you nearly died . . . and then what would we have done?*

And not "we" as in the Brotherhood.

Not even "we" as in he and John. More like . . . "me."

Shit, why did he keep coming back to this corner with this male?

It was just too stupid. Particularly as he stood over the guy, watching as more color came into that mangled face, and his breathing grew less labored, and the bruising faded even further . . . all thanks to Layla.

"I'd better go," he said, without leaving.

That one eye, the blue one, just kept staring up at him. Bloodshot, with a cut across the brow above it, the thing shouldn't have been able to focus. But it was.

"I have to go," Blay said finally.

Without leaving.

Damn him, he didn't know what the hell he was doing—

A tear escaped from that eye. Welling up along the lower lid, it coalesced at the far corner, formed a crystal circle, and grew so fat it couldn't hold on to the lashes. Slipping free, it meandered downward, getting lost in dark hair at the temple.

Blay wanted to kick himself in his own ass. "Shit, let me get Doc Jane—you must be in pain. I'll be right back."

Qhuinn called out his name, but he was already turning away.

Idiot. Stupid-ass idiot. The poor male was there suffering on a hospital bed, looking like an extra on *Sons of Anarchy*—last thing he needed was company. More painkillers—that was what he required.

Jogging down the corridor, he found Doc Jane logged in at the clinic's main computer, entering notes into medical records.

"Qhuinn needs a shot of something. Come quick, will you?"

The female was on it, snagging an old-fashioned doctor's bag and going back down the hall with him.

While she went inside, Blay gave them some privacy, pacing back and forth in front of the door.

"How is he?"

Stopping and pivoting around, he tried to smile at Saxton—and failed. "He decided to be a hero . . . and I think he might have actually been one. But, God . . ."

The other male came forward, moving elegantly in his bespoke suit, his Cole Haan loafers making soft impacts, as if they were too refined to ever make much noise—even on linoleum.

He didn't belong in the war. Never would.

He would never be like Qhuinn, jumping out of safety into the thick of a fight, going up against the enemy with his bare, clawing hands to take down an aggressor and serve him his own balls for lunch.

It was probably part of the reason Saxton was easier to deal with. No extremes. Plus the male was intelligent, refined, and funny . . . had lovely manners, and lots of exposure to the very best in life . . . always dressed well. . . .

Was fantastic in bed . . .

Why did it sound like he was trying to convince himself of something?

As he explained what had gone down in the field, Saxton stopped right up close, his Gucci cologne a calming scent. "I'm so sorry. You must be a mess in the head over it all."

Annnnnd the male was a saint. A selfless saint. Never to be jealous?

Qhuinn wasn't like that. Qhuinn was jealous and possessive as hell—

"Yes, I am," Blay said. "A total wreck."

Saxton reached out and took his hand, giving it a subtle squeeze and then retracting his warm, smooth palm.

Qhuinn was never that discreet about anything. He was a marching band, a Molotov cocktail, a bull in a china shop who didn't care what kind of mess he made in his wake.

"Does the Brotherhood know?"

Blay shook himself. "I'm sorry?"

"What he did? Do they know?"

"Well, if they've heard about it, it wasn't from him. John looked upset and I asked him—and that's the way I heard the story."

"You should tell Wrath . . . Tohr . . . someone. He should get credit for this—even though it's not his style to care about that sort of nonsense."

"You know him well," Blay murmured.

"I do. And I know you just as well." Saxton's expression tightened, but he smiled nonetheless. "You need to take care of him in this."

Doc Jane emerged from the room, and Blay wheeled around. "How's he doing?"

"I'm not sure—what exactly did you think was wrong? He was resting comfortably when I went in there."

Well, shit, he wasn't about to say the male had been crying. But the fact of the matter was, Qhuinn would never have shown that kind of weakness unless he was in some serious pain.

"I guess I misread him."

Over Jane's shoulder, Blay happened to notice the way Saxton's hand passed through the thick blond waves that were sculpted up off his forehead.

It was the strangest thing . . . Sax may have been related by blood to Qhuinn, but at the moment, he looked a lot like Blay had for years.

Then again, unrequited was the same, no matter the features that reflected the emotion.

Crap.

FORTY-FOUR

own the hall, Tohr sat in a chair across from the hospital bed Wrath had been laid out in. It was probably time to go.

Had been a while ago.

For God's sake, even the queen had fallen asleep next to her mate on the bed.

Guess it was a good thing Beth didn't mind his kibitzing. Then again, they had come to an accord years ago, proving just what a Godzilla marathon would do for a relationship.

Over in the corner, on a huge round Orvis bed the color of oatmeal, George stretched out of the curl he'd been in and glanced up at his master. Getting no response, he put his head down and sighed.

"He's gonna be okay," Tohr said.

The dog's ears pricked and he gave two thumps of his feathered tail.

"Yup. I promise."

Taking a cue from the canine, Tohr repositioned himself, and then rubbed his eyes. Man, he was exhausted. All he wanted to do was dog-bed it like George and sleep for a day.

The problem was, even though the drama was over, his adrenal gland still piped up every time he thought of that bullet. Two inches to the right and it would have hit the jugular, turning Wrath's light out for good. In fact, according to Doc Jane and Manny, where that lead had been lodged by pure chance had been the only "safe" place—assuming the guy was with someone who could, oh, say, do a tracheotomy in a moving van with nothing but a section of hollow tubing and a black dagger.

Jesus Christ . . . what a night.

And thank the Scribe Virgin for that angel. Without Lassiter showing up to drive? He shuddered—

"Waiting for Godot?"

Tohr's eyes snapped over to the bed. The king's lids were low but open, his mouth cracked in a half smile.

Emotion came on thick and quick, flooding Tohr's neurotransmitters, stealing his voice from him.

And Wrath seemed to understand. Opening his free hand, he beckoned, even though he couldn't lift up his arm.

Tohr's feet felt sloppy as he stood up and approached the bed. As soon as he was in range, he knelt by his king and took that big palm, turned it over . . . and kissed the gigantic black diamond that flashed on Wrath's finger.

Then, like a pussy, he laid his head down on the ring, on his brother's knuckles.

All could have been lost tonight. If Wrath had not lived . . . everything would have changed.

As the king squeezed his hand back, Tohr thought about Wellsie's dying, and felt nothing but fresh dread. To realize that there were as yet others to lose was not reassuring in the slightest. If anything, it made the churning, ambient anxiety in his gut swirl faster.

You'd think after his *shellan*'s passing he'd be exempt from the grief pool.

Instead, it appeared that he just had a deeper bottom to look forward to.

"Thank you," Wrath whispered hoarsely. "For saving my life."

Tohr lifted his head and shook it. "It wasn't just me."

"It was a lot you. I owe you, brother mine."

"You'd have done the same."

That patented autocratic tone came out: "I. Owe. You."

"So buy me a Sam some night and we'll call it evens."

"You're saying my life is only worth six bucks?"

"You vastly underestimate how much I love a good longneck—" A big blond dog head shoved its way under his armpit. Glancing down, he said, "See? I told you he'd be all right."

Wrath laughed a little, then grimaced as if things hurt. "Hey, big man . . ."

Tohr moved out of the way so master and canine could reconnect . . . then ended up scooping the ninety-pound bale of hay-colored fur up and settling it next to the king.

Wrath positively beamed as he looked back and forth between his *shellan*, who was asleep, and his animal, who was ready to be his nurse.

"I'm glad that's our last meeting," Tohr blurted.

"Yeah, I like to go out with a bang—"

"I can't let you do shit like this anymore. You realize that, don't you." Tohr stared down at the king's forearms, tracing those ritualistic tattoos that spelled out his lineage. "You need to be alive at the end of every night, my lord. The rules are different for you."

"Look, I've been shot at before—"

"And it's not happening again. Not on my watch."

"What the hell is that supposed to mean? You going to chain me in the basement?"

"If that's what it takes."

Wrath's brows dropped low, and his voice grew stronger. "You can be a real prick, you know that."

"It's not a matter of personality. And it's obvious or you wouldn't be getting your panties in a wad."

"I'm not wearing any." The king cracked another smile. "I'm naked under here."

"Thanks for that picture."

"You know, technically you can't order me to do shit."

Wrath was right; you didn't tell the leader of the race a good goddamn thing. But as Tohr met the male's blind eyes, he wasn't talking to the ruler of them all; he was talking to his brother.

"Until Xcor is neutralized, we're not taking any risks with you—"

"If there's a Council meeting, I'm going. Period."

"There won't be. Not unless we want there to be—and right now? Nobody needs you anywhere but here."

"Fucking hell! I'm the king—" As Beth frowned in her sleep, he calmed his voice out. "Can we talk about this later?"

"No reason to. We're done on the subject—and every one of the brothers is behind me on this."

Tohr did not look away as he got hit with a glare that, in spite of those eyes being blind, was strong enough to burn a hole in the back of his skull.

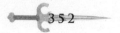

"Wrath," he said roughly, "look at what's next to you. Do you want to leave her on her own? You want her to have to mourn you? Fuck all of us—what about your Beth?"

It was a low-down dirty to play the *shellan* card, but any weapon in a fight. . . .

Wrath cursed and closed his eyes.

And Tohr knew he'd won when the male turned his face into Beth's hair and breathed in deeply, as if he were smelling her shampoo.

"Are we in accord," Tohr demanded.

"Fuck you," the king murmured against his beloved.

"Good, I'm glad that's settled."

After a moment, Wrath looked over again. "Did they get the bullet out of my neck?"

"They did. All we need is the rifle that goes with it." Tohr gave George's boxy head a stroking. "And it's got to be the Band of Bastards'—Xcor's the only one who would try something like that."

"We need to find where they live."

"They're cagey. Smart. It's going to take a miracle."

"Then start praying, my brother. Start praying."

Tohr replayed the attack in his mind yet again. The brazenness was off the chain—and suggested Xcor was capable of just about anything.

"I'm going to kill him," he said in a low voice.

"Xcor?" When he nodded, Wrath said, "I think you're going to have to get in line for the job—assuming we can tie him to the shooter. The good news is that as head of the B.o.B., he can be held accountable for his fighters' actions—so as long as one of his soldiers was at the trigger of that rifle, we can nail him."

As Tohr thought shit over, that grinding in his gut tightened to an unbearable level. "You said you owed me a favor—well, this is what I want. I want Xcor's death to be at my hands and no one else's."

"Tohr . . ." When he just stared straight ahead, Wrath shrugged. "I can't give him to you until we have proof."

"But you can stipulate that if he is responsible, he's mine."

"Fine. He's all yours—if we have proof."

Tohr thought about the expressions on the faces of the brothers out in the hall. "You need to make it official."

"Oh, come on, if I say—"

"You know what they're like. Any one of them crosses paths with that shithead and they'll peel him like a grape. Right now that male's got more targets on the back of his ass than a shooting range. Besides, a proclamation won't take long."

Wrath's lids closed briefly. "Okay, okay . . . stop arguing the point and go get a witness."

Tohr went over and stuck his head out of the room—and as luck would have it, the first person he saw . . . was John Matthew.

The kid was parked by the recovery room across the way, butt on the floor next to a worried Blaylock, hands on his head like there was a fire alarm going off in his skull.

Except he snapped right to and signed, *Is Wrath still all right?*

"Yeah." Tohr glanced down the corridor as Blay murmured a prayer of thanks. "He's going to be fine."

You looking for someone?

"I need a witness—"

I'll do it.

Tohr shot up his brows. "Okay. Thanks."

As John Matthew got to his feet, a loud crack sounded out, like his back was playing DIY chiropractor. And when he limped over, Tohr realized the kid had been injured.

"You have Doc Jane take a look at that?"

John bent down and lifted the pant leg of the scrubs he had on. His calf was wrapped in white gauze.

"Bullet or blade?" Tohr asked.

Bullet. And yes, they kept it as well.

"Good. How'd you fare, Blay?"

"Just a surface wound on my arm."

That it? Tohr thought. Because the fucker looked a little hollow—then again, it had been a long night and day for everyone.

"I'm glad, son. We'll be right back."

"I'm not going anywhere."

As John came over to the wide-open door, Tohr stepped aside, and then followed him in.

"How you doing, son?" Wrath asked as the kid approached him and bent down to kiss his ring.

As John signed, Tohr translated, "He says just fine. He says . . . if it would not offend, he has something he and Blay need you to know?"

"Yeah, sure. G'head."

"He says . . . he was with . . . Qhuinn at the house . . . after you were shot, before the Brotherhood arrived. . . . Qhuinn went out alone. . . . ah,

Blay spoke with the guy a little while ago. Blay said that . . . Qhuinn told him he'd engaged with . . . Xcor . . . so that—wait, John, slow down. Thanks . . . Okay, engaged with Xcor . . . so that you could get free in the van—"

Beth stirred, her eyes opening, her brows tightening as if she were catching the drift of the conversation.

"Are you serious?" the king blurted.

"He took on . . . Xcor . . . one-on-one—" Holy shit, Tohr thought. He'd heard the kid had gone out there, but that was it.

Wrath whistled under his breath. "That's a male of worth, right there."

"Wait, John, let me catch up. One-on-one . . . so that Xcor, who was waiting to attack the van, was neutralized. . . . He—John, that is—wants to know if there is some kind of official recognition that . . . you can give Qhuinn? Something to recognize . . . his above-and-beyond . . . service? And P.S.," Tohr spoke for himself, "me, personally? I'm so on board with that."

Wrath stayed quiet for a moment. "I'm sorry, let me get this straight. Qhuinn went out after the brothers arrived, right?"

Tohr got back with the translating. "John says no. It was on his own, unguarded, unprotected before they came. Qhuinn said . . . he had to do what he could to make sure you were okay."

"That dumb-ass idiot."

"Hero is more like it," Beth said abruptly.

"*Leelan*, you wake." Wrath became instantly focused on his mate. "I didn't want to disturb you."

"Believe me, just hearing your voice is heaven . . . you can wake me up with it anytime." She kissed his mouth softly. "Welcome back."

Both Tohr and John got busy looking at the floor as tender words were exchanged.

Then the king came back online. "Qhuinn shouldn't have done that."

"I agree," Tohr muttered.

The king focused on John. "Yeah, all right. We'll do something for him. I don't know what . . . but that kind of shit is epic. Stupid, but epic."

"Why don't you make him a Brother," Beth interjected.

In the silence that followed, Wrath's mouth dropped open, and it was a join-the-club reaction—Tohr's jaw did likewise, and so did John's.

"What?" the queen said. "Doesn't he deserve it? Hasn't he always been there for everyone? And he's lost all his family—yes, he lives here, but sometimes I get the impression that he feels like he doesn't belong. What better way of thanking him and telling him he does? I know no one doubts his strength in the field."

Wrath cleared his throat. "Well, according to the Old Laws—"

"Fuck the Old Laws. You're the king—you can do anything you want."

More pin-drop silence swept in, clearing out even the sounds of the HVAC system blowing warm air through the ceiling vents.

"What do you think, Tohr?" the king asked.

As Tohr glanced at John, he was struck by how much he wanted to bestow the honor on the closest thing to a son he had. But Qhuinn was the one they were talking about.

"I think . . . yeah, I think it could be a good idea," he heard himself say. "Qhuinn should be claimed, and the brothers respect him— Shit, tonight isn't the only time he's shined. He's a stellar fighter, but more than that, he's calmed down tremendously in the last year. So, yeah, I think he could handle the responsibility now, which is not something I might have said at any other time."

"Okay, I'll consider it, *leelan*. It's a wonderful suggestion." The king glanced back at Tohr. "Now, about that favor. Approach me, brother mine, and render thy form unto your knees—we have two witnesses now, which is even better."

As Tohr complied and grasped the royal hand, Wrath proclaimed in the Old Language, *"Tohrment, son of Hharm, are you prepared to have proscribed unto you, and you alone, the death of Xcor, son of an unknown sire, said demise to occur by your hands and your hands only in retaliation for a mortal affront against me this previous night—if said affront can be proven to be due to Xcor's direct or indirect order?"*

Placing his free hand over his beating heart, he said gravely, *"I am so prepared, my lord."*

Wrath looked at his mate. *"Elizabeth, blooded daughter of the Black Dagger Brother Darius, mated of myself, your king, do you hereby agree to witness my grant should I deign to bequeath it on this matter to this male, carrying forth the representation of this moment unto all others, placing also your mark upon parchment to commemorate this proclamation?"* When she answered affirmatively, he regarded John. *"Tehrror, blooded son of the Black Dagger Brother Darius, also known by the names John and Matthew, do you hereby agree to witness my grant should I deign to bequeath it on this matter to this male, carrying forth the representation of this moment unto all*

others, placing also your mark upon parchment to commemorate this procla-
mation?"

Tohr translated from ASL. *"Yes, my lord, he does."*

"Then by the power held sure and true by myself through mine father, I hereby command you, Tohrment, son of Hharm, to go forth and perform the now royal duty of retribution on my behalf—if it is so supported by requisite proof—returning in future with the body of Xcor, son of an unknown sire, unto me as a service to your king and your race. Your pledge is a credit to your bloodline, past, present, and future."

Once more, Tohrment bent to the ring that had been worn by genera-tions of Wrath's lineage. *"I am, in this and all things, yours to command, my heart and body seeking only to obey your sole authority."*

When he lifted his eyes, Wrath was smiling. "I know you'll bring that bastard home."

"You got it, my lord."

"Now get the fuck out of here. The three of us need some goddamn sleep."

Various good-byes were exchanged, and then Tohr and John were out in the corridor in an awkward silence. Blay had since fallen asleep outside that other recovery room, but he wasn't resting—there was a deep frown on his face, like he was brooding even in the midst of his REM.

A tap on his forearm had Tohr focusing on John.

Thank you, the kid signed.

"For what?"

Supporting Qhuinn.

Tohr shrugged. "Only makes sense. Shit, the number of times that guy's thrown himself into battle with all guns blazing? He deserves it— and that Brotherhood nomination stuff shouldn't be about bloodline, but merit."

Do you think Wrath will do it?

"I don't know—it's complicated. Lot of history to deal with—the Old Laws would have to be reworded. I'm sure the king will do something for him—"

Down the corridor, No'One stepped out of a doorway, as if she had been drawn by the sound of his voice.

The instant he saw her, he lost his train of thought, everything he had locking on her robed figure. Fucking hell . . . he was too raw to be around her, too hungry for life-affirming contact, too disinclined to make good decisions.

God help them both, but if he walked down to her, he was going to take her.

Out of the corner of his eye, he saw that John was signing something. It took every ounce of self-control to force his head toward the kid.

She was so worried about you. She's been waiting out here with us—she thought you had been injured.

"Oh . . . well, shit."

She loves you.

Okay, well, didn't that make him want to crap in his pants. "Nah, she's just . . . you know, a compassionate person."

John cleared his throat, even though his hands were doing the talking. *I guess I didn't know that you guys were this serious.*

Thinking of how upset the kid had been, Tohr waved away the comment. "No, I mean, it's no big deal. Honest. I know who I love—and who I belong with."

Except that brush-off didn't feel right, not on his tongue, not to his ears . . . not to the center of his chest.

I'm sorry about . . . you know, losing it before, John signed. *It's just . . . Wellsie's the only mother I had, and . . . I don't know. The idea of you with someone else makes me want to throw up—even though that's not fair.*

Tohr shook his head and dropped his voice. "Don't you ever apologize for caring about our female. And as for the love thing, I gotta say it again. In spite of what it looks like from the outside, I will love one and only one female for the rest of my life. No matter what I do, who I'm with, or how things appear, you can take that shit to the bank, son. We clear?"

John's rough embrace was difficult to bear—because letting down the kid had been a killer, and it was tough not to worry about doing it again in some way.

It was also hard because Tohr's convictions were heartfelt and honest . . . as well as Wellsie's doom. Weren't they.

God, was he ever going to find a way out of this mess?

As that panicky thought occurred to him, he shifted his eyes and looked down the way to No'One's slight, still form.

Behind her, Lassiter stepped out and just stared back at him, the disappointment in the guy's face so apparent, it was clear he'd somehow heard what had been said.

Maybe all of it.

FORTY-FIVE

As Tohr walked off toward No'One, John resumed tending his little patch of linoleum outside of Qhuinn's room.

On some level, he didn't want to see the Brother go down the hall to that other female. It seemed fundamentally wrong, as if one of the laws of the universe had decided to run in reverse. Hell, paralleling it with his own life, the idea that there would ever be another female aside from Xhex for him was anathema: Even though he was in constant agony without her, he still loved her so much, he was asexual.

Then again . . . she was still alive.

And you couldn't argue that the relationship hadn't been good for Tohr. He was back to the size he'd been when John had first met him, huge, hard, and strong. And come on, he hadn't walked into a death trap of a gunfight or leaped off a bridge in, like, months.

Good thing Qhuinn had taken up the slack on that one. Yay.

Besides, No'One was tough not to approve of: She was very non-bimbo . . . quiet. Unassuming. Not at all bad to look at.

There were so many worse candidates out there in the world. Gold diggers. Stuck-up *glymera* types. Spacy, big-breasted gigglers.

Letting his head fall back against the concrete wall, he closed his eyes as he heard the pair of them talking. Soon enough, the voices stopped and he assumed they'd taken off, likely to go to bed—

Okay, he was so not going there.

Left to his little lonesome, he listened to Blay's soft breathing and occasional repositioning of limbs, resolutely keeping his mind off Xhex.

Funny, this stretch of wait-and-worry felt like old times . . . he and Blay waiting on Qhuinn.

Man, they were lucky the guy had come back alive. . . .

As his memory coughed up images from that mansion on the river, he saw Wrath going down to the floor, and V with his gun up to Assail's head . . . and Tohr going body-shield over the king. Then he and Qhuinn were searching the house . . . arguing next to that sliding glass door . . . fighting over his best friend going out into the night, uncovered and alone.

You need to let me do what I can.

Qhuinn's eyes had been resolute and utterly unafraid, because he knew his capabilities, knew that he could go out on a Hail Mary and rough shit up, knew that even though there was a chance he wasn't coming home, he was strong enough and sure enough of his fighting skills that he would do everything possible to decrease that risk.

And John had let him go. Even though his heart had been screaming and his head had been ringing and his body prepared to block the way out. Even though it hadn't just been *lesser* new recruits out there, but the Band of Bastards, who were highly trained, very experienced, and brutal as hell. Even though Qhuinn was his best friend, a male who mattered to him in this world, someone whose loss would rock him for life. . . .

Shit.

John put his palms to the front of his face and gave himself a good buffing.

Except no amount of rubbing was going to change the revelation that was creeping up on him, unwelcome and undeniable.

He saw Xhex in that meeting with the Brotherhood back in the spring, when she had offered to find Xcor's lair: *I can take care of that—especially if I hit them in the daytime.*

She had been utterly hard eyed and clearheaded, sure of herself and her capabilities. *You people need me to do what I can.*

When it had been his best friend? He hadn't liked it, but he'd stepped aside and let the male do what he had to for the greater good—even though there was mortal danger involved. If something had happened to

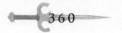

the guy and he'd died? John would have been crushed . . . but that was the code of soldier, the code of Brotherhood.

The code of males.

Losing Xhex would be so much worse, of course, because he was a bonded male. But the reality was, in trying to save her from some violent fate, he'd lost her completely: They had nothing left, no passion, no conversation, no warmth . . . little contact. And it was all because his protective urge had taken over.

It was all his fault.

He had mated a fighter—and then freaked when the risk-of-injury thing had gone from the hypothetical into the actual. And Xhex was right—she didn't want him dead or in the hands of the enemy, and yet she was allowing him to go out there every night.

She was letting him do what he could to help.

She wasn't permitting her emotions to try to stop him from executing his job—and if she had? Well, then he would have explained patiently and with love that he was born to fight, and he was careful with himself, and . . .

Kettle, black, much?

Besides, how would he have felt if someone had viewed his being mute as a rate limiter for fighting? How would he have reacted if he'd been told, in spite of all his other qualifications and skills, in spite of his natural talent and instincts, that because he couldn't speak, he wasn't allowed on the field?

Being female was not a disability in any sense of the word. But he had treated it as such, hadn't he. He had decided that because she was not male, in spite of all her qualifications and skills, she couldn't go out into conflict.

As if breasts suddenly made shit more dangerous.

John restarted with the rubbing, his head beginning to thump with pressure. His bonded side was ruining his life. Strike that—it *had* ruined his life. Because he wasn't sure, no matter what he did now, whether he could get Xhex back.

He was, however, certain about one thing.

Abruptly, he thought about Tohr and that oath.

And knew what he had to do.

As Tohrment walked toward her, No'One became breathless: His massive body was shifting from side to side to the rhythm of his gait, his burning eyes fixing on her as if he meant to consume her in some vital way.

He was ready to mate, she thought.

Dearest Virgin Scribe, he was coming to take her.

I want to fuck you.

Her hand went to the tie on her robe, and it was a shock to realize that she was prepared to open her clothing at this moment. Not here, she told her fingers. Somewhere else, though . . .

There were no thoughts of that *symphath*, no anxiety over whether it would hurt, no sense that she might regret this. There was just a resonant peace in the midst of her body's pounding need that this male was what she wanted; this mating was what she had waited so patiently for.

They were both ready.

Tohrment stopped in front of her, his chest pumping up and down and his hands curling into fists. "I'm going to give you the chance to get away from me. Right now. Leave the training center and I'll stay here."

His voice was warped, so low and deep that his words were nearly unintelligible.

Hers, on the other hand, was very clear: "I shall not depart from you."

"Do you understand what I'm saying? If you don't go . . . I'm going to be inside you in another minute and a half."

She kicked her chin up. "I want you in me."

A great growl rose up from him, the sort of sound that, had she heard it in another context, might have terrified her. But face-to-face with this magnificent, aroused male? Her body responded with a marvelous loosening, further preparing to accept him.

He was not gentle as he scooped down and picked her up, swinging her legs high and catching them in the crook of his arm. And he was not slow as he went forth toward the pool—as if the idea of getting them to a proper bed in the big house was simply too much to bother with.

Whilst he strode off with her captured like a prize, she stared up at his face. His brows were down hard, his mouth parted to reveal his fangs, his coloring high with anticipation. He wanted this. Needed this.

And there was no going back.

Not that she would have chosen to. She loved the way he made her feel in this moment.

Although she supposed it was treacherous to take compliment in the desperation with which he took possession of her. He was still in love with his dead mate. Then again, he did want her—and that was enough. That was, mayhap, all she would ever have—and yet, as she had told him, so much more than she could ever have prayed for.

Upon his will, the glass door to the pool's entry hall opened wide for them, and as it eased shut in their wake, she heard its lock slip into place. Then they were traveling fast through the anteroom, and rounding the corner into the pool proper, the warmth of that thick, humid air making her body even more languid—

In a coordinated sequence, the overhead lights dimmed and the blue-green glow of the pool gathered in intensity, casting an aquamarine illumination over everything.

"No going back," Tohrment said, as if giving her one last chance to end this.

When she merely nodded at him, he growled again and then put her down on one of the wooden benches, laying her on her back. He was true to his word. He didn't wait or hesitate; he arched over her and fused their mouths, bringing his chest to her own, positioning his legs in between hers.

Wrapping her arms around the nape of his neck, she held him close as his lips moved against hers and his tongue entered her. The kissing was glorious and consuming, to the point where she didn't notice he was undoing the tie of her robe.

And then his hands were upon her. Through the linen shift, his palms burned as they stroked her breasts and continued lower. Parting her thighs even farther for him, she pulled up the sheath and got what she wanted, his touch going to her core, massaging her, bringing her to that knife edge of release—but no farther.

"I want to kiss you," he growled against her mouth. "But I can't wait."

She thought he was kissing her?

Before she could respond, he lifted his hips from her and worked with rough urgency at the front of his leathers.

And then something hot and blunt was bumping . . . nudging . . . slipping against her.

No'One arched up and called his name—and that was when he took her: As her voice echoed to the high ceiling, his body claimed hers, pushing inside, making its way, hard yet satin soft.

Tohrment's head dropped down beside hers as they were joined, and then he stopped moving altogether—which was good: The sense of stretching and accommodating his size bordered on painful—not that she would have traded it for the world.

Groaning deep in his throat, his body started to move, slowly at first, then with greater speed, his hips swinging against hers as he gripped her outer thighs and squeezed. With the great wave of passion o'ertaking them both, every sensation was magnified, her mind at once fully present and totally blown away by the manner in which he dominated her without hurting her.

As the rhythm bordered on out of control, No'One held on to him for dear life, her physical form soaring even as it was pinned down under his, her heart shattering and being made whole in the same instant as the pleasure suddenly coalesced and then snapped. Indeed, her orgasm had her core gripping him and relenting in an alternating rhythm, the release entirely different from any of her previous ones—more intense, longer lasting. And it seemed to pitch him off the edge and into his own wild contractions, his pelvis shoving in and then jerking against her.

It all seemed to last forever, but as with any flight one took, they eventually eschewed the freedom of the sky and returned to earth.

Awareness was a gradual, unsettling burden.

He was still dressed, and so was she, the robe as yet draped upon her shoulders and arms. And the bench was cutting into her shoulder blades and the back of her head. And the air around her was not as warm as the passion had been.

How strange, she thought. Even though they had shared so much before, these moments just now had taken them up to and over a great divide.

She wondered how that would make him feel—

Tohrment lifted his head and stared down at her. There was no particular expression on his face, neither joy nor sorrow nor guilt.

He just looked at her.

"Are you okay?" he said.

As her voice appeared to have deserted her, she nodded, even though she wasn't sure what she felt. Physically, her body was fine—in fact, it continued to welcome the presence inside of its recesses. But until she knew how he was, she couldn't testify to anything else.

The last female he had been with had been his *shellan*. . . . And surely that was on his mind in this tense silence.

FORTY-SIX

Zohr stayed frozen right where he was, poised over No'One, erection still buried in her body, his sex twitching to keep going even as he put a lock on his lust.

He waited for his conscience to start screaming.

He prepared himself for an overwhelming desolation that he had been with another female.

He was . . . ready for something, anything to cough up out of his chest—despair, anger, frustration.

All he got was the sense that what had just happened was the beginning, not an end.

Shifting his eyes to No'One's face, he searched her features, looking for any indication that he'd swapped her for his *shellan*, probing his internal wiring for signs of alarm . . . bracing himself for some great explosion.

All he felt was a sense of rightness.

Reaching up, he brushed back a strand of blond hair from her face. "You sure you're okay?"

"Are you?"

"Yeah. I kind of am. . . . I mean, I truly am . . . okay. Guess I was prepared for anything but that, if it makes any sense?"

The smile that bloomed on her face was nothing short of the sun's radiance, the expression transforming her features into a beauty so resplendent, she took his ever-loving breath away.

So kind. So compassionate. So accepting.

He wouldn't have been able to do this with anyone else.

"Mind if we try that again?" he said in a soft voice.

Her cheeks flushed a deeper pink. "Please . . ."

The tone in her voice made his cock jump inside of her, her slick, tight heat stroking it on a oner, making him ready to roar and start pounding away again.

Except it wasn't fair to ask her to lie on that hard bench.

Tunneling his arms around her, he held her close to his chest and let his heavy thighs do the work of picking them both up. When they were on his feet, he kissed her again, tilting his head and working his mouth over hers as he palmed her bottom and braced himself to start moving. Using his arms, he lifted her up and down on his arousal, kissing what he could of her throat and her collarbones as he penetrated her at a different, deeper angle.

She was incredible, enveloping him, holding him tightly, the friction making him want to bite her just for the taste of her.

Faster. Even faster.

The robe was swinging wildly, and No'One must have hated the flapping as much as he did, because she abruptly dumped the thing, scraping it free of her shoulders and letting it fall to the tile. As her arms returned around his neck, she tightened her hold—which was just fine with him.

Digging in with his fingers, he got closer and closer to the end point—and it was the same with No'One. The sounds she was making, the incredible moans, her gorgeous scent rising up, her braid slapping—

Abruptly, he slowed down and snagged the tie that secured the plait of her hair, ripping it off and freeing the lengths. Shaking the thick waves out of their confines, he drew them over her shoulder and his own, blanketing them both.

Something about that undoing led to his own undoing: Two pumps later and his body pitched off its ledge, the release taking over everything until he cursed on an explosive breath.

Careening through the pleasure, he squeezed her hard and put his face into all that blond, breathing in, smelling the delicate shampoo that she used. Shit, the scent of her cranked him even higher, until his orgasm abruptly became the rough-and-tumble kind, racking his body, throwing his balance out of whack, rendering him temporarily blind.

It must have been the same for her—from a distance, he heard her call out his name as she locked her legs around his hips, melding them together.

Incredible. Absolutely incredible. And he rode out the pleasure for as long as it lasted—on both sides. When he finally stilled, No'One's head flopped onto his shoulder, her body collapsing against his chest, her lovely flesh going loose as her lovely hair.

Unbidden, one of his hands found her spine and followed it upward to the base of her neck. As his breathing eased, he just . . . held her.

Before he knew it, he was rocking them both from side to side. She weighed next to nothing in his powerful arms, and he had the sense that he could have kept them linked and against each other . . . forever.

Eventually, she whispered, "I must be getting heavy."

"Not at all."

"You're very strong."

Man, that did his ego good. Matter of fact, she hit him with anything like that again, he was going to feel like he could bench-press a city bus. With a jet plane parked on its roof.

"I should get you cleaned up," he said.

"What ever for?"

Okay, that was sexy. And it made him want to do . . . other things to her. All kinds of things.

Over her shoulder, he eyed the pool, and thought efficiency was actually the mother of invention.

"How about we take a dip?"

No'One lifted her head. "I could stay like this . . ."

"Forever?"

"Yes." Her eyes were low-lidded and glowing in the blue-green light. "Forever."

As he stared at her, he thought . . . she was so alive. Her cheeks flushed, her lips swollen from his being all over her, her hair lush and a little wild. She was vital and hot and—

He started to laugh.

Oh, for fuck's sake, he had no idea why—there was nothing funny about anything, but suddenly he was laughing like a lunatic.

"Sorry," he managed. "I don't know what the problem is."

"I don't care." She beamed at him, showing her delicate fangs and her even, white teeth. "It's the most beautiful sound I've ever heard."

Caught up in an impulse he didn't understand, he let out a whoop and took a lunge in the direction of the pool, throwing out a long stride, then another, then a third. With a mighty leap, he sent them both flying into the still, aquamarine light source.

They landed in the warm water as one, soft, invisible arms gathering them into a temperate cushion, and insulating them from gravity's heavy-handed pull, sparing them both any kind of hard landing.

As his head went under, he found her mouth and claimed it, kissing her under the surface as he planted his feet and pushed up so that they found the air. . . .

In the process, his cock found her core again.

She was right there with him, linking those legs of hers around his hips once more, echoing his rhythm, kissing him back. And it was good. It was . . . right.

Sometime later, No'One found herself naked, wet, and stretched out on the side of the pool on a bed of towels Tohrment had arranged for her.

He was kneeling next to her, his wet clothes clinging to his muscles, his hair glistening, his eyes intense as he stared at her body.

A sudden insecurity struck, chilling her.

Sitting up, she covered herself—

Tohrment captured her hands and gently put them at her sides. "You're spoiling my view."

"You like . . . ?"

"Oh, yeah. I like." He leaned over and kissed her deeply, slipping his tongue inside of her, easing her back down so that she was prone once more. "Mmmm, that's what I'm talking about."

When he eased back a little, No'One smiled up at him. "You make me feel . . ."

"What." He dipped his head and brushed his lips over her throat, her collarbone . . . the tip of her breast. "Beautiful?"

"Yes."

"That's what you are." He kissed her other nipple and sucked it into his mouth. "Beautiful. And I think you should ditch that damn robe for good."

"What will I wear?"

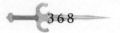

"I'll get you clothes. All the clothes you want. Or you could just go naked."

"In front of the others—" The hiss that curled out of him was pretty much the best compliment she had ever been given. "No?"

"No."

"Then mayhap in your room."

"Now, that I can get behind."

His lips drifted downward and to the side, until he ran a fang over her ribs. Then he was going across her belly, the kisses soft and lazy. It wasn't until he went even farther, lingering on her hip and then brushing very close to her sex, that she realized he had a purpose.

"Spread your legs for me," he urged in a deep voice. "Let me see the most beautiful part of you. Let me kiss you where I want to be."

She wasn't completely sure what he was suggesting, but she was powerless to deny him anything when he used that tone with her. In a haze, she brought up one knee, parting her thighs . . . and she knew when he looked at her, because he growled in satisfaction.

Tohrment moved around between her legs and stretched out, palming either side of her and widening her further. And then his lips were upon her, warm and silky and wet. The sensation of soft on soft kicked off yet another orgasm, and he took advantage of it, entering her with his tongue, sucking at her, finding her rhythm and taking her further.

Her hands dug into his dark hair as she rolled her hips.

And to think she had liked the sex. . . .

Little had she known that there was so much more to discover.

He was mind-shatteringly attentive and painstakingly thorough in his explorations, taking his time unless he was taking her to the height of pleasure. And when he eventually lifted his mouth, his lips were slick and reddened, and he ran his tongue over them as he stared at her from under his lids.

Then he rose up and gripped her hips, tilting them up.

His erection was impossibly thick and long, but she already knew he fit her perfectly.

And he did again.

This time she paid more attention to the sight of him than the feel of him. Rising above her, he moved in that powerful, potent way of his, pleasuring them both as he curled his hips up and back, moving himself in and out of her.

His smile was dark. Erotic. "You like to watch me?"

"Yes. Oh, yes . . ."

That was as far as she got as another wave of release crested and assumed control of her thoughts, her speech, her body . . . her soul, wiping everything clean.

When she finally quieted and was again able to focus, she recognized the strain in Tohrment's face, the tightness around his jaw and his eyes, the pumping of his chest. He had not found his release yet.

"Do you want to watch," he gritted out.

"Oh, yes . . ."

Withdrawing from her body, his arousal was as his lips had been, glossy and swollen.

With one big hand he gripped himself, and with the other he braced his weight against the floor so that he could stretch out over her lax, open body. Twisting his shoulders, he provided her with plenty of view as he stroked up and down, that blunt head of his appearing and disappearing in and out of his fist.

His breath grew louder and harsher as he showed her just how it happened for him.

When the time came, his shout rang out in her ears and his head shot back, his chin punching forward as he bared his fangs and hissed. Then with rhythmic pulses, jets sprayed out of him, hitting her sex and her lower belly, making her arch sure as if the satisfaction had been her own.

As he finally sagged, she extended her arms. "Come here."

There was no hesitation as he complied, bringing his chest to her own before he turned on his side to cushion her weight.

"Are you warm enough," he murmured. "Your hair is wet."

"I do not care." She snuggled into his body. "I'm just . . . perfect."

A rumble of approval came up his throat. "That you are . . . Rosalhynda."

At the sound of her former name, she jerked back, but he held her tight. "I can't keep calling you No'One. Not after . . . this."

"I don't like that name."

"Then another."

Staring into his face, she had the distinct notion that he was not going to budge on this. And he was also not going to refer to her as she had so chosen long, long ago . . . when that word was what she had felt she was.

Mayhap he was right, however. She suddenly didn't feel like no one.

"You need a name."

"I cannot choose," she replied, aware of a stout pain in her heart.

He looked up to the ceiling. Wound some of her hair around one of his fingers. Made a clicking sound with his tongue.

"Autumn is my favorite season of the year," he said after a time. "It's not that I'm chicking out or anything . . . but I like the leaves when they turn red and orange. They're beautiful in the moonlight, but more to the point, it's an impossible transformation. The green of spring and summer is just a shadow of the trees' true identity, and all that color as the nights grow cold is a miracle every stinking time it happens. It's like they're making up for the loss of the warmth with all their fire. I like . . . Autumn." He stared into her eyes. "You're like that. You're beautiful and you burn brightly—and it's time for you to come out. So I say . . . Autumn."

In the silence that followed, she was aware of a pricking at the corners of her eyes.

"What's the matter?" he rushed in. "Shit—you don't like it? I could pick another. Lihllith? How about Suhannah? What . . . Joe? Fred? Frickin' Howard?"

She put her hand upon his face. "I love it. It's perfect. I shall henceforth be known by the name you have given me, and the season of the year when the leaves burn—Autumn."

Lifting herself up, she pressed her lips to his. "Thank you. Thank you . . ."

As he nodded solemnly, she wrapped her arms around him, and held him tightly. To be named was to be claimed, and it made her feel . . . reborn.

FORTY-SEVEN

It was a long while before Tohr and Autumn reemerged from the warm, humid confines of their pool. Man, he was never going to go into that place again without thinking of it as "theirs."

Holding open the door into the corridor for her, he took a deep, easing breath. Autumn . . . the perfect name for a perfectly lovely female.

Walking side by side, they made their way to the office together, his feet leaving wet prints, because the damp pants he'd squeezed himself back into were dripping at the hems. She, on the other hand, left no trail, as her robe was dry.

Last time she was going to wear the damned thing.

Shit, her hair looked good all loose around her shoulders. Maybe he could get her to lose the braid, too.

When they stepped out into the tunnel, he put his arm around her, tucking her in against him. She fit well. She was smaller than . . . Well, Wellsie had been much taller. Autumn's head was lower on his pecs, her shoulders not as wide, and her gait was uneven, whereas his mate's had been smooth as silk.

But she fit. Differently, yes, but the lock and key of their bodies was undeniable.

Approaching the door that led up to the mansion, he dropped back and let her go up the stairs first. At the top, he reached past her, punched in the code, and opened the way into the foyer, holding the heavy panels wide for her.

As she pased through, he asked, "Hungry?"

"Famished."

"Then you go upstairs and let me wait on you."

"Oh, I can get something in the kit—"

"Nope. Don't think so. I wait on you." He took her around the base of the grand staircase. "You go up and get into bed. I'll bring the food."

She hesitated at the bottom step. "That's really not necessary."

He shook his head as he thought of all the exercise they'd gotten poolside. "It's very necessary. And you're going to humor me by losing that robe and getting in between the sheets naked."

Her smile started out shy . . . ended up spectacular.

And then she pivoted and flashed him her backside.

Watching her hips sway as she ascended got him hard. Again.

Bracing one hand against the carved banister, he had to look down at the carpet and compose himself—

A nasty curse brought his head around.

Bad word, good timing . . .

Striding across the mosaic of an apple tree in bloom, he leaned into the billiards room. Lassiter was on the couch, focused on the wide-screen over the fireplace.

Even though Tohr was half-naked and half-wet, he strode over, getting in between the angel and the TV. "Listen, I—"

"What the fuck!" Lassiter started motioning like his hands were on fire and he was trying to flap them free of flames. "Get outta the way!"

"Did it work?" Tohr demanded.

More cursing, and then the angel jacked to the side in an attempt to get at the screen. "Just give me a minute—"

"Is she free?" he hissed. "Just tell me."

"Aha!" Lassiter pointed at the boob tube. "You mother*fucker*! I knew you were the father!"

Tohr fought the urge to slap some sense into the son of a bitch. His Wellsie's future was at stake, and this dumb-ass was worried about Maury's paternity tests? "Are you kidding me."

"No, I'm damn serious. Bastard has three kids by three sisters—what kind of man is that?"

Tohr smacked his own head in lieu of the angel's. "Lassiter . . . come *on*, man—"

"Look, I'm still here, aren't I," the guy muttered as he muted the screaming and hopping up and down on Maury's stage. "As long as I'm still here, there's work to be done."

Tohr let himself fall into a chair. Propping his head in his hand, he bit down on his molars. "I don't fucking get it. Destiny wants blood, sweat, and tears—well, I've fed from her, we've—ah, sweated, for sure. Shit knows I've cried enough."

"The tears don't count," the angel said.

"How is that possible?"

"It just is, my man."

Great. Fantastic. "How much longer do I have to get my Wellsie free?"

"Your dreams are the answer to that. In the meantime, I suggest you go feed your female. I gather by your wet pants that you just gave her a helluva workout."

The words, *She's not mine*, rose up automatically into his throat, but he clamped down on them in the hopes that keeping them inside would help somehow.

The angel just shook his head back and forth, as if he were well aware of both the sentiment that had remained unspoken . . . and the future that was as yet unknown.

"Goddamn it," Tohr muttered as he got to his feet and started for the kitchen. "Goddamn me."

Some thirty miles away, at the Band of Bastards' farmhouse, the sound of wheezing drifted up into the stale air of the cellar, rhythmic, ragged, wretched.

As Throe stared into the candlelight aimlessly, he didn't feel good about where his leader was.

Xcor had been in one hell of a hand-to-hand contest toward the end of the engagement at Assail's house. He had refused to say with whom, but it must have been a Brother. And naturally, he had had no medical attention since then—not that they had much to offer in that regard.

Cursing to himself, Throe crossed his arms over his chest and tried to remember the last time the male had fed. Dearest Virgin Scribe . . . had it been back in the spring with those three prostitutes? No wonder he wasn't healing up . . . and he wouldn't until he was better nourished—

The wheezing shifted into a rough cough . . . then resumed at a slower, more painful rate.

Xcor was going to die.

That dire conclusion had been dawning with relentless vigor ever since that breathing pattern had changed hours ago. To survive, the male needed one of two things, preferably both: access to medical facilities, supplies, and personnel the likes of which the Brotherhood enjoyed; and the blood of a female vampire.

There was no way of getting him the former, and the latter had proven to be a challenge over the last few months. The vampire population in Caldwell was slowly increasing, but since the raids, females had been at an even higher premium. He had yet to find one who was willing to service them, even though he was able to pay handsomely.

Although . . . considering Xcor's condition, mayhap even that might not be enough. What they needed was a miracle—

Unbidden, an image of that spectacular Chosen he'd fed from at the Brotherhood's facility came to mind. Her blood would be a lifesaver for Xcor right now. Literally. Except obviously it was not obtainable on so many levels. How would he be able to reach out to her, for one thing. And even if he could connect with her, she would undoubtedly know he was the enemy . . .

Or would she? She'd called him a soldier of worth to his face—mayhap the Brotherhood had kept his identity from her to insulate her delicate sensibilities—

No more sound. Nothing.

"Xcor?" he called out as he sat up in a rush. "Xcor—"

At that point, there was another round of coughing and then the labored breathing resumed.

Dearest Virgin Scribe, he had no idea how the others slept through all this. Then again, they had been fighting for so long on nothing but human blood that sleep was their only chance for any kind of recharge. Throe's adrenal gland had overridden that imperative as of two in the afternoon, however; whereupon he had begun his vigil over Xcor's respiratory process.

As he reached for his cell phone to check the time, he struggled to focus on the numbers that were displayed, his mind frantic.

Ever since that incident between them in the summer, Xcor had been a different male. Still autocratic, demanding, and full of calculations that could shock and stun . . . but his stare was different when he looked upon his soldiers. He was more connected to all of them, his eyes opened to some new level of relating, the likes of which he hadn't appeared to have been aware previously.

Shame to lose the bastard now.

Rubbing his eyes, Throe finally got a read on the hour: five thirty-eight. The sun was probably just below the horizon, the dusk no doubt lingering in the sky to the east. It would be better to wait for the darkness to truly arrive, but he had no more time to waste—especially given that he wasn't sure what he was doing.

Shifting off his bunk, he rose to his full height, walked across the way and shook the mound of blankets Zypher was under.

"Go 'way," the soldier mumbled. "Still have thirty minutes . . ."

"You need to get the others out of here," Throe whispered.

"Do I."

"And you must stay behind."

"Must I."

"I'm going to try to find a female to feed Xcor."

That got the soldier's attention: Zypher's head lifted—down at the other end. "In truth?"

Throe shuffled to the foot of the bunk so they could meet eye-to-eye. "Make sure he stays here, and be prepared to drive him to my coordinates."

"Throe, whatever are you about?"

Without reply, he turned away and began pulling leather upon his personage, his hands shaking from Xcor's treacherous state . . . and the fact that if his prayer was answered, he would be in the company of that female once again.

Glancing down at his fighting clothes, he hesitated . . . dearest Virgin Scribe, he wished he had something with which to clothe himself other than leather. A lovely suit of worsted wool with a cravat. Proper shoes with laces. Underwear.

"Wherever are you going?" Zypher asked sharply.

"It matters not. What I find is the only important thing."

"Tell me you are taking weapons."

Throe paused anew. If for some reason this backfired, he might well need armaments. But he didn't want to frighten her—assuming he could in fact reach her somehow and get her to come to him. Such a delicate female was she . . .

Some concealed things, he decided. A gun or two. Some knives. Nothing that she could see.

"Good," Zypher murmured as he began checking his weapons.

Mere minutes later, Throe ascended from the basement, and burst out the kitchen's exterior door—

Hissing and throwing up his forearms, he was forced to jump back into the dark house. With his eyes stinging and tearing up, he cursed and went for the sink, running cold water and splashing it upon his face.

It seemed forever until his phone's display informed him that an exit was safer to attempt, and this time he opened the door with far less bravado.

Oh, the relief of the night.

Leaping out from his confines, he landed upon the good earth and filled his lungs with the cold, damp air of autumn. Closing his still throbbing eyes, he focused himself inward, and spirited himself away from the house, casting his component molecules north and east until he reformed in a field of meadow grass marked in the center with a large, flame-tipped maple tree.

Standing before the great trunk, underneath the red-and-gold leaf cover, he surveyed the landscape with his razor-sharp senses. This bucolic spot was far, far away from the battleground of downtown, and not even close to any compound of the Brothers or outpost of the Lessening Society—at least that he was aware of.

To be sure of his read on the site, though, he waited, as motionless as the big tree behind him, but not nearly as serene—he was prepared to engage with anything and anyone.

Nobody and nothing came upon him, however.

Some thirty minutes later, he lowered himself to sit cross-legged upon the ground, linking his hands together, and settling in.

He was well aware of the peril of this path he was embarking upon. But in some battles, you had to make your own weapons, even if you ran the risk of them blowing up in your face: There was grave danger in this, but if there was one thing you could count on with the Brotherhood, it was an old-fashioned protection of their females.

He'd had the jaw shots to prove it.

So he was banking upon the fact that, if he did reach the Chosen, she wouldn't know his true identity.

He was also forcing himself to push aside any guilt at the position he was putting her in.

Before he closed his eyes, he looked around again. There were deer at the far edge of the meadow by the forest of trees, their delicate hooves brushing through fallen leaves, their heads bobbing as they meandered along. An owl sounded off to the right, the hooting carried upon the light, cold breeze to his perked ears. Far in front of him, on a road that he could not see, a pair of headlights drifted along, likely a farm truck.

No *lessers*.

No Brothers.

No one but him.

Lowering his lids, he pictured the Chosen and recaptured those moments when her blood was going into him, reviving him, calling him back from the brink his life had trembled upon. He saw her with great clarity and focused on the taste and the scent of her, the very essence of who she was.

And then he prayed, prayed as he never had before, even when he had lived a civilized life. He prayed so hard his brows tightened and his heart pounded and he couldn't breathe. He prayed with a desperation that left a part of him wondering whether this was to save Xcor . . . or simply so he could see her once again.

He prayed until he lost his train of words and all he had was a feeling in his chest, a howling need that he could only hope was a strong enough signal for her to respond to, if she indeed got it.

Throe kept it up for as long as he could, until he was numb and cold and so exhausted his head hung no longer out of reverence, but out of tiredness.

He kept at it until the persistent silence around him intruded upon his quest . . . and told him that he had to accept failure.

When he finally reopened his eyes, he found that moonlight had sneaked under the canopy he sat beneath, the sun's opposite having arrived for its evening shift of watching o'er the earth—

His shout echoed loud as he jumped to his feet.

'Twas not the moon that was the cause of the light.

His Chosen was standing afore him, her robing of such a bright white, it appeared to throw off its own illumination.

Her hands extended forth as if to calm him. "I am sorry to startle you."

"No! No, no, it's fine—I . . . You are *here*."

"Did you not summon me?" She appeared confused. "I was not sure what called me forth. I . . . simply had this urge to come here. And there you were."

"I didn't know if it would work."

"Well, it did." At this, she smiled at him.

Oh, sweet Virgin Scribe in the great heavens above, she was beautiful, her hair all coiled up high upon her head, her form so willowy and elegant, her scent . . . ambrosia.

She frowned and looked down at herself. "Am I not properly covered?"

"I'm sorry?"

"You stare."

"Oh, indeed, I am . . . Please forgive me. My manners have been forgotten—because you are too lovely for mine eyes to comprehend."

That made her recoil ever so slightly. As if she were unused to compliments—or mayhap he had offended her.

"I'm sorry," he said—before wanting to curse himself. His vocabulary was going to have to expand past apologies. Fast. And it would help if he didn't behave like a schoolboy in her presence. "I mean no disrespect."

Now she smiled again, a stunning display of happiness. "I believe you in that, soldier. I suppose I'm simply surprised."

That he found her attractive? Good Lord . . .

Reclaiming his past as a genteel member of the *glymera*, Throe bowed low. "You honor me by your presence, Chosen."

"What brings you out here?"

"I wanted . . . well, I did not desire to risk any harm to you as I prevailed upon you for a favor of great weight."

"A favor? Truly?"

Throe paused. She was so guileless, so delighted at being called upon, that his guilt renewed tenfold. But she was the only savior Xcor had, and this was war. . . .

As he struggled with his conscience, it occurred to him that there was a way to make it up to her, though, a vow he could take in return for the gift, if she chose to give it.

"I would ask . . ." He cleared his throat. "I have a comrade who is gravely injured. He is going to die if we do not—"

"I must go to him. Now. Show me wherever he is and I shall be of aid to him."

Throe closed his eyes and could not draw any breath. Indeed, he even felt tears threaten. In a hoarse voice, he said, "You are an angel. You are not of this earth in your compassion and kindness."

"Waste not pretty words. Where is your fellow fighter?"

Throe took out his phone and texted Zypher. The response he received was immediate—and the time line for arrival ridiculously short. Unless, of course, the soldier had already gotten Xcor into the vehicle and was prepared to start driving.

Such a male of worth he was.

As Throe put his cell back into his pocket, he focused on the Chosen once more. "He is coming this very moment. He must be transported by vehicle, as he is not well."

"And then we'll take him to the training center?"

No. Not hardly. Not ever. "You shall be enough for him. He is weakened from too little feeding more than he is injured."

"Shall we wait here, then?"

"Aye. We wait here." There was a long pause, and she began to fidget as if uncomfortable. "Forgive me, Chosen, if I continue to stare."

"Oh, no need to apologize. I'm just awkward because it is rare that I hold someone's rapt attention."

Now he was the one recoiling. Then again, the Brothers no doubt treated any male in her presence as they had him.

"Well, permt me to persist," he murmured gently. "For you are all I can see."

FORTY-EIGHT

Shuinn emerged from the hidden door under the grand stairway at around six p.m. that evening. His head was still a little fuzzy, his footfalls more shuffle than step, his body aching all over. But, hey, he was upright, he was mobile, and he was alive.

Things could be worse.

Plus he had a purpose. When Doc Jane had come in to check on him just now, she'd told him that Wrath had called a meeting of the Brotherhood. Of course, she'd also informed him that he was off rotation and had to stay in bed in the clinic—but like he was going to miss the postgame wrap-up on what had gone down at Assail's? Negs.

She'd done her best to persuade him otherwise, naturally, but in the end, she'd dialed up and told the king to expect one more.

As he came around the carved post of the banister, he could hear the Brothers talking on the second floor, those voices loud and deep, overriding one another. Clearly, Wrath hadn't called shit to order yet—which meant there was time to grab a drink of the alcohol variety before going up.

Because, duh, that was precisely what you needed when you were rocky on your pins to begin with.

After some careful assessment, he decided that the distance to the library was shorter than that to the billiards room. Old-manning his way to the oak doors, he froze as soon as he got to the archway.

"Holy hell . . ."

There were at least fifty books of the Old Law crowding the floor, and that wasn't the half of it. Over at the trestle table beneath the leaded-glass windows, more leather-bound volumes had been cracked open and were lying with their guts exposed like soldiers shot dead on a battlefield.

Two computers. A laptop. Legal pads.

A creak from up high lifted his eyes. Saxton was on the rolling teak ladder, reaching for a book on the top shelf by the ceiling molding.

"Good evening to you, cousin," the guy said from his lofty perch.

Just the male he needed to see. "What's doing with all this?"

"You're looking rather well recovered." The ladder creaked again as the male descended with his prize. "All and sundry have been worried."

"Nah, I'm fine." Qhuinn went over to liquor bottles lined up on the marble-topped bombé chest. "So what are you working on?"

Do not think of him with Blay. Do not think of him with Blay. Do not think of him—

"I didn't know you were a sherry man."

"Huh?" Qhuinn glanced down at what he'd poured himself. Fuck. In the midst of the self-lecture, he'd picked up the wrong bottle. "Oh, you know . . . I'm good with it."

To prove the point, he tossed back the hooch—and nearly choked as the sweetness hit his throat.

He served himself another only so he didn't look like the kind of idiot who wouldn't know what he was dishing out into his own glass.

Okay, gag. The second was worse than the first.

From out of the corner of his eye, he watched Saxton settle in at the table, the brass lamp in front of him casting the most perfect glow over his face. Shiiiiit, he looked like something out of a Ralph Lauren ad, with his buff-colored tweed jacket and his pointed pocket square and that button-down/sweater vest combo keeping his fucking liver cozy.

Meanwhile, Qhuinn was sporting hospital scrubs, bare feet. And sherry.

"So what's the big project?" he asked again.

Saxton glanced over with a strange light in his eyes. "It's a game changer, as you might say."

"Ohhhh, supersecret king stuff."

"Indeed."

"Well, good luck with it. Looks like you've got enough to keep you busy for a while."

"I'll be at this for a month, maybe more."

"What are you doing, rewriting the whole goddamn law?"

"Just a part of it."

"Man, you make me love my job. I'd rather get shot at than do paperwork." He poured himself a third cocksucking sherry and then tried not to look too much like a zombie as he headed for the door. "Have fun with it."

"And you with your endeavors, dear cousin. I would be up there as well, but I have been given no time to accomplish too much."

"You'll get through it."

"Indeed. I will."

As Qhuinn nodded and then hit the stairs, he thought . . . Well, at least that exchange hadn't been too bad. He hadn't imagined anything X-rated. Or entertained visions of beating the motherfucker until he bled out all over his nice threads.

Progress. Yay.

Up on the second story, the double doors of the study were wide-open, and he paused when he got a gander at the size of the crowd. Holy crap . . . everyone was there. As in not just the Brothers and the fighters, but the *shellans* . . . and the staff?

There were literally forty people in the room, packed in like sardines around the pansy-ass furniture.

Then again, maybe it did make sense. After that goddamn sharp-shooter attack, the king was back behind his desk, sitting on his throne, all but risen from the dead. Kind of warranted a celebration, he supposed.

Before stepping into the fray, he went to take another haul of the sherry, but one whiff of the shit in his nose and his goiter went no-go. Leaning to the side, he tossed the stuff out into a potted plant, left the glass on the hall table and—

The instant they saw him come through the door, everyone shut up. Sure as if there were a remote to the room and someone had muted the picture.

Qhuinn froze. Glanced down at himself in case he was flashing something indecent. Looked behind him in the event there was someone important coming up the stairs.

Then he looked around the room, wondering what he had missed—

In the great, yawning absence of sound and movement, Wrath braced himself against his queen's arm and grunted as he rose to his feet. He had a bandage around his neck, and he looked a little pale, but he was alive . . . and wearing an expression so intense, Qhuinn felt like he was being physically enveloped.

And then the king put the hand that bore the black diamond ring of the race to his own chest, right in the middle, directly over his heart . . . and slowly, gingerly, with the help of his *shellan*, bent over at the waist.

To bow at Qhuinn.

As all the blood drained out of Qhuinn's head, and he wondered what the fuck the most important vampire on the planet was doing, someone started clapping slowly.

Clap. *Clap. Clap!*

Others joined in, until the entire assembly, from Phury and Cormia, to Z and Bella and baby Nalla, to Fritz and his staff . . . to Vishous and Payne and their mates, to Butch and Marissa and Rehv and Ehlena . . . were clapping for him with tears unshed in their eyes.

Qhuinn tucked his arms around himself as his mismatched stare bounced anywhere and everywhere.

Until it settled on Blaylock.

The redhead was over to the right-hand side, clapping like the rest of them, his blue eyes luminous with emotion.

Then again, he would know how much something like this meant to a fucked-up kid with a congenital defect whose family hadn't wanted him around for the embarrassment and social disgrace.

He would know how hard the gratitude was to accept.

He would know how much Qhuinn just wanted to escape from the attention . . . even as he was touched beyond measure at this honor he did not deserve.

In the midst of all he couldn't handle, he just looked at his old, dear friend.

As always, Blay was the anchor who kept him from being swept away.

As Xhex tooled up through the *mhis* on her bike, she found it hard to believe she was making the trip to the mansion under royal command: Wrath himself had extended the "invite"—and as much of an iconoclast as she was, she wasn't about to shut down a direct order from the king.

Man, she was nauseous.

When she'd first gotten the voice mail, she'd assumed that John was dead, having been killed out on the field. A quick Hail Mary text to him had been replied to immediately, however. Short and sweet. Just *Will u come @ nightfall?*

That was all she got back; even after she said yes, and had expected something further from him.

So yeah, she felt like throwing up because this was probably John putting an end to them officially. The vampire equivalent of divorce was rare, but the Old Laws did provide for an out legally. And naturally, for people at John's social level—namely, that of the blooded son of a Black Dagger Brother—the king was the only one who could give them dispensation to split.

This had to be the end.

Shit, she actually was going to throw up.

Pulling around in front of the mansion, she didn't park the Ducati at the tail end of the orderly row of muscle cars, SUVs, and station wagons. Nope—she left the bike right at the base of the stairs. If this was a royal divorce decree, she was going to help John put an end to their misery, and then she was . . .

Well, she was going to call Trez and tell him she couldn't come to work. Then she was going to lock herself in her cabin and cry like a girl. For a week or two . . .

So stupid. This whole thing between them was so fucking stupid. But she couldn't change him, and he couldn't change her, so what the hell did they have left? It had been months since they'd had anything but distance and awkard silence between them. And the trend wasn't reversing itself; the black hole was just getting deeper and darker. . . .

As she mounted the steps to the grand double doors, she was breaking in half, shattering sure as if her bones had turned brittle and were collapsing under the weight of her muscles. But she kept going, because that was what fighters did. They pushed on past the pain and took out their objective— and sure as shit she and John were killing something tonight, something that had been so precious and rare she was ashamed of them both for not finding a way to nurture it in the midst of the cold, hard world.

Inside the vestibule, she didn't step up immediately to the camera's eye. Never a prepper-upper kind of female, she nonetheless found herself brushing fingertips under her eyes and shuffling a palm over her short hair. A quick straightening of her leather jacket—and her spine—and she told herself to suck it up.

She had gotten through legions of things worse than this.

Through pride alone, she could marshal some self-control for the next ten or fifteen minutes.

She had the rest of her natural life to lose her goddamn composure in private.

With a curse, she hit the summons button and stepped back, forcing herself to look into the camera. As she waited, she straightened her jacket again. Stomped her boots. Double-checked that her guns were where they'd been holstered.

Played with her hair.

Okay, what the hell.

Leaning to the side, she gave that button another stab. The *doggen* here had high standards. You rang that bell, and it was answered within moments.

On the third try, she debated how many more times she was going to have to beg for—

The vestibule's inner door was thrown wide and Fritz looked mortified. "My lady! I am so sorry—"

A loud cacophony drowned out whatever else the butler said, and she frowned as she looked past the old male. Up over the *doggen*'s white head, at the top of the grand staircase, there was a tremendous crowd milling around and drifting off, as if a party had just broken up.

Maybe someone had just told everybody they were getting mated.

Good luck with that, she thought.

"Big announcement?" she asked as she stepped through into the foyer and braced herself for someone else's happy news.

"More a recognition." The butler put his weight, such as it was, into shutting the door. "I shall allow the others to inform you."

Ever the dutiful butler—discreet to his very marrow.

"I'm here to see—"

"The Brotherhood. Yes, I know."

Xhex frowned. "It was Wrath, I thought."

"Well, yes, of course the king as well. Please come up to the royal study."

As she crossed the mosaic floor and started her ascent, she nodded at the folks coming down . . . the *shellans*, the staff she knew, the people she had lived with for a mere matter of weeks, but who had become, in a short time, a sort of family to her.

She was going to miss them almost as much as John.

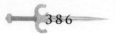

"Madam?" the butler asked. "Are you all right?"

Xhex forced a smile and guessed she had probably let out some kind of curse. "Fine, just fine."

When she got to Wrath's study, there was so much approval in the air, she practically had to push the shit aside to walk into the room: The Brothers were all thick chested with pride . . . except for Qhuinn, who was blushing so deeply he'd turned himself into a Roman candle.

John, however, appeared reserved—not looking at her at all, but at some middle ground right in front of himself.

From behind the desk, Wrath focused on her. "And now on to business," the king announced.

As the doors shut behind her, she had no fucking clue what was doing. John still refused to even glance at her . . . and, shit, the king had a wound on his neck—assuming he hadn't decided that white gauze at the throat was some kind of fashion statement.

Everyone shut up, settled down, got serious.

Oh, man, they had to do this in front of the whole Brotherhood?

Then again, what else could she have expected? The groupthink was so pervasive in this bunch of males, of course they'd all want to be present when things were finished.

She stood strong. "Let's get this over with. Where do I sign?"

Wrath frowned. "I'm sorry?"

"On the papers."

The king glanced over at John. Looked back. "This is not the kind of thing I'll be reducing to writing. Ever."

Xhex glanced around and then refocused on John, reading his emotional grid. He was . . . nervous. Saddened. And purposeful in such a powerful way, she was momentarily struck stupid.

"What the hell is going on here," she demanded.

The king's voice was loud and clear. "I have an assignment for you—if you're interested. Something that I have on good authority you can discharge with remarkable skill. Assuming you are open to helping us."

Xhex stared at John in shock.

He was responsible for this, she thought. Whatever wheels were turning in this room, he had set them in motion.

"What have you done?" she said directly to him.

That got him to look at her properly. Raising his hands, he signed, *There are limits to what we can do. We need you for this.*

Glancing at Rehv, she got a whole lot of grave coming back at her—

and nothing more. No censure, no girls-not-allowed. Same for the rest of the males in the room: There was nothing but calm acceptance of her presence . . . and her capabilities.

"What exactly do you want from me?" she said to the king slowly.

As the male spoke, she continued to look at John while hearing things like Band of Bastards . . . an assassination attempt . . . their lair . . . a rifle.

With each passing sentence, her brows cranked higher and higher.

Okay, so not about a bake sale or some shit. This was locating the heart of the enemy, infiltrating their secure domain, and removing any long-range weaponry that could have been used to try to kill Wrath the night before.

Thus providing the Brotherhood, if all went as expected, with the proof they needed to condemn Xcor and his soldiers to death.

Xhex put her hands on her hips—so they wouldn't start rubbing together with glee. This was right up her alley—an impossible proposition backed up by a principle she could get behind: revenge on someone who had fucked you.

"So what do you think?" Wrath asked.

Xhex stared over at John, willing him to look at her again. When he did not, she just reread his emotional grid: He was terrified, but he was resolved.

He wanted her to do this. But why? What the hell had changed?

"Yeah, it's something I'm interested in," she heard herself say.

As deep male voices growled approval, the king curled up a fist and banged it on the desk. "Good! Well-done. There's just one thing."

A catch. Naturally. "I work best on my own. I don't want eight hundred pounds of babysitter sneaking around behind me."

"Nope. You go by yourself—knowing that you have all our resources as backup if you need or want them. The one constraint is that you can't kill Xcor."

"No problem, I'll just bring him in alive for questioning."

"Nope. You can't touch him. No one can until we analyze the bullet. And then if we find what I think we will, he's Tohr's to kill. By official proclamation."

Xhex glanced over at the Brother. Jesus Christ, he looked totally different, as if he were a younger, healthy relation of the guy she had known since Wellsie had been killed. And given the way he was now? Xcor had a grave with his name on it already dug.

"What happens if I have to defend myself?"

"You have permission to do whatever you have to in order to secure your safety. In fact, in that event . . ." The king turned his blind eyes in John's direction. "I encourage you to bring every weapon you have to bear in your own defense."

Read: Use that *symphath* side of yours, girlfriend.

"But if possible," Wrath added, "leave as much undisturbed as possible, and Xcor aboveground."

"That shouldn't be a problem," Xhex said. "I don't have to touch him or any of the others. I can keep it just about the rifle."

"Good." As the king smiled and flashed his fangs, the others started talking in a rush. "Perfect—"

"Wait, I haven't agreed to anything yet," she said, shutting them all up as she looked over at John. "Not . . . yet."

FORTY-NINE

"**U**nhand me, you fool," Xcor blabbered as he felt himself lifted once again.

He was beyond finished with being manhandled: Up off his bunk he'd been resting on. Into the vehicle. Taken somewhere else. And now disturbed anew.

"Almost there," Zypher said.

"Leave me be. . . ." That was supposed to have come out as a demand. Instead, he sounded like a child to his own ears.

Ah, how he wished for his former strength, so that he could have pushed himself free, and stood upon his own legs.

But that time had passed. Indeed, he was well gone . . . and mayhap done for.

His dire condition was the result of no one particular injury from that fight with that soldier—it was the culmination of all of them, the wounds covering his head and his gut, the agony something rather like the beat of his heart, a force that existed and persisted within him, over which he had no control.

Initially, he had fought the tide under the masculine just-throw-it-off theory. His body had had other plans for him, however, and more sway than his mind and will did. Now it felt as if he was owned by this pall of disorientation and exhaustion—

Abruptly, the air he breathed was cold and clear, slapping some sense into him.

Struggling to focus his eyes, he was greeted by a meadow, a rolling meadow that rose to meet a magnificent autumnal tree. And there . . . yes, there under the branches that were cast in red and yellow was Throe.

Next to whom was a slim figure in a white gown . . . a female.

Unless he was seeing things?

No, he was not. As Zypher carried him closer, she became more distinct. She was . . . incalculably beautiful, with pale skin and blond hair that was twisted up upon the crown of her head.

She was vampire, not human.

She was . . . unearthly, an illumination spilling out from her form, one so bright it o'ershadowed the moon.

Ah, so this was a dream.

He should have guessed. After all, there was no reason for Zypher to take him into the farmland parts, risking their lives for some fresh air. No cause for any female to be waiting upon his arrival. No possibility that someone as fair as she would be out alone in the world.

No, this was just a product of his delirium, and therefore he relaxed into the iron arms of his soldier, recognizing that whatever his subconscious had coughed up was not going to matter at all, and he might as well let things play out. Eventually he would wake up, and mayhap this was a sign he had finally settled into a deep, healing sleep.

Besides, the less he fought, the more he could concentrate on her.

Oh . . . loveliness. Oh, virtuous beauty, the kind that turned kings into serfs and soldiers into poets. This was the sort of female worth fighting for, dying for, just to gaze for a moment upon her face.

Such a shame she was but a vision . . .

The first sign that something was off was that she seemed taken aback at the sight of him.

Then again, his mind was probably just going for realism. He was hideous uninjured. Beaten and starving? He was lucky she did not shrink away in horror. As it was, her hands lifted to her cheeks and her head shook back and forth until Throe stepped in as if to protect her delicate sensibilities.

Didn't that make him wish for a weapon. This was his dream. If she was going to be sheltered, he would take care of that. Well . . . assuming he could stand up. And she did not run away—

"He is failing," he heard her say.

His eyes fluttered back at the pure, dulcet sound. That voice was as perfect as the rest of her, and he concentrated hard, trying to get his brain to make her speak some more in his dream.

"Aye," Throe said. "This is an emergency."

"What is his name?"

Xcor spoke up at this point, thinking he should be the one to make his own introduction. Unfortunately, all that came out was a croak.

"Lay him down," the female said. "We need to do this with speed."

Soft, cool grass rose up to meet his broken body, cushioning him sure as if the palm of the earth was mittened in wool. And when he reopened the steel doors of his eyes, he got to watch her kneel beside him.

"You are so beautiful . . ." was what he said. What came out of his mouth was nothing more than a gargle.

And abruptly, he had difficulty breathing, as if something had burst in his interior, perhaps as a result of all the moving?

Except this was a dream, so why would that matter?

As the female brought up her wrist, he reached out a shaking hand and stopped her before she could score her vein.

Her eyes met his own.

In the periphery, Throe once again closed the distance, as if he were worried that Xcor would do something violent.

Not to her, he thought. Never to this gentle creature of his imagination.

Clearing his throat, he spoke as clearly as he could. "Save your blood," he told her. "Beautiful one, you save what makes you vital."

He was too far gone for the likes of her. And that was true not merely because he was badly wounded and probably going to die.

Even in his imagination, she was far too good for even proximity to him.

As Layla fell to her knees, she found it difficult to speak. The male stretched out before her was . . . well, injured severally, yes, of course. But he was more than that. In spite of the fact that he was on the ground and clearly defenseless, he was . . .

Powerful was the only word that came to mind.

Tremendously powerful.

She could tell nearly naught of his features for the swelling and the bruising, and the same was true of his coloring, because of all the dried blood. But in physical form, although he appeared to be not as tall as the Brothers, he was every bit as wide, and thick of shoulder, with arms that were brutally muscled.

Mayhap the contours of his body were the seat of her impression of him?

No, the fighter who had called her forth to this meadow was of equal size, as was the male who delivered the wounded here to her feet.

This fallen soldier was simply different from the other two—and in fact, they did defer to him in subtle ways with their movements and their eyes.

Indeed, this was not a male to toy with, but rather, like a bull, capable of crushing anything in its path.

Yet the hand that touched her was light as a breeze and even less confining—she had the distinct impression that not only was he not holding her here, but that he wanted her to go.

She was not about to leave him, however.

In the strangest way, she was . . . ensnared . . . held captive by a deep blue stare that even in the night, and despite the fact that he was fully mortal, appeared to be lit with fire. And under that regard, her heart quickened and her eyes clung to him as if he were at once indecipherable and capable of her understanding—

Sounds came out of him, guttural and incomprehensible because of his wounds, urging her to to proceed with haste.

He needed to be cleaned. Cared for. Nursed back to health over a matter of days, perhaps weeks. Yet here he was in this field, with these males who obviously knew more about weapons than healing.

She looked at the soldier she knew. "You must take him in to be treated after this."

Although she got a nod and an affirmation as a reply, her instincts told her it was a lie.

Males, she thought derisively, were too tough for their own good.

She refocused on the soldier. "You need me," she told him.

The sound of her voice appeared to put him further into some kind of thrall, and she took advantage of it. Weakened though he was, she had the distinct sense that he had more than enough power in his body to prevent her from bringing her vein to his mouth.

"Shhh," she said, reaching out and brushing his short hair back. "Be of ease, warrior. As you protect and serve the likes of me, allow me to return your service."

So proud he was—she could tell by the hard thrust of his chin. And yet he appeared to listen to her, his hand dropping from her forearm, his mouth parting, as if he were hers to command.

Layla moved fast, prepared to take advantage of the relative surrender—for no doubt he would soon retreat from the submission. Biting into her wrist, she quickly brought her arm over his lips, the drops falling one by one.

As he accepted her gift, the sound he made was . . . nothing short of breathtaking: A groan laced with infinite gratitude and, in her opinion, baseless awe.

Oh, how those eyes of his held on to hers, until the field, the tree, the other two males faded away, and all she knew was the male she was feeding.

Compelled by something she was disinclined to argue with, she lowered her arm . . . until his mouth brushed her wrist: This was something she never did with the other males, even Qhuinn at this point. But she wanted to know what it felt like, this soldier's mouth upon her skin—

The instant contact was made, that sound he'd uttered returned, and then he formed a seal around the twin points. He did not hurt her; even as big as he was, as starved as he was, he did not ravage her. Not at all. He drew with care, keeping always his stare upon her own as if he were safeguarding her, in spite of the fact that he was the one who needed protection in his current condition.

Time passed, and she knew he was taking a great deal from her, but she did not care. She would have stayed forever in this meadow, beneath this tree . . . linked to this brave warrior who had nearly given his life in the war against the Lessening Society.

She could remember feeling something like this with Qhuinn, this incredible sensation of destination, even though she had not been aware she was traveling. But this pull put what she had once experienced with that other male to shame.

This was epic.

And yet . . . why should she trust such emotion? Mayhap this was just a heartier version of what she had felt for Qhuinn. Or mayhap this was simply how the Scribe Virgin ensured the survivability of the race, biology o'errunning logic.

Pushing such blasphemous thoughts aside, she focused on her job, her mission, her blessed contribution that was her only opportunity to serve now that the Chosen's role had been so diminished.

Providing blood to males of worth was all that was left of her calling. All that she had in her life.

Instead of thinking of herself, of the way she felt, she needed to thank the Scribe Virgin that she had come here in time to do her sacred duty . . . and then she had to return to the compound to find other opportunities to be of service.

FIFTY

"What's changed, John."

In the bedroom he and Xhex had once shared, John went over to the windows and felt the cold wafting through the clear glass. Down below, the gardens were bathed in security lighting, the false moon glow making the grout around the terrace's slate slabs seem phosphorescent.

As he surveyed the landscape, there wasn't much to look at. Everything had been prepped for winter, the beds of flowers quilted in mesh covers, the fruit trees bagged, the pool now drained. Stray leaves from the maples and oaks at the forest's edge skipped across the mowed, browning grass, like they were homeless and in search of shelter.

"John. What the hell is going on?"

In the end, Xhex had not committed, and he didn't blame her. One-eighties were disorienting, and real life sure as shit didn't come with seat belts or air bags.

How did he explain himself? he wondered as he scrambled for words.

Eventually, he pivoted around, brought up his hands, and signed, *You were right.*

"About what?"

That would be everything, he thought as he started to sign.

Last night, I watched Qhuinn go out into the suck zone—alone. Wrath was down; we were scrambling; the Brotherhood hadn't come yet as backup— bullets were everywhere. The Band of Bastards had surrounded us, and we were running out of time because of the king's injury. Qhuinn . . . see, he knew he was better off outside the house—he knew that if he could secure the garage, we might be able to get Wrath out. And . . . yeah, it nearly killed me, but I let him go out there. He's my best friend . . . and I let him go.

Xhex went over and slowly lowered herself into a chair. "That's why Wrath's neck was all wrapped up . . . and Qhuinn was . . ."

He went up against Xcor, one-on-one, and gave Wrath the best shot at surviving. John shook his head at her. *And again, I let him go out there because . . . I knew he had to do what he could. It was the right thing for the situation.*

John paced around, then parked it at the foot of the bed, bracing his palms on his thighs, rubbing them up and down. *Qhuinn is a good fighter—he's strong and decisive. A heavy hitter. And because he did what he did, Wrath lived—so yeah, Qhuinn was right, even though it was dangerous.*

He looked over at her. *You're the same here. We need that rifle to declare war on the Bastards—Wrath has to have the proof. You're a hunter who can go out in daylight—none of us can do that. You also have your symphath abilities if shit gets critical. You're the right person for the job—even though the thought of you going anywhere near them terrifies me, you are the right one to send out to wherever they are.*

There was a long pause. "I don't . . . know what to say."

He shrugged. *That's why I didn't explain anything to you beforehand. I'm done with the talking, too. At some point, it's just hot air. Action matters. Proof matters.*

As she rubbed her face as if her head hurt, he frowned. *I thought . . . this would make you happy.*

"Yeah. Sure. It's great." She got to her feet. "I'll do it. Of course I will. I'm going to have to keep on top of things for Trez, but I'll start tonight."

John felt the pain receptors in his chest light up like a power grid— which told him how much he'd expected out of this olive branch.

He'd hoped it would bring them together.

A Ctrl-Alt-Delete that reset their system.

He whistled to get her eyes back on him. *What's wrong? I thought this would change things.*

"Oh, it's clear they already have. If you don't mind, I'm just going to go out—" As her voice caught, she cleared her throat with a cough. "Yeah, go talk to Wrath. Tell him yes, I'm in."

As she went for the door, she appeared to be totally discombobulated, her movements stilted and stiff.

Xhex? he signed—which did no good, because she'd turned away.

He whistled again, then popped up off the mattress and followed her into the hall. Reaching out, he tapped her on the shoulder, because he didn't want to offend her by grabbing at her.

"John, just let me go—"

He stepped in front of her and lost his breath. Her eyes were glowing with unshed red tears.

What's the matter? he signed desperately.

She blinked fast, refusing to let anything fall to her cheeks. "You think I'm going to be jumping for joy because you aren't bonded to me anymore?"

He recoiled so badly, he nearly fell over. *Excuse me?*

"I didn't know it could end, but in your case, clearly it has—"

Fuck that! He stamped his feet because he had to make some noise. *I'm completely fucking bonded with you! And this is both totally about us—because I want to be with you again—and totally not, because whether or not I am, this is still the right thing to do! You are the right person for the job!*

She seemed momentarily stunned, nothing but those quick lids of hers moving. Then she crossed her arms over her chest and stared up at him. "Are you serious?"

Yes! He forced himself not to jump up and down again. *God, yes . . . fuck, yes . . . everything I've got*—yes.

She glanced away. Looked back. After a moment, she said roughly, "I have . . . hated not being with you."

Me, too. And I'm sorry. As he took a deep breath, his heart eased enough so that it didn't feel like it was going break through his sternum. *I don't think I can ever fight side by side with you. That's like expecting a surgeon to operate on his wife. But I'm not going to stand in your way—and no one else is either. You were right in the first place—you've been fighting for longer than you've been with me, and you should be able to do what you want. I can't actually be there, though—I mean, look, if it happens, it happens, but I'd like to avoid that if we can.*

As her lids dropped a little, he had the sense that she was scanning him in the ways of her other side, and he squared his shoulders under the scrutiny: He knew what was in his mind, his heart, and his soul.

He had nothing but love for her.

He wanted her back.

He had nothing to hide.

And those terms he'd just spilled out were ones that not only he had thought long and hard about, but knew he could live with. This was not the off-the-cuff of a newly mated guy thinking life was going to be a breeze just because he had the girl of his dreams in his arms and a future so bright he had to wear shades.

Now, as he spoke, it was as a male who had lived for months without his mate; who had suffered through the strange death valley that came with knowing the one you loved was on the planet but not in your life; who had emerged out the other side of hell with a new understanding of himself . . . and her.

He was ready to meet real life head-to-head . . . and compromise.

He just prayed he wasn't the only one.

As Xhex stared up at John, she found herself blinking like an idiot. Shit on a shingle, she hadn't expected any of this: the personal call from Wrath, the opportunity presented to her . . . and definitely not what John was saying to her now.

He was utterly sincere, though. This was not a calculated ploy to get her back into his life—although she knew that without reading his grid. Not his way.

He meant every word.

And he was still bonded to her, thank God.

The problem was . . . she had been to this corner with him before. She had been ready for a good stretch of happy normal. Instead? The most important relationship she had had crashed and burned.

"You sure you're going to be okay with me heading into wherever they live and maybe fighting directly with them. Without backup."

If anything happens to you, I'm going to be Tohr. Straight up. One hundred. But fear of that is not going to get me to try to keep you at home.

"You were pretty adamant that where Tohr is is not a place where you want to be."

He shrugged. *But see, I'm already in it if we're not together. After you were injured, I think . . . I think I had this idea that if I could just get you not to fight, then I'd be safe from what he's going through—that I wouldn't be exposed to that shit because you wouldn't get stabbed or . . . yeah, worse. But come on, downtown Caldwell is not the safest place on the planet, and it's not like you're working around children with that job at Trez's. More to the point, I'm all in with you—whether it's old age, the number nineteen bus or a bullet from the enemy . . . anything happens to you and I'm fucked.*

Xhex narrowed her eyes. She could read his grid, but not every part of his brain, and before she opened up to him again and got her hopes up, it was critical to know that he'd thought this shit through. "What about afterward? Say I get the rifle and bring it back here and it turns out to be the weapon that was used—what if I want to go after them. Wrath is not my king, but I like the guy, and the idea that someone tried to snuff him makes me cranky."

John's stare didn't waver, leading her to believe he had in fact considered that outcome. *As long as I'm not on rotation with you, I'll be okay. If I have to come in as backup—well, that's just what it is, and we'll deal with it—I'll deal with it,* he corrected. *I just don't want to be in the same territory as you if we can avoid it.*

"What if I want to keep my job with Trez? Permanently."

That's your business.

"What if I wanted to keep staying at my cabin."

I don't really have a right to demand anything at this point.

It was, of course, everything that she had wanted to hear: no limits on her, free to choose, free to be equal.

And, God, she wanted to fall into it all. Being apart from him had been the shittiest stretch of darkness she'd ever been through. But the thing was, she was used to the chronic suffering. The only thing worse than it would be having to acclimate to this kind of hell all over again. She didn't think she could go through that—

I'm not doing this to "make up" with you, Xhex. I want that—fuck, yeah, I really want that. But this is how I expect things to be from now on. And like I said, words don't mean shit. So how about you get to work and see what happens. Let me prove to you by actions what I've spoken to you now.

"You realize that I can't go through another freak-out from you. I can't—it's too hard."

I'm so fucking sorry. As he signed, he also mouthed the words, the shame on his face biting into her chest. *So sorry—I wasn't prepared for how I'd react because I'd never considered the ramifications until I was knee-deep in them. I handled it badly—and I'd like you to give me the chance to handle it better. But on your time, at your choosing.*

She thought back a million years ago to Lash and that alley—when

John had given her her revenge, had allowed her to be the one to kill her own personal enemy. And that had been in spite of the bonded-male thing that had no doubt made him want to rip that evil fucker apart.

He was right, she thought. Good intentions didn't always work out, but he could prove how things were going to be over time.

"Okay," she said hoarsely. "Let's give it a go. Come with me to Wrath's?"

When John nodded once, she stepped in beside him.

Together they walked down to the king's study.

Each step they took seemed wobbly, even though the mansion was solid as a rock. Then again, she felt as though the earthquake that had been tossing her life around in a blender had suddenly stopped, and she didn't trust her balance or the steadiness of what was below her feet.

Before they knocked on the closed doors, she turned toward the male who had had her name carved in his back. The assignment she was about to accept was a dangerous one, something vital to Wrath and the Brotherhood. But its implications to her own life, and John's, seemed even more significant.

Stepping into him, she put her arms around his body and held on. As he returned the embrace, they fit just the same as they always did, hand in glove.

Goddamn, she hoped this worked out.

Oh, and yeah, nailing Xcor and his band of freaks?

Nice bonus.

FIFTY-ONE

The reality that the female in the white robe had not been a dream came gradually upon Xcor, rather like fog clearing over a vista to reveal contours and conceptions previously obscured from the buffering.

He was back in the van, lying on the seat that had carried him forth from their lair, his head pillowed on the meaty inner bend of his elbow, his knees bent and stacked one atop the other. Zypher was not behind the wheel this time. Throe was driving.

The male had been silent since they had left the meadow. Uncharacteristically so.

As Xcor stared straight ahead, he traced the subtle pattern in the fake leather cover of the seat Throe was in. It was a hard job, given that the only light he had was from the instrument panel up front.

"She was real, then," he said after a while.

"Aye," came the quiet response.

Xcor closed his eyes and wondered how it was possible a female like that actually existed. "She was a Chosen."

"Aye."

"How did you manage that."

There was a long pause. "She fed me when the Brotherhood had me in their custody. They told her I was a soldier, not identifying me as their enemy to spare her worry."

"You should not have used her," he growled. "She is an innocent in all this."

"What other option did I have? You were dying."

He pushed that fact out of his mind, focusing instead upon the revelation that that which was legend in fact lived and breathed. And serviced the Brotherhood. And Throe.

For some reason, the thought of his soldier taking the vein of that female made Xcor want to reach around the headrest and snap the male's neck. Except jealousy, however unfounded it was, was just one of his problems.

"You have compromised us."

"They will never use her as a locator," Throe said grimly. "A Chosen female? Entering the war in any fashion? The Brothers are too old-fashioned, and she is far too valuable. They will never take her out into the field."

Thinking things through further, he decided Throe was likely correct—that female was priceless in too many ways to count. Besides, he and his Band of Bastards set out at the crack of night every evening—they were far from sitting ducks. And if they encountered the Brothers? They would reengage. He was no pussy to run from his enemy—better to plan an attack, but that was not always possible.

"What is her name?" he demanded.

More silence.

As he waited for the reply, the reticence told him that he was right to be jealous, at least in one respect: Clearly his second in command felt the same way he did.

"Her name."

"I do not know."

"How long have you been seeing her?"

"I have not. I reached out to her solely on your behalf. I prayed for her to come and she did."

Xcor inhaled long and slow, feeling his ribs expand without pain for the first time since he'd gone up against that fighter with the mismatched eyes. It was her blood in him. Indeed, what a miracle she was: That sense of drowning in his own body had alleviated, the thumping in his head dulling, his heartbeat settling to a steady rate.

And yet the power coursing through him, drawing him back from the brink, did not bode well for him and his soldiers. If this was what the Brotherhood enjoyed on a regular basis? Then they were stronger not just by virtue of bloodline, but sustenance.

At least it did not make them unbeatable. Syphon's shot had proven that even the purebred king had his vulnerable points.

But they were even more dangerous than he'd thought.

And as for the female . . .

"Are you going to call upon her again?" he asked his soldier.

"No. Never."

No hesitation in that—which suggested it was either a lie or a vow. For both their sakes, he rather hoped it was the latter—

Oh, but what was he going on about. He'd fed from her only once, and she was not his—and never would be, for too many reasons to count. Indeed, thinking back to the way even the human whore in the spring had recoiled from him, he knew someone as pure and perfect as the Chosen wouldn't have anything to do with his likes. Throe, on the other hand, might have a chance—except, of course, he was not a Brother.

He was, however, enamored of her.

No doubt she was used to that.

Xcor closed his eyes and concentrated on his body, feeling it reknit, realign, rekindle.

He found himself wishing the same rejuvenation could occur on his face, his past, his soul. Naturally, he kept that impotent prayer to himself. For one, it was an impossibility. For another, such was a passing whimsy imparted by the vision of a beautiful female—who had no doubt been repulsed by him. In truth, there was no redemption for him or his future: He had struck a mighty blow against the Brotherhood and they would be coming after him and the Band of Bastards with all the force they could muster.

They would also be taking other actions: If Wrath was dead without issue, they would be scrambling to fill the throne with the closest male blood relation they could find. Unless the king was hanging at the edge of death by his fingertips? Or mayhap he had pulled through thanks to all that medical technology they had cultivated at their compound . . . ?

Ordinarily, thoughts such as these would have consumed him, the lack of answers twisting up hard in his gut and causing him to pace endlessly if he wasn't fighting.

Now, though, in the logy aftermath of the feeding, the ruminations were naught but distant screams of urgency that did not carry far and failed to energize him.

The female under the colored maple tree was what he dwelled upon.

As he retraced her features from memory, he told himself he was permitted this one night of distraction. He was in no condition to fight, even with her gift, and his soldiers were out carrying forth the mission against the *lessers*, so there was still some progress being made.

One night. And then upon the sunset of the morrow, he was going to cast her aside as one did with both fantasies and nightmares, thus returning to the real world to battle once again.

One night only.

That was all he would grant this futureless diversion of fancy . . .

Assuming, a small voice pointed out, that Throe kept his word and never again sought her out.

FIFTY-TWO

"**O**ne more?"

As Tohr returned his attentions to the silver tray of food, No'One wanted to decline the offer. Indeed, lying back against the pillows of his bed, she was *stuffed*.

And yet as he shifted toward her with another ripe strawberry held by its fluffy green crown, she found the fruit was too much to resist. Parting her lips, she waited, as she had learned to wait, for him to bring the food to her.

Several of the bright red berries had failed to meet his rigorous requirements, having been set aside on the edge of the tray. The same had been true for some of the slices of freshly cooked turkey, as well as parts of the green salad. The rice had all passed muster, however, as had the delicious sourdough bread rolls.

"Here," he murmured. "This is a good one."

No'One watched him watch her as she accepted what he provided. He was singularly focused on her consumption—in a way that was both touching and a source of fascination. She had heard of males doing this. Had even caught sight of her parents in such a ritual, her mother seated to the left of her father at the dining table, him inspecting each plate and bowl and glass and cup afore it was sent in her direction by him personally, rather than by the staff—provided the food was of high enough quality. She had assumed the practice was a quaint holdover from some earlier time. Not so. This private space here with Tohrment was the basis of exchanges such as that. In fact, she could imagine aeons ago, in the wild, a male returning with something freshly killed and doing likewise.

It made her feel . . . protected. Valued. Special.

"One more?" he said again.

"You shall make me fat."

"Females should have meat on their bones." He smiled in a distracted way as he picked up a plump berry and frowned at it.

As his words resonated, she did not take them to mean he thought her wanting in any fashion. How could she, when he had done nothing but pick through perfectly good food and weed out what he did not think was worthy enough for her?

"A last one, then," she said softly, "and then I must decline all other offerings. I am full to bursting."

He tossed the berry aside with the other rejects and snagged another, and whilst he all but growled at the poor thing, his stomach let out an empty howl.

"You must needs eat as well," she pointed out.

The grunt she got back was either grudging approval of the second berry or agreement—likely the former.

As she bit down and chewed, he rested his arms in his lap and stared at her mouth as if he were prepared to help her swallow if he had to.

In the quiet moment, she thought, oh, how he had changed since the summer. He was so much bigger—impossibly so, his once large body now absolutely mammoth. And yet he had not swollen up unattractively, his muscles expanding to this outer limit without any coating of fat upon them, his form pleasing to the eye in its proportion. His face had remained lean, but it was no longer drawn, and his skin had lost the gray pallor she had not recognized until color bloomed anew in his cheeks.

The white streak remained in his hair, however, evidence of all he had been through.

How often did he think of his Wellesandra? Was he as yet dwelling upon her?

Of course he was.

As her chest ached, she found it difficult to draw breath. She had always had sympathy for him, her pain receptors firing up when he was in extremis sure as if his loss was her own.

Now, though, she had a different kind of agony behind her sternum.

Mayhap it was because they were closer still now. Yes, that was it. She was commiserating with him at an even deeper level.

"Done?" he said, his face tilting to the side, the lamplight hitting it with gentle kindness.

No, she was wrong, she thought as she dragged another breath in.

This was not commiseration.

This was something altogether different from caring about another's suffering.

"Autumn?" he said. "You okay?"

Staring up at him, she felt a sudden chill tickle the skin of her forearms and skitter across her bare shoulders. Under the warmth of the covers, her body shimmied in its own flesh, going cold and then flushing with heat.

Which was what happened, she supposed, when your world was turned upside down.

Dearest Virgin Scribe . . . she was in love with him.

She had fallen in love with this male.

When had it happened?

"Autumn." His voice grew more forceful. "What's going on?"

The "when" couldn't be pinned down, she decided. The shift had occurred millimeter by millimeter, the engine of change driven by exchanges between them both big and small . . . until, similar to the way the lovely night fell and laid claim to the landscape of the earth, what began as imperceptible culminated in the undeniable.

He bolted up to his feet. "I'll get Doc Jane—"

"No," she said, holding out her hand. "I am fine. Just tired, and satiated from the food."

For a moment, he gave her his strawberry look, that discerning eye of his narrowing and locking on.

Clearly she passed muster, however, as he sank back down.

Forcing a smile to her lips, she motioned to the second tray, the one that still had the silver covers over its dishes. "You should eat now. In fact, perhaps we should get you some fresh food."

He shrugged. "This is fine."

He popped the berries that hadn't been good enough for her into his mouth as he revealed his dinner, and then ate everything that had been left behind on her tray as well as all that was on his own.

His attention diverted was a good thing.

When he was finished with his meal, and the remains of her own, he took the trays and the stands and put them outside in the hall.

"I'll be right back."

With that, he disappeared into the bathroom, and soon the sound of running water drifted out to her.

Curling onto her side, she stared at the closed drapes.

The lights went out and then his quiet padding came across the carpet. There was a pause before he got upon the bed—and for a moment, she worried that he had read her mind. But then she felt a cooling breeze against her and realized he'd lifted the covers. For the first time.

"Okay if I join you?"

Abruptly, she blinked back tears. "Please."

The mattress dipped down and then his naked body came over against her own. As he gathered her in his arms, she went willingly and with surprise into him.

That odd, ambient chill went through her again, bringing with it a sense of foreboding. But then she was warm, even hot . . . from his flesh against her own.

He must never know, she thought as she closed her eyes and rested her head on his chest.

He must never, ever know what beat within her heart for him.

It would ruin everything.

Winter

FIFTY-THREE

As Lassiter sat at the base of the grand staircase, he stared upward at the painted ceiling some three floors above him. Within the depiction of warriors astride stallions, he searched the painted clouds and found the image he was looking for, but did not want to see.

Wellsie was ever farther back in the landscape, her form even more compact as she huddled into herself in that field of gray boulders.

In truth, he was losing hope. Soon she would be so far off into the distance that they wouldn't be able to see her at all. And that was when it was over: she was done, he was done . . . Tohr was done.

He'd thought No'One was the answer. And, you know, back in the early fall, he had gotten psyched that all was resolved. The night after Tohr had finally bedded that female good and proper, she had arrived at the dining table without her hood or that awful robe on: She had been in a dress, a cornflower blue dress that was too big for her and lovely nonetheless, and her hair had been loose around her shoulders, a cascade of blond.

The pair of them had had an accord that came only after two people banged the crap out of each other for hours.

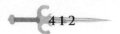

He'd repacked his clothes at that point. Hung around his room. Paced for hours, waiting to be summoned by the Maker.

When the sun had set again, he'd chalked it up to administrative delay. When the sun had risen once more, he'd started to get worried.

Then, he'd become resigned.

Now, he was in panic mode. . . .

Sitting on his ass, staring up at the figment of a dead female, he found himself wondering the same thing Tohr had so very often.

What more did the Creator want out of this?

"What are you looking for?"

As a deep voice interrupted him, he glanced across at the male in question. Tohrment had obviously come out from the hidden door underneath the staircase: He was dressed in black running shorts and a muscle shirt, and had sweat slicking his skin and dark hair.

Aside from the postworkout drips, the guy looked great. But that was what happened to 'em when they were well fed, well fucked, and unharmed.

The Brother lost some of that hale-and-hearty as their eyes met, however. Which suggested that he had the same worry just below his surface, lingering always, a chronic concern.

Tohr came over and sat down, toweling off his face. "Talk to me."

"You getting any more dreams about her?" No reason to proper-name the "her." Between the two of them, there was only one female who mattered.

"Last was a week ago."

"How'd she look." As if he didn't already know. He was frickin' staring at her right now.

"Farther away." Tohr took the towel from around his neck and stretched it taut between his fists. "You sure that maybe she isn't just fading into the Fade."

"She look happy to you."

"No."

"That's your answer."

"I'm doing everything I can."

Lassiter glanced over and nodded. "I know you are. I totally know you are."

"So you're worried, too."

No reason to answer that one.

In silence, the pair of them sat hip-to-hip, arms dangling off their knees, the metaphorical brick wall they were standing in front of blocking any horizon.

"Can I be honest with you?" the Brother said.

"Might as well be."

"I'm terrified. I don't know what I'm missing here." He rubbed the towel over his face again. "I don't sleep much, and I can't decide whether that's because I'm scared of what I'll see—or what I won't see. I don't know how she's holding on."

The short answer was that she wasn't.

"I talk to her," Tohr murmured. "When Autumn is asleep, I sit up in bed and stare into the dark. I tell her . . ."

When the guy's voice cracked, Lassiter wanted to scream—and not because he thought Tohr was being a pussy. More like it hurt that badly to hear the agony in that voice.

Shit, sometime in the last year he must have developed a conscience or something.

"I tell her that I still love her, that I'll always love her, but that I've done what I can to . . . well, not fill her void, because no one can do that. But at least try to live some kind of a life . . ."

As the male continued to speak in soft, sad tones, Lassiter was struck with a sudden terror that he'd led the guy wrong in some way, that he'd . . . shit, he didn't know. Fucked this up, made a bad call, sent this poor, sorry bastard in a wrong direction.

He reviewed everything he knew about the situation, starting from the ground floor, building the logic tier by tier, reconstructing where they were.

He could find no faults, no missteps. They had both done the best they could.

In the end, it appeared that was the only solace he could take—and didn't that just suck ass. The idea he might have even inadvertently harmed this male of worth was so much worse than his version of purgatory.

He should never have agreed to this.

"Fuck," he breathed as he closed his aching eyes. They had come so far, but it was as if they were chasing a moving target. The faster they ran, the farther they traveled, the farther away the end seemed to become.

"I've just got to try harder," Tohr said. "That's the only answer. I don't know what else I can do, but I've got to go deeper somehow."

"Yeah."

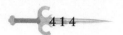

The Brother turned to him. "You're still here, right?"

Lassiter shot him a look. "If you're talking to me, that's a yes."

"Okay . . . that's good." The Brother punched up to his feet. "Then we've still got some time left."

Woo-hoo. Fantastic. Like that was going to make any difference.

Outside her private cabin, Xhex stood alone on the shores of the Hudson, her boots planted in the white snow, her breath leaving her nose in puffs that drifted off over her shoulder. The sunset's peach-and-pink glow rained down on the frozen landscape from behind her, the colors picked up by the sluggish waves in the center of the channel.

There wasn't much open water left in the river—ice was building up from the shores and closing in, threatening to strangle the surface as the cold endured through the season.

Without any command from her, her *symphath* senses pierced the gloaming, invisible tentacles that probed the thin, frigid air. She did not expect to get any hits, but she was so used to being receptive after these last couple of months, she found that side of her wanting to stretch and extend outward, if only for exercise.

She had not found the Band of Bastards' lair. Yet.

Right person for the job, huh. Frankly, the shit was getting embarrassing.

Then again, the reasons to handle everything carefully were too many to count: So much was riding on her getting a bead on them as quietly and unobtrusively as possible, and at least the king and the Brothers understood that.

John had likewise been endlessly supportive of her mission. Patient. Ready to discuss any angle or not bring it up at all when she was at the mansion—which had been on a regular basis as it turned out: Between seeing her mother, updating the Brotherhood and the king, or even hanging out a little, she was there two or three times a week.

Yet, when it came to John, things had never gone further than a polite meal.

Even though his eyes burned for her.

She knew what he was doing. He was keeping his word, holding back until she penetrated the B.o.B. so he could prove that he meant what he said. Except, as crass as it was . . . she wanted to be with him. And not as in separated-by-a-dinner-table "be with him."

It was an improvement over the summer and fall for them, to be sure—and not nearly enough.

Refocusing, she continued to search the environs for no good reason until all around her, darkness descended fast, the light draining out of the sky in the way of late December—which was to say, the shit flushed out like it was on the run, pursued by the cold.

Over to her left, at the mansion on the peninsula, lights came on rather suddenly, as if Assail had shutters on the inside of all his glass: One moment the property was unlit; the next it was like a football stadium.

Ah, yes, the gentlemale Assail . . . not.

The guy's hold on the drug scene in Caldwell was nearly secure, with no one of any significance left other than that big-fish supplier Benloise. What she couldn't figure out was who the vampire's troops were. He couldn't be operating a business that involved by himself, and yet there was never anyone coming or going from his house other than him.

Then again, why would he want his associates in his private space?

A little later, a car eased down the lane, heading out. That Jaguar of his.

Man, bitch needed to invest in an armor-plated Range Rover. Or a Hummer like Qhuinn's. The Jag was fast, and suited the motherfucker, but come on. Little traction in all this snow was never a bad idea.

The sports car slowed to a stop as it approached her, its exhaust curling around and glowing in the red tail lights like something a magician would call up onstage.

A window went down and a male voice said, "Enjoying the view?"

The temptation was to flip him off, but she kept her middle finger sheathed as she crunched through the drifts to him. At this point, Assail was not viewed as a "suspect," per se—he had done nothing but help the Brotherhood get Wrath out of there when the assassination attempt had gone down. But still, the attack had occurred at his house, and she wondered about where Xcor was getting his financial resources: Assail had had money even before he'd decided to be a drug kingpin, and wars required cash.

Especially if you were trying to fight the king.

Focusing her *symphath* side on the male, she read his grid and saw a whole lot of . . . well, lust, for one thing. He wanted her, but she was willing to bet that was not specific to her.

Assail liked sex with chicks. Fine. Got it.

Beneath that testosterone surge, however, she found a hunger for

power that was curious. It wasn't about taking down the king, though. It was . . .

"Reading my mind?" he drawled.

If only he knew what he was talking to. "You'd be surprised what I can find out about people."

"So you know I want you."

"I would suggest you don't go there. I'm mated."

"So I've heard. But where's your man."

"Working."

As he smiled, the lights of the dashboard picked up his features, highlighting them and making them even more handsome. But he wasn't just a pretty boy: There was a lick of evil in those heated eyes of his.

Dangerous male. Even though he looked like he was nothing more than a coiffed member of the *glymera*.

"Well," he murmured, "you know what they say. Too much time apart makes the heart grow—"

"Tell me something. You see Xcor around anywhere?"

That shut him up. And lowered his lids.

"I have no idea," he said after a moment, "why you'd ask me that."

"Oh, really."

"Not a clue."

"I know what happened at your house in the fall."

There was a another pause. "I wouldn't have thought that the Brotherhood mixed business with pleasure." When she just stared at him, he shrugged. "Well, frankly, I can't believe they're still looking for him. Matter of fact, it's a surprise that that bastard is still breathing."

"So you've seen him lately."

At that, his grid lit up in one specific sector—obstruction. He was hiding something from her.

She smiled coldly. "Haven't you, Assail."

"Listen, I'm going to give you some free advice. I know you're all leather wearing and tough and a self-actualized female of the world, but you don't want to have anything to do with that guy. Have you seen what he looks like? You're mated to a pretty boy like John Matthew, you don't need—"

"I'm not looking to fuck the bastard."

Her deliberately crass language made him blink. "Indeed. And, ah, good for you. As for myself, I haven't seen him. Not even that night he ambushed Wrath."

Liar, she thought.

When Assail spoke next, his voice was very low. "Leave that male alone. You don't want to get in his path—he's got less mercy than I have."

"So you think only the big boys should deal with him."

"You got it, sweetheart."

As he put the Jag in gear, she stepped back and crossed her arms over her chest. Too frickin' typical. What was it about the cock and balls that made males think they had a lock on strength?

"I'll see you around, neighbor," she drawled.

"I'm serious about Xcor."

"Oh, I can tell you are."

He shook his head. "Fine. It's your funeral."

As he drove off, she thought, Wrong pronoun there, buddy. Wrong goddamn pronoun . . .

FIFTY-FOUR

Autumn was dead asleep when she was joined in the bed, but even in her deep, nearly painful repose, she knew whose hands came upon her skin, and traveled over her hip, and eased up her stomach. She knew exactly who cupped her breasts and rolled her over.

For sex.

Cool air hit her skin as the covers were folded aside, and on instinct she parted her legs, preparing to welcome the one male she would e'er take within her.

She was ready for Tohrment. Had seemed in recent weeks to always be ready for him.

Handy—as he would have said. As he was always ready for her.

Her great warrior found his way between her thighs, opening them further with his hips—no, those were now his hands, as if he had had one plan and then changed his mind—

His mouth found her, locking on, then licking.

With her eyes still closed and her mind in that fuzzy netherworld that was neither sleep nor awakening, the pleasure was so intense she bucked and thrashed against his tongue, giving herself over to him with everything she had as he sucked and teased and penetrated. . . .

Except there was no orgasm for her. No matter how much he pleasured her.

Try as she might to capture the release, she couldn't fall off the edge, pleasure sharpening to the point of agony—and still she could find no climax, even as sweat beaded up her skin, and breath sawed in her throat.

Desperation made her grab his head and press him harder against her.

Except then he disappeared.

This was naught but a nightmare, she thought as she cried out at the denial. A torturous dream with erotic overtones—

Tohrment surged back at her, and this time it was his full body against her own. Tucking his arms behind her knees, he split her wide as he cranked her into a tight little ball underneath his great weight.

And then he entered, hard and fast.

Now she came. The instant he filled her with that long length of his, her body responded with a tremendous, cracking explosion, the orgasm so violent she bit her own lip with both fangs.

As blood flooded her mouth, he slowed his pounding to lap it up. But she didn't want slow. Using his arms to push against with her legs, she found her own rhythm against his shaft, riding him, taking him . . . until she soon found herself again on the verge.

And going nowhere.

In the beginning, it had been so easy for her to get what she needed when they mated. Lately, though, it was harder and harder. . . .

As she strained against him, pumping herself faster and faster, her frustration made her wild.

She bit him.

In the shoulder.

Scored him. With her nails.

The combination should have had him stopping and demanding more civilized behavior. Instead, with his blood flowing onto her, he let out a roar so mighty there was a crash in the room, as if it had rattled something off the wall.

Then he orgasmed. And thank the sweet Virgin Scribe for his release. As he jabbed into her and his erection kicked violently, she finally caught that elusive ride herself, her body rocking with him, the headboard banging.

Someone was shouting.

Her.

There was another crash.

The lamp . . . ?

When they finally stilled, she was soaking wet all over, throbbing between her legs, limp to the point of being boneless. One of the bedside lamps had indeed been knocked off its table, and as she looked across the way, she saw that the mirror over the bureau had cracked its glass.

Tohrment lifted his head and stared at her. In the light from the bathroom, she saw the damage to his shoulder.

"Oh . . . dearest . . ." She put a hand to her mouth in horror at the gaping wound. "I'm so sorry."

He glanced at himself and frowned. "Are you kidding me?"

When he looked back at her, he was smiling with a male pride that made absolutely no sense at all.

"I have hurt you." She wanted to cry. "I have—"

"Shh." He brushed a damp strand away from her face. "I love it. I *fucking* love it. Scratch me. Dent me. Bite me—s'all good."

"You are . . . nuts." To use a colloquialism she'd picked up on.

"I'm not finished is what I am—" Except as he went to move in her, she winced.

Instantly, he froze. "Shit, that was pretty rough."

"It was wonderful."

Tohrment propped his great chest up on his arms and withdrew so slowly and carefully, she barely felt it. And yet she started cramping somewhere inside. Or maybe that was another orgasm? Hard to know, as her body was so o'errun with sensation.

Either way, the delicious wear and tear was a good thing. They were so familiar with each other now, so comfortable with mating, and the incredible intensity they achieved was a result of the lack of barriers, and the freedom . . . and the trust they shared.

"Let me run you a bath to clean you up in."

"That's okay." She smiled at him. "I'm just going to relax here while you take a shower. Then I'll do the same in a bit."

In truth, she didn't trust herself to be naked in the bathroom with him. She was liable to bite him on the other side of his shoulders—and as much as she appreciated his carte blanche with the teeth, she would far prefer not to use the leeway.

Tohrment slid out of the mess of covers and stood over her for a moment, eyes narrowed. "You sure you're okay?"

"Promise."

Eventually, he nodded and turned away—

"Your back!" He looked like he'd had cat claws in him, great streaks of red cutting down his torso and spine.

He glanced over his bitten shoulder and smiled with more pride. "It feels great. I'm going to think of you when I'm out tonight, every time they pull."

As he disappeared into the bathroom, she shook her head to herself. Males were . . . well, nuts.

Closing her eyes, she cast the sheets from her skin and moved her arms and legs out from her body. The air was cool in the room, perhaps even cold, but in the aftermath, she was her own furnace, the remnants of passion practically steaming from her pores.

Whilst Tohrment showered, the flush gradually faded, however, as did the throbbing aftermath of the lovemaking. And then, finally, she found the peace she had been looking for, her body uncoiling, the lingering tension and ache easing.

With a stretch that felt all the better for her nakedness, she smiled at the ceiling. Never had she known such happiness—

From out of nowhere, that strange chill she had felt now and again since the fall came back upon her, a premonition she could sense but not define, a warning without context.

Cold now, she drew the covers around herself.

Alone in the bed, she felt stalked by destiny as surely as though she were in a forest at night, with wolves she could hear but not see padding around the trees . . .

Ready to pounce.

In the bathroom, Tohr dried himself off and leaned into the mirror. The bite mark on his shoulder was starting to heal already, his skin reknitting over the punctures, everything sealing up nicely. Too bad—he wanted the wounds to stick around for a while.

There was pride to be had in being marked like that.

Still, he decided to wear a Hanes T-shirt instead of a wifebeater under his jacket. No reason for his brothers to see it. That shit was private— between him and Autumn alone.

Goddamn . . . that female was incredible.

In spite of the stress he was under, in spite of that convo with Lassiter

on the staircase, in spite of the fact that he'd started to touch her only because he'd felt like he should, in the end, and as usual, it had been all about the sex, the raw, pounding sex: Autumn was like a vortex that he spun around, the erotic hold she had on his body sucking him in and then spinning him out to the surface for air . . . before claiming him once again.

In this, he was sad to say, he had moved on.

It pained him to admit that, and sometimes as he lay there afterward, the pair of them recovering their breath and cooling their sweat, that old familiar ache sharpened to a dagger point behind his sternum.

He didn't suppose he was ever going to lose that sensation.

And yet, every dawn, he sought her out and he took her . . . and he had every intention of doing the same in another twelve hours.

Coming out of the bath, he found her still on the bed. She had curled away toward the windows and was lying on her side with the sheets drawn around herself.

He saw her naked.

Utterly. Fucking. Naked.

The image made his body get instantly hard, his sex punching out from his hips. And as if she sensed his arousal, she moaned in an erotic purr and undulated. Reaching behind herself, she pulled back what covered her and moved her upper leg forward, exposing her glistening sex.

"Oh, hell," he groaned.

His body went to her without thought or decision, tracking her with such a locked-on focus that he wouldn't have even killed anyone who got in his way: He'd have just trampled them and waited to commit murder until he was finished taking care of business with her.

Getting up on the mattress, he took his cock in his hand and fit himself to her from behind, head to her core. He was careful as he entered her, just in case she was still sore, and then he waited, suspending himself above her to make sure she still wanted him again so soon.

When all she did was moan his name in satisfaction, he let his hips begin to pump.

Slick, smooth, hot . . .

He took her without apology and liked the freedom to do that. She remained slight of stature, but she was tougher than she looked, and in the last few months he had learned to let himself go, because he knew she liked it like that, too.

Shifting one of his hands to her hip, he changed the angle of her body so he could get in even deeper. And of course, there was another added bene to this position: He could see himself going in and out of her, watching the rim of his head make an appearance before going deep, only to return to the edge of her once more. She was pink and swollen, and he was hard and glossy thanks to her—

"*Fuck*," he barked as he started to come again.

He rode her while he released, feeling her orgasm with him, that sex of hers fisting him. And he watched the show until his eyes cranked shut—which was fine, because he could still see her on the backs of his lids.

After he was done, he nearly collapsed on her, but caught himself just in time. Dropping his head, he found his mouth close to the top of her spine, and he took advantage of the proximity, brushing his lips on her skin.

Knowing he should give her a break, he forced himself to ease back and pull out. Except as he slipped free, he had to grit his teeth at the sight of how ready she still was for him.

Planting his hands on her perfect cheeks, he spread her for his tongue. Shit . . . the taste of her and him together, the feel of her smooth, perfectly hairless sex against his mouth . . .

When she began to grow restless, as if she were on the verge, but not getting quite enough, he licked three fingers and slid them up inside as he continue to lap at her. That did the trick. As she called out his name and she jerked backward against his face, he smiled and helped her through the pulses that racked her.

And then it was time to stop. Period.

For the last week or so, he'd been all over her—which was the reason he'd forced himself to go to the goddamn gym today. She was looking tired, and the reason? She insisted on working during the nights, and he hadn't been able to leave her alone during the days—

Autumn shifted around so she was lying on her belly; then she put her knee out to the side and arched her back. For more.

"Jesus," he groaned. "How'm I supposed to leave you?"

"Don't," she said.

No asking twice on that one. He took her from behind again, lifting her hips, gripping them, and tilting her pelvis so he could get in deep. He ended up with a forearm around her midsection and his weight balanced on his other hand, working her, pounding her until their bodies slapped together and the bed made that noise again. He came on a curse, his orgasm exploding out of him as if he hadn't had sex in months.

And still he was hungry for her. Especially as she found her own release.

After things quieted, he curled them over onto the mattress, spooning her as he held her against him. Nuzzling his way under her hair to her neck, he worried about the way he was treating her in bed.

As if she knew he needed some reassurance, she reached behind and stroked his hair. "You feel wonderful."

Maybe. But he felt bad for the demands he was putting on her body. "Let me run you a bath now?"

"Oh, that would be wonderful. Thank you."

Heading back into the bathroom, he went over to the deep-bellied Jacuzzi, started the water running and then got the bath salts from the cupboard.

As he checked the temperature of the water and made a minute adjustment, he realized he liked taking care of her. Realized also that he'd found a lot of ways to do it. He looked for excuses to take her upstairs and feed her dinner in private. Bought her clothes off the Internet. Stopped by Walgreens and CVS to get her favorite magazines like *Vanity Fair*, *Vogue* and *The New Yorker*.

Always made sure there were Pepperidge Farm Milanos up here in case she got a craving.

And he wasn't the only one looking after her and showing her new things.

Xhex came to the house to see her at least once or twice a week. Together, the pair of them would go out to the local movie theater and watch films. Or head into the better parts of town so Autumn could see the nice houses. Or hit the late-night shops and stores—where they bought things with Autumn's own money that she earned working.

Bending down, he tested the water, tinkered with the temp again, and got her some towels.

On his side, it made him a little tetchy that she was out with the human crazies and the violent *lessers* and the untrustworthy winds of fate. But at the end of the day, Xhex was a straight-up killer, and he knew she would protect her mother if anyone so much as sneezed in their direction.

Besides, whenever mother and daughter went out, Autumn always returned with a smile on her face. Which in turn put a smile on his.

Christ, they'd both come so far since the spring. They were nearly two different people.

So what else was there?

Moving his hand through the churning water in the tub, he wondered with desperation what the fuck he was missing. . . .

FIFTY-FIVE

Two nights later, Xhex awoke with a strange conviction hounding her. Kind of like she'd swallowed her alarm clock during the day and the thing was going off in her belly.

Intuition. Anxiety. Dread.

No snooze button on that shit.

As she went and took a shower, she continued to be dogged by the sense that forces unseen and unknowable were coalescing, that the landscape was going to shift, that the chess pieces of various people were about to be moved by hands not their own, to places not part of their strategies.

The preoccupation stuck with her during the short trip into Caldwell proper; persisted as she got things started at the Iron Mask.

Unable to stand it any longer, she removed her cilices and went out into the city hours earlier than she usually did. And as she dematerialized from rooftop to rooftop searching out the Bastards, she had a feeling . . . tonight was the night.

But for what?

With that question weighing her down, she was especially careful to stay far from where the Brothers were fighting.

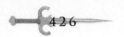

The fact that she had committed to giving them a wide berth was probably the biggest factor in her delay at finding that rifle. The Band of Bastards was out in the field every night, but as the skirmishes with the Lessening Society tended to happen only in the desolate parts of the city, it was hard to get close enough while retaining a distance from John and the Brotherhood.

Yeah, she had some grids that were new in her repertoire, but it was difficult to isolate who was Xcor—and even though that was academic, because she needed only one of those soldiers to slip up, get injured and have to be taken back to their lair in a car she could track, she wanted to know her larger target intimately.

Check out his secrets from the inside.

That she had gotten nowhere so far was driving her nuts. And the Brothers weren't crazy for it, either, although for a different reason: They wanted to just take the other fighters out, but Wrath had KO'd that one: They needed the rifle first, so the king had declared that renegade group of traitors off-limits until he got the proof he needed. Logically speaking, the proclamation made sense—no good would come out of slaughtering them all and then trying to calm the *glymera* with an oh-but-they-shot-me kind of thing. But the night-after-night was tough going.

At least they had one thing in their favor: It was unlikely that rifle had been destroyed.

The B.o.B. would want to keep that shit as a trophy, no doubt.

It was time to end this, however. And maybe this premonition thing she was rocking meant that she was finally going to.

On that note, and under the theory that doing the same thing over and over again and expecting a different result was insane, she decided to stop looking for Xcor.

Nope, tonight, Assail was going to be the one she was after—and what do you know, she located his imprint in the theater district . . . inside the Benloise Art Gallery, natch.

A quick shift down to street level and she got an eyeball full of cocktail party going on at the facility.

As the artsy set was perfectly capable of wearing leather and considering it business attire, she slipped in—

Hot. Cramped. Lot of egocentric accents echoing around.

Jeez, in a place like this, you couldn't tell the sexes apart—everyone had bird-wing hand gestures and nail polish on.

Two feet past the door she was promptly offered a flute of champagne—as if blowhards with delusions of being Warhol ran on Veuve Clicquot.

"No, thanks."

As the waiter, a nice-looking guy in black, gave her a little nod and sauntered off, she almost pulled him back just for the company.

Yeah, wow, there were so many arched eyebrows and pointed noses up in the air, you had to wonder if these folks even approved of themselves. And a quick glance around at the "art" told her that she and her mother were going to have to come here—just so Autumn could get a sense of how truly hideous and overindulgent some kinds of self-expression could get.

Dumb-ass humans.

With grim determination, she parried her way through all the shoulders, turning this way and that while sidestepping around other waiters. She didn't bother hiding her face. Rehv had handled all his deals by himself or with Trez and iAm, so no one here was going to recognize her.

And pretty quick, she identified the way to Benloise's office. It was just so damn obvi: Two goons dressed like waiters, but not carrying trays, were standing on either side of a nearly seamless door cut into the cloth-covered walling.

Assail was up on the second floor. She could sense him clearly. . . .

But getting to him was a thing: It was tricky to try to dematerialize into spaces unknown. There was probably a staircase on the far side of what was being guarded, but she didn't want to Swiss-cheese herself by re-forming in the middle of it.

Besides, she could always catch the guy on the exit. Chances were good he'd come in through the back, and would leave the same way: He was cagey, and his visit was not about the frickin' art.

Good thing, too, as it was difficult to see Q-tips glued to a Tupperware bowl mounted on a toilet seat as anything other than trash.

Heading deeper into the building, she slipped through a staff-only door and found herself in a concrete-floored, concrete-walled warehouse space that smelled like chalk dust and crayons. Up above, caged fluorescent lights were set into the high, unhung ceiling, and exposed ductwork and electricals burrowed through joists like moles in a lawn. Desks were set back, and file cabinets were out to the sides, the center of the space remaining clear, as if large installations were regularly rolled in from the rear alleyway.

The double doors straight ahead were made of steel and had security alarm contacts on them—

"May I help you."

Not an inquiry.

She turned around.

One of the bouncers had followed her inside, and he was standing with his feet spread and his blazer open like he had a gun in there.

Rolling her eyes, she waved a hand and put him in a temporary trance. Then, placing a thought in his mind that there was nothing unusual going on, she sent him back to his post—where he would relate to his big-ass buddy that, in fact, there was *nothing unusual going on.*

Not exactly rocket science with these Homo sapiens. But just to be on the safe side, she fritzed out the security cameras as she went toward the back doors. Shit. One look at the way the steel panels were wired and she decided not to push on through and risk an incident involving the police.

If she wanted to be in the alley, she was going to have to work for it.

With a curse, she headed back for the party. It took her a good ten minutes to weed her way through all the denizens of questionable taste and undeniable ego, and as soon as she was out in the night air, she dematerialized up to the roof and walked to the far side.

Assail's car was parked down in the alley below, facing out.

And she wasn't the only one looking at it. . . .

Holy. . . crap . . .

Xcor was in the shadows, waiting for the male as well.

Had to be him—whoever it was had a lockdown on his inner core to such a degree, there was little superstructure to be read: By habit or by trauma, or likely some of both, the three dimensions had shrunken in on each other until they formed such a gnarled, tight mass, it was impossible for her to get a bead on any emotion whatsoever.

Man, she'd seen imprints like this from time to time. They usually meant real trouble, as the individual was capable of anything.

For example, you'd need precisely this kind of knotted center to have the balls to make a run at the king.

This was her target. She *knew* it.

And now that she had locked into that mangled grid, she backed off, dematerializing to the roof of a tall building a block away. She didn't want to spook the son of a bitch by getting too close, and from here, she still had an adequate sight line to the Jag.

Shit, if only her radar had greater reach: She could go maybe a mile with her *symphath* side, but that was pushing it, her instincts strong, just short-range. So if he dematerialized a great distance away? She was going to lose him. . . .

As she waited, she wondered once again about Xcor's connection to

Assail. Unfortunately for that aristocrat, if he was funding the insurrection, even indirectly, he was going to find himself in the crosshairs.

Not a good place to be.

About a half hour later, Assail emerged from the gallery's ass and looked around.

He knew the other male was there . . . and he addressed some sort of comment to precisely where Xcor stood.

The cold breeze and ambient noise of the city killed the sound track of whatever exchange occurred between the pair, but she didn't need dubbing to get the gist: Assail's emotions shifted around until she had to approve of the dislike and mistrust he felt toward whoever he was talking to. The closed-up male, naturally, gave nothing away.

And then Assail took off. And so did the other grid.

She trailed the latter.

Like so many things in life, in retrospect, what happened to Autumn around eleven o'clock that evening made sense. The clues had been there for months, but as was rather often the case, when you were going about your life, you misinterpreted the guideposts, misread the compass needle's position, mistook one thing for another.

Until you were at a destination that was nothing you would ever have chosen, and not something you could get away from.

She was down in the training center, taking out a pile of hot sheets from the dryer, when the storm hit.

Later, much later, a lifetime later, she would remember with clarity the feel of that soft heat against her torso, the warmth burrowing into her gut and making sweat break out on her forehead.

She would remember forever turning to the side and putting the fluffy white sheets on the counter.

Because when she stepped back, her needing hit for the second time in her life.

At first, it just felt as though she were still holding on to the sheets, the warmth remaining with her, along with a weight upon her belly sure as though she was as yet carrying the load.

As perspiration dripped down the side of her face, she glanced over at the thermostat on the wall, thinking that it was malfunctioning or set too high. But no, it read seventy degrees.

With a frown, she looked down at herself. Although she wore naught

but a T-shirt and a pair of what they called "yoga" pants, it was as though she had on the parka she wore out with Xhex—

A curling cramp gripped her lower abdomen, fisting up around her womb, her legs wobbling until she had no choice but to allow herself to go down onto the floor. And this was a good thing, at least temporarily. The concrete was cold and she stretched out on it—until the next big crunch grabbed hold of her.

Pressing her hands into her pelvis, she balled up and strained, throwing her head back as she tried to escape whatever had o'ertaken her body.

And then it started.

Her sex, which had been throbbing a bit ever since Tohr and she had been together for those rough, intense matings before he'd left, gained its own proper heartbeat, the core of her begging for the only thing that would give it relief.

A male—

The sexual craving hit her so viciously, she couldn't have stood if she'd had to, couldn't have thought of aught else had she chosen to, couldn't have spoken intelligible words had she wanted to.

This was so much worse than it had been with the *symphath*.

And this was her fault . . . this was *all* her fault . . .

She hadn't been going over to the Sanctuary. It had been . . . Dearest Virgin Scribe, it had been months since she had tarried at the Far Side to regulate her cycle. Indeed, there had been no need to refresh herself for blood, because Tohr had been feeding her, and she hadn't wanted to miss even a moment with him.

She should have known this was coming—

Gritting her teeth, she panted hard through another peak. Then, just as it relented and she was about to yell for help, the door was thrown wide.

Dr. Manello stopped short, his face a mask of confusion. "What the—"

He sagged against the doorjamb, and abruptly covered the front of his hips with his hands. "Are you okay—"

As the craving crescendoed again, she caught a fleeting image of him going loose where he stood, but then her lids clamped down and her jaw locked and she was momentarily lost.

From a distance, she heard him say, "Let me get Jane."

Seeking more of the cold floor, Autumn rolled over onto her back, but as her knees wouldn't unhinge, she didn't have enough surface contact.

Back to the side. Then over onto her stomach, even though her legs wanted to recurl against her chest.

Pushing down with her hands, she tried to take control of the sensation and manipulate her position, tried to find another arch or breath or stretch of the arms or thighs to bring relief.

There was none to be had. She was at the center of a lion's den, great teeth of need biting into her, tearing at her flesh, racking her bones. This was the culmination of those hot flashes that she had mistaken for spikes of passion, and the bursts of chills that she had chalked up to premonitions, and the bouts of vague nausea that she had blamed on big meals. This was the exhaustion. The appetite. Probably the hot sex that she had been having of late with Tohrment.

As she moaned, she heard her name being said and thought someone was talking to her. But it wasn't until the craving ebbed that she could open her eyes and see that yes, in fact, she was not alone.

Doc Jane was kneeling before her. "Autumn, can you hear me?"

"I . . ."

The healer's pale hand brushed tangled strands of blond out of her face. "Autumn, I think this is your needing—would that be right?"

Autumn nodded until the wave of hormones resurged, robbing her of everything but the overwhelming need for sexual relief.

Which her body knew could only come from a male.

Her male. The one she loved.

Tohrment . . .

"Okay, okay, we'll call him—"

Autumn threw out a hand and grabbed the other female's arm. Forcing her eyes to work, she pegged the healer with a hard demand. "Do *not* call upon him. Do *not* put him in that position."

It would kill him. To service her in her need? He'd never do that—sex was one thing, but he'd already lost a child—

"Autumn, honey . . . that's his choice, don't you think?"

"Don't call him . . . don't you dare call him. . . ."

FIFTY-SIX

Qhuinn hated nights off. Absolutely despised them.

As he sat back on his bed, staring at a TV that wasn't on, it dawned on him he'd been watching nothing for close to an hour now. Still, getting the remote and picking a channel just seemed like a lot of fucking hassle for not much in return.

Damn it, there were only so many miles you could run down in the gym. Only so much surfing you could do on the Internet. A limited number of trips you could take up and down to the kitchen . . .

Yeah, and that last one was especially true, given Saxton was still using the library as his own personal office. That "supersecret king stuff" was taking him for frickin' ever.

Either that or he was getting distracted a lot. By a certain redhead—

Okay, not going there. Nope.

Qhuinn glanced at his watch again. Eleven o'clock. "Fucking hell."

Seven thirty tomorrow night was an eternity away.

Shifting his eyes to the flat wall across the way, he was willing to bet John Matthew was next door, locked in the same grind. Maybe they should head out and have a drink somewhere.

Then again, meh. Did he really want to go to the effort of getting dressed just to have a beer around a bunch of drunk, horny humans? At one point in time, it would have sexed him up. Now, the prospect of all that pathetic, alcohol-induced yearning depressed the shit out of him.

He didn't want to be home. Didn't want to be out.

Christ, he wasn't sure he even wanted to be fighting, for that matter. The war just seemed like a slightly more interesting slice of empty.

Oh, for fuck's sake, what was his problem—

His phone beeped beside him and he picked it up without any real interest. The text made no sense: *All males stay in main house. Do* not *enter training facility. Thanx, Doc Jane.*

Huh?

He got up, grabbed a robe, and went over to John's. The knock was answered immediately by a whistle.

Putting his head in, he found his buddy in the same position he'd just been rocking—except the plasma screen was on. *1000 Ways to Die* on Spike TV. Nice.

"Did you get that text?"

Which one?

"From Doc Jane." Qhuinn tossed his cell over. "Any ideas?"

John read it and shrugged. *Not a clue. But I've already worked out. You?*

"Yeah." He walked around the room. "Man, is it me or is time dragging."

The whistle he got in reply was a big fat *yup.*

"You want to go out?" he asked with all the enthusiasm of someone suggesting a trip to a nail parlor.

Movement on the bed drew his eyes around: John was up on his feet and heading for his closet.

Across his back, deep in his skin, the name of his *shellan* was carved in the Old Language:

$$\text{XHEXURIU}$$

Poor bastard . . .

As the male pulled on a black button-down and covered his bare ass in leather, Qhuinn shrugged. Guess they were going for a beer.

"I'll go get clothes and be right back."

Stepping out into the hall, he frowned . . . and followed a compelling instinct down to the open landing that overlooked the foyer.

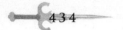

Leaning over the gold-leafed railing, he called out, "Layla?"

As the name echoed, the female emerged from the dining room. "Oh, hello." Her smile was automatic and meaningless, the expressional equivalent of a blank wall. "How fare thee?"

He had to laugh. "You're blowin' me away with all that happy joy-joy."

"I'm sorry." She seemed to snap out of her distraction. "I don't mean to be rude."

"Don't worry about it. What are you doing here?" He shook his head. "What I mean is, were you summoned?"

Had someone come home injured? Blay, for example . . .

"No, I have naught to do. I'm just waffling about as you would say."

Come to think of it, ever since the fall, she had been doing that a lot, just hanging around in the periphery, loitering as if she were waiting for something.

She was different, he thought abruptly. He couldn't quite put his finger on it, but lately she had changed: Grave. Less quick to smile. Serious.

To put it in human terms, he supposed she'd been a girl for as long as he'd known her. Now she was starting to look like a woman. No more wide-eyed wonder about everything this side of the divide had to offer. No more glowing enthusiasm. No more . . .

Shit, she looked a lot like he and John did. Worn out by the world.

"Hey, you want to come out with us?" he asked.

"Out? As in . . ."

"John and I are going to go have a drink. Maybe two. Maybe more. I think you should come with us. After all, misery loves company."

She linked her arms over her chest. "Is it so obvious?"

"You're still beautiful."

Layla laughed. "You're being charming."

"Lady in distress, you know the drill. Come out with us—let's just kill some time."

She looked around. Then she picked up her skirting and ascended the stairs. When she got to the top, she stared at him. "Qhuinn . . . may I please ask you something?"

"Long as it's not multiplication tables. I suck at math."

She laughed a little, but quickly lost the levity. "Did you ever think life would be so . . . empty? Some nights, I feel as though I could choke on the void."

Jesus, he thought. Yeah, he did.

"Come here," he told her. As she stepped into him, he pulled her in close, tucking her against his chest and resting his chin on the top of her head. "You are such a good female, you know that?"

"You're being charming again."

"And you are still in distress."

She relaxed in his arms. "You are very good to me."

"Back at you."

"It's not you, you know. I'm not pining over you anymore."

"I know." He rubbed her back as a brother would. "So tell me you're coming out—but be warned. I might just have to get you to tell me who you are missing."

The way she pulled back and ducked his eyes told him, yup, there was a male involved, and nope, she wasn't volunteering any information. "I shall need some clothes."

"Let's try the guest room. I think we'll find 'em there." He put an arm around her shoulders and led her down the hall. "And as for this Joe Shmoe of yours, I promise not to beat him—unless he breaks your heart. Then I might have to do some dental work on the bastard."

Who the hell could it be? he wondered. Everyone in the house was hooked up.

Maybe it was someone she'd met up north at Phury's great camp? But who would the guy be letting in?

Could it be one of the Shadows? Hmm . . . those bastards were males of worth, to be sure, the kind of thing that could definitely turn a female's head.

Man, he wished it was something else, for her sake. Love was hard, even if good people were involved.

In the guest room, he found her some black jeans and a black fleece. He didn't like the idea of her in some miniskirted nightmare—not just because it offended his delicate sensibilities, but he didn't need the Primale doing any cosmetic dentistry on *him*.

When they came out, John was waiting in the hall, and if he was surprised to be joined by the Chosen, he didn't show much of the reaction. Instead, he was kind to Layla, mouthing small talk with her as Qhuinn threw some proper clothes on.

About ten minutes later, the three of them dematerialized downtown—not to the bars, though: Neither he nor John was interested in escorting a Chosen into Screamer's or the Iron Mask. Instead, they ended up in the theater district, at a dessert place that was open until one a.m. and served liquor along with chocolate thingies draped in whatever topped with blah-

blah-blah on a bed of poached uh-huh, yeah. The tables were small, the chairs likewise, and they sat in front of the emergency exit in the back, hunkering down as the waitress continued to blabber about the specials, none of which were appealing.

The beer selection was mercifully short and to the point.

"Two black and tans for us," he said. "And for the lady?"

As he glanced at Layla, she shook her head. "I can't decide."

"Get both of whatever appeals."

"All right . . . I'll take the crème brûlée and the moon pie. And a cappuccino, please."

The waitress smiled as she wrote on her pad. "I love your accent."

Layla inclined her head graciously. "Thank you."

"I can't place it—French and German? Or . . . Hungarian?"

"Those beers would be great now," Qhuinn said firmly. "We're thirsty."

When the woman went off, he hairy-eyeballed the other diners, getting markers on their faces and scents, listening to the talk, wondering whether there was an attack coming. Across the way, John was doing the same. 'Cuz, yeah, it was so relaxing taking a Chosen out into the world.

"We're not very good company," he said to Layla after a while. "Sorry."

"I'm not either." She smiled at him and then John. "But I am enjoying being out of the house."

The waitress came back with the order, and everyone eased away from the table as glasses and plates and the cup and saucer were arranged.

Qhuinn snagged his tall glass as soon as the coast was clear. "So tell us about him. We can be trusted."

Across the table, John looked like someone had goosed him in the ass, especially as Layla blushed.

"Come on." Qhuinn took a pull off the black and tan. "It's obvious this is about a male, and John won't say a thing."

John looked over at her and signed; then flashed Qhuinn the bird.

"He says, duh, he's a mute," Qhuinn translated. "And if you don't know what that final gesture was, I'm not going to be the one to tell you."

Layla laughed and picked up her fork, cracking the hard top of the crème brûlée. "Well, I've been waiting to see him again, actually."

"So that's why you're hanging around?"

"Is it bad of me?"

"God, no. You're always welcome, you know that. Except who's the lucky guy?"

Or dead one, depending . . .

Layla drew in a deep, bracing breath, and took two mouthfuls of her first dessert—like the thing was a V&T. "Promise you shan't tell a soul?"

"Cross heart, hope to die, all that shit."

"He's . . . one of your soldiers."

Qhuinn lowered his glass to the table. "I'm sorry?"

She lifted her cup and sipped from the rim. "Remember when that fighter came into the training center back in the autumn—he'd been with you against the *lessers*? He was injured badly and you were taking care of him?"

As John sat up straight in alarm, Qhuinn swallowed his own case of the fucking-hells and smiled smoothly. "Oh, yeah. We remember him."

Throe. Second lieutenant of the Band of Bastards.

Holy shit, if she thought she was into him, they had a huge problem.

"Annnnnd," he prompted, forcing his voice to stay level. Good thing he'd put the Guinness down—he was stressing enough to crush the glass.

Then again, he supposed shit could be worse. Throe wasn't going to be able to get anywhere near her—

"He called me to him."

Layla started to pick at her moon pie, and good goddamn thing: He and John had both bared their fangs.

Humans, he reminded himself. They were out in public with humans. . . . Now was not the time for the canine display. But *fuck* . . .

"How?" he hissed—only to dial back. "I mean, you don't have a cell phone. How'd he reach you?"

"He summoned me." As she waved her hand like that was no big deal, he told his inner caveman to pipe down, sonny. There would be time to sort the *how*s out later. "I went and there was another soldier—injured badly. Oh, God, he was beaten so badly."

Tendrils of pure panic feathered across the back of his neck and pegged him in the chest, jacking his heart rate up. No . . . oh, shit . . . no—

"I don't understand why males are so pigheaded. I told them to bring him into the clinic, but they said he just needed to feed. He was having trouble breathing, and . . ." Layla fixated on the moon pie as if it were a screen, as if she were remembering every single thing that had happened. "I fed him. I wanted to care for him further, but the other soldier seemed in a hurry to take him away. He was . . . powerful, so powerful, even though he was hurt. And as he looked at me—I felt as though he was touching me. It was like nothing I've ever known before."

Qhuinn shot a stare over to John without moving his head. "What did he look like?"

Maybe it had been one of the others. Maybe it hadn't been—

"It was hard to tell. His face had been wounded so badly—those *lessers* are vicious." She reached up to her mouth. "His eyes were blue and his hair dark . . . his upper lip was twisted—"

As she kept talking, Qhuinn's hearing took a little TO.

Reaching over, he put his hand on her arm, stopping her. "Baby girl, hold up. That first soldier called you out to where?"

"It was a meadow. A field in the farmland."

As the final pint of blood drained out of his head, John started to mouth various curse words, and damn right with all that. The idea that Layla had been out in the night, alone and undefended, with not just Throe, but the heart of the beast?

Plus . . . holy hell, she had fed the enemy.

"What's wrong?" he heard her ask. "Qhuinn . . . ? John . . . ? Whatever is the matter?"

FIFTY-SEVEN

Across town, in the meatpacking district, Tohr outted both his black daggers in preparation to strike. Z and Phury were a mere block over from him, but there was no reason to call them—and not because he was rocking the whole death-wish shit again.

These two *lessers* up ahead were suffering from a fantastic case of the meanders; they were just ambling along like they had nothing better to do than wear down the soles of their boots.

The Society was overrecruiting, he thought, mining too deep into the pool of miscreant antisocials. And then once they were inducted, the SOBs weren't getting enough training or support—

Against his side, his phone vibrated as a text came through, but he ignored it as he broke into a jog. The snow cover helped muffle the sound of his shitkickers, and thanks to the cold air blowing into him, he had no scent to give himself away—not that these fools would have noticed either.

At the last moment, however, something tipped them off and they pivoted around.

He couldn't have asked for a better response.

He nailed them both right in the neck, ripping through their carotids,

opening second mouths below their chins. As their hands shot up, he tore through the space between them and wheeled about, ready to escort them onto the ground if necessary—

Oh, but no. The pussies were already falling to their knees.

Whistling through his teeth, he signaled to the others as he outted his phone to call Butch for cleanup—

He froze. The text that had come in was from Doc Jane: *I need you to come home right now.*

"Autumn . . . ?" As his brothers came skidding around the corner, he looked up. "I gotta bounce."

Phury frowned. "What's happened?"

"I don't know."

He dematerialized on the spot, ghosting to the north. Had she hurt herself? Maybe down in the clinic working? Or . . . fucking hell. What if she'd been out in town with Xhex and someone had aggressed on her?

As he re-formed on the steps in front of the mansion, he all but broke down the doors of the vestibule. Good thing Fritz cut the need for a carpenter by answering the inner one quick.

Tohr blew by the butler at a dead run. He was damn sure the guy was talking at him, but there was no tracking that or any other conversation. Hitting the hidden door under the stairs, he fell into a pounding gallop as he shot through the underground tunnel.

His first clue as to what was wrong came as he burst out of the supply closet and into the office.

His body flipped out, the signals from his brain cut off by interference and a change of focus that made no sense: An erection, thick and long, punched at his leathers, his head swimming with a sudden, crushing need to get to Autumn and—

"Oh, fuck . . . no . . ." The ragged sound of his voice was cut off as a scream pealed out of some room down the corridor. High-pitched and horrid, it was that of a female in incredible pain.

His body responded instantly, trembling as an overriding need struck him. He had to get to Autumn—unless he serviced her, she was going to spend the next ten or twelve hours in hell. She needed a male—him—inside of her, taking care of her—

Tohr lunged for the glass door, arm outstretched, hand ready to shove the transparent, fragile barrier aside.

He caught himself just as he opened the way.

What the fuck was he doing? What the *fuck* was he doing?

Another scream echoed down to him, and he sagged as a wave of sexual instinct nearly brought him to his knees. As his higher reasoning browned out again, his thought patterns ground to a halt as all he could think about was mounting Autumn and easing her torment.

But as the hormones ebbed, his brain started cranking over again.

"No," he barked. "No, no fucking way."

Pushing himself away from the door, he scrambled backward until he hit the desk and grabbed onto the thing in preparation for the next onslaught.

Images of Wellsie's needing, the one when they had conceived their young, flickered through his mind, the onslaught as unrelenting and undeniable as his body's urges. His Wellsie had been in such pain, crippling pain. . . .

He'd come home just before dawn, hungry, tired, thinking he was going to enjoy a good meal and some bad TV before they fell asleep against each other . . . but as soon as he'd entered through their garage, he'd had the same response he was fighting now: an overwhelming urge to mate.

There was only one thing that caused that kind of reaction.

Six months before that, Wellsie had made him swear, on the very basis of their sanctified mating, that when she went into her next needing, he would not drug her. Man, they'd had a fight over that. He hadn't wanted to lose her to the birthing bed; like a lot of bonded males, he would have rather they remain childless for the rest of their long lives together than for him to be left with nothing.

And what about you fighting? she'd yelled at him. *You face your own goddamn birthing bed every night!*

He couldn't remember now what he'd said to her then. No doubt he'd tried to calm her down, but it hadn't worked.

Something happens to you, she'd said, *I've got nothing either. You think I don't go through that crucible every fucking night?*

What had he said to her? Fuck him, he didn't know. But he could picture her face clear as day as she'd stared up at him.

I want a young, Tohr. I want a piece of you and me together. I want a reason to go on living if you don't—because that's what I'm going to have to do. I'm going to have *to keep living.*

Little had they known that he'd be the one left behind. That the young wouldn't be why she died. That all the things they had fought over that night hadn't been the right worries.

But life was like that. And as soon as he'd walked into their house,

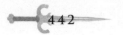

he'd wanted to call Havers, had even gone to the phone. But in the end, and as usual, he hadn't been able to deny her.

And instead of bleeding after the needing had passed, she'd found herself pregnant. *Incandescent* had barely described her joy—

The next scream was so loud, it was a wonder it didn't shatter the glass door.

Jane burst into the office. "Tohr! Listen, I need your help—"

As his hands clawed into the desk's edge to keep himself in place, he shook his head like a crazy man. "I'm not doing it. I'm not servicing her—no fucking way. I'm not doing it, I'm not doing it, I'm not doing it—"

Babbling, he was fucking babbling. He didn't even hear his own words as he started to lift up the desk and slam it down over and over again, until something hard and heavy got knocked onto the floor.

Somewhere in the back of his mind, he dimly thought it was too fucking ironic that he was losing it in this room again.

He'd found out Wellsie was dead in here.

Jane held her hands up. "No, wait, I need your help—but not in that way—"

Another wave of instinct made him grit his teeth and have to bow his upper body as he cursed.

"She told me not to call you—"

Then why was he here? Oh, fucking hell, the urge— "Then why did you text me!"

"She won't take any drugs."

Tohr shook his head—only this time it was in an attempt to improve his hearing. "What?"

"She's refusing the drugs. I can't get her to consent, and I didn't know who else to call. I can't reach Xhex—and no one else is close to her. She's suffering—"

"Drug her anyway—"

"She's stronger than I am. I can't even get her back on the bed without her lashing out. But that's not the point—ethically, I can't treat someone who doesn't let me. I won't do that. Maybe you can talk to her?"

At that point, Tohr's eyes got with the program and actually focused on the female. Her white coat was torn, one lapel hanging loosely like a flap of white skin. Clearly she'd been roughed up.

Tohr thought of Wellsie in her needing. When he'd gotten down to their room, it had looked like the place had been ransacked. The bedside table and everything on it knocked over and broken. The clock radio on the floor. The pillows off the mattress, the sheets split.

He'd found his female on the far side, on the carpet, in a ball of agony. She'd been naked, but flushed and sweating even though it had been cold.

He'd never forget the way she had looked up at him and, through her tears, begged him for what he could give her.

Tohr had mounted her fully clothed.

"Tohr . . . ? *Tohr?*"

"Have you quarantined the other males?" he mumbled.

"Yes. I even had to send Manny away. He was . . ."

"Yeah." The guy was probably calling Payne in from the field. Either that or spending a lot of meaningful time with his left hand: Once a male got exposed, he was perma-hard for some time, even if he left the vicinity.

"I also told Ehlena—and she said she's got to stay away. I guess sometimes one female's cycle can affect the others? And nobody wants to be pregnant around here."

Tohr put his hands on his hips and bowed his head, pulling his shit together. He told himself he was not some animal to take Autumn on whatever bed she was lying on. He was not. . . .

Shit, how much was he willing to trust that resolution? And what the hell was she thinking? Why the fuck wasn't she taking the drugs?

Maybe this was a ploy. To get him to service her.

Could she be that calculating?

The next scream was heart-wrenching—and pissed him off. In its wake, he told himself to turn around to the supply cabinet and put the thing to good use—except he couldn't leave Doc Jane. Sure enough, she'd make another attempt to help Autumn and get shanked again.

He looked over at the healer. "Let's go down together—and I don't care if she consents or not. You're going to put her out of that misery even if I have to pin her to the fucking floor."

Tohr took a couple of bracing breaths, jacked up his leathers.

Jane was talking to him, no doubt spouting all kinds of ethical-this and ethical-that, but he wasn't hearing it.

That walk down the corridor took forever: With each step, his body's needs tightened up, transforming him into a bomb of instinct. By the time he got to the door of the recovery room she was in, he was bent over, clutching himself at the groin even in front of Doc Jane. His cock was pounding, his hips straining—

He opened the door. "Fuuuuck . . ."

His bones nearly snapped in two as half of him went to lunge forward and the other half had to hold himself back by the steel jamb.

Autumn was on the bed, on her stomach, one knee up to her chest, her other leg extended out at a tortured angle. Her shift was twisted tight around her waist, and soaking wet from the sweat, her hair a knotted mess tangling around her upper body. And there were spots of blood near her mouth—she'd probably bitten through her lip.

"Tohrment . . ." Her broken voice rose up. "No . . . go 'way. . . ."

He lurched over to the bed and put his face in front of hers. "It's time to stop this—"

"Go . . . 'way. . . ." Her bloodshot eyes met his without focusing as tears streamed down her spectacularly colored face, the hormones suffusing her skin with a peachy tint like she was an old-fashioned, hand-painted photograph. "Go—no—"

The grunt that cut off the word rose in volume to another scream.

"Get the drugs," he snapped at the healer.

"She won't take them—"

"Get them! You may need her consent, but I sure as shit don't—"

"Talk to her first—"

"No!" Autumn hollered.

All hell broke loose at that point, everyone shouting at each other until the next wave came and shut him and Autumn up, the two of them once again bowing under the pressure.

Lassiter's appearance registered in the heartbeat between the surge easing off and the next round of arguing: The angel stepped up to the bed and extended his palm.

Autumn calmed instantly, her eyes rolling back in her head, her limbs loosening. Tohr's relief, such that he had any, was that at least her suffering had eased off. He was still gripped by the need, but she was no longer killing herself.

"What are you doing to her?" Doc Jane asked.

"Just a trance. And it's not going to last."

Still, that shit was impressive. Vampire minds were stronger than human ones, and the fact that the angel could pull this kind of reaction out of her in her condition suggested he had some special tricks up his sleeve.

Lassiter's eyes met Tohr's. "You sure?"

"About what," he snapped. Fucking hell, he was on the verge of losing his mind here—

"Servicing her."

Tohr laughed in a cold burst. "Not in the cards. *Ever.*"

To prove the point, he lunged to the right, where a tray of syringes was on standby, clearly intended for Autumn. Nabbing two, he punched them into his thighs and shot himself up with whatever was in them.

Lots of shouting at this point, but it didn't last. The drug cocktail, whatever it was, took immediate effect and dropped him to the floor.

His last image before he passed the fuck out was of Autumn's fuzzy eyes watching him go down.

FIFTY-EIGHT

As Qhuinn and John stared at her with studiously blank expressions, Layla straightened in the hard chair she was seated in.

Glancing around the restaurant, she saw only humans calmly enjoying little confections similar to what were on her plates—so it was hard to understand what was wrong.

"Is it something outside?" she whispered, leaning forward. Generally speaking, she found that humans were much the same as vampires—just trying to live their lives without interference. But these two males would know otherwise.

Qhuinn looked at her and smiled in a way that didn't reach his eyes. "After you fed the male, what did you do? What did they?"

She frowned, wishing they'd tell her what was wrong. "Ah . . . well, I tried to talk them into bringing him back to the training center. I figured since his comrade had been treated there, he could be as well."

"Do you believe that his injuries could have been fatal?"

"If I hadn't gotten there in time? Yes, I do. But he was looking better when I left. His breathing was much improved."

"Did you feed from him."

Now the tone in Qhuinn's voice was dire. To the point that, had the boundaries of their relationship not been well set, she might have thought he was jealous.

"No, I did not. You're the only person I've done that with."

The silence afterward told her more than the questions did. The problem was not the humans around them in the restaurant or outside on the streets.

"I don't understand," she said angrily. "He was in need and I took care of him. You of all people should not discriminate simply because he is a soldier and not of noble birth."

"Did you tell anyone where you were going that night? What you did there?"

"The Primale gives us free rein. I have been feeding and caring for fighters for a long time—it is what I do. It is my purpose. I don't under-stand—"

"Have you had any contact with them since then?"

"I was hoping . . . in truth, I had hoped either one or both would ap-pear at the mansion in some official capacity so that I might see the wounded one again. But no, I haven't seen them." She pushed her plates away. "What is so wrong here?"

Qhuinn got to his feet and took out his money roll. Peeling off a couple of twenties, he tossed the bills onto the table. "We have to go back to the compound."

"Why are you being—" She dropped her voice as a few people looked over. "Why are you being like this?"

"Come on."

John Matthew stood up as well, his expression furious, his fists clenched, his jaw hard.

"Layla, come back with us. *Now.*"

To avoid a scene, she rose up and followed them out into the cold air. But she had no intention of taking orders and dematerializing like a good little girl. If the pair of them were going to behave like this, they were damn well going to tell her why.

Planting her feet in the snow, she glared at the two males. "What is wrong with you?"

Her tone of voice was one that even a year ago she would have been shocked to hear coming out of her own mouth. But she was not the same female she had once been.

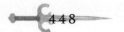

When neither of them replied, she shook her head. "I'm not budging from this stretch of sidewalk until you talk to me."

"We're not doing this, Layla," Qhuinn bit out. "I have to—"

"Unless you tell me what is going on here, the next time either of those soldiers contacts me, you'd better believe I'm going to see them—"

"Then you'd be a traitor, too."

Layla blinked. "I'm sorry—traitor?"

Qhuinn glanced over at John. When the male shrugged and threw up both his palms, there was a long stream of curses.

And then the earth fell out from beneath her feet: "I believe the male you fed is a soldier named Xcor. He is the leader of a rogue squadron of fighters colloquially called the Band of Bastards. And back in the fall, about the time you fed him, he made an attempt on Wrath's life."

"I'm . . . I'm sorry. What . . ." As she weaved on loose legs, John stepped in and held her up. "But how can you be sure . . ."

"I was the one who put those bruises on his face, Layla. I beat the shit out of him—so that Wrath could get home safely and have his gun-shot wound treated. That's our enemy, Layla—sure as the Lessening Society is."

"The other—" She had to clear her throat. "The other soldier, though, the one who took me to him. He was in the training center. Phury brought me to feed him—with Vishous. They told me he was a soldier of worth."

"They said that? Or allowed you to believe that."

"But . . . if he was the enemy, why harbor him?"

"That's Throe, Xcor's second in command. He'd been left for dead by his boss—and we were going to be goddamned if he was dying on our watch."

John took out his cell phone with his free hand and texted quickly, but Layla wasn't tracking anything. Her lungs were burning, her head swimming, her gut twisting.

"Layla?"

Someone was calling out to her, but the panic that claimed her was the only thing she could connect with. As her heart hammered, and her mouth opened wide for air, a blackness descended upon her—

"Fucking hell, Layla!"

Working the rooftops of Caldwell, Xhex kept on Xcor at a distance, tracking him from alley to alley and district to district as he went up against slayers. From what little she saw, the male was an incredibly efficient fighter, that scythe of his doing some serious fucking work.

Damn shame he was a megalomaniac with delusions of the thronal variety.

At all times, she stayed a minimum of a block away. There was no reason to press her luck and run the risk of his tweaking to the fact that he was being followed. She had a feeling he knew, though. If the way he handled the enemy was any indication, he'd be smart enough to assume that Wrath and the Brotherhood would send emissaries out after him, and it wasn't like he was in hiding. He was an individual with a pattern within a limited geographic space: He fought in Caldwell. Every fucking night.

Hello.

As snowflakes began to swirl in the air, the male in question moved position, falling into a jog with his right-hand man, Throe, by his side. Staying on them, she dematerialized to another building. And another. And a third. Where were they going? she thought, as they left the fighting sector. . . .

Half a mile or so later, Xcor paused down at street level, clearly trying to decide between left and right. As Throe came up next to him, angry words were exchanged. Maybe because Throe recognized they were headed in the wrong direction?

While they argued, she glanced at the sky. Checked her watch. Shit. Xcor was going to dematerialize at the end of the night, and that was how she was going to lose him. With her instincts roaming only so far, he was going to get out of range fast when he ghosted away.

But at least she had his grid now. And sooner or later, either he or one of his soldiers was going to get injured and have to be driven out of the city. It was inevitable—and that was how she was going to get them: a scattering of molecules she couldn't track. But a car, a van, a truck, an SUV—that was her way in. And shit knew they were months overdue for a goddamn injury.

Abruptly, Xcor went on the move again, heading around the building she was up on top of, calling her back into action. With grim intensity, she crunched through the crusted snow of the rooftop, circling with him, jogging by HVAC vents and other mechanicals. When she got to the other side, she—

John Matthew.

Shit, her John was not far. What the hell—

He'd told her he was staying home tonight because he was off rotation.

Who was he out with? Qhuinn had given up his man-whore ways . . . wrong part of the city for that, anyway. This was the theater district.

Dematerializing to the lip of the building, she looked down. Across the street, at the head of an alleyway, John was standing in the shadows, with Qhuinn and . . . Layla. Who was up off the ground in the former's arms, looking like she'd passed out?

Shiiiiit. Lot of drama down there. Big drama—the kind that was threatening to fritz out the Chosen's emotional grid altogether.

Scattering her molecules, Xhex re-formed in front of John, startling the bunch of them. "Is she okay?"

We're waiting for Butch, John signed.

"Is he on his way?"

He's tied up across town on cleanup. But we need him now.

Clearly. Whatever had happened here was deep.

"You can put me down now," Layla said gruffly.

Qhuinn just shook his head and kept holding her up off the snow.

"Look, iAm's not far." Xhex took out her cell and flashed it. "Will you let me call him?"

"Yeah, that'd be good," Qhuinn replied.

As she hit up the Shadow, she stared at John while the phone rang. "Hey, iAm, how's you? Yup. Uh-huh—how'd you know? Yeah, I need a set of wheels in the theater district, stat. . . . You are so the man, iAm." She ended the call. "Done. ETA is less than five minutes."

Thank you, John signed.

"What is it?" Qhuinn said as Layla started to stiffen.

Xhex narrowed her eyes on the Chosen's face as the female's grid lit up . . . with arousal. And shame. And pain.

"He's here," the Chosen whispered. "He's not far at all."

John and Qhuinn instantly went for their weapons—which was a good trick on the latter's part, given that he still had Layla up in his arms.

Who the hell was she talking about—

"Xcor," Xhex breathed as she looked in the same direction the Chosen was focusing on. And then connecting the dots, she thought out loud, "Jesus Christ . . . Xcor?"

iAm picked that moment to pull up in a BMW X5, and a split second later, he was out and holding the door open.

Qhuinn lunged for the SUV, and Layla didn't put up any fight as she was shoved in there like an invalid.

"Take the vehicle," iAm told the males. "Use it as your own."

After an abrupt thank-you from Qhuinn, there was a brief moment of now-what as John looked at Xhex.

Bracing herself for some male chest thumping, she wanted to curse—

We'll take her back, John signed. *You stay here and do what you have to.*

Just like that they hopped into iAm's SUV and off they went.

"Do you need help?" iAm asked.

"Thanks, but nope," she murmured as she watched the red brakes flare and then disappear around the far corner. "I got this."

FIFTY-NINE

Xcor had sensed the Chosen female from blocks away. Drawn to her, he had changed direction and headed toward her—until Throe had gotten in the way and argued with him.

Which had been, in a manner of speaking, a good thing. It meant that the male was staying true to his vow to never see her again.

Xcor, on the other hand, had made no such promise—so he had pressed onward, leaving his soldier in the dust. Fates, but he had spent so many days staring up at the cobwebbed beams above his bunk, wondering where she was, what she was doing. How she was doing.

If the Brotherhood ever found out who she had been of aid to in that field, they would be furious—and Wrath, the Blind King, had long been known to live up to his name. Lo, how Xcor still regretted that his second lieutenant had brought her into this mess. She was guileless, an innocent seeking only to help, and they had made a traitor out of her.

She deserved better.

Indeed, it felt insane to pray for his target's mercy in her case. But he did. He prayed that Wrath would spare her if the truth ever came out . . .

Closing in on her, he'd dared not get too close . . . and he found her in the lee of a little café, draped in shadows that, no matter how hard his eyes strained, he could not penetrate.

She was not alone; she was guarded by soldiers—two of them male, one of them female.

Would she sense him? he wondered, his heart beating sure as if he were being chased. Would she tell them he was nearby—

A black vehicle came tearing up to the group, and what got out was something he'd only heard whispers about: Was that a Shadow? An actual living, breathing Shadow?

The Brotherhood had worthy allies, that was for sure—

With speed, his Chosen was carried to the car in the arms of the soldier he had fought with that night at Assail's.

Xcor bared his fangs, but kept the growl to himself. That another male was touching her made him violent to his core. That she might be injured in some way? Made him terrified to the point of tremors.

In the last moment, just before she disappeared into the backseat, she looked his way.

The moment of connection slowed time down until everything from the snowflakes that were falling to the blink of the neon sign beside her to the speed with which she was dispatched out of sight went into single frames, the photographs taken by his mind one by one.

She was not in a white robe, but rather human clothes that he did not favor. Her hair was still pulled up high above her neck, however, accentuating the spectacular features of her face. And as he breathed in, his sinuses hummed from both the cold and her delicate scent.

It was everything he remembered about her. Except now she was clearly in distress, her skin too pale, her eyes too wide, her hand shaking as she raised it to her throat as if to protect herself.

His fighting palm actually reached forward for her, as if there was something he could do to relieve her suffering, as if he could help her in some way.

It was a gesture that would have to remain forever in the shadows. She knew he was here, and that was probably why they were taking her away.

And she was scared of him now. Likely because she knew he was her enemy.

The two males packed in with her, the taller one getting behind the wheel, the one he'd fought slipping in beside her in the back.

Without his being aware of it, his palm sneaked inside his jacket, and found his gun. The temptation to flash into the path of that vehicle, kill the two males, and take what he wanted was so great, he actually shifted his position down the street.

But he could not do that to her. He was not his fath—he was *not* the Bloodletter. He would not torture her conscience for the rest of her days with such violence—because surely she would extrapolate and blame herself for the deaths.

No, if he ever had her, it would be because she came unto him of her free will. Which was an impossibility, of course.

And so . . .he let her go. He stepped not into the path of the motorcar to put a bullet through the forehead of the driver. He did not then rush forth, shoot the one in the backseat, and turn about to kill the female soldier who was, as of this moment, directly behind him by about half a block. He did not infiltrate the vehicle, lock the Chosen in and drive her off to somewhere warm and safe.

Whereupon he would take those dreadful human dressings from her skin . . . and replace them with his naked body.

Dropping his head, he closed his eyes and recalibrated his thoughts, reining them in, steering them away from the fantasy. Indeed, he would not even use her as a way to find the Brothers: that would be signing her death warrant sure as if he could actually write his own name.

No, he would not use her as a tool in this war. He had already compromised her too much.

Pivoting in the snow, he faced the direction of the one who was behind him. That the soldiers had left with the Chosen instead of fighting with him was logical. A female such as she was a highly valuable commodity, and they'd likely called in many reinforcements for the trip to wherever they were going.

Interesting that the one they had picked to stay behind was of the fairer sex. They must have assumed he'd give chase.

"I sense you clear as day, female," he called out.

To her credit, she stepped into the light of a doorway down the alley. With short hair and a tight, powerful build that was encased in leather, she was definitely a female fighter.

Well, wasn't this a night for surprises: If she was associated with the Brotherhood, he had to assume she was dangerous so this could be fun.

And yet, as she confronted him, she took out no weapons. She was prepared, though—indeed, her stance told him she was ready to do what she must. But she was not on the offensive.

Xcor narrowed his eyes. "Too ladylike to fight?"

"You are not mine to take."

"So whose am I." When she didn't reply, he knew there was a game afoot. The question was, what kind. "Nothing to say, female?"

He took a step toward her. And another. Just to test where the boundaries were. Sure enough, she didn't retreat, but instead slowly unzipped the front of her jacket as if she were ready to get at her guns.

Standing in that pool of light, with the snow falling around her and her boots planted on the white, fluffy ground, her black figure cut quite a picture. He wasn't attracted to her, however—mayhap it would be easier if he was. Someone with her intrinsic harshness might fare better in the face of his . . . face, as it were.

"You appear rather aggressive, female."

"If you force me to kill you, I will."

"Ah. Well, I shall keep that mind. Tell me, do you tarry here for the pleasure of my company?"

"I doubt there'd be much pleasure in it."

"Right you are. I am not known for my social graces."

She was tracking him, he thought. That was the reason she was here. In fact, he had had the sense since the earlier part of the night that there had been a shadow on him.

"I'm afraid I shall have to be going," he drawled. "I have a feeling our paths shall cross again, however."

"You can bet your life on it."

He inclined his head toward her . . . and promptly disappeared himself far away. Whatever her tracking skills were, she couldn't follow molecules. No one was that good.

Not even his Chosen could do that—and thank the Fates for it. For truth, the thought had long lingered in his mind that she might find him if she wished, her blood in him a beacon she could follow for quite some time.

But she hadn't done so, and she wouldn't. She was not of the war—

His phone went off just as he came back into his physical form on the shores of the Hudson far from downtown. Taking the black device out, he looked at the screen. The picture of an old-fashioned dandy was showing beside writing and numerals he could not decipher—which indicated his contact within the *glymera* was reaching out to him.

He hit the button with green lettering on it. "How lovely to hear from you, Elan," he murmured. "How ever are you doing this fine eve. They are?

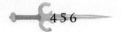

Indeed. Yes. I shall get back to you on a location—but tell them aye. We shall meet with them posthaste."

Perfect, he thought as he hit the red button. The splintering faction of the *glymera* wanted to meet in person. Things were finally starting to move.

About time.

Staring out over the river, he let his aggression flow, but the surge didn't last. Inevitably, his thoughts returned to his Chosen and that horrid expression on her face.

She knew who he was now.

And as all females did, she viewed him as a monster.

Riding in the back of iAm's SUV, Qhuinn kept a lookout on all sides of the vehicle in case they were being trailed. He'd also called in V and Rhage to flank the BMW on a just-in-case.

Not that he'd told them it was the Bastards he was worried about. They had assumed it was *lessers*, and he'd let them go with that one.

And John wasn't driving back to the compound—no reason to get anywhere near home base. Instead, they were going to head out into the 'burbs and go in circles, staying in the human-heavy neighborhoods until Layla had time enough to recover and dematerialize back to the mansion.

On that note, he glanced over at her. She was staring out the window beside her, her chest rising and falling way too fast.

But, yeah, finding out you'd helped the enemy—probably saved his life—was not the kind of thing anyone would handle well.

He leaned over and put his hand on her leg, giving it a squeeze. "It's okay, baby girl."

She didn't turn her head to him. Just shook it. "How can you say that."

"You didn't know."

"He stayed back in town. He didn't follow us."

Good to know. "You'll let me know if that changes."

"Absolutely." Her voice was dead. "In a moment."

Qhuinn cursed under his breath. "Layla. Look at me." When she didn't, he put his forefinger on her chin. "Hey, you didn't know who he was."

Layla closed her eyes, as if she wished she could return to whatever night she had met the guy and do everything over.

"Come here," he said, pulling her into an embrace.

She came stiffly to him, and as he rubbed her back, the tension in her muscles was legion.

"What if the king turns me out?" she said into his pectoral. "What if Phury—"

"They won't. They'll understand."

As she shuddered against him, he glanced up at John in the rearview mirror and shook his head at his best friend. Mouthing the words, he said silently, *Let's just drive her in. Xcor stayed back in town.*

John cocked a brow, and then nodded.

After all, blood sense didn't lie—although unfortunately, it was a sword that cut both ways. The good news was that the *mhis* V threw up around the compound would keep anyone on the outside from finding her—which was the reason Throe had been fed in the first place. And at least that connection with Layla was fading with every passing night, even with the Chosen's blood being so pure.

"I've got nothing of my own," Layla said roughly. "Nothing. Even my service can be taken away from me."

"Shhh . . . ain't going to happen. I won't let it."

Man, he prayed that wasn't a lie. And they damn well had to tell the king and the Primale right away: Their first stop, after they took her to Doc Jane's, was going to be Wrath's study. Those two just had to understand where she'd been coming from—she'd been manipulated by the enemy, exploited like any other resource into doing something she never would have volunteered for in a million years.

He wished he'd killed Xcor when he'd had the chance . . .

A good thirty minutes later, John turned off onto the rear road to the training center, and it was another ten before they finally pulled into the parking garage.

The first clue something was off came when Qhuinn stepped out onto the curb: His skin tightened up in a rush, his blood heating to a boil in his veins for no good reason. And then he popped a giant, throbbing erection.

Frowning, he glanced around. And John did the same as the guy cracked his door and got out from behind the steering wheel.

There was . . . some kind of mojo working in the parking lot. What the fuck?

"Ah, right, okay, let's get you to Doc Jane," Qhuinn said as he took Layla's elbow, and made sure the front of his hips was covered by the tails of his leather jacket.

"I'm fine. Honestly—"

"Then that's just what the good doctor will tell—"

As John opened the door to the place and they all stepped inside, Qhuinn lost his train of thought as a wall of hormones smacked right into him. Looking down at his pelvis, he couldn't believe he was suddenly about to orgasm.

"Someone's in her needing," Layla announced. "I don't think you two should go in—"

Far down the hall, Doc Jane all but jumped out of one of the examination rooms. "You have to leave—Qhuinn and John, you've got to go—"

"Who's—" Qhuinn had to close his eyes and slow his breathing down: The motion was causing his cock to rub against his button fly, threatening a messy explosion. "Who is—"

As some kind of wave intensified, he lost the ability to speak.

Fuck, it was like he'd just come through his transition and was surrounded by naked females in all-access positions.

"It's Autumn," Jane said, running toward them and ushering them back out into the parking lot. "Are you okay, Layla?"

"I'm fine—"

"She needs a quick physical," Qhuinn mumbled as he turned for the Shadow's car. "Just came close to passing out. Text me when you're done, Layla, 'kay?"

John was walking like a scarecrow as well—stiffly and without any coordination. Then again, when you had a baseball bat in your pants, you were hardly going to Fred Astaire around.

As the heavy steel door shut them out, things got a little better, and by the time they had driven through the series of gates, short of a raging hard-on, he was feeling more rational.

"Jesus," Qhuinn said. "Bottle that shit and the Viagra boys are out of business."

Behind the wheel, John whistled an agreement.

As the guy drove them around the base of the mountain and approached the main house from the front, Qhuinn squirmed in his leathers.

He hadn't done much sexually since . . . well, shit, almost a year ago, when he'd had some private time with that red-haired guy at the Iron Mask. After that, he hadn't had much interest in anything or anyone, male or female. He didn't even wake up hard anymore.

Hell, given the length of his dry spell, he'd begun to think that he'd just burned through his allotment of orgasms: Considering how much fucking he'd done after his transition, it sure as shit seemed possible.

But here he was, itching in his seat.

Next door, John was doing the same, moving this way and that. Jacking himself up, pushing back.

When the mansion finally made an appearance out of the *mhis*, Qhuinn dreaded going inside. There didn't seem anything even remotely sexy or appealing about heading up to his room alone, jerking off once or twice, and then resuming his vigil in front of a dark TV screen.

I've got nothing of my own. Nothing. Even my service can be taken away from me.

Layla was so right about that: Although everyone made him welcome here, the bottom line was, he was allowed to hang because he served a purpose for John, as *ahstrux nohtrum*.

Like Layla, however, he could be fired.

And as for his future? He was certainly never going to be mated, because he wasn't going to condemn some female to a loveless union, and he was never going to have any young—although, considering his mismatched eyes, maybe that was a good thing.

Bottom line, he was staring down the barrel of countless centuries with no real home, no true family, no blood of his own.

As he rubbed a hand through his hair and wondered whether there was any possibility his cock would magically deflate . . . he knew just what that Chosen meant when it came to empty.

SIXTY

Xhex needed intel. Stat.

When Xcor had dematerialized away from her, he'd gone outside the scope of her radar within seconds. And yeah, she had a bead on his direction, but only an asshole wouldn't camo the way to his hideout.

Sure enough, as she followed what she could of him, she found herself stuck on the shores of the Hudson not far from her house: The trail got cold at that point, and not because the frigid north wind was blowing down the river.

She kicked a random snowdrift and paced around. Retraced her steps back to the theater district. Scanned the rest of the city, going rooftop to rooftop.

Nothing.

She ended up back on top of that building where she'd seen John and the others, stalking around and cursing like a sailor. In the absence of physical clues, she was forced to go with the only other thing she had: the drama outside that dessert place.

Taking out her phone, she texted John and waited. And waited. And . . . waited.

Did they get ambushed on the way back?

She texted again. Hit up Qhuinn—and got no reply.

Damn it, what if something had happened? Just because Xcor had appeared to leave the city, that didn't mean he couldn't cycle around and intersect iAm's SUV. Meanwhile, she was here chasing her tail like an idiot—

Just as she was about to start another round of near-panicked texting, John hit her back: *@ hm safe. Srry wz dwn in clinic.*

Dialing back on her chick-out, she took a deep breath and texted back: *We need to talk about Layla. Let me come to the house.*

It was possible that Qhuinn wouldn't want to leave the Chosen in her condition, and Xhex didn't want John to drag his *ahstrux nohtrum* out just for a meeting.

Instead of waiting for a response, she flashed herself over to the mansion and strode up the steps and into the vestibule. The inner door opened immediately, and Fritz appeared frazzled.

"Good evening, my lady."

"What's wrong?"

The butler bowed and shuffled backward. "Oh, indeed. Yes. Whom are you here to see?"

There was a time when that wouldn't have been a question. "John. Is he at the clinic?"

"Oh . . . no. No, definitely not there. He is upstairs."

Xhex frowned. "Is there any problem?"

"Oh, no. Please, madam, go forth."

Bullshit there wasn't something going on. She crossed the mosaic apple tree at a jog and took the stairs two at a time. When she got to the second floor, she hesitated.

Even out in the hall, she could catch the scent of sex—a mixed bag of it, actually, suggesting there were multiples going on. Literally.

And didn't that make her feel like throwing up.

As she approached John's door, she braced herself for whatever could be on the other side. Layla was trained as an *ehros*, and Qhuinn had long been up for anything—and maybe this separation had led her mate into the arms of others.

With a dead heart, she knocked loudly. "John? It's me."

Closing her eyes, she imagined naked bodies freezing, people looking

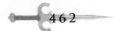

back and forth, John scrambling to get something to cover himself. There was no reading grids—she was too scattered to pull that off. No sorting through the scents, either—she was having enough trouble staying on her feet because she knew at least one of them was John's.

"I know you're in there."

Instead of the door opening, she got a text on her phone: *Am soz— busy. Can I cm find u l8r?*

Fuck that and the horse it rode in on.

Xhex grabbed the doorknob, twisted hard enough to break the thing off, and shoved her way—

Holy. Shit.

John was by himself on his bed, lying on top of twisted sheets, his naked body gleaming in the light that bled in from the bathroom. One hand was between his legs, his big fist locked on his thick cock . . . the other was gripping the headboard for leverage as he worked himself, his teeth bared, the muscles in his shoulders and neck standing out in stark relief as he strained.

Shiiiiit. His lower abdomen was slick from other orgasms, and yet he seemed starved for release.

Fevered eyes met hers as his hand stilled. *Go,* he mouthed. *Please . . .*

She quickly stepped inside and shut the door. This was not something anyone else needed to see.

Please! he demanded.

Please, indeed, she thought to herself, her own body responding, her own blood starting to pump.

Stepping over the crumpled discards of what he'd been wearing in the theater district, she could think only about how much she had missed the carnal side of him. It was as if she had been shut down during these long months—and yeah, it would have been far better for her to walk out, let him deal with his rock-and-a-hard-place by his lonesome, and reconvene later.

But, God, she had missed being his female.

I can't stop, he mouthed. *Autumn in her needing—got too close.*

Ah. That explained it. Except . . . "Is my mother okay?"

At Jane's, and yes.

God, that poor female. To have to suffer through that again after all she'd been through. But at least Jane would ease the suffering—assuming Tohr didn't. . . .

Right, she was so not getting close to that one.

Xhex, you have . . . to go. . . .

"What if I don't want to."

At that, his body undulated wildly, sure as if she were already touching him, and he orgasmed hard, his grip slipping up and down as he came all over the muscled expanse of his lower belly.

Well, wasn't that a very well-spoken answer: He wanted her, too.

Xhex stepped up to the edge of the bed and reached out, brushing his churning thigh with her fingertips. The light contact was enough to keep his release going, his hips thrusting up, his sex kicking, his warrior body contracting as the pleasure rocked through him.

Bending down, she shoved his pumping hand aside and captured him with her mouth, sucking him off, finishing him the right way as he thrashed in the sheets. And as soon as he was done, at least with that particular release, he stilled for only a nanosecond before sitting up and reaching for her.

She went to him with ease, kissing him as he pulled her on top of his body. His hands, those big, familiar hands, roamed everywhere . . . until they settled on her ass, and jacked her upward so he could nestle his face into her breasts—

With a quick slash of his fangs, he bit through her muscle shirt, and latched onto her nipple, sucking, and licking as she helped him out, pulling her jacket off, ditching her weapons, and—

John flipped her over onto her back and snarled soundlessly at her leathers.

Things didn't go well for them—which, considering how tough cowhide was, said something about all the get-naked that was happening. At least he knew better than to mess with her cilices, though.

As soon as they were in position, he pushed into her with a jab, and the sting of the stretch was enough to throw her right into a bone-bending orgasm. He followed, joining her, their bodies working each other while she cried out.

And still he kept riding her, the relentless pounding giving her more of exactly what she needed.

Baring her fangs, she waited until he paused for a moment—then she struck. Biting him hard, she shoved him over onto his back, forcing him flat on the mattress so she could straddle him. And as she held him down by the shoulders and drew against his throat, she resumed the fucking, her thighs lifting her up and pushing her down, working his erection.

John's surrender to her was complete. His arms stayed to the sides, his strength ceded to her, his body hers to use until she drained him dry up at his neck and down at his hips.

As she took him, his eyes stayed locked on her face, the love shining out of them so great, they were a pair of blue suns raining warmth all over her.

How in the world could she ever live without him . . .

Releasing his throat temporarily, she rode out the current orgasm, burying her face into his shoulder as things got so violent she couldn't keep contact with his throat. But she knew his vein was hers for the taking, as soon as it was over . . .

Man, life was complicated. But the truth was simple.

He was her home.

He was where she belonged.

Rolling to the side, she encouraged him to follow her, and he came with her as easy as water, as hot as fire. It was his turn to feed . . . and given the way his eyes zeroed in on her jugular, he agreed with her.

"Let me seal you first," she said as she went for her puncture marks.

He took her wrist and held her back, shaking his head. *No—I want to bleed for you.*

Xhex closed her eyes, her throat tightening.

It was hard to say where this was going to lead them, because she never would have predicted their split in the first place. But it was so damned good to be home . . . even if this was just a short stay.

Hours passed, the night waning and dawn arriving; and then the sun rose from the lip of the horizon, ascending to its noonday heights, washing the snow-covered mountain with light.

Autumn was unaware of any of this—and that would have been true whether she was down in the clinic or up at the mansion . . . or out in the snow.

In fact, she might as well have been directly in the sunshine.

She was on fire.

The blazing heat in her womb reminded her of the birthing of Xhexania, the agony rising to heights that made her wonder if death wasn't coming for her, before easing off just enough so she could catch her breath and prepare for the next peak. And as with labor, the cycling persisted, the moments of relenting becoming farther and farther apart until the pain of the need filled out the contours of her body and took over all movement, all breath, all thought.

It had not been like this before. Back when she'd been with that *symphath*, the needing hadn't been half this strong. . . .

Or half this long . . .

After however many hours of torture, she had no more tears left, no more sobs, not even any twitches. She just lay in stillness, barely breathing, her heartbeat sluggish, her eyes closed as her body was yet assaulted internally.

It was hard to pinpoint exactly when the tipping point came upon her, but gradually the throbbing between her legs and the burning in her pelvis drifted away, the rigors of the needing replaced with an abiding soreness in her joints and her muscles from all the straining she'd done.

When she could finally raise her head, her neck cracked loudly, and she groaned as her face hit a wall of some sort. Frowning, she tried to orient herself . . . oh, indeed, she was at the foot of the bed, pressed up against the short board at its end.

She laid her head back down for a while. With the boiling heat easing to a mere simmer, she began to feel cold, and she fumbled around for a sheet, or a blanket, or a cover of any sort. There was nothing—all was on the floor: She was naked on a bare mattress—clearly she'd ripped off even the fitted sheet.

Summoning what little energy she had, she attempted to push her torso up and lift her head. She made little progress. It was as if there was glue holding her down . . .

Eventually, she rose up.

The trip to the bathroom was as arduous and treacherous as a hike up a mountainside, but lo, the joy with which she beheld the shower and turned it on.

As temperate water fell generously from the spout anchored upon the wall, she sat down on the tile beneath it, tucking her heels up against her bottom, hugging herself around her knees. As she laid her head to the side, the gentle spray washed away the salt of her tears and her sweat.

The shivers turned violent shortly thereafter.

"Autumn?" came Doc Jane's voice from the room beyond.

Her rattling teeth prevented her from replying, but the shower said enough: The other female appeared in the doorway, and then ventured further into the bath, until she pulled back the cloth curtain and knelt down so they were eye-to-eye.

"How're you feeling?"

Abruptly, Autumn had to shield her face as she began crying.

Hard to know whether the outburst was because the needing had finally passed, or because she was so tired she had no boundaries left . . . or because the last thing she remembered before everything became a blur was the sight of Tohr driving those two needles into his thighs and falling to the floor.

"Autumn, can you hear me?"

"Yes . . ." she croaked.

"I'd like to get you back in bed if you're done washing up. There's a lot of heat in here, and I'm worried about your blood pressure."

"I'm c-c-cold."

"That's fever chills. I'm going to turn off the water now, okay?"

She nodded, because she didn't have the wherewithal to do anything else.

When the warm rain stopped falling, the rattling inside her skin got worse as the cold rushed in and traveled across her tender flesh. Soon enough, however, a soft blanket was draped around her shoulders.

"Can you stand?" When Autumn nodded again, she was helped up, dressed in a light sheath and escorted back over to the bed—which had magically been remade with fresh sheets and blankets.

Stretching out, she was aware only of the tears that seeped from the corners of both eyes, an endless, slow stream of them, hot against her cold face.

"Shhh, you're okay," the healer said, as she sat down on the edge of the mattress. "You're all right—it's over. . . ."

As a gentle hand stroked her wet hair back, the tone of Doc Jane's voice, more than the female's actual words, helped the most.

And then there was a straw sticking out of a soda can, brought close to her mouth.

One draw of that cold, sweet nectar and Autumn's eyes rolled back into her head. "Oh . . . blessed Virgin Scribe . . . what is that?"

"Ginger ale. And you're welcome—hey, not too fast."

After she'd finished the whole lot of it, she lay back again as a band was shuffled onto her arm and puffed up before being deflated. Next, a cold disk was pressed to her chest in a couple of places. A light was flashed in her eyes.

"May I have some more ginger ale, please?" she asked.

"Your wish is my command."

The healer did one better than that, returning not only with another chilly tin can and a straw, but some plain crackers that tasted like absolutely nothing and were total heaven in her belly.

She was making quick work of the sustenance when she realized the healer had sat down in a chair and was saying nothing.

Autumn stopped eating. "Do you not have any other patients?"

"Just one, and she was fine when she got here."

"Oh." Autumn picked up another of the crackers. "What are these called?"

"Saltines. Of all the drugs I dispense down here, sometimes there's nothing better."

"They're wonderful." She put the flaky, dusty square in her mouth and bit down. As a silence persisted, she said, "You want to know why I refused the drugs."

"It's none of my business. But I do think you need to talk to someone about it."

"A professional of some order?"

"Yeah."

"There is nothing wrong with letting nature take its course." Autumn glanced over. "But I begged you not to get him. I told you not to call him."

"I had no choice."

Tears threatened, but she forced them away. "I didn't want him to see me like that. Wellsie—"

"What about her."

Autumn jerked around in surprise, rattling the crackers, splashing soda out over her hand. In the doorway, Tohrment loomed, a great dark shadow that filled the jambs.

Doc Jane rose up. "I'll just go check on Layla again. Your vitals are good, and I'll bring a proper meal back with me when I come."

And then they were alone.

He didn't approach the bed, but stayed by the door, settling back against the wall. With his brows down tight and his arms linked over his chest, he was self-contained and explosive at the same time.

"What the hell was that all about," he said harshly.

Autumn put the crackers and the can aside, then busied herself folding and unfolding the edge of the blanket.

"I asked you a question."

Autumn cleared her throat. "I told Doc Jane not to summon you—"

"Did you think if you suffered I'd come and help you out?"

"Not at all—"

"You sure about that? Because what did you think Jane was going to do when you refused to be treated?"

"If you don't believe me, ask the healer. I instructed her specifically not to call upon you. I knew that that would be too much for you—how could it not be after—"

"This is not about my *shellan*. This has nothing to do with her."

"I'm not so sure about that—"

"*Trust* me."

After that, he didn't say anything else. He just stood there with that tense body and those hard eyes, staring at her as if he had never seen her before.

"Where are your thoughts?" she asked quietly.

He shook his head from side to side. "You don't want to know."

"Yes, I do."

"I think I've been fooling myself all these months."

As she felt the shivering from the shower return, she knew the cause was not a temperature imbalance in her bones. Not anymore. "How so."

"Now isn't the time for this."

As he turned to go, she had the very clear sense that she was not going to see him again. Ever.

"Tohr," she said in a rough voice. "There was no manipulation on my part—you need to believe that. I didn't want you to service me—I would never put you through that."

After a moment, he looked over his shoulder, his eyes dead. "You know what? Fuck all that. It's almost worse that you didn't want me in here with you. Because the other option is that you're mentally ill."

"I beg your pardon." Autumn frowned. "And I am utterly sane."

"No, you're not. If you were, you wouldn't have chosen to put yourself through that—"

"I just didn't want the drugs. Your extrapolation is extreme—"

"Oh, yeah? Well, brace yourself, you're really not going to like my next conclusion. I'm beginning to think you're with me to punish yourself."

She recoiled so sharply, her neck cracked again. "I most certainly am not—"

"What better way to steep yourself in misery than to be with a male who loves someone else."

"That is *not* why I'm with you."

"How would you know, Autumn. You've been making a martyr out of yourself for centuries. You've been a servant, a maid, a laundress—and you've been fucking me for the last few months—which brings us back to my point about clinical insanity—"

"How dare you judge my inner convictions," she hissed. "You know nothing of what I think or feel!"

"Bullshit. You're in love with me." He pivoted to face her and put up his palm to stop her commenting. "Don't bother denying it—you tell me in your sleep every day. So let's build a case. You clearly like to punish yourself. And you know damn well the only reason I'm with you is to get Wellsie out of the In Between. So don't I just fit your pattern to a T—"

"Get out," she snapped. *"Get out of here."*

"What—you don't want me to stay so you can make it hurt so good some more?"

"You bastard."

"You got that right. I've been using you, and the only person it's working for *is* you—God knows it's gotten me nowhere. The good news is that this whole thing"—he gestured back and forth between them—"is going to give you a terrific excuse to torture yourself even longer— Oh, don't bother with the denials. That *symphath* was your fault. I'm your fault. The weight of the world is all your fault, because you enjoy being the victim—"

"Get out!" she screamed.

"You know, the whole indignant routine is a little hard to take seriously, considering you spent the last twelve hours suffering—"

"Get out!"

"—when you didn't have to."

She threw the first thing within reach at him—the soda can. But his reflexes were so good, he just caught it in his big hand . . . and then walked it right back over to the rolling table.

"You might as well own the fact that you're a masochist." He set the thing down with deliberate finesse, as if he were daring her to pitch it at him again. "And I've been your drug of choice lately. But I'm not doing that anymore . . . and neither are you, at least not with me. This shit between us . . . it's not healthy for me. It's not healthy for you. And it's all we are together. All we'll ever have." He cursed low and hard. "Look, I'm sorry, Autumn. For the whole fucking thing—I'm really sorry. I should have stopped this long ago, long before it went as far as it did—and all I can do to make it right is to end it right now." He shook his head, his eyes growing haunted. "I was part of you self-destructing once, and I remember all too well the blisters that came from digging your grave. I'm not doing that again. I can't. You will always have my sympathy for everything you've been through, but I've got my own shit to deal with."

As he fell silent, she wrapped her arms around herself. In a whisper, she said, "All this just because I didn't want to be knocked out?"

"It's not just about the needing. You know it isn't. If I were you, I'd take Jane's advice and talk to someone. Maybe . . ." He shrugged. "I don't know. I don't fucking know anything anymore. The only thing I'm sure of is that we can't keep doing this. It's getting us both worse than nowhere."

"You feel something for me," she said, kicking her chin up. "I know it's not love, but you feel—"

"I feel sorry for you. That's where I'm at. Because you're just a victim. You're no one but a victim who likes to suffer. Even if I could fall in love with you, there's nothing about you to get truly attached to. You're just a ghost who's not really here . . . any more than I am. And in our case, two wrongs do not make a right."

At that, he turned his back on her and walked out, leaving her to reel in pain and loss, leaving her to confront his twisted vision of her past, her present, her future . . . leaving her alone in a way that had nothing to do with the fact that she was by herself.

The door, as it shut behind him, made no sound whatsoever.

SIXTY-ONE

As Tohr stepped out into the hall, he was crazed, incoherent, on the verge of a violent breakdown. Jesus Christ, he had to get out of here, get away from her. And to think he'd called her insane? He was a fucking madman at the moment.

When he looked up, Lassiter was right in front of him. "Not now—"

The angel hauled back and cocked him so hard, he didn't just see stars; he saw whole fucking galaxies of them.

As he hit the concrete wall behind him, the angel grabbed the front of his shirt and slammed him back again, rattling his molars.

When his vision finally cleared, that pierced face was nothing short of a demon's mask, the features distorted by the kind of anger that required a gravedigger's cleanup.

"You're an asshole," Lassiter barked. "A total fucking asshole."

Tohr tilted to the side and spit out blood. "Was it Maury or Ellen who taught you to judge character."

A long finger was shoved into his face. "Listen to me very carefully, because I'm going to say this only once."

"Wouldn't you rather hit me again? I know I'd get more out of it—"

Lassiter threw him into the wall again. "Shut up. And listen to me. *You win.*"

"Excuse me?"

"You've got what you wanted. Wellsie's condemned for eternity—"

"What the—"

The third slam cut him off. "It's over. Done." He pointed to the closed door of Autumn's room. "You just killed your chance when you ripped her apart."

Tohr lost it, his emotions detonating. "You don't know what the *fuck* you're talking about—you don't know *shit*! You haven't had a clue about any of this, not me, not her—not your job! What the fuck have you done here for the last year? Nothing! You've been sitting on your ass watching talk shows while my Wellsie's disappearing! You're a goddamn waste of time!"

"Really. Okay—you're so fucking brilliant, how about this." Lassiter released him and stepped back. "I quit."

"You can't quit—"

Lassiter flashed his middle finger. "I just did."

The angel turned away and stalked down the hall.

"You're fucking quitting! That's great—fucking great! Talk about staying true to someone's character, you selfish son of a bitch!"

All he got was another bird flipped over the shoulder.

With a vicious curse, Tohr made a move to go after the guy, but then stopped himself. Spinning around, he threw out a quick jab, punching the concrete so hard, he felt his knuckles break. And what do you know, the pounding pain in the back of his hand wasn't even close to the agony in his chest.

He was absolutely raw, inside and out.

Taking off in the opposite direction from that angel, he found himself at the heavy steel door that opened into the parking lot. With no clue what he was doing or where he was going, he sent it flying wide on its hinges, and marched out into the chilly air, going to the right, heading up the incline, passing the empty spaces that were demarcated with yellow paint.

He went all the way to the back, to the farthest wall, and sat his ass down on the cold, hard asphalt, his shoulders against the damp concrete.

As he breathed hard, he felt like he was in the goddamn tropics—likely the tail end of the needing's effect on his body: Even though he'd been out like a light from the drugs, he had had plenty of exposure, his balls aching as if he'd put them in a vise, his cock still hard, his joints sore as if he had strained even in the morphine haze.

Gritting his teeth, he sat alone and stared straight ahead, into the darkness.

This was the only safe place for him at the moment.

Probably for a while.

When Layla heard shouting, she poked her head out of the gymnasium to see who was yelling—and immediately ducked back inside. Tohr and Lassiter were having a set-to, and that was not anything she had to get involved with.

She had her own problems.

In spite of Autumn's needing, she had stayed down in the clinic for the night, knowing she had spent some time up at the Sanctuary recently, so there was no reason to worry about her cycle. More to the point, however, she had nowhere else to go. Qhuinn and John were no doubt talking to the king and the Primale at the main house, and soon enough she would be summoned to learn of her fate.

Faced with possible exile—or worse, death for aiding a traitor—she had spent the hours upon hours upon hours walking around the edges of the gym's honey-colored floor, passing the bleachers and the benches, and the entrances into the PT suite, and the doors out into the corridor. And then going back by them all again.

Her anxiety was such that it spooled out tension like a wool spinner, the twisted threads reaching up to encircle her throat and winding down to constrict her gut.

She thought relentlessly about Xcor and his second lieutenant. She had been used by them both—but especially the latter. Xcor hadn't wanted to partake of her vein. He had fought it—and when she had overridden him, there had been deep regret in his eyes because he had known exactly what position he was putting her in. The other soldier had had no such compulsion.

Indeed, she blamed him—whatever fell upon her head, it was his doing. Mayhap she would be reincarnated as a ghost and could haunt him for the rest of his nights . . . of course, that was assuming she would be put to death. And if she was not, what was she going to do? Surely they would strip her of her duties herein as well as her Chosen status. Where would

she go? She had nothing of her own, nothing that had not been provided at the behest of the king or the Primale.

Continuing on her loop, she confronted yet again the emptiness of her breathing days, and wondered what purpose she would serve in the future—

The door opened at the far end, and she stopped.

All four of them had come to find her: The king, the Primale, Qhuinn and John Matthew.

Straightening her spine, she crossed the gym down its middle, holding their eyes. When she got close enough, she curtsied down to the floor and did not wait to be addressed. Court manners were the least of her problems.

"My lord. I am prepared to accept all responsibility—"

"Rise, Chosen." A hand appeared in front of her face. "Rise and be at ease."

As she gasped and looked up, the king's smile was gentle, and he didn't wait for her to respond. Bending to her, he gathered her palm in his and helped her up from her supplication. And when she glanced at the Primale, his eyes seemed impossibly kind.

She just shook her head and addressed Wrath. "My lord, I fed your enemy—"

"Did you know who he was at the time?"

"No, but—"

"Did you believe that you were helping a fallen soldier?"

"Well, yes, but—"

"Have you sought him out again?"

"Absolutely not, but—"

"Did you in fact tell John and Qhuinn where he was when you were leaving town last night."

"Yes, but—"

"Enough with the *buts* then." The king smiled again and put his hand to her face, brushing her cheek lightly in spite of his blindness. "You've got a big heart, and they knew it. They took advantage of your trust, and used you."

Phury nodded. "I should have told you who you were feeding in the first place, but the war's a messy, nasty business, and I didn't want you to get sucked into it. It never dawned on me that Throe would seek you out—but I shouldn't be surprised. The Band of Bastards is ruthless to the core."

In a rush, she put her free hand up to her mouth, holding in a sob. "I'm so sorry—I swear to the both of you—I had no idea—"

Phury stepped in and drew her against him. "It's okay. Everything's okay. . . . I don't want you to think about this again."

As she turned her head to the side to rest it upon his heavy pectoral, she knew that wasn't possible. Unwittingly or not, she had betrayed the only family she had, and that wasn't the kind of thing someone could just shrug off—even if her stupidity was forgiven. And these past tense hours, when her fate had been unknown and her loneliness revealed to its fullest extent, were not going to be brushed away, either.

"The only thing I ask," Wrath said, "is that if he contacts you again—if any of them do—you tell us immediately."

She pulled free and had the temerity to reach for the king's dagger hand. As if Wrath knew what she wanted, he gave his palm over to her readily, the great black diamond flashing on his finger.

Bowing her head and placing her lips upon the symbol of the monarchy, she spoke in the Old Language. *"With all that I have, and all that I am, I so swear."*

As she made the pact with her king, in front of the Primale and two witnesses, an image of Xcor played across her mind's eye. She remembered every detail about his face and his warrior's body—

From out of nowhere, a shot of heat speared through her.

It mattered not, however. Her body might be a traitor; her heart and soul were not.

Straightening, she stared at the king. "Let me help you find him," she heard herself say. "My blood is in his veins. I can—"

Qhuinn cut her off. "Absolutely not. No fucking way—"

She ignored him. "Let me prove to you my fealty."

Wrath shook his head. "You don't have to. You're a female of worth, and we're not endangering your life."

"I agree," the Primale said. "We'll deal with those fighters. They're nothing for you to worry about—and now I want you to take care of yourself. You look exhausted, and you must be starved—go get yourself some food and have a sleep at the mansion."

Wrath nodded. "I'm sorry we took so long to come to you. Beth and I were down in Manhattan having some R and R, and we just arrived back at nightfall."

Layla nodded and agreed with everything else that was said, but only because she was suddenly too exhausted to stay on her feet much longer.

Fortunately, the king and the Primale left soon thereafter, and then Qhuinn and John took over, leading her back to the mansion, taking her to the kitchen, and sitting her down at the counter as they popped open refrigerator and pantry doors.

It was sweet of them to want to wait on her, especially given that they didn't know their way around even boiling an egg. The thought of food turned her stomach, however, making her gag.

"No, please," she said, waving away leftovers from First Meal. "Oh . . . dearest Virgin Scribe . . . *no.*"

As they fixed themselves plates of turkey and mashed potatoes and some kind of broccoli mix, she tried not to see or smell any of it.

"What's the matter?" Qhuinn said as he slid onto the stool next to her.

"I don't know." She should have been relieved that Wrath and Phury were so forgiving of her transgression. Instead, she was more anxious than ever. "I don't feel right . . . I want to help. I want to make amends. I—"

John began signing something from over by the microwave—but whatever it was, Qhuinn shook his head and refused to translate.

"What is he saying?" she demanded. When she got no response, she put her hand on the male's arm. "What's he saying, Qhuinn?"

"Nothing. John ain't sayin' no goddamn thing."

The other male didn't appreciate the shutout, but he didn't argue either as he prepared a second plate of food, no doubt for Xhex.

After John excused himself to go feed his *shellan*, the silence in the kitchen was broken only by the sound of Qhuinn's silverware against his plate.

It was not long before she was ready to jump out of her skin, and to keep from screaming, she began to pace around.

"You really should rest," Qhuinn murmured.

"I can't seem to settle."

"Try to eat something."

"Dearest Virgin Scribe, no. My stomach's a mess—and it's so hot in here."

Qhuinn frowned. "No, it isn't."

Layla just kept walking, faster and faster—and she supposed it was because she was trying to get away from the images in her head: Xcor looking up at her. Xcor taking her vein. Xcor's big body . . . his massive, warrior body laid out before her and clearly aroused from the taste of her blood—

"What the hell are you thinking about?" Qhuinn asked darkly.

She stopped short. "Nothing. Nothing at all."

Qhuinn shifted on his stool, and then abruptly shoved his half-eaten food away.

"I should leave you," she announced.

"Nah, it's cool. Guess I'm tetchy, too."

As he got up from the counter with his dishes, her eyes traveled down his torso and widened. He was . . . aroused.

Just as she was.

Remnants of Autumn's needing, clearly—

The heat wave came over her in such a rush, she barely had time to grab onto the granite counter to keep herself standing, and she coudn't respond as she heard Qhuinn shout her name from a distance.

Need gripped her body, fisting her womb, making her buckle under its force.

"Oh . . . dearest Virgin Scribe . . ." Between her legs, her sex opened, the blossoming having nothing to do with Xcor or Qhuinn or any outside force.

The arousal came from inside of herself.

Her needing . . .

It hadn't been enough. The visits to the Sanctuary hadn't been enough to keep her from being caught by Autumn's—

The next surge of yearning threatened to take her to her knees, but Qhuinn was there to catch her before she hit the hard tile. As he dragged her into his arms, she knew she didn't have much time to be rational. And knew the resolution that abruptly came upon her was at once utterly unfair and totally undeniable.

"Service me," she said, cutting off whatever it was he was saying to her. "I know you don't love me, and I know we won't be together afterward, but service me so that I can have something that's mine. So you can have something that's yours."

As the blood drained out of his face and his mismatched eyes bulged, she forged on, talking in fast gasps. "We both have no true family. We're both alone. Service me . . . service me and change all that. Service me so that we may each have a future that is at least partially our own. . . . Service me, Qhuinn. . . . I beg of you . . . service me. . . ."

SIXTY-TWO

Qhuinn was pretty certain he was in a parallel universe. Because there was no way that Layla was going into her needing . . . and turning to him to see her through it.

Nah.

This was just a mirror image of the way the real world was—a world where the biologically pure stuck to themselves so that they created generations of biologically pure and therefore superior young.

"Service me and give us something that is ours—" The hormones in her cranked up to a newer, higher level, cutting off her voice. It soon came back, however, with the same words. "Service me. . . ."

As he started to pant, it was unclear whether that was the sex in his blood, or the vertigo created by this unexpected cliff he was hanging off of.

The answer was no, of course. No, absolutely not, no children ever, certainly not with someone he wasn't in love with, certainly not with a virgin Chosen.

No.

No . . .

Fuck, no, shit, no, God, no, damn it to hell, *no* . . .

"Qhuinn . . ." she groaned. "You're my only hope, and I yours. . . ."

Well, actually, that wasn't true—at least the first part. Any other male in the house—or on the planet—could take care of this. And of course, right afterward, they would be answerable to the Primale.

Not a conversation he was going to volunteer for.

Except . . . well, she was right about the second part. In her delirium, in her desperation, she was voicing the same thing he'd been thinking for months now. Like her, he had nothing that was really his, no prospects of true love, no abiding reason to rise each sunset other than the war. What kind of life was that?

Fine, he told himself. Go get a goddamned dog. The answer to all that was *not* to lie with this Chosen.

"Qhuinn . . . please . . ."

"Listen, let me get you to Doc Jane. She'll take care of you the right way—"

Layla shook her head wildly. "No. I need you."

From out of nowhere, he thought, Young were a future that was your own. If you parented them well, they never truly left you—and they could not be taken away from you if you kept them safe.

Hell, if Layla conceived, even the Primale couldn't do shit, because Qhuinn would be . . . the father. Which in vampire terms was the ultimate trump short of the king—and Wrath wouldn't touch something private like this.

On the other hand, if she didn't fall pregnant, they would likely beat the ever-loving balls off him for soiling a sacred female—

Wait a minute. Was he actually considering this?

"Qhuinn . . ."

He could love a young, he thought. Love it with everything he was and ever would be. Love it as he had loved no other, even Blay.

Closing his eyes briefly, he went back in time to the night he had died and gone up to the door of the Fade. He thought about that image he had seen, that little female. . . .

Oh, Jesus . . .

"Layla," he said roughly, as he put her back on her feet. "Layla, look at me. *Look* at me."

As he shook her, she seemed to gather herself, focusing on his face as she gripped his upper arms with her nails. "Yes . . ."

"Are you sure. Are you positive—you need to be sure—"

For the briefest of moments, a completely lucid, rather ancient expres-

sion cut through her tortured, beautiful features. "Yes, I am sure. Let us do what we must. For the future."

He searched her face carefully, just to be sure. Phury was going to be pissed, but then, even Chosen had the right to choose—and she was picking him, right here, right now: As all he saw was an abiding resolution, he nodded once, picked her back up into his arms, and strode out of the kitchen.

His only thought, as he hit the bottom of the grand staircase, was that they were going to conceive in the next few hours, and both the young and Layla were going to live through everything: the pregnancy, the birthing, and those critical few hours thereafter.

He and Layla were going to bring into the world a daughter.

A fair-haired daughter with eyes that were shaped like his, and at first colored like the Chosen's . . . before they changed to be as the blue and green of his own.

He was going to have a family of his own.

A future of his own.

Finally.

As Xhex stepped out of the shower, she knew John had returned, because she caught his scent as well as the smell of something frickin' delicious. Reapplying the cilices she'd removed to get cleaned up, she wrapped a towel around herself and padded out into the bedroom.

"Oh, man, turkey," she said as he set up a lap tray for her.

Glancing over, his eyes lingered on her body like he wanted to eat her instead, but then he just smiled and went back to his ministrations with what he'd brought them both.

"This is perfect timing," she murmured as she got on the bed. "I'm starved."

After everything was set up properly, from the napkin to the silverware to the glass and covered plate, he brought the tray over to her, placing it across her thighs. Then he retreated to the other side of the room to have his own food at the chaise lounge.

Would he rather be feeding her by hand? she wondered as they ate in silence. Vampire males liked to do that . . . but she'd never had the patience for it. Food was energy for the body, not something to get all Valentine's Day about.

Guess they were both capable of closing each other out, weren't they.

And something was up: His grid was conflicted, to the point where his emotions were nearly frozen.

"I'll leave," she said sadly. "After I check in on my mother, I'll go—"

You don't have to, he signed. *I don't want you to.*

"You sure about that." When he nodded, she had to wonder, given what his grid was up to.

But come on, a couple of hours in the sack were not going to close the kind of distance they had been rocking lately—

Abruptly, he took a deep breath and stopped playing with what was on his plate. *Listen, I need to tell you something.*

She put down her fork and wondered how bad this was going to hurt. "Okay."

Layla fed Xcor.

"What the f— I'm sorry, did I hear you right?" As he nodded, she thought, Right, she'd known there was drama going down in the theater district, but she never would have guessed it was that serious.

She didn't know who it was. Throe tricked her—he reached out and found her and brought her to Xcor.

"Jesus . . ." Like the king needed another reason to kill that motherfucker?

Here's the thing. She wants to help find him—and with her blood in his veins . . . she can. She knew where he was last night—sensed him clear as day. She could really help you.

Xhex forgot all about the food, adrenaline rocketing through her body. "Oh, man, if I can just get her in range . . . How long ago did she feed him?"

The fall.

"Shit. Time's wasting." She burst up and went for her leather pants, picking them up off the floor. Damn it, they were split in half—

There are some others still in the closet.

"Oh, thanks." She went over and tried not to get depressed as she saw their clothes lined up together. God . . . "Ah, do you know where she is?"

Down in the kitchen with Qhuinn.

As John's grid shifted, Xhex stopped in the process of pulling a fresh set out. Narrowing her eyes over her shoulder, she said, "What aren't you telling me."

Wrath and Phury don't want to involve her. She offered to help and they shut her down. If you use her, they can't ever know you did—I can't state that more plainly.

Xhex blinked, her breath freezing in her lungs.

No one can know, Xhex. Not even Qhuinn. And it goes without saying that you've got to keep her safe.

As John met her stare grimly, she didn't care about any of that shit. Didn't even hear it.

With this piece of intel, he had just chosen her and her quest over both his king and the Primale of his race. Even more, he had potentially handed her the key to infiltrating the Band of Bastards—and sent her into the belly of the beast.

Talk about putting his money where his mouth was.

Xhex forgot about the leathers and walked over to him, taking his face in her hands. "Why are you telling me this?"

It's going to get you there, he mouthed.

She brushed back his hair from his handsome, tense face. "You keep this up . . ."

And what?

". . . and I'm going to owe you."

Can I pick how you repay me?

"Yeah. You can."

Then I want you to move back in with me. Or let me come live with you. I want us to be together properly again.

Blinking hard, she bent down and kissed him slowly, thoroughly. Words didn't mean shit. He'd been right about that. But this male, who'd been all about brick walls and obstacles in the spring, was clearing the way for her big-time now.

"Thank you," she whispered against his mouth, rolling everything she was feeling up into those two simple words.

John beamed at her. *I love you, too.*

After she kissed him once more, she stepped off from him, threw on a fresh set of pants, and grabbed her muscle shirt. Pulling it over her head, she—

At first she thought the hot flash that went through her was because she was standing directly under a heat vent in the ceiling. But as she moved and it stuck with her, she looked down at her body.

Glancing over at John, she watched him stiffen and glance into his lap. "Fuck," she whispered. "Who the hell's in her needing now?"

John went to check his phone, and then shrugged his shoulders.

"I should probably get out of here." *Symphaths* could generally control their fertility at will, and she'd always had luck with that. As a half-breed, however, she wasn't willing to take a chance on it with someone actually having their time next door. "You're sure my mother was over it when you went down to see Layla— Shit, I'll bet it's her. I'll bet it's the Chosen—"

A groan bled through the walls from over on the right. Where Qhuinn's room was.

The muffled thumping that followed could only mean one thing.

"Holy shit, is Qhuinn . . ." Except she knew the answer to that. Training her senses next door, she picked up on their grids. No romantic love between them—more like resolution on both sides.

They were doing what they were with a purpose she could only guess at. But why would they want a young? That shit was crazy town—especially given the Chosen's station . . . and his.

As another surge from the needing threatened to overtake her, Xhex lunged for her jacket and her weapons. "I really should go. I don't want to get exposed, just in case."

John nodded and went to the door.

"I'm going to go check in on my mother now. Layla's going to be busy for a while—but afterward, I'll talk to her and let you know how it goes."

I'll be here. Waiting to hear from you.

She kissed him once, twice . . . a third time. And then he opened the door and she left—

The instant she got out into the hall, the hormones hit her hard, knocking her off balance.

"Oh, hell no," she muttered, taking off for the stairs and then dematerializing down to the hidden door under the staircase.

The farther away she went, the more like herself she felt. But she was worried about her mother. Thank God they had drugs to soften the edges of that crucible.

Tohr couldn't possibly have serviced her. No way.

Emerging from the tunnel into the office, she strode out into the training center's long corridor. There was nothing peculiar in the air, and that was a relief. The fertility period was violent, but the good news was, when it was over, it got out of Dodge fairly quickly—although the female generally required a day or so to recover fully.

Putting her head into the main examination room, she found no one. Same with the two recovery rooms. But her mother was here—she could sense her.

"Autumn?" she called out with a frown. "Hello? Where are you?"

The reply came from somewhere much farther down, where the lectures used to be given to the trainees.

Striding toward the sound, she pushed her way into the primary class-room and found her mother seated at one of the tables that faced the blackboard. The lights were on overhead, and there was no one else in there with her.

Not good. Wherever the female was in her mind . . . was a not-good situation.

"Mahmen?" Xhex said as she let the door ease shut behind her. "How're you doing?"

Time to tread carefully. Her mother was as motionless as a statue, and just as put together, everything all arranged from her tightly braided hair to her carefully matched clothes.

That totally-put-together was false, however, nothing but external trappings of composure that just made her appear even more brittle.

"I'm not well." Autumn shook her head. "Not well. Not well at all."

Xhex walked over to the instructor desk and put down her weapons and her jacket. "At least you're honest."

"Can't you tell what is on my mind?"

"Your grid's shut down. So you're hard to read."

Autumn nodded. "Shut down . . . yes, that would cover it." Long pause, after which her mother looked around. "Do you know why I came in here? I thought the residue of the teaching would rub off on me. Not working, I'm afraid."

Xhex eased her ass down on the desktop. "Did Doc Jane check you out?"

"Yes. I am fine. And before you ask, no, I wasn't serviced. I did not want to be."

Xhex exhaled in relief. Aside from her mother's mental health, the physical risks of pregnancy and birth were not anything they needed to face right now—although maybe that was selfish.

Come on, though, she'd just found the female; she didn't want to lose her so soon.

As Autumn's eyes shifted over, there was a frankness in them that was new. "I need a place to stay. Away from here. I have no money, no job, and no prospects, but—"

"You can move in with me. For however long you want."

"Thank you." Those eyes moved away and lingered on the blackboard. "I shall endeavor to be a good guest."

"You're my mother. You're not a guest. Listen, what's happened?"

The other female stood up. "May we go now?"

Man, that grid was totally closed off. Battened down. Draped in self-protection. As if she'd been attacked, somehow.

Now was clearly not the time to push.

"Ah, yeah. Sure. We can go." Xhex shoved herself off the desk. "Do you want to check in with Tohr before you leave?"

"No."

Xhex waited for some kind of explanation after that, but none came. Which told her plenty.

"What did he do, *Mahmen*?"

Autumn lifted her chin, her dignity making her more beautiful than ever. "He told me what he thought of me. Quite succinctly. So at this point, I do believe he and I have nothing more to say to each other."

Xhex narrowed her eyes, anger curling up in her gut.

"Shall we?" her mother said.

"Yeah . . . sure . . ."

But she was going to find out what the fuck had gone down; that was for certain.

SIXTY-THREE

After the shutters rose from their sills, and night whisked away all the light from the sky, Blay left the billiards room, intending to check in with Saxton in the library and then go up to shower for First Meal.

He didn't make it much farther than the trunk of the mosaic apple tree in the foyer.

Stopping dead, he glanced down at his hips. A pounding erection had punched out of him, the arousal as unexpected as it was demanding.

What the . . . looking upward, he wondered who else had gone into her needing. It was the only explanation.

"You may not want the answer to that."

Glancing over, he found Saxton standing in the archway of the library. "Who."

But he knew. He fucking knew it.

Saxton swept his elegant hand behind himself. "Won't you come and have a drink with me in my office?"

The male was aroused as well, the slacks of his fine herringbone suit pulled out of shape at the fly—except his face didn't match the erection. He was grim.

"Come," he repeated, motioning with his hand again. "Please."

Blay's feet went to work, taking him into the chaotic mess that the library had been in since Sax had been given his "assignment." Whatever it was.

As Blay stepped inside, he heard the double doors click into place behind him, and searched his mind for something to say.

Nothing. He had . . . nothing. Especially as up above his head, on the ornate ceiling with its plaster molding, a muffled thumping started to sound out.

Even the crystals on the chandelier twinkled, as if the force of the sex was being transmitted through the floor joists.

Layla was in her needing. Qhuinn was servicing her—

"Here, drink this."

Blay took whatever was offered and threw it back like his gut was on fire and the shit was water. The effect was the opposite of any extinguishing, though. The brandy burned its way down and landed in a ball of heat.

"Refill?" Saxton said.

When he nodded, the snifter disappeared and came back much heavier. After he sucked back number two, he said, "I'm surprised . . ."

At how awful this felt. He'd thought all the ties between him and Qhuinn had been severed. Ha. He should have known better.

He refused to finish the thought out loud, however.

". . . that you can handle this disorder," he tacked on.

Saxton went over to the bar and poured himself his own tipple. "The detritus is necessary, I'm afraid."

As Blay walked over to the desk, he circled his brandy in his palm to warm it, and tried to talk in a sensible way. "I'm surprised you're not doing this more on the computers."

Saxton discreetly covered his work with yet another leather-bound volume. "The inefficiency of taking notes by hand gives me time to think."

"I'm surprised you need it—your first instinct is always right."

"You're surprised about a lot of things right now."

Only one, really. "Just making conversation."

"But of course."

Eventually, he looked over at his lover. Saxton had settled on a silk couch across the way, his legs crossed at the knee, his red silk socks peeking from beneath his precisely pressed cuffs, his Ferragamo loafers gleaming from regular polishing. He was every bit as refined and expensive as the antique he was perched on, a perfectly elegant male from a perfectly appointed bloodline with perfect taste and style.

He was everything anyone could want—

As that fucking chandelier twinkled overhead, Blay said roughly, "I'm still in love with him."

Saxton dropped his eyes and brushed at the top of his thigh, as if there might have been a tiny piece of lint there. "I know. You thought you weren't?"

As if that were rather stupid of him.

"I'm so fucking tired of it. I really am."

"That I believe."

"I'm so fucking . . ." God, those sounds, that muted pounding, that audible confirmation of what he had been ignoring for the past year—

On a sudden wave of violence, he pitched the brandy snifter at the marble fireplace, shattering the thing.

"Fuck! *Fuck!*" If he'd been able to, he'd have jumped up and torn that goddamn cocksucking light fixture off the goddamn cocksucking ceiling.

Wheeling around, he went blindly for the doors, tripping over books, messing up the piles, nearly knocking himself over on the coffee table.

Saxton got there first, blocking the way out with his body.

Blay's eyes locked onto the male's face. "Get out of my way. Right now. You don't want to be around me."

"Is that not for me to decide."

Blay shifted his focus to those lips he knew so well. "Don't push me."

"Or. What."

As his chest started to pump, Blay realized the guy knew precisely what he was courting. Or at least thought he did. But something had come unhinged; maybe it was the needing, maybe it was . . . Shit, he didn't know, and he really didn't care.

"If you don't get the fuck out of my way, I'm going to bend you over that desk of yours—"

"Prove it."

Wrong thing to say. In the wrong tone. At the wrong time.

Blay let out a roar that rattled the diamond-paned windows. Then he grabbed his lover by the back of the head and all but threw Saxton across the room. As the male caught himself on that desk, papers went flying, the confetti of yellow legal pads and computer printouts falling like snow.

Saxton's torso curled around as he looked behind at what was coming at him.

"Too late to run," Blay growled as he ripped open his button fly.

Falling upon the male, he was rough with his hands, tearing through the layers that kept him from what he was going to take. When there were no more barriers, he bared his fangs and bit down on Saxton's shoulder through his clothes, locking the male beneath him even as he grabbed those wrists and all but nailed them to the leather blotter.

And then he pushed in hard and let out everything he had, his body taking over . . . even as his heart stayed far, far away.

The cabin, as Xhex called it, was a very modest accommodation.

As Autumn walked around its interior, there was not much to get in the way of her path. The galley kitchen was nothing but cabinets and countertops. The living space offered little more than a view of the river, with only two chairs and a little table for furnishings. There were only two bedrooms, one with a pair of mattresses, another with a larger, singular sleeping platform. And the bathroom was cramped but clean, with a single towel hanging from the shower rod.

"Like I told you," Xhex said from the main room, "it's not much. There's also an underground facility for you during the daytime, but we have to access it from the garage."

Autumn came back out from the loo. "I think it's beautiful."

"Tha's okay, you can be honest."

"I mean what I say. You are a highly functional female. You like things to work well, and you don't like to waste time. This is a beautiful space for you." She cast her eyes around once more. "All the fixtures that carry water in and out are new. So are the radiators for the heat. The kitchen has plenty of space to cook on, with a stove that has six burners, not four—and is gas powered, so you don't have to worry about electricity. The roof is slate and thus enduring, and the floors don't squeak—so I assume the undercarriage is as cared for as everything else." She pivoted from one corner to the next. "From every angle there is a window to look out of, so you will never be caught unaware, and I see that there are copper locks everywhere. Perfect."

Xhex took her jacket off. "That's, ah . . . very perceptive of you."

"Not really. It's obvious to anyone who knows you."

"I'm . . . I'm really glad you do."

"Myself as well."

Autumn went over to the windows that faced the water. Outside, the moon cast a bright light down upon the snowy landscape, the refracted illumination reading blue to her eyes.

You're in love with me. Don't bother denying it—you tell me in your sleep every day. . . . And you know damn well the only reason I'm with you is to get Wellsie out of the In Between. So don't I just fit your pattern to a T.

"Mahmen?"

Autumn focused on her daughter's reflection in the glass. "I'm sorry, what?"

"Do you want to tell me what happened between you and Tohr?"

Xhex had yet to take off her weapons, and as she stood there, she was so powerful, secure, strong . . . She would bow before no male and no one, and wasn't that wonderful. Wasn't that a blessing beyond measure.

"I am so proud of you," Autumn said, turning around to face the female. "I want you to know that I am so very, very proud of you."

Xhex's eyes dropped to the floor, and she brushed a hand through her hair as if she didn't know how to handle the praise.

"Thank you for taking me in," Autumn continued. "I shall endeavor to earn my keep for the duration I am here, and contribute in some small way."

Xhex shook her head. "I keep telling you, you're not a guest."

"Be that as it may, I shan't be a burden."

"Are you going to tell me about Tohr."

Autumn regarded the weapons that as yet hung from those leather holsters, and thought the gleam of the gunmetal was very much like the light in her daughter's eyes: a promise of violence.

"You are not to be angry with him," she heard herself say. "What transpired between us was consensual, and it ended for . . . a proper reason. He did nothing wrong."

As she spoke, she wasn't sure what she really thought about it all, but she was clear on one thing: She was not going to create a situation where Xhex went after the male with all guns blazing—literally.

"Do you hear me, daughter mine." Not a question, a command—the first she had ever made that sounded as a parent to a young. "You are not to find cause with him, or speak of this to him."

"Give me a reason why."

"You know the emotions of others, correct?"

"Yeah."

"When was the last time you met someone who had made themselves fall in love with somebody else. Who had willed their feelings in a given direction, when in their natural state, their heart cleaved unto someone else."

Xhex cursed a little. "Never. It's a recipe for disaster—but you can still be respectful of the way you phrase things."

"Gift wrapping one's words does not change the nature of truth." Autumn looked back out to the snowy landscape and the river that was partially frozen. "And I would rather know what is real than live a lie."

There was silence for a while between them. "Is that enough of a 'why,' daughter mine."

Another curse. But then Xhex said, "I don't like it . . . but yeah, it is."

SIXTY-FOUR

Zohr sat in that parking lot for God only knew how long. Had to be at least a night and a day and then maybe another night or two? He didn't know, and didn't really care.

It was rather like being back in the womb, he supposed. Except his ass was numb and his nose ran from the cold.

As his epic anger faded and his emotions smoothed out, his thoughts became as a band of travelers, passing through sections of his life, wandering around the landscapes of different eras, doubling back for the reexamination of peaks and valleys.

Long fucking trip. And he was tired at the end of it, even though his body hadn't moved in hours upon hours.

Not surprisingly, the two places most revisited were Wellsie's needing . . . and Autumn's. Those events, and their respective aftermaths, were the mountains most climbed, the different scenes like vistas flashing in an alternating sequence of comparison until they blurred together, forming a pastiche of actions and reactions, his and theirs.

After all the ruminations, there were three resolutions he kept returning to, again and again.

He was going to have to apologize to Autumn, of course. Christ, that was the second time he'd taken a hunk out of her, the first being way back nearly a year ago at the pool: In both cases, his temper had gotten the best of him because of the stress load he was under, but that was no excuse.

The second was that he was going to have to find that angel and do another set of I'm-sorrying.

And the third . . . well, the third was actually the most important, the thing he had to do before the others.

He had to make contact with Wellsie one last time.

Taking a deep breath, he closed his eyes and willed some relaxation into his muscles. Then, with more desperation than hope, he commanded his weary mind to be free of all thoughts and images, empty of everything that had kept him awake for all this time, devoid of the regrets and the mistakes and the pain. . . .

Eventually the order was complied with, the relentless mental trekking slowing down until all that Lewis-and-Clark cognition shit ceased.

Impregnating his subconsciousness with a single goal, he let himself go into sleep and waited in his resting state until . . .

Wellsie came to him in shades of gray, in that barren landscape of fog and frigid wind and boulders. She was so far away now that the scope of his vision allowed him to see one of the crumbling rock formations up close—

Except it was not, in fact, made of stone.

None of them were.

No, these were the hunched figures of others suffering as she did, their bodies and bones gradually collapsing in on themselves until they were but mounds to be worn away by the wind.

"Wellsie?" he called out.

As her name drifted off into the limitless horizon, she did not look at him.

Did not appear to even recognize his presence.

The only thing that moved was the cold wind that abruptly seemed to marshal itself in his direction, blowing across the flat gray plain, blowing across him, blowing across her.

As it caught her hair, wisps formed around her—

No, not wisps. Her hair was ashes now, ashes that scattered on the invisible current and came at him, hitting him as dust that made his eyes water.

Eventually that would be all of her. And then none of her.

"Wellsie! Wellsie, I'm here!"

He called out to her to rouse her, to get her attention, to tell her he was finally ready, but no matter how much he yelled, or how much he waved

his arms, she did not focus on him. She did not look up. She did not move . . . and neither did his son.

Yet still the wind blew, taking infinitesimal particles from their forms, wearing them down.

In a gripping fear, he turned himself into a great monkey, caterwauling and jumping all around, screaming at the top of his lungs and flailing his arms, but, as if the rules of exertion applied even in this other world, eventually he lost his energy and fell down onto the dusty ground in a heap.

They were sitting in the same pose, he realized.

And that was when the paradoxical truth came to him.

The answer was at once all about what had happened with Autumn and the sex and the feeding—and yet had nothing to do with her. It was about everything Lassiter had tried to help him with—and yet none of that. It wasn't even about Wellsie, really.

It was him. All . . . him.

In his dream, he stared down at himself, and abruptly, strength came to him with a calmness that had everything to do with the seat of his soul . . . and the fact that the pathway out of his suffering—and hers—had just been illuminated by the hand of his Maker.

Finally, after all this time, all this shit, all this agony, he knew what to do.

Now, when he spoke, he did not yell. "Wellsie, I know you can hear me—you hang on. I need just a little longer from you—I'm finally ready. I'm just sorry it took me so long."

He tarried for only a moment longer, throwing all his love in her direction as if it might keep what remained of her intact. And then he withdrew, yanking himself free with a herculean burst of will that had his body jerking out of its position on the concrete floor—

Throwing out a hand, he kept himself from landing on his face, and immediately got to his feet.

As soon as he stood, he realized that if he didn't take a piss immediately, his bladder was going to explode and take no prisoners with it.

Striding down the ramp, he punched into the clinic and hit the first bathroom he came to. When he emerged, he didn't stop to check in with anyone, even though he could hear voices elsewhere in the training center.

Up at the main house, he found Fritz in the kitchen. "Hey, my man, I need your help."

The butler jumped up from the grocery list he was making. "Sire! You are alive! Oh, blessed Virgin Scribe, all and sundry have sought out—"

Shit. He'd forgotten there were implications to going off the grid.

"Yeah, sorry. I'll text everyone." Assuming he could find his phone? Probably down in the clinic, and he wasn't going to waste time going back there. "Listen, what I really need is for you to come with me."

"Oh, sire, it would be my pleasure to serve you. But mayhap you should go unto the king first—all have been so worried—"

"Tell you what. You can drive and I'll borrow your phone." When there was a hesitation, he dropped his voice. "We've got to go now, Fritz. I need you."

The call to service was precisely the motivator the butler needed. With a low bow, he said, "As you wish, sire. And mayhap I shall pack you up some refreshments?"

"Good idea. I need five minutes."

When the butler nodded and disappeared into the pantry, Tohr rounded the base of the stairs and took the red-carpeted steps two at a time. He stopped rushing when he got to John Matthew's door.

His knock was answered immediately, John pulling open the way with a jerk. As the kid's face registered surprise, Tohr put his hands out in self-defense, because he knew he was going to get hollered at for disappearing again.

"I'm sorry that I—"

He didn't get a chance to finish. John threw his arms around Tohr and held him so hard, his spine cracked.

Tohr was right there with returning the favor. And as he held the only son he had, he spoke in a low, clear voice.

"John, I want you to get off rotation tonight and come with me. I need you . . . to come with me. Qhuinn can as well—and this is going to take all night—maybe longer." As Tohr felt the nodding against his shoulder, he took a steadying breath. "Good, son. That's . . . good. There's no way I would do this without you."

"How you doing?"

Layla opened her heavy eyes and looked up Qhuinn's body to his face. Standing next to her side of the bed in his room, he was fully dressed, big and remote, awkward though not unkind.

She knew how he felt. With the intense fire of the needing having passed, those hours of straining and pounding and clawing were done and dusted, a strange footnote that appeared to be already fading in her memory like a dream. When the two of them had been gripped in the fist of

the experience, it had seemed as if nothing would ever be the same, that they would be forever changed and transformed by the volcanic eruptions.

But now . . . the quiet return of normalcy appeared to be just as powerful, wiping the slate clean.

"I think I'm ready to get up," she said.

He had been so good about feeding her from his vein and also bringing her food, and she had stayed on bed rest for at least twenty-fours afterward, as was the tradition up in the Sanctuary after the Primale had lain with a Chosen.

It was time to get moving, however.

"You can stay here, you know." He went over to his closet and began to arm himself for the night. "Rest some more. Relax."

No, she had done enough of that.

Pushing herself up on her arms, she waited to feel light-headed, and was relieved when she didn't. If anything, she felt strong.

There was no other way to put it. Her body just felt . . . strong.

Shifting her legs off the side of the mattress, she put her weight on her bare soles and slowly rose up. Qhuinn came instantly to her side, but she didn't need the help.

"I think I'll have a shower," she announced.

And after that? She didn't have a clue what she was going to do.

"I want you to stay here," Qhuinn said as if reading her mind. "You are going to stay here. With me."

"We don't know if I'm pregnant."

"All the more reason to take it easy. And if you are, you're going to keep on staying with me."

"All right." They were, after all, going to be in this together—assuming there was any "this" to be had.

"I'm going out to fight now, but I have my cell phone with me at all times, and I've left you one on that bedside table." He held his up and pointed to the one by the alarm clock. "You call or text if you need me, clear?"

His face was dead serious, his eyes focusing on her with an intensity that gave her an idea of how accomplished he probably was in the field: Nothing and nobody was going to get in his way if she called for him.

"I promise."

He nodded and went for the door. Before he opened the way out, he paused and seemed to be searching for words. "How will we know if you . . ."

"Miscarry? I'll start cramping, and then I will bleed. I saw it happen on the Other Side a number of times."

"Are you in any danger if you do?"

"Not that I ever saw—not this early."

"Should you stay on bed rest?"

"After the first twenty-four hours, if it's going to take, it does—whether I am inactive or not at this point, our die is already cast."

"Let me know?"

"As soon as I do."

He turned away. Appeared to stare at the face of the door for a moment. "It's going to stick."

Of that he was far more confident than she, but it was gratifying to learn of his faith, and his desire for what she wanted.

"I'll be back at dawn," he said.

"I shall be here."

After he left, she attended to herself in the shower, passing the bar of soap over her lower belly again and again. It seemed odd to have such a potentially momentous thing occurring in her own body, and to be as yet unaware of the particulars.

They would find out soon enough, though. Most females bled within the first week if they were going to.

When she got out from beneath the spray, she toweled off and discovered that he'd thoughtfully left another of her robes upon the counter, and she drew it on, along with some underthings in the event that a termination event occurred.

In the main bedroom, she sat down on the duvet to pull on her slipper shoes, and then . . .

There was nothing for her to do. And the silence and stillness were rotten companions for her anxiety.

Unbidden, the image of Xcor's face returned to her once again.

With a soft curse, she feared she would never forget the manner in which he had regarded her, his eyes staring up at her as if she were a vision he couldn't fully comprehend, yet would be e'er grateful for having seen but once.

Unlike memories of the needing, the sensations she had felt when that male had focused upon her were as incandescent as the moment she had lived them, unfaded through the months that separated her from that meeting. Except . . . had she simply imagined it all? Was it possible that the recollection was strong simply because it was fantasy?

Clearly, if the needing was anything to go by, real life faded fast.

The desire to be wanted did not, however—

The knock on the door made her gather herself. "Yes?"

Through the panels, a female voice replied, "It's Xhex. Mind if I come in?"

She couldn't imagine what the female was doing seeking her out. Still, she liked John's mate, and she would always entertain his *shellan*.

"Oh, please do—hello, this is a welcome surprise."

Xhex shut them in together, and awkwardly looked everywhere but upon her face. "So, ah . . . how are you feeling?"

Indeed, she had the sense a lot of people were going to be asking her that in the coming week. "Well enough."

"Good. Yeah . . . good."

Long silence. "Is there something I may help you with?" Layla asked.

"As a matter of fact, yes."

"Then by all means, tell me and I shall do whatever I can."

"It's complicated." Xhex narrowed her eyes. "And dangerous."

Layla put her hand over her lower belly as if to shelter her young in case there was one. "Whate'er do you seek?"

"On Wrath's orders, I'm trying to find Xcor."

Layla's chest constricted, her mouth opening so she could breathe. "Indeed."

"I know you're aware of what he did."

"Yes, I am."

"I also know you fed him."

Layla blinked as the image of that cruel, strangely vulnerable face came to her anew. For a split second, she had the absurd instinct to protect him—but that was ridiculous, and not something she would sustain.

"Of course I will help you and Wrath. I'm glad the king has reconsidered his earlier stance."

Now the female hesitated. "What if I told you Wrath couldn't know about it. No one could, especially not Qhuinn. Would that change your mind?"

John, she thought. John had told his mate what had transpired.

"I realize," Xhex said, "that I'm putting you in a terrible position, but you know what my nature is. I'll use anything at my disposal to get what I want, and I want to find Xcor now. I have no doubt that I'll be able to protect you, and I don't have any intention of getting you anywhere near him. I just need the general area where he settles at night, and I'll take it from there."

"Are you going to kill him?"

"No, but I'm going to give the Brotherhood the ammunition to do so. The weapon that was used to shoot at Wrath was a rifle with a long-range scope—not the kind of thing anyone would take into the field on a normal night. Assuming they haven't destroyed it, they'll leave it behind when they go out. If I can get ahold of it, and we can prove what they did, things are going to take their natural course."

Kind eyes, she thought . . . the male had had such kind eyes when he'd stared up at her. But in fact, he was the enemy of her king.

Layla felt her head nod. "I shall help you. I shall do anything I can . . . and not say a word."

The female came over and put a surprisingly gentle hand on her shoulder. "I hate putting you in this position. War is an ugly, ugly business that specializes in compromising good people such as yourself. I can feel how this is tearing you up, and I'm sorry that I'm asking you to lie."

It was lovely of the *symphath* to offer concern, but her conflict was not with giving false testimony to the Brotherhood. It was the fighter she would be helping to kill.

"Xcor used me," she said, as if trying to convince herself.

"He's very dangerous. You're lucky to have come out of meeting him alive."

"I will do what is right." She glanced up at Xhex. "When do we leave?"

"Right now. If you're able to."

Layla called upon deep recesses of strength. Then nodded. "Allow me to get my coat."

SIXTY-FIVE

ours later, as Marissa sat at her desk at Safe Place, she answered her cell phone and couldn't keep the smile off her face. "It's you again."

Butch's Boston-accented voice was full of gravel. As usual. "When are you coming home?"

She looked at her watch and thought, Where had the night gone? Then again, it was always this way at work. She came in as soon as the sun was safely below the horizon, and before she knew it, the light was threatening in the east, and driving her back to the compound.

Into the arms of her male.

Hardly a chore, that was.

"About forty-five minutes?"

"You could come now. . . ."

The way he drawled those words suggested an altogether different meaning to that verb than "return home." "Butch—"

"I didn't make it out of bed tonight."

She bit her lip, picturing him naked in the sheets that had been messy when she left. "No?"

"Mmm, no." He drew out the syllables—at least until his breath caught. "I've been thinking about you. . . ."

His voice was so deep, so raw, that she knew exactly what he was doing to himself, and for a moment she closed her eyes and indulged in some seriously beautiful mental pictures.

"Marissa . . . come home. . . ."

Snapping herself together, she pulled out of the spell he knew damn well he was weaving around her. "I can't leave quite now. But I'll start getting ready to check out—how about that?"

"Perfect." She could hear the grin on his face. "I'll be here waiting for you—and listen, all kidding aside, take as long as you need. Just come back here first before you go to Last Meal? I want to give you an hors d'oeuvre you won't forget."

"You're pretty unforgettable already."

"That's my girlie. I love you."

"I love you, too."

As she ended the call, that big, fat, happy smile stayed on her face. Her mate was a traditional kind of male, "old-school," as he called himself, with all the biases that came with that mental set: Females should never pay for anything, open a door, pump gas into their cars, step through a mud puddle, carry something larger than what could fit in a sandwich bag . . . you name it. But he never got in the way of her job. Ever. That was the one area of her life where she called the shots, and he never complained about her hours, her workload, or her stress level.

Which was just one of the many reasons she adored the Brother. The displaced females and children who stayed at Safe Place were a kind of family to her, one that she was the head of: She was in charge of the facility, the staff, the programs, the resources, and, most important, everything and everybody who was under its roof. And she loved her job. When Wrath had given her the charter to run the charity, she had nearly balked, but she was so glad she had fought through the fear to find her professional purpose.

"Marissa?"

Glancing up, she found one of the newer counselors standing in her office's doorway. "Hi, there. How was group tonight?"

"Really good. I'll be filing my report in about an hour—right after we finish making cookies down in the kitchen. I'm sorry to interrupt you, but there's a gentlemale here with a delivery?"

"Really?" She frowned at the calendar on the wall. "We don't have anything scheduled."

"I know, so I haven't unlocked the door. He said you'd know him, but he didn't give his name. I'm wondering if we shouldn't call the Brotherhood?"

"What does he look like?"

The female reached a hand up over her head. "Very tall. Big. He's got dark hair with a white stripe in front?"

Marissa jumped up so fast her chair let out a squeak on the floor. "Tohrment? He's alive?"

"I'm sorry?"

"I'll handle this. It's okay—you head back to the kitchen."

Marissa shot out of her office and went down the front set of stairs. Pausing by the main entrance, she checked the security monitor that V had installed, and then immediately yanked open the door.

She threw herself at the Brother without thinking. "Oh, God, where have you been! You were lost for nights!"

"Not really." He returned her embrace gently. "I was just taking care of some business. But it's all good."

She stepped back, but held on to both his thick biceps. "Are you okay?"

Everyone at the mansion knew that Autumn had gone through her needing, and she could imagine how hard that had been on him. And she'd hoped, as they all had, that the growing relationship between the Brother and the quiet, fallen aristocrat would heal him. Instead, he'd disappeared after she'd come out of her fertile time, and Autumn had moved out of the house.

Not a happy outcome, obviously.

"Listen, I know you take donations, right?" he said.

Respecting the fact that he hadn't answered her question, she stopped probing. "Oh, we absolutely do. We'll take anything—we're experts at adaptive reuse around here."

"Good, because I have some things I'd like to give the females, maybe? I'm not sure you can use any of it, but . . ."

He turned and led the way over to the Brotherhood's van, which was parked at the head of the driveway. Fritz was in the passenger seat, and the old butler hopped out as she approached.

For once, he did not have a cheery smile on his face. He did bow deeply, however. "Madam, how fare thee?"

"Oh, very well, Fritz, thank you."

She fell silent as Tohr slid the side panel back—

One look inside and she stopped breathing.

Illuminated by the van's overhead light were neat piles of what appeared to be clothes in laundry baskets, cardboard boxes, open duffels. There were also skirts and blouses and dresses still on their hangers, draped with care on the floorboards.

Marissa looked at Tohr.

The Brother was silent and staring at the ground—and clearly not about to make eye contact. "Like I said, I'm not sure you can use any of it."

She leaned in and fingered one of the dresses.

The last time she had seen it, it had been on Wellsie.

These were his *shellan*'s clothes.

In a voice that cracked, she whispered, "Are you sure you want to give this away?"

"Yeah. Throwing it all out just seems like such a waste, and she wouldn't approve of that. Wellsie would want them to be used by others—that would be important to her. She hated waste. But, yeah, I don't know about the whole female-size thing, though."

"This is very generous of you." She studied the male's face, realizing it was the first time since he'd come back after the killing that she'd heard him say the name. "We will use all of it."

He nodded, his eyes still avoiding hers. "I included unopened toiletries, too? Like shampoo and conditioner, her moisturizer, that Clinique soap she liked? Wellsie was really fussy about that kind of stuff—she tended to find something she liked and stick to it—she was also big into backups, so there was a lot when I cleaned out our bathroom. Oh, and I also have some of her kitchen things—those copper pans she preferred, and her knives? I can take that to a human Goodwill if you—"

"We'll take anything you have."

"Here's the cooking stuff." Tohrment went around and opened the back to show her. "And I know you don't allow males inside, but maybe I could put it all in the garage?"

"Yes, yes, please. Let me go and get some extra hands to help us—"

"I'd like to carry it in myself, if you don't mind."

"Oh yes, of course . . . yes." Shaking herself, she jogged over and punched in the code on the keypad by the garage doors.

As the left side trundled open, she went over and stood by the butler as Tohrment went back and forth at a steady pace, carrying his mate's possessions with care, creating a tall, orderly pile right by the door that led into the kitchen.

"He's packing up the house?" she whispered to Fritz.

"Yes, madam. We've worked all night—John, Qhuinn, myself, and him. He did their rooms and the kitchen, whilst the other males and I worked on the rest of the house. He's asked me to return with him after this coming sunset so that all the furniture and the art can be moved to the mansion."

Marissa put her hand up and covered her mouth so that her shock was less apparent. But she needn't have worried about her reaction making Tohr uncomfortable; the Brother was solely focused on his task.

When the van was empty, he closed everything up and came around to her. Just as she was trying to marshal appropriate words of gratitude, of profound respect, of deepest sympathy, he cut her off by taking something out of his pocket—a velvet bag.

"I have one more thing. Give me your hand?" When she extended her palm, he loosened the cord at the neck of the thing. Tilting it upside down, he poured out—

"Oh, my God!" Marissa gasped.

Rubies. Big red rubies set with diamonds. Lots of them—a necklace—no, a necklace and a bracelet. Earrings, too. She needed both hands to hold it all.

"I bought these for her back in nineteen sixty-four. From Van Cleef and Arpels? It was supposed to be for our anniversary, but I don't know what the fuck I was thinking. Wellsie wasn't a big fan of jewelry—she liked art more. She always said that jewels were fussy. Anyway, you know, I saw these in a magazine at Darius's—in a *Town and Country*. I thought they would go well with her red hair, and I wanted to do something over-the-top and romantic just to prove I could. She didn't really care for them, but every year afterward, every single year without fail, she took the set out from the gun safe and put it on. And every year—every single year—I got to tell her that they didn't hold a candle to how beautiful she was—" He stopped short. "I'm sorry, I'm totally rambling."

"Tohr . . . I can't accept these. This is too much—"

"I want you to sell 'em. Sell 'em and take the money and use it to expand the house in the back. Butch was saying something about you needing more space? I think they've got to be worth a quarter of a million, maybe more. Wellsie would have loved what you're doing here—she would have supported it, volunteered with the females and the kids, really gotten involved. So, you know, there isn't a better place for these to go."

Marissa started to blink really fast—it was either that or have tears fall. It was just . . . he was being so brave. . . .

"Are you sure," she said roughly. "Are you certain you want to do all this?"

"Yeah. It's time. Holding on to it hasn't brought her back and never will. But at least it can help the females in this house—so none of it's wasted. It's important to me that the things we bought together, had together, used together . . . aren't, you know, wasted."

At that, Tohr leaned in and gave her a quick hug. "Be well, Marissa."

And then he closed up the van, helped the butler into the driver's seat, and, with a final wave, dematerialized into the waning night.

Marissa looked down at the fortune in her hands, then back up at the van Fritz was cautiously reversing out of the driveway. As the *doggen* went, so she followed, walking down to the street, putting the gems back in their little bag. While he K-turned, she lifted her arm and waved. He did the same.

Wrapping her arms around herself to ward off the chill, she watched the tail lights fade.

With the weight of the gems still in her hands, she pivoted around toward the house and pictured the expansion she could do out into the rear yard, creating more rooms for more females and their young—especially underground, where it was safe during the day.

Her eyes misted over again, and this time there was no stopping the tears from hitting her cheeks. As the facility in front of her grew wavy, the future became clear: She knew exactly who she was going to name the new wing after.

Wellesandra had such a nice ring to it.

SIXTY-SIX

ayla had never been out close to dawn before, and she found it interesting to note that there was a real change in the air, a vitalization she could sense but not see: The sun was indeed powerful, capable of illuminating the whole world, and the gathering illumination made her skin prickle in alarm, some instinct bred deep in her flesh telling her now was the time to be heading home. Yet she did not want to go.

"How you doing?" Xhex asked from behind her.

For truth, it had been a long evening. They had been on the outskirts of Caldwell for hours, circling in the darkness, tracking Xcor and his fighters— which had proven easy enough to do. Her sense of the male was clear as a spotlighted location, her tie to him from that feeding months ago as yet unfaded. And on his side . . . Xcor appeared to be so caught up in his fighting that he did not know she was on the periphery; certainly if he was aware of her vicinity, he did not approach her, and nor did the other soldier.

"Layla?"

She glanced over at the female. "I know right where he is. He hasn't moved."

"That isn't what I'm asking about."

Layla had to smile a little. One of the big surprises of the night had been the *symphath*—whom she actually no longer felt comfortable defining as such. Xhex was razor-sharp mentally, and strong as a male physically, but there was a warmth to her that was at odds with those traits: She had never once left Layla's side, hovering like a *mahmen* over a young, ever solicitous and careful, as if she knew that so much of this was foreign work under troubling circumstances for her charge.

"I'm fine."

"No, you're not."

As Layla refocused on the signal of her blood some two blocks away, she stayed quiet.

"I'm sure you're already aware of this," Xhex murmured. "But you really are doing the right thing here."

"I know. He's changing positions."

"Yeah, I can sense that."

Abruptly, Layla turned toward a lofty, glowing beacon to the west: the highest skyscraper in the city. As she focused on the lights that blinked white and red at its apex, she imagined him standing in the gusting cold atop the monument, staking his claim to the city.

"Do you think he's evil?" she asked roughly. "I mean, you can sense his emotions, yes?"

"To a point I can."

"So . . . is he evil?"

The other female exhaled long and slow, as if she regretted what she had to share. "He wouldn't be a good bet, Layla. Not for you, not for anyone—and not just because of the Wrath issue. Xcor's got some sinister shit in him."

"So he is a dark soul."

"You don't need to read him to know that. Just think about what he did to your king."

"Yes. Yes, indeed."

From Qhuinn to Xcor. Fabulous track record for picking males—

"He's moving fast," Layla said urgently. "He's dematerialized."

"This is it. This is where you come in."

Layla closed her eyes and shut out all of her senses except the instinct to find her own blood. "He's moving north."

As previously agreed, the two of them traveled a mile and reconvened; traveled another five miles and reconvened; traveled another ten, and an-

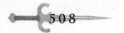

other ten . . . with Layla's instincts acting as a compass, steering their course.

And all the while time was of the essence, dawn racing in, a dangerous glow lodging in the seat of the sky and getting stronger.

The final leg of their race found them in a wooded forest, a good mile to a mile and a half away from where he had stopped—and at last gone no farther.

"I can get you closer," Layla murmured.

"He's not going anywhere?"

"No, he's not."

"Then you go. Now—go!"

Layla took one last look in the direction he was in. She knew she had to depart—for if she could sense him, he could perhaps sense her as well. The expectation, of course, was that if he did, he would not be able to react fast enough, that her disappearance to the *mhis*-protected environment up north would stop her trail and stymie him completely, not just giving him no inkling of her destination, but scrambling his blood sense so totally, he would be sent in a different direction like light bouncing off the surface of a mirror.

Fear made her heart skip, and she held on to the sensation, recognizing it as more real than her assessment of the time they'd been together when he had fed from her.

"Layla? Go!"

Dearest Virgin Scribe, she had condemned him to death this night—

No, she corrected. He had done that to himself. Assuming that rifle was found in and among the Band of Bastards' living arrangements, and that it proved what the Brothers thought it would, Xcor had set the wheels of his doom in motion months ago.

She might be the conduit, but his actions were the electrical charge that was going to stop his heart.

"Thank you for giving me this opportunity to do the right thing," she told Xhex. "I'll go home right now."

With that, she dematerialized away from the wooded glen, zeroing in on the mansion, making it into the vestibule just as the light was beginning to sting her eyes.

It was not tears doing that. No, those were not tears—it was the coming dawn.

Tears shed for that male would be . . . wrong of her on too many levels to count.

*   *   *

"We need to go, buddy."

John nodded as Qhuinn spoke to him, but he didn't move. Standing in the middle of Wellsie's kitchen, he was suffering from a kind of culture shock.

The cupboards were bare. The pantry was empty. So were all the drawers and the two closets. The bookcases over the built-in desk. The desk itself.

Walking around, he circled the table that was in the alcove, remembering the dinners Wellsie had served on it. Then he ambled down the long stretch of granite countertop, imagining her bowls of bread dough draped with dish towels, her cutting boards with piles of diced onions or sliced mushrooms on them, her canister of flour, her crock of rice. At the stove, he almost bent down to breathe in the aroma of the stew and the spaghetti sauce and the mulled apple cider.

"John?"

Turning away, he walked over to his best friend . . . and then kept going, heading out into the living room. Shit, it was like the place had been bombed in a way. The paintings had all been stripped from the walls, nothing but their claw-shaped brass hangers left where they had been hung: Everything in a frame had been moved over to the far corner, the works of art leaning up against each other, separated by thick terry-cloth towels.

The furniture had likewise been shifted all around, the lot of it sorted into arrangements of chairs, side tables, lamps—God, the lamps. Wellsie hadn't liked overhead lighting, and that had meant there were, like, a hundred lamps of different shapes and sizes in the house.

Same with rugs. She'd hated wall-to-wall, so there were Orientals—*had* been Orientals—lying everywhere on hardwood and marble. Now, though, like everything else, they had been rolled up with their pads and organized into a cordwood-like stack against the long wall in the living room.

The best of the furnishings and all of the artwork were going to be brought north to the mansion, the staff securing a U-Haul truck for the relocation. What was left over would be offered to Safe Place, and, if declined, forwarded on to Goodwill or the Salvation Army.

Man . . . even after the four of them had worked for ten hours straight, there was a lot left to do. This first big push, however, seemed like the most critical part.

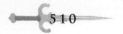

From out of nowhere, Tohr stepped into his wandering path, stopping him short. "Hey, son."

Oh, hey.

As they clapped palms and then shoulders, it was a relief to be on the same page again after months of estrangement. The fact that the Brother had brought him here to help with all this had been a measure of respect that had surprised him and touched him deeply.

Then again, as Tohr had said on the trip out here, Wellsie had been as much John's as anyone else's.

"I sent Qhuinn back, by the way. Figured this is an extenuating circumstance—and I gotchu."

John nodded. As much as he loved his friend, it felt right for him and Tohr to be in the house together alone, even if just for a few moments.

How'd it go at Safe Place? he signed.

"Really well. Marissa was—" Tohr cleared his throat. "You know, she's just a lovely female."

She totally is.

"She was really happy about the donations."

You give her the rubies?

"Yeah."

John nodded again. He and Tohr had gone through what little was in Wellsie's jewelry collection. That necklace, bracelet, and earrings had been the only things with any intrinsic value. The rest was more personal: little charms, a couple pairs of hoops, a set of tiny diamond studs. They were going to keep all that.

"I meant what I said, John. I want you to use the furniture if you want. The art, too."

There's a Picasso in there I really like, actually.

"It's yours, then. All of it, any of it, is yours."

Ours.

Tohr inclined his head. "That's right. Ours."

John walked around the living room again, his footsteps echoing up and around. *What made you decide tonight was the night*, he signed.

"It wasn't any one thing. More like a culmination of a lot of stuff."

John had to admit he was glad for that answer. The idea that this might have somehow been solely tied to Autumn would have made him angry—even though that would have been unfair to her.

People moved on. It was healthy.

And maybe that lingering anger was a sign that he needed to let go a little more as well.

I'm sorry I wasn't better about Autumn.

"Oh, no, it's okay, son. I know it's tough."

Are you going to mate her?

"No."

John's brows jumped. *Why not.*

"It's complicated—actually, no. It's pretty simple. I blew up the relationship the night before last. There's no going back."

Oh . . . shit.

"Yeah." Tohr shook his head and looked around. "Yeah . . ."

The pair of them just stood there side by side, their eyes tracing the mess they had created out of the order that had once been. The state of the house was now, John supposed, rather like where their lives had been after Wellsie had been killed: blown apart, hollow, everything in wrong places.

It was more accurate than what had been before, though. False order, preserved out of a refusal to move on, was a dangerous kind of lie.

You're really going to sell the property? he signed.

"Yeah. Fritz is calling the Realtor as soon as the business day gets rolling. Unless . . . well, if you and Xhex want it, it goes without saying—"

No, I agree with you. Time to let it go.

"Listen, I want to see if you can take the next couple of nights off? There's a lot still to do here, and I like having you with me."

Of course. I wouldn't miss this for anything.

"Good. That's good."

The two of them stared at each other. *I guess it's time to go.*

Tohr nodded slowly. "Yeah, son. It really is."

Without another word, the pair of them stepped out of the front door, locked up . . . and dematerialized back to the mansion.

As his molecules scattered, John felt like there should have been some kind of proclamation or exchange between them that was momentous, some conversational flag in the sand, a grave, milestone-y recitation of . . . something.

Then again, he supposed the healing process, in contrast to trauma, was gentle and slow . . .

The soft closing of a door, rather than a slam.

SIXTY-SEVEN

Several nights after Autumn arrived at Xhex's cabin, a towel changed everything.

It was just a white hand towel, fresh from the dryer, destined to be rehung in the aboveground bathroom and used by either one of them. Nothing special. Nothing that Autumn hadn't handled either at the Brotherhood mansion or up in the Sanctuary over the course of decades and decades and decades.

But that was the point.

As she held it in her hands, feeling the warmth and the soft nap, she began to think of all the laundry she had done. And the trays of food she had delivered to the Chosen. And the bedding platforms she had made. And the stacks of johnnies and scrubs and towels . . .

Years and years of maid service that she had been proud to do . . .

You've been making a martyr out of yourself for centuries.

"I have not." She refolded the towel. And unfolded it again.

As her hands made work for themselves, Tohr's angry voice refused to yield. In fact, it got even louder in her head as she went out and saw the floors gleaming from her hand-polishing, and the windows sparkling, and the kitchen neat as a pin.

That symphath *was your fault. I'm your fault. The weight of the world is all your fault—*

"Stop it!" she hissed, clamping her hands on her ears. "Just stop it!"

Alas, the desire to become deaf was thwarted. As she limped around the small house, she was trapped not by the confines of the roof and walls, but by Tohrment's voice.

The trouble was, no matter where she went or what she looked at, there was something she had scrubbed or straightened or buffed right in front of her. And her plans for the night had included more of the same, even though there was no demonstrable need for any more cleaning.

Eventually, she forced herself to sit down in one of the two chairs that faced the river. Extending her leg, she looked down at the calf that had not looked right or worked right for such a very long time.

You enjoy being the victim—you're all about it.

Three nights, she thought. It had taken her three nights to move into this place and slip right into the role of maid—

Actually, no, she had started in as soon as she had woken up after that first sunset.

Sitting by herself, she breathed in the lemon-scented fragrance of furniture polish and felt an overwhelming need to get up, find a rag, and start wiping tabletops and counters. Which was part of her pattern, wasn't it.

With a curse, she forced herself to stay seated as a replay of that horrid conversation with Tohrment churned through her brain again and again. . . .

Immediately after he had left, she had been in shock. Next had come great waves of anger.

Tonight, however, she actually heard his words. And considering she was surrounded by evidence of her behavior, it was hard to dispute what he had said.

He was right. Cruel though the expression of the truth had been, Tohrment was right.

Although she had couched it all in terms of service to others, her "duties" had been less of a penance, more of a punishment. Every time she had cleaned up after others, or bowed her head under that hood, or shuffled off to stay unnoticed, there had been a satisfying lick of pain in her heart, a little cut that would heal nearly as quickly as it was inflicted. . . .

Ten thousand slices, over too many years to count.

In fact, none of the Chosen had ever told her to clean up after them. Nor had the Scribe Virgin. She had done it herself, casting her own existence in the mold of worthless servant, bowing and scraping over millennia.

And all because of . . .

An image of that *symphath* came back to her, and for a brief moment she remembered the smell of him, and the feel of his too slick skin, and the sight of his six-fingered hands on her flesh.

Yet as bile rose up in her throat, she refused to give in to it. She had given him and those memories far too much weight for far too many years . . .

Abruptly, she pictured herself in her room at her father's manse, right before she had been abducted, ordering around the *doggen*, unsatisfied by everything around her.

She'd gone from madam to maid by her own choice, pitching herself between the two extremes of unqualified superiority and self-enforced inferiority. That *symphath* had been the binding agent, his violence linking the ends of the spectrum such that in her mind one flowed from the other, tragedy overtaking the entitlement and leaving in its wake a ruined female who had made suffering her new status quo.

Tohrment was right: She had punished herself ever since then . . . and denying the drugs during her needing had been part and parcel of that: She had chosen that pain, just as she had picked her low station in society, just as she had given herself to a male who could never, ever be hers.

I've been using you, and the only person it's working for is you—it's gotten me nowhere. The good news is that this whole thing is going to give you a great excuse to torture yourself even longer. . . .

The urge to attack some manner of dirt, to scrub with her palms until sweat beaded upon her brow, to work until her back ached and her leg screamed was so strong, she had to grip the arms of the chair to keep herself where she was.

"*Mahmen?*"

She twisted around and tried to pull herself out of the spiral. "Daughter mine, how fare thee?"

"I'm sorry I've gotten home so late. Today was . . . busy."

"Oh, that is fine. May I get you something to—" She stopped herself. "I . . ."

The force of habit was so strong, she found herself holding on to the chair again.

"It's okay, *Mahmen*," Xhex murmured. "You don't need to wait on me. I don't want you to, actually."

Autumn brought a shaking hand up to the tail end of her braid. "I feel quite undone this evening."

"I can sense that." Xhex came forward, her leather-clad body strong and sure. "And I know why, so you don't have to explain. It's good to let things go. You have to if you want to move forward in your life."

Autumn focused on the dark windows, picturing the river beyond. "I don't know what to do with myself if I'm not a servant."

"That's what you need to find out—what you like, where you want to go, how you want to fill your nights. That's life—if you're lucky."

"Instead of possibility, I see only emptiness."

Especially without—

No, she would not think of him. Tohrment had made it more than clear where their relationship stood.

"There's something you should probably know," her daughter said. "About him."

"Did I speak his name?"

"You don't have to. Listen, he's—"

"No—no, do not tell me. There is nothing between us." Dearest Virgin Scribe, that hurt to say. "There never was—so there is nothing I need to know about him—"

"He's closing up his house—the one he and Wellsie stayed in. He spent all last night packing up stuff, giving her things away, getting the furniture ready to move out—he's selling the place."

"Well . . . good for him."

"He's going to come see you."

Autumn burst up from the chair and went to the windows, her heart thumping in her chest. "How do you know."

"He told me so just now, when I went to make a report to the king. He said he's going to apologize."

Autumn put her hands up to the cold glass, the pads of her fingers going numb quickly. "For what part, I wonder. The insight that he was right about? Or would it be the honesty with which he spoke when he said he felt nothing for me—that I was merely a vehicle to free his beloved? Both are true, and therefore, short of his tone of voice, there is naught to offer apology for."

"He hurt you."

"No greater than I have been before." She retracted her hands and

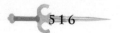

began rubbing them together for warmth. "He and I have crossed paths twice now in our lives—and I can't say I wish to continue the association. Even though his assessment of my character and my flaws is correct, I need not have that elucidated again, even gilded by syllables of 'I'm sorry.' That sort of thing sticks with one well enough the first time."

There was a length of silence.

"As you know," Xhex said quietly, "John and I have been having problems. Big ones, the kind of shit I couldn't live with even though I loved him. I really thought it was all over—what convinced me otherwise was not what he said, but what he did."

Tohrment's voice came back: *You know damn well the only reason I'm with you is to get Wellsie out of the In Between.*

"There is one difference, my daughter. Your mate is in love with you— and at the end of the day, that means everything. Even if Tohrment lets his *shellan* go, he will never love me."

The good news is that this whole thing is going to give you a great excuse to torture yourself even longer.

No, she thought. She was done with that.

Time for a new paradigm.

And though Autumn had no idea what it was, she was damn sure going to figure it out.

"Listen, I have to hustle," Xhex said. "But I'm hoping this won't take long—I'll come back as soon as I can."

Autumn glanced over her shoulder. "Do not rush on my account. I need to get used to being on my own—and I might as well start tonight."

As Xhex left the cabin, she was careful to lock up behind herself—and wishing she could do more for her mother than just turn a dead bolt: Autumn's emotional reorientation was extreme, the female's interior grid turned upside down on itself.

But then, that was what happened to people when they finally got a clear picture of themselves after aeons of sublimation.

Not a happy place. And it was hard to witness. Hard to leave behind— but Autumn was right. There came a time in everyone's life when they realized that in spite of how hard they'd been running from themselves, everywhere they went, there they were: Addictions and compulsions were nothing but marching bands of distraction, masking truths that were unpleasant, but ultimately undeniable.

The female did need some time to herself. Time to think. Time to discover. Time to forgive . . . and move on.

And as for Tohrment? There was a part of Xhex that really wanted to take whatever had been said to her mother out of his hide. Except she had been around him, and he was suffering in ways that a bruised jaw couldn't compete with. Tough to know how much of it was the shit with Autumn and how much was Wellsie—her instinct told her they'd all find out soon enough, however: The Brother had only started by dismantling that house and giving away Wellsie's clothes.

His end game was pretty damn clear.

Then they'd see just how much he cared about Autumn.

On that note, Xhex dematerialized and headed to the east. She had spent the entire day on Xcor's home turf, never getting closer than a quarter mile away: The male's grid had been clear to her as soon as she'd gotten within range, and she'd been careful to get beads on those of his soldiers as well before she'd headed north to the mansion and reported to the king.

And now she was back under the veil of the night, moving slowly through the forest, throwing out her *symphath* senses.

Closing in on the area where the grids had been concentrated during the daylight hours, she dematerialized at clips of a hundred yards, taking her sweet time, using the pine boughs as cover. Man, shit like this made her really appreciate evergreens, their fluffy branches not just concealing her, but providing a snowless ground cover that hid her footprints as she went from trunk to trunk.

The empty farmhouse she eventually came across was exactly what she would have expected. Made of coarse old stone, it was sturdy and had few windows—the perfect bunker. And of course, the irony was that with its snow-covered roof, and its cheery chimneys, the place looked like something off a Christmas card.

Ho-ho-ho, Season's Beatings.

As she cased the environs, the van that was parked off to the side seemed to belong somewhere else, an unwelcome shot of the modern in what appeared to be a resolutely antiquated picture. And the same was true for the electrical lines that came in and were anchored at the rear corner.

Xhex ghosted to that back flank. It was impossible to know whether

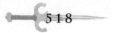

or not the power was live: No lights had been left on, the house dark as the inside of a skull.

The last thing she wanted to do was trigger an alarm.

Except a quick look at the glass of a window had her frowning. No shutters—unless they were on the inside? More important, no steel bars. Then again, the underground would be the priority, wouldn't it.

Going around, she looked in every window, then dematerialized up to the roof to check the dormers on the third floor.

Totally empty, she thought with another frown. And not well fortified.

Back down on ground level, she took out both her guns, grabbed a deep breath, and . . .

Re-forming inside the house, she was in full attack mode, her back to the corner of the empty, dusty living room, autoloaders up in front of her.

The first thing she noted was that the air was as cold inside as out. Did they not have heat?

Second thing was . . . there was no sound of an alarm.

Third: No one appeared from out of nowhere, ready to defend the territory.

Didn't mean this was a lickety-split sitch, however. What was more likely was that they didn't give a crap about anything on this floor or above.

With care, she dematerialized over to the doorway of the next room. And the next. The logical location of basement stairs would be the kitchen—and what do you know, she found what she assumed were them right where she expected them to be.

And gee-fucking-whiz, the door keeping her out was sporting a brand-new solid lock made of copper.

It took her a good five minutes to pick the bitch, and by then her nerves were twitchy. Every sixty seconds she stopped and listened hard, even though her *symphath* side was out in full force the whole time, her cilices left behind at the cabin.

When she finally worked the lock, she opened the door but a crack—and had to let out a dry laugh: The hinges squealed loud enough to wake the dead.

It was a reliable, old-fashioned trick—and she was willing to bet every door and window in the place was likewise unoiled; stairs probably creaked like an old woman if you put any weight on them, too. Yup, just like folks had done before electricity had been invented—a good ear and a lack of WD-40 was an alarm that never needed a battery or a power source.

Putting her penlight between her teeth so she could keep a gun in each hand, she searched what she could see of the rough wooden staircase. Down at the bottom there was a dirt floor, and she flashed herself to it, pivoting quickly into a defensive stance.

Lot of bunks: three sets of uppers and lowers with a single off to one side.

Clothes in big sizes. Candles for light. Matches. Reading materials.

Cell phone charging cords. One for a laptop.

And that was it.

No weapons. No electronics. Nothing that offered any true identification.

Then again, the Band of Bastards had started out as nomads, so of course their personal effects were few and very portable—and this was part of the reason they were so dangerous: They could relocate at the drop of a hat and leave no meaningful footprint behind.

This definitely was, however, their inner sanctum, the site where they were relatively vulnerable during the day—and they did protect themselves accordingly: The walls and the ceiling and the back of the door were covered with steel mesh. No getting down here, or out of here, but through that opening way above.

She went around slowly, looking for trapdoors, a tunnel entrance, anything.

They'd need an ammunition storage facility somewhere in here: Even as mobile as they liked to be, there was no way they could go out night after night buying just enough bullets to get them to the dawn.

They'd need a cache.

Refocusing on the single cot, she guessed it was Xcor's, as their leader, and it didn't take a genius to figure that if there was any hiding place, it would be in his area—he had just the kind of suspicious mind to not fully trust even his own soldiers.

Investigating the bed with her light, she searched for triggering mechanisms either to an alarm or a bomb or a trapdoor. Finding none, she sheathed her guns for a moment and lifted up the metal frame, moving aside. Taking out a miniature handheld metal detector, she scanned the dirt floor and . . .

"Hello, boys," she murmured.

Her handy-dandy piece of equipment picked up a perfectly square outline that measured about four by two and a half feet. Kneeling down, she used one of her knives to displace the soil around the peripheral edges. Whatever it was, was buried deep—

Xhex froze as her acute hearing informed her that a car had pulled up.

It was not one of the Bastards or their cohorts, however. The emotional grid was far too uncomplicated.

A *doggen*, arriving with provisions?

Flashing up to the head of the stairs, she shut the door as much as she could without reengaging the lock and then went back to the buried box. Moving at triple time now, she kept one ear pinned on the footsteps creaking around on the first floor. . . .

On the long side of the delineated rectangle, she used her knife point to probe the packed dirt for a handle. Finding nothing, she repeated the investigation on the short—

Bingo. Brushing the earth away, she gripped a circular ring, put the penlight back between her teeth and heaved with everything she had. The lid weighed as much as a car hood, and she had to swallow her grunt—

Wow. Talk about an arsenal.

In the large box below there were handguns, shotguns, knives, ammunition, munitions cleaning supplies . . . all of it in a well-ordered, obviously watertight environment.

Among which was a long, black, hard-plastic rifle case.

She took the thing out and put it on the dirt floor next to her. One look at the lock and she cursed. Fingerprint activated.

Whatever. The damn thing was big enough to house one or maybe two long-noses. So it was coming with her.

With quick, sure hands, she shut the lid, kicked dirt back over it, and patted the surface so it was packed hard once more. Covering her tracks took less time than she thought, and before she knew it, she was moving the bunk into place again.

Picking up the case with her left hand, she listened. The *doggen* was moving around upstairs, the female's grid as unremarkable as it had been when she had arrived: She had heard nothing, knew nothing.

Glancing around, Xhex thought it was unlikely that the maid had the key to get down here. Xcor would be too cagey for that. But still, it wasn't safe to just hang out. Even if they gave the *doggen* the run only of the upstairs, one of the Bastards could get injured in the field at any time, and though she had no hesitation in fighting any one of them, or every fucking one, if the rifle was in fact in this case, she needed to get the weapon out immediately.

Time for a meet-and-greet.

As she dematerialized up to the head of the stairs, her weight on the top step released a creak from the wood.

On the far side, the *doggen* called out, "Sire?" There was a pause. "Wait, I shall assume the position."

What. The. Fuck?

"I am ready."

Xhex palmed the doorknob, opened the way, and stepped out, expecting to find some kind of Kama Sutra nightmare going on.

Instead, the older female was standing in the corner of the kitchen facing the juncture of the walls, with her eyes covered by her hands.

They didn't want her to be able to identify them, Xhex thought. Smart. Very smart.

Timely, too, as she would have had to waste precious minutes screwing with the female's head. Further, that "position," as it were, was going to save the *doggen*'s life later, when Xcor eventually found out that his lair had been infiltrated while they were gone.

If you didn't see anyone ever, there was no way you were protecting an intruder.

Xhex shut the door, and the lock triggered itself, reengaging. Then she dematerialized right out of there, carrying the gun case against her chest.

Good thing it wasn't that heavy.

And God willing, Vishous was going to be off rotation for the night.

SIXTY-EIGHT

Back at the Brotherhood compound, Tohr held the basement door open and stood aside as John passed by and hit the stairs.

Descending after the other male, Tohr's body was stiff, especially his back and shoulders. His nightly workouts as a furniture mover were finished, though. After a final three-hour push this evening, his and Wellsie's house was officially empty, and on its way to being entered into Caldwell's MLS system. Fritz had met with the Realtor during the day, and the price they had set was aggressive, but not crazy. If Tohr had to carry the costs of the place for another couple of months, or even through the spring, that was fine.

Meanwhile, the furniture and rugs had been moved into the mansion's garage; the paintings and etchings and ink drawings were up in the climate-controlled part of the attic; and the jewelry box was in Tohr's closet above the mating dress.

So it was . . . done.

At the bottom of the stairs, he and John set off at a resolute pace that took them through a cavernous room and by the massive boiler that not only kicked out enough heat to keep the main part of the house warm, but threatened to fry his face and body as he strode into its orbit.

Continuing onward, their footsteps were loud, the air cooling fast as they left the boiler's range and hit the second half of the basement. This part was cut up into storage rooms, one of which would soon hold the balance of his and Wellsie's furniture, another of which was V's private workspace.

No, not *that* kind of work.

He used his penthouse for that shit.

Vishous's forge was down here.

The sound of the Brother's fire-breathing monster started off as a low hum; by the time they turned the final corner, the dull roar was loud enough to drown out the sound of their shitkickers. In fact, the only thing that cut through the din was the *tink-tink-tink* of V pounding a hammer on red-hot black metal.

As they stepped into the doorway of the cramped stone room, V was hard at work, his bare chest and shoulders gleaming in the orange light of the flames, his muscled arm rising up to strike again and again. His concentration was fierce—and it should be. The blade that strip of metal was becoming would be responsible for keeping its owner alive, as well as getting the enemy good and dead.

The Brother looked up as they appeared, and nodded. After two more strikes, he put down his hammer and cut the oxygen feed to the fire pit.

"What's doing?" he said as the great growl settled into a purr.

Tohr glanced over at John Matthew. The kid had been a star throughout the whole process, never faltering in the grim work of dismantling a lifetime's worth of keepsakes, mementos, and collections.

So hard, this was. On the both of them.

After a moment, Tohr looked back at his brother . . . and found himself at a loss for words—except V was already nodding and getting to his feet. Removing the heavy leather gloves that went up to his elbows, he stepped free of his station.

"Yeah, I've got them," the brother said. "Back at the Pit. Come on."

Tohr nodded, because that was all he had to share with anyone. Still, as the three of them filed out and walked in sad silence back for the stairs, he clapped his hand on John's nape and kept it there.

The contact comforted them both.

When they emerged into the kitchen, there was too much Last Meal

chaos for any of the staff to really notice them—so fortunately there were no questions, no kind inquiries, no guesses about why they were all looking so serious.

Out the butler's pantry. Hop across to the hidden door beneath the staircase. Down into the tunnel to avoid the cold of the winter.

As they hung a right and headed in the opposite direction from the training center, he couldn't believe on some level that this was happening. His shitkickers even faltered a couple of times, like maybe they were trying to pull him away from this last piece.

He was resolved, however.

At the door that led into the Pit, V punched in the code and opened the way up, indicating that they should go first.

The place where Butch and V bunked in with their *shellans* was the same as always—except neater now that there were females cohabitating there: The *Sports Illustrated*s were in an orderly pile on the coffee table; the kitchen didn't have empty bottles of Lag and Goose all over the counters; and there were no more gym bags or biker jackets hanging off of everything.

V's Four Toys still took up one whole corner, however, and the massive plasma-screen TV remained the biggest thing in the place.

Some things would never change.

"She's in my room."

Tohr wouldn't ordinarily follow the guy into his private space, but this was not ordinary.

V and Doc Jane's room was small and had more books than bed in it, stacks of physics tomes and chemistry volumes crowding the rug until you could barely walk on it. The good doctor made sure the place wasn't a total pigsty, however, with the duvet all pulled up nice and neat, and the pillows angled carefully against the headboard.

Over in the corner, Vishous opened the closet and reached up to the top shelf, straining even with his height for . . .

The black velvet–wrapped bundle he brought out was big enough and heavy enough to require both hands, and he grunted as he eased back and carried it over to the bed.

As he put the thing down, Tohr had to force himself to keep breathing.

There she was. His Wellsie. Everything that was left of her on earth.

Lowering onto his knees before her, he reached forward and undid the satin bow at the top. With hands that shook, he pried the velvet bag open and pushed it down, revealing a sterling silver urn that had art deco etchings on its four sides.

"Where did you get this?" he said, running a forefinger down the bright, shiny metal.

"Darius had it in a back room. I think it's Tiffany, from the thirties. Fritz polished it up."

The urn was not part of their tradition.

Ashes were not meant to be kept.

They were supposed to be set free.

"It's beautiful." He glanced up at John. The kid's face was pale, his lips tight . . . and in a quick, slashing movement, he brushed under his left eye. "We're ready to do her Fade ceremony, aren't we, son."

John nodded.

"When?" V asked.

"Tomorrow night, I think." As John nodded again, Tohr said, "Yeah, tomorrow."

"You want I talk to Fritz and set it up?" V asked.

"Thanks, but I'll take care of it. John and I are going to do it." Tohr refocused on the lovely urn. "He and I are going to let her go . . . together."

Standing over Tohr, John was having a difficult time keeping it together. Hard to know what was getting to him more: the fact that Wellsie was actually in the room with them again, or that Tohr was kneeling before that urn as if his legs weren't working right.

The past couple of nights had been a brutal exercise in reorientation. It wasn't that he hadn't known Wellsie was gone; it was just . . . dismantling everything in that house had made that fact so loud, there was a constant screaming in his head.

Goddamn it, she was never going to know that he'd made it through his transition, or that he was a halfway decent fighter, or that he'd gotten mated. If he ever had a child of his own, she'd never hold it in her arms, or see a first birthday, or get to witness first steps or first words.

Her absence made his own life seem less full, and he had the awful feeling that that was always going to be true.

As Tohr bent his head, John went over and put his palm on the guy's heavy shoulder, reminding himself that however hard this was for him, what Tohr was going through was a thousand times worse. Shit, though, the Brother had been strong, making all those out and safe decisions about

everything from pairs of jeans to pots and pans, working steadily in spite of the fact that he had to be raw on the inside.

If John hadn't respected the fuck out of the Brother before, he sure as hell did now—

"Vishous?" came a female voice down the hall.

John wrenched around. Xhex was here?

Tohr cleared his throat and pulled the velvet bag back into place. "Thanks, V. For taking such good care of her."

"V? You got a minute?" Xhex called out. "I need to— Oh, shit."

As she stopped herself, like she'd tweaked to the vibe in the bedroom from where she was out in front, Tohr got to his feet and nodded at John with a smile too generous to comprehend. "You'd best go to your female, son."

John hesitated, but then V stepped up and put his arms around his brother, whispering low words.

Giving the males some privacy, John went down to the living room.

Xhex was not surprised to see him. "I'm sorry, I didn't mean to interrupt anything."

It's okay. His eyes went to the carrying case in her hand. *What's that?* Even though he knew . . . Holy *shit*, had she gotten the—

"That's what we need to find out."

In a sudden panic, he looked her over carefully, searching for signs of injury. There were none, though. She had gone in and come out in one piece.

John didn't mean to do it, but he lunged forward and grabbed her hard, holding her against his body. As she embraced him in return, he felt the rifle case press into his back, and he was just . . . really fucking glad she was alive. So fucking glad—

Shit, he was tearing up.

"Shh, John, it's okay. I'm safe. I'm all right. . . ."

While he shuddered, she held him with the strength and power in her body, keeping him together, blanketing him with exactly the kind of deep love that Tohr had lost.

Why some people were lucky and others were not seemed the cruelest kind of lottery.

When he finally pulled back, he mopped up his face and then signed, *Will you come to Wellsie's Fade ceremony?*

There was no hesitation. "Absolutely."

Tohr says he would like the two of us to do it together.

"Good, that's good."

At that moment, Vishous and Tohr came back out, and both Brothers immediately locked eyes on that case.

"You are fan-fucking-tastic," V said with a kind of awe.

"Hold your ass-kissing—I haven't opened it yet." She held the thing out to the Brother. "Fingerprint lock. I need your help."

V grinned in an evil way. "Far be it from me to not come to the aid of a lady. Let's do this."

As the pair of them took the gun case over to the kitchen counter, John pulled Tohr aside. Nodding at the velvet-covered urn, he signed, *Do you need me any further tonight?*

"No, son, you stay with your female—I've got to go out for a little bit, actually." The guy stroked the velvet. "I'm going to put her in my room first, though."

Yeah, okay. Cool.

Tohr hugged him hard and fast, and then went out the door into the tunnel.

From over in the kitchen, Xhex said, "How are you going to— Well, yeah, that'll work."

The smell of burning plastic had John twisting around. V had removed his glove and put his glowing forefinger up against the locking mechanism, acidic smoke rising from the contact in nasty curls of dark gray.

"My prints tend to do the job on just about anything," the Brother said.

"Clearly," Xhex murmured, her hands on her hips, her taut body bent forward. "You ever barbecue with that thing?"

"Only *lessers*—and they ain't good eatin'."

Staying back, John stared across the way and just . . . Well, he was just amazed at the female. Who the fuck did shit like this? Going into the B.o.B.'s secured hideout. Rifling through, looking for a rifle, natch. Coming back like she'd done nothing more incredible than order a Starbucks.

As if she sensed his eyes on her, she glanced over.

Opening himself up emotionally, so that there were no barriers at all, he revealed to her everything he was feeling—

"Got it," V announced, retracting his glowing hand and regloving it.

Turning the gun case toward Xhex, the Brother said, "How'd you like to do the honors."

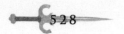

Xhex refocused and cracked open what she had brought home, the mangled locking mechanism falling apart.

Inside, there were a pair of rifles nested in black egg-crate padding, along with long-range scopes.

"Bingo," she breathed.

She'd done it, John thought. He was willing to bet his left nut that one of those guns was going to prove to be the rifle that shot Wrath.

She'd frickin' done it.

From out of his gut, a massive groundswell of pride rose, warming his entire body, stretching his lips into a smile so wide his cheeks hurt. Staring at his female, and the mission-critical evidence she'd brought into the fold, he was willing to bet he threw shadows, he was beaming so much.

He was just so incredibly . . . proud.

"Pretty goddamn promising." V closed up the case. "I've got the equipment we're going to need at the clinic—along with that bullet. Let's do this."

"One minute."

Xhex turned to John. Walked over to him. Took his face in her hands. As she stared up at him, he knew she was reading every bit of everything he had in him.

Rising up onto her tiptoes, she pressed her lips to his and spoke three words he hadn't expected to hear again anytime soon.

"I love you." She kissed him again. "I love you so much, my *hellren*."

SIXTY-NINE

On the other side of the Hudson, down south from the Brotherhood compound, Autumn sat in the cabin in darkness, still occupying the same chair she'd settled into at the beginning of the night. She had long since willed the lights off, and the lack of illumination around her made the snow-covered landscape appear bright as day under the moon's glow.

From her vantage point, the river was a wide, motionless expanse, even though it was iced in only at its shores.

From her vantage point, she had seen little of the view before her, having dwelled instead on the stages of her life.

Many hours had passed since Xhex had checked in with her, the moon shifting position, the black shadows thrown by the trees pinwheeling around over the white ground. In many ways, time had no meaning, but it did have an effect: The longer she spent mulling over things, the more clearly she saw herself, her earlier realizations no longer a shock, but instead something she steeped herself in. . . .

Something she began to change herself with—

At first, the dark slash that cut through the wintry vista seemed to be

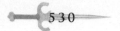

just another shadow cast by a tree trunk at the edge of the property. Except then it moved.

It was alive.

It was . . . not an animal.

It was a male.

A sudden shot of fear jerked her upright, but her instincts rushed forward and told her immediately who it was. Tohrment.

Tohrment was here.

Her first thought was to go down into the underground retreat and pretend she hadn't seen him—and considering how he waited on the lawn, giving her plenty of time to identify him, he seemed to be offering her that out.

She was not going to run, however. She'd done enough variations of that to last for several lifetimes.

Rising from the chair, she went to the door that opened toward the river and unlocked it, pushing it wide. Crossing her arms over her chest against the cold, she tilted up her chin and waited for him to come forward.

And he did. With an expression of somber purpose, the Brother approached slowly, his heavy boots crunching through the crusty top layer of the snow. He still looked the same, still tall and broad, with his thick, white-striped hair, and his handsome, grave face marked with lines of distinction.

How odd of her to measure him for some kind of metamorphosis, she thought.

Clearly, she was ascribing her own transformation to anyone and everyone.

As he stopped in front of her, she cleared her throat, easing the tickle of the bitterly frigid air. She did not speak first, however. That was his due.

"Thank you for coming out," he said.

She just nodded, unwilling to make whatever cursory apology he was about to offer easy on him. No, no more easing his way—or others'.

"I want to talk for a bit—if you have some time?"

Given the way the cold wind cut through her clothes, she nodded and stepped back inside. The interior of the cabin hadn't seemed particularly warm before; now it was tropical. And cramped.

Sitting back down in her chair, she let him choose whether to stand or not. He picked the former, and did so directly before her.

Upon a deep, bracing breath, he spoke clearly and succinctly, as if he had mayhap practiced his words: "I can't apologize enough for what I said to you. It was utterly unfair, and unforgivable. There's no excuse for it, so I'm not going to try to explain it away. I just—"

"You know what?" she cut in evenly. "There's a part of me that wants to tell you to go to hell . . . to take your apology, and your weary eyes, and your heavy heart, and never, ever get anywhere near me again."

After a long pause, he nodded. "Okay. I get that. I can totally respect that—"

"But," she cut him off again, "I've spent all night sitting in this chair, thinking about that candid soliloquy of yours. Actually, I've thought of little else since I left you." Abruptly, she glanced out at the river. "You know, you must have buried me on a night like tonight, didn't you."

"Yes, I did. Except it was snowing."

"It must have been hard to get through the frosted ground."

"It was."

"Blisters to prove it, yes, indeed." She refocused on him. "To be honest, I was fairly close to ruined when you left my recovery room at the training center. It's important to me that you realize that. After you departed, I had no thought, no feeling, nothing but breathing, and only because my body did that on its own."

He made a noise in the back of his throat, as if, through his regret, he couldn't find the voice to speak.

"I have always known that you love only Wellsie, and not just because you told me so yourself in the beginning—but because it was evident all along. And you're right: I did fall in love with you, and I did try to keep it from you—at least consciously—because I knew that it would hurt you in an unbearable way—the idea that you had let some female get that close . . ." She shook her head as she imagined how that would have impacted him. "I really wanted to spare you any more pain, and I honestly wanted Wellsie to be free. Her disposition was nearly as important to me as it was to you—and that was not about punishing myself, but because I truly loved you."

Dearest Virgin Scribe, he was so still. Barely even breathing.

"I've heard that you're disposing of the home you had with her," she said. "And have done likewise with her things. I am guessing it is because you are trying a new route to release her unto the Fade, and I hope it works. For the both of you, I hope it works."

"I came here to talk about you, not her," he said softly.

"That's kind of you, and know that I am turning the conversation onto you not because I feel like a victim of some unrequited romance that has

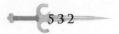

ended badly, but because our relationship in this era has always been based upon you. Which is my fault, but also the nature of the cycle we have completed."

"Cycle?"

She rose up, wanting to put them on equal footing. "Just as the seasons come full circle, so have we. When we first crossed paths, it was all about me, my selfishness, my focus on a tragedy I had lived through. This time it was all about you, your selfishness, your tragedy that you had lived through."

"Oh, Jesus, Autumn . . ."

"As you yourself pointed out to me, we can't deny the truth, and shouldn't attempt to. Therefore, I suggest that neither of us tries to fight it any longer. We are of an accord as of now, our transgressions one against the other wiped clean by deeds and words that neither of us can take back. I will always regret the position I put you in with your dagger so many years ago, and you don't have to tell me that you feel deep sorrow as you stand before me now—I can see it written in your face. You and I . . . it's a full circle, and it is completed."

He blinked, his stare holding hers. Then he brought his thumb over his eyebrow and rubbed at his forehead like it hurt. "You're wrong about that last part."

"I fail to see how you can argue with the logic."

"I've been doing a lot of thinking, too. I'm not going to fight with you about it, but I want you to know I was with you for more than just Wellsie. I didn't realize it at the time—or I couldn't let myself . . . I don't fucking know. But I am rock solid that it was also very much about you, and after you left, that became clear—"

"You don't have to apologize—"

"This isn't an apology. This is about waking up and reaching for you and wishing you were next to me. It's about ordering extra food for you, and then remembering that you're not around to feed it to. It's about the fact that even as I was packing up my dead mate's clothes, I had you in my mind, too. It wasn't just Wellsie, Autumn, and I think I knew that after your needing and that's why I snapped. I spent a day and a half sitting on my ass, staring into the dark, trying to figure this all out—and I don't know . . . I guess I finally found the courage to be really fucking honest with myself. Because it's hard when you've loved one person with every-thing you've got, and she's gone, and someone else comes and treads all over her territory in your heart." He put his hand up to his chest and struck at his sternum. "This was hers and hers alone. Forevermore. Or at least so

I thought . . . but shit didn't work out that way, and then you came along . . . and circle be damned, I don't want to be finished with you."

Now it was her turn to feel poleaxed, her body going numb as she struggled to comprehend what he was saying.

"Autumn, I'm in love with you—that's why I came here tonight. And we don't have to be together, and you don't have to get over what I said, but I wanted you to hear that from me. And I also want to tell you that I'm at peace with it, because . . ." He took a deep breath. "You want to know why Wellsie got pregnant? It wasn't because I wanted a young. It's because she knew that every night when I left the house I could get killed in the field, and as she said, she wanted something to keep on living for. If I had been the one to go? She would have carved out a life for herself, and . . . the strange thing is, I would have wanted her to do that. Even if it included someone else. I guess I've realized that . . . she wouldn't have wanted me to mourn her forever. She'd have wanted me to move on . . . and I have."

Autumn opened her mouth to speak. Nothing came out.

Had she really heard him say all that—

"Halle-fucking-lujah!"

As she let out a cry of alarm and Tohr unsheathed a black dagger, Lassiter stepped out into the middle of the room.

The angel clapped a couple of times, and then held his palms up to the heavens like an evangelist. "Finally!"

"Jesus," Tohr hissed as he put his weapon away. "I thought you'd quit!"

"Okay, still not that guy who was born in a manger. And believe me, I tried to file my resignation, but the Maker wasn't interested in what I had to say. As usual."

"I called for you a couple of times and you didn't come."

"Well, first I was flat-out pissed off at you. And then I just didn't want to get in your way. I knew you were up to something big." The angel came over and put his hand on Autumn's shoulder. "You okay?"

She nodded and managed something close to an *uh-huh.*

"So this is good, yeah?" Lassiter said.

Tohr shook his head. "Don't force her into anything. She is free to choose her path, as she always has been."

At that, he turned and went to the door. Just before he opened the way out, he glanced over his shoulder, his blue eyes locking on hers. "Wellsie's Fade ceremony is tomorrow night. I would love you to be there, and will understand completely if you don't want to come. And, Lassiter, if you're

going to stay with her, and I hope you do, make yourself useful and get her a cup of tea and some toast? She likes the sourdough bread done on both sides, with sweet butter, preferably the whipped kind, and a little straw-berry jam. And she's Earl Grey with a teaspoon of sugar."

"What—do I look like a butler?"

Tohrment just stared at her for the longest time, as if he were giving her a chance to see just how sure and steady and grounded he was—solid in a way that had nothing to do with his weight, and everything to do with his soul.

He had, in fact, been transformed.

With a final nod, he stepped out into the snowy landscape . . . and dematerialized into thin air.

"You got a TV in here?" she heard Lassiter ask from the kitchen as cupboards were opened and shut.

"You don't have to stay," she mumbled, still shocked down to her shoestrings.

"Just tell me you have a television and I'm a happy guy."

"We do."

"Well, what do you know, it's my lucky day—and don't worry, I'll keep us entertained. I'll bet I can find us a *Real Housewives* marathon."

"A what?" she said.

"I'm hoping it'll be New Jersey. But I'll take Atlanta. Or B.H."

Shaking herself, she went to look at him, and could only blink as she was blinded by all the lights he'd turned on.

Oh, wait, that was just him, glowing.

"Whatever are you speaking of?" she asked, finding it incredible that the male would be talking about human TV at a time like this.

From over at the stove, the angel smiled darkly and gave her a wink. "Just think—if you let yourself believe in Tohr and open your heart to him, you can get rid of me forever. All you have to do is give yourself to him, mind, body, and soul, baby girl, and I'm as good as gone—and you won't have to worry about what a Real Housewife is."

SEVENTY

The following evening, as soon as night fell, Assail, son of Assail, stalked through his glass house, heading for the garage. As he passed by the mansion's rear door, he glanced at the glass that had been replaced back in the fall.

The repair was neat as a pin. To the point that one could not tell that anything violent had ever transpired.

The same could not be said about the events that had gone down that horrid night. Even as calendar days churned by, and seasons shifted, and moons rose and fell, there was no repairing what had happened, no way of patching up that mess.

Not that Xcor wanted to, he supposed.

Indeed, tonight he was finally going to get a sense of exactly how much damage had been done.

The *glymera* were so fucking slow, it was ridiculous.

Initializing the alarm system with his thumbprint, he went into the garage, locked up, and walked around the Jaguar. The Range Rover on the far side had huge tires with clawlike treads—his newest purchase having

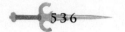

finally been delivered last week: As much as he loved the XKR, he was tired of feeling as though he were driving a greased pig on ice.

Once inside the heavily modified SUV, he hit the garage door and waited; then he reversed, K-turned, and waited again until the door was down.

Elan, son of Larex, was a right little shit, the kind of aristocrat who truly set Assail's teeth on edge: too much inbreeding and too much money had insulated him too utterly from the realities of life. The male was no more capable of forging his way without the trappings of his station than a babe out in the cold.

And yet by the exigencies of fate, that male was in a position now to effect more change than he was worthy of: Following the raids, he was the highest-ranking non-Brother on the Council, but for Rehvenge—who was so entangled with the Brotherhood, he might as well have had a black dagger strapped on his chest.

Therefore, Elan was the one calling tonight's little "unofficial" get-together.

Which would again not be including Rehvenge. And which was going to likely be about an insurrection.

Not that someone as highbrow as Elan would call it such. No, traitors who wore cravats and silk socks tended to couch their reality in much more refined terms—although the wording would change naught . . .

As Assail sped along, the trip to Elan's house took a good forty-five minutes even though the highways were all salted and the streets plowed. Naturally, he could have saved himself time by dematerializing, but if things got out of hand, if he were to be injured and unable to disappear himself, he needed to make sure he had effective cover and escape.

He had taken for granted safety only once, and long ago. Never again. And, indeed, the Brotherhood were highly intelligent. There was no telling whether this nascent cabal would be raided tonight or not—especially if Xcor were to make an appearance.

Elan's retreat was a gracious brick house, Victorian in derivation, with lacelike woodwork marking its every peak and corner. Located in a sleepy little hamlet of only thirty thousand humans, it was set well back from the lane it was on, and had a river snaking down one side of the property.

As he got out, he did not fasten the tortoiseshell buttons on the front of his camel-hair coat or put on gloves. Nor did he do up his double-breasted suit jacket.

His guns were close to his heart, and he wanted access.

Closing in on the front door, his fine black boots clapped over the shoveled walkway and his breath left his mouth in puffs of white. Overhead, the moon was bright as a halogen light and fat as a dinner plate, the lack of clouds and humidity allowing its true power to rain down from the heavens.

The drapes on all the windows had been pulled, so he could not see how many others had arrived, but it would not surprise him if they were already assembled, having dematerialized to the site.

Imbeciles.

Punching the doorbell with his bare hand, the entry was immediately pried wide, a formal *doggen* butler bowing at the hips.

"Master Assail. Welcome—may I take your coat?"

"No, you may not."

There was a hesitation—at least until Assail cocked a brow at the servant. "Ah, but of course, my lord—please come this way."

Voices, all of them male, flooded his ears as the cinnamon scent of mulled cider eased into his nose. Falling in behind the butler, he allowed himself to be led into a grand living room that was crammed with heavy mahogany furniture as per the period of the house. And in and amongst the antiques, there were a good ten males attending upon the host, their trim forms dressed in suits with ties or cravats at the throat.

There was a noticeable dip in conversation as he made his appearance, suggesting that at least some of them did not trust him.

It was likely the only wise thing about the group.

His host broke away and approached with a smug smile. "How good of you to come, Assail."

"Thank you for having me."

Elan frowned. "Where is my *doggen*? He should have taken your coat—"

"I prefer to leave it on. And I shall take that seat over there." He nodded to the one corner that would provide the most visual access. "I trust we will be getting started soon."

"Indeed. With your arrival, we await only one more."

Assail narrowed his eyes on the subtle line of sweat that dotted the skin between the male's nose and upper lip. Xcor had chosen the correct pawn, he thought as he went over and eased himself into his chair.

A sharp draft announced the arrival of the final guest.

As Xcor strode into the room, there was a hell of a lot more than a lull in the chatter. Every one of the aristocrats fell silent, a subtle rearrangement of the crowd being effected as they each stepped back.

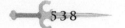

Then again—surprise! Xcor had more than a plus-one with him.

The entirety of the Band of Bastards filed in on his heels, forming a semicircle behind their leader.

In person and up close, Xcor was precisely as he had always been: rough and ugly, the kind of male whose countenance and stance suggested his reputation for violence was based on reality, not conjecture. Verily, standing in the midst of these weaklings, in their environment of luxury and civility, he was ready and perfectly capable of cutting down everything that breathed in the room—and the males at his back were just the same, each dressed for war, and prepared to bring it to bear at a mere nod from their liege.

Regarding the lot of them, even Assail had to admit they were impressive.

What a fool Elan was—he and his *glymera* gadabouts had no clue of the Pandora's box that they had opened.

With an officious cough, Elan stepped forward to address all and sundry as the one who was in charge—even though he was dwarfed not only by the soldiers' heft, but their very presence.

"I believe there are no introductions necessary, and it goes without saying that if any one of you"—at this point, he eyed his fellow Council members—"speaks of this meeting, there will be reprisals the likes of which shall make you wish for the raids to return."

Whilst he spoke, he gathered a certain momentum, as if assuming the mantle of power, even if it was provided by someone else, was a sort of masturbation for his ego.

"I thought it was important to bring all of us together this night." He began to pace, clasping his hands at the small of his back and leaning forward to address his shiny shoes. "From time to time in the last year, the esteemed members of the Council have each come unto me and expressed not just their catastrophic losses, but their frustration with the current regime's response to any meaningful recovery."

Assail's brows popped at the word *current*: This uprising had progressed further than he'd guessed if that was being thrown around. . . .

"These discussions have taken place over a period of months, and there has been an unwavering consistency to the complaints and disappointments. As a result, and after much deliberation with my conscience, I have found myself for the first time in my life eschewing the race's current leader to the extent that I am compelled into action. These gentlemales"—at that ludicrous term, he waved an open hand to the collection of fighters—"have expressed similar concerns, as well as a certain willingness to—how shall I put it—effect a change. As I know that we are all of one mind, I thought we might discuss our next steps."

At this point, the assembled dandies decided to piss on the conversational guidepost, reiterating, in their own interminable words, precisely what Elan had just stated.

Clearly they felt it was an opportunity for them to prove to the Band of Bastards how serious they were, but he doubted Xcor was moved by any of the hot air. These members of the aristocracy were fragile, expendable tools, each one of them limited in use and easily broken—and Xcor had to know this. No doubt he was going to work them until he didn't need them, and then he was going to snap their paltry wooden handles and cast them aside.

As Assail sat back and listened, he had no particular love or regard for the monarchy. But he was clear on the fact that Wrath was a male of his word—the same could not be true of any of these *glymera* yahoos: This whole group, with the exception of Xcor and his males, would kiss the king's ass until their lips went numb—right up until they caused his death. And after that? Xcor would serve himself and himself alone—and to hell with anyone else.

Wrath had stated that he would allow commerce with the humans to continue unfettered.

Xcor, however, was the type who would not permit any other seats of power to rise up—and with all the money there was to be made in the drug trade, sooner or later Assail would have a target on his back.

If he didn't have one already.

". . . and my family's estate is lying fallow in Caldwell—"

When Assail rose up from his chair, all the eyes of the fighters flipped to him.

Stepping forward through the crowd, he was careful to show his hands, lest they believe he had taken out a weapon.

"Please excuse the interruption," he said without meaning it. "But I must leave now."

Elan began to sputter as Xcor's lids lowered.

Addressing the true leader in the room, Assail spoke clearly. "I shall make no reference to this meeting, either to the individuals here in this room or to any others, neither about the statements that have been made nor who has attended. I am not a political individual, nor do I have designs on any throne—I am but a businessman seeking only to continue to prosper in circles of commerce. In leaving this meeting and resigning herewith from the Council, I am acting accordingly, seeking neither to promote nor obstruct any of your agenda."

Xcor smiled coldly, his eyes locked and loaded with deadly intent. "I shall consider anyone who departs this room to be mine enemy."

Assail nodded. "So be it. And know that I will defend my interests as appropriate against interlopers of any kind."

"As you wish."

Assail left without hurry—at least until he got into his Range Rover. Once inside the SUV, he was efficient in locking the doors, starting the engine, and taking off.

Driving along, he was alert, but not paranoid. He believed Xcor meant every word he'd said about marking him as an enemy, but he was also aware that the male was going to have his hands full. Between the Brotherhood, who were no doubt more than formidable foes, and the *glymera*, who were going to be like herding cats, there was much to consume his attention.

Sooner or later, however, the male would focus on Assail.

Fortunately, he was ready now, and would stay that way.

And waiting had never bothered him.

SEVENTY-ONE

As Tohr emerged naked and dripping from the shower, the knock on his bedroom's door was loud and a little muffled, as if it had been made by the heel of a hand, instead of a set of knuckles—and after so many years of being a brother, he knew it could have been made by only one male.

"Rhage?" He put a towel around his waist and walked over to open the way up. "My brother, what's doing?"

The guy was standing out in the hall, his incredibly beautiful face solemn, his body clad in a white silk robe that fell from his broad shoulders and was tied at the waist with a simple white rope. Across his chest, his black daggers were holstered by white leather.

"Hey, my brother . . . I, ah . . ."

In the awkward moment that followed, Tohr was the one to break the tension. "You look like a powdered doughnut, Hollywood."

"Thanks." The brother stared down at the carpet. "Listen, I brought you something. It's from Mary and me."

Opening his big palm, he held forward a heavy gold Rolex, the one that Mary wore, the one that the brother had given her when they'd been mated. It was a symbol of their love . . . and their support.

Tohr took the thing, feeling the warmth that lingered in the metal. "My brother . . ."

"Look, we just want you to know we're with you—I added back the links so it'll fit your wrist."

Tohr slipped the thing on, and yeah, it clipped just fine. "Thank you. I'll return it—"

Rhage snapped out his arms and gave the kind of bear hug that he was known for—the sort that put a strain on your spinal cord and made you have to reinflate your rib cage afterward just to make sure you hadn't punctured a lung.

"I got no words, my brother," Hollywood said.

As Tohr clapped him on the back, he felt the dragon tattoo seethe, as if it, too, were offering condolences. "It's okay. I know this is hard."

After Rhage left, he was just shutting his door when there was another knock.

Peering around the jamb, he found Phury and Z lined up side by side. The twins were wearing the same robing and tie that Rhage had on, and their eyes were just the same as Hollywood's Bahama blues: sad, so damned sad.

"My brother," Phury said, stepping up and embracing him. When the Primale eased back, he held out something long and intricate. "For you."

In his hand was a five-foot-long grosgrain white ribbon on which a prayer for strength had been carefully and beautifully embroidered in gold thread.

"The Chosen, and Cormia, and I are all with you."

Tohr took a moment to fan out the strip, and trace the Old Language characters, reciting the ancient words in his head. This must have taken hours, he thought. And many, many hands. "My God, it's beautiful. . . ."

As he forced back tears, he thought, Fan-fucking-tastic. If just the warm-up to the ceremony was getting to him like this? He was going be a goddamn mess when it actually happened.

Zsadist cleared his throat. And then the brother who hated touching others leaned in and put his arms around Tohr. The embrace was so gentle that Tohr had to wonder if it was from lack of practice. Either that or Tohr looked as fragile as he felt.

"This is from my family to yours," came the soft words.

The brother offered forward a small piece of parchment paper, and Tohr's fingers shook as he opened it. "Oh . . . shit . . ."

In the center was a tiny handprint in red paint. A young's. Nalla's . . .

There was no greater or more precious thing to a male than his offspring—especially if it was a female. So the palm print was the symbol that everything Z had and all that he was, now and in the future, was pledged in support of his brother.

"Fuck," Tohr said simply as he took a shuddering breath.

"We'll see you down there," Phury stated.

They had to close the door.

Tohr backed up and sat down on his mattress, laying the ribbon across his thighs and staring at the child's print.

When another knock sounded, he didn't look up. "Yeah?"

It was V.

The brother seemed stiff and awkward, but then, he was probably the worst out of all of them when it came to mushy shit.

He didn't say anything. Didn't try any of the hugging bullshit, either, which was just as well.

Instead, he placed a wooden case next to Tohr on the bed, exhaled some Turkish smoke, and went back for the exit like he couldn't wait to get out of the room.

Except he stopped before he left. "I gotchu, my brother," he said to the door.

"I know, V. You always have."

As the male nodded and left, Tohr turned to the mahogany case. Freeing the black steel clasp and lifting the lid, he had to curse under his breath.

The set of black daggers was . . . breathtaking. Taking one out, he marveled at the fit against his hand, and then saw that there were symbols etched into the blade.

More prayers, four of them, one on each side of each of the weapons.

All for strength.

These daggers were really not for fighting—they were too valuable. Christ, V must have worked on these for a year, maybe longer . . . although of course, as with everything the brother made down in that forge of his, they were deadly as hell—

The next knock was Butch. It had to be.

"Ye—" Tohr had to clear his throat. "Yes?"

Yup, it was the cop. Dressed as all the others were, in that white robe with the white rope tie.

As the brother came across the room, there was nothing in his hands. But he hadn't come empty-handed.

"On a night like tonight," the guy said roughly, "I only got my faith. That's all I got—'cuz there're no mortal words to ease where you're at—I know up close and personal."

He reached up behind his neck and worked at something. When he brought his hands forward once more, he was holding the heavy gold chain and even heavier gold cross that he never, ever took off.

"I know my God is not yours, but can I put this on you?"

Tohr nodded and dropped his head. As the linchpin of the male's awesome Catholic faith was hung around his neck, he reached up and touched the cross.

It had incredible weight, all that gold. It felt good.

Butch bent over and put a squeeze on Tohr's shoulder. "I'll see you down there."

Fuck. He had nothing to say anymore.

For a while, he just sat there, trying to hold it together. Until he heard something at the door. A scratching, as if . . .

"My lord?" Tohr said as he forced himself to his feet and went across the way.

You opened the door for the king. No matter what state you were in.

Wrath and George came in together, and his brother was characteristically blunt. "I'm not going to ask how you're holding up."

"I appreciate that, my lord. Because I'm pretty fucking ragged."

"Why wouldn't you be."

"It's almost harder when people are kind."

"Yeah. Well. Guess you're going to have to suck some more of that shit up." The king worked at something on his finger. And then put forward—

"Oh, fuck, no." Tohr threw his hands up and out of the way even though the male was blind. "Uh-uh. No way. No fucking way—"

"I order you to take it."

Tohr cursed. Waited to see if the king would change his mind.

Got nowhere on that one.

As Wrath just stared straight ahead, Tohr knew he was going to lose this argument.

With a dizzying feeling of total unreality, he reached out and took the black diamond ring that had only ever been worn by the king.

"My *shellan* and I are there for you. Wear that during the ceremony so that you know my blood, my body, my beating heart are yours."

George chuffed and wagged his tail as if backing his master.

"Fucking hell." This time, Tohr was the one who reached for his brother, and the embrace was returned sharply and with power.

After Wrath left with his dog, Tohr pivoted around and leaned back against the door.

The final knock was soft.

Steeling himself so that he at least appeared to be a male, even though he was feeling like a pussy on the inside, he found John Matthew out in the hall.

The boy didn't bother signing anything. He just reached out for Tohr's hand, and pressed . . .

Darius's signet ring into Tohr's palm.

He would have wanted to be here for you, John signed. *And his ring is all I've got of him. I know he'd want you to wear it during the ceremony.*

Tohr stared at the crest that was stamped in the precious metal and thought of his friend, his mentor, the only father he'd really had. "This means . . . more than you can imagine."

I'll be right beside you, John signed. *The whole time.*

"Right back atchu, son."

They embraced, and then Tohr shut the door quietly. Going back over to the bed, he looked down at all the symbols of his brothers . . . and knew that when he faced this crucible, it was with all of them with him—not that that had ever been at issue.

Something was missing, though, in all of this.

Autumn.

He needed his brothers. He needed his son. But he needed her, too.

He hoped what he'd said to her would be enough, but there were some things you couldn't come back from, some things that there was no healing from.

And maybe she had a point about the cycle thing.

He prayed there was more to it than that, however. He truly did.

As Lassiter stood in the corner of Tohr's room, he kept himself invisible. Good thing. Watching that in-and-out of males had been rough. How Tohr had managed to get through it in one piece was a flipping miracle.

But this was finally coming together, the angel thought. Finally, after all this time, after all this—well, *shit*, frankly . . . things were finally turning in a good direction.

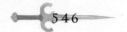

After spending the previous night and day with a very quiet Autumn, he had left her at sunset to stew in her thoughts, putting his faith in the fact that she was replaying that Tohr visit over and over in her head and finding nothing but sincerity in what had been said to her.

If she showed tonight, he was home-fucking-free. He'd done it. Well, okay, fine—*they* had done it. In truth, he had been a sideline player in all this . . . except for the fact that he kind of fucking cared about the pair of them. And Wellsie, too.

Across the way, Tohr went to the closet and seemed to brace himself.

Taking out a white robe, the Brother put the thing on and then returned to the bed to gird his waist with the magnificent ribbon Phury had brought. After that, the guy picked up the folded piece of parchment Z had given him, tucked it into the tie, and drew on a white holster—into which he slid V's two spectacular black daggers. The signet ring went on his left middle finger, the black diamond on the thumb of his fighting hand.

With the unfamiliar sense of a job well-done, Lassiter thought about all the months he'd been back on earth, recalling the way he and Tohr and Autumn had all worked together to save a female who would in turn . . . well, in different ways, free each of them.

Yeah, the Maker had known what was up when this assignment had been made: Tohr was not the same. Autumn was not the same.

And Lassiter himself was not the same: It was simply impossible for him to disconnect from this, to be all blasé, to act like nothing mattered—and the funny thing was, he really didn't fucking want to pull out.

Man, there were a lot of purgatories getting expunged tonight, he thought ruefully, both real and figurative: When Wellsie transitioned unto the Fade, he was going to finally get out of his prison. And with her release, that meant Tohr's burden was lifted so the both of them were free.

And as for Autumn? Well, with any luck, she'd allow herself to love a male of worth—and in turn be loved back—so after all these years of her suffering, she could finally begin to live again; she would be reborn, resurrected, come back from the dead. . . .

Lassiter frowned, a strange alarm beginning to ring in his head.

Looking around, he half expected some *lessers* to be rappelling down the side of the mansion or landing out in the gardens from a helicopter. But no . . .

Reborn, resurrected . . . back from the dead.

Purgatory. The In Between.

Yeah, he told himself. Where Wellsie was. Hello?

As an odd, disembodied panic gripped him, he wondered what the fuck his problem was—

Tohr froze and looked over into the corner. "Lassiter?"

With a shrug, the angel figured he might as well make himself visi. No reason to hide—although, as he took form, he kept his dread to himself. God . . . what the hell was wrong with him? They were at the finish line. All Autumn had to do was show up at the Fade ceremony—and, going by the way she'd been laying out clothes as he'd left to come here, it was pretty clear she wasn't just going to be scrubbing floors at that cabin all night long.

"Hey," the brother said. "I guess this is it."

"Yeah." Lassiter forced a smile onto his face. "Yeah, it sure is. I'm proud of you, by the way. You've done well."

"High praise." The guy fanned his fingers out and looked at the rings. "But you know what? I really am ready to do this. Never thought I'd say that."

Lassiter nodded as the Brother turned and headed for the door. Just before Tohr got there, he stopped at the closet, reached into the darkness, and pulled out the skirting of the red gown.

As he rubbed the delicate fabric between his thumb and forefinger, his mouth was moving like he was talking to the satin . . . or his former mate . . . or, shit, maybe it was just to himself.

Then he released his hold on the dress, letting it settle back into the quiet void it hung in.

They left together, Lassiter pausing to give a last measure of support before breaking off and paving the way down the hall of statues.

With each step closer to the stairs, that alarm bell got louder, until the sound of it reverberated through the angel's body, his stomach going sour as his legs grew sloppy.

What the *hell* was his problem?

This was the good part, the happily-ever-after. So why was his gut telling him that doom was waiting in the wings?

SEVENTY-TWO

As Tohr stepped into the pitch-dark hallway outside of his room, he accepted a quick hug from the angel and then watched the guy walk off toward the glow at the second-floor balcony.

Damn, his breath sounded loud in his ears. And his heart rate was the same.

Ironically, it had been just like this when he and Wellsie had been mated, his nervous system all a-twitter. And funny, the fact that his physiological response was identical in this context proved the body was a one-note machine when it came to stress, the adrenal gland firing in the same way, regardless of whether the trigger was good or bad.

After a moment, he began to walk down the corridor toward the grand staircase, and it was good to feel all the symbols of his brothers on him. When you got mated, you went into it alone: You came up to your female with your heart in your throat and your love in your eyes, and you didn't need anyone or anything else, because it was all about her.

When you were performing her Fade ceremony, on the other hand, you had to have your brothers with you, not just in the same room, but as close as you could get them: The weights on his hands and around his neck and the tie about his waist were all that were going to keep him standing. Especially when the pain came.

As he got to the head of the stairs, he felt the floor under his feet go into a wave, the great swell beneath him shifting his balance right when he really fucking needed it to stay in place.

Down below, the foyer had been draped in vast bolts of white silk that fell from the ceiling molding, so that everything, from the architectural features to the columns to the fixtures to the floors, was covered up. All the electric lights had been turned off throughout the mansion, and massive white candles on stanchions along with fires in the fireplaces made up for the deficit.

Every member of the household was standing around the edges of the great space, the *doggen*, the *shellans*, the guests all dressed in white, according to tradition. The Brotherhood had formed a straight line off from the center starting with Phury first, who was going to officiate, and then John, who was going to be part of the ceremony. Wrath was next. Then V, Zsadist, Butch, and Rhage on the end.

Wellsie was in the middle of it all, in her beautiful silver box, on a small table that had been draped in silk.

So much white, he thought. As if the snow had sneaked in from outside, and was breeding in spite of the warmth.

It made sense: color was for matings. For the Fade ceremony, it was all about the opposite, the monochromatic palette symbolizing both the eternal light the dead would be subsumed in, as well as the intention of the community to someday join with the deceased in that sacred place.

Tohr took one step, and then another, and then a third. . . .

As he descended, he looked at the upturned faces. These were his people, and they had been Wellsie's. This was the community he was continuing with, and the one she had left.

Even in the sadness, it was hard not to feel blessed.

There were so many with him in this, even Rehvenge, who was now so much a part of the household.

And yet Autumn was not among them; at least, not that he could see.

Down at the bottom, he fell into a bracing stance before the urn, his hands clasped in front of his hips, his head lowered. As he settled into his body, John joined him, assuming the same pose even though he was pale, and his hands couldn't seem to still.

Tohr reached out and touched John's forearm. "It's okay, son. We're going to get through this together."

Instantly, the jerky movements stopped, and the boy nodded as if eased a little.

In the ticking moments that followed, Tohr thought dimly that it was amazing how a crowd this size could be so quiet. All he could hear was the crackle of the lit fires on either side of the foyer.

Over to the left, Phury cleared his throat and bent down to a table over which a bolt of white silk had been draped. With graceful hands, he lifted the cover to reveal a mammoth silver bowl filled with salt, a silver pitcher of water, and an ancient book.

Picking up the tome, he opened it and addressed them all in the Old Language. *"On this night, we come herein to mark the passing of Wellesandra, mated of the Black Dagger Brother Tohrment, son of Hharm; blooded daughter of Relix; adoptive mahmen of the soldier Tehrror, son of Darius. On this night, we come herein to mark the passing of the nascent Tohrment, son of the Black Dagger Brother Tohrment, son of Hharm; blooded son of the beloved departed Wellesandra; adopted brother of the soldier Tehrror, son of Darius."*

Phury turned the page, the heavy parchment making a soft noise. *"According to tradition, and in hopes it will be both pleasing to the Mother of the race's ears, and of solace to the bereaved family, I call upon all who tarry herein to pray with me for the safe carriage of those who have passed unto the Fade. . . ."*

So many voices rose up as Phury commanded sentences and had them repeated, female and male tones mixing together such that the words were lost to Tohr and all he heard was the pattern of somber speech.

He glanced over at John. Lot of blinking going on, but the boy was holding back the tears like the male of worth he was.

Tohr swung his eyes back to the urn, and gave his mind free rein to play through a slide show of images from all different parts of their shared lives.

His reminiscing ended on the very last thing he had done for her before she'd been killed: put those chains on the tires of that SUV. So she'd have traction in the snow.

Okay, now he was blinking like a motherfucker. . . .

The ceremony became a blur at that point, with him saying things when prompted, and staying silent the rest of the time. He found himself glad that he had waited this long to do it. He didn't think it would have been possible to get through all this at any other moment.

On that note, he glanced over at Lassiter. The angel was glowing from head to foot, his gold piercings catching the light around and within him and magnifying it back tenfold.

For some reason, the guy didn't look happy. His brows were squeezed

together as if he were trying to crunch numbers in his head and coming
up with a sum total he didn't like—

*"I would now ask the Brotherhood to pledge their condolences to the be-
reaved, starting with His Majesty Wrath, son of Wrath."*

Tohr decided he was seeing things and refocused on his Brothers. As
Phury stepped away from the little table, Wrath was discreetly led forward
by V so that he was standing over the bowl of salt. Drawing up the sleeve
of his robe, the king unholstered one of his black daggers and drew the
blade up the inside of his forearm. As bright red blood rushed to the surface of the cut, the male extended his arm and let drops fall.

Each one of the Brothers did the same, their eyes locking on Tohr's as
they reaffirmed without words their shared mourning for all he had lost.

Phury was the last, with Z holding the book as he completed the ritual. Then the Primale picked up the pitcher and spoke sacred words as he
poured water from it, turning the pink-stained salt into brine.

"I would now ask Wellesandra's hellren *to disrobe."*

Tohr was careful to take out Nalla's palm print before untying the
Chosen's sash, and he put both down on top of the robe after he'd removed it.

"I would now ask Wellesandra's hellren *to kneel before her for one last
time."*

Tohr did as commanded, falling to his knees in front of the urn. In
his peripheral vision, he watched Phury walk over to the marble fireplace
on the right. From out of the flames, the brother withdrew a primeval iron
brand, one that had been brought over from the Old Country long ago,
one that had been made by hands unknown, long before the race had had
a collective memory.

The terminal part was about six inches long and at least an inch wide,
and the line of Old Language symbols was so hot it glowed yellow, not red.

Tohr assumed the proper position, curling his hands into fists and
easing forward so that his knuckles were planted on the heavier white cover
that had been laid on the floor. For a split second, all he could think about
was the mosaic depiction of the apple tree that was underneath him, that
symbol of rebirth that he was beginning to associate only with death.

He had buried Autumn at the foot of one.

And now he was saying good-bye to Wellsie on top of one.

As Phury stopped beside to him, Tohr's breath began to come in
punches of air, his ribs jerking tight and popping open.

When you were mated, and you got your *shellan's* name carved in your

back, you were supposed to bear the pain in silence—to prove that you were worthy of both her love and the mating.

Breath. Breath. Breath . . .

Not so with the Fade ceremony.

Breath-breath-breath . . .

For the Fade ceremony, you were supposed to—

Breathbreathbreath—

"What is the name of your dead?" Phury demanded.

On cue, Tohr dragged in a giant pull of oxygen.

As the brand was laid to the skin where her name had been carved those many years ago, Tohr screamed her name, every ounce of pain in his heart and his mind and his soul coming out on a oner, the sound shattering through the foyer.

The scream was his final good-bye, his pledge to meet her on the flip side, his love made manifest one last time.

It went on forever.

And then he was sagging so badly, his forehead was on the floor, while all across the top of his shoulders, his skin burned as if it was on fire.

But this was just the beginning.

He tried to drag himself up, but his son had to help him, because he had lost all muscle tone: With John's help, he reassumed his position.

His breath took over once again, that rhythmic, shallow panting pumping him up, restoring his energy.

Phury's voice was rough to the point of hoarseness. *"What is the name of your dead?"*

Tohr grabbed another hectare of oxygen and got ready to do it again.

This time, the name he screamed was his own, the pain of losing his blood-born son cutting him so deep he felt as though the inside of his chest was bleeding.

He screamed longer the second time.

And then he flat-out collapsed on his arms, his body spent—even though it was still not over yet.

Thank God for John, he thought, as he felt himself get repositioned.

From up above, Phury said, *"For to seal unto your skin e'ermore, and to bind our blood with yours, we shall now complete the ritual for your beloveds."*

No panting this time. He didn't have the energy.

The salt stung so badly he lost his vision and his body convulsed, his limbs jerking uncontrollably until he fell over on his side, even though John was trying to hold him upright.

Indeed, all he could do was lie there in front of all of these people, many of whom were crying openly, his pain their own. Tracing the faces, he wanted to comfort them in some way, spare them what he had gone through, ease their sorrow. . . .

Autumn was at the far end, by the billiards room archway, standing in the flesh.

She was dressed in white, her hair twisted back from her face, her delicate hands up to her mouth. Her eyes were wide and red rimmed, her cheeks wet, her expression one of such love and compassion, it instantly made the pain fade.

She had come.

She had come for him.

She still had love . . . for him.

Tohr started to weep properly, his sobs exploding out of his chest. Reaching for Autumn, he held his hand forward, beckoning to her, because in this moment of letting go, after this seemingly endless, painful journey, along which she and she alone had joined him, he'd never felt closer to anyone. . . .

Even his Wellsie.

Reborn, resurrected . . . back from the dead.

Across from where Tohr was writhing in pain from the salt wash, Lassiter grit his teeth not because he was commiserating, but because his head was driving him nuts.

Reborn, resurrected . . . back from the dead—

Tohr began to sob, his heavy arm stretching, his hand opening . . . and reaching for Autumn.

Ah, yes . . . Lassiter thought, the final part of it. Fate had demanded the blood, and the sweat . . . and the tears, not for Wellsie, but for another. For Autumn.

This was the final part, these tears spilled by the male for the female he had finally allowed himself to love.

In a rush, Lassiter looked up to the ceiling, to the painted warriors with their fierce steeds, to the deep blue background—

The sunbeam seemed to come from out of nowhere, piercing through the stone and mortar and plaster of what was above them all, the bright light so strong even Lassiter had to wince as the illumination arrived to claim a female of worth from a hell that was not of her doing. . . .

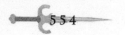

Yes, yes, there in the center of the dome, with her young in her arms, Wellsie appeared as brilliant and vibrant as a rainbow, lit from without and within, color returned unto her, life renewed because she was saved, because she was free—and so was her son.

And just before she was subsumed, from the loft of her heavenly heights, she looked upon Tohr, and looked upon Autumn, though neither of them saw her and nor did the crowd. Her expression was nothing but love for the pair, for the *hellren* she had had to leave behind, for the female who would spare him his own torment, for the future the two would have together.

Then with an abiding, peaceful expression, she lifted her hand in a good-bye to Lassiter . . . and was gone, the light consuming her and her son and carrying them away to the place where the dead were at home and at rest for all of eternity.

As the light faded, Lassiter waited for his own burst of illumination, his own claiming sun, his own return for a final time to the Maker.

Except . . .

He was still . . . right where he was.

Resurrected, reborn . . . back from the dead . . .

He was missing something here, he thought. Wellsie was free, but—

At that moment he focused on Autumn, who had gripped the skirting of her white robe and taken a step forward, toward Tohr.

From out of nowhere, a second bolt of great light broke through from above—

But it came not for him. It came . . . for *her.*

Lassiter's mind made the connection with the speed and shock of a lightning bolt: She had died long ago. Taken her own life . . .

The In Between. Different for each person. Tailor-made.

Everything went into slow motion as the second truth was revealed: Autumn had been in her own In Between the whole time, traveling to the Sanctuary and serving the Chosen for all those years, then coming down here to earth to complete the cycle that had begun back in the Old Country with Tohrment.

And now that she had helped him save his *shellan* . . . now that she had let herself feel for him and let go of her sorrow at her own tragedy . . .

She was free. Just as Wellsie was.

Fucking hell! Tohr was going to lose another female—

"No!" Lassiter screamed. "Noooooo!"

As he broke out of the lineup and lunged forward, trying to stop the connection between the two of them from being made, people started shouting, and someone grabbed onto him, as if to keep him from getting in the way. But it didn't matter.

It was too late.

Because the pair of them didn't have to touch. The love was there, and so was the forgiveness of deeds past and present, as well as the commitment in their hearts.

Lassiter was still lunging forward, in midair, when the final beam of light claimed him, catching him in flight, plucking him out of the present and pulling him upward, even as he still screamed at the cruelty of fate.

His entire purpose had culminated in condemning Tohr to another round of tragedy.

SEVENTY-THREE

For truth, Autumn had not been sure she would come unto the mansion . . . until she did. And she had not been sure how she would feel about Tohrment . . . until she saw him searching the crowd and knew he was looking for her. And she did not completely open her heart to him . . . until he reached out for her, his control breaking the moment he locked eyes with her.

She had loved him before now—or had thought she did.

But she had not been all the way there. The critical part that had been missing was a sense of herself not as somebody who was unworthy and had to be punished, but as an individual with value and a life to live beyond the tragedy that had defined her for so long.

As she stepped forward, it was not as a servant or a maid, but as a female of worth . . . one who was going to go to her male, and embrace him, and be joined with him for as long the Scribe Virgin deemed.

Except she didn't make it.

She was not even halfway across the foyer when her body was struck by some kind of force.

She could not comprehend what o'ertook her: One moment she was striding toward Tohr, answering his silent plea that she come to him, crossing over the floor, zeroing in on the one she loved. . . .

And the next, a great light fell upon her from some unknown source, halting her in her tracks.

Her will commanded her body to continue to Tohr, but a greater force laid claim to her, and take her it did: With a pull that was as undeniable as gravity, she was drawn up from the earth, into the light. And as she was lifted upward, she heard Lassiter screaming, and saw him surge forward as if he wanted to stop her departure—

That was what energized her to flail against the current. Struggling fiercely, she fought with all she had, but there was no freeing herself from what had captured her: No matter how she battled, she could not alter her ascension.

Down below, chaos reigned, people racing forward as Tohr dragged himself up off the floor. As he regarded her, his face was a mask of confusion and disbelief—and then he began to leap up as if he were trying to catch her, as if she were a balloon, the string of which he sought to palm. Someone grabbed him as he lost his balance—John. And the Primale rushed to his side. And his Brothers . . .

Her last image was not of any of them, not even of Tohrment, but of Lassiter.

The angel was beside her, rising as well, the light consuming them both until he disappeared and so did she, until she was nothing at all, not even conscious. . . .

When Autumn came to once again, she was in a vast white landscape, one so wide and so long that it had no horizons.

Before her was a door. A white door with a white knob and a glow around its jambs as if there was a bright light awaiting her on the other side.

This had not been what had greeted her when she'd first died.

Back years and years ago, when her consciousness had returned to her after she had inflicted that dagger upon her own stomach, she had found herself in a different white landscape, one that had trees and temples and rolling lawns, one that was populated by the Scribe Virgin's Chosen females, one that she had gone on to live in without question, accepting her fate as not one of her choosing, but the inevitable result of her choices down below.

This, however, was not the Sanctuary. This was the entrance unto the Fade.

What had happened?

Why had she—

The explanation came to her in a rush as she realized that she had finally let the past go and opened her heart to embrace all that life had to offer . . . thus freeing herself from her own In Between—even as she had been unaware she had been within it.

She was out of the In Between. She was . . . free.

But Tohrment was down below.

Her body began to shake, rage shooting through her, the anger so deep and abiding she wanted to claw through the door and have a harsh word with the Scribe Virgin or Lassiter's Maker or whoever the sick bastard was who dealt out fates.

After having traversed the great distance from where she had first started, only to find that the prize was nothing but another sacrifice, she was livid to the point of violence.

Not holding anything back, she let herself go, throwing herself at the portal, beating at it with her fists, tearing at it with her nails, kicking at it with her feet. She uttered curses that were vile and called the holy forces names that were villainous—

When arms shot around her waist and began to drag her back, she attacked whoever it was, baring her fangs and biting into the thick forearm—

"Fucking hell! Ouch!"

Lassiter's indignant voice cut into her temper, stilling her body until she just heaved to catch her breath.

The damn door was utterly uninjured. Uncaring. Unmoved.

"You bastards," she hollered. "You bastards!"

The angel turned her around and shook her. "Listen to me—you're not helping here. You need to calm the *fuck* down."

With a force of will, she pulled herself together. And then promptly sobbed. "Why? Why are they doing this to us?"

He shook her again. "*Listen* to me. I don't want you to open that door—just stay here. I'm going to do what I can, okay? I don't have a lot of pull, I may not have any at all—but I'll give it a fucking shot. You stay right where you are, and for the love of God, do *not* open that thing. Once you do, you're in the Fade and I can't do shit. Are we clear?"

"What are you going to do?"

He stared at her for a long moment. "Maybe I'm finally going to be an angel tonight."

"Wha— I don't understand . . . ?"

Lassiter reached forward and cupped the side of her face. "You two have done so much for me—hell, we've all been in our own In Betweens, in a way. So I'm going to offer up everything I've got to save the pair of you—we'll see if it's enough."

She clasped a hold on to his hand. "Lassiter . . ."

He stepped back and nodded to her. "You stay here and don't get your hopes up. The Maker and I have not had the best relationship—I may just get incinerated on the spot. In which case, no offense, but you're screwed."

Lassiter turned away and walked into the whiteness, his big body disappearing.

Closing her eyes, Autumn tucked her arms around herself and prayed for the angel to work a miracle.

Prayed with everything she had . . .

SEVENTY-FOUR

Down below on earth, Tohr felt as though he was losing his ever-loving mind. Lassiter was gone. Autumn was gone.

And a terrible sense of logic was making him wonder why he hadn't guessed at the mechanisms they'd been working under for the past year.

Wellsie had been trapped in the In Between by him.

And Autumn . . . had been trapped in the In Between by herself.

Then by loving him, and forgiving not just him but herself, she had been freed—so just like Lassiter, she had been granted what she had not even known she was in search of: She had been given at long last the entrance to the Fade, that which she had been denied when she had taken her own life in a fit of terror and agony.

Now she was free.

"Oh . . . Jesus . . ." he said as he let himself fall into John's strong arms. "Oh . . . fucking hell . . ."

Now, like his Wellsie, she was gone from him, too.

Bringing a hand up to his face, he rubbed hard, wondering if maybe he'd wake up from this . . . like maybe this was just the worst nightmare his subconscious could possibly dream up . . . yeah, like he'd wake up at any moment and drag himself out of bed to get ready for the Fade ceremony, where in the real world this would not be the outcome . . .

There was only one problem with that theory: His back was still stinging from the salt and the branding. And his brothers were still milling around, talking over each other in a panic. And somewhere, somebody was yelling. And all around, the glow from candles provided plenty of light to tell who remained in the foyer and who had left. . . .

"Oh, fuck . . ." he said again, his chest suddenly so empty he wondered if he hadn't had his heart removed and not noticed.

Time passed, and shit sank in, and he was taken into the billiards room. A drink was pressed into his hands, but he just let it sit on his thigh, his head falling back as John Matthew comforted Xhex and Phury talked to Wrath and some plan was made for the king to go confront the Scribe Virgin.

At which point V stepped in and volunteered to hit up his mother.

Which was promptly shot down. Only to have Payne's offer to go with the king accepted.

Blah, blah, blah . . .

He didn't have the heart to tell them all it was a foregone conclusion. And besides, he'd already been through the mourning process once—so he had a core competency in recovery, right?

Yay.

For godsakes, what the fuck had he done in an earlier life to deserve this? What the hell had he—

The sound of the doorbell going off was a dim noise behind him. Nonetheless, everyone froze.

Anybody who knew about the mansion was already here.

Humans couldn't find them.

Lessers shouldn't have been able to.

And the latter was also true for Xcor—

That doorbell let out its throaty demand once again.

On a oner, all the brothers as well as Payne and Xhex, and Qhuinn, John, and Blay, outted weapons.

Fritz was bodily prevented from going over to the vestibule; Vishous and Butch did the duty of checking the screen.

And even though he didn't give a crap whether it was the Scribe Virgin herself on the other side, Tohr focused on the foyer.

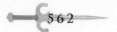

A shout went out, an excited shout with a Boston accent. And then there were lots of shouts, a legion of them, too many to decipher.

Someone in a white robe came in with V and his boy.

Whatever—

Tohr jacked up onto his feet, sure as if someone had hooked his ass up to a car battery.

Autumn stood under the arches of the room, her eyes dazed and her hair a flyaway mess, as if she had been through a wind tunnel—

Tohr plowed through big male bodies, shoving people out of the way to get to her. And when he did, he skidded to a halt. Grabbed her shoulders. Looked her over from head to foot. Shook her hard to get a sense of how corporeal she was.

"Is it . . . truly you?"

In response, she threw her arms around him and held on so hard, he couldn't breathe—and thank fuck. Because that meant she was real, right? It had to be . . . right?

"Lassiter . . . Lassiter did it. . . . Lassiter saved me. . . ."

He tried to track what she was saying. "What . . . what are you— I don't understand any of this—"

The story came out several times in different iterations, because his mind just wasn't tracking anything. Something about her making it up to the Fade, and that angel coming out and telling her . . .

"He said he would give everything he had to save us. Everything . . ."

Tohr pulled back and touched Autumn's face, her throat, her shoulders. She was as real as he was. She was as alive as he was. She had been . . . saved by that angel?

Except Lassiter had said he would be free if this worked.

The only possible explanation was that he had traded his future . . . for theirs.

"That angel," he whispered. "That godforsaken angel . . ."

Tohr bent down and kissed Autumn as deeply and for as long as he could. And as he did, he resolved to honor Lassiter, and himself, and his female as best as he was able, for however many years he had on the earth.

"I love you," he said to her. "And just like Lassiter, I'm going to give everything I've got to give to the two of us."

As Autumn nodded and kissed him back, he felt more than heard her say, "I love you," back.

Gathering her up in his arms, he held her close and closed his eyes, his body shaking from too much to describe. But he knew the score, and he was good with it.

Life was short, no matter how many days you were granted. And people were precious, each and every one, no matter how many you were lucky enough to have in your life. And love . . . love was worth dying for.

Worth living for, too.

SEVENTY-FIVE

As dawn approached at the end of the darkened night, and the moon sunk low in the sky, Xcor left downtown Caldwell. After that ridiculous meeting with the *glymera*, he and his bastards had reconvened at the top of their skyscraper, but he hadn't been able to stomach any strategizing or talk of the aristocrats.

Upon ordering his soldiers to return to their newest home base, he escaped into the cold night air alone, knowing precisely where he had to go.

To the meadow, the moon-washed meadow with the big tree.

As he re-formed in the landscape, he saw it not covered in snow, but vibrant with fall's colors, the oak's branches not bare, but lush with red and gold leaves.

Marching through the snow, he mounted the rolling earth, stopping when he came to the spot where he had seen the Chosen for the first time . . . and taken her blood.

He remembered every bit of her, her face, her scent, her hair. The way she moved and the sound of her voice. The delicate structure of her body and the frightening fragility of her smooth skin.

He yearned for her, his cold heart crying out in prayer for something that he knew fate could never provide.

Closing his eyes, he planted his hands on his hips and lowered his head.

The Brotherhood had found them at that farmhouse.

The rifle case that Syphon used to keep the tools of his assassin's trade was gone.

Whoever had taken it had come and gone during the previous night. Which meant at sunset, they had packed up their few things and scattered for a new location.

He knew the Chosen had been the cause of it. He could think of no other way their lair could have been located. And another thing was clear: The Brotherhood were going to use the rifle to prove with surety that the bullet driven into Wrath months ago had been from a weapon of theirs.

How thorough of them.

Indeed, Wrath was such a good little king. So careful not to behave rashly and without cause—and yet he was obviously capable of using any weapon at his disposal.

Not that Xcor would find blame with the Chosen—not at all. He did, however, have to find out if she was safe. He simply had to be reassured that though his enemies had wielded her, they had not mistreated her.

Oh, how his wicked heart churned at the idea that she might have been hurt in any way. . . .

As he considered his options, a cold wind blew in from the north, trying to cut him to the core. It was too late, though. He was already sliced in the heart.

That female had slashed him in a way no war wound ever could, and from the likes of her, he was never going to heal up.

Good thing he didn't ever allow his emotions to show, for it was best that no one knew his Achilles' heel had finally, after all these years, come to find him.

And now . . . he would have to find her.

If only to put his conscience, such as he had one, at ease, he was going to have to see her again.

SEVENTY-SIX

Quhinn didn't know *what* the fuck was up. People fucking poofing it in and out of the fucking foyer, shit going south . . . until Autumn came the fuck back.

If there had ever been a time to drop the f-bomb, tonight was it.

But at least it ended okay, with all being recovered, and the ceremony completed: With Autumn standing beside Tohr, John had been branded twice, once for Wellsie, once for the lost brother he'd never meet. And then, after the salt had sealed those wounds, the crowd had gone up to the highest point in the house where Wellsie's urn had been opened and revealed to the air, her ashes lovingly carried up and out to the heavens by the gusts of a rare easterly wind.

Now, everyone was heading back down to the dining room to eat and recharge; after which they'd no doubt go off to pass the fuck out in their rooms as soon as they could politely disengage.

Everybody was just about done, himself included, and that conviction had him turning to Layla as they reached the foyer. "How you doing?"

Man, he'd been asking her that nonstop for three days straight, and each time, she'd told him she was fine, and hadn't started to bleed yet.

She wasn't going to bleed. He was sure of this, even if she had yet to believe it.

"I'm good," she said with a smile, as if she appreciated his kindness.

The good news was that they were getting along really well. He'd been worried after the needing that things would get weird or some shit, but they were like a team that had run a marathon, reached a goal, and were ready for the next challenge.

"Can I get you some food?"

"You know, I am hungry."

"Why don't you head up, have a lie down, and I'll bring you something."

"That would be lovely—thank you."

Yup, it was nice the way she smiled at him in that uncomplicated and warm way, the one that made him love her like family. And as he escorted her back over to the base of the stairs, it was good to smile at her in the same manner.

All that simple-and-easy ended as he turned around. In the library, through the open doors, he saw Blay and Saxton talking. And then his cousin stepped in and pulled Blay into his arms. As the pair of them stood together, body on body, Qhuinn took a deep breath and felt a little death of his own come to him.

He guessed this was how it ended for them.

Separate lives, separate futures.

Hard to think that they had started out *in*separable—

Abruptly, Blay's blue stare found his.

And what Qhuinn saw in it caused him to falter: Love shone out of that face, unadulterated love untempered by the shyness that was very much a part of his reserve.

Blay didn't look away.

And for the first time . . . neither did Qhuinn.

He didn't know whether the emotion was about his cousin—it probably was—but he'd take it: He stared right back at Blaylock and let everything he had in his heart show in his face.

He just let that shit fly.

Because there was a lesson in this Fade ceremony tonight: You could lose the ones you loved in the blink of an eye—and he was willing to bet,

when it happened, you weren't thinking about all the reasons that could have kept you apart. You thought of all the reasons that kept you together.

And, no doubt, how you wished you'd had more time. Even if you'd had centuries . . .

When you were young, you thought time was a burden, something to be discharged as fast as possible so you could be grown-up. But it was such a bait-n-switch—when you were an adult, you came to realize that minutes and hours were the single most precious thing you had.

No one got forever. And it was a fucking crime to waste what you were given.

Enough, Qhuinn thought. Enough with the excuses, and the avoidance, and the trying to be someone, anyone else.

Even if he got shanked, even if his precious little ego and his dumb-ass little heart got shattered into a million pieces, it was time to stop the bullshit.

It was time to be a male.

As Blay started to straighten, like a message had been received, Qhuinn thought, That's right, buddy.

Our future has come.

EPILOGUE

The following evening, Tohrment rolled over and found Autumn's body in the sheets. She was warm and willing as he mounted her, her thighs splitting for him, her core welcoming him as he sank in deep and moved inside.

They had fallen asleep together, sinking into the kind of rest you had when a journey was over and home had finally reappeared on the horizon.

"Give me your mouth, my female," he said softly in the dark.

As her lips yielded to him, he let his body take over, the release not an earthquake, but more of a wave, an easing of tension rather than a chaotic explosion of stars. And as he continued to ride her in that gentle rhythm, making love to his Autumn, he was reassuring himself that she was real—that they were real.

When it was over, he willed on a single light on the bedside table and traced her face with his fingertips. The way she smiled at him made him totally believe in a benevolent Maker.

They were going to be mated, he thought. And he would add her

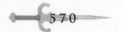

name, the one he had given her, to his back, right below Wellsie's. And she would be fully his *shellan* for however long they had together.

"Do you want something to eat?" he whispered.

She smiled some more. "Please."

"I'll be right back, then."

"Wait, I'd like to come with you. I don't know what I want."

"Then we'll go down together."

It took some time to actually make it out of the bed, get dressed in pj's, and wander down the hall of statues to the stairwell.

Autumn paused at the top, as if she were remembering the night before and leery of getting anywhere near the space—like she might get sucked up into the Fade again.

With a nod of understanding, he swung her up into his arms. "I'll carry you."

As she stared up into his face, she put her hand to his cheek, and didn't have to speak. He knew exactly what she was thinking of.

"I can't believe Lassiter saved us, either," he said.

"I don't want him suffering."

"Neither do I. He was a good guy. A real . . . angel, as it turned out."

Tohr started the descent, taking careful steps because he had a precious load. Down at the bottom, he paused for a moment to look at the depiction of the apple tree on the floor. He had let go of two females at the foot of one . . . and now he was in the position of carrying one of them back over it—thanks to that angel who had somehow pulled off a miracle.

He was going to miss that son of a bitch; he really was. And he was going to be eternally grateful for—

The doorbell chimed, loud and clear.

Frowning, Tohr glanced over at the grandfather clock by the door to the butler's pantry. Two in the afternoon? Who the hell could—

The chime went off again.

Striding across the mosaic floor, prepared to call for his brothers if he had to, he peered at the monitor—

"Holy . . . *shit*."

"Who is it?"

Tohr put Autumn down, freed the locking mechanism to the inner portal and put his female behind him in the event any daylight shone in.

Lassiter walked in like he owned the place, that swagger back in full force, his smile as wide and naughty as ever, his blond and black hair marked with fresh snowflakes.

As Tohr and Autumn stared at him with their mouths open, he held up two oversize McDonald's bags.

"I brought us all Big Macs," he said happily. "I know you dig 'em, remember?"

"What the . . ." Tohr tightened his grip on his *shellan*, just in case . . .well, shit, with the way things were going lately, anything could happen. "What are you doing here?"

"It's your lucky day, motherfucker." The angel did a little spin, piercings glinting, Mickey D's bags flaring out. "Turned out there were three of us being tested, and I passed as well. The instant I pledged myself for you two, I was free—and after I thought about it for a while, I decided I'd rather be on earth doing good works than up there in the clouds. 'Cuz, you know, I've kinda gotten a ball rolling, and this compassion shit looks good on me. Besides, no *Maury* in heaven."

"Which is what distinguishes the place from hell," Tohr pointed out.

"Too right." The angel jogged his load of high-calorie, high-fat. "So what you say? I got fries, too. No sundaes. I didn't know how long it would take for someone to open the door for me, and I didn't want them to melt."

Tohr looked at Autumn. Then they both looked at the angel.

As one, they stepped in and embraced the guy, and what do you know, the son of a bitch held them back.

"I'm really glad this worked out," Lassiter whispered in all seriousness. "For you two."

"Thanks, man," Tohr said in return. "I owe you one. . . . Shit, I owe you everything."

"You did a lot of it yourself."

"Except for that last bit," Autumn pointed out. "That was you, Lassiter."

"Meh. Who's counting. Between friends, you know."

The three of them eased back, and then after an awkward moment, they walked into the dining room. As they sat down at one end and Lassiter began passing out the goods, Tohr had to laugh. He and this angel had started with the golden arches . . . and here they were again.

"Much better than that cave, right?" Lassiter murmured as he handed over fries.

Tohr glanced over at Autumn and couldn't believe how far they all had come. "Yeah. Really, totally . . . completely much better."

"Plus this place has cable."

As Lassiter winked at them both, Tohr and Autumn started grinning.

"It does, angel. It so does . . . and anytime you want the clicker, it's yours for the taking."

Lassiter barked out a laugh. "Damn, you really are grateful."

Tohr stared at Autumn and found himself nodding. "You bet your ass I am. Eternally grateful . . . I am . . . Eternally. Grateful."

On that note, he kissed his female . . . and bit into his Big Mac.